WILD SWANS

JUNG
CHANG

Here is
LEON URIS'
eagerly awaited new novel—
a sweeping epic that probes behind today's
headlines to uncover the true, moving
story of the "terrible beauty" that is Ireland.

TRINITY

brilliantly re-creates Ireland's struggle for
independence—a saga of glories and defeats,
triumphs and tragedies—as lived by
a young Catholic rebel, Conor Larkin, and the
beautiful and valiant Protestant girl
who defied her heritage to join herself to him
and his cause. Moving from
Conor's tiny Donegal village, with its
close, loving family ties, its warm friendships,
its fierce loyalties, to the Bogside
slums of Londonderry, to the teeming port
city of Belfast, Uris paints a searing
portrait of a beleaguered people divided by
religion and wealth. On the one side,
the impoverished Catholic peasantry;
on the other, the Protestant aristocracy—
railroad tycoon Sir Frederick Weed and his
headstrong daughter, Caroline, and the
arrogant Hubble clan, landed
gentry wielding tyrannical power
over life and death.

Books by Leon Uris
Ask your bookseller for the books you have missed

ARMAGEDDON
* THE ANGRY HILLS
* BATTLE CRY
* EXODUS
* IRELAND: A TERRIBLE BEAUTY, with Jill Uris
* MILA 18
* QB VII
* TOPAZ
* TRINITY

* Available from Bantam Books, Inc.

TRINITY

LEON URIS

BANTAM BOOKS
TORONTO · NEW YORK · LONDON · SYDNEY

*This low-priced Bantam Book
has been completely reset in a type face
designed for easy reading, and was printed
from new plates. It contains the complete
text of the original hard-cover edition.*
NOT ONE WORD HAS BEEN OMITTED.

TRINITY

*A Bantam Book / published by arrangement with
Doubleday & Company, Inc.*

PRINTING HISTORY

*Doubleday edition published March 1976
12 printings through April 1977
Literary Guild selection March 1976
The Franklin Library edition March 1976*

Bantam edition / August 1977

2nd printing . September 1977	8th printing .... April 1978
3rd printing . September 1977	9th printing .... June 1978
4th printing . September 1977	10th printing ...... August 1978
5th printing . September 1977	11th printing .. February 1979
6th printing . September 1977	12th printing .... June 1979
7th printing .... February 1978	13th printing . November 1979
14th printing .... June 1980

A limited edition of this book has been privately printed.

*Design of Bantam cover from Doubleday hardcover jacket
created by Alex Gotfryd.*

*Bantam Books are published by Bantam Books, Inc. Its trade-
mark, consisting of the words "Bantam Books" and the por-
trayal of a bantam, is Registered in U.S. Patent and Trademark
Office and in other countries. Marca Registrada. Bantam
Books, Inc., 666 Fifth Avenue, New York, New York 10019.*

PRINTED IN THE UNITED STATES OF AMERICA

23 22 21 20 19

THIS BOOK IS DEDICATED TO
MY WIFE, JILL,
WHO IS AS MUCH A PART OF THESE PAGES
AS THE IRISH PEOPLE

I wish to express my heartfelt appreciation to my associate, Diane Eagle, whose research and devotion constituted a tremendous contribution, and to the Denver Public Library.

There are others, tens of dozens, whose interviews and expertise made this work possible. Sheer weight of numbers precludes my thanking them all. Unfortunately, some of these cannot or do not wish to be acknowledged, for the story of Ireland goes on. Those who did help me know who they are and have my everlasting gratitude.

CONTENTS

CONTENTS

"There is no present or future—only the past, happening over and over again—now."
—EUGENE O'NEILL
A Moon for the Misbegotten

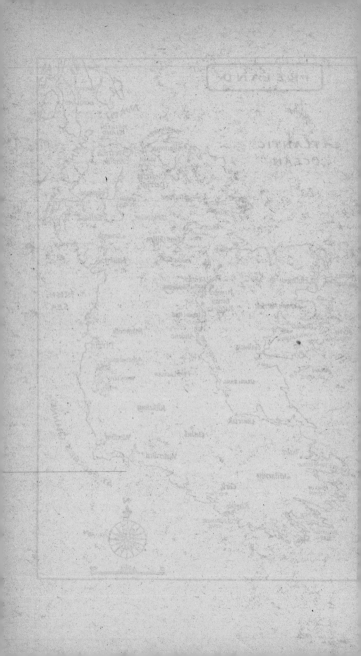

PART ONE
Ballyutogue

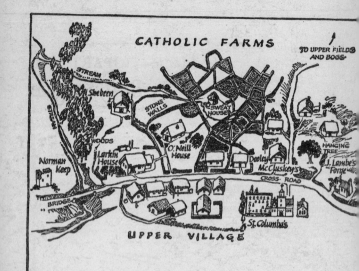

CATHOLIC FARMS

TO UPPER FIELDS AND BOGS.

STREAM

Shebeen

STONE WALLS

SWEAT HOUSE

WOODS

Norman Keep

Larkin House

O'Neill House

Dooley

McCluskey's

HANGING TREE

J. Lambe's Forge

BRIDGE

CROSS ROAD

St. Columba's

UPPER VILLAGE

PROTESTANT FARMS

WOODS

ROAD TO DERRY

LOUGH FOYLE

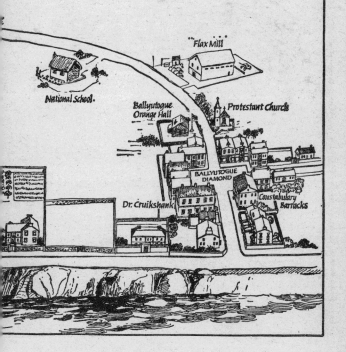

BALLYUTOGUE

→N

Flax Mill

National School

Ballyutogue
Orange Hall

Protestant Church

BALLYUTOGUE
DIAMOND

Dr. Cruikshank

Constabulary
Barracks

CHAPTER ONE

MAY 1885

I recall with utter clarity the first great shock of my life. A scream came from the cottage next door. I rushed into the room, as familiar as my own home. The Larkin kids, Conor, Liam and Brigid, all hovered about the alcove in which a mattress of bog fir bedded old Kilty. They stood in gape-mouthed awe.

I stole up next to Conor. "Grandfar is dead," he said.

Their ma, Finola, who was eight months pregnant, knelt with her head pressed against the old man's heart. It was my very first sight of a dead person. He was a waxy, bony specimen lying there with his open mouth showing no teeth at all and his glazed eyes staring up at me and me staring back until I felt my own ready to pop out of their sockets.

Oh, it was a terrible moment of revelation for me. All of us kids thought old Kilty had the magic of the fairies and would live forever, a tale fortified by the fact that he was the oldest survivor of the great famine, to say nothing of being a hero of the Fenian Rising of '67 who had been jailed and fearfully tortured for his efforts.

I was eleven years old at that moment. Kilty had been daft as long as I could recall, always huddled near the fire mumbling incoherently. He was an ancient old dear, ancient beyond age, but nobody ever gave serious consideration to the fact he might die.

Little Brigid began to weep.

"Hush!" her ma said sharply. "You'll not do any crying until Grandfar has been properly prepared. The house has been surrounded by fairies just waiting to pounce and your weeping will encourage them to break in and snatch his soul from us."

Finola struggled to her feet, going into a flurry of activity. She flung open the windows and doors to let

5

the evil spirits out and quickly covered the mirror to hide his image.

"Liam, you be telling the news. Be sure to go to the byres and the beehives and let the cattle and bees know that Kilty Larkin is gone. Don't fail or the fairies will take his soul." She wrung her hands and sorrowed. "Oh, Kilty, Kilty, it was a good man you were." And then she turned to me. "Seamus!"

"Yes, ma'am," I answered.

"Get to your ma. I'll need her good hands to help lay him out. Conor!"

Conor didn't respond, just looking on at his grandfather. She joggled him by the shoulder. "Conor!"

"Aye, Ma."

"Go up to the bog and get your daddy."

Brigid had fallen to her knees and was crossing herself at a furious pace. "Off your knees and be helping me, Brigid," Finola commanded, for the corpse was a woman's work.

Liam bolted first into their own byre. I could see him through the half door speaking to the Larkin cows as Conor backed away from the alcove slowly, his eyes never leaving his grandfather.

Outside, I punched him lightly on the arm. "Hey, if you come to my house first, I'll go to the bog with you to fetch your daddy." We scampered over the stone wall which separated our cottages. My own ma, Mairead O'Neill, as all the mothers of Ballyutogue will be remembered by us bent over her eternal station at the hearth. As we tumbled in she was hoisting the great copper pot by pulley chain over the turf fire.

"A good day to you, Mrs. O'Neill," Conor said. "I'm afraid we are in sorrow."

"Kilty Larkin croaked," I said.

"Ah, so it is," my ma sighed, and crossed herself.

"And sure Mrs. Larkin will be needing you to lay him out."

My ma was already out of her apron. "Conor, you stay here with your brother and sister tonight," she said.

"I was hoping to mourn at the wake," he answered.

"That will be up to your ma and daddy. Are you carrying salt?"

"Oh, Lord, we all forgot in the excitement."

Ma went to the large salt bowl in a niche on the side

of the fireplace and doled out a pinch for my pocket, for Conor and for herself to ward off the evil spirits.

"I'm going to the bog with Conor," I said, bolting behind him.

"Be sure you tell the bees and cows," she called after us.

"Liam is doing that."

Our village started at an elevation of three hundred feet above Lough Foyle and our fields crept up into the hills for another five hundred feet, all sliced into wee parcels of a rundale. Some of the plots were hardly larger than our best room and very few people could really tell what exactly belonged to whom. Each plot was walled off, making a spider web of stone over the mountainside.

Conor ran like he was driven on a wind, never stopping until he cleared the last wall gasping for breath. He sat sweating, trembling and sniffling. "Grandfar," he said shakily.

Now Conor Larkin was twelve, my closest friend and my idol, and I wanted very much to be able to say words of comfort but I just could not manage much at all.

My earliest memories had to do with the Larkins. I was the youngest of my family, the scrapings of the pot. My sisters were all grown and married and my oldest brother, Eamon, had emigrated to America and was a fireman in Baltimore. The middle brother, Colm, at nineteen was eight years older than myself when Kilty died.

Conor and I waited for a time, for seldom was the day as clear and the view as splendid. Ballyutogue, meaning "place of troubles," lay grandly on the east side of Inishowen several miles north of Derry in County Donegal.

From where we stood we could see it all . . . all the stolen lands that now belonged to Arthur Hubble, the Earl of Foyle. The vista this day sparkled so we could make it out all the way over Lough Foyle to County Derry and up and down the coast from Muff to Moville. Directly below us at loughside was the Township and on either end of it the long, perfectly proportioned rectangular symmetry of lush green Protestant fields, each holding a finely built stone farmhouse of two stories and a slate roof.

The Upper Village where we Catholics lived was "in

the heather" with its crazy patch-quilt labyrinth of stone walls creeping up the savage hills.

Conor was biting his lip hard to fight off the tears.

"Do you think he's in purgatory yet?" I asked.

He shook his head to say he didn't know, then scooped the ground, picked up a rock and slung it down the hill. I threw a rock too because I usually did what Conor did.

"Come on, runt," he said, and turned and trotted up the path into the mountain bogs. It was nearly an hour when we arrived. The bog warden directed us to the area where Tomas Larkin and my own daddy, Fergus O'Neill, would be clamping turf. At this point the cut of the bog was deep. Four-man teams worked their slanes with the precision of machines, digging out and slicing bricks which were raised up by pulley and stacked like cottages to dry. When the water finally oozed out of them weeks later, they had lost most of their weight and were ready for burning. The dried bricks were loaded on a string of donkey carts and taken to a warehouse in the Township.

Our people got fifteen per cent of the turf for working the bogs, with the balance either going to Derry to fire up his lordship's factories or sold to Protestant farmers, shops and homes. Conor was already working the bogs from time to time and in a year or so I would be joining him during the dry clamping season in May.

Tomas Larkin was not hard to spot, being half again the size of my daddy, who dug alongside him. A great show of a man he was. On seeing Conor he set his slane aside and waved broadly, then immediately sensed his son's intensity.

"Grandfar," Conor cried, running into his daddy's arms.

"Aye," Tomas Larkin sighed from a terrible depth, "aye." He sat himself on the ground, taking Conor onto his lap. I envied the Larkins so. I truly loved my own daddy, of course, and my ma and Colm and my sisters, but in thinking back I never have a remembrance of an embrace. None of the families in Ballyutogue were much for showing outward affection except the Larkins. They were different in that way.

The word drifted around the bog in scarcely a whisper and one by one the slanes were set aside and the men filed past Tomas and Conor and doffed their caps and moved on down the mountain.

The long walk back was dirgelike and wordless with
Conor holding tight to his daddy's hand and both of them
clench-teethed. It seemed half of forever before we
reached the crossroads where Conor and I waited every
morning to have the milk collected. Here at the three-
hundred-foot level the Upper Village began with the main
road twisting down to Ballyutogue Township and the
lough. It was a neat, square, solid Protestant Ulster town
below with an array of merchants, flax and flour mills, the
dairy and their homes. In the diamond, the town center,
the Royal Irish Constabulary barrack and crown offices
attested to the omnipresence of Her Britannic Majesty.
All of it down there, the town and the Protestant farms,
was once O'Neill land either grabbed by Lord Hubble's
ancestors and planted by imported Scots or doled out as a
reward to the soldiers of Oliver Cromwell's army.

At the crossroad stood the one prosperous Catholic
merchant, Dooley McCluskey, himself, proprietor of a
public house and wee inn. The Protestants were rabid
in defense of temperance and wouldn't dirty their hands
running such an establishment. However, McCluskey's
was beyond the eyes of their roaring preacher men and
those thin-lipped, pinched Presbyterian wives. Why, we've
seen temperance Presbyterians so tore they could be put
to sleep hanging on a clothesline.

Most of the Catholic drinking was in the nature of
poteen, a white mountain dew stilled in illegal stills which
could be broken down and moved in minutes ahead
of the excise tax collectors and the Royal Irish Constabulary. The actual partaking was done in a shebeen, a
converted byre buried in our village. Tradition in Ballyutogue and many other towns of Inishowen was that the
stilling and selling of poteen be given to widows who had
no other means of livelihood.

Across the road from McCluskey's stood our second
mighty establishment, St. Columba's Church, named for
the blessed founder of Derry and overseas missionary who
converted thousands of heathen English and Scots to
Christianity centuries before. Just about half of the holy
places in Donegal and Derry were named for him.

To look at St. Columba's you'd think we were in the
shank of prosperity. Why, St. Columba's was half again
the size and double the beauty of the Protestant Lord
Houses in the Township. Coming from our own stark

cottages, it seemed like a preview of heaven. You'd be
given to wonder how and why people living on a diet of
potatoes and salted herring would be putting up such
grandiose monuments to the Almighty.

For generations we were not permitted to worship
in our traditional manner. Penal laws by the British
forced us to hold secret mass in caves and hidden places
in the high pastures. When the religion was emancipated
earlier in the nineteenth century, mother church went on a
building spree despite the fact that it kept the peasants
in a state of dire poverty.

Father Lynch (God bless County Tipperary which
gave him to us) ruled the parish like an avenging angel.
The first thing I ever learned after the name of my ma
and daddy was the awesome power the father held. It
was total, for it included priestly infallibility and ownership of our most private thoughts. Nothing was to be
withheld on pain of his never ending array of punish-
ments. We were so starved for a learned man, someone
who could simply read and write, much less represent
a mystical conduit to the beyond, that the people of the
village bestowed on him the status of a ruling baron.
For better or worse Father Lynch gave us a vague dream
to cling to, to alleviate the pain of our dismal existence.
I discovered the meaning of fear at the receiving end
of his wrath for breaking the rules of his autocracy.
Father Lynch's supply of holy reproachables was
bottomless . . . utterly inexhaustible.

Kilty Larkin, the deceased, had been excommunicated
for taking part in the Fenian Rising of eighteen and
sixty-seven. His son Tomas rarely set foot inside St.
Columba's because of it. It took a powerful man to
defy the Church in our tight existence but he was that
and more, the uncrowned chieftain. The priest took
umbrage because there could not be two rulers of one
parish.

Let me tell you, Sunday mass was a sorry sight with
better than half the village men standing against the stone
wall opposite the church like cattle about to be driven
down the chute, waiting in discomfort for a reprieve that
never came.

At the last possible minute they'd drag in, a line of
beaten curs, and fill the last two or three rows, fall to
their knees, cross themselves and beat their chests for

the sole purpose of exoneration for another week. They'd
perspire as a group, hating the chore, but of no mind
to stir waves with their neighbors or the priest.

Dooley McCluskey never failed to reach his establishment first after the mass, just ahead of the stampeding
herd in desperate need of a drink.

Coming down from the bogs and common pastures,
we had to pass St. Columba's. A great hush would fall
as we tried to sneak past the church, hoping that the
father might otherwise be occupied with a bit of solitary
meditation. Some of the men would slip over the wall,
using its cover to crawl through the ditches. A few were
able to get through until the new curate, Father Cluny,
arrived on the scene.

From a strategic position that cut off escape, Father
Lynch would signal to Father Cluny, who then sounded
the bloody angelus . . . bong, bong, bong . . . and we'd
drop to our knees like felled trees while Father Lynch
flushed out would-be fugitives like a covey of quail . . .
bong, bong, bong, bong, bong, bong, bong, bong, bong
. . . out came Father Lynch like a skinny reed, pinched
and puckered and droning in monotone . . . "the angel
of the Lord declared unto Mary" . . . to our inaudible
mumbled response . . . "and she conceived of the Holy
Ghost . . . hail, Mary, full of grace, the Lord is with
thee; blessed art thou among women . . ."

. . . and they'd steal a glance with aching heart and
with mouths dry as the bottom of a bird cage as Tomas
Larkin defied his way into Dooley McCluskey's public
house. It was said that McCluskey was so stingy he would
rather peel a potato in his pocket than share it. Despite
this he found it solid practice to stay on the good side
of Tomas Larkin and offer him a nightly drop, for Tomas
could stop the brawl or get repayment for breakage far
better than the Constabulary. . . .

On the night of Kilty's death, the men trudged on to
the village after another losing bout with the angelus.
Tomas emerged from McCluskey's with Conor just as I
was dusting off my knees. Father Cluny, the curate,
recently out of Maynooth Seminary in County Kildare,
padded nervously up the church path toward us. He
was reasonably likable, for a priest, and his presence
meant we had someone to teach us to read and write.
He was awkward, already too heavy from eight pounds

of potatoes a day and too little physical work, and he had quickly taken to aping Father Lynch's gestures, approaching us with hands tucked in cassock, then greeting us with a kind of pious papal wave.

"Your sorrow is shared by myself and Father Lynch."

"I'll thank you for that," Tomas answered.

"Might I be having a word with you?" the curate asked.

"Aye."

Father Cluny indicated by raised brow that the conversation was of a private nature and Tomas likewise indicated he was not sending us off. The priest seemed to have suddenly run out of courage, reinforcing his wind with a number of deep sighs. "There is a matter you must know," he began. "In his last moments, your beloved father got sudden apprehensions and desired to rescind his excommunication from mother church and sought absolution."

"Kilty . . . absolution. Aye, you're daft, man."

"Nae, it's the truth. Father Lynch himself performed the rite less than a week ago."

"Go on with you. Kilty would have drunk snake poison first. And why isn't Father Lynch here himself to deliver this blasphemy?"

The curate popped perspiration. "Knowing the feelings between you, we thought it best if I delivered the news."

"Nae, I don't believe it." Flicking it off, Tomas started away, leaving Father Cluny pawing the air and sputtering.

"Daddy," Conor said, "it's true."

Tomas stopped in his path and turned, looking queerly.

"It's true," Conor repeated.

"My God. I do think you're serious," he said.

"For the sake of the village and your family and in respect for the dead, I beg of you not to interfere when we bring Kilty to St. Columba's and hold a requiem mass."

"Kilty? A requiem mass?"

"He came back to the Church of his own free wish and those wishes should be honored."

"But, man, what are you telling me! How could such a thing like this have happened?"

"On the days I was teaching the lads in your cottage I came to know Kilty. I would stay on and visit with him . . . mind you, just talking . . . nothing underhanded. Indeed, it seemed to comfort his distress. A week ago,

sensing his end was near, he was stricken with a desperate
need to confess . . ."

"I don't believe you, Father Cluny. You were sent on
a dirty mission by that toothache of a man, Father
Lynch, and no doubt with the prodding and blessings
of my own wife . . . murping him up with fear!"

"As God is my judge," Father Cluny muttered,
flushing and backing off, "as God is my judge. Curse me
as you will, my duty is clear when a man begs absolution,
and it was no more than his immortal soul I was seeking
to save."

"Ohhhh," Tomas groaned, "it's all too foul . . . pin-
pricking him with innuendoes of hell, deftly prodding
your holy blather until you stripped him of the one dignity
he had left."

"It wasn't like that at all, Daddy," Conor interjected
strongly. "There were times, right up to the last day,
that Grandfar would see things clearly. I told him you
would go off into a fury but he insisted on absolution.
'Conor,' he said to me, 'in the unlikely event there is going
to be a life after death, I don't want it to be like the
life I've had before death.' Grandfar said he just didn't
want to take the chance of having to suffer again like he
did on earth."

"Why didn't you tell me! Creeping behind my back in a
bloody conspiracy!"

"Because, Daddy, we knew you'd try to stop it."

"And surely I would have! Taking advantage of a sick,
daft old man."

"Daft or no, Grandfar was entitled to his last wish."

"And you stood against your daddy!"

"Nae, Daddy. I stood for Kilty."

It grew terrifyingly quiet. I tell you now that Tomas
Larkin appeared twice as big as normal. I'll never forget
the look of him as he glared at us each in turn. His face
spoke of neither anger nor hatred, but utter contempt.
Contempt that a very strong man can dispense to the
weak. He left us heading up the hill with Conor racing
after him.

"Daddy!"

"Get home with you, Conor," he said softly.

"Daddy!" Conor pleaded.

"Just go home, lad. I need to be alone."

CHAPTER TWO: Kilty Larkin looked ever so grand laid out in the best room. There was none the equal of my mother, Mairead, in County Donegal when it came to scrubbing up and shaving and tidying a corpse for the waking. Moreover, she was the midwife of the Upper Village, having attended the birth of all the Larkin kids. It seemed she spent half her nights bringing new wanes into the world. Until the Protestant doctor came to the Township, she was often called down into Protestant homes to attend difficult births.

When we arrived at the cottage, Kilty's bed was burning in the yard as a further measure to ward off the fairies and inside he was stretched out on a wooden slab, held up by four chairs and covered saintlike with a fine white linen sheet . . . except for his face and his hands and his two big toes, which were tied together to keep him from returning as a ghost. Candles flickered about his head and a new pair of boots were at his feet to help his walk through purgatory. His eyes had been closed restful-like with a new carved stone crucifix on his chest and rosary beads entwined in folded hands. Never having seen old Kilty at prayer when he was alive, he surely looked like St. Columba himself, all stretched out and lovely.

The women of the village and the older folk who no longer worked in the fields were the first to arrive and Finola greeted them at the door.

"I'm sorry for your troubles."

" 'Tis a powerful loss."

"May he be dead for a year before the Devil hears of it."

"How are you keeping, old dear?"

"Bravely . . . bravely," Finola managed.

Moving on to the deceased, they "oh'd" and "ah'd" over the grand job my ma and Finola had done. "I've never seen him looking so much like himself."

They knelt, intoned a quick prayer and drifted to the fringes of the room. Brigid had filled dozens of small clay pipes with tobacco which had supernatural qualities

14

at times like this, and offered them about with a plate of snuff to hasten Kilty's journey and resurrection.

Three lambs had been slaughtered and an immense stew boiled in the great pot and a dozen loaves of fadge, a potato bread, browned on the baking boards and likewise our own kitchen throbbed into action, for the gathering would be large.

There were many foods we avoided because it reminded the elders of our poverty during the great famine and cheese was foremost among them, but cheese was always present at a wake, heaped unsparingly into wooden bowls. Finola flitted from greeting the mourners to the fire to the guests, prodding them to eat. Plunging into the cheese, they intoned, "We will sup this meal with a spoon of sorrow."

All the hill farmers lived in various stages of poverty, but the Larkins through defiance and stronger men always had more than the rest. Wealth, by our standards, was measured by the amount of butter one put on one's bread. There was a tiny patch of bog just beyond the first row of stone fences where a number of souterrains had been built to store and keep butter from becoming rancid. Liam arrived with two large pails of it, making it obvious that no expense was to be spared at this waking.

Finola was gifted with magic at the churn, a churn which was crafted minutely to her exact specifications, and her secret of pouring the skim milk to break the lumpiness was said to be a formula learned from the fairies. Her butter was velvet . . . rich, creamy, smooth, sumptuous, unadulteratedly glabrous.

Now, aside from the known fact that Conor was my closest friend and idol, one of the rewards of hanging around the Larkin cottage was a daily slice of bread and butter. "Don't be afraid of the butter," she would tell me and I would heap it on so that it was thicker than the bread itself. On it went in great swathing strokes like the Protestants troweling mortar between the stones of their houses.

Seeing Liam enter with those two enormous pails, I thought it would be an appropriate time to kneel at Kilty's feet and say a few Hail Marys. Just as I finished my prayers, a donkey belonging to the poteen-making widows was led into the room with creels filled with

bottles of mountain dew. The stew was thickening to a
boil and the room swelled with tobacco smoke when
who should arrive but Dooley McCluskey, that legendary
skinflint, still in his apron and bowler hat, his eyes always
screwed up in a squint from peering in the dark to see
that nobody cheated a drink. And what do you know!
Dooley McCluskey came with a dozen bottles of whiskey,
all legal, with government stamps on them, and from that
stingy man no greater compliment could be paid Kilty
Larkin. It was getting so crowded you could hardly pass a
straw between the people who were spilling over into the
byre and the yard.

Just like that, the noise outside screamed to a dead
halt and the silence rode in on a wave clear through the
cottage as Tomas Larkin appeared. He looked neither
to the left nor right nor acknowledged the whispered
condolences. The visitors parted like biblical floodwaters
as he moved toward his daddy and stood over him.

Knowing that Kilty sought absolution, a terrible tension
invaded the room. Would Tomas fall to his knees or rip
the place asunder? Well . . . he just sat alongside Kilty
laying his hand on his daddy's hand gently and the whole
place heaved a simultaneous gasp of relief. Conor came
to him and they gave wee sad smiles to one another. . . .
"Aye," Tomas said, ". . . aye." Dooley McCluskey took
off his bowler, held it over his heart and thrust a bottle of
whiskey in Tomas' direction which he nearly half did in
on a single go and then he took a pipe from Brigid,
patted her head and retreated into a corner.

The room sighed again.

It was the signal for Finola to commence keening.
She emitted a horrendous, piercing shriek that shivered
the place and dropped to her knees and crawled toward
the corpse. "Kilty! Kilty! I knew you were leaving us, for
I saw the banshee last night with my own eyes!"

Well now, that sobered things up. A frightened murmur
arose.

"Indeed!"

"Where, old dear?"

"I'll tell you," Finola gasped, afeared with the thought
of the terrible event. . . . "I was going into the byre . . .
there"—she pointed—"to feed the chicks. I remember a
glance to dear Kilty when I saw the sky graying up . . .

just like the day old Declan O'Neill took his leave from us. . . ."

"Aye," was the universal response of recollection, with universal signs of the cross and a magnetic inching closer to the now entranced mourner.

"Graying as it did, I struck a light and on me toes turned up the lantern, and as I did, I was thrown into a chill by a blowing dagger of ice and bringing on a fright for my unborn baby. The lantern blew out all by itself and I trembled to light it six times over, and each time it doused out, plunging the byre dark as a tomb!"

Jaysus, the room got quiet.

Palms was damp and mouths so dry that tongues was sticking to teeth.

"And then," she moaned weirdlike, "a glow came on all by itself. I turned ever so slow from the lantern and seen a shimmer at the far end of the byre. Fearing to go closer, I could not make out the body of it but over the face was . . . a shroud . . ."

"Hail Mary," someone said.

"The hair was long and raven mixed up with streaks of red and on the shroud . . . blood stains and teardrops."

"The banshee of Dooreen O'Neill! Sure and didn't I see the very same sight myself on the passing of my beloved Caley!" one of the poteen widows cried.

A spattering of screams and cries erupted but Finola overrode them. "She gave out a cackling laugh and said over and over . . . 'Kilty . . . Kilty . . . Kilty . . . Kill-tee . . . Kill-tee' . . . and as she did she kept reaching out for me and then . . . she melted . . . right into the ground. . . ."

"Sure it was the sign!"

"Kilty!" Finola screamed. "Sweet Kilty Larkin! God love you, Kilty! Oh, you've got away from us, sweet Kilty!" Weeping now, she kissed his feet. . . .

"Grandfar!" Liam cried, and soon the four of them, Finola and her three children, erupted into unabashed grief of the most intense order as Tomas sat in his corner quietlike nipping away at Dooley McCluskey's whiskey. Finola keened with a fervor that could have caused a thunder plump, clutching at the linen sheet that covered Kilty and howling in incoherent anguish.

Liam became hysterical, shrieking until he doubled over and convulsed. His daddy snatched him up, set him on his

lap and wrapped his great arms about him until the
writhing dulled to sobs.

Finola keened until the cottage was in a fever . . . for
she was the greatest keener of the entire east coast of
Inishowen and her lamenting for the dead so powerful
she was in the most heavy demand for wakes. Since the
death of her own parents she had not had close family to
keen over for a number of years and she was letting it all
out, intent on sending Kilty to the hereafter on a rainbow
of glory.

Conor and Brigid soon howled themselves into exhaustion and joined Liam on Tomas' lap, but Finola carried on
in the throes of exquisite agony. Being as I was quite little
and Tomas' lap quite big, I squeezed my way on too.

Swept up by her frenzy and struck fuzzy by the poteen,
a smattering of others, including my ma, were on their
knees keening with more wailing coming from that
cottage than from two thousand head of cattle on Fair
Day in Derry.

Finola's face had gone white as the paint on the priest's
house and her hair was a dishevelment of kelp, and wide
streaks from the gush of tears smeared her cheeks, dripping down her nose and chin and the corners of her lips,
and she sweated like she was being boiled in the big pot.
The belly holding her baby convulsed so jerkily I thought
surely it would be born at the feet of the deceased.

"You've had enough of your first wake," Tomas said,
"all of you scat to Seamus' house and go to sleep."
Conor's protest was overridden sternly and we were
ushered out with orders not to return.

With the rest of my brothers and sisters gone I had
only to share my sleeping place with Colm, who would be
waking and chasing girls through this whole night. We
had a space where the chickens roosted at night on a
huge soft mattress of bog fir, large enough to hold the
four of us. We tucked in close together. Although Conor
was my closest friend, I always recall trying to be next to
Brigid when we slept together for, although I loved
Conor, Brigid had a different feeling which I recognized
even then. I suspected that wanting to rub up against
Brigid had something to do with the sins Father Lynch
warned us of but I simply pretended not to know it was a
sin because it felt so good. Anyhow, Liam and Brigid
were soon dead out but Conor and I kept thrashing.

"Conor?"

"Aye."

"You asleep?"

"Nae."

"What you suppose is happening now?"

"Sure I don't know."

"Can you sleep at all?"

"Nae. My head's dinnling."

And after a time I said, ". . . Conor, you asleep?"

"Nae."

"Do you suppose your daddy would be fierce with us if we went back and hid up in your loft? What I'm thinking is, Kilty was your only living grandfar and I just know he'd want you to keep the waking with him."

There was a contemplative silence to weigh the pros and cons after which Conor intoned the magic words . . . "Let's go, runt."

We slipped out of my house with extreme care and with the stealth of cattle rustlers on his lordship's estate slithered over the wall. It was so boisterous now that we would have gone unnoticed if we were a pair of charging bulls. Conor threw the ladder up to the window opening of the loft and we scampered in, diving into the hay and burying ourselves and squeezing our quickened breath to a quiet.

The loft was the sleeping place for the Larkin kids. Aside from the window there were two other openings down into the cottage. A ladder through a trap door into the best room and, on the opposite side, another ladder into the byre housing the cattle, horse and chickens. The Larkins made the pigs live outside. From the loft we had a splendid view of all the doings.

With the heavy lamenting over for a time, the older folks tucked in their niches, smoking away on clay pipes, playing cards and telling stories. Some of the young wanes scampered about stuffing pepper into the teapots and tobacco jars, setting off sneezing seizures, while outside the bachelor boys and spinster girls snuck into the shadows to play kissing games and perform mock marriages. There was a group of troublemakers too gawky to mix with girls who amused themselves by a water fight right in the best room, and just near the corpse a group of older men engaged in a dexterity contest, holding a broom handle in both hands and leaping back and forth through

it. Directly opposite them, on the far side of the corpse, a
dozen women knelt in prayer and keening. The water
fight took on a heightened dimension with the addition of
potatoes as missiles which buzzed alarmingly close to the
worshipers. Just outside, Donall MacDevitt, Finola's
cousin from the next village, passed around a bottle of
ether to a group lifting weights and leaping a stone wall.
In a matter of minutes they were tore out of their minds,
staggering crazy and doubled up laughing like maniacs
and thinking they was birds trying to fly off the roof or
over the wall, bashing themselves fearfully but feeling
nary a thing. Someone broke out a fiddle and bagpipe and
them that wasn't singing revolutionary songs kicked up
their heels in a jig, and the widow women were getting
their juices stirred looking over the eligibles in a way that
spelled no good at all. Arguing broke out over arguable
subjects, which covered just about anything. . . . Ah, it
was a grand wake, a grand wake indeed. Had he not been
dead, Kilty would have been the proudest man alive and
surely he was making an impression on St. Peter and all
the angels for having so many darling friends.

"Shhhh," Conor said, nudging me. Someone was
climbing the ladder from the outside. We burrowed into
the hay, leaving only room for our noses to breathe and
our eyes to see. Sure it was Billy O'Kane helping Bridie
O'Doherty into the loft and in no time at all they were
thrashing about and giggling and his hands were reaching
under her petticoats. Me and Conor clutched each other
to keep from breaking out laughing. Just as suddenly,
Billy and Bridie stopped their spooning and dived under
cover as they heard someone else coming up the ladder,
and just that quick, Maggie O'Donnelly and my own
brother Colm had entered the loft and were having at it.

Fortunately the wake was off bounds for Father Lynch
and Father Cluny, but we all knew they were stationed in
some shadowy place within earshot to amass evidence of
bawdiness, nudity, dirty language, ether drinking, kissing,
or worse . . . and all the other things in their endless
catalogue of carnal sins.

Father Lynch had so much as forbidden boys and girls
to walk on the same side of the road together, always
hovering like a sharp-eyed gannet over every gathering,
watching for members of the opposite sex touching, giving
endearing glances and, by Christ, he could tell if anyone

was even thinking about it. His blackthorn stick put a
lump on many a head as it struck into the haystacks of
Ballyutogue like God's own lightning rod.

It was a good thing he wasn't in the house of Tomas
Larkin this night because the loft was getting severely
crowded. Our amusement turned to awe at the things they
were starting to do to each other. Just as it was getting
the most interesting, a fearsome thing happened. Some
hay tickled my nose so that I burst into a sneezing spell.
Heads popped up all over the loft.

"Jaysus!"

"Holy Mother, have mercy!"

"Tell the priest and I'll kill you, Seamus," my very
own brother said to me.

They poured out of the loft like it was on fire. However, the entertainment soon continued as our attention
was drawn down to the byre where Dinny O'Kane and
Bertie MacDevitt were bashing each other around to a
fare thee well . . . winging in punches that clouted off
their noggins with accompanying grunts. Their blows had
little aim and less power but the cows were getting upset
and would be giving off sour milk for a week.

It was only a matter of time for this fight to have
occurred, for there was bad blood between the O'Kanes
and MacDevitts as a matter of historical tradition.

Those two had gone into a partnership that was bound
to end in disaster. One day, when in a brotherly mood,
they decided to buy a horse together. The animal had to
be purchased early in the spring for the plowing and then
sold after the last harvest to carry their families through
the winter. Therefore the buying and selling of a horse
was serious business.

In order to pay for his half of the horse, Dinny O'Kane
went over the water to work at the Liverpool docks
during cattle shipping season and, for his half, Bertie
MacDevitt harvested Dinny's crops.

Figuring they knew just about everything about horseflesh between them, they set out to swindle a tinker horse
trader at the Carndonagh Fair and laughed up their
sleeves all the way home.

However, Dinny felt he got the worst end of the deal
because he had to work in England and, to add insult,
Bertie got first use of the horse by a flip of the coin.

Now, wouldn't you know. The nag no more than

finished plowing Bertie's fields when it up and died of the heart. From then on the complications became monumental.

The two of them reeled about the byre, more jarred by the poteen than by each other's blows, with O'Kanes and MacDevitts squaring off all over the place and the O'Neills leaning toward the O'Kanes and the O'Dohertys favoring the MacDevitts. It was shaping up into an epic when the peacemaker arrived in the person of Tomas Larkin. He seemed as big as the two of them together, wrapping his right arm about Bertie's waist and lifting him off the ground and at the same time holding Dinny off at arm's length.

"Gentlemen, gentlemen," Tomas warned.

The two combatants continued to swing at the air, careful not to make contact with Tomas while hurling appropriate observations at each other.

"I'll be after banging your heads together if you don't stop," Tomas said, but brush fires had erupted all over the byre.

"Very well. I'm turning the matter over to Father Lynch."

Hostilities screeched to a halt. Tomas and his gladiators sat down in the hay, gasping for breath and mopping up their cuts.

"I'll settle on Tomas' word if you will," Dinny panted.

"Only in the name of peace and for the memory of the departed do I agree," Bertie said, "for you're a loathsome . . ."

"Now, now, now," Tomas interrupted.

"Well?" Dinny said.

"Well . . . all right . . ."

Tomas shook his head. "Aye, it's bending my mind. 'Tis a problem for Solomon. Is there a wee drop about so I can illuminate my thoughts?" A stupendous slug disappeared down his throat and he wiped his mouth with an "ah." "In my eyes a partnership should share disasters as well as rewards."

"What did I tell you," Dinny said, poking a fist under Bertie's nose.

"Shut up till I'm finished," Tomas explained. "I will lend you my horse, Dinny, to plow your fields on the condition that Bertie brings in your crops."

"But we've no horse to sell later, Tomas!"

"Aye, and that is because you both went to the fair with larceny in your hearts to cheat the tinker . . ."

"But . . ."

"But . . ."

"That is my decision, gentlemen. And if you follow my advice, I'll see to it that everyone in the village contributes a share of crops so you'll make the winter . . . on the condition you buy no more horses together because the two of you couldn't tell if you were looking at a horse's arse if it shit on your boots."

After performing his saintlike miracle, Tomas got to his feet, pulled Dinny and Bertie to theirs and suggested it would be wise if they shook hands in front of him. . . .

"They're starting the rosary."

Energy had run low in the outpour of communal grief and, laced with ether, liquor and exuberance, it was high time for everyone to get on their knees and pray. Finola crawled once more to Kilty's corpse and, as she did, I felt nausea overtaking me. I always got sick when they got to reciting "Mary's Crown."

If I am barred from heaven it will be because of the rosary, for even though I tried not to think unkind thoughts about it God knows everything, including my true feelings, and He knows the most torturous hours of my life were spent in its recitation and it is an established fact that no one will ever be made to say it over my dead body.

I brushed the hay off me as I got to my knees, blowing off sighs of anguish as I did.

"Aw, you don't have to say it, Seamus," Conor said.

I was too scared not to.

"We can pretend to be asleep or even go back to your house."

"Nae," I groaned, "God will know, anyhow."

"Don't go getting sick," Conor warned.

I crossed myself . . . "I believe in God the Father almighty creator of heaven and earth and in Jesus Christ His only son our Lord born of the Virgin Mary suffered under Pontius Pilate was crucified and was buried on the third day He arose again from the dead . . ."

I finished this part ahead of everyone so I could round up some wind. The candles below fought for a last gasp of life, bounding crazy shadows off the worn shiny face of Kilty Larkin, and outside the wind crept up from the

lough and as it drifted through the loft I knew that
weather would not be far behind. As they droned on my
stomach got queasier so I closed my eyes and gritted and
prayed through clamped teeth . . . one sign of the cross,
four Lord's prayers, six Glory be to the Fathers, five
sorrowful mysteries and fifty three Hail Marys' worth. . . .

"The first sorrowful mystery," Finola moaned, "the
agony in the garden."

They were the weary down there, the craggy-faced,
knobby, leather-handed toilers rehearsing their own
demise, yielding in pitiful weakness to the scythe of
mystery kept poised a lifetime at their jugulars . . . too
simple and too tired to protest . . . too frightened to seek
the truth . . . succumbed in silence, for without it . . . what
was there left to believe?

Five minutes . . . ten minutes . . . fifteen minutes . . .
beat the heart, nod the head . . . drone, drone, drone.
Who knew what they were saying any longer? Who ever
really knew except the priest and you don't question him.

I was determined to be good this night for the soul of
Kilty Larkin and I concentrated till my head hurt, thinking about the agony of sweet Jesus, and I made myself
feel his pain because that was what I was supposed to do,
and the reason for that was because Jesus was so good
and I was a sinner. I was going to taste the salty sweat
and buckle under the cross and the blood was going to
drip from my crown and squirt out of my wrists like it
never did before.

Oh shit, my stomach was starting to go and Conor
would be mad.

Outside the sky was blackening like it did the day they
crucified our blessed Lord Jesus and now God Himself
was looking down on the Larkin cottage and God was
looking at me because He knew I hated the rosary. I was
getting scared of feelings I couldn't hide even though God
was looking right at me, so I tried more and more to feel
the pain of Jesus.

"Our Father, who art in heaven . . .

"Hail, Mary, full of grace."

How many does that make? I think thirty-four but I
shouldn't count because that is a sin because you're
supposed to love the rosary. . . .

"Glory be to the Father and the Son and the Holy
Ghost."

Twenty minutes . . . twenty hours . . . twenty-three minutes . . . nod the head . . . beat the heart . . . sometimes it all blurs together and it isn't so bad.

At least once a week I threw up during the rosary. The harder I tried to think of Jesus and his suffering the more I threw up. I just didn't know what to do.

Thirty minutes . . . forty minutes . . . forty years in the wilderness . . .

"Jesus, you're pale, Seamus. You going to vomit?"

"I . . . I'll try not . . ."

"Stop praying."

"I have to finish, Conor. We're at the act of contrition and if I say a good one maybe God won't punish me."

"Why would God want to punish you?"

"For hating the rosary. . . ."

"Aw, you got nothing to fear. My daddy said God never made up the bloody rosary in the first place, and in the second, He isn't even listening."

Conor scared me when he spoke like that. "Don't say no more. If you do I'll have to confess for hearing you."

"Aw, my daddy says God's got more important things to do than listen to a little pisser reciting Mary's Crown."

I clamped both hands over my ears so I wouldn't hear any more. . . . "Oh, my Savior, I am truly sorry for having offended you because you are infinitely good and sin displeases you. I detest all the sins of my life . . ."

Conor grabbed my wrists and pulled my hands away from my ears. "What sins! You're only eleven years old!"

I jerked away from him and dove into the hay and held my breath, closing my ears very, very hard. . . . "I detest all the sins of my life," I prayed with crazy fervor, "and I desire to atone for them through the merits of your precious blood; wash from my soul all stain of sin so that, cleansed in body and soul, I may worthily approach the Most Holy Sacrament of the Altar . . ."

When Conor pulled me up I was sobbing and shaking and he held me like I was himself on his own daddy's lap. "Take it easy, runt . . . I'll take care of you."

In the best room the gathered throng came to their feet in infinite weariness and most of them took leave, trudging stooped to their own cottages with only the family and dearest friends left to continue waking with the corpse.

CHAPTER THREE: I was still quaking from my latest calamity with the rosary when that familiar brigade of rain charged up the hill from the lough and assaulted the cottage.

The Larkins had fled to Donegal at the beginning of the century and after eighty-five years still kept the County Armagh manner of thatching their roofs by scalloping, whereas we had the simpler method of roping the thatchings with sally rods. Despite the fierceness of the weather, never a drop found its way through the Larkin roof. We were content as field mice in the harvest bin, dozing off at a rapid pace, when a flurry of excitement in the best room sent us crawling once more to the trap door.

No less a personage than Daddo Friel, the first storyteller of all Inishowen, had arrived. Conor and I knew very little of the world beyond, only hearing of it second-hand at the fairs or from wandering tinkers, or when our kin returned from working "over the water" in England. The only thing we had to read was a tattered volume of catechisms.

The arrival of a shanachie, a storyteller, was a powerful event for us, for it was he who kindled the flames of boyhood dreams. Daddo Friel was a most honored member of that special breed, able to speak with clarity of events that had taken place hundreds of years before.

He was lame and nearly sightless in his right eye and his left was just as bad. Tomas led him to Kilty. He felt over the corpse with knowing and tender hands. "Aye, there was a lad . . . there was a lad," he said, and two salty tears made their way through the crevices of his face.

"Tomas, get him out of those wet clothes. He's soaked clear through," Finola said.

In a few moments the turf fire was renewed and old Daddo was made comfortable and warmed by a measure of poteen and another one more, also. Hearing of his presence, the gathering increased, waiting for his dialogue, which came in a clear voice that belied his age.

Daddo always began his personal recollections in 1803, the year he was born. The date was immortalized by the

26

hanging of Robert Emmet for an attempted insurrection. Emmet stood right up to the British, delivering an immortal and inspired speech from the dock. You'd think by the way Daddo was reciting it he had been in the courtroom at the time instead of weaning at his ma's tits.

From Emmet he brought up the great and magic name of Daniel O'Connell, recounting the times Kilty and himself walked so much as a hundred miles to hear "the liberator" speak at monster rallies before more than a million people. Because he was a shanachie of stature, nobody bothered to check his mileage or the real size of the crowds.

Next came the Fenian Rising of '67 and the year and four months he and Kilty spent in the Derry bridewell being tortured from sunup to sundown and what affronts Daddo didn't have for the British he had for mother church which excommunicated the pair of them.

When Daddo Friel got going on the Catholic Church and all the bishops, he made everyone nervous, including myself, who had heard enough heresy for one day. But Daddo had seen both sides of eighty years, coming and going, and when a man is that old you just listen respectfully.

Although he was in full glory and would be captivating his listeners for several more hours, I couldn't hold off sleep any longer. His voice and the voice of the rain began to run together and my eyes grew awfully heavy.

When I woke it was morning. Conor had fallen asleep at the trap door trying to inhale every last word. I crept to the window. It was a real Ulster bleezer outside, with the wind blowing so stiff it caused the rain to fall almost horizontal. In the best room a mess of bodies were strewn about, some curled up near the fire and others stretched on the table and chairs or propped up against the wall. Likewise, the byre was filled with guests packed in the empty stalls.

Tomas Larkin himself sat motionless close to Kilty, his eyes so shot they looked like they belonged to a salt mackerel.

My heart bolted suddenly on realizing that all three ladders to the loft had been removed and we were prisoners. I woke Conor and whispered our predicament. We waited, hoping Tomas would take leave, giving us a chance to get down unnoticed. Finola plodded behind him so that her big belly pressed against his back. She stroked his hair. I liked this so much about the Larkins, the fondness they had for touching each other.

"Dirty weather," Tomas said without looking up.

"Are you feeling sorely toward me about Kilty taking absolution?"

He shook his head. "Maybe not. Nothing less than I should have expected. It's done . . . it's done."

"Don't get your anger up against Father Lynch. It will do no good . . . and besides, Tomas, the father isn't all that hard."

"Hard? The softest thing about that man is his teeth."

"Tomas," she pleaded, "you'll not be making a scene at the mass."

He looked up, smiled and patted her hand. . . . "Don't worry," he said.

Finola sighed with relief, then grabbed her stomach. "The baby's been kicking up a riot. I think it wants to come early. Ah, now look at you. I've seen better-looking specimens laid out at a wake. Get yourself to the sweat house and have a steam. I'll start a fire for you . . ."

"Nae, I'll not let you go out in that rain." Looking up to the loft, he stabbed us with his eyes. "All right. Down with the both of you."

Caught red-handed, we hung from the trap door and dropped into the best room with a thud, coming to rigid attention before him.

"If I recollect," Tomas said, "you were sent next door to sleep. Well?"

"Aye, Daddy," Conor gulped.

"Well!"

"We just couldn't sleep."

"But surely the rosary put us to sleep," I added quickly.

"Fire up the sweat house," he commanded, "and it better be hot or I know two lads who are going to get the skinning of their lives."

We rushed off, relieved by our reprieve. The sweat house was a small round corbeled stone affair shaped like a beehive, owned commonly by a number of families, and used to manufacture intense heat to ease the pain of rheumatism, the constant ailment of the damp weather.

We stacked a heap of straw in the fire pit and set a dozen bricks of turf on it, then laid on an iron grate and covered that with a bed of river rocks. The straw soon

fired the turf, turning the place into an oven. Tomas
Larkin entered naked, hunched over sitting on a creepie,
and groaned the miseries out of him as we fanned the
fire furiously until the turf held an angry glow. When it
was hot enough to boil the Devil we lifted a bucket of
water together, coughing and sweating for Tomas' benefit
to show him how earnest we were. We poured it over the
rocks, sending up a sizzling vapor and a heat so intense it
nearly melted our fingernails. Tomas gushed poteen and
sweat like a spring thaw, then crawled out of the low
opening and flung himself into the icy pond that fronted
the sweat house, beating on his chest.

"Ah, that's grand! Grand!" he bellowed.

Having seen the smoke rise, neighbors in as bad or
worse condition staggered in for a communal roasting.

Thus the second day of the wake commenced with
callers arriving from distant towns. By afternoon the
winds had swept the weather toward Scotland, leaving a
fast-moving line of broken clouds that allowed teasing
glimpses of sunshine.

The placidness was punctured by the arrival at the
crossroads of a sidecar being driven by a splendid oversized Connemara pony. It was convoyed down the village
road by a bevy of prancing children while a dozen others
piled into the cart. It halted before the Larkin cottage,
creating uncommon commotion. Kevin O'Garvey was
helped down from his carriage by a half dozen pairs of
solicitous hands. The guardian and protector of the tenant
farmers himself had come all the way from Derry to pay
final respects to Kilty Larkin.

CHAPTER FOUR: Often as not, my ma would end a
dissertation with the words, "Seamus my darling, when
you're old enough to grow a beard, may you be half the
man of Kevin O'Garvey."

Looking him over, you'd never have a clue to his
importance. He was short as my daddy, who was the
shortest man in the village, and appeared even shorter
because of a potbelly. There was no hair at all in the
middle of his head, being fringed on top by a horseshoe
thatching of gray stubble which popped straight up when

he removed his high bowler. His eyes were poorly, encased in thick spectacles. A morning coat of fine tweed set him apart from us in manner of dress, but close inspection betrayed a fraying of the velvet collar and a general encroachment of shabbiness of his whole attire.

Kevin O'Garvey was our champion, head of the Land League for Counties Donegal and Derry, which had lifted the onus of serfdom from the tenant farmers. As the League began winning too many rights for us it was naturally declared illegal and when Charles Stewart Parnell, himself, was jailed in Kilmainham in Dublin, Kevin O'Garvey was interned in the Derry bridewell. It was a familiar place for him, having been guest of the Crown twice previously for membership in the Fenians, the secret republican brotherhood.

Kevin O'Garvey getting to be Kevin O'Garvey wasn't all that easy, starting life as he did as a foundling, a kiss of death for many children. He survived to be raised in the most fearsome orphanage in Ulster. By seven, he was hired out, as orphans were, to a poor farm operated by Lord Hubble's estate for slave wages, and by the time he was nine he was doing time in the borstal for stealing, boozing and cursing the Crown.

Back and forth from workhouse to borstal, he was well on the way to becoming an incorrigible when fate took a hand. O'Garvey was sent on trial to a Protestant solicitor in Ballymoney, a town no bigger than a wide spot in the road, which had gained a measure of prosperity as a railhead for the iron mines. Working as a stableboy, he began an inspirational story, teaching himself to read and write by candlelight, an ordeal that led to the ruination of his eyes. So bright a penny he was, the solicitor took him into his office and in no time at all he was deviling legal briefs of the highest quality. Kevin went on to become one of the rare Catholic lawyers in Ulster, returning to Derry and giving his life to the betterment of croppy and slum dweller alike.

Law was something queer to us, as foreign as African tribal rites. Although we were under it, manipulated and maligned by it, it was ever kept as a grandiose and mystical force beyond our knowledge. All those connected to law—the Crown and the courts and the soldiers reading edicts—were bullies forcing us into a game played by their rules and spoken in a language only they understood.

We knew little about our rights and nothing at all about
the ability to use law. Law remained a bludgeon owned by
Lord Hubble and the Protestants, and we'd no manner of
defense against their judges all dressed up like princes
and their documents all covered with seals.

And then Kevin O'Garvey came along, able to read
their statutes and pick them naked. Having someone to
defend the croppies at their own game came as a shock to
the British. After making the fool of their barristers, he
tied the courts into knots, twisting and maneuvering their
petty rules against them. Don't you know he became a
bone in their throats. They tried pretty near everything,
bribery, harassment and finally jail, but queer things
would happen whenever he was put behind bars, like his
lordship's hunting lodge mysteriously burning down. The
authorities didn't like us having either knowledge or
access to their laws, but they disliked the results of tam-
pering with Kevin O'Garvey even more.

After paying amenities to the Larkins and old Kilty, he
was engulfed and listened to the endless woes with endless
patience.

On the second night of the wake Conor and I decided
it would be prudent not to tempt the wrath of Tomas
twice in so short a time, and went to my byre to sleep
slightly before the rosary was to start. Liam and Brigid
were already dead to the world and my brother Colm,
destroyed by drink, ether and chasing the night before,
lay on his back with his mouth gaping like a nesting
birdlet begging for a worm and snoring so loud we
thought he'd wake Kilty from the dead.

Voices came from the best room and natural curiosity
brought us to the half door for a peek. All huddled
around the fire and puffing away at their pipes were my
daddy Fergus, Tomas, Daddo Friel and Kevin O'Garvey,
as impressive a gathering as you'd ever want to see in
Ballyutogue. Conor and I whispered back and forth excitedly. We were certain that it could only mean a highly
secret meeting on republican matters.

Then, just like his eyes could see through stone walls,
Tomas flung the door open, tumbling us into the best
room. "You'd think these lads would be dead from the
lack of sleep," he said.

"I'm sure they're just following your example," Kevin
retorted.

Knowing we wouldn't sleep now, Tomas glanced to
Kevin, who nodded to say it was all right for us to remain.
It was high honor indeed. On the other hand, nothing of a
republican nature was ever kept from us. Our earliest
heroes were escapees from the Crown hidden in the village
and spirited to the next underground station.

"Bring us a bottle from the widows," Tomas ordered
Conor, and to me he pointed to a corner. "Make yourself
even smaller than you are."

When Conor returned we tucked away, keenly watching every puff and stare they made at the fire. The bottle
was passed, swigged in turn, and followed by a great
Irish sigh of remorse.

"Kilty got away from us at a bad time," Kevin said.
"Even as half a man he held a powerful image."

"Aye," my daddy agreed, "we'll not see the likes of
him passing this way again."

"You'll have to keep on taking up the slack for him,
Tomas," Kevin said.

Tomas shook his head. "I'm not willing or able to carry
Kilty's burdens."

"You've already been doing it since he suffered his first
stroke. Whether or not you like it or want it, everyone
will be turning to you now. You'll not close your door on
them any more than I've been able to."

"It's the Larkin fate," Daddo said, "the Larkin fate."

"I don't know," Tomas opined. "It's one matter to
settle village quarrels or tell a man who he should coor
his horse with. But taking up Kilty's war against the
British . . . nae, it's not for me."

"You've got to, Tomas. We're coming into a new era.
For the first time in seven hundred years the tenant
farmer has the right to vote and it's going to be up to
you to see that everyone in these parts does."

"You're digging with the wrong foot," Tomas answered.

"There's a new atmosphere sweeping England. An
atmosphere of reform."

"They must have gotten wind about the revolution that
took place in France last century," Tomas retorted.

"Gladstone is of a different breed than the aristocracy,"
Kevin continued.

"Gladstone, my old sow's tits," Tomas interrupted.
"Scratch under his skin and you'll find an Englishman
complete with an English heart. There's not been one

born yet who understands that we're anything but a race of apes. What has their bloody Parliament ever doled out but cleverly worded destitution . . ."

"Stop your jibbering," Daddo snapped. "Can't you see that Kevin is attempting to tell us something?"

It never failed to amaze me how Daddo, near blind and ancient as he was, could feel the mood of a person by the pitch or quiver of his voice or even the length of silence between thoughts. Indeed, he was right again, for what we witnessed was Kevin O'Garvey in a rare moment of hesitation.

"What are you trying to say, Kevin?" Daddo repeated.

"I'm running for the House of Commons for the East Donegal seat the next election."

Well, you would have thought those fairies who had been hovering about waiting to snatch Kilty's soul suddenly turned on our best room and struck everyone into stone. It was that shocked. Kevin was unnerved by the sound of his own voice. The bottle passed silently but swiftly from hand to hand. Conor and I turned blue from holding our breath in tension.

"Jaysus," my daddy mumbled at last.

First to regain his senses, Tomas emitted a low whistle. "And I suppose," he said, "Lord Hubble will finance your campaign and all the Prods and Orangemen will carry you to London on their shoulders and Major Hamilton Walby, who's held the seat for thirty years, will be waiting to usher you in and dust it off."

"I never thought I'd get it without a fight but we've enough votes if you stop leaning on your shovel."

"And if it looks like you're going to prevail over Major Walby and the Earl and all that bunch," Tomas went on, acting the Devil's advocate, "what about mother church?"

"I've not thought too much about it," Kevin answered, backing down.

"I can see it clear as the lough in the full moon," Tomas went on. "All up and down Inishowen there's that old republican stirring. O'Garvey for Commons and pretty soon his lordship is drumming his fingers on the table top nervouslike after figuring out the croppies may have enough votes. Quick! Right to the heart of the matter. His lordship and a few other lordships with the same problem will be paying our Cardinal a little social visit in Armagh. 'Ah, Your Eminence, we extol the continued emancipation and betterment of the Roman Church. This must not be allowed to be deterred or reverted.' They'll be ladling out good will drippings on His Holiness like they was the liberator, Daniel O'Connell. 'Your Worship, we've been considering the next great steps forward ... new legislation in your behalf ... a new college ... new privileges ... new subsidies and increased gifts from ourselves for your various good works. Her Majesty's Government is all for that, you know. *However,* this program would be put in jeopardy by *atheist* Fenians trying to compel their way into Parliament and you *know* what *that* would mean to mother church. *Fenians!* The very sort excommunicated by yourself. Now, Your Worship, it would be a pity to see all the gains you've made go to waste. We respectfully submit you have a chat with your bishops and offer them a word to the wise.' And Father Lynch and all the Father Lynches will be condemning you from every pulpit in Donegal. Have you enough votes to overcome Jesus, Mary and all the saints?"

My daddy was red-faced and I tried to crawl inside my own stomach. I'd never heard so much revilement of the Lord in two days running. Tomas had worked himself into a small rage but Kevin and Daddo had been at war too many years to be jolted.

Few men, including the priest, could admonish Tomas, Kevin being one of them, Daddo the other, and he was between the two. My daddy sort of drifted out of range of the discussion, merely shaking his head at the implications of it. Kevin refilled his pipe with deliberate slowness, allowing Tomas' boil to slow to a simmer.

"If the wind is out of your bagpipe," Kevin said at last, "let me try to put over what kind of stakes we're shooting for. Parnell calculates he can take an Irish Party into the British Parliament holding some seventy seats. Seventy seats, mind you, unquestionably the balance of power between the Liberals and Conservatives. His price for cooperation with Gladstone's Liberals will be a Home Rule Bill for Ireland ..."

"You're putting too much on Parnell," Tomas cut in. "In the end Parnell is a rich Protestant, a landowner. Oh, he's got a good line of gab all right, but what he's doing is using us and our misery in his own personal drive for power."

It was not fair to say that Kevin looked Tomas in the

eye, being that much shorter, but he flushed with anger. "I'll thank you to shut up, Tomas Larkin! Parnell has done more for this country than all the Roman collars put together."

"Well, that's not saying a hell of a lot!"

"I'm going to tell you once who Charles Stewart Parnell is and don't you forget it . . . he's an Irishman."

"Same like Smith O'Brien and Isaac Butt," Daddo said, "who spent many an hour guiding me and Kilty in Young Ireland and the Land League. They was Prods, too . . . to say nothing of Wolfe Tone and Robert Emmet, who was executed in the Liberties of Dublin on the very same year I was born. Hanged he was, and drawn and quartered and his blood sucked up off the pavement. He was a Prod but he was Irish."

"God love you, Kevin," Tomas said, switching to the conciliatory, the icy logic and the cold approach, "there's not an iota of sense to this entire exercise. It's a dirty game you're playing with yourself and a dirty illusion you're holding up to us. So what if you do go roaring into London at the end of your rainbow with seventy members of Parliament and you force Gladstone to pass a Home Rule Bill . . . tell me . . . tell me one honest thing . . . will the House of Lords veto it . . . yes or nae?"

"It's not the point at all."

"Then what the hell is the point!"

"Continuing the war on a new field of battle . . . taking the first step in a new direction open to us . . ."

"You've no more chance of getting a fair hearing in their chambers than winning the straw game at the Derry Fair."

"Nae," Daddo said with his old voice now showing its wear. "Kevin's got to do battle in his way like we all did before him in our own way. Are you telling Kevin that all the fighting he's done and all the rights he's won have been for naught?"

"I would never tell Kevin O'Garvey that," Tomas said, "but I'll tell him this. In the end there is only one thing Lord Hubble and the Crown understand . . . withhold his rents . . . rustle his cattle . . . assassinate his gombeen men . . . boycott his fields when he needs our labor. But don't get yourself into his parlor and try to play his parlor games. It will never be his laws that make our life bearable, but our time-honored methods."

"Up to this point his time-honored methods have been a hell of a lot more effective than our time-honored methods," Kevin retorted. "There is a sin in all of this, Tomas, and that sin is for you to tell me to stop trying."

An uncertain silence fell on the room. My daddy set new turf in the fire while the other three sort of hung in mid-air with their thoughts. Tomas took up a slow pace that increased in sulkiness, then gave to tugging at his hair and cracking his fist in an open palm in frustration. As he did, the others closed in tighter to the fire, waiting for his last words. He stopped, held his arms apart as though he could devour them in one sweep, then waved his hands about as though trying to pick thoughts from the air.

"What we are," he said, "is consumed by the pair of Irish fantasies. We have submitted as a people to a Christ fantasy that has dulled our minds to think for ourselves and kept us on our knees pleading guiltily to a terrifying God whom we are not permitted to know as an intimate . . . but only to perpetuate a vaguely defined, unquestioned myth of a land beyond the mountains. And . . . the republican fantasy that fills us with false, childlike courage when we're bragging about our manhood in the shebeen, telling each other what brave lads we are. Glorifying deeds that were never done and feeding ourselves republican saltpeter for a liberation we'll never live to see. Never! For God's sake, never, facing up to what is real. We're never out of our fantasies long enough to look at ourselves and say, 'This is what we are. The fields are real. The rents are real. Kilty's death is real as was his pain in life.' Nae, but we have to smother in the sauces of fantasy, hovering fairies, the smile of Mary and her promises of the hereafter, the jail breaks that never took place. You deal in fantasy, Daddo, you're the shanachie."

"Aye," the old man answered. "The problem being that most of the poor bastards aren't Tomas Larkins. Strip the fantasy away from most men and women and they won't be able to make it through this dirty life. All a dream is, is a bit of poteen to dull the pain. Is it all that bad? And are you telling me, Tomas, that Conor over there is not to be allowed to have a few dreams of his own?"

Tomas came to us awesomely. "I'm telling Conor that I'm not the son of Kilty, only his follower. I'm telling

him that the only thing that matters for his daddy is
to farm his land well, pay his debts, feed his children,
and pass his fields along in good order. Wrap yourself
in Irish fantasies, lad, and it will end up crushing your
chest like a giant boulder rolling amok down the mountainside and tumbling the cottage."

I watched their four soiled and weary faces, hoping
that a spark would ignite them, but they had stripped
each other of their wild Irish dreams, and even as Tomas
told Kevin he would support him there was no celebration
in it.

"You've my pity," Tomas said, "for the day Home
Rule becomes a threat you'll have a reality all right
enough. Howling Orange mobs whipped to hate and
screaming for our blood. Is that fair enough, Daddo?"

The old man's blinded eyes stared foggily into infinity.
And tears of reality fell.

CHAPTER FIVE: My daddy and Tomas left to see
Kevin O'Garvey off. The Larkin house was still overrun
with wakers so we were told to bed Daddo down before
our hearth. Conor fetched another bottle of poteen from
the widows while I made up a mattress of hay, covering
it with Ma's prize goose-down quilt she'd got with her
egg money from a tinker at the Muff Fair before I
was born. I puffed up the fire till Conor returned and
directed a bottle into Daddo's hands.

"Your daddy was the biggest dreamer of them all no
matter what he says," Daddo said to Conor. "I knew
Tomas from his first scream as a newborn . . . sure, he
was no more than half the size of Seamus there when
me and Kilty was carting him clear over Donegal to
hear Daniel O'Connell."

Yet another healthy measure of poteen found its
way down that ancient gullet on the path well worn by
many a gallon before it.

"Help me to the straw," he said.

Conor and I moved him onto the mattress, his joints
creaking like they were loosely welded. We propped his
back up against the wall and dimmed the lantern,
leaving only a wee glow from the turf fire. Being so

little had its advantages. I nestled close to him while
Conor pulled up a creepie.

"The biggest dreamer of them all," he repeated slowly,
undoing the wrappings around his hands and revealing
a mass of rheumatic swollen knuckles. He splashed
them with poteen, rubbing it in and grunting as he
attempted to flex his fingers.

"Tomas is no less a Larkin than Kilty even though
his ways are different. I knew all the Larkins. I knew
your great-grandfar, Ronan, as well as your great-
uncles. The family fled to Inishowen from Armagh
shortly before I was born . . . that would be the year of
eighteen and three, the selfsame year they hanged
Emmet in Dublin."

We became duly entranced by the spell as the ancient
shanachie ascended on a wisp of reverie with his
thoughts prancing about like a mischievous fairy. With
merely the two of us, myself and Conor, as his honored
listeners, he fished about for that moment in time to
begin the odyssey of the Larkins.

*

By the end of the seventeenth century the Irish had
dissipated their energy fighting a dozen rebellions against
the British rule. The O'Neill clan had been the most
troublesome, rising no less than three times during the
1600s alone. Most of their land had already been seized
by the British aristocracy, who dispossessed them and replaced them by the importation of tens of thousands of
Scots. Ulster was colonized in the form of a plantation to
protect the Crown against the Catholic natives.

Oliver Cromwell zenithed the slaughter against the
Irish and, after crushing yet another O'Neill rising, took
whatever land was left of the ancient pale around Inishowen and Ballyutogue for back pay to his officers and
soldiers. When Cromwell was finished with his work the
Catholics owned less than five per cent of their own
country and the most of them were banished west of the
River Shannon . . . to hell or Connaught.

In order to break any future spirit of rebellion and to
assure their conquest, a future Dublin Parliament of
British Protestant ascendancy would pass a set of penal
laws which were to reduce the Catholics to chattel status
without human rights.

No Catholic was permitted to own land.

No Catholic was permitted to vote.

No Catholic was allowed to hold public office.

No Catholic was allowed to work in the civil service.

No Catholic was allowed to own a weapon.

No Catholic was allowed to own property of value over £5.

No Catholic was allowed to be educated in or out of Ireland.

No Catholic could earn more than one third of the value of his crops.

No Catholic was permitted to practice as a lawyer, doctor, trader or professional.

The Catholic religion was largely forbidden, with no facility to train new priests, and foreign-educated priests were outlawed.

All Catholics were compelled to pay a tithe to the Anglican Protestant Church.

This brought on secret masses. Priests returning from the Continent were hunted down, hanged, drawn and quartered in the diamonds of Ulster townships.

*

Conor snitched a puff of the pipe he filled and lit for Daddo.

"England's darkest hour," Daddo said. As though he had heard those words spoken himself, he recited Edmund Burke. "The penal code was a contrivance for the impoverishment and debasement in the Irish of human nature itself as bad as ever invented from the perverted ingenuity of man." Daddo puffed and sighed. "Those were his very thoughts and, what is more, a Lord Chancellor once ruled that law doesn't presume that any such person as an Irish Roman Catholic exists. Well, they did us in so good that the most destitute beggar in London wouldn't have traded places with an Irish farmer."

Daddo held the poteen bottle before his face as though he could really see it. "And they wonder why we drink so much, as if it weren't the only way to stave off total madness from what they imposed on us. But lads . . . even in our most dire straits we kept the old language alive and never ceased the writing of music and poetry, and we clung as fiercely to our religion as we did to the bottle . . . as you know, I was a hedge teacher for your daddies."

*

A large part of the Scottish immigration to Ulster was a fleeing from English religious persecution. The Presbyterian soon found himself under many provisions of the penal code as an inferior "non-Anglican." This triggered a Scots-Irish exodus from Ulster to the New World, where they became a blood stock of the American pioneer movement, soldiers in the Revolutionary Army, forefathers of many great Americans, including a number of their Presidents, and a backbone of the emerging Canada.

Those Presbyterians who remained in Ulster were liberal of mind and of a kindred spirit with the suffering Catholics. They were among the first republicans.

To protect themselves from perverse landlordism, they banded together to fight the gentry and his agent. Steelboys, Peep o' Day Boys, Heart of Oak Boys all rode the night, bent on chilling the marrow of the oppressor and keeping rents and rights within humane limitations.

Toward the end of the 1700s a dramatic change had come over the Dublin Parliament. Inspired by the principles of the French Revolution, a new breed of ascendancy—upper-middle-class Protestants, including descendants of Cromwell—began to consider themselves as Irishmen first. No longer acting as a rubber stamp for the Crown, they sought their own liberation from England. In a spirit of reform, the Dublin Parliament proceeded to roll back and repeal the vile penal code. By the 1790s Catholics were allowed to bid on land leases.

So great was their starvation for land, the Catholics bid on leases, throwing caution and reality to the wind, willing to mortgage their souls to obtain it. They began underbidding the Presbyterian so that his privileged position eroded. It created a sense of anger, fear and panic, and Peep o' Day Boys who had ridden against the landlord now began to ride against the new threat—the Catholic native trying to regain his land.

Catholic Defenders answered outrage for outrage and committed more than a few of their own. Ulster became a battleground of forays between a land-starved Catholic peasantry and an entrenched Presbyterian peasantry.

*

"It was about this time that the Larkins of Armagh came into the picture," Daddo said. "Your great-grandfar, Ronan, being the leader of the Defenders in that county. In the year of seventeen and ninety-five a showdown fight took place between the Peep o' Day Boys and the Defenders. It occurred near Armagh Township in a place called the Diamond, and was a most furious battle. Thirty of our lads were killed, including two Larkin brothers. Ronan never called the fight but had to come in to save our forces and, sad to relate, the Prods carried the day.

"So sweet was their victory, the Prods likened it to King William of Orange's victory over James at the Boyne a hundred years earlier, and in honor of it they changed the name of their band to the Orange Society . . . a name that was to ever make our skins crawl.

"So we were split forever from our former Presbyterian brothers. The British aristocracy used them freely to apply the ancient principle of divide and rule."

*

The alliance for Irish liberation was a queer one. The intellectual and political front was led by ascendancy Anglicans joined in the countryside by the Catholic peasantry. These two factions allied loosely under the banner of the United Irishmen. It was led by a hopeless dreamer and maverick, Theobald Wolfe Tone, who had renounced his own ascendancy class.

Thousands of Irishmen, remnants of defeated armies, had historically fled to the sympathetic shores of France. Paris of the 1790s was filled with the opiate of rebellion. Here Wolfe Tone pleaded the Irish cause. Catholic France had a certain affinity for Catholic Ireland, enough to become a reluctant ally on the eve of the United Irishmen insurrection of 1798.

Catholic emancipation had become a goal of the United Irishmen. After the peasant land wars, the Presbyterians of Ulster stood in dire fear of their own survival. As the rising grew, thousands of them in the Orange Society joined the Crown through the Yeomanry, going after the Catholics with murderous vengeance.

In the south of Ireland there was a short-lived rebel victory at Wexford. The rebellion collapsed in short order with a French-supported invasion turning into a fiasco by a gale at sea which debilitated their fleet. Two years later in '98 a French force landed. It was surrounded and captured.

*

"In Ulster the Presbyterians in the British Yeomanry conducted a blood orgy so revolting that one British commander resigned in disgust. Every village diamond in Ulster was crimson from the drippings of the whipping post," Daddo said, commencing to embellish the gory doings of the Orange Society among the English forces. "Floggings to get the names of Defenders and United Irishmen left victims crippled for life. Lord Cornwallis, who learned about losing revolutions in the American colonies, was making certain his sword would never be surrendered again. The madness to crush the Catholics was heightened by the arrival of regiments of Welsh and Hessians from Germany, determined not to be outdone by Presbyterian butchery."

My heart and my stomach were both feeling it as Daddo related the horror in crushing the rising. Daddo hummed a tune but his voice was so crooked we could barely make it out, then recognized it as one of the songs we heard so often when the Prods celebrated around the Twelfth of July.

"Poor croppies, ye know that your sentence was come
When you heard the dread sound of the Protestant
*   drum.*
In memory of William we hoisted his flag
And soon the bright Orange put down the Green rag.
Down, down, croppies, lie down.

"When it was over, Wolfe Tone had been captured and killed himself in jail. They say some fifty thousand was killed. Not on the battlefield but mostly in cold-blooded murder. Ronan Larkin and his brothers fled to hiding in the Mourne Mountains."

*

A new and permanent order had been born out of the rising. The Presbyterians were alienated forever from the Catholics. They had proved their worth and loyalty to the Crown and established that Ulster principle of fanati-

cal loyalty to the British monarchy. The tragedy was
that two peasantries had been driven into sectarian conflict with no one the winner except the British aristocracy
who had stolen the land in the first place.

*

"Ronan was ultimately betrayed by an informer.
Remember me, lads, when I say informers are the bane
of Irish life. Beware of them for all your days. He was
brought down in chains from the Mourne to Armagh
Township and its bloody whipping post in the diamond.
They lashed him with the cat-o'-nine so fiendishly you
could see the bare bones of his body through the shredded
flesh. And then they crowned him with boiling tar."

"Jaysus," I whispered.

Conor never said anything when he was aroused. His
eyes only narrowed and his whole being tightened up
ominously.

"They left him with the life oozing from his body,"
Daddo continued, "planning to return the next morning
to complete the punishment. He was to be drawn and
quartered and then decapitated and his head stuck on
a pike to display as an example for any future rebellious
croppies."

*

During the night the last of his band, including the
two surviving brothers, stole back, overpowered the Yeo-
men on guard, cut Ronan down from the whipping post,
flung him into a cart and raced away. Somehow, he
continued to live.

The three Larkin brothers found their way by the underground to Inishowen and Ballyutogue just as 1800
came into being. There was no decent land to be had,
so they took leases above the seven-hundred-foot level so
high in the heather it was little more than shelf rock.
They busted the rock, clearing plots and using it for
walls. Then they carried up topsoil two buckets a man
at a time, mixed it with seaweed and kelp till it became
fertile. In the meantime, they survived by poaching on
Lord Hubble's fishing rights on Lough Foyle, becoming
the first proficient fishermen in the area. By the second
year, a crop was brought in and over a period of time

they were able to increase the size and holding of their leases through monumental toil.

*

"Ronan was never a total man after his beating and he sired only three boys, Kilty being the oldest among them. Kilty . . . aye, there was a lad. He was born scrapping."

Daddo was caught up in a sudden burst of enthusiasm which enveloped us too. As Kilty lay next door on the final night of waking, his legend was being birthed by a wizened shanachie drinking up the warmth of the fire with us two young wanes. During my days I was to hear the feats of Kilty Larkin over and over but never again would it be like that first moment of revelation.

"You've heard tell that only pigs can see the wind but I tell you Kilty Larkin could see it. He rode in and out on the wind, raiding like an invisible scythe, and never once did they touch him.

"When Kilty took over the land at the passing of Ronan he already had a number of ideas. Just like that he refused to pay the tithe to the Anglican Church. The Constabulary came, dirty turncoat Irishmen that they are, and extracted the payment from his crops. Shortly thereafter their commander mysteriously disappeared, to be washed up on Dunagree Point two weeks later. This was a signal that a new dawn had come."

For years no tenant would fix up his home or improve his fields, for if he did his rent would be raised on the grounds that his lease had become more valuable. Kilty studied the Protestant farms below, figuring they had better methods. He adopted what he could and beautified his cottage as well, separating the pigs and chickens from the main house and whitewashing his walls and fences. Sure enough, the land agent near doubled his rent.

This sort of a landlordism led directly to a local war. The Constabulary was not up against a sloppily organized band of fence busters but a skilled and fierce raiding force that knew how to inflict damage. The first culmination was a master stroke by Kilty in organizing a boycott against the Earl of Foyle's fields at harvest. Outside labor was imported from Scotland and the harvest was carried out under the protection of Constabulary guns.

The Earl's fields were vast and the Constabulary spread too thin. Before troops could arrive to reinforce them, the imported labor had been thoroughly terrorized, crops were burned and informers assassinated. Lord Hubble's losses ran into the thousands.

Retaliation came in the form of evictions, rent raises and public floggings.

"It was the eve of July 11 in eighteen and forty-three that Kilty rose to an epic moment," Daddo said with his voice now tuned to near singing. "The Prods was all swacked to the eyeballs, celebrating King William's holidays. Kilty set up a beautiful decoy. An informer he had suspected was fed false information about a planned raid to take place right at the Earl's castle at Hubble Manor. They fell for it, moving in Constabulary and troops, leaving the road to Derry wide open.

"The likes of it were never seen from the ancient Celtic cattle raid of Cooley to this day . . . me . . . myself . . . riding on the lefthand side of Kilty with a a full moon lighting our way.

"The cattle pens at Derry was bulging at dockside waiting for shipment to England. We struck so hard my bootlaces tore apart, busting open the pens and stampeding. Within an hour we had run over two thousand head of Lord Hubble's finest into Lough Foyle and drowned 'em, and disappeared on the wind.

"The informer who had fed his masters incorrect information met a terrible fate at their hands. Other informers became very hesitant about stepping forward with information. Well they knew all along it was Kilty Larkin but they were afraid of jailing him and twice as scared to let him stay free."

Daddo cackled a laugh at the memory of the event, no doubt enhanced in his mind by the passing of time.

"Kilty became the first tenant to ever sit down and negotiate. And he broke the tithe. Mind you, it was the days before any of the fancy protective leagues. Aye, there was a lad. Years later, me and Kilty became Fenians. The rising never amounted to much and we was excommunicated for our troubles just like Ronan and his brothers had been excommunicated for being United Irishmen."

His mind drifted. . . . "The Church always buttered its bread with British droppings. . . ." Daddo suddenly became dry and paused for lubrication, now tired, and all the magic thoughts went floundering. . . . "Oh, what a grand raid that ever was . . . Conor . . ."

"Aye," Conor said, coming off the creepie, kneeling before the shanachie, who reached his hand out and touched over his cheek and hair and grunted a laugh of sorts. "The shadow of Kilty has been a heavy burden for your daddy but he had dreams of his own, the same as you do. It was the famine that killed his dreams. No matter what we were before, we were never the same after the famine nor have we ever lived a day without the fear of it. . . . Conor . . ."

"Aye, Daddo."

"Tomas is apt to be touched with the madness tonight. I've felt it coming over him. All the Larkins had the madness . . . Ronan . . . Kilty and your daddy as well. He'll be under the spell this night."

Conor pulled away, his eyes already searching beyond the cottage for his daddy.

*

Conor made a hand leap over the wall between the cottages and was greeted by the drone of the rosary. He shoved the door open tentatively. The best room was filled with kneeling wakers, all beating their fists against their hearts in cadence, with mumblings calling to the saints who were surely watching from a place of glory, unknown.

Conor's eyes played over them, searching for his daddy. Finola knelt near the corpse, her face hidden in her hands, completely spent from a second shrill of keening. She lifted her eyes slowly, making contact with her son in a way that needed no further amplification.

Conor backed out quietly. The night was unusually plentiful with stars as he trotted down the path past a dozen cottages, then set off up the side of the hill toward the shebeen.

The shebeen sat in blackness and there was nothing to be heard from it. Conor shoved the door open. As it groaned apart, heavy whiskey odors were set free.

"Daddy."

With no answer greeting him, he groped inside, feeling about for the taper which sat on a post, and managed to light it. The room glowed reluctantly from the smallness of the flame.

Tomas Larkin crouched on a barrel, all doubled over like a defeated bull, staring as blind as Daddo Friel and completely unaware of another presence. Conor came above him.

"Daddy."

Tomas looked up and blinked, giving no recognition of his boy. "Kilty," he whispered with a tinge of horror shaking his voice, "the potatoes all turned black. They rotted right before me eyes. My God, Kilty, what are we going to do?"

"Daddy, it's me, Conor. You're just off in a bad dream."

"Oh, Jesus help us. We're going to die. All of us are going to die."

CHAPTER SIX: The Catholic fields of Ballyutogue were still of a May morning as the bells of St. Columba's tolled for Kilty Larkin.

His coffin was lifted from its four supporting chairs which were then kicked over in accordance with custom that also dictated the coffin leave the cottage feet first.

Finola had to remain at home, for a pregnant woman might surely have a stillborn if she attended a funeral and obtained the curse of the dead.

Being that there were no other Larkin men than Tomas, the friends and neighbors rotated as pallbearers, carrying the coffin on their shoulders and switching around every several yards. Tomas walked directly behind them, his hands and forehead resting on Kilty's box. His children marched at his side. Behind Tomas a dozen men carried spades and behind them the entire village formed an entourage.

Father Lynch approached the procession wearing a black vestment for death which had been embroidered along with his other vestments by the women of the village. Chanting and sprinkling holy water, he turned and led the way to the church.

Tomas stepped aside as the coffin passed the churchyard gate with the mourners pouring in behind. A sense of pending altercation heightened as the priest and his curate tried to get the church filled and the doors closed. Conor shoved Brigid and Liam inside and edged back toward his daddy, who remained motionless by the gate.

"I'll not be going in," Tomas said. "Fetch me at McCluskey's after the mass and I'll say good-by to Kilty at the grave."

Father Lynch made toward Tomas with his face pinched tight as a walnut shell. Conor was waved away and joined a number of villagers at the door who were now poking about curiously but minding to keep a respectful distance. Father Lynch snarled an authoritative warning to stay back.

"We're waiting for you," he said in a hiss to Tomas.

"Nae . . . I'll not attend this mass."

"Have you lost your mind?"

"I'm doing what Kilty would have done had he been in his right senses. Here's your money for the mass."

The priest's trained hand snapped in the fee with the speed of a striking asp, then edged ever so much closer. "Tomas Larkin. The sin you're about to commit is grave and dangerous. If you don't come in I'll not hold the mass."

"In that case," Tomas answered softly, "your sin will be as grave as mine. I know it's disappointing to you after having waited so long for the sweet victory of Kilty and Tomas Larkin both inside St. Columba's at the same time . . . one laid out and the other on his knees praying for his immortal soul. But God won't know who we are anyhow, because we've priests here who don't even know how to pray in the Irish language . . . it's that English they are."

"You'll never rise high enough to see purgatory. Now get in there and take his coffin out of my church."

"Very well . . ."

Father Lynch grabbed his sleeve quickly. "No, wait. This is no good at all. If you come I'll say the mass for no fee . . . provided you don't tell anyone."

"No, I'll take him. He'll be happier sleeping in the hills, anyhow."

The priest knew the faith of his people was bottomless. They obeyed meekly. Yet with all that faith there was one thing more powerful and that was their memory. Everyone knew Kilty had received absolution. Never having had his authority challenged, Father Lynch was in a quandary. Moreover, he was taken with a spell of un-cluttered fear and broke into a sweat.

The assemblage crept closer over the yard. The father could sense their breaths. "For the sake of the departed soul," he said loud enough to be heard, "and for the peace and comfort of your innocent wife and children . . ."

"And to save the face of the priest," Tomas interrupted, and turned and walked away.

"As representative of Jesus Christ I am imposing on you, Tomas Larkin, eternal damnation in this life and for-· er after and you're never to come sniveling to me for absolution, for I'll not give it!"

The villagers bounced back in horror.

Tomas slowly retraced his steps, shaking his head. "Ah, Father, you are a blister," he said, and beat a path to McCluskey's.

The enraged man turned slowly to his mesmerized flock, who retreated into the church openmouthed. Fighting to regain control of himself, he started praying at the moment for the day, months or years away, that Tomas Larkin would come whimpering and crawling, prostrating himself, begging atonement. As he made down the aisle he told himself he was a merciful and forgiving man who would not glory in the vengeance, but nevertheless, he would pray for the time. And then, deciding to have the last word on the matter, he would not give a lengthy mass over Kilty nor would he go out to the graveyard and say any special words there. Slipping the fee into his pocket, he mounted the steps to the pulpit and faced a congregation that dropped to its knees in unison as though they had been felled by a single shot.

CHAPTER SEVEN: It was not that Dooley McCluskey was irreverent of the dead. For an ordinary funeral he would have closed his public house until after the mass. However, Kilty's passing brought up a large delegation of Protestants from the Township. Most of them would no more enter St. Columba's than a good Catholic would allow himself to be seen inside St. Andrew's Presbyterian

or St. George's Anglican. After all, one could not just
leave one's neighbors standing about idly. And besides,
he had donated a dozen bottles at the wake and was
surely entitled to make up the loss.

As Tomas adjusted his eyes to the low-ceilinged pit
of drink, their hats came off and their heads bowed
slightly. One by one they offered an awkward consolation.
Luke Hanna, the flax mill foreman who had years of
dealing with both Kilty and Tomas, acted as senior
spokesman. He intoned praises that Kilty had never heard
during his life. They had been adversaries most of their
lives but the kind of adversaries who were able to pro-
claim the public house as mutual sanctuary and drink
together without fussing.

Luke Hanna's litany was a mixture of relief that the
old bastard was out of his hair and sorrow over the passing of such a powerful man.

"I saw the doings with Father Lynch," Luke said, shoving a whiskey to Tomas.

"Ach, that man has the smile of last year's rhubarb."

"Are you in trouble with him?"

"It's my wife I'm after fearing now."

Tomas' cup was running over with free drink to the
delight of Dooley McCluskey. Tomas was just verging
on the staggers when Conor entered. "They're digging
the grave, Daddy," he said.

He wiped his mouth with the back of his hand and let
go of a thunderous belch and followed his son out.

Father Lynch had abolished some of the more grisly
graveside customs such as thrusting the dead man's hand
into a pail of milk to make the cream rise. However, he
reinstated a loathed tradition of separating the men and
women, burying each sex in its own section. The priest
left the final prayers and sprinkling of holy water at
graveside to Father Cluny, wishing no second confrontation with Tomas.

While the men alternated at digging, most of the others
wandered about the cemetery visiting graves of relatives,
clearing weeds and smoking pipes. A half dozen women
keened over the coffin but not in the terrible lamenting
of the wake. It was a lyrical weeping and a soft feeling of
each other's rhythm of prayer so that it all harmonized
in the creation of a primitive melody.

After Tomas arrived, the coffin was set down into the

ground and covered. Each mourner passed by in turn and placed a rock on it until the pile became a small cairn. In twos and threes the men drifted to McCluskey's public house and the women back to the village.

Fergus O'Neill balanced himself cross-legged atop Kilty's cairn. Bertie MacDevitt stood alongside playing the flute, his lips still puffed from the fight with Dinny O'Kane, while Fergus spoke his recitation.

"Tora loo, tora loo,
I'll set me here till darkin',
A soldier of the green is croaked,
So weep for Kilty Larkin.

Tora loo, tora loo,
The Fenians he was sparkin',
That lad who killed the hated tithe,
God love ye, Kilty Larkin.

Tora loo, tora loo,
The neighbors kept embarkin',
Through famine's hell, he kept his land,
Farewell, ye, Kilty Larkin."

After fifteen more verses the poem was done and over the years it would be enhanced by a hundred more. Kilty had received the hero's reward of a song in his honor. Fergus and Tomas remained and Bertie played until his lips pained too greatly to continue. Finally Conor and Liam and Brigid quit and trudged home and Tomas was alone by his father's cairn until dusk fell over Ballyutogue.

In the wee hours of the night Conor pushed open the door of McCluskey's. All who remained standing were his father and Luke Hanna and two other Protestants, with McCluskey keeping account of each pouring. Conor tugged his daddy's coat. Tomas' eyes looked like a red tide and it appeared to his son he was halfway into the spell again.

"Daddy, I'm after taking you home."

"Out with you!" Tomas bellowed.

"Well, I have to know when you're coming home," Conor persisted.

"When I finish drinking, that's when."

"I'll wait."

"I repeat. Out. I cannot enjoy my pints with a small boy hovering about me."

"I'll stay in the corner and I'll be quiet."

"Is it a thrashing you're sporting for!"

"I have to wait. I promised Ma I'd bring you home."

Tomas drew his arm around as if to give the boy the back of his hand but Conor merely stared unintimidated and with a tinge of disgust. Tomas dropped his hand and sulked, groaned and grumbled, scratched his hair and jaw and finally wilted under Conor's glare. "Ach, Christ," he moaned, setting his glass down and timidly following the boy into the night.

He drank the cool tinged air into his lungs and steadied himself on Conor as they plodded silently with naught but the sounds of the wind and the smells of the fields for company.

"I guess Ma has heard about my little conversation with Father Lynch?"

"She has."

"Oh, I can see the look on her face now. It will sour the cream for a fortnight."

Tomas steadied himself before the cottage, emitting little beepings of self-pity punctuated by pained Irish groans. "Conor, my boy. Why don't you tell Ma I passed out in the public house? Aye, that's it. I passed out and Fergus came and fetched me and put me to sleep in his place."

"Ma will never believe you passed out. Everybody knows how much drink you can hold."

"Won't work, eh?"

"Uh-uh."

"Well then. Let's just sit in the byre until the old head stops dinnlin'."

Tomas stumbled along the walls telling the cows to hush, then wilted into the hay as Conor lit the lantern.

"Daddy, everything's going to be all right. You've done nothing out of turn."

"It's a good lad you are. They'll be writing songs for you one day."

"Shouldn't you be going to bed?"

"Aw, I'm not ready to face that in there, yet."

Tomas rubbed his head hard to wipe out electric circles of confusion now racing through him, tilting him, nauseating him, breaking his skull with throbs, blurring his vision, muddling up his words.

"Daddy, I know how you loved Kilty and I'd grieve the same way after you."

Tomas slumped over on his back and thrashed in agony. "And I'd keep you alive like Kilty did for me. Oh, God . . . oh, God . . ." The breaths were loud and tortured and the cattle rustled with nervousness. "Kilty!" he cried. "Kilty!"

The sobbing of his father nearly tore Conor's heart. He cried, watching the giant shake, Tomas' great back bulging with strain and sounds coming from him the likes of which Conor had never heard before. Finally it slowed to soft pathetic little gasps.

"It's no use, Kilty. The potatoes have all turned black . . . we're going to die . . . we're going to die . . ."

CHAPTER EIGHT: "Isn't he a grand-looking sight," Finola said, entering the byre.

"He's feeling sorely," Conor apologized.

"No doubt of that," she said, bending over laboriously to get a closer look. "I've seen better-looking faces eating hay."

"He's not faking, Ma," Conor said, "he's truly destroyed."

"Ach, we'll be saying penance for his nonsense till All Saints' Day. You'd better stay here and see he doesn't drown in his own bile, and if he gets too noisy just give him a pail of water in the face." She paddled off contemptuously.

"Conor."

He looked up to the loft where Liam had stuck his head into the opening and Brigid rubbed her eyes. "Is Daddy back?"

"Aye."

Liam shinnied down the ladder and looked his father over. "Sure he looks like somebody gave him a fair bash in his lug."

"Aw, he's just resting," Conor snapped.

"I'll stay with you. We can take turns watching him,"

Liam said, becoming excited over the prospect of being his father's protector.

"I'll take care of him myself. Go on back to sleep."

Liam clenched up at what was unmistakably a command. "I ought to stay too."

"Go on!"

Liam contemplated making a stand but retreated meekly under his brother's authority. Conor dimmed the lantern and arranged a place for himself. Tomas' hands worked open and closed in a twitchlike grab at the straw, writhing slightly. He moaned incoherently.

He sat for ever so long, dozing as he did but always waking up alert each time his daddy moved. Tomas was wending his way down a torturous road and not a body could help him.

With sharp suddenness, an air of ultra silence enveloped the byre so that Conor was aware of the loudness of his own breath. This was followed by a swift pierce of wind shooting through the place, drawing the boy up in a shiver, and the flame of the lantern danced precariously, then doused, pitching it into total blackness. Conor groped about, the cows groaned uneasily as though a stranger had made his way in.

An unaccountable light, more of a radiation, bubbled from one of the stalls at precisely the location Finola had seen the banshee. Conor felt seized by a fit of fright.

The light flickered up unevenly as if it were trying to find its way out of the stall.

"Who's in there?" he managed with quivering tone.

"Only me," came an answer.

The boy's mouth ran dry. He recognized the voice but only vaguely, and was in no temper to think things out. He crawled on hands and knees to try to get a better vantage, and as he did the light emerged into the open, glowing eerily around the figure of a man.

"Who . . . who . . . are . . . you?"

A sardonic laugh came in answer.

"Oh, something crazy is happening," Conor said, springing to his feet, thinking of running out. But that would mean leaving his daddy. Perhaps, scream at the top of his lungs. A translucent figure stepped closer.

"Have a look, Conor."

The boy placed himself defiantly between the advancing shadow and his prostrate father, squinting the faintest glimmer of recognition. It was someone he knew all right but for the life of him could not place. He saw an outline of a robust man, dressed for the fields, sinewy-armed and with a large mop of curly black hair. It was the head of hair Conor fixed on, for he'd seen its likes, but what he had seen was stone white on an old and wilted man.

The ghost smiled, sporting a mouth of big bright teeth. No, it was not the same man at all, for the one he was thinking of had not a bar in his grate . . . he was toothless.

"Granted, I've changed a mite," the man said, "but you should know me."

The voice! The voice! "Daddo?" Conor ventured.

"Good lad."

Conor slowly put his hand out directly before the man's face.

"What are you doing that for?"

"Can you see me?"

"Of course I can see you."

"But you're next to blind."

"Oh, that. Considering when you saw me last I was forty years older than now."

"But it was only last night!"

"Now, if we're to continue this discussion, you've got to accept certain facts, such as my presence. I wasn't always feeble and sightless, you know. Not any more than Kilty was. Unfortunately, that's all you remember of both of us. Forty years ago we was a pretty scrappy pair. I was never the lad Kilty was. Why, he could break rocks with his bare hands, he was that strong."

Conor backed off suspiciously as the man advanced. It could have been Daddo in younger times. The longer he studied, the greater the similarity. Daddo proceeded to make himself comfortable, producing a large jug of poteen from nowhere and swigging it heartily. He shook his head as he studied Tomas Larkin and offered Conor the jug. Conor nearly choked in a coughing fit trying to hold the vile stuff down but at the same time he was complimented at being treated as a man.

"Did he ever tell you about the great hunger?"

"Nae, not really."

Like most of the kids, he had heard about the famine in snatches, tales from the shanachies, whispers about the turf fire on a winter's night. Famine sayings, famine foods, famine fears . . . it was all in loose and mysterious threads. When talk of it heightened, Tomas Larkin invariably closed up. The better part of a half century had passed but the memory and effects were still in every cottage and field of Ballyutogue.

"We live," Daddo said, "with a number of rooms inside us. The best room is open to the family and friends and we show our finest face in it. Another room is more private, the bedroom, and very few are allowed in. There is another room where we allow no one in . . . not even our wives and children, for it is a room of the most intimate thoughts we keep unshared. There is one more room, so hidden away that we don't even enter it ourselves. Within we lock all the mysteries we cannot solve and all the pains and sorrows we wish to forget. When Kilty died, it unlocked the last of these rooms inside Tomas Larkin and all the bitterness escaped."

Conor looked to his daddy, who seemed peaceful enough now. Still cautious of Daddo's appearance as the work of fairies, he remained alert. Daddo did not seem to have evil intent but the situation called for caution.

"Tomas was about your age at the time of the great hunger and quite like yourself. Kilty and I were very close. I lived in the next village at the time and rode with him as his most trusted lieutenant, so I knew every last bit of what happened. To understand how such a thing could have happened, you have to know what was going on in those days. . . ."

*

After the crushing of the Wolfe Tone's United Irishmen Rising of 1798, the British were determined not to have to contend with any further liberation-minded Dublin Parliaments.

To this end, William Pitt, the British Prime Minister, engineered an Act of Union for the sole purpose of total political suppression of the Irish.

Cornwallis, the Viceroy of Ireland, embarked on a campaign of rank chicanery designed to coerce the Dublin Parliament into dissolving itself after five hundred years. When it was done, the Cross of St. Patrick was added to the British Cross of St. George and the Scottish Cross of St. Andrew, all fixed on a single banner known as the Union Jack to fly over a so-called United Kingdom.

For their participation in the scheme, the Irish bishops had their loyalty purchased by the British with promises of Catholic emancipation.

A major seminary was established at Maynooth under English eyes and supervision to create a British version of Catholicism that would eventually diminish the old Celtic and Norman versions.

The Act of Union was a shotgun wedding. With the death of their own Dublin Parliament, any chance of guiding Irish destiny was removed from Irish hands. A small Irish delegation with a smaller voice was lost in the enormity of Westminster. England was able to rule Ireland through Crown servants from the infamous Dublin Castle.

Over a quarter of a century went by after the Act of Union before the first Irish Catholic was able to take a seat in Westminster. It took the enormous person of Daniel O'Connell to achieve it. As he dominated the Irish political struggle, the goals of emancipation seemed attainable. O'Connell then devoted his life to a second goal, repeal of the Act of Union . . . a divorce from England. This was not to be realized.

*

"So you see," Daddo said, "why the upcoming election is so very important. For eighty-five years of this century we have been fighting for Home Rule, a Dublin Parliament and the end of the Act of Union."

Conor nodded in understanding. "Why did the crop fail?" he asked.

"It was bound to happen, sooner or later," Daddo answered, standing and stretching a mite. He took to stalking about, for he never failed to become aroused when he spoke of it.

"All the fancy political jabber didn't do much for us," he said. "The croppies remained among the most wretched and destitute peasants in the world and, adding to our miseries, mother church was bent on helping the British attempts to Anglicize us. They no longer prayed in the old language. In the schools and the books there was never a mention of Irish history or legends. It was the shanachies and hedge school teachers like my own daddy, repeating his tales from village to village and giving secret lessons, who saved the culture."

Daddo abruptly stopped his pacing as the sorrow of it rose in him and his eyes misted. He slumped and recited now in monotone.

"We'd bring in the potato crop in September, same as now. If it was a very good year, we could barely scrape by, but the blue months always were on us by midsummer and food ran low. Those who had anything to pawn would pawn it. The rest went further and further into debt to the gombeen men. We were never out from under the shadow of starvation and, what with the rents, the tithe to the Anglican Church and the absence of human rights, the cattle and pigs got better treatment because we were lower than animals in British eyes.

"Ireland of 1800 was a country of eight million. Two to three million had no land or jobs and wandered aimlessly, scrounging the countryside. When they went into the cities there was no work to be found, for the British didn't put in factories or ports or businesses or roads or schools . . . except for the Prods in Ulster. The cities were portraits of squalor inundated by tens of thousands of beggars, young and old, whose only alternative was a final damnation of the workhouse. This was the Ireland of British creation."

The two of them remained silent for a time, Conor trying to digest it and Daddo pondering that eve of disaster.

"When I was a lad people married young. They were content with a few wee acres chipped off the family lease. The farms grew smaller and smaller until barely a leasehold on Inishowen ran over fifteen acres.

"The thin line of existence had become the potato. An entire family could exist off a few acres and the only tool needed was a simple spade to dig the lazy bed on almost any kind of land. An average man ate between eight and twelve pounds a day with the skins going to feed the chicks and pigs. With that and the turf for heat, we had the elements of survival.

"As the population grew larger and the farms smaller, the land became overworked and played out. Total dependence on a single food crop was a courtship to catastrophe.

"Tomas Larkin, lying there so still, had the spirit crushed out of him by the famine same as the Irish people were crushed."

CHAPTER NINE

SEPTEMBER 1845

"Daddy! Uncle Aidan! Uncle Cathal!"

Kilty Larkin and his two brothers, digging up the last of the potatoes in their lazy bed, turned from their work to see young Tomas racing up the hill, waving and shouting as he did.

"Daddy! Uncle Aidan! Uncle Cathal!"

Kilty tossed a handful of spuds into the big basket sitting on the runners of the sidecar and stretched to his limits, which was high indeed. The three brothers consumed a fair portion of ground just to stand on, they were that large. As he wiped his brow a gust of wind set his hair flowing, giving him the look of a red-bearded Moses. His son stumbled up the last yards. "Ho there, Tomas, slow down with you."

"Ma," he gasped, "she wants you to come right away, all of you."

"Aye, what is it?" Cathal asked.

"Something strange is happening to the potatoes."

"Now what could be happening? They were healthy-looking enough yesterday."

Tomas shook his head and bit his lower lip hard for fear he'd cry.

"What's going on?" Kilty demanded.

"They just started turning black right in front of our eyes."

The brothers stared at one another puzzled, then all turned and moved out together on the verge of a run. There was already a small gathering of women and elders when they reached the large stone and turf clochan used for crop storage. Kilty's wife Mary, Aidan's Jenny and Cathal's wife Siobhan were among them.

Kilty shoved through to Mary. Her face was screwed up with fright as she gripped his arm hard and pointed wordlessly to the clochan. He entered with his brothers following. The bulging bins emitted a sharp rancid odor.

He scooped up a handful of potatoes and squinted in the half-dark. They had gone black and sogged into a dripping mush between his fingers. He poked deeper into the bin. They had all turned. The three of them pawed through bin after bin clear down to the end of the building. It was the same.

"Mother of Jesus!" Aidan cried.

"For Christ's sake, talk softly," Kilty snapped. The three gathered close in a head-to-head huddle.

"What do you make of it?" Cathal asked.

"Sure I don't know," Kilty said.

"Do you think it could be the blight?" Aidan mumbled.

"Sure I don't know," Kilty repeated, "I've never seen the likes of this."

"I remember Daddy telling about how it hit in Armagh once. One day the crop was pulled up sound and looking good and just like that they turned."

"Let me see," Kilty said, thinking fast. "Cathal, slip out of here quiet as you can with a sack. Take some chickens and a piglet and isolate them in a stall away from the other animals and feed them some of these."

"Right."

"Now, let's go out and look bravely for God's sake."

Just as they emerged three of the neighbor men arrived, all reporting that the same had happened to their stores. As the gathering grew in numbers and mounted in confusion all eyes began to turn to Kilty. He remained almost aloof, speaking softly and assuringly, and for the moment everyone seemed calmed. Only Mary, his wife of fifteen years, was able to read the desperation whirling about behind that impassive expression.

In a few hours Cathal had an answer. The animals which had been fed the black potatoes were dead. Kilty dispatched his brothers and Tomas north to Moville, inland to Glencaw Hill and south to Muff to gather in the titular clan heads. When they all arrived deep in the night the church was filled with weeping and praying women and sullen, terrified men.

The meeting took place at an ancient abandoned Norman keep a mile beyond the village with all the men of Ballyutogue present as well. Daddo Friel was first to report that the harvest in his village of Crockadaw had started rotting a day before.

After a long moment of utter silence came a burst of confused yelling. Kilty assumed control, waylaying a rising flood of fear.

"When we break up, I want each of you to appraise his own situation and let me know exactly what you must have to make the winter and get the spring planting in. When I have all the information, I am appointing myself and Daddo as a committee of two to go to Derry and meet with the chief estate agent, MacAdam Rankin himself personally."

"A fat lot of good that dirty bastard will do us."

"I am going to insist that everyone shut up. We've had our differences with MacAdam Rankin before but we've never been faced with a total loss of our basic food. Even Rankin has to realize we'll do his lordship no good if we all starve."

It all seemed logical enough. The Earl of Foyle had to have tenants in order to make and keep his fortune. He would have to react in such a manner as to save his own goose.

"Let me know your absolute needs," Kilty repeated forcefully, "and Daddo and I will negotiate for enough to keep body and soul together. In the meantime you are to make no loans from the gombeen men and for God's sake avoid spreading panic."

Fortified by the rock strength of Kilty, they left on a note of hope.

The Larkins consisted of three families numbering twenty lives. Kilty was the elder, the true son of Ronan who had fought the rising of '98 and made land yield a harvest where none had grown before. He and Mary had four children, three boys and a small girl, with Tomas, at fourteen, the eldest. Tomas was large and strong in the manner of the Larkins but dawdled and dreamed and spent every possible waking hour sitting at the knee of the shanachie and the traveling hedgerow teachers.

Cathal, the middle brother, was sorely burdened by an absence of a male heir, having four daughters to the age of seventeen and none married.

Last was Aidan with six wee wanes from nine years down to infancy.

They were close and their closeness gave them added strength in crisis. The family council talked things over with quiet sureness. The immediate problem was sufficient food to make the winter after the rents. There would be enough from their share of the crops to hold on but by spring there would be no money for seed and to meet other expenses.

It was decided that one of them should cross the water to England and work the docks and late harvests. Kilty was the most likely to have good earnings and, otherwise, the only logical choice.

Aidan had no replacement in his fields and it was nearly the same with Cathal. Two of his daughters could help him but could not run his acreage alone if he were gone.

Young Tomas was almost capable of turning in a man's day's work if he got his head out of the clouds. Kilty imparted the importance and responsibility in assuming the place of the head of the house and the boy agreed he would do so.

All in all the Larkins appeared in good shape with not much more than the usual struggle. But then reports from the neighbors and nearby villages came in and prospects for the others were bleaker.

Armed with a detailed need of the tenants within the Earl of Foyle's pale, Daddo Friel and Kilty set off for Derry to see MacAdam Rankin.

It boiled down to meeting the emergency with deferred payments. They would convince Rankin to let the tenants keep a number of livestock and other crops to use as food in lieu of the potatoes.

The Catholic tenants of Inishowen and nine Earls of Foyle had had bloody bouts for two and a half centuries but all of that was in the past. The penal laws were long gone and a spirit of reform and compromise swept in from England. It had been well over two years since Kilty had taken to night riding. Negotiations were no longer out of the ordinary.

Kilty and Daddo were in a mood of optimism. After all, it was eighteen and forty-five and they would be dealing with civilized men.

CHAPTER TEN: Tomas rolled over on his back, shattering the air with a long spell of snoring that halted

Daddo's tale. The shanachie utilized the pause to fortify himself and once again offered the jug to Conor. After his last swig Conor had felt a bit sick to the stomach and respectfully declined. Tomas tossed about, finally flattening out on his stomach so the roar dimmed to a whistle.

"What happened when you and Kilty went to Derry to see the estate agent?"

Daddo laughed sardonically. "We saw him all right. MacAdam Rankin."

"Rankin? Of the same clan that still manages the land?" Conor asked.

"The very same Rankins. But MacAdam was *the* Rankin. So crafty he could draw blood from the wind. A good number of our people trusted him, he was that clever. After all, they argued, he had agreed to pay our tithe two years before if Kilty stopped night riding."

"What did he say to you?"

"He bled from every pore trying to charm us off our perches. He said how sorely sorrowed he was. He had communicated with the Earl himself to return to Ulster, and was praying for some kind of help from the government. But all the time he made this show of sympathy he was measuring us for a box because he'd made up his mind long before the blight what he wanted to do with the croppies."

Daddo shook his head, still disbelieving MacAdam's treachery. "While he spoke to us with utter sincerity he was pushing plans for us to have an early meeting with Jesus and Mary. Conor, if you're ever to remember one thing, it's never to sit and negotiate with those people. They're like goats looking through the hedge, with more tricks than the lowest tinker and honor unbefitting a sow.

"MacAdam had an older brother, Owen, a sour brew of a man incapable of managing the estate himself, who was kept around as a willing hangman. And there was a nephew, Glendon, zesting for the day he would take over. It was an ugly crew, the afterbirth of three generations of estate agents. Satanic, pure satanic . . ."

*

During these months the Earl of Foyle, Lord Morris Hubble, and Lady Beatrice resided in Daars, their southern manor house near Kinsale. Daars had won a measure of renown as the most fashionable drawing room for the colony of high-ranking retired British naval officers and a troupe of nomadic gentry.

News of the potato blight dominated most of the conversation. In fact, a number of untimely departures from Kinsale had all but ruined the yachting season.

In response to his inquiry, MacAdam Rankin assured his lordship that everything was under control at Hubble Manor. The agent suggested a number of precautionary measures be initiated. In any event, Rankin wrote, there was no need for his lordship to rush home by subjecting himself to that torturous coach trip up the length of the country.

The Rankin family had been in the earldom's service as estate agents for nearly a century. In the decade that MacAdam had managed affairs he had been granted an ever wider range of confidence and authority. It was an arrangement that left Lord Morris and Lady Beatrice free to enjoy the social graces at Daars and London.

The Earl returned Rankin's message, giving him permission to move forward on his proposals, and suggested he would be booking his normal passage, a packet sailing from Queenstown to Londonderry several weeks in the future.

Although Rankin had delayed Kilty Larkin and pacified the Catholic tenants, his greatest concern was a spreading sense of panic that could be followed by outlaw activity.

The stoic older brother, Owen, was dispatched to Dublin Castle with a number of specific requests. Contacts and friends of the earldom within the ruling circles had been established for generations and he was certain to receive quick consideration.

Young Glendon sailed for London to participate with other agents and gentry in making the ascendancy views known to the government.

Rankin put his solicitors into motion preparing a mass of legal instruments to have at the ready for action against the Catholics.

The earldom's most potent asset was its large settlement of loyal Protestants in and about Ballyutogue dating back some two hundred years. Presbyterians had come as planters from the Scottish Lowlands and the Anglicans later took acreage as payment for service to Cromwell.

Yet they were isolated from the main body of Ulster Protestants and it created in them a feeling of being surrounded by those hostile neighbors up in the heather.

The anatomy of Protestant fear was a handy tool in MacAdam Rankin's kit, one that could easily trigger them to fever pitch. Failure of the potato crop afforded the wily estate manager an opportunity he was not about to overlook.

*

"You see," Daddo said, "the blight was one of the few things to happen of a non-sectarian nature, ruining their potatoes as well. Although they never carried our burdens and poverty, the Prods were now in serious trouble. MacAdam Rankin plunged into their Orange Halls and their churches promising that the Earl would carry them through and at the same time warning they should prepare for the worst from the croppies. The Prods never needed much convincing over that issue. They were still pissing and moaning and preaching about and living with the horrors of a Catholic rising two centuries earlier.

"Just to tidy things up, Owen Rankin returned from Dublin Castle with permission to reactivate the East Donegal Yeomanry. And what a lovely bunch of lads they were. It was a unit of the reserve militia that had outflogged, outdissected, outrazed and outtortured every battalion in Ulster from Cromwell through the United Irish Rising. In their isolation, their fears had always been translated to sadistic frenzy.

"In exchange for the Earl's support, MacAdam strongly suggested that every able-bodied man take up arms to protect the land and his privileges. They hauled out the old banner, dusted it off, unfurled it and raised it over the Ballyutogue barrack and piped and drummed croppy hate songs so that nary a Catholic missed the point."

"I don't mean to be interrupting you," Conor said, "or disputing your points, but how'd you ever know what was going on in Dublin Castle or the Orange Halls?"

Daddo stared across the stall, startled at first, then dismayed. "Are you doubting my veracity, Conor?"

"Well, not exactly," he answered, "but all of this is getting a bit queer, what with you being forty years younger than you actually are and you being so transparent I can see to the other side of the byre right

through your body, telling me about events you could
have hardly known about . . ."

"Enough!" Daddo stood waving his hand in disgust.
"Do you think I'd go to the trouble of sitting here
through the night if I didn't want you to know? And besides"—his voice dropped off with a tinge of mystery—
"a shanachie has certain ways of finding things out."

"From the fairies?"

"I'm not after telling you my secrets but I'll not be giving the confidence of my heart to a doubter. If you don't
mind, I'll be taking my leave . . ."

On that cue the image of him shadowed and began
to wave before Conor's eyes. "Don't go!" Conor cried.
"Please!"

Daddo stopped his fading and pouted. "There are
things you're not to question such as what you're seeing
and what you're hearing."

"It's only that my daddy and Kilty always told me to
question everything, particularly never to let the priest
get away with too many miracles. But honest, Daddo, I
never meant to compare a shanachie with a mere priest,"
he added quickly.

"Well now, you're thinking brightly," Daddo said,
"therefore I'll continue," and he picked up the threads
without so much as a pause.

"When he was in Dublin, Owen Rankin obtained official orders to increase the size of the Constabulary. Oh,
they were the bane of our life. There was never enough
land for all our sons and being forced to join those devils
was often the only way to make a living. We hated the
Constabulary because the Crown was using us against our
own people. The blight presented a perfect incentive for
recruitment. Hundreds of families hovering on the brink
were suddenly wiped out. A small enlistment bonus, Constabulary wages and bribes and a faint hope of protection
by a son in the police was all that was needed to turn it
into the size of an army. It was an ideal situation for
the British of having Catholics to do their dirty work.

"By now Kilty was onto MacAdam Rankin's game. In
the past he had held us together but this time it was
different. Never were people so terror-stricken. Then all
hope of staging a rising ended when some treacherous,
informing turncoat revealed the locations of our arms.
Panic invaded every house. Gombeen men prowled the

land and the more desperate threw themselves at their mercy, taking out loans with impossible interest rates, and while others fled to the swollen ranks of the Constabulary, hundreds were crossing to look for work in England."

*

The British initiated a series of moves to cool off soaring food prices in Ireland, lifted the protective tariff on corn importation and brought in large shipments of American Indian corn but most of it fell into the hands of speculators.

Poor laws based on workhouses had been in effect in Ireland for several years to attempt to cope with the chronic unemployment. Although the workhouse was a part of English life it was particularly repugnant to the Irish, whose existence was communal, and presented little more promise than a death sentence.

Other plans included large-scale public works, mainly the building of roads.

What was missing was a major policy, a supreme decision for Ireland. In England itself, the nation was in the throes of a social upheaval brought on by an immoral class system riding the waves of the Industrial Revolution.

So what of it if the Irish were in trouble?

At best they were considered a quaint folk, a lying, lazy, ignorant, drunken ingrate race certainly unworthy of life on the plane of a civilized Englishman to whom they were disloyal.

As Ireland's fate was pondered, the colonizers who had squandered the country now exerted every possible pressure to salvage their necks.

*

After a long silence, Conor knelt to hear his daddy breathe, he had become so quiet.

"Don't worry," Daddo said, "he's deeply out of it."

"Aye," Conor said, yawning.

"Are you too sleepy, yourself?"

"No. I want to hear it all," Conor said.

"Then come sit near me like you usually do so I won't have to talk too loud."

Conor came over the hay on his hands and knees and settled at Daddo's feet.

"When your great-grandfar Ronan Larkin came to

Ballyutogue from Armagh around 1800, England had been fighting wars which had ravaged many of the fields of Europe and the needs of the army were great. Every acre in Ireland was transformed to planting grain, for that was where the money was. In doing so, a great deal of the pastureland was wrecked.

"After Waterloo, the demand for grain dropped and the estates earned less and less. Huge holdings of the aristocracy fell into ruin. Many of the gentry were living way over their heads and many had contracted enormous gambling debts. The estates were encumbered and mortgaged to the hilt.

"The MacAdam Rankins and their kind lived from a percentage of their collections and were out to milk every last drop. Ireland's greatest curse has been the landlord, and at the moment of the blight landlordism reached its foulest hour. The issue before the British government was not the survival of the people they had conquered but the survival of the aristocracy they had planted on our soil.

"Other than the potato failure, the crops had been good that year and there was plenty of food in the country to feed us all, provided it was allowed to remain in Ireland, but the encumbered gentry had to sell abroad."

*

The government adopted a position of laissez-faire . . . business as usual with no official interference.

Winter looked the croppy dead on with him holding his bins of rotten food. The estate agents sped up rent collections and soon the cattle pens of Londonderry and the other Irish port cities bulged with meat for export to England.

The deep frosts had made themselves known, first curling leaves, then stripping birch trees and browning the hills. Ballyutogue shivered. It was not until then that Morris Hubble, the Ninth Earl of Foyle, landed in Londonderry.

CHAPTER ELEVEN: The Hubbles seemed to forget, from one year to the next, that the Irish Sea could be every bit as nasty as the Irish roads. No amount of

charm, wit and attention was able to quell the Countess'
nausea. She swooned off the packet and was whisked to
Hubble Manor where she retired immediately to her
apartment and declared herself indisposed.

The Earl of Foyle's annual homecoming was a premier
event on Inishowen. In addition to the flurry of activity,
the usual deluge of social and official invitations and pleas
for audiences, this year's tense conditions created more
than the normal commotion.

As he was settling in, sorting things out, and giving
Lady Beatrice a chance to recover, young Arthur arrived
from Harrow for the holidays with a pair of schoolmates.
This would be the time for bucking up the relationship
with his son.

After three daughters, Arthur's late-in-life birth had
come as a welcome relief, for the line of the ascendancy
was assured. At an early age, the boy showed uncharacteristic fragility for a male Hubble. He was not exactly
his father's pride. In fact, Arthur was so much of a disappointment, Lord Morris wondered if he would even be
able to carry his own weight in the family regiment later.

Morris spent a number of years in frustration attempting to instill manliness into his son. The hard games filled
with good physical going. As the father pressed harder,
the son shrank away, seeking the solace of his mother and
sisters. The Earl's harpooning sarcasm only made Arthur
retrench further. Before he was eight he stammered and
was given to attacks of shortness of breath which increased in intensity when he returned to Hubble Manor
and stood before the imposing figure of his father.

But there would be no more sons. Sobered by this
reality, Morris Hubble, who considered himself an enlightened man, tried to make peace. What he desired in a
son and what he had been given were two different matters. He began to muffle his roars until they were mere
sighs of disgust and controlled burblings. Although signs of
outward disenchantment were kept subdued, the boy's
lack of physical aggressiveness, his stammering and de-
fensiveness and downright prettiness, never failed to churn
the Earl's stomach.

Well, at least Arthur showed a keen mind and he
seemed to do well in school. As the only son, he was the
sole heir and born to the title of Viscount Coleraine.
Adopting distance as the most sensible way to exist, Mor-

ris was grateful that Arthur had come home with friends.
The annual "getting-to-know-one-another father and son
frolics" could be kept to a bare minimum.

The residential wing of Hubble Manor began to fill
with the staggered arrival of three daughters, their husbands and a half dozen grandchildren. The young ladies
had married astutely. Although the Hubble gentry had
been established on Inishowen for two hundred and fifty-
odd years, Lord Morris and all his predecessors considered the earldom a parcel of English land and his own
identity totally English. They were there to carry on responsibilities in a place that was not quite a colony, but
not quite not a colony. Ulster, the seat of their wealth and
power, came in for little personal loyalty, for it remained
an alien land and Ireland an alien planet. Keeping England's presence in Ulster was what mattered and two of
his daughters were meticulously united with their own
kind in the game of self-perpetuation. Beatrice had carefully managed to keep them from straying off to the lure
of the British court.

In the case of the middle daughter, Lady Beverly, a
clever marriage had been effected with a wealthy family
of Ulster Scots who had risen dramatically through linen
mills in Belfast. In England, Beverly's in-laws might have
been considered a comedown, but out here, alliances with
the Scottish element were not treated as that much of a
drop in caste. The Industrial Revolution was creating vast
new fortunes and one had to consider the realities of the
time as well as the reality of their physical separation
from the motherland. Given a few years, Beverly's husband would attain knighthood and, with proper guidance,
a peerage was not out of the question.

The arrival of her daughters and grandchildren was
just the antidote Lady Beatrice needed to gossip her way
out of confinement.

*

Morris Hubble had been elevated from Viscount Coleraine to Earl of Foyle a dozen years earlier, inheriting an
estate sagging under debts incurred by his father's gambling and obscene expenditures on women. The old Earl
passed on, basking in the Indies in the arms of an extremely young, beautiful, black mistress. He had lived in
supreme style and died from an unmentionable disease,

the pain of which had been removed by a heavenly veil of opium.

One of Morris Hubble's first moves had been to oust Owen Rankin from the top estate position, replacing him with his younger brother, MacAdam, a brain of the first order. It permanently embittered Owen, who seemed permanently embittered to begin with. The move changed the earldom's fortunes dramatically.

Lord Morris continued on to become the first of his line to adopt the new principles in dealing with his tenants. The O'Neills and their traditional allies, whose ancient lands were taken to carve out the earldom, had remained the most belligerent clan in Ireland. This condition was worsened by the isolation of the earldom on Inishowen. Croppy violence had been a way of life and was clearly demonstrated when Kilty Larkin ran two thousand head of Hubble cattle into Lough Foyle.

Showing the whip seemed to make little impression on the croppy. Peasant reform had swept Europe in the backwash of the French Revolution with some of its messages finally seeping through to the British Isles. As an age of reason dawned, Lord Morris chose negotiation and won considerable respect plus an era of peace by his agreement to pay the tenants' tithe. Actually, MacAdam Rankin got the entire tithe amount back through subtly manipulated rate raises.

Although he endowed MacAdam with greater responsibility as time passed, he continued to control his affairs scrupulously. Despite their close association, the Earl kept aloof, demanding stringent protocol. It was his lordship's custom to consult with no one except MacAdam, usually in homecoming sessions that lasted many hours.

As their marathon meeting wore on, Lord Morris made his way steadily and unruffled through the massive ledgers, looking up now and then for a question whose answer was invariably on the end of the manager's tongue.

Morris seemed blended into the great library, which was divided into stunning ranks of volumes eternally at attention. Volumes which had been bound and tooled by two generations of craftsmen imported from Florence, who lived and worked on the estate for that sole purpose. The reputation of the library was that of the greatest single place of enlightenment in the cultural desert that existed clear down to the boundary of Dublin.

Behind the severely polished rosewood pedestal desk,
he was framed by a bay window bearing the Hubble coat
of arms in stained glass depicting the Red Hand of Ulster
and a three-headed mythical blue griffin emblazoned with
the Latinized motto: "One More Charge for the Glory of
the King." At the opposite end of the forty-seven-foot hall
hung an immense oil of Ireland's Britannic liberator, King
William of Orange, a work of the court artist of the period, Sir Godfrey Kneller. In keeping with Ulster tradition,
he had replaced Queen Mary with a white steed. The
painting had been miraculously salvaged when a wing of
the original castle was razed during one of the peasant
risings.

Though in his late fifties, the Earl still showed the figure
of a young fusilier officer attired in a dandy frock coat
of striped valencia worn over a vest of Chinese silk. His
sturdy, shapely legs were embraced by white leather
breeches, and his hair, without a speck of gray, was a
mass of curls to the top of his collar length with sideburns
trimmed at lip level. The only sign of oncoming years
was the eyeglass brought up into play to read some of the
more finely written papers.

By contrast, MacAdam Rankin was a small, nippy man
in unpressed bulky kerseymere leaning to the Scottish aus-
terity.

Four imperial cane trunks sat alongside the desk containing the necessary books and records. After the last
ledger had been scrutinized, the two men stared at each
other in forlorn silence interrupted only by the clinking of
their spoons in their teacups. The sparkle of the stained
glass was diffused in graying light. Lord Morris snapped
open his tiny jeweled snuffbox and indulged.

"What caused it?" he asked at last.

MacAdam shifted his aching back and shrugged. "The
Peel Commission says it's a fungus of sorts. There have
been potato failures in America and on the Continent
in the past several years but nothing like this. My own
theory is that germs that caused it must have done their
breeding due to the heavy rains before harvest."

Morris tapped his fist on the desk with repetitious futility, then popped from his chair and literally flung himself into the bay window seat glaring glumly to the outside.

"It's like an armed camp," he said with annoyance.

"It's always like an armed camp in one form or another," Rankin answered, likewise rising for a stretch and wiping his reddened eyes.

"I had come to hope that bloodshed on Inishowen was a thing of the past."

"The good Lord knows you've done more than your share to prevent it."

Lord Morris paced, hands clasped behind him. He traversed the length of the library, settling before the mantel and the portrait of King Billy.

"I hope your lordship realizes I felt bound to increase our police forces as a precaution."

"Yes, but are we able to trust the Constabulary? They're over ninety per cent Catholic."

"They'll do as they're ordered," MacAdam snapped. "Besides, with conditions as they are, any one of them would sing on his mother for a few shillings. The proof is that we've uncovered most of their hidden arms through informers. We'll have no risings from Kilty Larkin this time."

As the two men edged closer to the heart of the situation, they eased into a more comfortable seating arrangement about the fireplace, now measuring each new probe with a stab of anxiety for that awesome decision that lay just ahead. Rankin praised God the ports remained open to allow them to sell to England and ventured that over half the estates in Ulster would have gone under, otherwise.

"What is the latest on government plans?" Lord Morris asked. "I mean, concerning the tenants."

"Road building. If you can get them to work, mind you. If you can get them to work. There's talk of soup kitchens."

"Well, just how hungry do you suspect they are going to get, Mr. Rankin?"

"M'lord, my experience is that they've probably stolen enough of the crops and have them hidden in the hills."

"But what if real hunger becomes widespread?"

"I say that's the government's responsibility."

"Mr. Rankin, in the bundle of petitions, didn't I come across one asking for permission to fish the lough between Carrowkeel and Drung?"

MacAdam had hoped the document would be passed over without notice. Blotches of red cropped up on those parts of his face not hidden by hair. Lord Morris was up off the sofa standing below William of Orange so that both of them seemed to be inquiring. "Well?" Lord Morris said.

"I cannot recommend it," the agent answered.

"Not even in the event of a severe food shortage?"

"M'lord, we've villages of loyal Protestants planted there for two hundred years for the very purpose of protecting the estate's fishing rights."

"Is there not enough to go around in the event of a severe food shortage, Mr. Rankin?"

"Not at the expense of loyal subjects."

"I think I see your point but this is apt to become a crisis, perhaps a total emergency."

As MacAdam Rankin arose, the very nature of the man underwent a change from docile servant to a man suddenly clothed in righteous rage. The eyes of him watered as he spewed forth and punctuated the air with an angry pudgy forefinger. "These folk have inhabited an island for two thousand years. Two thousand years with no tradition as sailors, nor boatbuilders, nor explorers, nor fishermen. They were here a thousand years piling stones on top of each other without mortar before we showed them how. My own maternal forefathers were planted here on Inishowen to preach the true gospel and teach the King's language. But they rejected the true God, choosing instead to hide in caves and carry on their heathen rituals! God knows we tried to convert them but they rejected our Lord! You cannot make men of character out of pure sloth!"

The piercing of his voice suddenly boomeranged back to his own ears and he stopped, catching sorely needed breath and somewhat astounded at his own outburst.

"What we have here, Mr. Rankin, might well be a matter of life and death."

"It is a matter of life and death, m'lord. Theirs or ours. If we allow these people to go down to Lough Foyle and build fishing villages, we'll never get rid of them. They'll continue to breed like flies so that in ten years the lough will be played out, just like the land is played out now."

MacAdam retraced the entire length of the library to the fourth of the trunks, which had remained locked, and he opened it, unfolding a large familiar map and spreading it on the desk. Lord Morris knew it instantly as a plot map of the confusing rundale leases of the Catholic tenants. It was different in that large areas had been shaded with a darker color.

"The solution lies in a single word, the same as we've talked of for years," MacAdam said, "and the word is 'consolidation.' If we can remove the tenants in these shaded areas it would mean immediate conversion of several thousand acres of poor cropland into rich pastureland, unburdened with mouths to feed except those of the cattle. No tithe wars, no risings, no rent collections, no moonshining, no idolatry. Just pastureland and thousands upon thousands of head of cattle plumping up for a ready market in England."

Without further word Lord Morris knew the rest of the trunk contained eviction orders requiring only his signature. His face saddened and he sank behind his desk. "What about those people?" he rasped, pointing to the trunk.

"What about them, m'lord? They've despoiled the land with their ignorance and breeding habits and they have forfeited themselves of our mercy by their rejection of God and the Queen."

All the trappings of his aristocracy suddenly drained from him. "Just how many does that represent?"

"Twenty per cent of the tenants to begin with. There will be more by spring. M'lord, I get no satisfaction of this. Yet the figures do not lie. Overpopulation is so great that within a few years almost every available acre would have been planted into potatoes just to feed them. That is why the earnings have been declining so steadily. We must think of the blight as a blessing in disguise, a message from the Almighty to save this land for the deserving."

MacAdam Rankin was a pragmatic man and his outburst of religious zeal seemed out of place. Yet Ireland, and Ulster in particular, had its pragmatism centered in the Bible as well as the sword. Total belief that their interpretation of God and God's word was the only one, their complete righteousness, their piety through devoutness, all of this was basic Presbyterian Ulsterism, so MacAdam Rankin was keeping strangely in character even for a thick-skinned businessman.

For a fleeting instant it crossed Lord Morris' mind to call a congress of the landowners and shut the ports and feed the people. The idea went as quickly as it came.

Ireland had been raped to the brink of bankruptcy and any such notion would have resulted in massive fore-closures on unpaid mortgages. The Earl's own notes were calling for payments of several thousand pounds which simply could not be met unless crop and cattle went to England.

"You've had the authority all along to sign these eviction notices, Mr. Rankin."

"I don't mind evictions in the normal course of duty, m'lord, but I cannot take responsibility for something like this. It is a basic decision affecting the course of your own life and, after all, you are the Crown here. If you'll affix your signature, I'll do the rest."

"Thank you, Mr. Rankin," he said harshly. "I'll call you when I want you."

MacAdam Rankin nodded and bowed slightly. "Thank you, m'lord."

Morris Hubble was quickly overtaken with a roaring headache as he brooded into infinity while nibbling at his fist. A servant entered and trod about in a whisper, light-ing the candles as darkness overran light. Their flames glowed up the polished mahogany grains of the high rows. He tossed about the room in muted pain and appeared somewhat wild-eyed. And he searched the stacks for a word of consolation, his hand mystically stopping at a small volume of Alexander Pope. The flame light licked close to the page as he read aloud in agonized monotone.

"Religion, blushing, veils her sacred fires,
And unawares Morality expires.
Nor public flame nor private dares to shine;
Nor human spark is left, nor glimpse divine!
Lo! thy dread empire Chaos! is restor'd,
Light dies before thy uncreating word·
Thy hand, great Anarch! lets the curtain fall,
And universal darkness buries all."

After a short eternity he lifted the first batch of evic-tion orders from the trunk, all properly bound in red tape. He unknotted it, taking up the top document His hand trembled so that he had to lay it flat on the desk to read it. It described a pathetic little lease of sixteen acres scattered around the hills in nine separate plots. One Grady MacGilligan. No doubt a toothless number with eyes bleary from drink and emitting unwashed odors. All of it was vivid: the cottage, the flabby woman leading a cow past the fire, the squalling mob of children, the crucifixes and omens, a best room filled with scrambling chickens.

Morris unsheathed the quill from its holder and dipped it in the inkwell. As the first scratch of his signature sounded he looked up startled. "What the devil!"

Young Arthur stood near the desk.

"What are you doing sneaking in here!"

The boy's cheeks flushed. "I'm s-s-s-sorry, Father. I knocked b-b-b-but you didn't answer."

There he goes with his bloody damned stuttering! Morris threw the quill down. "Well! What do you want!"

"I only w-w-w-wanted to b-b-b-borrow a b-b-book."

At that instant Lady Beatrice appeared. "There you are, dear," she sang. "We saw Mr. Rankin leave. Everyone is gathered in the family room. Brooke is going to read us a few chapters of the new Charles Dickens, *The Life and Adventures of Martin Chuzzlewit.*"

"Is there nothing better to read to our grandchildren than that damned radical!"

Beatrice arched her back and her eyebrows at the same time while Morris battled for control of himself, blurting out an apology for his outburst as he did. "Sorry. I've a lot to do yet tonight. Please go on without me. I'll just take a light supper here."

"Very well."

"And, Beatrice," he called as she reached the door. "There is a change of plan. We shall be leaving Hubble Manor within the fortnight. Arrange to send some of the staff ahead and open the town house in London. We shan't be returning to Ireland for some itme."

"Morris, are you quite serious?"

"Don't . . . argue . . . with . . . me . . . Lady Beatrice," he emphasized, "don't argue with me."

She remained in place, utterly perplexed, then turned on her heels. "I'll talk to you later when you are in a civil mood," and departed, banging the door closed.

Arthur crept closer to the desk. "F-F-F-Father, is there anything . . ."

"No, my son," he groaned. "Just try to understand someday . . . and be generous."

CHAPTER TWELVE: Tomas remained ever so peaceful, barely budging for two hours, during which time Daddo had talked himself dry. The shanachie went so often to the jug that himself was getting a bit fuzzy. He stretched, brushed the hay off and strolled unevenly to the byre door. The night had turned entirely sweet with a warming zephyr rushing up the hill. He drew a bucket of water from the well and dunked his face, then settled on a place on the wall worn smooth by generations of Larkin backsides.

Conor followed him to the bucket, then the wall.

"Did you know," Daddo said, "that there's a star for every Irish lad and lass who's had to cross the water?"

"Nae, I didn't know that."

"Neither did I," Daddo said, "I just made it up. But there must be. I waited here, right in this very spot, while Kilty was making his farewells to Mary and his brothers. When the fishing rights were denied and our arms uncovered, we fell into a fearsome funk, knowing it would be days, weeks at the most, until evictions would begin. That was more than Kilty could stay and bear.

"They came out of the cottage, Mary, Kilty, Aidan, Cathal and your daddy Tomas, walking to the crossroads like a funeral procession, stuffing in the hurt. Kilty stopped, mustering all his courage and said, 'You'll go no farther.'

"Tomas was about your age then, perhaps a bit older. He asked if he could go with us to the diamond in Ballyutogue. Kilty nodded and took his hand. At the edge of town we were suddenly run off the road by a pair of racing carriages spattering us as they rushed past and pulled to a halt before the Anglican church. The yard was crowded with people waiting for his lordship's arrival. As we stopped to watch, Hubble and his son, the same scrawny specimen who is now the Earl, passed within touching distance of us. In a queer kind of instant Kilty and the Earl stared eye to eye, then he quickly disappeared inside with the rest of the folk piling in after.

"The weather didn't let us down. It was one of those

thunder plumps pouring down hard enough to split rocks. It was as though every Irishman in heaven was weeping for us.

"We reached England on a cattle boat and got a bit of work unloading it in Liverpool but that was all. The only jobs open were for dustmen, working in the sewers. So we unplugged sludge beneath Liverpool by day. Now your grandfar had always been quick and splendid with his fists so he was able to get a job keeping peace in a dangerous public house in Liverpool's Irish town."

Daddo came off the wall, preening a bit before Conor. "Forty years ago," he said, "as you see me now, I had a voice that could lilt a bluebird out of an arbutus tree. Aye, I could turn a ballad that would make an angel weep. While Kilty kept peace, I sang and told tales for a farthing or ha'penny. Between the sewer and the public house we managed to save a few quid, getting the money back to Ireland when we could, through traveling priests.

"The quickest wages we could come by in spring was scything the winter wheat, where a man was paid by the acre. The size of Kilty always caught the eye of the foreman when we answered calls for work. Scything five or six acres a day might have soon done in a normal man, but Kilty Larkin, with thoughts of Mary and his wee wanes beating through his brain, cut down six to eight acres a day, day in and day out, working so furiously it took two teams of bundlers to stay up with him. The pair of us lived off less than sixpence a day, sleeping in the ditches to save room rent.

"After the winter wheat harvest was in, thousands of desperate Irishmen were roving England looking for work at any price. We was as welcome as the blight."

Daddo looked to the sky for a moment, shaking his head and grunting, still not believing what had happened forty years before.

"We were utterly desperate," he continued with a voice still echoing the urgency, "so we concocted a desperate plan. We followed county fairs and carnivals with me hawking up business and Kilty taking on all comers in a winner-take-all bare knuckle fight. Maybe you wondered why his hands were so crippled and his face so busted. It was over a hundred fights that did it. More than once it would go on for three or four hours, with teeth coming

out and so much blood you couldn't make out his features. He lost a few fights, all right, but he had to be
beaten unconscious before he quit."

"Oh, Grandfar," Conor whispered.

Daddo stopped his story and looked long over the tired
land. "Eighteen and forty-six," he whispered with obvious pain, "was the year that God abandoned Ireland. The
blight struck again and the potato crop was a total loss."

                                    *

Evictions went on with methodical repetition. Four or
five times a week a small legion of Constabulary paraded
into Ballyutogue behind Owen Rankin, who oversaw it
with fanatical lust while his brother, MacAdam, continued
to link up shaded plots on his map.

The police deployed around the victim cottage. A
squad then moved in and threw the family out. Screams
and prayers met deaf ears. Resistance met swift, merciless
subjugation.

Owen Rankin read the riot act, a warning that Queen's
business was about to ensue and must not be interfered
with. Next he read the eviction notice. The man, his wife,
his parents and his children watched in helpless terror as
their home was bashed in with battering rams and tumbled to make it uninhabitable, and what was burnable was
razed. They sat in stunned little huddles with their belongings on a single cart as the Constabulary re-formed
and marched on to the next cottage and the next.

Owen Rankin read the riot act before a dozen, ten doz-
en, ten hundred with the echo of the battering ram re-
verberating around Ireland by the tens of thousands. Cottages jammed with homeless refugees. When these were
tumbled, hundreds of thousands burst out onto the roads,
open to the elements, scavenging the hills as pack animals.

                                    *

"Kilty managed to keep his family alive. Aidan was the
youngest brother with the largest family and some of the
poorest land. Even working as one large family unit, it
became apparent that he was going under. Night after
night they'd talk it over, begging him to split up the family between Mary and Cathal, and give up his own land.
He was draining the others to keep him afloat and everyone's chances would be better if he did.

"Aidan and his wife, Jenny, could never quite bring themselves to agree and one morning a platoon of Constabulary had surrounded the cottage and Owen Rankin was reading the riot act. It was a particularly sweet moment for the Rankins, for they had craved vengeance on the Larkins for years. Well . . . Owen never got to finish because Aidan went into a rage, unearthing a hidden musket, and blew his face off.

"He and Jenny held the Constabulary off for three hours until he was shot dead and she wounded. The Constabulary broke in and she and the six wee wanes were hauled off screaming and struggling as the cottage was tumbled."

"What happened to her, Daddo?"

"They were carted off to Derry and taken before a magistrate. She was charged with being an accomplice to the murder of Owen Rankin and interfering with Her Majesty's police."

*

The winter of 1847 was a bitter recurrence of icy rains. Hunger was joined by the lethal ally of disease.

Young Tomas took the responsibility of finding his Aunt Jenny and her children. The walk to Derry was over twenty miles. Gangs of bony, ragged, evicted farmers, their wives and children, worked on public projects for a few pennies a day, dragging about, keeling over in the chill and wet, making roads to nowhere.

MacAdam Rankin had obtained a large government grant and set his work gangs to building high stone walls to seal off the Earl's fields and fishing areas. Famine walls. Even as the gangs toiled they were berated by their British overseers as useless for not attending to their farms.

As Tomas neared Derry, the open fields were filled with thousands of beggars squatting without food or shelter. Ancient men and women of forty and little old men and women of four and five. These had been driven out of Derry by gangs of "bang beggars," other wretches who were beggars themselves now earning a few pence a day to keep the beggar population from growing.

The poor law and workhouse system had been particularly alien to the Irish, for it spelled a final loss of hope and dignity within the hollow cavernous halls. Tomas

arrived there as the first stop on his search. The workhouse was now a mob scene, besieged by hundreds of
screaming, maddened human skeletons pleading to be allowed in, crawling over each other to get to the soup
kitchen where they were slopped like pigs. In the workhouse yards fever sheds held hundreds more dying, too
far gone to do much more than moan their agony, low.

The boy passed from row to row, mat to mat for hours,
looking in vain. He roamed Derry for four days in utter
futility until hunger began to overtake him. As a last
desperate measure he found an old retired priest who had
known his grandfather, Ronan, in County Armagh,
who was able to ascertain that Jenny had been taken to
the bridewell as a convicted criminal and confined in the
black hole. The children had been removed to a foundling
home.

For another three days Tomas was driven from the
prison but persisted until one of the wardens promised
to find out. He got the word that his Aunt Jenny had
been found dead four days after her imprisonment. No
one seemed to know or care how she died but, being
profoundly religious, it was doubtful she took her own
life. Perhaps grief, perhaps her wounds, perhaps . . .
something else.

The search for the children was even more frightening,
for if anything was feared more than the workhouse, it
was the foundling home. The old priest took Tomas into
his own home and after another agonizing week got permission for him to get inside the orphanage. Hundreds
upon hundreds of children lay on the floor in rags in the
odorous, damp gray light. Their skins spotted and bleeding from advance stages of scurvy, lice-ridden and burning
with fever. The institution workers were no longer sound
of mind, having worked themselves into exhaustion. The
smell of death intermixed torturously with monologues
to a God who apparently did not hear. The children of
Aidan and Jenny Larkin were not found or heard of
again.

Tomas retreated back to Ballyutogue. Dozens of dead
now lay in the ditches. Winter was only half through.
Communal life, a key to past survival, had been destroyed
by the evictions and, with it, life itself.

People of the villages, too proud to die in front of their
neighbors, staggered up to the scalps, the bog caves, to

meet their end. Once the husband crossed the water or died, the end came swiftly for the balance of the family.

They would lie in their awful agony huddled together, covered with whatever rags they could carry . . . the ma, the babies, all still and moaning with no more than skin stretched over bones and filled with stinking sores and bloated from dropsy. Often, one or more would be dead for days and just remain among the others.

An only alternative was emigration for those who could scrape fare together. Although the Irish were British citizens according to laws enacted by the British, the people in England were hostile and of a temper to keep them out.

British authorities channeled the fleeing Irish to Canada and America by whatever means and no matter in what condition. Cattle boats were rushed into passenger service and they poured out of Ireland by the hundreds of thousands. This was the opening round of the most penetrating of all Irish tragedies, the export of her greatest resource, her people.

*

"Me and Kilty were on hard times in England. Communication was near impossible. The few available priests spent every waking hour writing letters but getting one from Ireland was a mighty chore. Finally a message did reach Kilty telling him to get home.

"The situation with the Larkins grew more desperate. A decision was made that the last of their money should go to buy passage for Cathal and his family to America. Three days before they were to sail it was discovered that the ship was fictitious and the passage money taken as a swindle by gombeen men.

"MacAdam Rankin, moving feverishly to finish his chores, chartered a ship and offered free passage in a move to clear the rest of the croppies from the earldom. Most of the boats were no more than floating coffins but what Rankin chartered turned out to be the worst death ship of the entire famine. Half the passengers died en route and, among them, Cathal's two youngest daughters."

Daddo walked to the byre door again and pointed to Tomas sleeping in the hay. "One by one, your daddy lying there watched his sister and brothers and his mother die and put them under with his own hand. All of them died with green mouths like so many of our people did. Green mouths from eating grass.

"And then the fever got him. The boy lit a turf fire and set himself near it with a few roots and berries and waited for his end. That was how Kilty found him."

CHAPTER THIRTEEN: Daddo and Conor returned to the byre as the first half-light edged over the lip of the lough. Daddo's voice was ever so weary from the sorrows and length of his tale. After he made himself comfortable he bade Conor lie down and rest his head on his lap and, stroking the boy's hair softly, hastened to bring his story to a close before the daylight should cause him to vanish.

"When Kilty had passed through his awful grief he set about the business of surviving with his only son, your daddy, Tomas. By trial and error they got to know every edible plant that grew wild in the high mountains. There was the odd rabbit on a lucky day and ways of stealing from the Prods, even though they were armed for a war. In short time Kilty realized that if they were to come through it they had to fish the lough.

"A fragile curragh was hidden in the tall grass near Three Trees. By night they would row with whispering stealth to one of the rock islands between Red Castle and White Castle, with navigating as treacherous as St. Brendan finding his way to the New World. Many the time I'd row the night with them. After living through that ordeal we'd nearly have our heads bashed off making the approach to the rock . . . bobbing up on the high swells, then sweeping in like a bolt. Footing was slippery as the snot off your nose. We'd run the curragh ashore and hide it in the crags just before daylight.

"We'd make our way around the island and do most of our work on our bellies, laying low to avoid being spotted by the Constabulary patrols. We'd clean mussel from the rocks, set lobster traps and fish the day with horsetail hand lines. Maybe the saints would bless us and we'd net a sea gull or migrating bird. If we got entirely skunked there would still be the mussel and edible seaweed."

Daddo blew a long breath. "Oh, Lord, Conor. All I seem to remember for almost three years is seaweed and mussel. The taste of it is in my mouth to this very day. Famine food. We would fill our bellies while out there on the island so's we could take back what was left for the neighbors. We'd wait for the cover of darkness just lying there. It would turn into a nightmare when the winds and tides blew high. Many the day we'd cling to the rocks, our arms around each other to keep from getting washed away with the sea bashing over us, choking us half to death and pounding us to pudding. With blessed darkness we'd make our way in, being tossed about like seeds in the wind."

With his head on Daddo's lap, Conor could no longer contain the tears which had been seeking an outlet all through the night and he cried softly as the shanachie came to the closing of his story.

"In America, Cathal and his wife Siobhan and two living daughters joined the shanty Irish in a shantytown near the railroad tracks. The women worked as domestics in fine Boston homes for fifty cents a day. Their masters were not unlike our aristocracy. Cathal did what he had to do. The railroads paid a dollar a day and almost everything they earned was sent back to keep their kin alive. It was the Irish fleeing the famine were the navvies who put down the railroads and canals in the New World."

*

The British wearied of Irish famines by the fourth straight crop failure and relief was nearly at a halt. The door to England was shut in Irish faces. In the fifth year of the great hunger Ireland had been decimated by a million deaths of starvation and disease and yet another million by emigration. Those fortunates who reached America kept those in Ireland existing. The American people generously poured millions of dollars into Irish relief.

*

"Cathal never returned to Ireland. Once a man leaves, he gives all his love to his new country, for what he had left was bitter vetch. Sure, they sing sentimental songs, weeping crocodile tears as they do, and they wear the green once a year in their parades . . . but they never come back.

"There came a time in all of this that even MacAdam Rankin and his kind realized too many good farmers had gone. Those who survived were able to increase their holdings and laws changed so that there was a chance to buy land.

"That is why you have to realize why thirty-two acres of this land has the Larkin name stamped on it forever and why your daddy stands so proudly upon it. . . ."

*

Daylight streaked into the byre, inching into the stall and over Conor's face. The warmth and brightness of it brought him out of his deep sleep. He sat up quickly. Daddo and Tomas were both gone! He sprang to his feet, looking about in confusion.

"Ah, there's the sleeping beauty," Finola said from her milking stool. "I thought you'd never wake up."

"Where's Daddy?"

"He's off to the bogs and high time he decided to do a day's work."

Conor pranced out to the yard, looking around perplexed. He dunked his face, sprinted to the wall, leaped it and broke into the O'Neills' best room.

"Daddo!" he cried.

The old man was seated at the table digging into a pot of mush.

"Daddo!"

"Just because I'm blind doesn't mean I'm deaf as well. Who's doing all the shouting at me?"

"It's me, Conor."

"Blessings of the day to you, Conor."

Conor slipped to the table opposite him and studied him queerly. Sure, it was not the same man he had talked the night away with. It was just plain old Daddo.

"Daddo . . . where were you last night?"

"Taking my rest of course."

"Did you not go any place special?"

"I'm too old to be dancing around; besides, I'm feeling sorely over Kilty."

"Did you . . . I mean . . . Jaysus, I don't know what I mean. Daddo, let me ask you this. Were you once a fine ballad singer?"

"Aye, lad, aye. There's legends about the saintly quality of my voice. You know that, surely."

"And . . . and did you go to England with Kilty during the great hunger?"

"Of course. Everyone knows I did."

"And did you steal fish from the Earl's islands?"

"Like any adventurous man hereabouts has done. And why, may I ask, the grand inquisition?"

Conor cradled his face in both hands, attempting to get things in proper order. "Oh, it's a puzzlement."

"What's a puzzlement?"

"I think I'm getting things all mixed up. Stories and dreams and things."

"Oh, I see," Daddo said. "A visit from the fairies during the night, perhaps?"

Conor scratched his head. "It was so real."

"Then you did get a visit. But sometimes, Conor, we know little bits and pieces of things all along, only needing a fairy to fit them all together. If that's what happened, you're likely onto a special gift with the possibility of being a shanachie one day yourself."

Conor looked to the door and his legs quickly followed his eyes to it. "Good-by, Daddo! Have a grand journey home!"

He raced like fury to the crossroads, then stopped short at the churchyard, entering reverently. Kilty's grave was still a mass of flowers and little clay pipes. Conor fell to his knees and crossed himself.

"Oh, Grandfar, it was a great man you were. I'll be a Larkin you'll be proud of one of these days."

Conor did not stop running for almost a mile until he caught up to the line of men trudging toward the bogs with his daddy, as usual, at the head of them.

"Daddy! Daddy!"

On seeing his boy Tomas became alive with joy. "Slow down with you, Conor. You're always running too hard."

"Can I come and work the bogs with you today?"

Tomas put his arm around his son's shoulder and they continued upward. "Sure now," he said, "that would be grand."

END OF PART ONE

PART TWO

The Orange Card

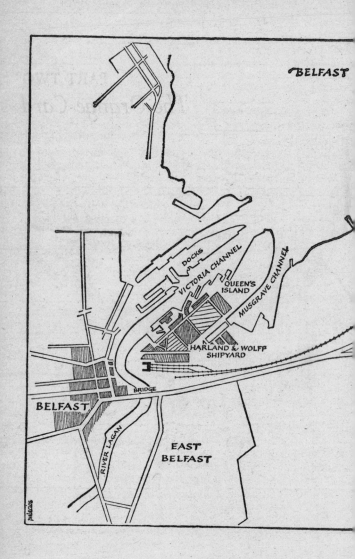

BELFAST

DOCKS

VICTORIA CHANNEL

QUEEN'S ISLAND

MUSGRAVE CHANNEL

HARLAND & WOLFF SHIPYARD

BRIDGE

BELFAST

RIVER LAGAN

EAST BELFAST

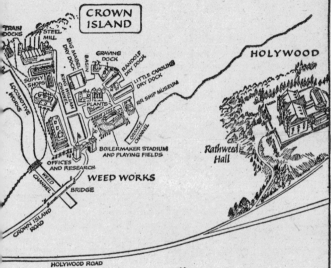

LOUGH

CROWN ISLAND

TRAIN DOCKS

STEEL MILL

HOLYWOOD

BIG MABEL DRY DOCK

GRAVING DOCK

RANDOLF DRY DOCK

BASIN

LITTLE CAROLINE DRY DOCK

KING WILLIAM CHANNEL

SUPPLY SHOPS

LOCOMOTIVE WORKS

PLANTS

RR SHIP MUSEUM

ORANGE CHANNEL

Rathweed Hall

BOILERMAKER STADIUM AND PLAYING FIELDS

OFFICES AND RESEARCH

WEED WORKS

WEED CHANNEL

BRIDGE

CROWN ISLAND ROAD

HOLYWOOD ROAD

N

BELFAST LOUGH
AND
WEED WORKS.

CHAPTER ONE

JUNE 1885

Major Hamilton Walby, M.P., M.M., M.V.O., C.I.E., was a bluster of a man. Belying his sixty-three years, he rode his white Arabian with ramrod erectness, surveying his realm at a fast trot as though he were perpetually on the verge of breaking into a cavalry charge.

The squire of Lettermacduff Township and Borough was contemptuously proud that his was the most thoroughly Anglicized community in County Donegal. Nearly every constituent was an inheritor of Cromwell spoils.

The first of the Walbys to come to Ireland had been Isaiah, who in 1649 won a measure of renown as a Cromwell officer. Captain Isaiah distinguished himself during the massacre at Drogheda in which several thousand Catholics, women and children no exception, were slaughtered in holy vengeance. The Drogheda murders were sanctified by Oliver Cromwell himself, who declared it "a righteous judgment of God upon barbarous wretches." In the three hundred-odd years that followed, this opinion of the natives remained largely unchanged by succeeding generations of Walbys.

As his reward, Captain Isaiah Walby was given a grant of some four thousand acres of land usurped from the O'Neill clan, and a Crown charter for the Borough of Lettermacduff. Isaiah peopled it with soldiers of his old regiment, parceling out land grants and, after making further seizures, selling that to worthy Englishmen at threepence an acre.

Major Hamilton Walby, the present squire, continued an unbroken tradition of family service to the Crown. He purchased a commission in the army and the privileges that went with rank. In the Ulster Rifles he got his taste of action in suppression of the great Sepoy Mutiny in

India. It was a particularly gory affair distinguished by a brand of savagery on the part of rebel and Crown alike that would have done old Isaiah proud. The manner of executions became grisly and highly ingenious. The Ulster Rifles, successors of a notorious Yeomanry, were determined not to be outdone. Condemned sepoy mutineers were piped out to the parade ground with great pomp in cadence to the jaunty music of some old Orange or Ulster marching air. After a proper reading off the sepoy would then be strapped to the muzzle of a cannon and a round blown off. This method of execution became so popular that it was literally stolen by less inventive regiments until it became a universal punishment.

Lettermacduff Borough proved to be among the most prosperous settlements, resembling a bit of transplanted English countryside, and no Irish property was more loyal to the Crown. The Walbys built a modest fortune on flax. Each new squire in turn became a pillar of the community.

Prior to the Act of Union, the family had been members of the all-ascendancy Anglo Parliament in Dublin during the seventeenth and eighteenth centuries. After the Union, the East Donegal seat in the House of Commons at Westminster became a family possession. Major Hamilton Walby, alone, had served for nearly three decades. With the Walbys in Commons and the Hubbles in Lords, the political well-being of the loyal settlements was thoroughly attended to. Then came the audacious news that a Fenian and Land Leaguer, Kevin O'Garvey, was challenging the squire's seat.

Enraged by the utter cheek of it, Hamilton Walby erupted so furiously that his personal physician feared the squire was going to have a seizure of apoplexy. For a week the color of his face rarely faded below sunrise purple. He finally sputtered to a low gasping calm when his son-in-law and closest confidant, A. J. Pitkin, returned from Dublin Castle with comforting news. With so many new voters eligible for the next election, most of the districts would be subject to review and a Crown commission would make required necessary boundary adjustments. It was never put into so many words but certain districts such as Walby's East Donegal could be nudged into the proper column with a bit of fixing.

Major Walby, with Pitkin at his side, was invited to closed-door commission meetings to offer his advice in the matter. In company of sympathetic friends from the Castle, Walby drew out new boundaries which would guarantee a loyal majority and his continuation in the seat. In adopting his proposals the East Donegal boundaries were jiggled about and redrawn, so that land corridors reached out into the hinterlands as elongated fingers to encompass the most remote Protestant pockets of population. At the same time, numerous Catholic towns and villages, which had always been inside the district, were lopped off and placed outside so their votes would be nullified.

Without public hearings or consideration of O'Garvey's proposals, the commission departed and dispatched their conclusions by post. East Donegal had been gerrymandered into a grotesque configuration resembling an octopus. No justification was required of the commission and no appeal allowed.

Relieved that the Castle had come through for him, as it should have, Hamilton Walby was content to oversee his borough and remain in communion with his renowned garden of Ulster roses.

Until that time, few croppies in East Donegal believed there was a chance for Kevin O'Garvey. Yet, instead of the desired results, the blatant gerrymander had a powerful adverse effect. Defying the ravages of age, Daddo Friel heralded O'Garvey's candidacy in village after village and Tomas Larkin followed in his steps. As news of this activity filtered back to the squire, he became increasingly irritated, then suspicious.

"It's becoming a bloody damned nuisance," he told A. J. Pitkin after another disturbing report of a meeting with over a hundred croppies in attendance right in his own borough. "I thought we put this nonsense behind us with the new boundaries, Pitkin. What do those people think they're doing?"

"One would gather," Pitkin answered after the usual double clearing of his throat, "they actually believe they've sufficient strength to win."

"Balderdash, pure rot. I mean, after all, you were right there at the commission with me. They acted completely down the line on our proposals."

Atwell Pitkin sputtered in a manner which meant that

unpleasant news was not far behind. A.J. was a good
chap, that sort of thing, but not the staunchest of men.
He had been selected to marry Heather Walby because of
his legal and accounting skills. The squire arched his brow
ominously, wilting his son-in-law under his sternest military
glare.

Pitkin blanched and his voice upped in pitch. "We have
a small doubt whether our majority is clear cut," he said.

"What!" A cup clattered about the desk from the crack
on the table.

"Now, now, Major, mind the old blood pressure."

"*I* [fist on table] *want* [fist on table] *to* [fist on table]
know [fist on table] WHAT THE HELL IS GOING ON!"

After clearing his forehead of its sudden outpour of
moisture, Pitkin pulled himself together, trying to stem
the growing rage opposite him. "I had a shadow of doubt
so I went back over the tenants' lists supplied by his lordship, as well as the available public records. As you well
know, Squire, the Catholics are extremely lax in registering births and deaths. Well, we are all aware of that, are
we not?"

The Major's eyebrow was scrinched so it looked as if
it was going to touch his mustache. "Carry on, Pitkin."

"With all their comings and goings and their breeding
habits, well, one can't be certain of their actual numbers,
can one?"

Hamilton Walby's face was turning that awful color
again. He bellowed for his son-in-law to get to Dublin
Castle and reopen the matter of the district boundaries
with the commission. Pitkin then dropped the other shoe.

"As a matter of fact, Squire, I contacted them immediately."

"And?"

"They said we'd better leave well enough alone," he
mumbled.

"What did you say?"

"I said they said we'd better leave well enough alone."

"The Castle told you that!"

"Well, sir, it seems that the only way we can extend
the boundaries to take in more loyal subjects is to reach
clear down to the outskirts of Londonderry. The problem
with that is that Londonderry is reaching out to Ballyutogue for the same purpose. You see, the Liberals are

liable to get wind of all this and come to Ireland and investigate . . . er . . . irregularities."

"Irregularities? What irregularities? The whole bloody
mess was perpetrated by the bloody Liberals in the first
place with their bloody reform. It's the end of the Empire, that's what."

After his hot blows Hamilton Walby generally went
about his business with cold dispatch. Pitkin was ordered to
seek an audience with the Catholic Bishop, Gerald Nugent.
As a matter of practical policy, Lord Hubble endowed the
Bishop's good works generously, a policy also subscribed
to by the Major. Neither Bishop Nugent nor the Cardinal
at Armagh needed to be reminded that legislation favor-
able to the Church was in Walby's and Hubble's hands. Support for that legislation could be counted on only so long
as a quid pro quo was maintained.

Pitkin's request was twofold. The Bishop proved most
cooperative. An accurate census was needed and the best
way to obtain it was through His Grace's parish priests.
Secondly, the Bishop's priests should be instructed to inform their parishioners in no uncertain terms that flirta-
tion with Fenian agitators would be construed as sinful.

The census came back in quick order and, despite the
gerrymandering of the district, it turned up some sobering
figures. The number of Catholics and Protestants with
the right of franchise was only a few hundred votes apart.
A.J. tried to mollify the Major with the argument that the
Catholics would be too disinterested to exercise their vote
and, furthermore, Bishop Nugent's message would soon be
at parish level.

"Everyone knows," Pitkin stated as fact, "those people
do what their priests tell them."

Hamilton Walby wasn't so sure but the old days with the
Ulster Rifles had told him there could be no flinching in
the face of the enemy. Damned if he'd be forced into any
change of stance. He would carry on as usual, attending
some of the fairs and making the perfunctory visits to the
Anglican congregations in the district. Yet even as he
practiced bullheaded nonchalance he could not completely shake the feeling that the family heirloom, their seat
in Commons, might be in danger and God forbid if he
were the first Walby since the Act of Union to lose it.

Things came to a head at the Buncrana Fair. It was

a large annual event attended by nearly everyone on the Inishowen Peninsula. Although the area was heavily Catholic, the fair drew great numbers of Presbyterian farmers from Ballyutogue. While the squire did his usual stint of judging flowers and horseflesh, Kevin O'Garvey held a rally at the far end of the grounds.

Curiosity over the Fenian Land Leaguer brought scores of Presbyterians near the speaker's platform, which was heavily guarded by Tomas Larkin's people. Trouble was likely because the Constabulary had refused to provide protection, stating that O'Garvey's permit to speak was not properly executed. Despite the possibility of a riot, Kevin decided to hold the rally because he knew that his chances to address Protestant crowds would be limited.

He marched to the platform convoyed by an escort of tough croppies, many of whom had once been night riders, and he seemed even smaller than he was. That image disappeared as he launched directly into the heart of matters affecting every farmer in the area. He was a Land Leaguer and a solicitor and he knew all the tricks of the agents and estate owners. Connivance used on the Protestants was far more subtle than that against the croppies, such as manipulation of flax prices, which took money out of the pockets of every man listening.

Any notions of harassment or stampede dispelled to rapt attention as O'Garvey issued a challenge to Hamilton Walby to come up to the stand and explain the matter of providing money for the gombeen men to loan to farmers at abnormal interest rates. After throwing a hundred Presbyterian farms into debt because of flax prices, Walby's agents had made them loans and when these were defaulted he had annexed hundreds and hundreds of their acres, Presbyterian acres, to his personal squiredom.

When the message of O'Garvey's speech got back to the squire, his loyal legions were further shattered to see the Major and his entourage gallop away from the fair without finishing his judging chores.

The charges had gone unanswered and the loyalists were in a quandary.

*

Luke Hanna, a craggy old sort of about the Major's age, had managed Lord Hubble's flax mill for two decades.

A. J. Pitkin led Luke through the scented splendor of the squire's rose garden but was suddenly held at bay by a pair of nasty characters, Walby's pit bull terriers. The Major looked up from his digging, pacified his pets, set his tools aside and tugged off his gloves.

"Good of you to come, Hanna."

The three made to the gazebo. Walby knew that Luke practiced temperance only part of the time and ordered refreshments of a substantial nature. One of the dogs staked claim to the Major's lap, fixed on Luke and growled low at his every move.

"Bang on, Hanna," Walby said. "I asked you here because I want to use you as a sounding board. As you know, the next election will have some novel aspects to it."

Luke held his hands up in a begging-off gesture. "I'm no politician."

"Ah, but you are a deacon in your church and the Grand Master of your Orange Lodge. You know what the chaps are saying and thinking."

"Just what are you after finding out, Squire?"

"Hummm, any whispers of discontent, that sort of thing."

"Shall I be blunt?"

"Candor, I believe, is the order of the day here, what, Pitkin?"

"Candor, indeed," Pitkin concurred.

The squire's eyebrow arched as Luke pondered his words and the dog was petted until he stopped his rumbling.

"The lads are thinking it's high time you gave us the time of day," Luke said.

"I think that calls for an explanation," Pitkin said.

"Well now, take this incident at the Buncrana Fair. There were some pretty harsh charges, Squire. Maybe they should have been answered."

"Rubbish," Walby snapped. "You certainly don't expect me to engage in a name-calling contest with a gang of rowdies. Well, do you?"

Luke shrugged and fortified himself.

"See here, Hanna," Pitkin said indignantly, "certainly no one believes that pack of Fenian lies."

"It's like this, gentlemen. Makes no difference to our

lads. Nothing Kevin O'Garvey tells them is going to change a single vote. Our lads are loyal to the end. However, they're after thinking some of that loyalty should be returned by yourself."

Walby and his dog growled together in practiced rhythm. Pitkin and he had discussed the possibility of recruiting Orangemen to harass O'Garvey's meetings. It seemed a bit dicy in that they had to steer clear of anything that might cause outside observation. A riot that would bring in journalists could well drag up the business of the voting boundary changes.

"You are certainly not suggesting that the squire hasn't represented loyal interests in Parliament?" Pitkin snipped.

"Well, let me see if I can tell you what I'm telling you," Luke retorted. "We've gone along with the Major unflinching and unfailing. Times have taken a turn, like maybe the Major needs us just as much as we need him. So what I'm telling you is this. You've not gone out of your way to give us a little praise in the past. I think you'd better consider your partnership with us in the future. Just because we're not Anglicans doesn't mean we're not good, loyal Protestants."

"I see," Walby said.

Luke managed to suppress his delight. This was apt to be a painful comeuppance for the squire, who was going to be forced to come out of his enchanted little borough and solicit the same men he'd spent a lifetime ignoring. Sure they were loyal and sure they were Protestants but Luke knew how the squire considered them. Dissenters, that's what. Any non-Anglican was a dissenter, an inferior.

"You'll find the strongest way to influence our lads is through our preachers, who never let our people forget their duty to the Crown, both in the Church and in the Orange Order. In my opinion, you ought to consider taking part in the Twelfth of July and Apprentice Boys celebrations this summer. Let yourself be seen around, if you know what I mean."

When it suited his purpose Hamilton Walby could turn livid. Otherwise, he owned an extremely shrewd mind capable of evaluations in a clear and quick manner. He remained placid, for what Luke told him was entirely clear.

"Don't you feel that because of the lack of personal contact in the past your chaps are apt to think my sudden rash of appearances might be somewhat . . . er . . . transparent?"

"They will consider it to mean you finally recognize their importance," Luke answered directly. "The new political order of things, one might call it."

Sensing his master's discontent, the dog growled and was booted from his lap for his trouble. Walby didn't like the bloody alliance, not a bit. And what if he refused to make an ass of himself and parade about in their idiotic costumes? Indeed, what of it? Who would they vote for? The Fenian?

As though Luke were reading his mind, he smiled and delivered the coup. "If you don't get out and march with the lads, they might put up their own candidate."

With that question answered, the Major turned to Pitkin and in true commanding-officer style ordered him to get cracking on a program of appearances.

"Like I said when I came," Luke said, "I'm no politician but you'd also better consider the fact that your constituency has expanded." Luke jerked his thumb in the direction of the hills.

"Are you suggesting, Hanna, that the squire go up there and mingle with the Catholics?"

"Isn't that carrying this democratic business a bit far?" Walby said.

"Right or wrong, they've got the vote," Hanna answered. "I think it would show a great deal of character on your part to face them man to man and let them know you're a man of your own convictions."

"But they haven't the vaguest idea of fair play," Pitkin said, "they'll make a shambles."

"I've got to disagree," Hanna said. "I've been dealing with them all my life without trouble."

"Never, sir, never!" Hamilton Walby cracked.

"Hear, hear," Pitkin echoed.

*

"Never" turned out to be three days of agonizing.

The new demands to practice egalitarianism for the first time in one's life was confusing.

The Presbyterians had been trying to gain an equal status with Anglicans for generations. History on the matter was quite clear that in the beginning of the plantation of Ulster the Presbyterians were in league with the Catholics. They turned to the Crown when it suited their own purposes and ever since had tried to force an alliance down the Anglicans' throats.

Walby detested the zealous evangelical nature of the Presbyterian Church as crude, pompous, downgrading and highly imaginative. The squire had studiously arranged to be in England during their summer marching season and avoid all that Orange rowdyism.

Despite their shortcomings, Walby could rationalize that they were palatable. They were now completely loyal. They were British, in a manner of speaking. They were Protestants. A low order, mind you, but Protestant nonetheless. An accommodation with them was required to keep the Irish properties safe for the Crown. East Donegal was his personal segment of that duty and responsibility.

While one might live with the Presbyterian thing, the Catholic thing was incomprehensible. Hitherto, a visit to their Bishop had sufficed. Those church people knew how to play the game. But now he was faced with the repugnant prospect of actually soliciting Catholic votes to return to a seat in Commons that was his and his alone.

Few blue thoughts and utterances about Gladstone and the Liberals failed to cross Walby's mind and lips. Those people were conspiring to destroy the Empire. Since when does a colonizer give the natives the right to vote? It was ridiculous enough to form the Act of Union which permitted the Irish Catholics to sit in the British Parliament. Lord, everyone knew Parnell and his wretches were out to destroy the Union and impose Home Rule. What between heaven and earth could be more devastating than a Dublin Parliament peopled by Fenians who had neither the right nor the ability to rule themselves?

Through all his agonizing, one ideal prevailed. The unthinkable disaster would be to bring eternal shame to the family name by losing the seat. Things were a bit up in the air now but a good officer assesses his losses, regroups his forces and attacks.

And then his agonizing was done.

*

Bong! Bong! Bong! sounded the angelus, the men trudging through the crossroad fell to their knees as though they had been cut down by the blast of a blunderbuss. "Hail, Mary, blessed art thou . . ."

Tomas squinted into the muffled light of Dooley McCluskey's public house, the odor of the place pure heaven after a day in the fields. McCluskey slid Tomas' nightly measure over the bar to him.

"How are you keeping, Dooley?"

McCluskey grimaced. "Poorly, Tomas. The constipation," he moaned. "I've a monumental case of knots in me puddin'." He nodded to the dark corner where Luke Hanna held forth alone with a bottle.

"Ho there, Luke. What brings you to these parts this time of day?"

"I've been waiting for you." He refilled Tomas' glass. "Here, throw that across your chest."

"Sláinte."

"Sláinte," the salute was returned.

Luke shook his head, disbelieving what he was about to say. "The squire wants to hold a political meeting with the lads in your village."

"Aw, don't glink me, man."

"I'm not glinking you."

"Surely?" Tomas said.

"Aye, it's a fact."

Dooley, who was generally the soul of discretion, emitted a whistle.

"Jaysus," Tomas said. "About the only time we ever see Hamilton Walby is when he comes galloping through our fields after those poor dear little foxes. Does the man really think he's going to win votes in these parts?"

Luke scratched his jaw. "It's like this, Tomas. You know where I stand and I know where you stand. It might not do any good. On the other hand, what harm is there? So long as the new laws require certain accommodations, they ought to be arranged peacefully."

"That makes sense," Tomas said. "And I suppose the squire is prepared to give the same courtesy to Kevin O'Garvey."

"Ah, I knew you was going to bring that up. Tomas, all of this is new and there's only so many shocks the likes of Hamilton Walby can stand at one time. Don't push things too fast, man. Let's have his meeting here and see what happens after."

Tomas shrugged. "Why not? Tell the squire he'll be most welcome."

Dooley McCluskey then launched a sincere appeal that the meeting take place at the crossroad under the great old oak known as the "hanging tree." It would be far better than the Norman keep, he reckoned, because, with a gathering of that size and nature, thirst would not be far behind.

Luke and Tomas spat on their hands and shook to consummate the deal, then made outside where the angelus groaned on.

"How come you let yourself get mixed up with the squire?" Tomas asked.

Luke hitched his belt and stretched in the cool evening air. "Doesn't matter, does it? I mean, who's sitting in Westminster, Walby or O'Garvey? You and me, Tomas, know it's all a game of words. There's nae going to be a Home Rule in our lifetime so long as the House of Lords remains in England and it has the right of veto. I'll still be going to the mill six days a week and you'll be doing the same up in your fields. Nothing is really going to change."

Tomas had told Kevin about the cruel disillusions of brave new dawns. He and Luke Hanna knew the realities. "Aye," Tomas said, "that's a fact, Luke, that's a fact."

CHAPTER TWO: Sir Frederick Weed pounded out his steps with a tenacity attributed to one of his larger marine engines. The entourage strung out behind him broke into a half trot to keep up as he reached the midway point of his personal, fortnightly inspection tour. The main graving dock stood in dead center of the sprawling industrial monolith where he disappeared into the hold of the ship undergoing major repairs.

The inspection tour had become a classic of sorts with flash consultations and on-the-spot decisions with his engineers and foremen. A flood of orders and memos spewed out to his aide, Kendrick, and a string of male secretaries who perspired to a man despite the chill in the air.

Out of the hold he plunged into his newly expanded marine engine plant, a mastodon of five acres under roof. Sir Frederick had wagered heavily on the concept of a triple expansion engine designed to increase boiler pressures which drove his new twin screw ships to mercurial speeds of up to eighteen knots. Unheard of! But this was an age of unheard-ofs and now his architects were planning ships of ten thousand tons!

Weed knew a large number of the thousands of employees by first name. As he moved along he feigned camaraderie, constantly politicking as he lent a "sincere" ear to this complaint or that suggestion, shoving off again with the backslap, the handshake, the word of mock encouragement. His blocklike build of former athletic days had somewhat blubberized but he still cut a figure of respect and his cigar bellowed as though it were smoke from an eternal flame.

Out of the marine engine building the inspection party paraded to King William Channel, which divided the complex in half. Sir Frederick never failed to stop in the middle of the high bridge. From here he could see it all, the graving docks, the dry docks, the great roofed structures housing plating sheds, foundries, sawmills, warehouses, support shops, factories. On the south side of the channel four chimneys of his steel mill fractured the sky in what was Belfast's most familiar landmark, and next to that, the new locomotive works. All that went into Weed Ship & Iron Works could be seen as it nestled mightily on Belfast Lough. King William Channel had been constructed as an artery off the River Lagan and Crown Island; dredged and reclaimed, it now spread to its third thousandth acre of factories, parks and playing fields all bearing the name of Weed. It was as mighty, indeed, as the Harland & Wolff complex on the Victoria Channel a half mile to the south.

Sir Frederick devoured the sight from mid-bridge. "Beautiful," he said, "bloody fucking beautiful."

On both sides of the channel it looked like Queen Victoria's birthday with the snappy fluttering of thousands of

Union Jacks, Red Hands of Ulster, buntings and pennants. In a manner of speaking, the Queen's birthday was celebrated all year round, for just beyond the Weed Works rose that monotony of red brick called East Belfast, the most loyal Protestant bastion in the entire Empire.

Forty separate Orange Lodges were attributed to the Works. Riveters' Lodges, Boilermakers' Lodges, Warehousemen's Lodges, Joiners' Lodges, Plumbers' Lodges, Teamsters' Lodges, Shipwrights' Lodges, Carpenters' Lodges. There was even a gentlemen's lodge of executives led by Sir Frederick himself, to guide the policies of the others. Of the 9,640 jobs, 9,217 belonged to Protestants from East Belfast and the Shankill. Of this number, over 8,500 were members of the Loyal Orange Order.

The steel mill boasted open-hearth Siemens-Martin furnaces with sufficient capacity to produce everything the shipyard and locomotive works required, plus most of Ireland's rails and a hog's share of other steel needs.

Beyond the rolling mill, Sir Frederick had created a research department, for this was the heyday of ships and railroads. Infinities were being overtaken in rapid order. New designs and breakthroughs in engine, hull and boiler design spiraled world shipping. The zenith was not in sight. Sir Frederick Weed was not apt to be caught short or wanting in the rage of ideas. He was the man most responsible for making Belfast a world-class shipbuilding center and his railroading zeal was not far behind.

The steam-powered Industrial Revolution found ultimate expression in an outpour of British genius. A great industrial exhibition to showplace Britain's wares to the world was inspired by Prince Albert and held in Hyde Park's Crystal Palace in the year of 1851. "Victorian," as the name to identify the age, was born here and the stage was set for an epoch of unparalleled progress. The Crystal Palace itself was a masterpiece of Victorian technology and spearheaded the first important use of prefabrication.

As steam yielded more and more secrets, a plethora of advancements avalanched from British inventive titans. Steam hammers, steam shovels, steam pile drivers, steam-powered hydraulics and lifting jacks. It put high-speed, steam-driven tools into the hands of the world's builders and steam-driven farm machines out on the land. High-speed steam turbines drove mammoth vessels over the seas and other steam turbines created power in land stations. New methods of purifying iron opened the way for fabrication and tubing of steel and this went into girders for buildings and bridges of undreamed-of magnitudes. Architects and engineers added such new wonders to the world as the magnus Thames Embankment and the Liverpool dock complex.

Steam sired the transportation revolution that burst the British from their island restraint to the class power of the world with ships and rails to match her statesmen and guns. The Rocket, the first practical modern steam engine, led the way on land to match her mastery of the seas.

A lion's share of the world's shipping tonnage carried the Union Jack and every continent hosted gangs of British navvies, the laborers whose industry awed the world as they set down British rails and canals.

Flamboyant symbol of the era was Isambard Kingdom Brunel, who built the Great Western Railroad and twenty-five others, engineered the first underwater tunnel, fathered the broad-gauge railroad, launched the first ironclad ship and the first ocean-crossing steamer, followed by an armada of the largest, fastest boats ever known, began railroad telegraphy, sired jet propulsion and engineered the building of tunnels and aqueducts and piers and dry docks and rail bridges and suspension spans of staggering precipitous audacity. Brunel, the "Little Giant," whose demands inspired dozens of world-shaping inventions.

Thomas Brassey completed wrapping the world in British rails, building an exotic roll call of lines in India and Norway and Canada and France and Argentina and Italy and Australia and Poland and Mauritius. The Calcutta-Ganges, the Warsaw-Galatz, the Vienna-Trieste.

These and the others were all the Queen's men.

Not least of the breed was Frederick Murdoch Weed. A young Scotsman, he had won minor laurels as a naval architect and marine engineer at the great yards of Clydebank.

Intrigued by the series of innovations brought on by the American Civil War, he crossed the ocean to study and became particularly fascinated by the quick change from ironclads to the steel blockade runners built by the Confederacy.

His brain became a fountain of ideas but he was constantly frustrated by the entrenchment of the establishment in Glasgow, Liverpool and Newcastle. Greener fields had to be sought and, in keeping with the giants of the day, fertility of mind ran hand in glove with daring enterprise. He looked over the Irish Sea and liked what he saw. There had always been a small but substantial shipbuilding industry around Belfast. Harland & Wolff had established a yard and prospered. This made the thought of cutting his own ties with the mother island more palatable. The Belfast City Corporation was continually expanding and reclaiming land at the mouth of the River Lagan for this purpose and there existed an excellent nucleus of skilled shipworkers who had immigrated from Scotland.

Starting with the capital of a few thousand pounds, Weed bought out a small yard covering eight acres on the newly reclaimed Crown Island. He attacked with the same fury that had marked his glory days as a rugby great.

Frederick Weed's first daring came when he doubled the length of the conventional oceangoing steamer/sailer without widening the beam. In the beginning his long narrow needles were guffawed over as Weed's coffins. He was never to be laughed at again. Innovating with above-deck iron superstructuring and a unique hull design below the water line, the ships not only proved more stable but were the quickest afloat.

As the orders poured in, Crown Island continued to reclaim, doubling and tripling in size. Weed converted from iron to steel ships with spectacular results. His genius at shaping steel alloy and prefabrication kept him well up in the pack. By 1878, the year he received his knighthood, he had established his own marine engine plant as well as his own steel mill, and had become the largest single employer in the province of Ulster. He systematically looted the Clyde of its best engineering and building talent at every level. Liverpool's decline as a shipbuilding center was quickly reflected in Belfast's growth. The median and core of his work force were tightly embedded in East Bel-

fast, which was often referred to as the "second plantation of Ulster."

*

Final stop on the inspection tour was the research and
design department. After a quick walk through his half
acre of architects, scientists and draftsmen, he was alone
with its chief, Walter Littlejohn, a foremost metallurgist.

The weightiest problem confronting shipbuilders had
merely been dented. The most costly and time-consuming
part of the process in metal ships had proved to be the
casting and hand riveting of each plate. For nearly three
years Walter Littlejohn had devoted himself and a number of his staff to Sir Frederick's mania for finding a
method of welding ships without rivets.

The most recent in the series of experiments had been
concluded a few days earlier in the recurring pattern of
failure. Over sixty new alloys had been tested in an effort
to create stronger steel. The best of the formulas was
rolled and fused into the hull of a hundred-ton experimental ship. It was towed to Rathlin Island where the
North Channel ran hard between Ireland and Scotland.
The boat was anchored in an exposed cove, and for two
breathless months held together under a fearful pounding. Then she broke apart as the others had done.

Sir Frederick whipped through Littlejohn's report. He
brushed the fallen cigar ashes from it, his eyes watering.
"Goddammit, Littlejohn, I could have sworn we had it
this go-round."

Walter Littlejohn was weary and discouraged and it
made him appear more pallid than usual. His thin lips
were lost under a drooped mustache. He shrugged to
Weed's questioning look.

"Same old story, Sir Frederick. The steel proved to be
too brittle without rivets, yielding point too low, and our
welding techniques are simply not advanced enough."

"I thought we had it with the new torch."

"The properties of acetylene are still in question. Perhaps, if we could come up with a more perfected torch . . ."

"Perhaps, perhaps, perhaps," Sir Frederick said, "perhaps if the dog hadn't stopped to take a shit he would
have caught the rabbit."

Littlejohn became an instant recluse as Weed skimmed the report again.

"I say a higher percentage of nickel and manganese. What do you say?"

Littlejohn doffed his specs, rubbed both eyes with the heels of his hands, allowing his mind to grow deliberately vacuous.

"Well, what, what, what, what?"

The scientist threw up his hands.

It was fist-on-desk time. "I know, by Jesus, there's a way of doing it and I can't stomach any more of this fucking frustration."

"Haste," Walter Littlejohn replied, "is the enemy of research."

"Oh, Jesus, Littlejohn! This is 1885. All up and down the Clyde they've got wind of our program. Some son of a bitch is going to beat us to it."

Littlejohn scratched his head aimlessly. "Alloying steel is still an infant field," he repeated for the umpteenth time to the restless bull who charged at his cape. "Unless someone accidentally spills the proper contents of the proper bottles and creates a miracle formula we are still a decade away from finding the ultimate hardness of steel. And even if we do find it we are still more years away from a concurring hull design and methods of fusion."

Weed wagged his finger beneath the man's nose. "If some son of a bitch beats us to it, I'll die. I want this fucking ship more than anything in my life."

"We shall continue to do our best," Littlejohn mumbled.

*

Sir Frederick's brougham was waiting outside the research department and clip-clopped him back to the main administration building where he plunged into a final round of work.

The last paper Kendrick had placed on his desk renewed his rage. A Select Committee of the House of Commons had finished a study on the growing problem of industrial waste in the United Kingdom's manufacturing and mining centers. Belfast, they concluded, was the worst in the British Isles, where the air had reached hazardous levels of pollution actually endangering persons with respiratory ailments. Furthermore, industrial discharges (particularly from Weed's steel mill) into Belfast Lough were putrefying the water. Sir Frederick's solicitor wished to have his comments to attach to the minority opinion.

He snatched up his pen and scrawled "HORSESHIT!" over its cover. Kendrick came in with a tray of tea and as he cleared Sir Frederick's desk of papers glared wordlessly at the commission report.

"Just return it," Weed ordered.

"No further comment, Sir Frederick?"

"Oh, very well, take this down. 'This is the same kind of nonsense a Select Committee attempted to pull twenty years ago on the linen mills. It is contemptuous bullying by the Liberals to impede progress, combined with a long-standing conspiracy to snuff the life out of Belfast. If they want to clean up filth, let them go after their own in the Midland cities. Belfast's progress will not be compromised or waylaid by political chicanery, et cetera, et cetera, et cetera.' "

He walked to the window. Belfast was not to be seen through the pall. "Polluting the air and water, indeed! What do they want these people to do here, starve?" The six o'clock whistle screamed. The yard disgorged its thousands. Legions of begrimed, tweed-capped marchers in ragged rhythm passed on their way to those melancholy regiments of red brick. Sir Frederick nodded patronizingly as his army tipped their caps en masse in homage. Halfway through their march he returned to his desk.

"When is Brigadier Swan's train due?"

"Half seven," Kendrick answered.

"Good. Send a carriage for him. I'll see him at the hotel."

"Very well, sir," Kendrick said, and left.

With a stout cup of tea laced with brandy, Sir Frederick slowly banked the fires of his feverish mind, then allowed his thoughts to drift to the newest thrust of his empire.

When the decision had been made several years back to open his own steel mill, Weed bought out a number of small iron mines in mid- and north Ulster. This began his involvement with the narrow-gauge railroads which operated in the mines. Fascination with trains led to standard gauge and this in turn led to designing and building a prototype locomotive which won note as the Red Hand Express.

He looked restlessly beyond the mid-Ulster termination points of his Belfast & Portrush Line until it became his latest obsession to own the first trans-Ulster railway. Belfast to Sligo. After that, who knew?

Weed assigned his strong right arm, Brigadier Maxwell Swan, to test the waters. Arthur Hubble, the Earl of Foyle, controlled a combination of bits and pieces of short lines out in the west. An inquiry was made of Glendon Rankin, who ran the Earl's affairs. The response was noncommittal but warm. Maxwell Swan was dispatched to Londonderry to negotiate.

Sir Frederick glanced at the clock. Swan would be back in Belfast in a little over an hour. He broke into a sudden burst of laughter as he felt a rush of exhilaration. All the energy of that shouting brain poured into thoughts of cutting the ribbon.

SIR FREDERICK WEED INVADES WESTERN ULSTER!

CHAPTER THREE: As Sir Frederick Weed pressed his courtship and love affair with railroads, acquisition of a fleet of private cars followed. A confirmed Americanophile, Sir Frederick had long adored George Pullman's Palace cars and the opulent work of Webster Wagner. Manning Fitch, who designed the luxury cabins on Weed's steamers, was dispatched to America, commissioned and licensed to study and blueprint their work. Weed's private cars were executed right at the Works. In addition to the executive car, there was Sir Frederick's personal car, a scandalously lavish affair, a car used to transport his rugby team on its annual tour of the English Midlands and three lesser cars. With a Red Hand Express engine up front, the train served as the commander-in-chief's land flagship.

The train passed through Templepatrick toward Monkstown, where rolling and evergreen land began to flatten near the sea and thicken with cottages and people, indicating that the outer fringes of Belfast had been reached.

A single passenger was aboard.

The lone man in the dark polished mahogany and Spanish leather splendor of Sir Frederick's Belfast & Portrush executive car was Brigadier Maxwell Swan, D.C.L., D.S.C., C.V.O., C.V.E., Retired. What made his otherwise middling appearance so acute was a bald, clean-shaven head holding a most penetrating pair of azure eyes which radiated constantly.

Swan, an Ulsterman, had retired from the army after a quarter-century service, still in his forties, somewhat of a mystery figure, moving silently through the backwaters of the Empire to potential hot spots. His role had been to ferret out brewing insurrections and nip them in the bud. Movements were hush-hush as he maneuvered behind the scenes of the Indian Mutiny, the Maori wars in New Zealand, at Peking, and in the African territories to finish off the Ashanti.

Swan's final years of Crown service were spent in Dublin Castle where he proved a master in the use of the informer to penetrate secret and rebellious societies. His counteroperations were merciless, clean and final. Small wonder that Sir Frederick grabbed him on retirement and placed him in charge of labor matters.

A divine Ulster principle was to keep its working class a decade behind the mother island. Swan went into deadly combat against poaching trade unionists and other agitators, building a penetrating espionage system which no one could escape.

It was simpler to do in Belfast. The entire work force was jammed into East Belfast and the Shankill where tribal existence was almost totally ritualized by the Orange Order and the Reformation. Few men could stand up to the wrath of an Orange Grand Master, the preacher and his neighbors by refusal to join.

Using the Orange Order as his power base, the Grand Master was endowed with special powers of hiring and firing as were many of the preachers. It was Swan who encouraged Sir Frederick to patronize the Orange and even join himself through formation of a "gentlemen's" lodge.

While the Orange had a surveillance grip, the ministry pounded home the gospel that these Ulster folk were a special folk gifted with the twin virtues of godliness and industriousness and had been chosen to do God's work in Ireland. Fathers passed their Orange bowlers to their sons and purchased apprenticeships in the yard to assure family continuance. Poor little intellectual thought, liberal ideas, curiosity or content was allowed to penetrate the twin-shrouded bastions of East Belfast and the Shankill.

When sniffings of trouble did emerge from these areas, a simple ploy was used over and over with unerring success. Fear of the Catholics, the anti-God heathens, the sloths, was kept as a razor blade pressing their wrists. Loyalty, Orange loyalty, Protestant loyalty, Crown loyalty, anti-union loyalty was rewarded by the job upon which their livelihood depended. Deviation from that total loyalty could infer that the Catholic might get their jobs.

Swan showed all of Ulster how to apply the cardinal principle of divide and rule by keeping the Catholic and Protestant working classes separated and hating each other. He was flint and his operation textbook. Generous donations to the proper causes were coldly effective. His special peace-keeping squads of ex-pugilists, toughs, informers, detectives and spies were no less effective. Peace reigned at the Weed Ship & Iron Works and Belfast remained years behind the unionization of the English Midlands.

Maxwell Swan advanced in swift order until he was a permanent fixture at Sir Frederick's right hand. Always the background figure, he carried out the black work which allowed Frederick Murdoch Weed to create a public image of charity and gregariousness.

*

Choppy Belfast Lough came into view at Newtownabbey. The train hugged the coastline to the northern suburbs, slowing into the harbor build-up where the aroma of tobacco and coffee and hemp hung both pungent and dingy. As the Red Hand Express hissed into the York Road terminal Swan caught a glimpse of the smokestacks of the Ship & Iron Works across a conglomerate of channels and docks and warehouses and factories.

He snapped his brief bag shut, buttoned on a caped

Inverness coat and stepped directly from the private car to a waiting carriage at platformside.

Hotel Antrim was a single jewel in Belfast's otherwise drab hostelries. Located on Victoria Street a few blocks from Donegal Square and the Linen Hall, it sat in the heart of Belfast's cultural, government and commercial matters.

Sir Frederick had purchased the hotel as part of the Belfast & Portrush Railroad holdings and renovated it to a standard of luxury unmatched in Ireland. The entire fourth story was converted to his intown residence, housing himself and containing suites to accommodate visiting ship and rail executives, dignitaries, aristocracy and nobility.

His personal quarters consisted of ten rooms decorated from a warehouse of leftovers from his principal residence, Rathweed Hall in the Holywood Hills.

Weed spread himself out in the drawing room, disposing of a pair of stiff Bushmills while his man quietly picked up strewn jacket, cravat, hat, gloves, cane and shoes and replaced them with a smoking jacket and slippers. As he poured his third drink, his daughter Caroline flowed in begowned and bejeweled.

Ah, Caroline! He smiled inwardly and outwardly. Caroline his joy, Caroline his bane. Caroline, the sole offspring of widower Weed. She had grown splendidly handsome in her twenty-eighth year but it had been a monumental undertaking to get her that far.

When her mother died years earlier, Caroline had gone on a continental tear which ended up in a short, disastrous marriage. Perplexed in his efforts to tame her and thwarted in his efforts to get her married and produce suitable male heirs, Sir Frederick toyed with the idea of a second marriage for himself. Yet he could not cross the bridge on that point, his love for his daughter a powerful countergravity.

During Caroline's annulment she returned to Belfast and calmed somewhat, showing good hard traits, indicating she might be cut from Weed's mold after all. He wanted the future in her hands and the hands of her sons. Caroline continued to be independent and self-indulgent but she developed a keen business mind and each time she saw those four smokestacks from the balcony of the Antrim there could be little doubt of her own ambition. Sir Frederick was getting nervous about the business of heirs but one had to tread softly on that subject.

The two exchanged affections. Tonight it was a ballet troupe from Russia, a real coup for Belfast, arranged largely because of Caroline's patronage. Most of the cultural meanderings did Sir Frederick in with boredom unless they involved personal attention and a bit of a chase with an actress or diva. He sponsored culture because Caroline adored the scene and it had spiraled her to a social lioness and kept her in Belfast.

"Who's the lucky chap tonight?" he asked.

"Marquess of Monaghan, father, mother, two daughters and that son."

"Oh, them."

"Are you joining us, Freddie?"

"Better shrink off to the old study," Weed said, winking. "I'm expecting the Brigadier back from Londonderry. Mind terribly?"

"Of course not," she answered, working a long opera glove up her slender arm and making a final primp in the mirror. "Any word how Max managed?"

"No, and I'm damned keen. He's been gone most of the week."

"Well, that could only indicate that he's been in some good stiff negotiations," she said.

"Hope so, hope so."

He grunted out of the chair slowly, the whiskey having found its mark, and gently pecked her cheek.

"Wait up for me, Freddie," she said. "I'll have a headache about twenty minutes after the final curtain. I'm dying to know what happened. Oh, by the by, reception tomorrow night at Rathweed Hall. There are a couple of ladies in the troupe you might like to give some attention to before they get off to Dublin."

"Ballerinas? Too damned skinny, most of them."

Another whiskey sent Sir Frederick's head nodding to his chest in a massive marble tub while his man stood close at hand to see that he didn't slide below the water line. A sharp knock on the bathroom door sent his eyes popping open. Maxwell Swan entered as Sir Frederick dashed himself with cold water to clear out the fuzz.

The Brigadier seated himself at tubside, propped his feet and rocked his chair back to a tilt and nipped at a sherry.

"Well, Max, when do we cut the ribbon to Londonderry?"

"Better have a drink," Swan answered. A long exchange into those compelling eyes told Weed the story.

"What the hell went wrong?"

"Almost everything."

"Goddammit! Get me the hell out of here!" he roared, fighting his way out of the water like a surfacing whale. Robed in a toweled sheet, he plopped like an ancient Roman on the bedroom settee and hunched forward, fixing a glare on his assistant.

Swan cast about for a starting point. "We made an assessment that Glendon Rankin was running a pretty archaic operation of the Hubble earldom. Of course, we both knew that Lord Arthur scarcely sets foot in Ulster and that Rankin was the one to negotiate with. I mean, we both felt Rankin had the latitude and authority to conclude a deal with us."

"Yes, yes."

"Knowing that Lord Arthur would likely go along with Rankin's proposals, et cetera, et cetera."

"Yes, yes, yes, yes."

"Well, Sir Frederick, something new has been added. Lord Arthur's son Roger has plunged into the business up to here," he said, indicating eye level.

"The Viscount Coleraine? Good Lord, I thought he was off in the service somewhere . . . India . . . China . . . someplace."

"To the contrary. Young Hubble has been out of the military for two or three years and has become extremely active. I venture to say he's about ready to take the whole thing over, pack and packet."

"Hubble? Roger Hubble? Sort of an arsy-tarsy chap as I remember. Besides, isn't he awfully young?"

"Obviously you haven't seen him in some time."

Sir Frederick pondered. "Well, come to think of it, it's been five or six years. How old do you suppose he is now?"

"Oh, thirty, thereabouts."

"Sprouted brains, has he?"

"Shrewd as Disraeli. He'll have Glendon Rankin out to pasture before the end of the year."

"By God, that's interesting," Weed said. "The Hubbles have had that awful Rankin family running the earldom —oh, Lord, for generations."

"Precisely the point," Swan answered. "Roger Hubble is extremely keen on converting it from a medieval fiefdom bang into the new economic scheme of things. He came right out and said he can't carry on by tenant farming as his major source of income and he's moving quickly and quietly into any number of things, linen, minerals, diverse factories. At the same time, I'm very impressed with the consolidations he's made on the land by conversion of huge acreages into flax and cattle."

"You know, Max," Weed said, "just tonight, Caroline went to the ballet with old Monaghan. That sputtering old archaic fart is determined to hang onto every last acre mortgaged to the bloody sky until he is absolutely impoverished."

"Well, young Hubble smells the end of the landed estates all right," Swan concurred.

"I gather you dealt directly with him then?"

"For the first two days there was a pretense of going through Glendon Rankin. Roger Hubble was only trying to find out what we were up to without having to make comment or commitment. After that, it was the two of us as though Rankin weren't even alive."

Sir Frederick fished about under the towel to free his hands and light a flame to the end of his cigar. "You say he's shrewd."

"Quite."

"Then why the hell is he balking about selling those dirty little bits and pieces of railroad? They're no damned use to him as they sit and he must know he'd turn a tidy profit by unloading them."

"He's completely suspicious of your motives," Swan said.

It made its mark. Weed growled his way into a robe, mentalized to the french doors, and looked down on the expansive thoroughfare. "Goddammit, Max, I want that trans-Ulster railroad more than I've ever wanted anything in my life."

The Brigadier remained passive in light of the variation on an old theme. Before that, Weed had wanted to build a twelve-thousand-ton ship more than anything in his life, and before that he wanted to build a welded ship more than anything in his life, and before that it was a locomotive that could do sixty miles an hour ... more than anything in his life.

He turned back into the room. "Go back to Londonderry and double the present offer. If he refuses, it's war!"

"Won't work, Sir Frederick."

"Horseshit. Enough money always works."

"He's got some overriding concerns," Swan said, "says he doesn't want any *weeds* growing in the West."

"I'll ... break ... his ... bloody ... balls. ..."

Maxwell Swan scratched the back of his hairless neck hard with a forefinger as though it had been attacked by a mosquito and waited for his boss to repeat the threat of warfare and castration. When the paintings on the wall quit their quaking, Sir Frederick realized Hubble had him blocked. An agonized interval of reality ensued during which he sought his aide's pragmatic advice.

"Only way I see it is by an alliance," Swan said.

Weed's face went from sour to a puckish smile. "I see," he said, gleaming. "We take young Hubble in and then"—he clapped his hands together—"stamp him out later."

Swan shook his head. "He's too clever for that. If you merge, count on it being permanent."

If there was a single plank in Sir Frederick's timber it was a cherishing of his own independence as sole purveyor of personal power. The Brigadier knew that. The suggestions must have been drawn from some other kind of evaluation.

"You know you're talking against my grain, Max."

"I'm so aware," Swan answered. "I didn't want to break things off with finality. Hubble is intrigued and excited by your interest. I left an open end. He's going down to Daars shortly to see his father. It might be a good idea if you were to invite him to stop in Belfast on the way."

Sir Frederick had long come to read that very special glow in Maxwell Swan's eyes. "What's going on in your fucking head, Max?"

Swan managed what could reasonably be construed as a smile. "Caroline and Roger Hubble," he said.

CHAPTER FOUR:

What an eventful day it was when himself, Major Hamilton Walby, came up to the crossroad to speak to the croppies. It marked the first time in six hundred years of British occupation and rule that the villagers of Ballyutogue were to have a democratic meeting with them.

It was also my twelfth birthday, which meant that I could be the same number of years as Conor, for a few months at least, until he became thirteen.

The hanging tree was indeed an appropriate location for the grand event. No one knows the exact number who were strung off its limbs but sure it ran into the hundreds, if not thousands, and it stood as a constant reminder of the Crown's presence as well as our centuries of oppression.

Our lads were hanged in great droves when the Elizabethan conquest set down the mighty O'Neill clan. They were hanged in even greater numbers by the squire's ancestor, Isaiah Walby, during the Cromwell wars. They were hanged in the Jacobite war against William of Orange. They were hanged in penal times for practicing the Roman religion and during the peasant land wars and by that savage Yeomanry during Wolfe Tone's United Irish Rising. I note in passing that the Yeomanry introduced floggings, beheadings, boiling oil and pikings as well, on this very spot. Most recently it was the Fenians. Our lads were also hanged in between those other times for various acts of disloyalty such as resisting the Constabulary who had come to evict them, or stealing our own crops in order not to starve.

Every year there was an extensive debate over whether or not we should chop down the hanging tree. We wasn't any too sentimental over its past history but it was the only decent tree left in these parts. Daddo Friel tells of a time there was a great stand of oaks all over Inishowen and land with topsoil two feet deep. The forest was stripped and the oaks carted

off to be used in building the English fleet against the
Spanish Armada. Erosion of the soil came soon after.
In fact, Daddo says, the only thing not carted off by
the British were the rocks and they would have surely
been taken, too, had they been worth anything.

The Larkins, whose voices usually prevailed in such
matters, said the hanging tree should stand as a constant
reminder of who we were—as if we didn't already
know—so for better or worse it continued to give shade
to our two most powerful institutions, St. Columba's
Church and Dooley McCluskey's public house.

*

The squire arrived on the most splendid Arabian
I ever saw, cutting a spectacular figure in a red morning
coat, high silk hat and boots polished to a fare thee
well. He rode in alone as if to convey to us that he
was both brave and filled with conviction. It was a
well-taken point. Several hundred of us croppies, a
grubby lot by comparison, milled about at arm's length as
Father Lynch blathered over him like he was receiving
the Pope himself.

Tomas and my daddy took the squire around for
handshakes and socializing but in truth we were looking
him over and he was looking us over like creatures
from different planets. Due to Tomas' words before the
meeting, we all understood it was to be an orderly
affair. It was leisurely, like of a Sunday after mass, with
some of the men partaking in the public house and others
visiting kin in the graveyard or just sitting around against
the wall tossing stones and flipping coins. Some of the
women hovered in the background, minding not to get too
close because politics was men's business.

Conor and I staked out places right up against a
platform built for the occasion. As the meeting began
there was a slow drifting of the crowd toward the
speaker. The gathering pressed in tighter because it
was hard to make out the squire's words. You'd think
that a man educated in Trinity College in Dublin
could speak his own language more plain. It became
so quiet you could hear a butterfly.

"We are embarking on a splendid new age," the
squire began, "which began at the onset of this century

when the cross of St. Patrick was added to the crosses
of St. Andrew and St. George to become the Union
Jack which we so gloriously hail. The United Kingdom
marked us as a single people under a single king."

I WAS BARELY TWELVE YEARS OLD WHEN HAMILTON
WALBY SAID THAT. MEANING NO DISRESPECT, I WAS
STILL OLD ENOUGH TO REALIZE FROM THE OPENING
REMARK IT WAS GOING TO BE A HARD DAY FOR BOTH
SIDES. WE WEREN'T ONLY NOT UNITED BUT SEPARATED BY
PLANETS AND STARS AND MILKY WAYS AND UNIVERSES.

"The Act of Union that made us a United Kingdom
brought to Ireland your magnificent British heritage . . ."

NOW, WHAT WE'VE BEEN SAYING FOR TWELVE YEARS
OF MY LIFE AND FIVE HUNDRED YEARS BEFORE THAT
IS WE'VE NEVER FELT IT A GREAT HONOR TO BE
CONSIDERED BRITISH.

"A time in which the greatest series of reforms and
democratic legislation ever initiated by a Parliament . . ."

WELL NOW, DON'T YOU KNOW THE IRISH HAD A
DEMOCRATIC SOCIETY PRIOR TO THE YEAR OF 1171
UNDER THE CELTIC SYSTEM OF ORDER WHEN YOU
GRACED OUR LAND WITH YOUR PRESENCE? AND DON'T
YOU KNOW THAT A BACKWARD BRITISH ARISTOCRACY
HELD ANY NOTIONS OF LIBERTY IN CHECK EVEN AFTER
THE IDEAS OF THE FRENCH REVOLUTION SWEPT OVER
AND FREED EUROPE?

". . . now this unparalleled system of justice has
been fully extended to cover all of Her Majesty's
subjects . . ."

LIKE, KATY BAR THE DOOR, WHEN IRISHMEN
ATTEMPTED TO FLEE TO ENGLAND DURING THE FAMINE.
AH, THE FRUITS OF BRITISH JUSTICE, THE PENAL LAWS,
EVICTIONS FROM OUR LAND, THE TITHE TO THE
ANGLICAN CHURCH, TO RECALL A FEW.

". . . through a series of social welfare opportunities
never before extended to the average citizen . . ."

WORKHOUSES, CHILD LABOR, DEBTORS' PRISONS,
EMIGRATION IN COFFIN SHIPS.

". . . to massive public works . . ."

BUILDING FAMINE WALLS, ROADS TO NOWHERE.

". . . under the Act of Union, full religious freedom
was restored . . ."

AFTER IT WAS TAKEN FROM US FOR CENTURIES AND

RETURNED TO US AS AN ANGLICIZED VERSION STRIPPED
OF ALL ITS GAELIC MAJESTY AND WONDERMENT.

". . . schools . . ."

BEYOND THE MEANS OF ANY CROPPY IN THIS VILLAGE
WHERE THEY TEACH NO IRISH LANGUAGE OR IRISH
HISTORY OR IRISH MARTYRS OR IRISH FOLKLORE.

". . . total political expression."

WON BY THE BLOOD OF DANIEL O'CONNELL THREE
DECADES AFTER IT WAS PROMISED BY BRITISH LEGIS-
LATION. WHAT WE REALLY GOT WAS GERRYMANDERED
BOUNDARIES AND CLASS-PRIVILEGED FRANCHISE.

"Of course, that is only a thumbnail sketch of the
past. What interests you and me, hereabouts, is a
continuation of land reform. Let me say right off, I
stand foursquare in favor of legislation that will give
each and every one of you the right to purchase land
of your own in unlimited quantity."

I SWEAR I THOUGHT I HEARD KILTY AND RONAN
LARKIN GROANING FROM THEIR GRAVES. IT WAS A
SHOCKER, ALL RIGHT. LOOKING UP AT THIS MAN IN
THE PLATFORM AND HIM TALKING TO US LIKE THAT
WITHOUT AN IOTA OF REALIZATION THAT IT WAS NO
LOFTY PRIVILEGE TO BE ABLE TO BUY BACK LAND WHICH
HAD BEEN STOLEN FROM YOU . . . EXCEPT IN THE MIND
OF A HORSE THIEF.

"The heart of the matter, gentlemen, is this. The union
with Britain must be preserved at all costs. Without
British markets, where would we sell? We would be
without privileged tariff and trade regulations we enjoy as
British subjects. No greater disaster could befall us."

INDEED, SQUIRE, WHAT COULD POSSIBLY BE MORE
DISASTROUS TO THE IRISH THAN TO BE FREE MEN IN
THEIR OWN LAND, WHAT GREATER DISASTER?

"Where would we sell our cattle and our linen?
Where indeed without British ships to convey our
product and a British Navy to protect our interests? Well
then, we not only receive the benefits of the most advanced culture in the world but we are poised to enjoy
even greater rewards in the immediate future. Your own
Church fully agrees on the matter. Your shepherd, your
spiritual guidance is quite clear, *QUITE CLEAR, IN-
DEED.*

"Having the vote constitutes a heavy responsibility.

The question before us is, do we continue to prosper in an orderly manner as a single, united people or do we court tragedy and chaos through Home Rule? All the benefits, all the gains of British citizenship, all the glory of the Empire, all the glorious tomorrows . . . are these to go for naught? I say it's a time for us fellow British to close ranks and stand together. I ask that you do one thing so that you can cast your ballot with a clear conscience, and that is, consult your priest . . ."

Major Hamilton Walby bumbled to conclusion. He looked into a mass of faces locked in sorrow. He was greeted with neither rudeness, anger nor applause. Tomas asked if there were any questions. There were none. In an instant the men flaked off quietly, seeming a mite wearier as they trudged up the road to their fields.

In a moment there was only Conor and me and Father Lynch left under the hanging tree with the squire. His teeth were locked together in anger as he strode to and mounted that beautiful horse. He glared up the road where the men were making their way up to the heather. I'm sure he had that same look on him at other times when he rode at the head of a company of Ulster Rifles about to charge into some ungrateful natives elsewhere in the Empire.

He mumbled something unintelligible, spurred and galloped off.

*

The Lambeg drum was a Scottish concoction which gave off a shattering, horrendous boom. It was designed to break the courage of the enemy upon hearing it. The Lambeg was a monster affair, five feet in diameter and two feet thick, and the drum head was beaten with heavy bamboo rods lashed to the wrists of the drummer by leather thongs.

It bore illustrated paintings of some Protestant victory over the croppies or a glorification of King Billy or a portrait in memory of a departed brother. No Orange Lodge would be without their Lambegs. The Bally-utogue Total Temperance Lodge was no exception.

There existed a phenomenon in our area that took place each evening around the time of the angelus. Some said it was the work of fairies, for there was no other logical explanation. A strange and sudden calm would descend followed by a queer reverse wind which blew up from the Township, carrying the most minute sounds. At that time of evening the Lambeg could shatter rocks from nearly two miles distant.

RAT A TAT TAT A TAT TAT! RAT A TAT TAT A TAT!

Conor and me would be meeting our daddies at the crossroad as they came down from the fields. The Lambeg drums seemed to be going all the time.

The four of us would just stare down to the town.

"The louder they beat their drums, the more scared they are," Tomas said.

"Aye, and that's a fact," my daddy added.

"You see, lads, they got to beat the drum to prove to themselves and each other they aren't scared and that we ought to be."

"I don't understand you at all, Tomas Larkin," I said.

"Aye, Daddy," Conor added, "why should they be scared? I mean, the Constabulary is working for them."

"Well, Kevin O'Garvey scares them. Mostly, the thought of equality scares them."

There had been rumors that the squire didn't have much use for the Orange Order, but that must have been before our meeting. No sooner had he ridden away from the hanging tree than he was spending half his waking hours in Orange Halls all over the district. I guess he must have been scared, too, because they were sure falling all over each other.

RAT A TAT TAT A TAT A TAT! RAT A TAT TAT A TAT!

And those fierce voices flowed up to us on the twilight winds.

It's old but it's beautiful,
Its colours they are fine,
It was worn at Derry, Aughrim,
Enniskillen and the Boyne,
My father wore it when a youth
In bygone days of yore,
On the Twelfth I proudly wear
The sash my father wore.

Bong! Bong! Bong! sounded the angelus. Bong! Bong! Bong!

Me and my daddy would drop reverently to our knees as Tomas made for Dooley McCluskey's and Conor just stared in the direction of the Ballyutogue diamond.

"The Angel of the Lord declared unto Mary."

"And she conceived of the Holy Ghost. Hail, Mary . . ."

RAT A TAT TAT A TAT A TAT!

The Protestant boys are loyal and true,
Stouthearted in battle and stout-handed too,
The Protestant boys are true to the last,
And faithful and peaceful when danger has
*   passed. . . .*

"Pour forth, we beseech thee, O Lord, thy grace into our hearts that we, to whom the incarnation of Christ thy Son . . ."

RAT A TAT TAT TAT A TAT A TAT!

Then Orangemen remember King William
And your fathers who with him did join,
And fought for our glorious deliverance,
On the green, grassy slopes of the Boyne.

". . . by the message of an angel, may by his passion and cross be brought to the glory of his resurrection through the same Christ our Lord."

RAT A TAT TAT TAT A TAT A TAT!

Begone, begone, you Papist dogs,
We'll conquer or we'll die. . . .

"Amen."
Amen.

CHAPTER FIVE: Brigadier Swan rapped once from his adjacent office, entered and set the report on Sir Frederick's desk.

"By God, that was fast," Weed said. "Don't tell me how you managed it; I don't want to know."

"I won't."

Weed rubbed his hands together gleefully, then snipped the red tape with a pair of sterling silver scissors. HIGHLY CONFIDENTIAL: COMBINED ASSETS, HOLDINGS, EARNINGS AND NET WORTH OF FOYLE ENTERPRISES LTD., A. HUBBLE —EARL OF FOYLE, R. HUBBLE—CHIEF EXECUTIVE & HEIR.

"How'd you manage it?" Weed asked.

"Same old infallibles. Two main contacts: one chap in Dublin Castle, one in Inland Revenue. One malcontent, a former senior clerk recently dismissed by Rankin's office."

"Lovely."

"I think you'll find what you want on the last four pages."

Sir Frederick balanced his specs on nose end and bent over the report.

Landed Holdings
24,000 acres in rangeland and pasturage. Herd numbering 3,300 head with annual average shipment to England of 1,500 head.
4,000 acres in flax.
2,200 acres of woodlands, hunting and recreational grounds, formal and informal gardens adjacent to Hubble Manor.
Major fishing patents, Lough Foyle & River Foyle.

Leased Lands
90,000 acres on 30-year leases to Roman Catholic tenants. Since Roger Hubble has joined Foyle Enterprises actively, a secret plan has been initiated to reduce and stabilize Catholic tenant acreage at 50,000. This is considered the desired figure needed to support the earldom's agricultural goals. The balance of this land will either be sold to the more productive Catholics or annexed to the earldom's pasturage.

    a. All marginal and encumbered farms will be foreclosed, purchased or otherwise eliminated. This will reduce over-population and weed out the "weaker strains" of Catholics. Most of this acreage has been poorly farmed primarily to feed outsized families and has made no meaningful contribution to the earldom's agricultural scheme. Conversion of this land into pasture will allow the earldom to increase its cattle herd, which is the major agricultural income earner.

    b. Remaining Catholic acreage will be refined and geared to create a pool of raw material to feed into the earldom's enterprises.

With the hue and cry of liberalism and land reform prevailing from Westminster and Catholic agitators, Lord Roger has proceeded with great care and deftness. His own estimation is that it will take a decade to achieve all land goals. The old cottage-tumbling tactics have been replaced with highly sophisticated and subtle legal maneuvers, a skill in which Roger Hubble appears to excel.

20,000 acres leased to Protestant tenants.

This is a stable and desirable population, 90% Presbyterian, largely stemming from plantation immigrants of 1600. Their farms are larger, their land more productive. Because of the earldom's geographic isolation, this loyal population is deemed a necessity.

In addition there are some 35,000 acres owned by freeholders dating back to the Cromwell era. These are 90% Anglicans. The Borough and Township of Lettermacduff is squired by the Walby family. Farms run up to 600 acres, are enormously prosperous and the population stable, industrious and loyal. Their production is entirely attuned to the earldom's policies.

Four coastal villages with mixed Anglican/Presbyterian freeholders. Established originally to protect the earldom's fishing patents from poaching Catholics. An annual royalty to the earldom is paid to exercise Protestant fishing rights on Lough Foyle.

Other Real Property

Hubble Manor

Daars—summer estate, Kinsale, County Cork.

Town house, Hubble Square, London W.1.

7–8,000 acres, Warwickshire, England, mostly in wheat on sharecrop leases.

Extensive holdings connected with mining interests, Powys County, Wales (Precise figures unavailable).

Hubble Square, London W.1. This prime London property was developed in the early eighteenth century by Erskine Hubble, 6th Earl of Foyle. Approximately half the sixty town houses on the square were built by Hubble for short-term leases. All land was retained by the family on the 100-year leaseholds of privately built residences.

Industrial Holdings, Fully Owned, Traditional

Ballyutogue Flax Mill & Linen Industries
Londonderry Woolen Mill
Foyle Fisheries

Recent Acquisitions, Fully Owned

The Little Northern Line (Portrush, Coleraine & Limavady)
Witherspoon & McNab Shirt Factory, Londonderry. One of the three largest in the U.K.
Doles & Doles Distillery, Milford

Norton Department Store, Liverpool
Limavady Crystal

Controlling Interest
Londonderry Shipyard, Londonderry
Caw & Train Graving Dock, Foundry & Machine Works,
Londonderry L & L Packet Line. The Londonderry & Liverpool operates eight passenger/freighters in the 800- to 4,000-ton classes, including two transocean vessels. The line accounts for about 50% of Londonderry's import/export tonnage.
The Donegal Line (Londonderry to Sligo)
The L.C. & D. Line (Londonderry, Claudy & Dungiven)

Shareholders or Minority Partnerships
County Tyrone Mines, Inishowen Quarries, Cavan Mines,
Canadian Zinc & Lead, Ltd.
The Hubbles have traditionally held directorships in Londonderry and various Irish banking institutions and numerous semi-public trust type organizations.

To the best of our determination, the family has no sizable encumbrances. Numerous bank loans are in the nature of financing acquisitions or for capital expansion. Although cash reserves are limited, cash flow is extensive. Roger Hubble's diversifications have taken a great deal of pressure off traditional dependence from tenant rent revenues. Marginal or money-losing operations such as the L.C. & D. Railroad and Limavady Crystal have more than been compensated for by the earnings of Witherspoon & McNab, etc.
Under Roger Hubble the Foyle Enterprises have slowly changed from static to mobile. The earldom must be considered extremely sound.
It is very difficult to come to an exact figure, but best estimations are that the combined holdings represent a net worth of between £ 2,500,000 to £ 3,000,000. Net income to the family after taxes, loans and new investments is in the neighborhood of £ 200,000 annually.
To summarize, Lord Roger has adopted a completely modern view of things. One might think, on the surface, he has moved too rapidly with changes but he has obviously been considering it all for a long time and, once he took control, he boldly cut away the dead wood. Industrial growth and shrinking the holdings of the small farmers will probably be at a much slower rate in the future.

Sir Frederick dusted the ashes from the report and looked up to Swan, smiling. "By God, you just can't beat old gold. They must be a clever bunch, managing this in that destitute part of the world."

"It seems that Morris Hubble led Ireland in fore-closures during the famine in order to earn money to finance loan sharks. His gombeen men are alleged to have gobbled up well over a million acres in foreclosures for literally nothing. After the dust of the famine had set-tled, his lordship resold it at a hundred-fold profit."

"The famine, eh? Well, that's turning disaster into tri-umph. Looks like this Roger is a chip off the old block. Max, send him a warm invitation to drop in and see us on his way to Daars. No, no, hold it. I'll do it myself."

*

One could count on a single hand the number of peo-ple whom Frederick Murdoch Weed was unable to intimidate . . . and have three fingers left over. There was Maxwell Swan and there was Caroline Weed. There were no others. The taming of Caroline had been an unfulfilled mission.

Her mother, Livia, had been a delicate creature, seem-ingly an unlikely mate for the bullish Frederick Weed, but he had absolutely adored her. Livia had passed on eight years earlier in an influenza epidemic, leaving the family without a male heir.

Caroline was twenty at the time, continentally edu-cated, deliciously pampered, and had already collected a small pyramid of the bleached bones of jilted suitors. Al-though the girl had inherited her mother's splendid looks, what she had the most of was her father's lust and inde-pendence.

Sir Frederick tried to make up for the loss of his wife by attempting to turn Caroline into hostess and companion and to arrange the marriage that would bed her down and produce desperately desired male children.

Caroline rebelled in olympian fashion, bolting to France and burying herself in a bohemian attic. Her father thrice vowed she could die in poverty, thrice relented and thrice revowed in a transchannel chase and capture gamble that spanned three years.

Sir Frederick was considering the desperation measure of taking a second wife for the purpose of a son, when fate intervened in the form of Marco de Valenti, a charm-

ing but tattered Italian grandee on the prowl for moneyed
English and American ladies. The aristocratic roustabout
caught Caroline's fancy in Florence. A short, heady conquest followed. Caroline was induced to convert to Catholicism in a ritual questionably administered by a young
priest with a worldly weakness for money. Barely off the
altar of that oath, she found herself at a second altar exchanging marriage vows. All of it happened within a
week.

What had caught her fancy about the man in the first
place disappeared almost immediately. He proved to be a
peacocking bore, a gross lover and whatever svelteness he
possessed was overpowered by an omnipresent aura of
garlic. Caroline fled her bridal bed.

Having endured many a lean year, Marco de Valenti was
not easily dissuaded. Caroline raced north into Switzer-
land with her heels being yapped at by a heart-clutching,
forehead-slapping, symphonic arm-waving outpour of the
jilted groom. She managed to get him off the scent in St.
Moritz and fired a frantic HELP, DADDY cable, then holed
up and rehearsed a scene of high drama in which she
would whimper for forgiveness and bleed with remorse.

Her father arrived, flushed with victory, and assayed the
damage. Count Marco de Valenti was a persistent chap who
had to be fended off with a barrage of pounds sterling.
Never one to be caught wanting in pressing his advantage,
Sir Frederick agreed to bail her out but set down firm conditions. In exchange for getting her out of the mess
Caroline would have to return to Ulster, resume her duties as mistress of Rathweed Hall, find a suitable mate of
British stock and end the continental horseshit, once and
for all.

In a final glorious tantrum, Caroline Weed denuded her
hotel suite of drapes, obliterating breakfronts, vases and
other delicate furnishings to the tune of four hundred quid
accompanied by language never heard before in that fine
old hostelry. The entire performance was witnessed by
Sir Frederick doubled over in laughter.

Caroline limped back to Rathweed Hall and went into a
prolonged period of self-purge. Getting her unattached
from Marco de Valenti proved not all that simple. In the
matter of her conversion to the Catholic faith the Count
was proving the least noble Roman of them all. There was

not only de Valenti's pecuniary appetite to be appeased but the Weed anonymity to be preserved. It would not sit well in the Orange and Anglican circles of Ulster's strangling atmosphere if word got around that Weed's daughter had married a papist.

The Brigadier was given holy orders to obtain a quiet annulment. Formidable roadblocks lay ahead and they had to play it by Vatican rules. Swan by-passed the lower echelons, going directly to the Irish Cardinal. From there a trail of payoff money was sprinkled down to Rome where he bought the best canon lawyer in that holy city, who in turn greased his way to a direct petition to the Vicariate Tribunal. The Tribunal then sought a decision of the Sacred Rota, which handled the dissolution of marriages for the Vatican.

Even with open purse and inside contacts, the theological word games went on for nearly three years before Caroline's case was presented to the Sacred Rota. By any standard this was still considered uncommon speed. Swan had proved a brick.

Caroline Weed was burned with ultimate humiliation. When summoned to Rome to face a panel of priests on the Sacred Rota, she was questioned for days on end about every minute detail of her relationship with de Valenti. Every sexual expression, diversion and perversion was unearthed. No intimacy could be protected on pain of rejection of the petition. She was grilled into exhaustion by minds which functioned in sharply honed ecclesiastical mazes and traps. No personal mortification was spared.

At last Caroline pleaded ignorance of what the marriage involved, pretense in going into the marriage, holding secret reservations so that her vows had been given dishonestly and, finally, admission that she had no intention of having children.

Three years and twenty thousand pounds later the annulment was granted and she was mercifully excommunicated from the Catholic Church. Through this process of humility, Caroline Weed was to become humanized. Swan's work was so clean that there were only a few vague whispers about what had happened and these soon died out as she grew to the archsymbol of culture, charity and gaiety in Belfast.

The girl was a woman now. She and her father indulged

each other's frailties with unstated understandings. Caroline's new affairs were carried on with utter discretion in her beloved Paris in the company of artists, writers and musicians.

•

Caroline and Sir Frederick enjoyed one of their rare quiet tête-à-têtes at the Hotel Antrim, unburdened by business or social doings. After dinner they retired to the billiard room.

"English or snooker, Freddie?"

"Billiards will do, a fiver a frame too rich for your blood?"

"You're on."

Caroline quickly ascertained that his mind was not on his game. She reeled off two easy frames and was well on the way to a third. After she missed her shot, he chalked and stalked up to the table. He lined up a winning hazard, then halfway through his backstroke she said, "You and Max are plotting to exile me to Londonderry, aren't you?"

He nearly rammed the cue through the cloth. "Nothing of the sort. All I have asked is that you be reasonably decent to Viscount Coleraine during his stay. If we can get his thinking turned around I'll have a railroad at both ends of Ulster, and you know how much I want that."

"Oh, Jesus, Freddie, you're a wretched liar. . . . Let me see what we have on the table here."

"You've deliberately upset my game . . . deliberately."

"It seems I'm always upsetting this particular game of yours," she said.

"Put the damned cue down, I'm through," he said.

"You owe me ten, fifteen if you want to concede this game."

He peeled off the bills and grunted in mock disgust as she naughtily tucked the money in her bosom and winked.

"See here, Caroline . . . I am a reasonable man."

"You are the most unreasonable man in Europe."

"Well, I suppose the Viscount Coleraine did cross my mind, vaguely."

"Then let him uncross your mind, vaguely."

"Before you go into full gale force I urge you to give

this serious consideration. I mean, just sort of look the old boy over."

"I've thought about it," Caroline said seriously, "but every time I see a glimmer of possibility I think about that awful, grotesque, prehistoric mausoleum, Hubble Manor. We were there ten years ago and I've still the smell of mildew in my nostrils. Oh, God, Freddie, to think you'd condemn me to that dreary hole."

"Well, do the bloody place over!"

"Do what over? Londonderry? Roger Hubble? The whole damned west is a cultural blob, a nightmare. And from what I remember of Roger Hubble, he's a silly, bloody prig who snorts when he laughs."

Sir Frederick sighed painfully. "Why am I to be eternally cursed because your poor fragile, lovely mother could bear no more children?"

"Oh, Freddie, put the fiddle down."

"I'm not asking you to fall desperately in love with him for God's sake. Just marry the bastard, produce a few heirs, then bugger off to Paris and orgy with the entire bohemian colony for the rest of your life."

"You are a low, filthy, shocking, disgusting man."

"Horseshit!"

The door slammed after her and slammed again as he followed into the hall and into her bedroom before she could lock him out. "For God's sake, Freddie, no heart attacks, no let's remember we are rapidly aging, no tears, no requiems for Mummy, no threats of poverty and, please, no horseshit that you want this more than anything in your life."

Denuded, he shrugged and softened almost into an object of pity. "But I suppose I do want it more than anything," he said.

"Yes," she answered sympathetically, "I think you really do."

"Forgive me for saying this, Caroline, but there are times I wish that de Valenti had kept you still long enough to father a son. I get a feeling of depression, sometimes. Caroline, you're all of it to me, the entire thing. I want it to belong to your sons. Is that wrong? Please don't force me to get married again." He opened the door to leave.

"Freddie."

"Yes, pet."

"What would you do if you knew I married unhappily?"

"That's not fair to ask."

"But I am asking."

"If you keep closing your mind, killing off your suitors before you even get to know them, you're not giving me much choice but to start a second family. Caroline, how can you make a happy marriage or an unhappy marriage with someone you refuse to know? But, to answer your question, what do we really have but loyalty to each other and sense of family continuity? I think if you were faced with a poor marriage I might ask you to go through with it long enough to assure our ascendancy and tell you to find your pleasures where you can."

She sagged to the edge of her bed. "Yes, you are being reasonable. I was hoping it could go on like this always. You've had the indecency to create an empire and lay its riches at my feet. Why should your instincts be any less than that of a salmon going upstream, or the she-wolf trekking above the tundra to have her cubs? Freddie, I love you. It's awful of me to deny you the only thing you've ever asked."

His hand touched her shoulder and she pressed her cheek to it.

"Who knows," she said, "Hubble might be a good old shoe, at that. I wish that damned place of his weren't so . . . oh, Freddie, get the hell out."

CHAPTER SIX: Rathweed Hall sat candescently opulent on a high knoll in the Holywood Hills just beyond the grasp of East Belfast. It was walled off from that depressing sight by a magnificent mixed woods of Sitka spruce, whitebeam, alder, yew and aspen. The main house was set to afford an alleyway of visibility down on Weed Ship & Iron, then over Belfast Lough.

It was not that large as stately homes went, a tidy thirty to forty rooms, depending how one counted, contained in a modest compound of three hundred acres of rolling hills and forest. Yet it was second to none in

Ireland and often compared to the *petit* palaces of The Loire in France.

Disdaining the filigree, dark woods, ponderousness and exaggeration that marked Victorian décor, Lady Livia and later Caroline had thrown it open to air and light, using the ultimate product of imported artisans from a half dozen diverse cultures.

Livia established the home's Italian pre-eminence in white Paonazzetto marble, delicately veined and hued with pink and purple strands, a dazzle that shouted its name and uniqueness to all of Ulster. The main floor, halls, stairs, salons and columns ran heavily to Paonazzetto, then deepened dramatically into darker breccias and verde anticos in the master suites on the upper floors. What might have been a preponderance of marble was broken by twenty thousand square feet of Savonnerie carpets, each designed to offset its particular area. The grand-drawing-room floor was covered with a thirty by seventy silken-sheened, gold- and silver-threaded "Polish" carpet executed in Persia.

All of the second- and third-story ceilings, doorways and many of the walls were cast in bluish and alabaster-shaded friezes after the Francini Brothers' school and in continuity told the entire mythology of Scotland and Ireland.

An original set of Cole wallpaper murals was commissioned depicting Ulster scenics. These covered the walls in the less formal rooms, children's rooms, gun room, billiard room, morning room, game rooms, smoking room and library. The scenes were executed in woodcuts. After the single printing for Rathweed Hall, the blocks were destroyed.

Caroline added France. To upholster the large collection of Chippendale originals, she convinced François Bony, the leading Paris designer of the day, to scour the Far East for Chinese damasks and rare brocades of the Mongol and Manchu periods.

Interspersed amid a breath-taking assortment of Venetian gilt mirrors hung an even more breath-taking and seemingly endless array of Gobelin, Karcher and Boucher tapestries. Everything was selected to give a feeling of pastel euphoria, each Grecian vase, each free-standing candleholder, each artifact. The only part of the house leaning toward the weighty were the massive Viennese lacquers in Sir Frederick's personal quarters.

In accordance with time-honored tradition, few of the gentry spent their money in Ireland. Sir Frederick did acknowledge his adopted country in the form of three dozen Cork crystal chandeliers. The one in the main foyer weighed over a ton and was hung from special hidden steel beams cast at the Works. The china was Limoges in a formal setting for seventy and the main silver Garrard, in his own pattern.

Yet there was almost no formal garden, no stable other than that used for transportation, no portrait of the Queen, no chapel, no flagstaff and not a single coat of arms in what was an ultimate display of reverse snobbery.

No sooner had Sir Frederick come to Ulster and opened his first modest dry dock of the present shipyard then he decided he had to have a Turner painting of a ship for his office. Finances were close in those days and the particular oil he craved was costly. A large gambling win enabled him to purchase "Steamboat in Shallow Water," which foreran what was to become the most illustrious personal art collection in Ulster. Later, when his interest expanded to railroads, another Turner, "Railway in the Snowstorm," one of the first oils ever done of a train, was acquired.

Art begat art with the usual Weed zeal. Forays to Venice and Spain burst Hieronymus Bosch and Goya into his life. In bizarre contrast to the clean villa lines of the house and its understatements came a legion of tortured naked bodies, satanists, monsters in the throes of perversions, black masses, grotesque satires of semi-men/semi-beasts. Bosch's "Garden of Thorns" and Goya's "The Wounded" fell into the priceless classification. His greatest coup and personal landmark as a collector was discovery of six original sketches which Goya used in his eighty-etching masterwork, "Los Caprichos."

Lady Livia complained that the place was at war with itself and was taking on the appearance of a lunatic asylum. Her gentle rebellion was ignored until she was on her deathbed when he promised to put things in proper order. Sir Frederick kept his word and built the first of Rathweed Hall's two notable outbuildings, a small museum to house the major part of the collection.

The building, nearly a peer of the art work within, was magnanimously open to the public on the Queen's birthday and numerous other occasions during the year.

Caroline's Francophilia brought in a new burst of art. During her off-again, on-again affair with Paris she was caught up with both the new wave of art and the artists. They were her friends and she often modeled for them. More than one was a lover. They were unknowns and their work went for minuscule prices. Often as not Caroline had first selection before they went on auction at the Hôtel Drouet for a few hundred francs. Sir Frederick had no use for that "horseshit junk" and refused to hang it. Caroline's personal quarters became a clutter of Manets, Monets, Sisleys, and Pissarros. A chap named Degas used her as a model for a dozen wire sculptures of "The Lithe Dancer" series and another fellow, Renoir, painted her twice, "Young Woman in the Forest" and "The English Lady," which she acquired by modeling for the other. The most serious of her lovers, Claude Moreau, did her nude in a passionate outpour of oils, sketches and water colors.

It was not until a French shipbuilding colleague, Gustave Caillebotte, contacted Sir Frederick with an offer to buy back Caroline's entire collection at an obscene profit that he took notice. The offer aroused his suspicion and an investigation bore out that something indeed was doing with this new art out of Paris. He hung the Renoir of her (one of his few slender models) in the gallery, then found himself spending inordinate amounts of time immersed in it. One day in a table-thumping decision he declared he was turning over one entire corridor of the gallery to Caroline's "French horseshit."

When all was considered, one would have thought Rathweed Hall had taken a lifetime but not so for the relentless Frederick Weed. With agents dredging the world and an army of experts and artisans in tow, it was completed in a biblical-like designation of seven years.

Roger Hubble, the Viscount Coleraine and heir to the earldom of Foyle, arrived at the lair. The foxes were immediately at play but it was difficult to say who was stalking whom.

*

Roger Hubble possessed all the expected attributes. Had reasonable, sandy, ruddy, good English looks. A bit too tall and a bit too slender, a touch of gangliness seemed to give off a boyish flavor. He was pleasant enough with a minimum of annoying traits: too fast at flashing his teeth into a fixed smile and a few jerky body motions at times when he ought to be standing still. Otherwise, he was palatable in manner. What Caroline and Sir Frederick sized up was an excessively ordinary chap, showing none of those special qualities Maxwell Swan had perceived. Surface politeness and lack of content prevailed in the opening day. Roger was properly impressed by Rathweed Hall, the Weed Ship & Iron Works and the Weed domination of the Belfast scene. He remained totally nondescript at a stag dinner in his honor at the Patrician Club, and if Caroline had tingled any amorous nerves in him, he failed to show it.

It was precisely this inconclusiveness that began to intrigue both father and daughter Weed. Obviously something was stewing behind Hubble's dull gray eyes. Sir Frederick preferred men like himself, out-in-the-open chaps. This one seemed to be making assessments and judgments without revelation. Once or twice Caroline noted a swift expression of frightening intensity that seemed out of context with his character, after which he'd slip back to what he seemed to be, decent and mediocre. There was just enough riddle to keep the venture going.

On the second day Sir Frederick invited Roger to join him for a trip to his rail testing site on the Newtownards Peninsula. Not least among Weed's capabilities was that of master salesman. The Red Hand Express engine was gaining serious attention beyond Ireland. As part of the selling job he scheduled his rugby team for a tour of the English Midlands each year and transported them about on a private train piloted by the latest model of the Red Hand.

Rails, like steamships, were on the rise and Britain led the world outside America. England's experimental line, the Liverpool & Manchester, had been nibbling about the Weed Works and although an order from them would be prestigious, Sir Frederick had larger game in mind. Britain and the Continent counted their new rail lines in tens of miles. America and Canada counted theirs in the hundreds and thousands.

A year hence there was to be the largest industrial fair ever, in Chicago, the nation's rail center. Sir Frederick was determined to come in and challenge Baldwin and all the other great American locomotives for his share of the business.

It posed a heady problem, calling for an ingenious compromise engine that mollified two different railroading philosophies. The normal British engine was a smaller and more refined piece of machinery built to travel short distances. Working parts of the British engine were covered and more precise and had to be stringently maintained. People and farms in England were closer together so that rail right of way was meticulously controlled with fencing. The rails were solidly seated in such a manner that engines could hit switches and curves at full speed with safety and didn't even carry headlamps.

Contrary to this, the American distances were reflected in engine bigness. Trains often traveled in the open parts of the West for hundreds of miles between stops. Therefore, right of way was exposed, rails were more raggedly laid and engine maintenance not nearly as strict.

It was the long-haul, high-speed American goliath versus the British jewel.

The Red Hand engine was an attempt at a compromise, a mid-sized affair still with enough precision for British rails, yet hardy enough for the long run. The Red Hand had spectacular success in the Australian outback, which gave Weed's people hope it could handle the American and Canadian prairies.

Selling was the one thing the Americans understood. Sir Frederick knew that the real key lay in a single word, SPEED. He was determined to bring into Chicago a compound engine that had set a record by breaking the ultimate barrier of a hundred miles an hour.

It seemed within grasp. The basic design, a Pacific-type configuration originally built for New Zealand, had been successfully modified by Littlejohn. The four-wheel pilot truck and two trailers delicately balanced the forty-five feet and sixty tons of sleekness. Her six sets of drive wheels ran seven feet in diameter with the stroke meticulously increased from fourteen to sixteen inches, still a bit more than half the stroke on the largest American leviathans.

Saddle tanks had been removed from the engine and replaced with a water tank in the tender car holding three thousand gallons along with six tons of coal. Again, this was about half the fuel and water of the American standards.

What made it a feasible competitor was the compound formula, two uses of steam by recycling from a double cylinder, a system the Americans could not match.

It was now possible for the Red Hand to travel the same long distance as an American counterpart, pull the same load using half the coal and water, and at higher speed.

Littlejohn reluctantly gave in to some of the ragged American requirements. Some of the moving parts were left exposed so the engineers could slop on oil. Valves and driving apparatus were shifted so the driver would be on the right side of the cab. Littlejohn was perplexed over why the Americans insisted on driving on the wrong side. It seemed utterly idiotic but they had to go along with the idiosyncracy.

Three earlier sets of time trials had brought about more modifications so that Red Hand #367 was breaking ninety miles an hour regularly on the Greyabbey-Portaferry straightaway under the brilliant hand of Driver Cockburn and Fireman Henry Hogg.

Things were getting agonizingly close.

The party milled about at the beginning point of the test site. Sir Frederick circled his creation with his crew and Littlejohn. He spoke to Driver Cockburn in hallowed undertones with the confidential air of a trainer giving a jockey instructions. A final imparting of wisdom, a wish of luck and he made off to the observation tower. From its platform there was a view of the greater part of the three-mile clocking section. A telegraphic communications system tied the starting and finishing lines to the tower. The suffocating calm was broken only by the clicking key announcing first a delay, then that the run was under way. The gallery raised their field glasses and telescopes to a man. Rhythmic puffs of smoke through the distant trees heralded the assault on the record.

"Here she comes!"

The first of five runs was shrill-whistled in and as the Red Hand hit the starting line a cluster of watches with sweep second hands made rough note.

The engine billowed into view around a mild bend, then bore down the straightaway. As she passed below, the tower shook from the impact of iron on iron. A black pall of soot blew upward, attacking the lungs of the onlookers, who had their ears covered against the rush of deafening sound. The Red Hand seemed to hurl herself at that ultimate time barrier looking for her own breaking point, then vanished, vanished, vanished.

Gripping quiet ensued until it was punctured again by the telegraph key which Sir Frederick was able to read along with the telegrapher.

"Ninety-six point two."

Deflation, then a restless renewal of hope as the return run was under way. Eighty-nine point three.

Depression.

It would be the third run that would make or break. Even the stoic Littlejohn clutched the rail dry-lipped and heart-throbbing, for the naked eye told that an extraordinary run was taking place. Sir Frederick chomped through his cigar as the Red Hand blew past. He paced insanely for confirmation that the official clocker matched his own time and that they had inched over the goal. Ninety-eight miles flat.

They all groaned as he threw up his hands and roared. The final two runs were academic. Taunting doldrums set in and the circle around Sir Frederick widened to give him flailing room. He shut himself in a small office in the executive car on the return trip to the Works. Speaking not a word, he whisked off at the siding inside the yard to his office and slammed himself in. After allowing him ten minutes to simmer to a mere sizzle, Brigadier Swan braved entry.

"Fucking son of a bitch!" Weed greeted his aide. "Fucking son of a bitch! We had it there, right there. Cockburn choked up, that's what! He has the heart of a cur. All he had to do was open a few bloody valves a half turn, a quarter turn. Heartless, gutless bastard! They just don't make men any more, Max. I want their resignations, immediately."

Swan laid two sheets of paper before Sir Frederick.

"What the hell is this?"

"Their resignations. Both Cockburn and Henry Hogg want out."

Weed ripped the papers and threw them in the wastebasket. "Well, they'll not get off that easily. What, what, what possible explanation did Cockburn have? What possible excuse for that performance?"

"None whatsoever. He said everything was wide open."

"A likely story."

"He says the train won't go any faster, Sir Frederick. He pushed it well over its limit today."

Weed paced. "Of course it won't go any faster. I told that bastard Littlejohn to increase the stroke to two feet. Four dirty little inches more. I told him from the moment I saw the plans six months ago. 'Two-foot stroke, Littlejohn.' Those were my words, as God is my judge. Where the fuck is Littlejohn!"

"He prefers not to see you for a day or two."

"Oh, he does, eh? And I suppose you've got his resignation as well?"

"No, I don't, but he did say that if you mentioned the two-foot stroke to tell you that the train would have been scattered all over County Down today. He says you're lucky it didn't do it on the third run anyhow."

"Horseshit! All I get is horseshit!" He hung his head and tears formed. "Do something about Cockburn and Hogg, will you, Max? Bonus, pat on the back. Send them down to the fishing lodge, let them hook a few salmon. Tell Littlejohn and the boys we'll meet first thing in the morning. See if 367 can take one more modification. Otherwise we've got to get cracking on a new job. Time is running against us now."

Swan nodded and began his retreat. "Oh, by the way, your house guest is in my office pawing at the air."

"Oh, Hubble. Jesus, forgot about him. Well, have him come in."

He slumped behind his desk, studying 367's specifications for the thousandth time, searching desperately for a place to give her one more nudge. He didn't want to have to start from scratch this late. Roger Hubble entered and showed a mouthful of sympathetic teeth. I'll shit, Sir Frederick thought, if he says, "Blast the luck."

"Sorry about the bad luck," Roger said, "blasted nuisance."

"Yes," Sir Frederick rumbled, arising once more and pacing to quell the fires. Restraint had never been his forte and, although Swan had warned him not to come on too strongly at Hubble, two days of nothingness, plus the fate of Red Hand 367, had him down to nerve ends.

Roger was perched in a deep window seat staring into the complex of the yard, when Weed stopped his touring and wheeled about abruptly. "Why in the hell are you refusing to sell me the Donegal Line and that dirty little L.C. & D.!"

Roger greeted it calmly.

"Do you mind very much if we talk about it?" Weed continued.

"Well, I suppose we're going to talk about it whether I mind or not," Roger answered.

Weed returned to his desk, separated his coattails sharply and found the proper file. "See here, Hubble, both lines are pitifully run down, the rolling stock is dilapidated. We've offered you three times what the whole bloody works is worth and, moreover, we're bailing you out of a nasty situation."

"I thought I made it perfectly clear to the Brigadier, the lines are not for sale."

"I suggest that is most unfortunate. Why, even on a partnership basis, I am prepared to sink in thousands to rehabilitate them. It seems to me, sir, you might consider the welfare of your own part of Ulster. This *is* for the good of the west, you know."

Roger moved slowly out of the window seat to the desk, sat himself opposite Sir Frederick, stretched his legs and cast a most serious look of inquiry. His gray eyes sought and found Weed's, both men probing, neither flinching. "Really?" Roger said.

"Most certainly, sir. Any school child can see that the west can only stand to benefit by a trans-Ulster line."

"As you wish," Roger said.

One of Sir Frederick's pudgy hands scratched the back of the other pudgy hand. "I have an inkling you are being cynical, Lord Roger. See here, are you questioning my motives?"

"Of course I am," he answered, unfolding himself and returning to the window.

The first hints of Maxwell Swan's assessment of Roger Hubble were starting to come through. Bloody cold number indeed, Weed thought. "Exactly what are you suggesting?"

"That concern for the west of Ulster is absolutely the furthest thing from your mind. It's a lot of rubbish."

Weed betrayed his shock but stifled his anger. "Please go on," he said.

"Certainly," Roger answered. "Well, you see, one of the tragedies we have here in Ireland is that, outside of Belfast, Britain hasn't invested a shilling into industrializing. We've become a land of medieval fiefdoms about to decay. In our own small way, we in Londonderry are the natural commercial hub of the west. Our shaky little industry and port properly function as railhead, distribution center, et cetera, for the population clear down to Galway. What we will have to contend with in a trans-Ulster railroad is a bald-faced attempt to pillage Londonderry, destroy its natural function, steal its assets and reduce it to a drone of Belfast."

"See here, your cheek is matched only by your imagination," Sir Frederick said, attempting to blow himself up to indignation but quite defensive as one would be who was caught in the act.

"Spare me that, Sir Frederick," Roger said. "You and I know that if a trans-Ulster becomes a reality your first step will be to undercut our sea freight rates. You'll make it cheaper for England to ship into Belfast and then you'll take it by rail to and from Londonderry. The first thing that will go under will be Londonderry's shipping lines because Belfast will be controlling all freight movement. Our port will become derelict and what little competition we offer in shipbuilding will vanish. Belfast will replace our natural function with Weed ships and Red Hand engines."

The evening whistle interrupted, followed by the mass movement of workers. Tonight Sir Frederick did not take up his usual station before the window to receive the homage of his legions.

"There's the reason for it all," Roger said, pointing

to the passing workmen. "Belfast is the heart of Protestant Ireland, Londonderry is hinterland. In order to retain an ironclad position Belfast has to monopolize jobs and industry. You can't allow Londonderry or Catholic Ireland to siphon off any of the prosperity. It's all a Belfast plot to lock it up, rails, ports, factories. When you have destroyed competitive possibility by your boundless gluttony and reduced us to dependency, we'll have to exist on your crumbs. You do see my point of view, do you not, Sir Frederick?"

What Frederick Weed saw was a direct confrontation with a man as ruthless as himself. "Your thesis is mad, utterly without merit," he said.

"Perhaps," Roger agreed. "Let us say my suspicions are absolutely unfounded. Nonetheless it has crossed my mind. I can't take a chance later on that I made a wrong guess, can I?"

"The problem with you people in the west is that you're a bit frenzied out there. You're apt to go into fantasies."

"Oh, no doubt we're nervous in our isolation. But after the next election you good people here in Belfast won't be so ready to write Londonderry off."

Writing the west off had long been part of the scheme. "I'm not sure I follow you," Weed said cautiously.

"Parnell is going to beat the spots off us. We both know that. Good Lord, we may even lose the Commons seat within the earldom. When Parnell and the Pope's brass band go marching into Westminster he's going to tie it up into parliamentary knots."

"Yes," Weed conceded, "he's a clever son of a bitch all right. I wish I had him working for me, I can tell you that."

"So what are your plans, Sir Frederick?"

"We're thinking beyond the election. Parnell's victory, as nothing else, will bring every diverse Protestant element into unity out of the common fear of Home Rule. We've begun the Union Preservation Party. It's one answer."

"And throw up a wall around Ulster?" Roger interrupted.

"That's right. Cold reality is that the three southern provinces of Ireland are lost. By your own definition, they have decayed under a defunct land system. The south is topheavy with Catholics."

"Then the game," Roger said, "is to keep Parnell from getting Ulster, right?"

"That's the game," Weed said softly. "We are making preparations to turn loose the preachers to brand R for Reformation on the forehead of every newborn. We'll lean on our pious Presbyterian brothers in Scotland for support. We'll twist the balls off Westminster."

"How?" Roger asked. "How?"

"By letting them know the Empire begins and ends here in Ulster. Lose Ulster, lose it all. We'll force a permanent union with England . . ."

"Even if it means taking Ulster out of Ireland?" Roger pressed.

"Is that what you want to hear, Lord Roger?"

"I want to know how you intend to hold Ulster. We are still outnumbered by Catholics here, are we not?"

Weed became uncomfortable. He knew full well what Roger Hubble was getting at.

"Shall I tell you what you have in mind, Sir Frederick?"

"Please do. . . ."

"You are ready to cut down the size of Ulster, are you not? You are planning for an Ulster where you won't be outbred and outnumbered by Catholics, and that means giving up the west."

"I'm not so sure that we're ready to cede anything," Weed fenced.

"But it's crossed your mind . . . letting go of the west, hasn't it?"

"Of course it has. A small, isolated Protestant community might not be held in a sea of hostile natives. That is one of the reasons we are racing to establish Belfast's pre-eminence . . . before the fall. We have to set boundaries of a workable Ulster, one we can hold."

"And Londonderry is expendable?"

"For a workable Ulster, it might well be."

"Ah then, Sir Frederick," Roger said without missing a beat, "I suppose you are fully prepared to go before a convention of Orange Grand Masters and advise them that their holy city, Londonderry, has been written off by Sir Frederick himself . . . and for business reasons. What do you think they'll say about good old Sir Frederick then?"

"What's your bloody point!" Weed snapped, unable to
contain the rise of anger.

"I suggest you can tell the Jew he can never go to
Jersualem and the Moslem he can never go to Mecca,
but God have mercy on you if you tell the Orangeman
he cannot parade around Derry's walls."

Frederick Weed paled before the man he had so sorely
understimated. He felt a rush of strange sensation that
might have been fear. He knew by the eager, zealous
fire in those gray eyes that Hubble would take him on in
his own Orange bailiwicks.

"Are you trying to blackmail us into keeping Londonderry?"

"Of course I am," Roger purred. "You've locked in
with England to save yourself and we're locking in with
you for the same reason. You have your points to sell—
bastion of the Empire, loyalty, industrial importance. We
have our point also. We are the holy city of Londonderry,
without which there can be no workable Ulster. You
blackmail England into a union, we blackmail you."

"You don't go in for any horseshit, do you, Hubble?"
Weed said.

Roger changed his dire mood to boyishness abruptly,
shoved his hands in his pockets and bounced off his toes
with a sigh. "It's all part of Ulster and Ulster being part
of England. What we are doing is planning a future in
which an Irish province is to be severed from Ireland.
Whatever method, whatever pretext . . . threats against
our motherland, religious rage, whatever."

Roger asked if Sir Frederick minded if he helped himself to a cigar. The brand carried Weed's personal band
but Roger knew it to be Villar y Villar, Barquinero
Havanas or perhaps Exceptionales Rothschild. He clipped
the ends, lit up and blew meditatingly.

"We're all hung in this thing together, you know. Londonderry, Belfast, all together."

Weed did not answer but he knew that Roger Hubble
had joined that elitist group, now three in number, whom
he could not intimidate.

CHAPTER SEVEN: An informal dinner was attended by two dozen of Sir Frederick's cronies, fellow industrialists and gentry in his "gentlemen's" lodge of the Orange Order. A like number of executives and engineers came from Weed Ship & Iron. Caroline, the lone female, played hostess.

It was held in the Sunhouse, one of Rathweed Hall's celebrated outbuildings, a one-eighth scale-size replica of the great Crystal Palace that had housed the industrial exhibition in London three and a half decades earlier.

The Sunhouse contained a small theater which allowed the late Livia and, later on, Caroline to hold private concerts, recitations, lectures and theatrical presentations, and himself to stage boxing and wrestling matches. It also served as an Orange Hall, the most pretentious in Ulster, for Sir Frederick's "gentlemen's" lodge.

Texture of the conversation at Sir Frederick's table was a bitter grousing over the upcoming election, which had been reduced to a single question, the Irish question.

The old dander was up in Ellery Chillingham, Marquess of Monaghan, and Thurlow Ives, the largest owner of power looms in Belfast. A toilet room cartoon was passed around depicting "Paddy," the Irish anarchist, an apelike creature, prodding Parnell into knifing noble Britannia, who in turn protected a fragile, weeping Hibernia. This set the acid tone . . . Gladstone Liberal sellout . . . papist agitators daring to run for Parliament . . . taxation on Belfast industry if Home Rule became a reality . . . should have kept Parnell in prison when they had him there . . . since when does one give one's natives the right to vote . . . one more land act and our Irish properties would be done for . . . and all this under the direction of Rome . . .

"If we can't control the Irish rabble in our home islands," Lord Monaghan wheezed, "how the devil can we expect to control them in India and elsewhere? I say the battle line is here and here we must hold."

"Hear, hear," Thurlow responded, rapping glass with spoon. "Hear, hear."

149

Sir Frederick strangely said little. Roger watched his behavior curiously.

"Splendid chutney," Ives complimented Caroline, chewing his cud. "Do have your chef send Martha the recipe."

"Just mango and Bengal Club from Harrod's," she replied.

Weed sank deeper into thought as Lord Monaghan puffed up for a second go at Parnell.

After dinner the party sojourned to the Sunhouse's main room, a convertible theaterlike affair under a high glass dome. A boxing ring had been erected with a proper number of tables about it to accommodate the guests. Tobacco smoke set up a sporting atmosphere during the serving of cognac. Entertainment would be supplied by a stable of Jamaican fighters en route to London, who would be opposed by the best of the local lads. Caroline took a seat between Roger and her father closest to the ring and lit up a small cigar. Roger contained his chagrin.

The first fight was announced. A pair of lighter-weight pepper pots displayed great pugilistic skill, pecking away at each other without inflicting serious damage during the scheduled six rounds. In the second bout the Jamaican took a fearful thumping, spurting blood down on their table. He rallied gamely to cries of "Good lad" but had to be dragged bodily from the ring at the end of ten rounds. Roger was far more fascinated by Caroline's presence than by the fights. During the final event he became completely fixed on her. The last Jamaican was a powerful heavyweight of tawny color who entered the ring shining with perspiration which accented arms and body of muscled magnificence. His black eyes were deeply set behind tobacco-brown cheeks and peered deadly.

Upon introduction, he bowed in each direction, then looked directly at Caroline, who looked directly at him. He bowed to her, expanding his chest and bending his lips up slightly. She watched with delicate eyes every nervous tapping together of his gloves, each deeply sucked breath, each bounce off the toes as the rules were explained. His opponent was a well-known Belfast war horse, a squat docker with a middling record and body full of tattoos.

Black lay against white as they clinched and grunted and snorted behind the thuds of their punches. Caroline's eyes narrowed to a half-shut wild kind of trance as they wrestled over her, sweat mingling with sweat, each straining to hang on with a desperation to stave off annihilation. Her face twitched ever so slightly each time the black man was hit, when he grimaced, when blood spurted down his nostrils, when his eyes rolled white after a sharp clout. Her breath quickened and deepened as they squared off and slugged.

It came to a sudden end when the Belfaster walked into a right hand that nearly decapitated him and he sank to the canvas, seemingly in slow motion. Applause, cries of "Well done" and "Bully" as the black man walked around the ring again, bowing, woozed, puffed, gnarled. His last bow was a contemptuous one for a mutual orgasmic instant in Caroline's direction. Roger Hubble was enthralled.

"Nightcap?" Sir Frederick said, closing himself in his den with Roger.

"Very good."

"Lovely sport," Sir Frederick said. "I think the big nigger will do right well in London. Cheers."

"Cheers."

"Frankly, I liked it better under the old London rules, bare knuckles, fight to the finish. Queensberry has made a child's game of it."

Yes, Roger thought, no doubt Caroline would have liked that better too. "I must say, Sir Frederick, you were a bit pensive earlier, I mean about the election."

"Lord Monaghan is a damned fool. He and all the others continue to give it that stiff upper lip horseshit and divide our strength by putting up candidates in places where there is no possibility of winning. It's the same way he hangs onto his bloody land. His sort won't take an honest look at what's going on. Well, they'll all wake up the day after the election."

Most of his life, Frederick Weed had talked down to people. It was quite difficult to get around to squaring off with someone who was an unfearing equal. "Roger," he began slowly, "I've given a lot of thought to our conversation of yesterday. About the need to salvage Londonderry in the Ulster scheme. I'd like to come out and visit you, look things over, see if there are ways we can work together."

"I'd be delighted," Roger answered.

"I mean the Union Preservation Party is just getting off the ground. It might be well to include some new thinking about the west in the master plan."

Roger nodded, acknowledging his victory modestly.

"Suppose I invite myself up to Hubble Manor over Apprentice Boys Day. Do you have a real fire-breathing preacher out there? One to set a keynote to the future? I mean the kind who can turn a congregation into a whimpering mass?"

"Oh, we've nothing of the Belfast tent variety. Solid Presbyterians, solid Anglicans."

"I've a man for you, Oliver Cromwell MacIvor. He'll stir all the righteous juices. A real pious pulpit pounder. Why don't you arrange to have him preach at the Cathedral?"

Roger smiled slightly. "The baptism of the west?"

"Yes, something like that."

"On one condition," Roger said.

"And what is that?"

"That you bring Caroline with you."

"I think you'd better arrange that bit of business yourself," Sir Frederick said.

*

Rathweed Hall's museum ran directly off the main terrace, a square building with an open center court. Each corridor ran a hundred and thirty feet in length, covered with a glassed lancet archway to draw natural light. The flooring, different in each corridor, had been created by Doulton Ceramic in London, and at the end of each corridor was a stained glass window executed after old Bosch designs.

Roger was impressed by Caroline's in-depth knowledge of the Weed art collection. Nearly everything about her was impressive; even that which he had found shocking was shockingly impressive. Roger was annoyed. How did one treat a female as clever as oneself? He had an awful feeling that Caroline never relinquished her upper hand, was always in control and damned well did what she pleased. The bastion seemed too ominous for storming.

They turned into the corridor of the museum containing

her collection of French Impressionists, just as the Ulster sun made an unusual appearance.

"Feel the sun," she said. "Why don't we sit in the courtyard and save the best for last? The light will be beautiful in there in about ten minutes."

"Right you are," Roger answered.

They reached the inner court through one of the massive bronzed doors to a voluminous fountain taken from a defunct Lombardy castle and remodeled into a series of reflecting pools in gold and silver mosaic. The garden was laced with immaculately cast copies of Greek statuary.

The fountain was for wistfulness. Roger divided his time, fascinated by its gyrations, and studying the handsome chestnut-haired creature near him on a marble bench. Roger would be pressing on to Daars tomorrow, to see his father. If he intended making an opening gambit, he thought, he'd best get on with it.

"See here, Caroline," he said, "I've studied your financial statement and no doubt you've studied mine. I'm certain we're mutually impresssd. Should we encourage anything further between us, or drop it?"

"Living with Freddie, I'm quite used to abruptness," Caroline answered. "To bring you up on the latest, Freddie is more impressed with you than I am."

"Temporarily, I hope. You know you are damned intimidating. Do you make all men feel inept?"

"Nearly all," she answered bluntly.

"A sport with you, I gather."

He clasped his hands behind him and walked down the series of pools. Caroline realized she was about to run him off like all the others. She hadn't found him terribly interesting or exciting, yet she didn't want to run him off. It would be wrong to anguish Freddie. On paper, Roger was the best possible match . . . only . . . oh, Lord, he needed so much work. Only a gamble of marriage would really tell if he were capable. She walked up behind him.

"I'm glad you came," she said, "and I'd like to encourage your friendship."

Roger accepted it as unmeaningful politeness. "Caroline," he said, "I've a problem with this situation. I haven't the slightest notion of how to go about charming you."

His hands shoveled his sandy hair back and he threw his arms apart in a gesture of frustration. "You see," he continued, "most of my thirty-two years has been spent in boys' schools, on men's teams, male clubs, the regiment. I'm not a homosexual, mind you, but with tenure in all those smelly changing rooms, I've lived under an axiom that hard sport and a cold shower take care of one's erection. My experience with women to date has been limited and in rather bawdy situations."

"What a charming confession," Caroline said.

"It's not that I won't be able to acquit myself, not at all, I assure you. When the proper time comes, I'll do my job quite well, thank you. You see, Caroline, to be blunt, I've not given sex a great deal of consideration until I met you. What I mean to say is, I gather it is rather important to you."

"Just what do you mean, Roger?"

"Well, er, you have dabbled in it now and then?"

"I was married once for a short period and have otherwise been well attended to and, in turn, have returned that attention. There have been rumors, of course. What would you like to know, Roger?"

"Well, one hears about a certain penchant you have for . . . foreigners."

"The rumors are well founded and quite true," she said. Roger reddened and sputtered.

"Just how important is sex to you?" she said.

"I should think," he said with rising voice, "it will be quite important once one gets the gist of it. You see, since I left the regiment I've been in a horrible crush getting business matters in order."

Caroline was amused by his candor. She took his hand and led him back to the museum and into the gallery of French Impressionists, stopping for a short, instant education before each new artist.

Roger stared at the small oil bearing the plate, "The English Lady," looking from her to the painting several times as though it was his unique discovery. "Remarkable, utterly beautiful. Who is this Renoir chap?"

"A dear friend. Roger, just what have you heard about my penchant for foreigners?"

"Not much, really. One would gather you have had several lovers . . . Frenchmen . . . artists."

"Do you consider that vulgar?"

"No. One's past is one's own business. If you want to know the truth, I've always envied my father and his mistress."

"Clara Townsend-Trowbridge?"

"Yes, Clara."

"What attracts you?"

"Her being an actress. Their living in a kind of sin. And she does have an exquisite bosom. I like their bang-up relationship filled with all sorts of hush-hush nuances. They excite each other. It's lovely to watch."

"Then you don't look on my sisterhood as tarnished and damaged merchandise."

"On the contrary, indeed. I can't think of anything more depressing than getting involved with a virgin, either of body or mind. The problem is, how does a chap fresh out of the regiment cope with a woman capable of tying him into knots?" He continued to look at the painting with his hands in motion and rocking off his toes and heels. "Did you know these chaps well?"

"Very. From time to time I was the only one about who could afford to keep them in canvas and oils."

"They must have adored you as a model."

"They said they loved my lithe English body. Would you like to see it?"

"Your body?"

"Some paintings."

Roger clasped his hands behind him and showed teeth. "I suppose that would be quite proper."

"Come along."

Roger Hubble had never seen or smelled a room so deliciously white and sensuous, a marble cloudlike setting broken in transparencies of voile and mirrored walls. Within view of the boudoir, an open-laced tile grille screen of tiny blue Persian mosaics peered into a sunken tub alive with oils and scents. He mumbled something about what a lovely place to take a bath and his eyes came to rest on a wall of nudes done by a man of talent who was obviously much in love with the model. The poses were unabashed, a luring panorama of carnality.

"Do you like them?"

"Hardly a fitting description. They're smashing."

"Claude Moreau," she said.

"Did you love him very much?"

"He was a loathsome bastard."

Roger stepped close, nearly touching the pictures, then turned to her as she stood in the center of the room in willowy magnificence. Her fingers drew the drawstring of her blouse and she undid the buttons, with deliberate pain.

"Perhaps you'd like to see for yourself if Moreau got a proper likeness."

Roger lowered his eyes and fluttered his hands helplessly. "You're mocking me, Caroline. You know I can't handle you and you're making sport. You've no right to do that."

"Lift your eyes, Roger, and tell me what you see?"

He did. She was naked to the waist.

"Would you like to touch me?"

"I may not be as roaring a lover as your Frenchman, but I'm not your fool. I won't be treated like an uncoordinated puppy. If and when I want you it will be in my own middling manner."

Caroline smirked to squash the put-down. "Oh, for God's sake," she said, "go take your cold shower."

*

Sir Frederick insisted Roger continue to Kinsale in his private car, a gesture with unmistakable connotations. They agreed to meet six weeks hence at Hubble Manor to take part in Londonderry's Apprentice Boys celebrations. Sir Frederick would bring his new minister to deliver the service at the Protestant Cathedral. The time would be well used to further explore matters of mutual interest.

The private car was precisely what one would expect of Frederick Weed. Modeled somewhat after George Pullman's own in America, its appointments made it a rolling extension of Rathweed Hall. Aside from the main brocaded parlor and dining areas, the car held a small office, two bedroom suites, a kitchen and a separated "opera box" for the privacy of the ladies aboard.

Roger pouted alone, lost in the splendor after a back-thumping farewell from Sir Frederick. Although Roger was pleased with the way things were going with Weed, he found himself dejected over Caroline. He had never allowed himself to be taken in by a woman, never painfully desired any particular woman or even craved a short affair with a woman he could not dominate. He was properly perplexed.

"There you are, Roger."

He assembled himself into an air of indifference as Caroline entered from the far end of the car. "Do you mind a passenger as far as Dublin? I've a shopping list a yard long."

Roger's impulse to seize her in his arms was contained. It would be just what she would expect and she would play him for an idiot. He made a gesture which denoted that it was her daddy's train.

In a moment her luggage was aboard and the train inched out of Victoria Station into the garishness of southwest Belfast. After a brief stop at Lisburn, it angled toward the coast.

"I could be induced to come to Kinsale with you," Caroline said at last.

Roger stifled his surprise and pleasure, then countered with a deliberately cold tack. "Damn the luck," he said, feigning sympathy and futility, "but I have someone joining me at Daars. Quite frankly, I would have preferred you. Perhaps you'll visit Hubble Manor with Sir Frederick in August."

Caroline stiffened at the rebuff so carefully couched; it was impossible to tell whether he was speaking the truth or making a chess move. Whatever, she had learned what her father learned: not to underestimate the man.

CHAPTER EIGHT

DAARS AT KINSALE, COUNTY CORK, JULY 1885

"Lord Arthur's carriage has just turned the bottom of the hill."

"Thank you, Cronin," Clara said, "we'll take tea in his lordship's apartment."

Clara went out to the side porch and watched as the

carriage slowed on its steep ascent. Daars crested the tallest hill of Summer Cove, its gardens and grounds sloping downhill with a grand view sweeping the curve of the bay to Kinsale. From there one could see past Charles Fort to the open water, where a small fleet of billowing sails raced for the sanctuary of the harbor ahead of a blow.

In a few moments Arthur Hubble, Tenth Earl of Foyle, turned the carriage off the main road into the side entry where a pair of stable hands took the mount and assisted him down.

"You're in early," Clara said. "Did you have a good sail?"

He clasped his hands behind him, jutted a bearded jaw and tromped up the steps to the porch. "Gusty and nasty," he said, passing her.

Clara waited till he was dried out and warmed. "We got the wire, dear. Roger will be on today's Cork Mail from Dublin. He should be in in time for supper."

Arthur grunted his discomfort. Clara knew he cared for his son and Roger did make his visits infrequent, but anxiety would always rise. Arthur disliked all the business decisions. Moreover, Roger's particular visit at this time of the year meant he was coming to fetch his father and spirit him back to Hubble Manor for Apprentice Boys Day. It usually brought on a recurrence of stuttering. She was thankful that Roger was coming to Daars by himself without that dreadful bore, Glendon Rankin. The estate agent had been edged into the background since Roger left the military and got his teeth into the earldom's affairs. Although Rankin would not be coming, he had sent a distressing letter in advance of Roger that caused even more tension than usual.

Cronin set the tea service, then laid out a little stand of barbering tools and retreated. Clara pinned a bib around Arthur's neck and meticulously combed his beard, snipping and trimming him to bandbox perfection, a skill acquired during her days as an actress.

He slipped the desk drawer open and reread Rankin's epistle. It began with a torturous history of the Rankin family's devotion to the earldom which spanned a century and a half of service. Rankin did not fail to repeat the ultimate sacrifice of his uncle, Owen, who had been shot dead in the line of duty while evicting a resisting tenant. The letter went on to say that Lord Roger had been a welcome addition to the firm. Then came the cautions in carefully chosen words, the fear that Roger's move away from land and into industrialization was becoming reckless.

The split between son and agent was deeply philosophical and widening. Roger would be bringing more ideas with him for major new investments.

The reason manufactured linen product is in such heavy demand is because cotton has not fully regained its markets from its lapse during the American Civil War. But, your lordship, cotton is gaining and the linen industry could depress overnight. I've seen it happen before. It's dangerous to keep selling off solid land for this kind of speculation.

Rankin then lamented the radical ideas of land reform that had swept Europe but insisted the condition didn't apply to Ireland. Without an overseer to tell him what to do the Catholic farmer would simply create chaos.

The letter was finished with all Rankin's valves opened and bleeding. A chilling prognosis was set down on the thesis that, the more the earldom became involved with factories, the greater the chance for total calamity. Cities were flooded with jobless Catholics living in conditions that bred epidemics and crime and fostered papist and anarchist ideologies. Cities would demand Hubble involvement in the bottomless problems for schools, hospitals, workhouses, charities. Why indeed, Rankin argued, should the earldom be dragged into an urban potato blight?

Lord Arthur groaned at the miserable prospect of the next few days as he returned the letter to the desk. Clara applied bay rhum to his face, frictioning it into his scalp, and for the instant pure pleasure outweighed pure dread. A just-so application of brilliantine over the beard to highlight it and a combing and mirror. He studied the finished result with admiration.

A week's worth of London *Times* had arrived. They read, bantering gossip back and forth, but Arthur was clearly unhappy.

"Artie."

"Yes, angel."

"Is there any way you can talk Roger out of our going up to Hubble Manor next month? You stood firm on the issue two years ago and the place didn't go to seed."

Clara having hit the real nub of his discontent, he buried his face deeper into a paper.

"It's so dreary up there," she continued, "and I really don't enjoy being locked away like the family idiot. Those people are so damned sanctimonious. You'd think you were the only member of Lords living with his mistress."

"C-C-C-C-Clara."

"Now, Artie, you don't have to stutter. I've told you that for years."

"I'm not reciting Shakespeare on the London st-st-st-stage and I can st-st-stutter if I please."

"It's the only thing we argue about. They make me feel like a whore. Hubble Manor is as dark and grim and moldy as those righteous Ulstermen and they make me feel like a whore."

"I don't want a performance, if you please."

"I shan't say another word," she said, springing to her feet. She stood several inches above him normally and more so when he sat. "I don't see why you have to dress up like a clown in that ridiculous bowler and orange collar. You look like a low comic out of a Soho music hall. Ballyutogue Total Temperance Lodge, indeed, and there you are, the Earl of Foyle with a cemented strychnine smile on your face, parading about in the company of those unwashed farmers, uncouth roughnecks and their pimply preachers."

"Have you quite f-f-f-f-finished?"

"I shan't say another word."

"That dreary, moldy, sanctimonious place happens to pay for a lot of expensive habits you've developed, my dear."

"Oh, you are boring me, Artie."

"Once a year I am called upon for a little ceremonial pomp from the place which pays our passage. This year the political situation requires my presence more than ever. Some bloody Fenian is having a go at old Walby's seat. You've simply no right to make annual warfare over something so simple."

"If it's all that simple, then why do you become a wreck every time Roger is about to arrive?"

Little Lord Hubble came out of his seat, lips aquiver and perspiration popping. He tried to speak but was unable, and walked unsteadily into the adjoining bedroom and stared unseeing down to the bay. He had stood before his father once in that awful library in Hubble Manor and his father's eyes had been red and glassy and next to him a trunk filled with executed eviction orders . . .

. . . Arthur Hubble spent a lifetime avoiding twinges of conscience about famine walls, death ships, evictions and starvation but he never allowed any such twinges to overcome his appetite for self-indulgence.

He had long resigned himself to the fact that he had no stomach for running the earldom. He became the only earl in the line not to serve in the proper regiment or do the proper civil and colonial service. Instead, he had married early and left a pregnant wife for the Navy. When his own father, Morris, had begun to fail he put everything into the hands of MacAdam Rankin and, later, Glendon Rankin.

As Roger grew up, Arthur pushed him into the responsibilities early so that he might continue the pursuit of pleasure uncluttered. What he had totally miscalculated was Roger's zeal, a zeal that matched his own father's. Roger was taking things over with near total disregard for the past binding of the earldom to the land. Now Roger was forcing him into the terrifying decisions he had so skillfully evaded.

"Artie," Clara said, coming up behind him, "I'm sorry."

"You're quite right, Clara. I'll not be bullied into going up to Ulster. I'm standing firm."

She nestled up to him to comfort him, knowing the little lord was not telling the truth but making him feel for the moment that he was brave enough.

*

Roger had hoped for a few days of sailing and blue shark fishing before getting down to business but realized that would not be possible. Arthur's one mastery over his son was at golf. When Arthur five-putted the second hole and four-putted the sixth, followed by an onslaught of stuttering, Roger knew he'd better get on with it.

A horseback ride was suggested at breakfast, which Arthur knew to be the signal for a father and son talk. His own father, Morris, used the horseback ride for their father and son talks. Now he was doing it with Roger. Only Roger was taking the role of the father and Arthur the son again. As they rode off from Daars Arthur felt he was a boy about to be given a lecture and bucking up.

South of Summer Cove they galloped through meadows blanketed yellow with mule's ears. At Rinncurran the cliffs and point filled up with brick and ivy of Charles Fort where its defenses looked to a narrows passing to open sea. The fort had been built in the middle of the seventeenth century on the site of a Barry Og castle and down through the generations many new masters added on and it grew into a rambling affair. Part of it was still in use as a British garrison.

Lord Arthur was recognized and waved through the gate ceremoniously. They led their mounts to an abandoned decaying barrack and turned them loose in an overgrown enclosure, then climbed the steps to a promontory wall of the old outer perimeter. Hoping to throw Roger on the defensive, he grimly passed Glendon Rankin's letter to his son. Roger read it and handed it back.

"I'm afraid old Rankin's time has come," Roger said crashingly. "I intended to speak to you about his settlement."

Arthur went dry with shock. "I shouldn't be too hasty . . . obviously I've come to depend on you heavily but it takes time, a long time, to understand all the intricacies, and the Rankin family has been in it for over a century."

"Glendon Rankin hasn't the foggiest notion of what is happening today," Roger answered tersely.

"What I am saying, Roger, is that when you have completely saturated yourself in Foyle Enterprises your own participation will increase accordingly. We simply don't throw away a century of Rankin experience."

Roger steamrollered over his father's notes of caution. "There have been three major reform bills in the last decade," he said, "and after this next election there will be total reform madness. Glendon Rankin is nothing but a rent collector. He hasn't a prayer of coping with the new laws or the Land League and he can't continue bullying his way by outdated methods."

"Now, Roger, it's far too early for you to have all the answers."

Roger explained his concept of controlling everything from planted seed to finished linen to be shipped on Hubble ships and sold in Hubble stores. It was a concept that carried through similarly in wool, cattle and mines. He was getting rid of thousands of acres of low-rental-yield land and was converting it into great ranches. On the industrial side, Londonderry was ideal because there was a chronic shortage of jobs and labor remained the cheapest in the British Isles.

What Roger explained was largely beyond his father's grasp. Moreover, Arthur had gotten wind of the budding friendship with Frederick Weed and was wary of it. He knew Weed to be a bully and a pirate. Roger's seeming naïveté over Weed was annoying.

Lord Arthur slapped his riding crop into an open hand and walked out farther along the wall. "This direction you're plunging into is full of trouble."

"We've got to get out of the landlord business or sink with it," Roger said. "That's the reality of the day."

"Frankly, Roger, I find myself becoming most distressed about certain social aspects of this entire movement."

"I'm not sure I understand," his son answered.

"We are coming to the end of a century in which we have seen a great deal of—how shall I put it?—enlightenment. I've been doing a lot of reading these days, looking into some of the new philosophies coming from the Continent. The entire Industrial Revolution contains a dark underside. It's not only what Rankin says about the vice and evils of urbanization. Frankly, I don't particularly like the ugly specter of us engaging in child, orphan and female labor and through our factories making a direct contribution to the squalor of the cities."

Arthur felt good after having said that. It was a spirited statement reflecting a position of social consciousness. He studied the puzzlement on his son's face with a smack of contentment. Good to put him in his place, Arthur thought. Too damned cocksure. Needs a trimming.

"Do you know what I think, Father?" Roger said.

"About what?"

"About your pangs of conscience and new worldly enlightenment. I think you are a bloody hypocrite."

"I beg your pardon."

"I said you are a bloody hypocrite. Our fortune is based on ruthless colonization, land seizures and exploitation of the cheapest labor in the world. What do you think the price of a nine-year-old Catholic shepherd boy is and what do you think a peasant woman gets for cottage industry linen?"

"There's a difference, Roger."

"What difference?"

"Land and peasantry is a natural way of life that has gone on unchanged for centuries. No matter who owns the land, the peasant is the same everywhere. Factories and cities are man-made and all the vice that goes with them is man-made. Rankin is right about that."

Roger bristled. "My God, man, my God. I do not believe what I hear. You are seeking enlightenment. Well, I'd better enlighten you about what I've found studying the estate records. Do you have the vaguest notion what they contain?"

"Rankin has always represented the earldom's interests . . ."

"You don't know because you've avoided those books like leprosy. Just because you appointed a surrogate doesn't absolve you of the filth he's done in your name."

"I f-f-f-forbid this discussion to continue . . ."

"Forbid, do you? Well, you're not getting off this wall until you hear," Roger said, coming around to face his father, his neck swollen with anger as he shouted: "Your allowance, your greed, have kept us pinned to the wall since the minute you became Earl of Foyle. Bloody extravagance piled on bloody extravagance. Two worthless racing stables, a villa in the South of France, Clara's obscene shopping sprees, ten-thousand-quid yachts; your tailor bills alone would clothe half of Londonderry. But all of that was quite all right because you didn't allow yourself to know what Glendon Rankin had to do to keep your bloody allowance coming. He took it out of the hide of your tenants, that's what. For every ten pounds of seed he sold in the spring, he collected fifty in the autumn. For every expired lease he extorted bribes for renewals. He was in league with every gombeen man in Donegal, cutting himself in on outrageous interests and manipulating crop prices. Have you the slightest idea of how many people have been evicted under your humane regime? How many bills of ejection Rankin signed in your name? Oh there's more, Father, much, much more . . ."

Arthur's riding crop lashed out but Roger stopped it harmlessly with his forearm. "You're being ridiculous, Father. You hit like a woman."

Arthur turned into a trembling mass as his son grabbed him and shouted in his face.

"You're no better than me or your father, the famine Earl whom you despise. No better at all, so spare me your tuppenny philosophies in the future."

"Have you quite d-d-d-done?"

"No! As of now I'm directing the enterprise . . . everything. You'll get your bloody allowance but I don't want your meddling. It's either me or you can go hang yourself with Glendon Rankin."

"Roger," Arthur whimpered, "Roger," he cried, clutching his son's arms desperately. "My son . . . you're not serious . . ."

He removed his father's hands, firmly. "I'm afraid I insist we reduce this to an understanding in writing."

"My own son . . . blackmail!"

"Indeed not, Father. I shall resign immediately. I shall do so steeped in the joyous knowledge that Glendon Rankin will have you in bankruptcy within three years."

"All right . . . all right . . ." Arthur whispered. "I'll think about it. I'll give you an answer."

"No, Father. You've spent your entire life in idle thought and evading reality. You'll give me your answer here and now."

"I'm appalled, totally, utterly astonished!"

"You shouldn't be," Roger said coldly. "This has been coming since you rushed me into the breach years ahead of my time. You pushed me here, Father. You pushed me here in order to keep blood off your doorstep."

There was no way out for Arthur except to leap from the wall. A bugle from the fort pierced the air, adding to his sense of frenzy. Echoes of a master sergeant letting go with a barrage of exaggerated commands found their way up to them. Roger remained imperturbable, without bluff or bluster. It was neat surgery. What little fight his father had was dissipated. Arthur now spoke in a whine.

"What on earth shall I tell Glendon Rankin?"

"A simple document with your signature will suffice. I'll do the rest."

"Very well." He passed Roger like a man freed from a trap and looking for air to breathe.

"Father, there is another matter."

Arthur turned.

"The political picture is grim. When I was in Belfast I was asked if you would be available for some appearances during the Twelfth of July celebrations. I tentatively accepted on your behalf."

"You've no right to do that."

"I said the picture is grim."

"Londonderry and Hubble Manor is bad enough. I haven't been to Belfast for the Twelfth in fifteen years. Besides, what on earth would I do for an entire month until Apprentice Boys Day in Londonderry?"

"Hamilton Walby is in serious trouble. Your presence for the month is required."

In the last gasp of independence he was ever to make against his son, Arthur Hubble rose to what anger he was capable. Roger knew the protest was based on the fact he'd miss the best of the Kinsale social season and would have to incur Clara's wrath. "I shall not," Arthur said pointedly, "subject myself to a month of drum beating, pedantic speeches and hysterical hymn howling. I . . . shall . . . not . . . go!" With that he walked down the crumbling steps to the enclosure and mounted his horse.

Roger followed, reaching down and lifting the gate handle. "We'll be leaving day after tomorrow," he said matter-of-factly. "I cabled Mother in London. For appearances' sake, it will be best that the two of you attend to your public duties together during this period. Mother will be joining us in Belfast. I suggest you arrange a trip for Clara to Paris or Italy."

Roger spurred away, leaving father and horse immobile.

CHAPTER NINE: In the end, Lord Arthur went quietly.

In Belfast on the Twelfth of July he rode in a long line of open carriages filled with Anglo ascendancy aristocrats in a deliberate reminder of Ulster's connection to the motherland. Thousands of Orangemen from hundreds of lodges were piped by dozens of bands along a well-grooved route to Finaghy Field where an ominous annual tone was set and Protestant Belfast was again pitched to a hairline away from a riot.

The return trip to Belfast came as a bitter disappointment to Roger, who had anticipated a renewal of velvet combat with Caroline. She had left for Paris and the idea of her wallowing among the Claude Moreaus disturbed him deeply.

With the glorious Twelfth done, the Hubbles retreated to their lair outside Londonderry, where Roger and Arthur went about shoring up Hamilton Walby's fences and the business of getting rid of Glendon Rankin.

Rankin got his summons in the form of a cold, impersonal letter. He would receive a reasonable life pension and use of a Scottish summer retreat belonging to the Earl. Exile without confrontation. It was the same kind of tactic he had used to rid the earldom of unwanted tenants and enemies.

Rankin knew what the rest of it would be. Many unsolved crimes and abuses against tenants would be dug up from the past and attributed to him in an effort to purge the records. After he had departed, rumors hinting of his frauds would be circulated. Roger Hubble would then magnanimously make a public statement that he wished to bring no dishonor to the family who had served the earldom so well and let matters die without an investigation. Glendon Rankin, who had served as hangman, knew the victim had no chance even if the victim were himself. In the end, he too went quietly.

Lord Arthur's appearance at Hubble Manor, his rush to Hamilton Walby's aid and preservation of the union

167

with England was on every Protestant lip. As Apprentice Boys Day loomed, hospitality and housing tents were erected on the grounds of Hubble Manor and Londonderry set the stage to renew the battle for Ulster. The undercurrent of the summer's seething bubbled on the surface from great deep wells of righteous anger all set to spew forth on the holiest of Orange days.

*

Four days before the great event, Inishowen was flagellated by a three-day storm that seemed to indicate that the Almighty himself had taken personal note of the situation in Ulster and was roaring a judgment of approval. Hubble Manor buttoned down under the lashing as flinching, cringing flashes and crashes revived every ghost story known about the castle.

Lord Roger labored in the library unannoyed by the crackle and batter, and looked up from his desk as a knock persisted on the door. "Come in."

It was his father who approached him, obviously disturbed.

"Yes, Father?"

"Someone has arrived."

"Who?"

"A Reverend MacIvor."

"MacIvor? I don't believe I know the name."

"You'd better see him. Very strange sort," Arthur said.

Roger followed his father into the main foyer. A man of perhaps five and a half feet stood dead center. Outside, a fresh salvo of thunder stretched the manor's timbers. The man was cloaked in grim Presbyterian gray, Inverness cape and a wide-brimmed terai hat of soft felt. Although escorted in by an umbrella-bearing servant, he bore effects of the rain. His face was shiny from it and it dripped from the edges of his hat. Roger advanced. The man's face was baby smooth and he was thin-lipped. His eyes darted out a constant challenge.

"My son, the Viscount Coleraine," Arthur said.

"Oliver Cromwell MacIvor," the preacher answered in a resonant baritone that belied his diminutive stature.

"I don't seem to recall," Roger said. "Have you come with an Orange Lodge?"

"I was to have arrived with Sir Frederick Weed. I am early."

"Oh yes, forgive me," Roger said.

"I was attending to the Lord's work on the way and came separately."

"You are most welcome. Father, the reverend was invited here at the request of Sir Frederick. He is to preach at the Cathedral. Your bags?"

"They have been attended to."

"Have you had supper?"

MacIvor gave off an odd cynical smile. "When you get caught up in the Lord's work, you sometimes forget."

"Well then, why don't you get yourself dry and we'll send something up. It will be quite comfortable by the fire. May I join you?"

"As you wish," he answered, following a servant up the stairs.

A half hour later Roger halted before the preacher's apartment and knocked. A low, unintelligible moan from within was heard rising and falling on the pitches of the storm. Another sharp knock went unanswered. A gasping, strangulating sound sent Roger bursting into the room.

Oliver Cromwell MacIvor sat before the fire swaying back and forth like an old Jew at prayer with the rattling in his throat ranging from a choking wheeze to a gurgle.

"Are you quite all right?" Roger inquired.

The answer was unintelligible. Roger moved in to get a look at the preacher's face. It was glistening with sweat and his eyes rolled back, showing white.

"Reverend MacIvor!"

He was snapped from his trance and leaped to his feet. "Who told you to come! You interrupted! Get out! Get out!"

Roger backed away curiously.

"No . . . wait," MacIvor said, falling back to his chair. "Forgive me." He looked up and tears fell down his cheeks. "Do you know what it's like to have the Lord speaking to you? No, of course you don't. No one does. Kindly . . . kindly take your leave . . ."

When Roger departed, Oliver Cromwell MacIvor went to the water basin calmly, dunked his face, then did in the meal ravenously, quite enchanted with his performance.

*

The awesome Lambeg drums resounded from village to village like tribal messages on the dark continent. Kilted Orangemen stood before Orange Halls in the towns and villages and hamlets bombarding the countryside. During the summer-long marching season no place was immune from the drums' tattoo and no place too remote from the cocky jigsteps of the dancing marchers.

They had poured into Belfast by the tens of thousands for the Twelfth of July to celebrate their victory over the Catholics at the River Boyne in 1690. The marching season moved to its climax in their holy city of Londonderry where they would worship their savior, William of Orange.

They came by rail from Coleraine and County Tyrone and County Donegal and County Fermanagh and up from Dublin. They came by chartered boat from Belfast and Counties Down and Antrim, and Canada and England and Scotland where the Glasgow Orangemen were the most fanatic of all.

Londonderry was under siege again, this time by the heirs of her ancient defenders. When all the houses of all the brothers were filled, encampments resembling ancient tented regiments spread along the hills of the Waterside district and the grounds of Hubble Manor.

Every house and cottage of a loyal family flew the Union Jack side by side with the Red Hand of Ulster. Hundreds of archways were erected on main thoroughfares of the cities and the diamonds of the towns and these wore flower chains and bore portraits of beloved King Billy and beloved Queen Victoria and proclaimed, GOD BLESS THE EMPIRE and GOD SAVE ULSTER and REMEMBER 1690 and GOD SAVE OUR QUEEN.

The clans made their pilgrimage to the holy city for the holy day to revel in centuries-old victories over papists and croppies at the River Boyne and Enniskillen and Aughrim and the Diamond and Dolly's Brae. Now, at the sanctum sanctorum, Derry's walls.

Up the east coast of Inishowen on both sides of the River Foyle, bonfires inflamed the skies to satanic hues. In Londonderry about Irish Street and the Waterside and the old walled city, "The Protestant Boys" banalized the air, and for a penny a good Orangeman could kick the Pope in effigy for a worthy charity.

With an election coming up and the natives given the right to vote, the annual renewal of Protestant passion took on the air of a holy war.

CHAPTER TEN: I was dinnlin' with excitement when my daddy told me I was to go to Derry with him for a meeting of all the Irish Party candidates of three counties. I sped along the familiar route from our best room, across the yard and over the wall toward the Larkin cottage. The voices of Tomas and Finola raised in argument brought me to a halt before their byre.

"A dirty time to be calling you into Derry," Finola said, "with all those crazy Orangemen ready to go on a rampage."

"I think Kevin O'Garvey called the meeting deliberately," Tomas answered. "He wants us to get a good whiff of the Protestant temper this year."

"As if we didn't know it with those drums of theirs beating all day and half the night. And as if we couldn't hear them singing those awful songs from the public house. It's almost unsafe to go to church . . . a fact you wouldn't be familiar with."

"Aw, woman, your voice could split rocks."

"As if it weren't bad enough to lug yourself into Derry, you've just got to take Conor with you, don't you?"

"He's going to be hearing the drums for the rest of his life, woman. The sooner he learns what they're about, the better."

"And I suppose Liam won't be hearing them? Do you think it's fair taking Conor and leaving Liam so long as you're insisting on dragging children to Derry? What about Liam?"

"Someone's got to do the work. Conor's got privileges as the oldest."

"Go tell that to Liam. He's upset and rightly. It's the third time you've gone off with Conor this summer and left him."

"I'll hear no more of it," Tomas said in that tone that

denoted the end of a conversation. Though Conor was
my dearest friend, Finola's words were true. Liam was
always left out by Tomas and sorely hurt by it. Conor
felt bad about being so privileged. More than once he had
tried to convince his daddy but Tomas had a blind spot.
There was no question about who was his favorite.

When a decent time elapsed I inched into their best
room with the announcement that I would be going to
Derry too. It was greeted with coolness, then Tomas
told me and Conor to coor the horses to the large
communal wagon. It was a big four-wheeled high-stake
job for hauling crops and was used occasionally for
personal transportation. Not exactly his lordship's coach
and four but it would get us to Derry.

Daddo Friel, who had been traveling the district cam-
paigning for Kevin O'Garvey and had been staying at the
Larkin house, was also waiting for the journey to Derry.
Tomas led him out of the cottage door, lifted him in his
arms and swung him aboard the wagon where Conor and
I made him comfortable in the hay. We got close on
either side of the old dear because it was a rare treat to be
riding with him for so long a distance and him answering
all the questions we could think up.

My daddy threw in a sack of food and got up
alongside Tomas on the driver's seat, then they faced their
wives standing as glum as if we were all taking a final
trip to the hanging tree. My ma and daddy were not
much for public demonstrations but the Larkins usually
hugged and kissed before taking a journey. Tomas merely
waved, released the brake and slapped the nags into
motion.

Three nights before, the Constabulary had carried out a
sinister and successful raid on the widows' poteen still
and destroyed it, then closed up the village shebeen. The
place was in a terrible dry state so we had to stop at
Dooley McCluskey's for a few bottles of legal whiskey for
the journey.

Tomas stopped in the shade of the hanging tree as my
daddy jumped down and went into the public house. The
crossroad was filled these days with celebrating temperance brothers from the Township, as well as many
outside visitors, for the Orange doings.

"Seamus," Tomas called back to me.

"Aye."

"Better stick your head in and see after your daddy," he said. "Best to take no chances with this crowd around."

The barroom was thick with forbidden tobacco smoke and smelled of forbidden ale and forbidden whiskey. Half the good brothers were tore out of their heads. I made myself very little at the doorway, watching my wee daddy moving into the boisterous scene looking neither right nor left.

Dooley McCluskey was trembling with ecstasy over the speed he was raking in shillings. My daddy tapped his fingers nervouslike on the bar top trying to catch the skinflint's eye.

"We'll be needing six bottles," my daddy said, "half on Tomas' account and half on mine."

McCluskey deplored credit and never failed to moan about it, but seeing it was for Tomas Larkin, he grumblingly produced the bottles. Six was too many for him to handle so I ventured in to help.

"Hey, Paddy," a voice said behind my daddy. Oh-oh, that meant no good. It belonged to a stranger who had sidled up and measured my daddy as being too small to be much of a threat.

"Hey, Paddy," he repeated, "I seen you pulling up. If you go any slower, you'll be meeting yourself coming the other way."

Dooley licked dry and nervous lips as he slid the bottles over the bar. The room quieted, turning its attention to poor Fergus.

"Oh, it's a drinking man he is."

"Don't bother with him, Malcolm, there's not enough fat on him to fry an egg."

"If it wasn't for his ears his hat would be down on his shoulders."

"I hear he grew them whiskers because his brother took the razor to America."

"Don't you go falling down with all them bottles, Paddy."

My daddy handed me a pair of bottles, pretending not to hear, then loaded himself up. Well, then this Malcolm character blocked his path. As he did I edged back to the door.

"Up the long ladder and down the long rope . . . God

bless King Billy and go fuck the Pope. Ain't that right, Paddy?" this Malcolm character said.

"Out of me way," my daddy said softly.

"Oh, but not before ye say a Hail Mary."

The room was very quiet. Dooley McCluskey was crossing himself as my daddy and this Malcolm looked eye to eye and Malcolm was not joking. He was drunk and mean and large, a fearful combination. Just then I felt someone behind me. Thank God it was Tomas Larkin. The human blockade before my daddy melted with only Malcolm left to contend with. My daddy stepped around him and walked out untouched. A murmur of discontent arose over Malcolm's seizure of cowardice. He hitched up his pants and walked meaningfully toward Tomas.

"Hold it, Brother Malcolm," the voice of Luke Hanna called.

"Don't stop him, Luke," Tomas said. "I'd like to make the brother's acquaintance."

However, Brother Malcolm seemed only too happy to be talked out of it, grunted and snarled his way back to the bar. As Tomas went for him, Luke bisected his path.

"For Christ sake, Tomas," he said.

Tomas Larkin looked over the whole room with that devastating expression of contempt of his. "Get him out of here," he said to Luke.

"I will."

Luke followed Tomas outside and turned him around. "I'm sorry, Tomas," he said.

"You could have stopped it."

"Don't be angry, Tomas. They're like, well, kids at the first fair of springtime after a tough winter. They're just in a playful mood. I wouldn't have let anything happen."

"I know just what they're like," Tomas answered.

"Malcolm's not a bad lad. In his own home he's no meaner than me."

"Maybe. Maybe all of them are all right by themselves. But when they get into a crowd and they're wearing that bloody sash, they turn into a pack of animals."

"Now, just a minute . . ."

"A pack of bloody, dirty, devouring animals."

They was friends, most of the time, those two. At least they had learned how to live with each other. Both men were hurt. It was my daddy who led Tomas off, leaving Luke Hanna standing sorely under the hanging tree.

*

I fell into a magnificent slumber and remember entering Derry through a haze. Drums and bonfires broke the dark and silence of the night. We had passed through the enemy lines in the hills around the city. All the Scottish clans were in their encampments, their juices stirring for the battle on the morrow. And we was in the lowlands where our own septs had assembled with pikes and bowmen dressed in furs. Our king, holding a pair of wolfhounds at leash, called for his chieftains at the council fire to make plans to repel the usurpers.

CHAPTER ELEVEN: Although Kevin O'Garvey's house in Bogside was fine as any, Teresa O'Garvey kept a traditional potato patch in the front yard and pigs and chickens in the rear. The potato patch, a hangover from the famine, was a kind of safety blanket. The animals were kept because someone was always giving them to Kevin for legal fees.

Kevin built a second story over the stable which served as a hostelry for the constant stream of Land League petitioners in from the countryside. That is where we slept.

Excitement over being in Derry brought us awake before the rooster crowed. Our daddies and Daddo Friel were already gone. We scrambled into our clothing, touched our faces at the water pump, then made to the kitchen where a dozen or more visitors had gathered for mush and oatcakes.

Tomas told us to amuse ourselves for the day as they would be busy, and sternly admonished us to stay away from the Apprentice Boys celebrations. We left

the O'Garvey house with our pockets weighted down
under a tuppence each, faced with the decision of
whether to spend this unprecedented sum in a bakery
or the candy shop. As we walked beneath the wall
wrestling with our dilemma, music from the inner city
taunted us and the memorial column to the Protestant
Reverend Mr. Walker who had saved Derry from King
James during the siege hovered in stern reminder.
I could tell by the way Conor kept looking up what
was going through his head.

"I know what you're thinking," I said. "Our daddies
will blister the skin off us. Besides, it's too dangerous
up there."

The lure of it was overpowering for the likes of Conor
Larkin. "You can stay down here if you want," he said.
"I'll see you later."

"Conor! Wait! I'm coming with you."

I really didn't want to go but I didn't want to stay
equally as bad. Oh, Jesus, Patrick and Mary, my heart
was thumping right into my teeth as we raced uphill
on Bishop Street Without, me crossing myself every
ten steps of the way. Conor stopped momentarily under
Bishop's Gate and me hoping some miracle would
change his mind. It didn't.

"Act like a Protestant," he said.

"How? Look at the color of me hair. It's blazing.
They'll cut it off if they catch me."

"Aw, no matter if you lose your hair, so long as you
keep your head."

We passed into the forbidden land to Bishop Street
Within. What we saw was more Union Jacks and
Ulster flags than could have possibly existed. Shoving my
hands into my pockets in a most natural and unassuming
manner, I attempted to whistle my nonchalance but
my lips were too dry to even pucker. My courage increased
by the minute after realization we wouldn't be tarred
and feathered. We raced up to the top of the wall and were
able to look into a maelstrom of activity. Suddenly the
crowds all surged the length of Bishop Street, over the
diamond and down to Shipquay Gate, which was nearest
the river Foyle.

"Oh, look, Conor!" I cried, pointing to the bridge.

"Jaysus!" he said. "Jaysus!"

We quickly found ourselves the finest vantage point in all of Derry and stared bug-eyed.

A black mass of men spewed over Carlisle Bridge with the band ka-booming "Onward, Christian Soldiers." They led a line of gilded carriages holding high officials and aristocrats. I could recognize Lord Hubble and his son and Major Hamilton Walby. The carriages were followed by legions of swaggering Orangemen in black bowlers, black suits and black rolled umbrellas that went together with their black mouths. This black ocean and its black tide was punctuated with sprigs of orange lilies for the Orange Order and sweet Williams for King Billy, which they wore in their hatbands and lapels and their sashes, which told if they were purplemen or blackmen or scarletmen or bluemen, and on their breasts many-colored ribbons to boast about their military service to the Queen.

Bands and bands and bands followed. I counted seventy. Bands of pipes and drums and bagpipes and accordions came before the banner of each lodge. Although our reading wasn't too good we could make out the names of some of them. There was the Oliver Cromwell Lodge and Derry's Defenders and Sons of King William and the True Blue Boys of Coleraine and the Faithful Bakers of Belfast and the Loyal Dockers of Londonderry (they called Derry, Londonderry) and the Honorable Fighting Lads of Enniskillen and the Boys of the Empire and, sure enough, Ballyutogue Total Temperance. And other banners and paintings on their Lambeg drums reading, *Faith of our Fathers, Remember the Boyne, In Glorious, Loving and Revered Remembrance of Good King Billy.*

Oh, our eyes was burning and our brains was bursting from doing all that strange reading but after an hour we got the gist of it because it was the same thing over and over.

There was a preacherman leading every lodge. Alongside him another man holding a velvet cushion and on the cushion a Bible inside a glass case and the glass case topped with a crown. Alongside the Biblebearer another man walked with a drawn and polished sword. And all along I thought we were the ones who were the crazy Christians.

They kept coming over the bridge and down Foyle
Street near the waterfront, then into the walled city at
Shipquay Gate and up the hill and through the diamond
past a reviewing stand which now held all the lordships.
Once past the diamond, they broke up with some of
them mounting the steps of the wall until the wall held a
solid mass. They became so packed they couldn't move
but they kept marching in place, setting up a thumping
with their steps. They ranged over the top of Bogside's
shantytown of thin-clad shacks.

Half of them was singing one thing and half of them
another in a mess of discord. Conor and me crept up
close to where about twenty Lambeg drums were in a
row and they were beating like crazy men. The leather
thongs around their wrists cut into their flesh and soon
the drumheads was colored with their blood.

> The time has scarce gone round, boys.
> Two hundred years ago,
> When rebels on old Derry's walls
> Their faces dare not show.
> When James and all his rebel band
> Came up to Bishop's Gate,
> With heart in hand and sword and shield,
> We caused him to retreat.
>
> For blood be flowed in crimson streams,
> Full many a winter's night,
> They knew the Lord was on their side,
> To help them in the fight,
> They nobly stood upon the walls,
> Determined for to die,
> Or fight and gain the victory,
> And raise the crimson high.

Whistling and hooting and screaming and their drums
never stopping, they reached in their pockets and showered
farthings and ha'pennies down on Bogside. I began
trembling so that Conor had to cover me with his arms.

"Papist pigs!"
"Down with Parnell!"
"No Home Rule!"
"Fuck the Pope!"

At last, at last, with one broadside,
Kind heaven sent them aid.
The boom that crossed the Foyle was broke,
And James he was dismayed.
The banner, boys, that floated
Was run aloft with joy,
The dancey ship that broke the boom
And saved Apprentice Boys.

Then fight and don't surrender,
But come when duty calls,
With heart in hand and sword and shield,
We'll guard old Derry's walls.

Don't you know I'd had enough of Prods for one day.
I longed to get off the wall and down to the safety
of Bogside and my daddy, but Conor Larkin was
hypnotized by the growing frenzy and dragged me by
the hand all over the place. Oh, Jesus, my hair felt red.
The Orangemen broke into small disorganized groups,
some on the wall, some in the streets dancing and singing
crazy.

Movement began toward the Anglican Cathedral
where all the dignitaries from the reviewing stand were
making their way under Constabulary escort.

"Look," Conor said, "there's the Earl of Foyle again
and the whole mess of them."

"Oh, Conor, please, please, let's get out of here."

But Conor was inching closer to the Cathedral like
it was a giant magnet and it spelled no good at all.
The yard was filling with high persons tipping their
top hats and bowing to the ladies and shaking hands
solemnly, then moving inside the church.

"We're going in," Conor said.

I grabbed the iron rail and locked my arm through it.
Conor pulled on me. "Come on, runt," says he, "we'll
sneak in the back." Seeing as he really meant to go
inside, I held on for dear life. "Aw, Seamus, once we
get into the belfry they'll never know, and I bet we can
see the whole inside of the Cathedral from there."

"Conor," I pleaded, "you know it's a mortal sin to go
inside that place. On top of everything else we've done
today, we'll be in purgatory for ten thousand years."

He let loose of me and walked to the belfry alone.
For reasons entirely unknown to myself I was at his
side and he smiled and jabbed my ribs as we crept our
way toward never-never land.

*

The service droned on in uninspired English. Lord Arthur Hubble sat behind the altar in a row of deacons'
seats filled this day with gentry, Orange Grand Masters,
aristocracy, military and government grandees. Arthur appeared outwardly placid, in contrast to his inner churnings.
The horrible month would soon be over and he could
flee to Clara away from the nightmare of Ulster.

He glanced down at Roger, sitting in the family pew.
Roger had swallowed the Rankin mouse whole and was
launched on adventures that terrified Arthur. Next to him,
Frederick Weed, that gruff, overpowering man, also
acted like a contented cat.

Arthur shifted in his demi-throne uneasily. Beside him
the awful Reverend O. C. MacIvor breathed orgasmically,
adding to his discomfort. The whole business of bringing
this person to the Cathedral seemed vulgar.

O. C. MacIvor sensed Lord Hubble's uneasiness. Despite his smooth face and deceptively angelic appearance,
he made an art of causing people around him to squirm.
He studied the contents of the Cathedral like a wolf
closing in for the kill.

Born Enoch MacIvor, he had changed his name just as
he changed everything to serve his cause. Today was to
be his giant step, yet, if he were unnerved, he did nothing
to reveal it. He smiled smally and nodded to his benefactor, Sir Frederick, down there amid the power and
wealth.

For now he would bide his time and serve that power
and wealth until it otherwise suited him. There would be
no more sermons in wind-whipped tents with penny collections, no more freak shows of bringing fake "repen-
tant Jesuits" to Belfast, no more low gimmickry by putting on pseudo black masses to terrify his flock, no more
faith-healing tricks, no more kidnapping underaged
Catholic converts who had seen his light, no more bilking
widows, no more phony degrees in theology. From this
day forth he would preach in proper Lord's houses and

those high and mighty mucky-mucks down there would grow to respect ... nae ... fear him.

They stare at me, he thought. They wonder, do they, just what can this little man tell them? Well, just wait, dear souls, just wait.

". . . shall most happily yield the pulpit today for the Apprentice Boys message to Brother Oliver Cromwell MacIvor, who has traveled to us from Belfast for this momentous occasion," the Anglican Bishop said anciently, and retreated from his pulpit.

Oliver Cromwell MacIvor stood. The smallness and boyishness of him set up a murmur. He moved forward slowly, deliberately, toward his destiny. Frederick Murdoch Weed gave a quick thumb-up and tapped Roger on the shoulder and winked.

MacIvor's frock and breeches were of severe cut in century-old styling, that of a frugal Scottish preacher inundated with Reformation zeal and piety. He scanned his audience with lassitude, manipulating them with theatrical gesturing. When absolute attention had been drawn to himself, he thunderclapped. . . .

"Satanism reigns!" His voice boomed and rolled in waves over the congregation, startling them. "History shows us a recurring cycle of satanism and revival . . . satanism and revival. Since the great Reformation there has been a continuing struggle against evil, and when we have been pushed to the brink angels have come forth to save us, to cleanse us, to resore purity to our land."

Doubts dispelled. With rolling R's of Reformation, the thud of *Gawd,* a rhythm poured out of him clipped with deliberate intonations in an accent that was entirely the invention and innovation of O. C. MacIvor. With consuming power in his telling he wove a fascinating folklore, pitting Reformation goodness against Catholic evil in that game of kings and queens in the struggle for the English throne. Roger thought it all a bit pedantic but was equally puzzled by the grip MacIvor held on his audience.

"When the devils in the Vatican tried to plunge us into darkness, Oliver Cromwell spewed forth a great fountain of holiness and washed this sin-ridden land."

MacIvor stepped away from the pulpit, walking from one side of the altar to the other, swinging around to face

the row of notables, wringing his hands and bowing his
head in personal humility, invoking wrath, softening to let
the congregation into his confidence as friends and peers,
then scorning them. He had them guessing. . . . Will he
strike hard or soft? Will he praise or will he condemn? It
all seemed in his power, an unusual power, a sucking power, a chewing-up power, a soothing power.

"Where Rome has the power, there is a foul stench in
the air and depravity in the streets. For Rome is a cesspool! Papacy means eternal night, the destroyer of
democracy and freedom!"

His voice came down from the peaks, dropping to a
softness that forced everyone to strain. Through these half-
whispered passages Oliver Cromwell MacIvor gave out bits
of confidence that he had a special relationship with the
Lord and that through him was the best, if not the only
way, to be redeemed. All of the fine vocal coaching and
theatrical training and all of his touring on a southern
evangelical circuit in America was coming to brilliant fruition.

"Now, friends," he soothed, "in the quiet of my meditation I have prayed for guidance and there have been
times that I have received unmistakable communication.
I know one thing, friends. I know why you're here. Do
you know why you're here? Do you think it's an accident?"

He stopped, pointing to mid-Cathedral. "Do you know?"
And then he pointed to Roger Hubble. "Do you know?"
Both Roger and the Bishop reddened. MacIvor's fist
thumped the pulpit now that he had singled out a powerful man among them. "God has come to me in the night
and in revelation has told me that you are his chosen people! And God has told me to command you to save His
most noble creation, the Reformation! Arise, you warriors
of God, arise."

Tears came to Oliver Cromwell MacIvor's eyes. "How
well He picked *His* battle site. The siege of Derry of sixteen and eighty-nine was not an idle moment in history.
God brought inside Derry's walls simple, honest, hard-
working, devout Protestant, Reformation folk and He said
. . . 'here is my cause.' God caused those thirteen sainted
Apprentice Boys to shut the gate in the face of the papist

army! And . . . within these sacred blood-stained walls
. . . sons . . . died in the arms of mothers. Mothers . . . in
the arms of their husbands and the old in the arms of the
young. The young, angelic of soul and pure of heart,
lifted their eyes to God and their parting words were in
praise of God. Thousands of our cherished ancestors perished under that cruel and inhumane papish revilement.
Despite the treachery of the apostate Lundy, who bargained with the enemy, they refused to be broken. Despite
the starvation, despite the cruelty of wind and rain, they
. . . *knew* . . . they had to stand and fight Gawd's battle.
And Gawd looked down and said, 'Yea . . . you are mine
and I am yours.' And you know what Gawd did then,
don't you? Gawd broke the boom over the River Foyle,
ending the blockade, and delivered *His people!*"

For the first time in that venerable old house of the
Lord there was applause and people leaping to their feet.

". . . and later, friends," MacIvor said, riding the waves
of excitement he had created, "at the Boyne, where the
apostate James and his papist mob cringed awaiting battle, our beloved King William, wounded in his right
hand, took up his sword in his left hand and on an ala-
baster steed plunged without fear into their ranks. James,
shivering and cowering, turned and fled, and his mob fled
behind him, ending Roman rule forever!"

"Hallelujah!"

"God save King Billy!"

"Remember Derry's walls!"

"Jesus! I see . . . *Jesus!*"

Unabated screaming broke out until he held up his
hands, screeching them to a halt. He then cut loose over
their backsliding ways and their abandonment of their
ancient charge. He orchestrated a beratement that turned
their hallelujahs to whimperings and cringing. Now was
the moment that he, MacIvor, would lead them back onto
the path of righteousness. The Hubbles, father and son,
were totally abashed at the man's control over them all.
MacIvor swelled for the climax of his great aria.

"We are the inheritors of the magnificent victories at
Boyne and Derry. Our freedom, our clean, decent, Protestant ways, our privileged position, our Parliament have
all been sanctified by the holy waters of the Boyne!

God praise our savior, William of Orange, who bestowed upon us liberty . . . justice . . . *holiness* . . . Glory, Glory, Glory!"

"Jesus, save me!"

"Father, I'm coming back!"

"Hallelujah!"

"God save Brother MacIvor!"

As the screaming caromed off the Cathedral's beams and kept swelling. O. C. MacIvor walked up and down the center aisle dispensing blessings, touching hands, shouting banalities, then returned to the pulpit and held his hands wide to encompass all *his* newly won children.

"Let us pray," he said to the relief of the Bishop. The flock slowly came weak-kneed to their feet in turmoils of fear and adoration, the righteous juices of the men boiled and the paper flowers on the women's hats trembled as they bowed their heads.

"Won't you visit us, Lord. Now, You promised me You would. We're Your people and we're sorely troubled. The dark cloud of popery has descended again on our beloved Ulster. At this very moment as we sing to thee, to our democracy, our freedom, to our kindly and humble Christian ways and to our beloved Queen, agents of the Pope plot our demise even here in our sacred city of Londonderry. Oh, Lord, bless Your Christian soldiers and give them strength to gird for immortal battle against the satanic evils of the anti-God papists. . . . Amen and amen."

*

Conor and I had heard every word. There was an opening inside the belfry that led just above the choir loft and we had snuck in and curled up in balls under the rail, occasionally peeking over. We slipped back into the belfry and made down the steps with our legs wide apart so as to keep the stairs from creaking. Softly, softly, softly, round and round the tower. At last we reached the bottom. I lifted the latch. *The door had been locked!* Mary help me! Conor tried it and it was just as locked. There was a second door but we were certain it led right into the Cathedral behind the altar.

"We'd better stay put until the church is cleared out," I whispered.

"It won't do," Conor answered. "Suppose they lock that one as well? We're apt to die in the belfry."

"Oh, Jesus, I'm scared."

"That will do no good," Conor said. "If you're to keep your head as well as your hair, you'd better start using it."

"Mine eyes have seen the glory,
Of the coming of the Lord,
He is trampling out the vintage,
Where the grapes of wrath are stored."

"Surely you can sing to the glory of our Gawd with greater fortitude," that awful preacher shouted. "Sing up there in the balcony so He can hear you! Sing so He will come to Ulster to save us! Sing, brothers, sing, sisters, sing!"

"Conor," I said, "I'd rather wait and take a chance of finding a way out later."

"Maybe," Conor said, "but how will we find it in the dark?"

"Conor, I'm scared."

The decision was made for us when a curious caretaker who must have heard our voices opened the tower door and a big and awesome specimen he was, standing about eight feet tall and totally blocking our way.

"Run for it!" Conor cried, flinging open the other door. And there we were, sacrificial lambs on an Anglican altar.

"Glory, glory, hallelujah!
Glory, glory, hallelujah!
Glory, glory, hallelujah!
His truth is marching on. . . ."

The preacherman's voice like to shook the place down. "Ah, I can hear you folks in the balcony and you're singing much better than the folks on the main floor. Are you folks on the main floor going to allow the folks in the balcony to outsing you?"

Just as he turned we banged right into him and before anyone could get their wits we scrambled down the altar and the women screamed like we was a couple of mice turned loose in his lordship's scullery. Conor took off down the center aisle and with me biting at his tail.

"Stop them!"

An old usher in an orange sash blocked our path.
Conor Larkin lowered his head and butted him in the
belly on the dead run and down he went croaking for air,
and we hurdled his body and rattled desperately at the
door and, when it gave, we stumbled over the vestibule
and down the front steps.

"Act natural," Conor said.

We managed to do so for a few steps but out they
poured after us, yelling like we had stolen their golden
candlesticks. We fled like summer comets over the northern sky, zigzagging through the crowds of badly tore
drunks still celebrating. Fortunately their reflexes were
not of the same caliber as ours. We made Bishop's Gate
with blinding speed, putting distance between ourselves
and the mob from the Cathedral. The run from here,
thank God, would be downhill.

I tripped! I knew my face had gotten a bash off the
pavement because my head was dinnlin' and I fell when I
tried to get up and there was no wind in me to even call
Conor's name. I tried to crawl and saw the terrible sight
of Conor disappearing.

"You dirty little papist son of a bitch!"

I made myself into a shell as best I could. I thought
my ribs were busted from the kicking I was getting. I must
have fallen flat because I looked up and he was leaning
over me swinging his fists and shaking me at the same
time. Just when I thought I would never live to grow a
beard, I caught a glimpse of Conor holding a big rock
in his hand. He swung it and the beating stopped as the
man fell unconscious beside me.

Conor dragged me to my feet. I saw the man. His face
was half caved in like and he was groaning and spurting
blood from his mouth and nose. Conor held me up as I
tried to run, limping.

They were after us again screaming and rocks were
clattering around our feet. Conor fell. He had been hit
in the back. I pulled him up and we sort of hung
onto each other, limping and them gaining. Oh, God,
Daddy! God, Ma! Conor . . . we're going to die . . .
Conor . . .

And then a miracle happened! Suddenly the mob
stopped and melted back and I saw stones and rocks

coming at them. Oh, glory be, they were good Catholic rocks from the Bogside covering us! With no time to spare, we made it in.

The two of us sat gasping and crying at the community well, then dragged ourselves to the water for a repair and to conjure up a suitable story for our daddies. I didn't know what we could tell them. We were both very bloody and our clothes all torn. We discussed running away and sending them a letter, perhaps even emigrating to Boston. We must have sat for an hour until a priest came and took us by the hands and led us back to Kevin O'Garvey's.

We stood before Tomas almost as frightened as when we ran through the Cathedral.

"Some kids heard we had a tuppence each and a whole gang of them . . ."

"Aye, must have been ten or twelve."

"And big."

"Aye, real big ones."

"Well, they got after us, you see, with clubs."

"And knives."

"And I think one even had a gun."

"Are you sure that's what happened, lads?" Tomas said.

Conor lowered his head and shook it, and mumbled something.

"What did you say, Conor?" his father asked.

Conor repeated it but he still couldn't be understood.

"Would you say it again so's I can hear you?"

"We went into the Protestant Cathedral," he said, and both of us started bawling.

"All right," Tomas said, "find a pair of ash branches, return here and lower your pants."

We did as we were told and bent over bare-assed and waited. Tomas, looking doubly huge as he always did when he was mad, flexed the ash rod in his fist and hovered above us. I think, for once, even Conor was in prayer.

"Are you sorry!" Tomas demanded.

"Aye, I'm sorry," I said, "I've never been sorrier . . . ever . . . never . . . ever . . . never."

"And you, Conor Larkin?"

"Nae, Daddy. I'm only sorry their church is so filled with evil."

You could hear the man sigh across half the Bogside,

then toss the stick aside and slump in the hay and hold his head and fight off tears with hysterical laughter. "You like to scared us out of our heads. Button up your silly pants and come here."

I don't think I ever felt anything as warm and good and gentle as sitting on Tomas Larkin's lap with his great arm about me. "Aye," he sighed again and again. "Aye, and now you know. That bunch up there is enough to drive a man back to the Roman Catholic faith, they are."

*

At the Cathedral, the Reverend Oliver Cromwell MacIvor lathered at the defilement of the church by the two little papist devils. Churning the congregation into a frenzy, he led them outside, his booming baritone penetrating the air with "Onward, Christian Soldiers." They fell in behind him and sang with him in their wrath. He marched to the diamond and conducted an open-air service with hell-fire oratory striking out like prongs from the pitchforks of avenging devils. The crowd turned to a mob and the cry went up for papist blood. They swarmed out of the diamond seeking a place to vent their rage, first buzzing in aimless circles, then seething in the direction of Bogside, swelling as they went, to a rampage.

CHAPTER TWELVE: My daddy rushed into O'Garvey's stable, jabbering excitedly that the Protestants had gone berserk. Tomas and Fergus were to report to the Bogside Defense Committee which had been activated for Apprentice Boys Day. Conor and I were to go into the center of Bogside where it would be safer. Only then did we become aware of the growing excitement outside.

"I'm coming with my daddy," Conor said.

Fergus O'Neill was as gentle a soul as ever graced Inishowen. For the first time in my life I saw him turn on someone. "You'll go to a safe place with Seamus!" he shouted. "We've had enough of your bloody nonsense for one day. Get moving!"

Conor didn't budge. The answer was written on his face, a message of bedrock stubbornness.

"And don't you go standing up for him, Tomas. I'm not going to let that boy get his head broken and have to explain it to Finola."

"Fergus, for God's sake . . ."

"Nae, nae, nae! I'll not be talked out of it!"

"You'll have to tie him up and cart him off," Tomas said. "I'll never give an order to any son of mine to break and run at a time like this."

Seeing the two dug in against him, my daddy flung himself on a bale of hay and held his head in his hands. "Mairead pleaded with me not to take the kids to Derry. And I promised Finola on the holy cross I'd not let this kind of thing happen. Man, there's a crazy mob out there after lynching us."

"The mob will never go away, Fergus," Tomas said. "If Conor doesn't face it today it will be there tomorrow as well."

My daddy waved his hands around desperately and wrung them together. "To hell you say. Get it off of my neck, man. I took the responsibility and I've got to live with one of those women."

"I'm going with my daddy," Conor repeated.

"Oh, Jaysus," my daddy moaned.

I have never personally been noted for my bravery except for those times when Conor was with me. I didn't like the notion of having to defy my daddy or of facing that crazy gang of Prods, but there it was . . . a moment when a boy has to be like a man. How could I have continued living next door to Conor after I left him? You know what I mean, don't you? I closed my eyes, clenched my fists and blurted, "If you try to stick me in a safe place, I'll escape and find Conor. I can throw rocks as good as any kid in Ballyutogue. That's a fact. Ask Conor. Go on, ask him."

Kevin O'Garvey poked his head in, "You'd better be reporting to the Defense Committee. It's getting clear ugly out there . . . and get those boys back to safety."

It remained very quiet for a long time.

"Saints and martyrs," my daddy said bitterly. "All we produce in this country is saints and martyrs. God help us, Tomas, if we've done the wrong thing."

"I know," Tomas said.

"We'd better all go together," my daddy said, "our

Defense Committee man is down on William Street."
We left the stable as we lived our lives, beside each other.

Outside the walled city, William Street was a main
artery between Bogside and the commercial center down
by the waterfront. The Defense Committee knew out of
past experience that William Street was always an avenue
of approach during a riot. We were dispatched to the
intersection of William and Rosville streets where a
makeshift barricade of overturned teamster wagons and
piles of junk was being thrown up. Conor and I joined a
party of boys gathering up loose rocks, then tearing up
the street for paving stones. At the same time Tomas and
Fergus worked a few blocks away, evacuating several
streets of old pensioners. They were mostly debilitated,
unable to defend themselves, and lived in an area that
traditionally got the first bashings of a riot.

Bowie Moran, a hoary old Bogside veteran of a dozen
riots, was commander at our barricade and issuing orders
like a general of the Crown. By the time our daddies
returned, our wall seemed formidable and the pile of
rocks and stones was stacked high. There were several
dozen men and boys, many armed with clubs and a feeling
that we would be safe.

For an instant there was a murmur of relief as several
loads of Constabulary spilled up William Street. "Don't
get your hopes up," Bowie said, "they'll be worthless as
tits on a boar hog as soon as any fighting starts."

Just like that, I melted! The black mass of humanity we
had seen earlier in the day was storming up from the
Strand, filling the street from curb to curb. As Bowie
Moran had predicted, the Constabulary faded from sight.
Sounds of their howling was even less humanlike than
their earlier celebrating. Most of them carried ax handles
or barrel staves with big spikes on the end. They flailed
at store windows, poured in and hurled merchandise
into the streets, then set everything afire.

They inched past our barricade with neither side
opening up, then went at the evacuated houses, battering
their way in. In a few moments the air stunk up with
columns of black smoke. Some of our lads wanted to
take the fight outside the barricade but Bowie made them
hold fast. The Constabulary, he said, was just waiting
to pick off our strays.

By dusk every Catholic business around William Street was in a shambles and an entire block of thirty houses had been burned to the ground. Having finished off the undefended properties, they turned toward the barricade and came at us in waves, hauling missiles and screaming.

"Death to the papist pigs!"

"Down croppies!"

"Fuck the Pope!"

"Murder the traitors!"

About this time, quite frankly I peed in my pants and was wishing Fergus had talked Tomas into removing us earlier. It was like . . . well . . . in a dream of sorts . . . wave after wave running up and bombarding us.

"Bottle bombs!" Bowie cried.

The burnables on the barricade went up in flames and we staggered back, coughing and trying to stamp out the fires. In they poured! A fusillade of stones landed right in our midst. I was screaming over my daddy, who had fallen, and was trying to drag him back. The full terror crashed on me as I saw Tomas Larkin laying on his back awful still with blood pouring from his head. Above me the black wave was on our barricade and a crossfire of missiles blotted out the sunlight. Some men pulled Tomas and my daddy back to safety. As the Orange pierced our barricade they were met with paving bricks. Blood was all over the street and men running around holding their heads and groveling or laying still. Others flailed at each other maniacally.

Conor stood at Bowie's side fighting like he was ten men and I've got to say I was doing some pretty fancy rock throwing myself. We pressed them back and caught their next wave cold but they came again.

Tomas Larkin, half dead though he was, stormed out in front, picking Prods up over his head and hurling them back through the air. He was a wild man and turned us all into the same, as we burst over the barricade and chased them down William Street, which was now littered with dozens of their wounded. They regrouped and came back one more time, bending us back to the snapping point. We were saved by a roving squad of the Defense Committee who were experts with slingshots and inflicted terrible punishment.

Although our position was never assaulted en masse

again, we could hear the sounds of smashing glass and
screams until darkness brought a new kind of terror. The
night wore on with tantalizing slowness and was filled
with vile curses from the Orangemen and small sneak
attacks. From the top of Derry's walls a torrent of
missiles and torches poured down endlessly on the
Bogside, burning several more rows of shacks.

The Prods were able to make momentary penetrations
through the other barricades but the mobile squad of
slingshotters did a nasty piece of work on them.

British troops had been sitting in their barracks across
the river all night. They were even more worthless than
the Constabulary. The soldiers didn't move in till dawn
when it was realized the Bogside Defense Committee had
broken the Orange backs. I guess no one expected it.
When the authorities counted casualties, the Prods had
received more than they dealt out and the sport was
called off.

William Street stood ankle deep in shattered glass
and debris and other approaches to the Bogside were
worse. Eighty houses had been burned out, five Catholics
killed and hundreds injured. The Army and Constabulary
clamped a lid on Bogside to make certain we wouldn't
break out and go after Protestant areas.

It was the look in the eyes of our fathers that was the
saddest of it all. They had brought us to Derry to show
us Orange hatred but they had not expected this. They
were admitting to us that this was our legacy, the tarnishing of dreams, the finality of what was real in Ireland.

As for Conor and me, it was the moment we lost our
innocence forever.

CHAPTER THIRTEEN: The response to the Reverend
MacIvor's sermons had been overwhelming both in the
Cathedral and later at a rousing open-air meeting in the
diamond. It proved to be just the shot in the arm needed
in the face of a growing croppy threat, that reaffirmation
of the ancient cause and a clarion call for a crusade. A
number of the Orangemen had growled discontent lately

over the growing defensive nature and siege mentality of their own Presbyterian preachers and the wishy-washy thin-blooded Anglican Church.

MacIvor was a no-nonsense fundamentalist of fire and verve, a Godlike man, a holy man. Major Hamilton Walby, who had once disdained this sort of evangelism, saw its inspirational effects and realized it could be converted into a tremendous and desperately needed political asset. Walby implored MacIvor to remain in the district for several more meetings. O. C. MacIvor agreed, for he was now in the business of making spiritual loans to be collected at great interest in the future.

By the time the riots had broken out, the Hubbles and Weed were safely back at the Manor. Lord Arthur left for Daars that same night on the gallop.

For two days before the Apprentice Boys celebration, Lord Roger and Sir Frederick tested the waters of a general scheme devised to tie Londonderry to Belfast in the event Ulster went its separate way from Ireland in the future. Some broad ideas were agreed on in principle of a nature that paved the way for serious negotiations.

Then a coolness set in. Roger had obviously been annoyed over Caroline's failure to show up. The thought of her on a fling in Paris grated him. It hit bottom on Apprentice Boys Day, which proved an extremely unpleasant affair, due in large part to Weed's orchestration of the event.

Sir Frederick sensed that his delicate talks with Roger might slip away and decided to take the bull by the horns before leaving for Belfast.

An hour before departure he was postured in his suite totally relaxed and waiting for an opening. Roger gave him none and time was running out. "See here," he said, "I've a notion you've something on your chest and before I go tooting off I'd like to leave here knowing we've come to some solid understandings."

"Nothing, really nothing," Roger retorted.

"Come on, old man, you're in a snit about something. Caroline?"

"Not at all," Roger answered too quickly.

"What is it then?"

"I guess we'd better have a go," Roger allowed, "if

we're to continue our dialogue. I am distressed over that preacher you brought here and I am distressed over the riots he created singlehanded."

Weed smiled. "I shouldn't be if I were you. You must have heard all the praise you've come in for."

"That's exactly what distresses me. Why should people be rejoicing over all that bloodshed?"

"Because they're aroused, Roger. Because they heard what they wanted to hear. Because they don't feel so abandoned now."

Roger shook his head. "Gives one leave to wonder. They're treating him like a messiah. Good Lord, where did you ever find that horrible creature?"

Sir Frederick shrugged, undressed and caressed a cigar. "You know how it is in Belfast. Anyone with a gift of gab and ten quid can rent a tent and get himself certified Baptist, Presbyterian, Methodist, or whatever in a matter of a few months."

"The man incited a riot," Roger said, still in disbelief.

"Regrettable," Weed mumbled insincerely. "Roger, I don't want to seem presumptuous but you are just taking your first political steps out of swaddling clothes. As well as you know the province, it's still in an incubated, isolated and sterile state of mind. You've sensed the need to join up in the struggle to hold Ulster, but I don't think you quite understand that in this day and age we simply can't call out the military when we get in trouble. Gladstone and all that bloody Liberalism have changed that. We have to depend on masses of people, repugnant as it may be. Our base of power is Protestant unity, the Orange Order, if you will. What our good Ulster folk lack in culture and sophistication they make up in assumed piety. It's a simple sort of mentality which has to be kept fed and happy with a few crumbs of old-fashioned Jesus sprinkled on their daily porridge. MacIvor, repulsive as he may be to you and me, knows how to say exactly what they want to hear and there is no better way to keep those people unified than to put them in a state of righteous outrage . . . the holy grail . . . the crusade . . . that sort of nonsense."

A servant entered to say that Sir Frederick's private train had arrived at a siding near the Manor. Roger curtly ordered the man out and shoveled at his hair, dismayed. "This may be common practice in Belfast, but I will not condone deliberate use of the riot here."

Sir Frederick came from his chair, buttoned his vest and walked to Roger, placing a patronizing hand on his shoulder. "Like it or not, the Oliver Cromwell MacIvors are the most potent weapon in our arsenal."

Roger walked off, then came back in gray-eyed anxiety. "Did you ever stop to think what would happen if Oliver Cromwell MacIvor were to decide to take over?"

Weed laughed. "That's entirely impossible. He's completely under my control, completely beholden. He knows that."

"For the time being, maybe. You said yourself he's a cunning, ambitious, ruthless and gifted devil. I watched him closely for three days. He hates us. Until two days ago he couldn't buy his way into Hubble Manor or the Londonderry Cathedral. He hates us because he knows we see through him and his hogwash and he knows we are only using him to serve our purposes. But I tell you that somewhere in the back of that warped, black little mind he aspires to win the whole game, take it all over."

"That's a bit dramatic, what? When you come down to it he's a little more than a talented rabble-rouser and, if it ever comes to a choice, the people would have enough sense to stay with us. They do know where their bread is buttered."

"But do the people really have enough sense?" Roger questioned. "You heard the rubbish they ate up. It's frightening to think of the hypnotic appeal he has them under and that it could be turned on us."

"Dear Roger, I assure you the day will never come when the military and the industrialists can't control an O. C. MacIvor. We'll use him only so long as he works his passage in our behalf."

"Let me assure you just as earnestly that, once he gets his teeth into power, you're going to find him dangerous. He'll have the mob in his pocket and there will be nothing we can do about it. You go along with him now because you think it's for the good of Ulster. Frankly, I think you're flirting with the Devil."

Weed broke into his most gregarious smile. "Of course I'm flirting with the Devil," he said. "That's what Ulster is all about."

Roger remained unnerved until the string of servants removed Sir Frederick's luggage. Weed flipped his cigar in the fireplace. "Colonization is a hard game," he said, "but look what we have at stake in Ireland. Are you willing to give it up or do what is necessary?"

"When does the price become too high? We are knowingly making one repugnant alliance after another with madmen like MacIvor in order to perpetuate an archaic Reformation myth to control the mob, and we're deliberately using hatred and physical violence as a political weapon."

"Cheer up," Weed said, "that's what we've been doing in one form or another for centuries."

"And we're creating a mongoloid race. That's what scares me . . . these Ulstermen with their insane religious fervor. It ridicules common sense."

"Well, the whole thing here ridicules common sense," Frederick Murdoch Weed reckoned. "If that's what we've got to do, then that's what we've got to do, unless you know another way to keep the earldom as part of Ulster and Ulster as part of England."

Roger threw up his hands. "I sometimes think we are slowly getting strangled in the web of our own intrigue." They walked the long corridor and down the broad stairs. Sir Frederick thanked the personal servants assigned to his comfort and complimented the housekeeper and chief chef, leaving an envelope stuffed with his appreciation. Roger walked to the carriage with him.

"We'll be needing you in the party," Weed said. "I do hope we continue to stay in touch."

"To preserve the Union . . . yes, I'll be at your service."

"And, Roger, don't fret too much about the riots. After all, it's a blood sport and as long as they believe the blood is spilled in noble endeavor, what's the harm?"

"Have a good journey," Roger said, nodding to the driver. He watched the carriage make its way between the long rows of aspens and disappear through the main gate.

CHAPTER FOURTEEN: I've seen better-looking faces on potatoes than Conor and me and our daddies

wore. We were beat and bruised. Neither Conor nor I
could lift our right arms, we were that sore from
throwing stones. The next days were filled with work,
dismantling the barricades, cleaning up the mess, getting the homeless moved into communal shelters to be
taken care of. It was a time filled with weeping and
rage. Martyrs' funerals were given for the five murdered
Catholics with all of Bogside marching behind their
coffins and all the tragic pomp and inflamed speeches
that went with it.

British troops were in evidence everywhere and stray
bands of Orangemen prowled as we sifted through the
ashes in a tentative calm. From Bishop Street Without
to Iniscarn Road and from William Street to Brandy-
well, the lads of the Bogside Defense Committee manned
a perimeter.

The main meeting we had come to Derry for had to
be delayed because of the riots and it was just as well
because the four of us were in no condition to face the
women back home.

The old Royal Fever Hospital of famine fame at
Bligh Lane and Stanley's Walk had long been an
abandoned derelict when lack of a decent meeting hall
in the Bogside caused a consortium of organizations to
revitalize it. Renamed Celtic Hall, it became a communal hub, headquartering the Irish Party as well as the
Land League. Its auditorium was small, holding no
more than a few hundred souls, but what a sight. There
were buntings and green banners with golden harps and
even a wee band playing only slightly off-key songs of
the risings.

Conor and I got there early, saving seats in the first
row so we could sit at our daddies' feet. The spirit
that had successfully defended us two nights before
spilled over infectiously. Kevin O'Garvey chaired the
meeting with all the candidates grandly arrayed behind
him and when each was introduced from Donegal or
Tyrone or County Derry, there was a roar and the
band played and they spoke in terms of great optimism
about the election. There were official reports from
various committees, announcements for future rallies
and a passing of the hat for funds.

Things were all warmed up by the time Kevin

O'Garvey introduced the main speaker, who had
traveled all the way up from Dublin, and an impressive
man he was. His name was Michael Roche and he
was dressed to fit his name, a Dublin dandy. A high-
ranking member of the party, Roche was said to be a
close confidant of Parnell himself. Although he was a
Catholic, he was obviously cut from different cloth
than the Bogsiders and tenant farmers. The Roches
were an aristocratic old Norman family who had been
among the great Irish earls, but when he spoke, he
spoke our language.

Stinging, dazzling and shouting to the last row, he
proclaimed, "We are going to win sixty to sixty-five
seats and this time we'll not be shoved around like
poor relatives. The Irish Home Rule Party will stand as
the balance of power between the Conservatives and
Gladstone's Liberals and, by God, we're going to make
the ruling power pay the price for our support!"

Well, that got things going, it did, stirring up the
crowd to outbreaks of cheering.

"If you'll note the cut of my nose and hear the
manner of my voice you'll know I'm just another
'Paddy.' Don't let the fancy clothes and name fool
you . . . I'm as much a mick as any man in this
hall, and I tremble in awe before no Englishman. I
repeat to you from my own experience in Westminster
that no Englishman will ever really understand us, but
as long as we have to deal with them, Gladstone is the
best dog in the litter. Gladstone knows the reality of
Irish Home Rule. We will no longer be those shanty,
quaint little folk ignored by Her Majesty's councils and
ministers. Under Charles Stewart Parnell we will be the
shapers of our own destiny!"

Well, I'll tell you, this got the old blood rushing,
with Michael Roche being urged on by the grungy lot
of us. He climbed the hill of gains we had made
through the Land League and our never ending struggle
against the Crown and exhorted the ragged legion before him to double and triple their efforts in the days
to come. When he finally got to sitting down, he
did so to a standing ovation.

When Kevin was able to restore order, he called
for questions. It seemed like Michael Roche had the

answers before the questions left our lips, he was that
smart. As things were coming to an end Tomas Larkin
stood. It became very quiet because he was big and
the hall was little and everyone had heard of his heroics
at the William Street barricade.

"There is still one single question," Tomas said, "that
has been hanging fire since the beginning. It is a question
I cannot answer when it is asked of me and a question
that brings despair. Even if we get a Home Rule Bill
for Ireland, what in the name of God is going to prevent
the House of Lords from vetoing it?"

"I'll answer that!" someone called from the rear.

Necks craned. There was another dandy back there.
Michael Roche leaped up on a chair and shouted for
attention. "Gentlemen! Your attention! This morning I
received a message by telegraph at my hotel from
Parnell, who expressed his dire concern over the riots
here. He said in his message that he would get up to
Derry today if it were humanly possible. Gentlemen! It
is my extreme pleasure and honor to introduce my close
friend, the man whom Ireland has summoned and who
has answered that summons. I give you our leader . . .
CHARLES . . . STEWART . . . PARNELL!"

Oh, holy Mother, I never thought I'd live to see himself! There he came, walking calm as you please down
the middle of the hall like Jesus on the waters. Erect!
Tall! Aloof! Beautiful! Holy Mother, he was beautiful,
like Jesus himself! Everyone was standing on chairs and
screaming at the top of their lungs and men started
crying and jumping up and down and him as calm as
on a Sunday stroll shaking hands all outstretched to
him, and nodding like a king, the greatest of our chieftains exalted by his warriors and himself showing such
emotionless dignity.

By the time he was halfway down the hall with
stewards trying to clear the way, the yelling took shape.
"Parnell! Parnell! Parnell!"

"Parnell! Parnell! Parnell!" It swelled like a mighty
choir, reaching up and shaking the timbers, and straight
on out to heaven. The crescendo was maddening as he
was helped up to the platform and waved as his homage continued wildly.

"Parnell! Parnell! Parnell!"

He raised his hands for silence and in a moment you could hear a fairy whisper.

"Who addressed the question?" he asked, speaking very British.

"Tomas Larkin of Ballyutogue."

"The son of Kilty?"

"Aye."

"I am indeed honored," Parnell said. Can you ever believe that! Charles Stewart Parnell standing so close I could reach out and touch him and him saying that he was honored to meet Tomas!

"It's like this, Tomas, and all the rest of you who have pondered the same question. It's not a one-day battle. No one single bill of legislation will end the struggle. It is war, a war that will only cease when Ireland has achieved total independence. There were battles yesterday fought by Wolfe Tone and O'Connell, battles for land and religious freedom. Home Rule is today's battle, today's strategy in that war. What we will achieve by this election is to make Ireland and the Irish question the most important single issue in British politics. We shall use every parliamentary tactic at our disposal and take full advantage of the present air of liberalism. One veto, or two or three, by Lords will merely delay but certainly will not derail the drive for Home Rule."

Sure that was clear enough, even for me to understand. Parnell spoke softly and to the point about every kind of problem that was asked of him. His logical and quiet determination was inspirationally contagious. Conor had been gaping openmouthed like a hungry eaglet. When the meeting adjourned, he was the first to reach Parnell, and although there was a great deal of commotion around him, a magic thing happened before my eyes. Conor Larkin and Charles Stewart Parnell seemed to be all alone in the hall and speaking to each other without words, each seeming to have reached something very deep inside the other. He reached out and took Conor's hand and Conor grimaced from the pain and I guess it was then Parnell saw the rest of the cuts and bruises. He knew at once.

"Are you the son of Tomas Larkin?"

"Aye, my name's Conor."

"I'm staying at the Donegal House. Why don't you drop by, say in an hour, and we can have a chat."

"Oh, I couldn't do that, sir, not without my friend Seamus."

"Of course I meant the both of you."

I was so excited I nearly threw up as we approached the Donegal House. The lobby was filled with political persons and petitioners and callers but don't you know, Michael Roche himself was on the lookout for us and whisked us right past everyone and into Charles Stewart Parnell's parlor.

And there we were standing alone before him. I had an urge to drop to my knees and pray but I edged up close to Conor and tried to answer his questions sensibly. He and Conor talked, it seemed endless, almost ten full minutes when Parnell took something from the desk.

"I'd like you to have this book, Conor, and of course share it with Seamus."

Conor licked his lips and strained to read the cover. He shook his head and handed it back. "It would be a waste to give this to me," he said.

"Well, you do plan to read well enough someday, don't you?"

"Aye, I do, Mr. Parnell."

"Keep it for that time. It's called *The Rights of Man* by an American named Thomas Paine. It has some very important ideas you ought to know about."

He shoved the book back into Conor's hands and Conor lowered his eyes near to tears. "Mr. Parnell," he whispered, "whatever are you taking up your time for on a nobody like me?"

And Charles Stewart Parnell reached out and touched Conor with his left hand and me with his right. "That's one of our greatest problems here in Ireland. We've felt like nobodies for too long. You're very much somebody, Conor Larkin. . . . Do you understand me, lad?"

"Aye, I do," he said.

As Conor backed out of the room I could not resist the urge that swept me to Parnell. I threw my arms about him and said, "God bless you, Mr. Parnell."

We lay in the hay all night hanging onto that moment, never wanting to let it go. Conor thumbed through the book, picking out words he knew. Very late Tomas came

to check our wounds and tuck us in. There was a sadness
in the man. He had brought Conor to Derry to disenchant
him, to show him ugly realities. But the fires were lit in
Conor and they would never be dimmed for all his life,
and his daddy was sorely distressed.

CHAPTER FIFTEEN: Sir Frederick rapped briskly
on the door with the head of his cane. Caroline opened it
widely in anticipation. The warmth of her bear hug revealed that she was relieved over his arrival. Times have
changed, he thought. In the old days he would have had to
dredge through the Left Bank, usually turning her up in
some God-awful four-story walkup. Although her apartment at the Ritz was more in keeping with her status, it
was hardly in keeping with her old bohemian spirit. She
wore unusual pallidness and seemed on nerve's edge.

Caroline had not written for her father to come to Paris, nor had she written for him not to come. The undertones and between-the-lines had disturbed him sufficiently
to bring him over. After establishing himself in a suite
down the hall and devouring the always craved-for French
cuisine, he wove slowly toward the heart of her discontent.

"Found any good works?"

"They're getting scarce," Caroline answered. "The entire Impressionist school is becoming a victim of its own
success. Too many bad imitators about now. The prices
on Corot and Ingres are simply scandalous."

"Hummmm." He probed on with circumventing nonsense. Caroline grew irritable. "How've you been amusing yourself?"

"I damned well haven't and you know it," she snapped.

"What's up, Caroline?"

She strode to the french doors, unlocked them and
stepped out on the balcony. He trailed after her. The splendor of Place Vendome and its bustling colonnade over the
way came into full and glorious view.

"I can't believe that all the artists have suddenly abandoned Paris," he said.

"It seems they've all grown older," she said, "and so

have I." She fidgeted with the boxed hedge plant. "I guess I am getting along. I find young men extremely boring, pushy, bragging about a manhood they haven't achieved and most likely never will, and they're awful lovers. Their head-on cavalry charges will never be replaced by finesse. Even faithful old Claude Moreau spends his days in dreary cafés that I once found glowing and he prattles on endlessly about things I once found either earth-shaking or amusing. The climb up his stairs is too long, the bed too hard and the water too cold. In fact, Claude's foot is perpetually propped up on a chair and pillow from the gout, which he incessantly irritates by voluminous consumption of cheap red wine. He's a bloody alcoholic. Oh, Freddie, I've been miserable."

They joined forces in the heaving of a sigh.

"What do you suppose we ought to do?" he said.

"Quit running, I guess."

A chill sent them back into the parlor. Her first words of capitulation should have brought him some sort of vicarious pleasure but he had known all along that one of the most potent aspects of their love was his respect and admiration of her independence. He deplored seeing her defeated.

"I suppose my entire life game has been predicated on running away from you," she said. "So long as I was able to justify it, no matter how ridiculously, I found it all very funny. Funny, so long as self-indulgence in the fleshpots and self-centered brattishness could be rationalized. What has happened is a sudden loss of content in life. I'm no longer overjoyed and giddy riding the merry-go-round and I no longer take delight out of earning your ire. It seems that the time has arrived for me to earn my passage and everything indicates that Roger Hubble is my passage."

Weed loosened his vest, cravat and collar uncomfortably. "I said once that I'd let you go into a poor bargain but I'm not going to see you get into anything that's going to make you unhappy."

"It's not Roger Hubble making me unhappy, only what he symbolizes, the end of folly, the crossing over and coming of age of Caroline Weed."

"Do you think you can have a good go with him?"

"If I take it on, Freddie, I'm going to make it work."

"I guess it's the end of a game I've rather enjoyed myself," Weed said. "Hate to admit it but it's been good fun. I wish I could say I feel exalted about your decision."

"Freddie, I do want to earn my passage. It's just the realization of it that's come as a shock."

He nodded. "Once this all settles in, I think you'll know you've come to a sound decision. He is quite an unusual man."

"Can I tell you something? He scares me just a little. All the while he's acting out trivia, he's really seeing right through me and letting me play my ridiculous little games."

"I know what you mean," her father said. "The Brigadier saw it in him first. He's always further down the road waiting for you to catch up. In the long haul I think we're both going to need Roger. He has subtle touches of restraint, delicacy in his negotiations, a hand on the pulse of the times and an eagle eye on the future. He's thinking; his bloody mind is a trap. You'll never find him charging around like the Weed bulls. Watch him, the man is going to be one of the key persons in calling the plays for Ulster."

They allowed the reality of it to sink in over tea.

"Now that the Rubicon is about to be crossed," she said, "I might even allow myself to get excited over the prospect."

"Good!" Sir Frederick said. "That's the way it ought to be. Well then, let's give it a go, shall we?"

*

The journey to Hubble Manor was ostensibly arranged to conclude a formal closing of negotiations which had been carried on between Lord Roger and Brigadier Maxwell Swan. The Caw & Train Graving Dock, Foundry & Machine Works was a modest affair geared to the refitting and repair of ships servicing Londonderry and northwest Ireland with occasional callers from storm damage. The factory part of the yard monopolized ironwork for three counties. Sir Frederick made a generous offer to buy out everyone's interest except Lord Roger's, thus making them equal partners. Part of the transaction called for Weed to modernize Caw & Train, for, like most of Londonderry's industry, it verged on antiquity.

His purchase of half a graving dock was more allegorical

than practical. The gesture gave off an unmistakable reading that Sir Frederick and the other Belfast industrialists recognized Londonderry's right to its own markets. It further made an unwritten statement that the west was now locked into Belfast in any Ulster political scheme. This spelled a smashing victory for Roger Hubble and set up an atmosphere to allow future partnerships between the two ends of the province.

No sooner was the signing final than the two began to sniff about the possibility of establishing a modern roundhouse and engine repair facility in Londonderry. That hinted of a possible future merger of railroads into a trans-Ulster line.

Although everything was handled in subtle terms, there could be no mistaking hidden meanings accentuated by the presence of Caroline Weed. Roger took it in stride. All that was rumbling under the surface was treated with understatement. It marked the first time that father and daughter Weed had ever been so maneuvered. Roger neither gloried nor bullied at gaining the upper hand.

Hubble Manor and Londonderry showed Caroline little more than borderline palatability. The castle contained the same dank collection of relics she remembered from years before. Pocketbooks would be severely stretched and years would be required to make it habitable in her eyes. Moreover, nothing on earth could ever take Londonderry out of the provinces. If Ulster was a cultural desert, Londonderry was the furnace on the desert floor. It did offer some semblance of challenge. Redoing Hubble Manor could be made pleasurable and the idea of trying to civilize Londonderry had its interesting aspects. Caroline slowly accepted the situation with no intention of turning tail. What proved to be the stupefying stumbling block was a total lack of response on the part of Roger. He continued to be a charming host as well as an unrevealing one. It became clear to Caroline she would have to be the aggressor.

Late one afternoon she wandered into the Long Hall, a part of the original castle which had survived fairly well intact through fires and sackings. The Long Hall was a gargantuan open-beamed cavern of quasi-Gothic bravissimo, its history hung in oversized oil paintings depicting the entire line of the earldom.

"There you are," Roger called from the far end. "How on earth did you find your way in?"

"Back door was open, it was raining outside, and Freddie taught me as a little girl to always come in out of the rain."

Roger sniffed at the dankness and gloom. "Afraid the place needs a bit of cheering up. I don't think it's been used since my father abandoned the old homestead."

"Intimidating bunch," Caroline said, nodding down the line of paintings that ran the hundred-and-fifty-foot length that had earned the hall its name.

"Rogues' gallery," Roger said, "scoundrels."

He strolled a few paces and stopped before Calvert Hubble, the First Earl of Foyle, patriarch of the dynasty. They looked up to a classical depiction of a hard-riding warrior at the head of the charge. "Nothing small about Lord Calvert," Roger said. "When the main Elizabethan fleet landed at Kinsale to finalize conquest of the wearisome Celts and turncoat Normans, Calvert slipped away, doing a long dash up the coast and into Lough Foyle, claiming every inch of land he overran."

Roger popped off his toes, filling the air with gestures that Caroline had rather come to enjoy.

"Calvert was given a barony for his services, hardly enough to whet his appetite. His fertile mind helped convince the King that Ulster should be planted. Purchasing land at a penny an acre, he established an earldom, then sold boroughs complete with towns for five hundred quid each. A thousand pounds got an entire barony. A good farm of O'Neill land carried the price tag of a fiver. One could hardly turn it down, and in poured thousands of loyal Scots.

"This greedy chap soon owned land patents on both sides of the Foyle, controlled the lough's fishing rights and was exacting a toll on every ship in and out of Londonderry. Moving ever eastward, Calvert created the title of Viscount Coleraine which I wear with some apprehension. Viscount Coleraine was planted for future male heirs to claim the settlements around Coleraine and the mouth of the River Bann as part of the earldom. Alas, it was in the stars that he ran bang into the Chichesters, who were gobbling up land patents east to west as he was doing west to east. They say Lord Calvert foamed at the mouth like a werewolf the day Chichester was awarded the fishing rights on the Bann and Lough Neagh."

Caroline laughed so heartily she sounded for an instant like her father.

"Undaunted by the setback," Roger continued, "Calvert pressed on. To secure the defense of the earldom he conjured up another ingenious scheme: convincing the King to lease the entire city of Derry to the London guilds. The Honorable Irish Society was created to run the program and the city was renamed, Londonderry, a name still not recognized by the natives. As overseer of England's first colony, Lord Calvert controlled or manipulated every commercial, agricultural, military, political and financial dealing until his untimely death from drink and debauchery at the age of forty-four."

"I have the feeling," Caroline said, "you would like to shock me if you could."

"Shock you, good Lord, no," Roger said, walking away quickly. "Fact is, I've been generous to Calvert. Come this way," he said, trying to avoid the sensations of her closeness. "Here is my personal candidate for Hubble of Hubbles, Sidney, number three. To look at that brisk, noble bearing, you'd never believe him an asthmatic wart, nonetheless a stunning general. He was Cromwell's man for western Ulster, in which capacity he conducted three of the most notable massacres in Irish history. Having no money in the British Exchequer to pay for the Cromwellian follies, the Catholics were deported west of the River Shannon, as you know, and three million acres of their land was lifted, of which Lord Sidney grabbed a hundred thousand for himself. He wisely doled out large parts of it as back pay to Cromwell's soldiers and thereby established a private army within his earldom. The yeomanry that emanated from these stout lads has gained a frightening reputation . . . not without reason."

The rest of the line were lesser men in varying degrees. They came toward the front entry of the Long Hall, which had been locked for years. "My grandfather, Lord Morris, the famine Earl," Roger said, "and my father, Lord Arthur, the only Hubble in a sailor suit." Suddenly Roger had run out of nervous outpour and stood awkwardly.

Caroline approached a badly damaged wrought-iron

screen that covered most of the width of the entry vestibule. "This is magnificent," she said, "it ought to be restored."

"Never thought much about that," Roger answered.

She touched the screen, looked up to its soaring height, then turned to him deliberately. "Perhaps I ought to do it for you," she said.

"Oh, I see," Roger replied uncomfortably.

"Roger, you once told me you hadn't the slightest notion on how to go about charming me. I now find myself in the same position about you. You are an enigma, an evasion. Now that you have the Weeds eating out of your hand, what do you intend to do?"

Roger Hubble blushed, avoided her stare and edged into a dusty thronelike, high-backed carved chair. "As a matter of fact," he said, "I've given the matter a great deal of consideration."

"And what have you decided?"

"You are pampered beyond belief, shrewd and domineering, and I don't want to spend the rest of my life in a fencing match with you. I don't want to look into your eyes wondering what sort of cunning little things are whirling around in your brain. To quote the good Sir Frederick, I can jolly well live without all that female connivery. Nor will I be taunted into a jealous rage every time you look pantingly at the sweaty muscles of some half-naked workman. I shall not become a boudoir acrobat in competition out of fear of a band of unknown libertines and Lotharios."

The old Caroline returned, arching her back mightily. "And if you must know, I don't want your bloody title and I don't want to spend the rest of my life making this stricken monstrosity fit for human habitation and there's nothing that God-awful wonderful about you!"

"You're quite right, Caroline," Roger answered softly. "Nothing is all that attractive, that's the point."

"And as for Londonderry!"

"You're exactly right about that, too. You don't belong exiled in the colonies. I'm sure you noticed there are no portraits here of the Hubble women. They've been chosen for demure qualities and breeding possibilities. As for me, I think I'd also fare a lot better with someone rather simple, quiescent and bovine."

"You bloody bastard!" she shrieked, and tugged at the gated section of the screen to free herself from the place.

"I'm afraid we'll have to let ourselves out at the other end," he said.

She whirled around, "Bastard!" and she stormed past him. It was a very long hall, long enough so that humility, a quality that had escaped the Weeds, found its way into her. She slowed to a stop midway and stood trembling with anxiety until he came up behind her. "I don't know what kind of woman you think I am," she said shakily, "but I'd never go into a marriage without turning all my love into my husband."

"It's decent of you to say, Caroline, but I'm a conventional sort. I could never tolerate my wife's outside affairs. When you come right down to it, I'm a bit of an old shoe."

"Like hell you are," she said. "Roger, I know you're the boss."

He shrugged. "Oh, only because I'm being a bit forceful to someone who finds it novel, but I don't fancy playing Baptista to your Katherine. *The Taming of the Shrew* was never my favorite Shakespearean theme."

Her hands reached out and clutched at his arms and she pressed exquisitely close. "Let's try it and see how it goes," she pleaded, "please, you're exciting the hell out of me."

Roger's gray eyes mellowed and were at ease for the first time since she had known him. He nodded haltingly. "I think I'd like that," he said.

The Hubble hunting lodge, Knockduff, sat handsomely in the Urris Hills on the opposite side of Inishowen between Lenan and Dunree Heads with a haunting view to Lough Swilly.

With all his insecurities as the man to be her lover, Roger Hubble was only human. In the end he was not about to let her go . . . nor was she about to give him up. The full essence of partnership became silently but totally understood in a merger of two powerful forces completely respecting one another and willing to submit to the other's areas of superiority. To adore, magnify, absorb and drink in each other's strength instead of resenting and attacking it. The final cementing was a kind of fear. Now that they had come this far alone and found

this together, fear of losing one another ended the playing of games between them for all times.

As a wedding present to his father-in-law, Lord Roger
merged his rail lines with Sir Frederick's, creating the
first trans-Ulster line, and the Viscountess Caroline entered the Hubble pale to begin her reign.

CHAPTER SIXTEEN: We approached the harvest
walking insecure. The election had settled over us thick
and threatening. Rumors came swift as strokes of summer
lightning and were filled with menace. There was talk of
the bottom falling out of wool, grain and cattle prices and
of cutting trade benefits and imposing tariffs on Ireland.
Rumors fell of rent raises and evictions. While Father
Lynch and other agents of God and the Crown kept u a
tirade against the pagan Fenians, Major Hamilton Wa.by
turned into a demagogue, patterned after the Reverend
O. C. MacIvor. Trouble with the squire was, the angrier
he got the more he garbled his words to incomprehensibil-
ity. The early low-keyed campaign had degenerated into an
exercise in bigotry. Home Rule, Kevin O'Garvey and
Parnell became the filthiest blasphemies in the language.

Harvest was always a time of anxiety, for it meant a
summing up of the year's labor and an end to evading
how we would survive the winter. What Hamilton Walby
had succeeded in doing was implanting fear of reprisal
that would follow an Irish Party victory.

The Royal Irish Constabulary, who paid impoverished
farm boys next to nothing and had established the bribe
and informer as a way of life, found Hamilton Walby and
Roger Hubble very generous these days. An unslack noose
was on our necks in the unearthing of real or imagined
seditionists and other arrests of a political character.

We were shaken. The likes of Tomas Larkin and Daddo
Friel had their hands full to maintain unity. As election
time drew near, a very ugly threat surfaced when "distrainment," a practice which had passed from the scene
decades ago, suddenly reappeared. Distrainment was the
impounding of a man's cattle and tools if he was late with
rents or loan payments. The Constabulary would act solely

on the word of the landlord and often without legal process. When a man's cattle and tools were taken, he was forced to take out a loan from a gombeen man at exorbitant interest rates in order to pay the ransom and continue his livelihood. Often as not cattle were moved to impoundment sites miles from the tenant's home. The cattle would not be fed for the time of impoundment. That, plus droving it back to its original village, sometimes accounted for such a loss of weight that the grain used to refatten it amounted to loss of the entire profit on the animal.

It took Kevin O'Garvey and the Land League over two weeks of legal haggling to put a stop to distrainment but by that time the message to us was clear and the damage done.

Next came notification that all the voting places in our district would be located in town diamonds or otherwise situated in the middle of heavily populated Protestant areas. In the old days landlords used colored ballots to monitor the vote and God help the tenant who went against him. Although colored ballots were outlawed for this election, forcing us to vote in the midst of hostile neighbors amounted to about the same thing.

A week before the election, a final intimidation was tried. Signs were posted in every Catholic community offering several hundred temporary jobs of a week's duration in the stone quarry and as navvies on the rail lines, roads and canals. The catch was that the only men being hired were those eligible to vote, and the period of work would keep them away from their village during voting day. Our men would be shipped as far as Sligo and Meath although there were hundreds of unemployed men in those places to fill the jobs.

When it was all added up the plan was to remove over five hundred votes from the district, enough to assure Hamilton Walby's victory. Only the village idiot could fail to see through this bald-faced bribe but our economic situation was such that few could resist it. Our people reckoned that in one way or the other Walby would steal the election anyhow, so they might as well pick up the extra week's work. This was a small-scale repeat of 1800, when the British bribed the Dublin Parliament to dissolve itself and agree to an Act of Union with England. At that

time it had been done by creating new Irish peerages in
the House of Lords and meaningless seats in the House
of Commons. Today's bribe was not nearly as grandiose,
but it was the same dirty business.

There was only one way to combat this. Tomas Larkin,
Daddo, and all the Irish Party captains got together and
ended their meeting with the decision that any man reporting for the jobs would face total ostracism. If
Hamilton Walby reached back in time for his tactics, we
reached further back. Ostracism was the ultimate weapon
we held over our people. Punishment of turncoats by a
communal boycott within our close life structure was an
ordeal that few men could bear up under. It could mean
a lifelong sentence of total silence from his neighbors.

That was the atmosphere on the eve of Ballyutogue's
first free election after centuries of British rule.

Conor and I went with Tomas down to the diamond in
what was the longest, loneliest walk of my life. The tension was overpowering. We knew that the squire and the
Orangemen weren't going to go down gracefully and we
were braced for anything. The rest of the men of the
Upper Village stayed back at the crossroad waiting to see
if Tomas would get through. Fear stalked everyone. Our
people were confused over the entire voting process, like
it was an added burden they didn't want to carry.

Only the night before, Tomas confided he had been
offered a bribe, one that would double the size of his farm
with good land free and clear of debt. I think the reason
he told us was to let us know that he had more to lose
than anyone by casting his vote.

When the three of us arrived, the diamond looked like
an Orange rally without drums. Silence, ugly penetrating
silence, greeted us from burning eyes all teared up with
hatred. The voting place stood over the diamond in the
magistrate's chamber, that very same courtroom that had
been dispensing justice to the croppies for almost two
hundred years. We stood fast until the clock tolled the
hour that the voting place was to open, then started across
the diamond.

Strange to see Luke Hanna coming toward us. He had
always been a reasonable man but in the end he was a
senior among the Grand Masters and reverted to kind. He
and Tomas stood eye to eye for an eternity. Luke was puz-

zled, obviously not expecting Tomas to appear. The bribe
had been rejected and he couldn't believe it. He and the
squire had sorely miscalculated in believing they had
found his price.

"What's on your mind, Luke?"

"You'd better consider some of the disadvantages of
what you are about to do, for the sake of your own
people," Luke said hastily.

"Stand aside," Tomas said.

Luke Hanna panicked, knowing he had to knock off
Tomas Larkin so the others would turn back like sheep.
A riot was out of the question, for there was too much
to keep hidden from an inquiry later on.

"We'll not be buying flax this year," Luke said. "And
don't any of your lads be looking for work as drovers
and at the docks."

Luke faded under Tomas' glare, retreated a step, then
grabbed at Tomas as he walked past. "Don't be a fool,
Tomas. I've seen a master plan where they're going to
take over one third of your fields. If your people vote
today, they mean to go through with it and it will all be
on your head if you go in there."

Around the diamond the Orangemen closed slowly like
a lynch mob. Tomas looked at them almost smiling. "No
blight that ever destroyed our fields can match the human
blight that came to us from across the Irish Sea. Why
don't you people declare war on your ignorance?"

Those were Tomas Larkin's words as he entered the
magistrate's courtroom, signed his name and asked for his
ballot. Conor and I watched him drop it into the box with
our very own eyes. When he was done he stood outside
next to the doorway facing that seething gang with arms
folded, the calmest and strongest man who ever lived.

And then they came down from the crossroad. My
daddy, Fergus, and Billy O'Kane and Grady Mulligan.
They came at first in twos and threes and then in dozens,
over the diamond and into the voting room.

*

It would be days before the results were known. It
went well in Ballyutogue although there were flare-ups in
other places. We buttoned up in our cottages to face the
winter. Despite their threat of no work, there was the

usual annual employment over the water, and those on the
razor edge of survival made their weary trek.

The storm of the particular night when the news came
was average, being no better or worse than a normal
November deluge. About a dozen women including my
ma had gathered in the Larkin cottage to make lace on
finished linen, a nightly chore that put a few more pennies
in the pot. They came together in large numbers so as to
save candles.

Tomas and Fergus mended some harnesses for a while,
then broke out the homemade glink board. Glink was the
one game my daddy could do better than Tomas, and
howled with delight every time he trapped a spoof or
pulled off a double barness. There was only a single book
of study for Conor and me, catechisms naturally, which
we read for the millionth time.

Just like that a commotion was heard outside so loud it
was clear over the storm. I reached the door first. Sure it
was Kevin O'Garvey's carriage with half the village on his
tail screaming and yelling like banshees. He spilled into
the best room sopping wet and panting, having ridden
fiercely through the night all the way from Derry to tell
us the news, laughing and crying at the same time and
screaming that he had won!

Don't you know that mass hysteria erupted on the spot
and that was followed shortly thereafter by mass drinking.
You never heard tell of a wake like the one we held that
night for Major Hamilton Walby, the squire of Lettermacduff.

*

In November of the year of 1885 Kevin O'Garvey was
elected to the British Parliament as one of eighty-six
members of the Irish Party to gain seats. The issue of
Irish freedom after centuries of British occupation would
never be submerged again.

Parnell's star had zenithed. The aloof man who spoke
loudest by listening, the unemotional exterior which wept
within at injustice, the shy man whose moral strength was
powerfully evident, the Protestant who fought the
Catholic cause, the Anglo-ascendancy landowner who led
the landless, the Cambridge-educated genius who alone
was able to rally and control an effective conglomeration

of wild Irishmen. Charles Stewart Parnell, indeed, was the uncrowned king of Ireland.

CHAPTER SEVENTEEN: The Parnell victory set off an inflamed reaction within Ulster's Protestant community much along the lines predicted by Frederick Weed. He had made his preparations well to unify the divergent elements. With the nucleus of a Union Preservation Party already formed by himself and a few hundred gentry in gentlemen's lodges, it virtually exploded from the Orange Halls of the province.

The Orange Society now girded to fill its predestined role. From its spawning during the peasant land wars of a century earlier it had fallen into disrepute. Rowdy behavior by rowdy men earned the snubs of gentry and government. Throughout its checkered history, however, the spirit of Orangeism which called for the debasement of the Catholic native permeated the Protestant community.

Although outlawed at times, the Orange Society continued to thrive actively under thin disguises as benevolent societies and drinking clubs. As the decades of the 1800s rolled by and sectarian hatred became a permanent fixture in Ulster life, the Orange Society changed its tarnished image from a gang of thugs to a Reformation-oriented bulwark against the papists. Secret chapters formed within the British military while legal expansion spread to England, Canada and Scotland. Respectability was gained with an influx of preachers, Anglos and aristocracy. The once haughty landlords and industrialists saw the old order slipping; they could no longer call out the military and run roughshod over natives. A new center of power was needed, power from masses of people, and the Orange Order was ready made to supply it. From them was born the political arm, the party to preserve the connection with England, the Unionist Party, bringing together all Protestant elements under a single banner.

Sir Frederick sped to London after the election to enlist support. Into the mounting storm rode Lord Randolph Churchill. He was amenable to making a tour of the province and landed with Sir Frederick in Larne at the beginning of 1886. Young Churchill, a confirmed ultraconservative imperialist in his mid-thirties, loathed Gladstone and all that liberalism. He had hatred enough to spare for Parnell, the Irish anarchist, who was now maneuvering and dealing with both British political parties for his own ends.

The brilliant but highly unstable aristocrat reasoned that if he could bring about the defeat of an upcoming Irish Home Rule Bill the Gladstone government would fall. This would return his own Conservative Party to power and, in addition, bury Parnell's aspirations for decades.

The heart of the Churchill motivation was ruthless, unsparing personal ambition. To that end he shrewdly calculated that the Orange card was the one to play, to travel to Ulster and harp on ancient Protestant paranoias in a community which was reeling and enraged by Parnell's sweeping victory. Protestant Ulster opened its arms.

*

Caroline chose the isolation of the savagely wild and mystic Bere Peninsula in southwestern Ireland for her honeymoon over the conventions of Venice, Spain and the like. It was occultly wild, beyond her own visions of it. Roger recognized that through Caroline a door had been opened which he had thought was closed to him for life. He was quick to grasp the experience, expose himself and even press for discoveries on his own. The way was open wide for long periods of talking, of lovely self-examination, and this set the stage for deeper and more daring joint adventures.

Their idyll jolted to a temporary halt with the untimely appearance of Sir Frederick. After choking on his chagrin, he pleaded that the situation was so urgent that they should return to Londonderry to pull things together in the west while he toured the east with Churchill. In repayment for his indiscretion he promised to send them off afterward to an exotic place in North Africa, a place to fulfill their most erotic fantasies, one that even Caroline was unaware of.

The Churchill crusade became spectacular beyond expectations. Monster rallies in Belfast's Ulster Hall and through the eastern counties ignited short-fused passions.

Back in England sentiment mounted for the Ulsterman's cause. Staunch members of the Liberal Party who had favored Irish Home Rule were being shaken, their solid ranks wavering. Churchill pressed his advantages. His exit from Belfast signaled three days of rioting against the Catholic areas of the city.

Moving inland aboard Weed's private Red Hand Express, Lord Randolph found a magic key at Lurgan with a battle cry he repeated to adoring throngs in Portadown, Armagh and Dungannon.

"Home Rule will not come to you like a thief in the night," he repeated to the boiling Protestant masses. "I pledge that in this, your darkest hour, you will not be wanting for hundreds of thousands of English hearts and English hands who will cast their lot with you and share your fate. I say to you with pride, humility and resoluteness, ULSTER WILL FIGHT AND ULSTER WILL BE RIGHT!"

As Churchill's campaign hit full stride, ULSTER WILL FIGHT AND ULSTER WILL BE RIGHT blared from the newspapers throughout the United Kingdom. Roger joined the bandwagon in time for a rally at Ballymena and studied it with detached deliberateness. Churchill's wizardry had galvanized the entire span of the society, gentry and common man alike. After the meeting Roger locked in with his father-in-law and Churchill at the Castle of Lord Taggart-Royce, the Baron of Ballymena, where he made a plea that the final appearance should take place at Derry's walls. It was, after all, the most sacred symbol of the Orange/Protestant/Crown presence and what could better spell a triumphant finale? It seemed logical enough and Churchill agreed.

"We have certain unique problems out there," Roger continued, after having gained his first request. "Thinned-out population, communications lag and a sense of isolation . . ."

"I believe we call it siege mentality," Sir Frederick interrupted.

"Quite," Roger agreed. "What I should like to accomplish is an earth-shaking show of our determination to hold the west. It would be most profitable to call a special meeting at Hubble Manor in advance of the main rally. We could assemble all the leaders of the three counties to get them organized and heated up, that sort of thing."

Churchill had come to lean on Sir Frederick for advice, and cast a curious look in his direction. Once again Weed was impressed by his son-in-law's astuteness. It would be quite a feat to gather all the men of power and persuasion inside Hubble Manor and in one fell swoop see Roger take over political leadership of western Ulster. Roger would achieve in a single stroke what it had taken him years to accomplish in Belfast.

All right, lad, Weed thought, you're foxing me but I'll get a price. Blowing long of his cigar, he tooled up his answer. "Aside from Roger's vested interest, the idea makes sense. The west definitely needs a power base and a single strong leader of the new Unionist Party. Family considerations aside, Roger and Caroline are definitely the people to carry it out."

Men of ambition understood men of ambition. Mutual backscratching was in order. "Only one thing I would insist upon," Sir Frederick said. "To assure the success of the meetings, I would like to have the Reverend O. C. MacIvor as one of the principal speakers."

For the first time in their relationship, Sir Frederick thought he saw Roger wince, and he gloried in it.

"Rather raucous chap, I thought," Churchill said, "but he does cast a brand of magic on the crowd, I'll say that for him."

"Aye, and the best meetings you've had were with him. Well, what do you say, gentlemen?"

"Quite all right with me," Lord Randolph said.

"Roger?"

"Lovely . . . just lovely . . ." Roger said.

Viscountess Caroline plunged into preparations, although the workings of Hubble Manor were still strange to her. She gathered in the necessary army of cooks, servants, grounds keepers, carpenters, painters and stable hands. The Manor, and particularly the Long Hall, was cleared of mustiness and brightened up as much as time would permit. Tents for housing and receptions were repaired and a trainload of food run in from Belfast along with an orchestra, singers and actors for entertainment.

Roger girded himself for his new role by setting aside his long-standing distaste for the Orange Society. Invitations in the form of veiled summonses went to every Grand Master in the three counties. In a masterstroke

Lord Roger made every Protestant minister an automatic member of the new Unionist Party and they too were advised to attend.

With preparations continuing at breakneck speed, the Viscount and Viscountess Coleraine traveled to Cookstown to personally escort Lord Randolph into the west.

*

After "God Save the Queen" and the invocation, Viscount Hubble moved almost timidly from the head table to the rostrum, facing a throng of over six hundred persons. Above them from the open rafters hung a gigantic Union Jack at one end of the hall. This was matched by a gigantic Ulster flag at the other. Behind Roger a gigantic sign spanned the width of the hall, reading: ULSTER WILL FIGHT AND ULSTER WILL BE RIGHT.

Sir Frederick observed all of the preparations and the moment of truth with a twinge of envy. The speed and purpose of the partnership of Roger and his daughter had spiraled them to the forefront. The new Viscountess' debut had utterly dazzled the grim collection of Ulstermen.

But Sir Frederick had no inkling of the coup his son-in-law had in store. Lord Roger had almost shyly approached the lectern and gave formal welcome in such a manner as if to say, "It's a great day for you common folk because we're all in this together."

As Roger began to cite Hubble Manor's long history of sackings Weed saw him staking the claim of leadership based on old-line permanence. So far, so good. Then came Roger's first shocker. He calmly stated it was Lord Churchill's idea to hold the climaxing meeting of the tour in the historic Long Hall. In placing exaggerated importance on Hubble Manor he was establishing himself as the center of western Ulster's universe.

For although they had gathered in common purpose Roger left no doubt but that he and the gentry were the good fathers, protectors and leaders of the Protestant masses.

"I have been asked and humbly accept the honor of assuming leadership of the Unionists in the west."

It was neither Churchill's idea to hold the meeting here nor anyone's idea to place young Roger on the Unionist

Executive but no one was about to break the unity of the
gathering by negating his bold thrust for power and it
passed without comment.

Yet Sir Frederick wondered if Roger and Caroline were
in it together and what limits they might go to if they set
their minds to it.

"It is my extreme pleasure to introduce the first of the
speakers who will address you on the matter of economic
severance from England. He certainly needs no introduction to me because he is my father-in-law, and certainly
none to you, for who in Ulster has not heard of Sir
Frederick Murdoch Weed?"

As Roger finished a glowing tribute, Sir Frederick
squashed out his cigar and took a final sip from the
glass that contained gin and not water in full sight of
several dozen temperance ministers. He hunched and
growled his way to the rostrum, covering his chagrin at
Roger's coup, shaking Roger's hand to portray the unity
of east and west, of Ulster's wealth, power and ascendancy,
the captains of the ship.

"Let us not," Sir Frederick commenced, "entertain a
single illusion about the consequences of Home Rule. It
would mean the death blow to the Protestant ascendancy
in Ireland. We came to Ulster, your forefathers and myself," he said, identifying mightily with the common folk
as Roger had done before him, "and created a veritable
Eden from despicable clay. You've only to look at the
ignorance and squalor of the other three provinces of
Ireland to see who has done what here. Now these self-
same backward people led by Parnell and his alehouse
politicians and the Pope's brass band have the utter cheek
to say that they, who can't rule themselves, are going to
rule Ulster."

"Never!"

"No surrender."

"Ulster will fight!"

"God save Ulster!"

Half the crowd straggled to their feet but Frederick Murdoch Weed waved them down. Scanning their numbers,
he saw men recently bathed and cleansed at holy altars
all shining with goodness.

"Our good life, yours and mine," he continued, "has
been created through superior intelligence, traditions of

hard work, loyalty and purpose. That alien Dublin force without industrial ability is poised to deliver a death blow!"

Roger received pulsations. He looked up. His radiant, beautiful wife stood in one of the small side doorways. They smiled to each other and indicated mutual approval of the great event. Each new moment was building their own might and the first sweet taste of glory together was enthralling.

"Can you for a single moment," boomed Sir Frederick, "conjure in your minds a picture of a Dublin Parliament in the hands of Irish peasants? The commercial markets, the trade privileges, the tariff concessions we now enjoy as a member of the United Kingdom would vanish overnight and we would find ourselves in direct competition with England.

"Now, gentlemen, envision them in Dublin in their Parliament . . . envision them looking up to the border at Ulster's wealth. Who do you think is going to be taxed until bled white? We will! We in Ulster will pay the passage for those three miserable provinces!"

The men in the Long Hall became stricken. All of those easily tingled nerve ends out there vibrated and perspiration popped and the handkerchiefs to wipe that perspiration might have been taken for little white flags of surrender somewhere else. But not in the Long Hall.

"With a Dublin Parliament, not a single farm or estate would ever again be safe. The land for which your forefathers bled would be legislated to keep you in a grip of permanent serfdom. Home Rule would gerrymander voting boundaries in such a manner that Protestant Ulster would be made politically impotent. Home Rule would mean that not a single loyal Protestant would be employed in a government that would be stuffed with tens of thousands of their sort . . . bleeding payrolls and relief rolls with *your* tax money. You and your wives and little children would be confronted with a police force of *their* sort. You would be faced with *their* legal system and I don't have to tell you what kind of protection and justice you'd get from them! Is this the kind of Ulster your forefathers dreamed of when they came and tried to bring light to the heathen?"

Sir Frederick paused in deference to his own mounting

passion, mopped up his perspiration and glanced at his notes. He would now, he thought to himself, swat them squarely in the gonads.

His voice dropped from its bull range to a sincere tremble. "As a man," he began his finale, "employing thousands of our loyal people, I have pondered heavily for many a long hour in the throes of a recurring nightmare. Within days after a Dublin Parliament begins Home Rule they would be writing laws of parity to replace loyal Protestants in every factory in the province. Decent . . . loyal . . . God-fearing men would have generations of steadfast, abiding, unswerving obedience repaid by throwing them into the gutters. Before I would throw Protestant men out of work, I'd see my yard close first. I have made this position totally clear to every member of Gladstone's party. Democratic Ulster must remain free, with the help of God and our noble Queen!"

Dr. MacIvor prayed silently to himself to denote he was in exclusive communication with the beyond, clasping his hands together and nodding as that big voice from out there came through to him. Actually, he was biding time and smarting to himself. Sir Frederick had captured much of the thunder of the moment.

"Our great benefactor, Sir Frederick Weed, has told you what's going to happen to your lands and your jobs. I'm going to tell you what's going to happen to your souls. Oh, Gawd! Do not forsake us! We are alone and it is night and we are in the midst of hostile savages!"

"Amen!"

"Jesus save us!"

Jaws and fists clenched. New perspiration found its way out after the old.

"Home Rule," cried the preacher, "means Rome rule!" He repeated it three times in the event someone might not have heard.

"And Rome rule means that the first act of a papist-riddled Dublin Parliament will be to enact a tithe which you will have to pay from your sweat and honest labors into the coffers of the Catholic Church. A tithe for treasures to be stuffed into the Vatican vaults! A tithe for the building of ornate cathedrals over the length and breadth of Protestant Ulster! A tithe to pay for gold and silver priestly vestments!"

A portrait of horror was continued of schools being taught by priests and nuns, of colleges being taken over by Jesuits and little Protestant children being forced to kneel in pagan rituals. Graphic depictions of the harlot of Rome, that scarlet woman who would devour Protestant flesh like maggots, wrung them limp.

Lord Randolph Churchill had never heard the equal of the three speeches. He realized that he had come to Hubble Manor and Londonderry as the foil of a Hubble-Weed power play. He had been neatly boxed in by a trio of Ulster roughnecks. Although they were all using one another in the common pursuit of personal ambition, he made a note to be wary of this crowd and not let them suck on the Crown so blatantly. They were no gentlemen at all and God knew what lengths they would go to to keep their dirty little province British. It occurred to him frighteningly, as he surveyed the mob, that they'd bring over the whole British Army if need be, to save themselves under the guise of loyalty. Lord Randolph thanked his sponsors and, realizing the place was emotionally drained, keyed his remarks to soft, teary sincerity.

"I came to Ulster with saddened heart but I return to England feeling a great lifting. I am saddened to see Ulstermen drilling in the fields at night with wooden rifles in preparation for the defense of their God, their Queen and their liberty. Yet I am heartened that tens of dozens, nae, hundreds, of British officers have pledged to me that they will come forth and lead you in battle, if need be.

"It is my most profound prayer that the resounding of our voices will be heard in every corner of England and the Gladstonians will think mightily of the gravity and consequence of legislating an evil act of Home Rule. And I pray that your children and my own dear little sons, Winston and Jack, shall never be cursed with an Irish problem in their lives."

While Lord Roger and Sir Frederick gloated in their triumph, Churchill, the arch-Englishman, speaking with full English pomp, moved the place to patriotic tears. "Parnell has brought repugnant men into the sacred realm of Westminster. Men who are as foreign in their ways as Chinamen or niggers. Men who are completely dominated by him and who are dedicated to the destruction of the British Empire. You, gallant comrades in Ulster, stand on the forwardmost rampart of our great imperial adventure and you must not falter. I charge you to hold the walls just as you held the walls at Derry. There are two Irelands in spirit, in religion and in reality. The Ireland which is loyal to the Crown must remain in the Empire." Holding a hand aloft as though it were a full cup in a toast, he ended on a note of poetry. "Sail on, oh, ship of state . . . sail on, oh, Union great . . . shall Ulster from Britain sever? By the God who made us, never!"

*

Impact of Lord Randolph Churchill's sweep of Ulster reverberated throughout Britain. The press mounted a vitriolic campaign against the treachery of Parnell as the House of Lords closed ranks in preparation to veto any Home Rule attempt. Besieged Orangemen found vocal allies in England and zealous brethren in Presbyterian Scotland.

Anti-Irish sentiment, which was always close to the surface, erupted in England as public indignation swelled over the thought that loyal British subjects in Ulster were about to be sold out to the beastly Irish.

The Orangemen added threat on threat so that the possibility of a civil war in Ireland heightened the pressure.

At last the unity of the Liberal Party was shattered. In the end, ninety of Gladstone's backbenchers crossed the line to vote with the Conservatives to defeat a watered-down Home Rule Bill. The final vote was 341 to 311.

Gladstone's government fell. Randolph Churchill, the chief architect of that fall, was rewarded with the post of Chancellor of the Exchequer and leader of the Conservatives in Commons.

The Orange card had been played.

END OF PART TWO

PART THREE
The Booley House

ULSTER

N

ATLANTIC

OCEAN

BLOODY
FORELAND

Bunbeg

Letterken

Co

TRANS ULSTER RR

Killybegs   Donegal

Ballyshannon

LOWER
LOUGH
ER

CONNAUGHT

0   Miles   25

palacios

NORTH CHANNEL

SCOTLAND

Crockadaw
INISHOWEN
Lettermacduff
Moville
URRIS HILLS
Booley House
Ballyutogue
RATHLIN ISLAND
MAGILLIGAN POINT
LOUGH FOYLE
Portrush
Bushmills
Coleraine
Ballycastle
LOUGH SWILLY
Buncrana
Hubble
Manor
Lettershanbo
Castle
Muff
Limavady
Londonderry
(Derry)
TRANS ULSTER RR
Ballymena
Larne
Strabane
Carrickfergus
Ballyomalley
Cookstown
LOUGH
NEAGH
Antrim
Belfast
BELFAST LOUGH
Bangor
Holywood
NEWTOWNARDS PEN.
GREAT NORTHERN RR LINE
Newtonwards
Sixmilecross
Dunganion
Lisburn
STRANGFORD
LOUGH
Portaferry
Armagh
Downpatrick
Enniskillen
UPPER
LOUGH
ERNE
Monaghan
Newry
Cavan
LEINSTER

CHAPTER ONE

JUNE 1885

A week to the day that Kilty Larkin was put to rest, Tomas showed up at the O'Neill cottage in the wee hours of the morning with his three children.

"Finola's time has come," he said.

Mairead, who kept a calendar in her head for over two dozen pregnant women, frowned. "She's more than a month early. It must have been the excitement of Kilty's wake."

Fergus corralled the children into the sleeping place in his byre, settled them down and groped into his clothing. "I'll be right over to sit with you," he said to Tomas, as he had on all the other occasions. He grabbed his glink board and followed a few minutes after his wife.

As the hours dragged Tomas became uneasy. Bad experiences in the past were recalled with each sharp cry from the bedroom. Mairead was usually in and out with wry comments but this morning she never left the bedroom. By dawn both men had dozed, then crashed into hard sleep. Tomas was pried awake by a sharp shaking.

"Tomas . . . Tomas . . ." Mairead repeated.

"Aye?" he groaned.

"It's not to frighten you but we are having problems. I think you'd best send to town for Dr. Cruikshank." The rarity of the command from the midwife who had delivered tens of dozens of children without aid sent him spilling to his feet.

"What's wrong?"

"The baby is coming out wrong. I take it that the cord is around its neck. If we force it out, it may strangle and God knows it won't stay in much longer."

Conor was given the job. He climbed onto the old plow horse bareback and galloped from the Upper Village in the early mists. Its hoofs thundered in the day on the cobblestones of the diamond. He pulled up before the house of Ian Cruikshank, hitched the nag, approached the door, sucked in a deep breath, then boomed the knocker. The doctor's wife opened the door.

"It's my ma. She's having trouble delivering and Mairead O'Neill sent me to fetch the doctor."

"Who is it?" Ian Cruikshank called from the top of the landing.

"One of the Catholic children from the Upper Village. What's your name, son?"

"Conor Larkin and my daddy is Tomas and my ma is Finola."

"Aye," the doctor called down. "Go to the stable, Conor, and saddle up the black mare."

*

"Oh, God bless you, Doctor," Mairead said, whisking him directly to the bedroom. Liam and Brigid crept back to the cottage terrified by the presence of the doctor.

"Is Ma going to be all right?" Brigid whined.

"She'll be grand. We've had these little problems before, nothing of a serious nature," Tomas comforted. "Now get you back to the O'Neills' kitchen and fix us up some scroggins."

Bad news in Ballyutogue had neither to be seen nor smelled nor heard. It drifted in, felt on the winds, and as the sense of it grew, neighbors gathered about the Larkin cottage apprehensively. Some of the women attempted to make Tomas feel better by relating their own harrowing experiences at giving birth.

The shrieking from the bedroom intensified. Tomas cleared the cottage, save for himself and Fergus, and while Fergus prayed he thickened himself into fogginess.

For three years after their marriage Finola had been barren. Although it was difficult to provide for them, children continued to be the measure of a farmer's wealth and no greater disgrace could befall a woman than that of the sterile curse.

Finola spent every waking moment in prayer begging the favor of pregnancy. She consulted the village pishogue, the wise woman, who prescribed the peeling of ash rods, breaking potatoes at the fireplace, the correct passing of salt and all the other rituals not only to bear children but to keep the fairies from exchanging hers for a fairy child.

At the end of the second year Finola traveled to four different holy wells and on another occasion slept for two nights in a mountain cave said to have been the bed of Brigid, and swore to name her first girl after the blessed saint.

The first child was stillborn.

In the third year of the marriage she made the awesome pilgrimage to Crough Patrick, walking a hundred and fifty miles to the sacred mountain in County Mayo. There she joined tens of thousands of the devout in an all-night climb to the summit where Patrick had cast the snakes out of Ireland.

The trek up was made barefooted in the company of peasants and nuns and beggars and priests seeking favor or relief from daily suffering as they reasserted the depth of their faith. Stumbling along the route and dropping for prayer at the stations, she arrived with the dawn with bleeding feet and repeating in a fanatical frenzied stupor her desperate petition for children.

Finola Larkin was rewarded by a miracle, the healthy birth of Conor. Brigid and Liam were to follow later only after enormous difficulty between miscarriages and yet another stillbirth.

It was frighteningly far into the day when a haggard Ian Cruikshank emerged from the bedroom. "You've a son," he said.

Tomas listened intensely but heard nothing. A sensation of fright invaded him. "Why doesn't he cry?" Tomas whispered.

"He's very small and very tired."

"My wife?"

"She's very tired too. I should like to speak with you, man."

"Aye, come have a color of tea. You must be done in with hunger."

"The tea will be fine and perhaps a spot of whiskey."

"Aye, aye, come along."

Fergus already had the pot going. He plumped up the fire and disappeared. After a wash-up, Dr. Cruikshank took a creepie opposite Tomas at the fire and stirred his cup wearily. "The lad has problems," he said.

"What's wrong, Doctor?" Tomas thumped hoarsely.

"He came early, as you know, with lots of difficulties.

He's fluid in his lungs. Mairead O'Neill is fixing some warm stones to lay under him. You are to keep everyone away, even the children."

"What are his chances?"

"Fair. Perhaps you might want to send for the priest to say last rites, just in case."

Tomas' face tightened. "The bastards always get into your bedroom one way or the other," he said. "They're there on your wedding night after having played games with the poor woman's head, using every trick possible to choke them on fear and guilt. They use everything but reason. Even on the deathbed it's fear over love. Fear goes right into a woman's womb so ridiculously you have to wash away the sins of a day-old child."

"Don't you think you ought to put your own feelings aside, man? That woman in there's been through a terrible ordeal. What would it do to your marriage if you denied this?"

Tomas stood and shoved his hands into his pockets and stared glumly to the throng of black-kerchiefed women outside.

"What are you going to do?" Dr. Cruikshank pressed.

"Get the bloody priest! It always comes back to it, there's no escaping." He trudged to the door and flung it open. "Conor!"

His son was close at hand. Tomas closed him inside. "Slip out through the byre and say nothing to no one. Get Father Lynch."

"Ma?" Conor quivered.

"The baby."

Tomas put a new brick of turf on the fire which needed none at all and mumbled about sending a dressed lamb down to the doctor as payment.

"I want to ask you some questions about your wife's health," Ian Cruikshank said. "Has she had difficulties before?"

"Aye, all the births came hard. She's lost four by miscarriage and two to stillbirth."

"Has she ever consulted a doctor about this?"

"A doctor? There was no doctor between here and Derry before you came. The only thing we have an ample supply of is priests and the only advice she ever got was to pray."

"I'm afraid her problems can't be remedied by prayer."

"What do you mean?"

"Does she have unusual swelling during pregnancy? I mean to say, enlargement around the ankles and a puffing up about the eyes?"

Tomas nodded.

Ian Cruikshank grunted and leaned up near the fire, looking to and from Tomas a number of times. "We had a serious problem in there today, Tomas. I think we'd better talk about it." He held out his whiskey glass for a refill, popped it down and sighed uneasily. "As you know, I come up to the Upper Village on numerous occasions. There was a particular delivery a time back that became a case of either losing the child or losing the mother. The woman demanded hysterically that I send for Father Lynch. Tomas, the priest forced me to save the child and let the wife go on religious grounds. She was the mother of five. I had no choice with him hovering nearby. Do you know who I'm talking about?"

"Meara O'Malley?"

"Meara O'Malley," the doctor repeated.

"Oh, Jaysus, I didn't know . . . poor soul."

"We had the same situation in there today. Your wife doesn't know about it. When I realized what was happening I put her under for a few moments. I told Mairead O'Neill that it was Finola or the child. Actually, she had already guessed it. Mairead agreed with me that we were going to save your wife and she's sworn to carry the secret to her grave." Tomas buried his face in his hands as the doctor tried to console him. "She's to have no more children," he said at last, "it will kill her."

*

Tomas Larkin's immense hand gently drew back the swaddling clothes about the newborn. He seemed no bigger than a titmouse, all purple and gasping for life.

"Ah, look at the lad, wee Dary Larkin," he said, "another spade for the bog."

A crazy look spread over his wife's face, eyes rimmed in red and skin chalky and hair disheveled. "Never," she rasped.

Tomas took her hand and kissed it. "Finola love, the wee one is in danger but I know for sure we'll pull him through. As sure as I'm sitting beside you, the lad will live to grow a beard. Only now there's a bit of a problem,

and under the circumstances it would do no harm to see
that he has last rites."

She wailed pathetically, refusing to take comfort from
her husband.

"He will be all right," Tomas repeated to deaf ears
until he gave up.

Her weeping stopped. "We're paying for the sins you've
brought on this house," she said. "There is a curse on us
because of the blasphemies against the Church. God is
punishing us!"

Tomas dropped his head on the bedside, the door
groaned open. He looked up. Father Lynch assumed his
best grim posture for the moment of death and made
his way in. The gravity of the situation forced him to
conceal the inner flush of victory that God had scored
over Tomas Larkin.

CHAPTER TWO: There was poor little that could be
done with the grotty graystone exterior of Hubble Manor
but renovation of the interior was launched with typical
Weed fervor. After a two-month inventory, expendables
were hauled out to the delight of recipient museums,
workhouses and churches. The south wing, which contained most of the servicing facilities, was assaulted with
no less fury than that with which the army of James II
had attacked during the Williamite war. It was reduced
to a shell with rotted timbers and plasters carted off in a
trainload.

After an initial grunt of dismay, Lord Roger settled
back and enjoyed it as he enjoyed everything about his
wife. Caroline displayed all the organizational skills and
drive of her martinet father and this was enhanced by
exquisite taste. Even the cost of it was softened by an increasing number of mergers with Sir Frederick, who demonstrated tangible gratitude for his daughter's happiness.

She skimmed off three of the best architects from the
firm that had built Rathweed Hall and put them under
indefinite contract over a staff of talented underlings. A
new master plan was overlaid on the south wing. In
poured a legion of workmen, craftsmen, artisans, artists,

decorators and purchasing agents to scour London and the Continent for furnishings, materials, artifacts and art.

The south wing was anchored by a new kitchen of monstrous proportions designed by Sir Frederick's top naval architect, a prototype of the finest afloat on the Weed ocean liners.

Satelliting the kitchen, the south wing was pieced back together with modern stables, coach house, tack house, mews, hothouse, potting shed, wood store, coal store, poultry room, silver safe, pastry room, bake room, scullery, four pantries and larders, two refrigerated rooms, wild game room, smoke house, gun room, stillroom, housekeeper's office, knife room, shoe room, brushing room, china room, butler's pantry, under-butler's pantry, luggage room, dairy, linen room, wine cellar, liquor room, fish room, and a mammoth boiler and mechanical room also of marine construction.

A maintenance section was constructed containing a woodwork shop, upholsterer's shop, draper's shop, carriage shop, blacksmith forge, marble worker's shop, art studios and a sewing room employing a dozen seamstresses. The balance of the south wing contained twenty suites and rooms of living quarters for such higher-ranking servants as the chief chef, head coachman and maintenance overseer. Most of the other live-ins were scattered about the Manor in the proximity of the master quarters. Balance of the hundred and fifty staff, gardeners, gamekeepers, groundskeepers, stable hands and domestics were either cottaged away from the manor house or lived in Ballyutogue.

With work on the south wing in full swing, Caroline retained Victor Lessaux, student, associate and disciple of Viollet-le-Duc, the world's foremost master of castle restorations. Lessaux was charged with returning the Long Hall to its ancient glory and he in turn imported the necessary stonemasons, wood carvers and stained glass artisans. The partially destroyed wrought-iron screen covering the vestibule was proving to be the most difficult restoration. Lessaux convinced Lady Caroline that it should wait until last, when the rest of the hall was done. She reluctantly agreed, for she knew the screen was an enigma to the French master and decided to give him all the time possible to solve its mystery.

The junior architects and decorators drew up plans for suite-by-suite remodeling of the major living quarters in the north wing, plus some thirty rooms in the central wing, which consisted of the main parlors and drawing rooms, morning room, winter garden, music room, game rooms and formal dining hall. The library alone remained the single area left intact.

All of the newest in building materials were tested. Central heating, unheard of in that part of Ulster, was installed in master's areas complete with hot water boilers. In an imaginative and daring stroke that set even Sir Frederick gasping in disbelief, Caroline ordered lighting by electricity, the first in all of Ireland, generated on the grounds.

Housekeeping had become ordinary without a regular lady of the Manor during Lord Arthur's self-imposed exile at Daars. Cooking had never been anything but ordinary. The entire staff was retrained by experts brought over from London for the chore and a premier French chef and two assistants were contracted for from Paris.

As Caroline plunged into Londonderry's anemic cultural life, she pressed Lessaux to speed up work on the Long Hall. In Londonderry she guaranteed the lease on a dormant theater, refurbished it and booked in a number of concerts, plays, lectures and even music hall variety shows. Every troupe and virtuoso who came to Dublin and Belfast now traveled to Londonderry. Often as not a private performance was also given in the Long Hall.

Late one evening Caroline showed Roger the first set of completed drawings for a nursery in the north wing, her way of announcing her pregnancy. After the initial bouts with morning sickness she blossomed as though she were on a sacred mission of carrying a messiah in her belly. Considering her free-spirited past, few would have thought the idea of her mothering an heir would bring such a high sense of fulfillment. She reveled in the role. She didn't say so much to Roger but for the first time she was on a parity with her father . . . his equal . . . doing something inside her body that Sir Frederick could not accomplish.

Roger accepted the pregnancy without much ado. It was something that was bound to come along in due course. Sir Frederick proved the bell ringer, the exalted one. First flashes of joy were taken over by periodic panicking over his daughter's health. His concern brought him to Hubble Manor on fortnightly visits, thinly disguised as business. He fooled no one.

His concern deepened as she kept working at full speed into her sixth month. His latest visit found Caroline's boudoir converted into an office filled with floor plans, rotating foremen, samples of materials, cost sheets, payrolls and screaming French chefs. She wore thick practical eyeglasses as she pored over her paperwork, barely acknowledging her father's non-stop grousing. Sir Frederick, scarcely one to conceal an annoyance, became so blatantly obvious she was given no choice but to clear the air.

"Come on, Freddie, out with it," she said, noting he stormed in from Belfast on the brink of a roar.

He reached for a cigar, remembered her condition and replaced it in his jacket. She reached across the desk, took it from his pocket, unpeeled it, bit off the end, lit it and handed it back to him.

"You shouldn't do that, Caroline," he chided, snuffing it out immediately.

"Why not?"

"It's not good for the baby."

"Oh, Freddie, poppycock."

He grumbled, fishing about and jacking up his courage. "As a matter of fact," he began, "I had a chat with Dr. Chadwick a time back. Just happened to run into him at the Patrician Club, mind you. Obviously he asked for you and this led to . . . well, your condition. He quite agrees that all this activity of yours could prove quite harmful."

Roger caught the tail end of it as he entered the boudoir, bent over and kissed his wife's cheek. On the surface it seemed that Sir Frederick had little support for his argument, for Caroline had never looked so radiant.

"In another few weeks you'll be in your seventh month. You just can't go about climbing thirty-foot ladders and crawling through those awful tunnelways on your hands and knees where they're laying . . . pipes!" He turned to Roger for support. "Can she, Roger?"

"It seems that Caroline can't get her fill of sweaty workmen," he answered. Roger would have liked to add that pregnancy had blown the lid off his wife's wellhead of erotica and he might do well to keep her in that state permanently.

Weed caught their exchanges of endeared glances and gestures. "You are disgusting, the both of you." He rubbed his hands together and, in an old Weed trick, framed a question in such a manner that there could be only one answer, a foregone conclusion. "At any rate, you'll be off to a good private clinic in London shortly. Matter of fact, I had old Chadwick look into a few and . . ."

"Freddie," Caroline interrupted.

"Well, of course you *are* doing the final lap in London."

"The baby is going to be born right here in Hubble Manor," she said with soft finality.

"But . . . but . . . but . . . have you both gone mad! Roger, surely you're not going to let her push you around like this."

"Seems I've had as much success in telling Caroline what to do as you have. Besides, I rather like the idea. Ten generations of earls and viscounts have sired some fifty children, and this will be the first one to be born on Irish soil."

"I can't buy this sentimental horseshit. Caroline is nearly thirty and she's not some Catholic brood mare."

"The doctor says I'm sound as the pound sterling."

"Doctor, what doctor? That's another matter I wished to discuss. What possible doctor do you have out here?" he said with voice rising to falsetto.

"Ian Cruikshank, quite a capable chap," Roger answered.

"Cruikshank, Cruikshank, Cruikshank?"

"He's loads of experience, Freddie," Caroline said, "delivered most of the babies on this entire side of Inishowen."

"Well, I've never heard of this Cruikshank chap. Have you inquired into his schooling, his military service, his clubs? Where does this Cruikshank fellow practice?"

"Ballyutogue."

"Ballyutogue, are you saying Ballyutogue to me?"

"Yes, Freddie."

"Ballyutogue? A village doctor delivering my grandson?"

Sir Frederick's face froze as though he were in midseizure. Roger fortified his wife, grasping her hard on the shoulder as her father anguished to his feet. Half of Sir Frederick's rages were play acting, this was real. He continued to look at them stricken. "Are you insisting on this insanity?"

"The baby is going to be born right here," she repeated.

Confusion set in. There was nothing, absolutely nothing he could do about the situation. No vast sums of money to purchase his wishes, no threats to enforce them. "I'm . . . sending to Dublin . . . no, London, immediately to get some suitable men here to see that this . . . this . . . Cruikshank person does his job properly."

"Freddie, Freddie, he probably sees more difficult births in a single year than Chadwick sees in a lifetime."

"There! Exactly my point! You admit it's going to be a difficult birth."

"Nothing of the sort. I'm saying the man is capable in any situation."

"I demand," he said, with fist coming into play on the desk, "to know who's going to assist him."

Roger and Caroline looked at each other briefly. He patted his wife's shoulder, braced . . . "A midwife," he said.

"This Jesus-in-the-manger horseshit has gone far enough!"

"Freddie, please . . ."

"I shall not"—he thumped for emphasis—"return until you come to your senses. And as for you, Hubble, I am shocked and disappointed. Any disaster as a result of this folly will be clearly on your head."

Sir Frederick vanished, leaving loud evidences of his anger with an afterblow of bangings, clangings and thumpings. Roger started after him.

"Don't," Caroline commanded. "He's at his bully best now and there's no reasoning with him. Let him go beat his head against the wall. He'll be back."

Roger pushed his hair around, distressed. "It's his first grandchild, Caroline. Let me try to pacify him."

"No!" she said sharply.

"See here, you're going to end up as upset as he is over this."

She silently, adamantly put her thick glasses on and began to riffle through plans on the desk. Roger looked wistfully in the direction of Weed's departure. He was trapped between two of the most hardheaded bullies in Ulster acting out their lifelong diatribe. One step further

and he realized he could be obliterated in their love-hate
cross fire.

*

Caroline's final two months passed with neither she nor
her father yielding. Roger felt himself squeezed to the
outside, almost like a stranger. The Weed passions were
immovable. He spoke to Sir Frederick on business and
only through the medium of Brigadier Swan. A quiet
settled over Hubble Manor as father and daughter continued to be consumed by their own stubbornness. For
once, neither knew how to unknot the bindings and speak
out first or even send a signal. Cycles of silence turned
into cycles of tension as her time grew near. Once or
twice Roger determined to break the ice, to go to Belfast
himself, but Caroline's ultimatums contained finality.

The night which began with a slight but recognizable
cramp grew painful, and as the time between pains narrowed, Roger sent for Dr. Cruikshank, then retreated to
a special apartment prepared for the event. A number of
hours passed with Roger beside her holding her hand and
clocking the time between constrictions.

"Will you stay on, Roger?" she asked.

"As long as my stomach holds, and then I'll only be as
far away as the next room." He continued to stifle his
annoyance that Cruikshank had not arrived.

"Oh, Roger," she said, "you're a wonderful man. I'm so
glad about us. And I do adore the hell out of you."

"Come now, Countess, you say that to all the workmen."

"You're such a shy little boy when we play our games.
In the last month or so I've thought up some wonderful
things to do when all of this is over. For some mad reason, you excite me all the time. Something so . . . bloody
wonderfully English . . ."

"Caroline, you're embarrassing me." He leaned down
and whispered, "There are servants about, you know."

"I think they've already guessed about you and me,"
she said, taking his hand and putting it between her legs
and saying that they should make love one more time
here and now, and Roger turned crimson as she knew he
would and coughed away his chagrin. She tightened her
grip on him and writhed. It seemed far worse than the

last pain. Roger stole a glance at his watch, then sighed with relief at sounds of commotion in the hall outside.

Dr. Cruikshank entered, followed by a short squat woman. By dress and manner she was identified by Roger as a Catholic, most likely a tenant's wife.

"Sorry, m'lord," the doctor said, "had an emergency at the quarry."

Roger arched with a reaction that sent off the unspoken message, "what at the stone quarry could possibly be more important than the Viscountess?"

Cruikshank got the vibrations as he bathed his hands in a basin and returned vibrations of his own. "Had to amputate. Rockslide. Poor chap lost both his legs." The doctor's message was that if ordinary safety measures had been taken in his lordship's quarry there would have been no slide. As they unlocked their glances from each other, the doctor made to bedside. "How are we doing, Lady Caroline?"

She nodded affirmatively.

"How long between pains?"

"Just a bit under seven minutes," Roger said.

He dug through his bag, found the stethoscope and placed it on her belly and her heart. "We've a bit of time. This is Mairead O'Neill," he said. "She's brought hundreds of young ones in all by herself. Mrs. O'Neill is the finest midwife I've ever worked with."

Caroline nodded that she understood why he had made the choice but otherwise gave no greeting nor asked anything. Mairead was put in her station, even in this situation, but it did not matter to her. What seemed strange to her was the absence of questions she always heard from a first-time mother.

Caroline felt a pain coming. As it swept through her she tightened up and broke into perspiration but uttered not a sound, looking at the midwife as if to say, "You'll not hear me scream because I'm from as strong a breed as any woman you've ever met and I'll show you courage."

Mairead wiped Caroline's face and felt her pulse. "You'll do better for all of us and yourself as well if you loosen up, m'lady. It makes everything go a lot easier." After another series of pains failed to induce an outcry, Mairead looked at her with compassion. She leaned close out of earshot of the others. "You've nothing to prove or gain by your behavior. We're all the same when it comes to this. Let yourself go, darlin'."

"I can't," Caroline whispered. . . . "I can't."

The doctor drew Roger aside. "Everything looks fine," he said. "Mrs. O'Neill will be preparing your wife now, Lord Roger. I think you should wait outside."

"We've decided to go it together as long as I am able."

Ian Cruikshank grunted. Strange, he thought, but quite nice. Odd pair these, stubborn as hell but so in it together. He scratched his head, trying to think of cause, but acquiesced. "Well, stay out of our way."

The night blackened up outside and even as the pains intensified to excruciating thresholds, Caroline continued to refuse to cry out. In the seventh hour of her labor, Mairead tapped the dozing doctor. "It's coming," she said.

Roger was up and at bedside holding his wife's hand.

"Bear down, m'lady," Mairead said, "that's it, bear down now, love, bear down . . ."

"Freddie!" Caroline shrieked at the instant of Jeremy's birth. "Freddie! Freddie! Daddy! Daddy! Daddy!"

CHAPTER THREE: Having come to the most awesome decision of her life, Finola was determined to steel herself to go through with it, take all the necessary humiliation, for in her own eyes her sins were enormous.

The priest's presbytery was the finest house in the Upper Village and that was as it should be in the tradition of the Church. It was not in the mold of the simple cottages but a grand two-story home such as the more prominent Protestants owned in Ballyutogue. Widow O'Donnelly, the priest's housekeeper, admitted Finola and led her to a small but fine room of soft deep furnishings which members of the parish had purchased two years earlier.

"And how is wee Dary?" Father Lynch inquired of the new baby.

"You'll not see the likes of that one again in a hundred," she boasted of her favorite subject. "Dary will be a small child and more delicate than the others, but he'll be sound, I'll see to that. I never stop being grateful to the holy Mother for sparing his life."

Father Lynch accepted the gratitude on behalf of the Virgin. "And yourself, Finola? What urgent matter brings you here?"

She twisted her fine linen handkerchief nervously and struggled to keep her composure. "I've a lot on my conscience, Father. What I am about to tell you should have been confessed many times over the years."

Father Lynch grimmed up and braced.

"Father," she whispered, lowering her eyes and voice weakening with shame, "I have been the wife of Tomas Larkin almost twenty years and I have sinned all during the marriage." She squirmed, then blurted out, "I have always enjoyed pleasures of the flesh."

The priest shot to his feet, clasped his hands behind him and thrust his face heavenward. "I see," he sighed. "Would you kindly amplify that remark?"

"I've almost always enjoyed the sexual act," she whispered.

"That's quite unnatural, you know."

"I know."

"Exactly what is it you enjoy?"

"Everything," she whimpered.

Father Lynch pulled his chair up close and poked his face next to hers. "What you have told me is extremely serious. If I am to counsel you properly you must purge yourself here and now. Are you ready?"

"Aye . . . I am ready."

"Look at me, Finola." She did so out of the corners of her eyes and blushed with guilt. "We must go over this, item by item," he commanded.

It was degrading but if the gates of heaven were ever to open for her it had to be done. She confessed to one hedonistic pleasure after another, building a mountain of debauchery and mortal sins the likes of which he had never heard in his thirty-five years as an agent of God. Why, the woman reveled in everything! Nudity, pinchings, slappings, biting, licking, kissing, rubbing, even down to the reprehensible organs themselves. It appeared there was nothing the two didn't do, even taste each other! When Finola had drained herself, she sobbed. Father Lynch was ashen.

"These are unnatural acts under the influence of Satan!"
She wailed, he paced.

"I knew something might be wrong, Father, but so long as our purpose was to try to make babies and I couldn't help myself for enjoying it, I thought it really wasn't actual pleasure I was feeling but some kind of holy experience about the possibility of becoming pregnant."

"It's a curse," he said. "I know of many other women who have had these same carnal sensations but nothing as profane as you have spoken about."

"Oh, Father, what causes it?"

"It is God constantly reminding us of the original sin in the form of a woman," he answered. "What is so very serious is that you haven't confessed this before. Have you at least prayed that these sensations would go away?"

"Not with any great sincerity. I pretended I didn't know what they were."

He shook his head numerously. "At least you have enough faith left to seek atonement."

"Atonement is only part of the problem," she said. "It all came to roost with wee Dary's birth. As you know, it was a very difficult time. Dr. Cruikshank warned Tomas and later myself that it would be fatal for me to have any more babies."

Damn that Cruikshank! the priest thought. Always interfering with God's work, telling such rubbish to the women. Yet with all his power he was too wise to challenge the doctor. If he gave advice to ignore the doctor and the woman died, the repercussions would be terrible.

"I know it means violation of a holy duty," Finola said, "and I am perfectly willing to risk the consequences but Tomas takes the doctor seriously. Oh, Father, I know in my heart that God is punishing us for what Tomas did at the time of Kilty's passing . . ."

"What is the problem then?" he asked.

"Now that my health has returned and even though we fear having babies, both of us are very much desiring to be husband and wife in bed again."

The priest felt violated. After all she had told him, she still wanted to continue amassing sin upon sin. As his anger rose so did his determination to exorcise her of the demon which had seized her soul. "You have committed evil enough, attempting to cheat God by having experi-

enced pleasures of the flesh and to further that evil by
continuing to have carnal sensations year in and year out
without confessing them. It is evil enough to abandon
your duty to God and stop bearing children on the advice
of a Protestant . . . but there can be no graver mortal sin
than lusting after sex for the sake of sex!"

"What am I to do, Father! Tomas and I act like
strangers to one another."

"Tell me the truth. Do you still share the same bed?"

"That's the misery of it, we do," she wept. "Lying
there side by side without touching, knowing we are never
to have sex. He stays at the shebeen every night and
when he does finally come home he just falls into bed,
drunk. In the mornings there is hardly a word between us
any more." Finola gritted her teeth, trying to force the
next words out, but they stuck. She knew there were safe
times during the month for a woman to have sex with
her husband and she wanted to appeal to the priest for
dispensation to do it then, but it was clear by now he
would never condone such a thing, for he was disgusted
with her.

"Oh, Father, help me," she cried, falling to her knees.

He hovered above his victim, then pointed a bony
finger. . . . "The reason you have these unnatural and
evil desires is because of your neglect of mother church.
Instead of yielding to temptation, you should have been
confessing for years. You should have fortified your soul
and you should have filled yourself with the pain, the
goodness and the mercy of Jesus and Mary. You have
offended God, grievously!"

Finola Larkin howled.

"You are fortunate, woman, in that your Church is
all-forgiving. Are you ready to submit to the supernatural
redemptive powers of God?"

"I'll do anything!"

She remained on her knees as he considered the alternatives. "Your case is extreme. I must meditate for
guidance. In due course I will work out a course of
penance through prayer and offerings to the Church.
When I do, do you swear to adhere to it faithfully?"

"Yes, Father, yes."

"Through this devotion, you will eventually find the
strength to continue to live with Tomas in the only way
possible . . . as brother and sister. You are never again to

submit to him for sexual ravagement, for that sin would be final. Well, I'm waiting for your answer . . . it's that or hell!"

"I . . . I promise. . . ."

"Very well," he said. "Finally, because your sin is so grave I don't want to take chances that your penance wasn't sufficient. You must agree to give one of your sons to the Church. I am positive that by this action God will look favorably on your case, grant you quicker absolution on earth and shorten your time in purgatory."

"Tomas will fight having his son become a priest," she cried.

"That is your greatest chore, Finola Larkin. You must bring that man back to Jesus Christ on his knees."

"Father, he may choose to die first."

"Not if you do your duty. You are never to let him forget that it was his sins, his lechery, that brought you to this. In the end, when he returns to mother church, it will also give him the strength to forgo his lustful ways and live in peace with you as brother and sister."

Without offering her a hand to help her to her feet, he turned and walked to the door. "I must go meditate now. When I am done, I'll send for you and tell you what your penance is to be."

CHAPTER FOUR: In the autumn of eighteen and eighty-six a great event occurred in my life with the coming of a national school for the children of the out-lying villages. Father Lynch didn't take kindly to the intrusion on what he considered to be a personal domain, but was forced to hold his tongue because Bishop Nugent wasn't about to offend the British. He didn't have to worry because almost no one in the Upper Village contemplated going. Not only were the economics against it but much of the traditional Irish craving for knowledge died during the famine.

Our daddies had gotten their schooling from the hedge teachers like Daddo Friel's old man and Daddo himself, who traveled from village to village and held classes on the sunny side of the hedges. They were one part poet, one part Celtic scholar and one part regular teacher with the mission of keeping alive the ancient language and folk-lore. When they vanished from the scene, the Irish tongue vanished with them in our part of the country.

The only schooling Conor and I received was a weekly class from Father Cluny, the curate, and no great scholars were apt to evolve from him.

I was the scrapings of the pot, the last of the litter. It had its advantages. Aside from shepherding in the summer, I was generally useless around the farm and spoiled by my ma. There was no real reason for me not to attend the national school except for my parents' fear of me being thrown into a lough full of Protestant sharks, but I pouted and tempered until they gave in.

Conor had remained quiet about the school but there was no mistaking what was in his mind. When I told him the joyous news about myself, he was determined to make his own stand. We went up past the crossroad to the edge of the first fields and waited all afternoon. Conor sat with his back against the stone wall, more nervous and uncertain than he had ever acted before, as he looked up the path for his daddy.

Conor used to come here almost every day to meet Tomas until the last few months. Something queer was happening to the Larkins. Tomas was snapping at his kids and everyone knew he was taking more and more to drink. A lot of people thought he was still grieving over the loss of Kilty although that had happened over a year ago.

When he did come down from the hills that day his face broke into a smile on seeing Conor waiting for him again.

"Can we talk, Daddy?" Conor said.

"Sure, soon as I get in and clean up."

"I'd like to talk to you now."

"Well, if it's that important," he answered, sitting up on the wall, "what's on your mind?"

"Seamus is going to the new national school," Conor said.

"I know that. Fergus and I spoke of it at great length."

"Well, I was kind of hoping that, you know, our family and the O'Neills always do things together and maybe I should be going to school with Seamus."

I smiled grandly in the affirmative that it was my wish also, but I was wary over Conor's caution. He usually

plunged into the heart of matters without hemming
and hawing.

"It's not like cooring up a pair of horses to make a
plow team," Tomas said. "It's a completely separate
and independent decision for each family to make on
its own. The O'Neills are in a different situation. Seamus
has an older brother to help Fergus. Your hands are
needed by me."

"I talked it over with Liam. He doesn't want to go
to school and he's near as big as I am and could do
most of my work and I promise to keep up my part
and be no burden."

Tomas hardened. "You'd no right to discuss the
matter behind my back."

"It wasn't behind your back, Daddy. Liam wants my
chores. Half the time he's hanging onto me to do them
and he's never so happy as when he's up in the fields
with you."

Tomas came off the wall slowly, thinking deeply as
he did. He knew how persistent Conor could be and I
reckoned he didn't want to make a command out of it.
Conor's plea seemed logical. . . . "Well, now, I'm not
against school, mind you," Tomas said, seeming to
want to act reasonable. "On the other hand, there's
only so much schooling you need and you more than
likely know enough now."

"But I don't," Conor shot back. "All I know is
catechisms."

"What the hell do you think they'll teach you in that
school?" Tomas snapped, turning irate. "They know
nothing about Ireland, they care nothing about Ireland.
You'll be learning English history, English laws, saluting
the Union Jack and singing 'God Save the Queen.' They
won't so much as teach you the legend of Finn MacCool
or 'The Cattle Raid of Cooley.' There's only one reason
they're putting up national schools and that's because
they're after creating loyal British subjects."

"But, Daddy," Conor pleaded, "I want to learn how
to read so's I can read anything and I want to know
about adding and multiplying and what makes the
heavens and the seas. I swear I'll close my ears when
they're teaching British things."

"No . . . it's no good, lad, it's no good." He tried to

walk away but Conor was around in the front of him, blocking his path. "Ma said . . ."

"Your ma's tongue is like a yard of vinegar. She could start a fight in an empty house." He brushed past, then turned and softened a mite. "Conor, let me tell you something. You won't be needing all that education. Your bread is baked for life. You'll be coming into the land."

Tomas had given Conor his most precious gift, the farm. Since the famine it had been illegal to divide farms into smaller farms. The lease or ownership had to be passed on intact to a single heir. More often than not this inheritance was held by the parent as blackmail and competition between children could be fierce. As a rule the father would wait till the last possible instant before making a decision, usually when faced with his own death or the emigration of his sons.

"I said the farm will be yours," Tomas repeated.

Conor remained motionless and wordless as well. In that instant I knew something terrible was taking place between them.

"No matter," Tomas said, covering his hurt, "you'll wake up tomorrow knowing the importance of it and you'll just sing with joy, lad." He reached for his son as I had seen him do a hundred times, and waited for a return of his affection. None came. Tomas sagged back and seemed to age before my eyes. He continued down the path, then called back in a fit of anger. "You've had enough of Father Cluny, too! I don't want any more goddamned celibates teaching my kids!"

And he disappeared into Dooley McCluskey's public house.

CHAPTER FIVE: There were six of us Catholic kids from four villages at the first day of the national school and we found each other fast. As opening ceremonies were held in the yard under the Union Jack, we clung to one another trembling. A shiny new room greeted us, still smelling of paint and polish and filled with Protestant kids all starched and squeaking in their fine

dress and shoes. We slunk off to the rear of the class
and huddled together with a giant-sized picture of
Queen Victoria glowering at us, and awaited the
doomsday appearance of the teacher.

A tall, thin and seemingly delicate man stood before
us like a bishop about to announce our damnation. I
thought my heart was going to bounce out in the aisle
as he tapped a ruler on the desk.

"My name is Andrew Ingram," he said. "I am from
Scotland, Edinburgh. In a few days I'll know all your
names as well. I taught in a national school in Wales
for five years and asked to be transferred to Ireland
when I learned there were openings here. I never forgot
the beauty of Donegal from boyhood holidays and,
being Scottish as well, I do love my fishing."

Well, I'll tell you, he was obviously not a farmer and
it seemed to me he was far too soft for the likes of
Cromwell descendants, Ulstermen and croppies. Sure it
was only a matter of minutes before he was being
tested by Sandy Hanna, grandson of Luke, the biggest
and toughest kid in the school. Sandy seemed more than
adequate to withstand an ash-branch rodding from the
frail Mr. Ingram as he screeched chalk over his slate
that sounded like a bagpipe being tuned up.

Mr. Ingram stopped talking amid the giggles and
spotted Sandy Hanna. "You there."

Sandy ignored him and kept screeching away. Mr.
Ingram stepped down into the classroom, into the aisle
and over his desk. We dared not breathe, much less
move.

"What is your name?"

"Sandyhanna," he answered like it was one word.
More giggles in the form of tacit applause for Sandy.

"Sandy, you will kindly stand up when you are
addressing the class or myself." Sandy swaggered to
his feet as tall as the teacher and half again as broad
from pitching hay. "Tuck in your shirt," the teacher
said.

He made a meaningless gesture at his shirttail, then
folded his arms in defiance. Mr. Ingram smiled, kindly
like. I was starting to get a hint that his soft manners
were highly deceptive and, therefore, suspect. He
turned away from Sandy and spoke to the class. "I am
grateful for this opportunity so early in our relationship

to explain a few simple rules. Once we all understand them, and you in particular, Sandy, we're all going to get along just fine with no problems whatsoever." Oh, he was a cool number and by this time even Sandy Hanna was getting the idea. Mr. Ingram walked slowly and deliberately to him. Sandy was getting nervous but he had made his bed and had to stand his ground. As Mr. Ingram sized him up Sandy shifted from one foot to the other, gulping as he did.

"I don't believe in the ash rod or humiliations because I should like to assume we are all going to behave like ladies and gentlemen."

He was puzzling us, this Mr. Ingram, but he had our undivided attention as well. Sandy had slowly been wilted like a man receiving condemnation from the priest before the entire village.

"Sandy, you will kindly apologize to your classmates and assure me that you will behave. Otherwise . . . find your way home and return when you are ready to be a gentleman."

Confidentially, it was my opinion that Sandy wanted to apologize more than anything in the world but he had gotten himself in too deep. "I done nothing to apologize for," he said halfheartedly.

Mr. Ingram turned his back, went to his desk and sat down. "Leave the school," he said in the same soft voice he had used throughout.

Sandy didn't budge. This was it. All the kids' eyes burned on the pair of them as Mr. Ingram returned with that same deliberate calm. What we then saw was quicker than Father Lynch's blackthorn stick. He snatched Sandy Hanna's hand and in a motion worthy of Finn MacCool spun him around and had him in an arm lock, wrist lock and thumb lock with a single hand. Sandy screamed as Mr. Ingram shot him through the door like the mighty cannon of Athlone!

We were utterly, totally and completely mesmerized. It was all over for Sandy Hanna, who just stayed out in the yard and cried, then crawled back into the class begging not to be sent home, and then blurted out the most heart-wretching apology you'd ever want to hear.

We never had much trouble with discipline after that.

Each of us stood in turn and gave our names and village with Mr. Ingram's eyes playing on the six

shivering papists in the rear who had identified themselves in a dead giveaway with the names of O'Neill,
O'Kane, O'Connor, O'Doherty, O'Bannon and O'Toole.

"There is one more rule that each and every one of
you is going to understand clearly," he said. "We are a
family here, all of us." Then, leaving out the "O" and
"Mac" from the beginning of our names, he seated us
alphabetically.

I don't know what I can rightly say about my feelings
for Mr. Ingram. In my short time of life and in most of
my life afterward there always seemed to be someone who
needed to beat us down, be it the Orangemen or land
agents or gombeen men or Constabulary or our own
priests. Mr. Andrew Ingram was the very first person in
my life, if you don't count Charles Stewart Parnell, to ever
make me feel like an equal and very important human
being.

Most of the Protestant kids had had a fair measure
of schooling. We were very far behind. There was no
counting the extra hours Mr. Ingram spent to help us.
Pretty soon all the girls were in love with him and,
like I said, he never had much trouble again from the
boys. He had earned his spurs in Wales teaching the
kids of coal miners and they weren't exactly a soft
bunch.

A few months after his arrival there was some rumbling
and grumbling against him from the Protestant
ministers in the district and the Grand Masters of the
Orange Lodges. They didn't like some of the books
he was using because they were supposed to be filled
with evil ideas. They also objected to the fact he was
spending too much time on poetry and nature classes
and not teaching enough English history and Protestant
religion.

Dirty rumors spread around that he had left Wales
because he had gotten a girl into trouble. Other rumors
had it that he liked young boys and that was why he
was a teacher. A storm was rising and meetings were
being called. He rode it out with his own kind of quiet
dignity. The two times he was called before the school
board he tied his inquisitors into knots by his range of
knowledge and likewise exhibited an intimacy with the
Bible that petrified and silenced the preachers.

Mr. Ingram was extremely popular with the students

and had taken on many of their personal problems. He had singlehandedly established a neutral sanctuary where compassion and reason prevailed in a place that knew little of each, and we were terrified that we were going to lose him.

Then the Lord sent an angel in no less a form than Lady Caroline Hubble herself, who, with understatement, invited him to the Manor to tutor children of some of the foreign workmen. After it became known that Mr. Ingram attended plays and concerts in the Long Hall and gave a poetry reading there himself, opposition to him disappeared ... thank God.

*

I remembered everything I was taught in the national school because I had to learn it once for myself, then teach it to Conor. He waited for me every day at the crossroad and while things were still fresh in my mind we would hide out in the old Norman keep and go over the day's work. I would tell him about the goings on in the class so he'd feel a part of it and he came to know almost all of the kids from my description.

After a time Conor waited for me a bit farther down the road at Josiah Lambe's blacksmith shop. The smithy was a source of wonderment with its magic pools of fire silhouetting the brawny Mr. Lambe as he hammered and the sparks flew in the execution of highly secret formulas passed on by the fairies.

In village life the blacksmith was second in importance only to the priest. Mr. Lambe could certainly be that important except he was a Protestant. The Upper Village had lost its own blacksmith to emigration during the famine. At that time Josiah Lambe's father, who did the smithing for the Protestants, took on work for the Catholics as well. By unwritten code he always hired a Catholic as his assistant and another as his apprentice and thereby continued to work for both communities.

He ran Conor away from the shop twenty times but Conor returned a twenty-first and that happened to be the very day his apprentice took a job as assistant to the blacksmith in Clonmany. I was to find him operating the foot treadle on the double bellows and a week later Conor was making nails. He was so excited you would have thought he had given birth to them, personally.

"These are roseheads in this bin," he said, "and these are tenderhooks and horseshoe nails here, and scuppers." My, he was beaming. I praised him forcefully after intimate examination of his work. Of course I had seen all these nails before but not made by Conor.

Tomas didn't like it, but from a practical standpoint it was hard for him to object. Liam was capable of doing a full day's work in the fields and the money Conor began to earn was too important for the family to pass up so he eased into being Mr. Lambe's new apprentice.

Of a day late in the autumn we had a holiday from school. Not a holiday after a saint or even something like Christmas or an English holiday but a holiday sacred to the Ulster Protestant alone. I met Conor at the forge and went into town with him to help him make deliveries. When the last was done Conor took the horse to Mr. Lambe's house, stabled it and we walked back toward the Upper Village. As we reached the outskirts of town we heard sounds of powerful hymn singing coming from the Presbyterian church.

"The Prods are having a thanksgiving for their harvest," I said knowingly, "that's why school is closed."

"What are they thanking for?" Conor asked.

"I'm not quite sure I know."

"I don't get it. You know how nervous our daddies and mas get at late harvest, what with the rents due and winter coming."

I shrugged. "Mr. Ingram just didn't explain it."

"Listen to them singing, would you? It's queer if you ask me. Come on, let's have a look."

"Oh, Jaysus, no," I said, backing away. "The last time we got into a Protestant church, we like to got ourselves killed."

"Come on, runt," he said, tippy-toeing up the steps. After assuring myself escape routes were available and we could make a clean getaway, I followed to the front window and we stared in like two goats peering through a hedge. The sight inside made me gasp. Both sides of the altar were piled high with loaves of bread and sheaves of corn. There were turnips and cabbages and great pumpkins and carrots and parsnips and onions all shiny from scrubbing and baskets of nuts in fancy designs. There were big juicy apples and tomatoes and berries and all kinds of food we rarely saw and never ate. Arrayed below the altar was a stuffed pig, lambs and turkeys fancy dressed for a feast. The preacher had his arms spread and was praising God for the bountiful harvest and they sang out again about their rejoicing.

"Let's go," Conor said abruptly.

He shoved his hands in his pockets and walked to the road, retaining his fierce silence indicating he was deep in thought or hurting or both.

"Maybe their God is better than ours," I ventured.

"Like hell, it's the land they stole that's better."

I walked about a half step behind until we came to the schoolhouse. Conor stopped. His eyes watered and the muscles of his face quivered from tightly clenched teeth.

"I think you'd better blurt it out," I said.

"Blurt nothing."

"It's sticking out all over you, Conor, and I don't want to be spending the day with you if you're going to be mad all the time."

"Aw, go to hell."

"Hey, Conor, I know a secret way into the school," I said. Actually it wasn't so secret because Mr. Ingram always kept the back door unlocked. Conor followed me in tentatively, his eyes hungering as he played them over the desks and blackboard all filled with arithmetic problems.

"Here's where I sit," I said, "and right next to me is that girl I was telling you about who brings me apples and honey cakes and all those things to eat."

Conor ran his hand over the top of my desk, then slid into my seat and straightened himself, folding his hands as though Mr. Ingram were going to call on him.

"Hello there."

Conor jumped up startled as Mr. Ingram entered from his side office.

"Ah, a good day to you, Mr. Ingram," I said. "We was just passing by and my very closest friend Conor Larkin wanted to see my desk."

"Hello, Conor. I'm Andrew Ingram."

Conor shook his hand suspiciously. Mr. Ingram didn't have to ask why he wasn't attending school. He had already been to all the priests in the district to urge them to urge their parishioners to send more kids but met with little success.

"Conor reads and writes," I said proudly.

"I'm glad to hear that," Mr. Ingram answered.

"Seamus has been teaching me."

"I see. Well, you've a good teacher. Seamus is one of my star pupils. He'll be after my job soon."

"Not to worry about that, Mr. Ingram," I said. "I'm only doing this because Conor is my best friend."

"I'm very pleased, Seamus. One of the best things that can happen to a teacher is to produce his own missionaries. Is there any chance of you coming to school, Conor?"

"I'm afraid I'm too busy. You see, I'm the apprentice for Mr. Lambe and I work for my daddy as well. Besides, my daddy doesn't fancy the school. . . ." I tried to poke Conor to be quiet but he went on. . . . "He says you don't teach anything really Irish here."

"I see," Mr. Ingram answered, showing no irritation.

Even though Conor was trying to walk taller than he was, he couldn't help but look at the bookshelves which ran from floor to ceiling down one entire side of the room. Sight of them ate away at his show of pride, for his desire was unbearably apparent.

"Do you suppose I could lend you a book, Conor?"

"Which one?"

"Well, let's see here. Perhaps we can find something Irish, even in the Queen's realm. Here's one. *The Bardic Tradition of the Middle Irish Period.*"

"What's it about?"

"I'm sorry, I had the idea you knew all about Ireland. This is about the Irish court poets during the Middle Ages. I think that before one gets his teeth into the real red-blooded revolutionaries a foundation should be built on earlier Irish history. It is quite a history, you know. Do you think you'd like to take a try at it . . . it's not too difficult."

"It might be all right," Conor said as he accepted the book suspiciously. "I'll be sure to bring it back."

"No hurry. The door is always open. When you do return it, help yourself to another one. Just leave a note on my desk."

The door was open indeed! Conor walked down the rows of volumes feasting his eyes on the wonderland of it although he couldn't make out half the titles. He kept looking like he was in a dream, his hand irresistibly drawn to touching the books' spines.

"If you can spare the time," Mr. Ingram said, "oh, say an hour a week, you could stop by after school hours and the two of us can chat about what you're reading. Sometimes, when you're doing it by yourself, it can become complex and confusing and could stand a bit of explaining."

"I might."

"In that way I can also tell if Seamus is keeping your lessons up and maybe I can work out a few assignments for you."

Conor walked to the door but could not quite leave. He came back to Mr. Ingram and tried very hard to speak but he was too filled with the gift that had been bestowed. "I want to thank you very much," he said finally, then turned and ran out.

*

Conor Larkin always had magic in his hands. Since I could remember he was making toys of straw for the village children and straw costumes for weddings and celebrations and fine wood carvings and St. Brigid's crosses to ward off evil spirits and other omens to keep the home and byre safe from fire, fairies and ravagement. He made fishing lines and nets of horsehair tail and butterfly cages and was near as good as Tomas at repairing furniture and mending farm tools.

All of this talent leaped to life at Mr. Lambe's forge. Not only was he forging plowshares, spades, hinges and doing farrier work with horses, he was soon on advanced wheelwrighting and tinkering with fancy decorations that had Mr. Lambe scratching his head. Handles for hearth tools and hearth cranes took on beautiful scroll patterns and his trivets couldn't be matched, even in Derry. Everything that Conor made had his special touch on it and lucky the person who received a gift of utensils or candlesticks for his birthday.

Conor did not stand at the anvil and bang away like Mr. Lambe. He moved about it in the graceful manner of the master dancers of Inishowen in flight and he drew the metal out and twisted it like an artist at a canvas or a poet talking to the bluebird. It was to the everlasting glory of Josiah Lambe to encourage Conor even though the apprentice was catching up to the master.

As I watched him blossom in the blacksmith shop, I began to realize he didn't really want to come into the Larkin farm. Conor would never come right out and say

it in so many words for that would hurt his daddy.
Instead, he edged away from the family as he gained
skill at the forge and every spare minute was spent in
study.

On the other hand, Liam was ever at Tomas' side in the
fields, slaning turf at the bog, plowing, digging the lazy
beds for the potatoes. Liam Larkin had the land in his
soul but Tomas was unable to see it for his love of Conor.

What seemed so sad was that Conor and Tomas loved
each other as dearly as they ever had but they barely
spoke to one another. Here were two strong people almost
deliberately hurting one another through silence and
moving toward that point where there could be no turning
back.

CHAPTER SIX: Mr. Ingram asked everyone who had
a relative who had emigrated from Ireland to raise his
hand. Everyone in the class did. Mainly, the relatives were
in America. Us six Catholic kids had kin living in large
cities like Boston and Baltimore. The Protestants mostly
emigrated years before and had spread all over America
and many into Canada. For our most important term
assignment, Mr. Ingram had us write a long and detailed
letter or story to a relative and tell them about ourselves.

I can't recall my brother Eamon, who had left before
I was old enough to get to know him. The one photograph
we had was of him together with a bunch of firemen on a
picnic in the park and we could hardly make him out. We
didn't hear from him often, maybe once a year. I
especially remember the one letter we got telling of him
changing his name from Eamon to the American version
of Ed. Of course there was always a big package at
Christmas and, when my grandfar died, Ed sent money
for a fine tombstone as was the custom. You could tell
from the graveyard at St. Columba's who had relatives in
America.

I remember sitting near the fire trying to think of how to
start my letter and looking at my ma. I realized for the
first time how old she was getting. I watched her working
kind of bent over a little, for she didn't walk real straight
any longer. She smoored the fire constantly to keep it

alive and appease the fairies, for it is said that when the fire dies the house will soon be falling down. During the famine, neighbors would smoor the fires in the homes of those who had emigrated so it would be warm when they ended their exile and returned to Ireland. Of course they never did come back and the fires died out and the cottages came tumbling down. That is how I started my letter.

All of the women of Ballyutogue aged before their time. Endless chores in the house and out in the fields and byre kept them laboring like slaves from morning till night. They were the keepers of the customs, bringing their own new lives into the world and, in the case of my ma, hundreds of other wanes. When I asked her how many babies she had midwifed, she gave me her half-toothless smile and said, "Sure I can't count that high. I should have had a son in school like yourself when I started and then I'd know."

There were four-legged babies, too, the new animals in the byre and the driving of the cows past the fire for luck and the hanging of St. Brigid's crosses and rowan sprigs to ward off evil spirits and making certain a cricket was put in the handle of a scythe and mixing ashes with the new seed for luck. Maybe they couldn't read and write and count so high but they surely had to know a lot, women like my ma, just to keep up with all the old beliefs and make new lives and keep the old ones going.

When evening came and the men would be having at their jug at the shebeen or playing glink, the women would gather in a cottage and sit around the fire with a single candle or lantern and do the fancy lacework on the linen for his lordship's factory. Their eyes were always red-rimmed from the strain but the few pence they earned were sorely needed.

With the hours they worked and having the yearly baby, it was small wonder the grayness came and the teeth were lost and the stoop of weariness invaded long before its rightful time. There was little joy for these women. Even the joy that one felt as a haughty young girl being courted, and the joy of the moment of marriage, fled too soon.

The only path open was to plunge deeper into the fairy tales of their faith to keep them going, for it held out a promise of the hereafter and the long rest and the end of

suffering. So many of those who could not submerge
themselves into the fantasy of Jesus and Mary often went
the way of madness.

When the last crop was in and the rents paid, there was
an idle time, for our land was far too poor to work in
the winter months. It was needed to grass over to feed
the cattle and sheep. Winters were the time when the
babies were made and the wee wanes were harvested the
next year with the potatoes.

There were small respites during those long stormy
winter days and nights, the revelry of a new marriage
that matched the revelry of the wake. The bride went
through a mock kidnap by her husband, who rode in
gallantly on horseback and swept her off, and the invasion
of straw boys who broke into the merrymaking disguised
as washed-up seamen from a shipwreck. But the marriage
song soon dimmed with the coming of the first baby
and faded to nothingness and everlasting monotony with
the second and the third and the fourth. But on they
came, for to stop giving birth meant ostracism from the
dream of life hereafter with Jesus and Mary.

Us younger ones had a fortnightly ceilidhe of village
dancing and singing at the Norman keep. Half the lads
of our village could sing in any angel's choir and the other
half was just as talented at the pipes. Father Lynch laid
down stringent restrictions on all gatherings where both
sexes would be present and hovered about to make
certain that God's will was imposed. But try as he might,
he couldn't entirely, one hundred per cent keep the Devil
away.

Other gatherings of a more vigorous nature took place
at the shebeen and public house where the songs and stories
reeked of insurrection and poets went into gentle combat.

The Inishowen weather of storms within storms, and
storms in between storms, made it more difficult on the
men, who were idler than the women. Tomas Larkin had
his hands full to keep family feuds from flaring as tempers
grew short.

Conor and I alone seemed to fare well. I was as happy
in Mr. Ingram's class as Conor was at Mr. Lambe's
forge. For him it was a busy time repairing old tools
and making new ones, as well as filling the order for the
stone quarry.

Spring always seemed to rescue Ballyutogue just in

time. By the first of March the men were eager and tramping about the infields and outfields of the rundale, poking around to see if the ground was firm enough and always casting a weather eye toward the lough and praying it would be kindly. It indicated good luck if we turned the earth on St. Patrick's Day with the first ridge of potatoes planted by Good Friday. Tomas Larkin pretty much made the decisions in organizing communal work and marrowing together the labor pools. On his word, the year's labor began. "In the name of God," he'd say, spitting into the wind and throwing up some hay to ward off the storms, then turn the horses to the lucky side and plow the first row.

Tomas, my daddy and my brother, Colm, and later Liam, would take up their slanes, long thin spades, and make the lazy beds for the potatoes. I'd run water up to them. The lazy beds were dug by hand, a series of trenches and ridges designed to get full use of the slope of the hill but caring for the drainage to prevent rotting while at the same time making certain the rains carried down dead grass and humus as fertilizer. No plow could match a man's work and every lazy bed showed a slightly different individuality and technique.

With the lazy bed in, I'd gugger with my ma as Finola guggered with Brigid. It was women's and kids' work. I was too young for the slane and getting just old enough to be embarrassed working with the women. The gugger itself was an archaic sod-busting wooden tool that allowed seeds to be dropped into the holes. The women would gugger and the kids come up behind them, covering the holes with small forks.

> Four seeds in the hole,
> One for the rook,
> One for the crow,
> One for to rot,
> And one for to grow.

The crops followed in, one behind the other, in the ensuing weeks, and when summer was on us the youngest boys of the family went up to the mountains to shepherd.

Mairead and Finola kept close watch on that mystical animal, the pig, who alone in all the world was gifted by the fairies with an ability to see the wind. The pig was the gentleman who paid the rent, and his weight, welfare and size of litter were of utmost concern.

With the early crops in, the men would then move up to the bogs to clamp turf during the dry months starting in May, cutting and drying it and sharecropping enough for our own use. This time of year brought an annual tension. The next month was June and the beginning of the blue months, where all our superstitions and prayers were put into play. Food and fodder this time of year would be getting low. As July turned, a communal breath was held. On the Twelfth of July, the Orange celebration, there would be the first cutting of the hay and that was followed by the harvest—wheat, barley and oats in that order.

In blessed October the potatoes were lifted and, although the famine was thirty-five years behind us, no one ever forgot. If they were healthy after a week, we allowed ourselves an outbreak of relief.

Shortly thereafter, many of the men would be droving sheep and cattle to Derry, then crossing the water to find dock jobs in Liverpool or other menial labor in England. If all had gone well, if natural disaster had not struck, if surplus members of the family married or emigrated or moved to the city, if food and fodder held during the blue months and terrible loans didn't have to be made, the farmer would be able to make it for another year. The thin line of survival was so delicate it didn't really require a major disaster to wipe us out but the series of minor ones that never failed to come: loss of a few head, sickness, partial crop damage or some other unexpected assault on our meager resources which always put us in a position of trying to catch up. The only time any of us really got caught up was on that final visit to St. Columba's graveyard.

When the Rankins left the estate and it went under direct control of Viscount Coleraine, there was a feeling that a great burden had been lifted. We were dead wrong, of course.

Flax had been a good crop for us, grown communally in several of the larger outfields. Then the word was given by Luke Hanna that the Hubbles would no longer buy because they were putting in their own vast acreage, and the Protestants would supply the balance. He wanted us to grass over our flax land and increase our herds, but

in the transition the loss of revenue would be catastrophic.
Moreover, cattle was a lot riskier than flax.

Viscount Coleraine hadn't been in the business long
enough to see the effects of a boycott. As the old rumbles
of discontent and anger spread around the earldom,
Kevin O'Garvey, speaking for the Land League, was able
to impress on his lordship that other means had to be
found to make up for our loss. To his lordship's credit,
he smelled trouble and immediately got government funds
for road projects and doubled the jobs at the stone quarry,
then finally gave the Upper Village a contract to harvest
and prepare his flax fields.

Jaysus b'Jaysus, it was filthy, loathsome, disgusting
work. The stalks had to be pulled from the ground by
hand with us kids acting as gleaners to gather up what
the main body of men passed over. At the end of a day
you'd be so stooped it would take an hour to be able to
stand straight.

After tying the stalks into bundles, we set it in artificial
pools or dams to decay the cores. It remained in the
water for a fortnight and, as the cores rotted, it set up a
stink that would chase a banshee across the Irish Sea.
Then came the very job for the kids that convinced me
that I'd never make a farmer. We had to get into that
putrid, rancid, stinking pool which had turned slimy as
well, take out the sheaves, shake them and spread them
by hand to dry. It was worse than saying the rosary.

The men bundled it into stooks for further drying and
built up two-story huts awaiting Luke Hanna's carts from
the mill to collect it for spinning, weaving and bleaching
into linen.

I merely mentioned the flax harvest because of the
smell which I recall so vividly.

*

There were holy gatherings and traditional holidays
during which we'd have a chance to travel away from the
gimlet eyes of Father Lynch and dance complete with
touching your partner closely and game and bet and
drink and court and brawl. There were pilgrimages to holy
wells and holy beds but I didn't fancy that too much,
although our mothers took them seriously and forced us
to go along sometimes. St. Brigid and St. Columba were
very dominant in Donegal but, as in the rest of Ireland,

St. Patrick was by far the most important. Daddo Friel
said that some of the rituals we practiced as Catholics
were so old they were really begun by the Druid priests
of the Celts, such as the pilgrimage to Croagh Patrick
Mountain where the worshipers climbed one of the
highest peaks in Ireland barefooted. Only three people in
Ballyutogue had ever made that great journey to County
Mayo, Finola Larkin being one of them and, as everyone
knew, was rewarded by the birth of Conor because of it.

Conor and I would be walking on air the morning of
the monthly trading fair which was usually held on a
saint's day. At gathering day at Muff or Moville or
Buncrana or Culdaff we'd enter the grounds as cocky as
big swells from Derry.

There would be stalls of used clothing from Scotland
and kitchen and farm tools and boys looking for fights and
girls, and sometimes horse racing and illegal cock fights
and wandering troupes of bards and actors and ballad
singers and storytellers and piles of cloth and creels and
toys and straw men plying their gambling games.

Conor and I always had one important transaction at
the fair like buying a pair of secondhand shoes. We'd fill
our pockets with omens on gathering day in order to have
the luck of the fair and find a tinker and cross his palm
with copper and have our fortune told complete with dire
prophecies. They told us what to look for and what to
stay away from. Tinkers who weren't soothsaying were
plying their art as horse traders while their wives and kids
swarmed the grounds begging.

Daddo Friel told Conor and me that the tinkers were
not real genuine gypsies but our own Irish folk who had
taken to the road generations ago after their houses were
tumbled or after the defeats of the risings or from the
famine. Once each year they'd camp their wagons at the
crossroad near the hanging tree. We gave them safe
lodging and in turn they'd hardly steal a thing. In Ballyutogue we felt it was good luck to be kind to them. They
did the year's white-smithing of tin and sheet metal arts,
repaired the poteen stills and moved along. It was a dirty
life they lived. Dr. Ian Cruikshank had an annual Tinker
Day in which he'd examine the lot of them at no cost
whatsoever and supply them with medicine.

The second day was known as fair day. All the family
and clan feuds which had built up on gathering day were

apt to explode. As the crowds thickened, so did the
Constabulary. Peacemakers like Tomas Larkin were on
constant call. Sometimes it did no good at all and the
better brawls supplied fodder for next winter's conversation at the shebeen.

Trading on fair day would be fierce. In the spring we
were looking for a good horse and the women were after
cloth from the earnings of their egg money. In late spring
cattle was sold along with the first wool shearings in order
to make the first of two rent payments. The autumn fairs
were even more crucial. To have a prize cow or sheep
could mean the difference between a marginal year or a
highly successful one. There was the final auction of beef
that wasn't under contract to his lordship and hiring
ourselves out as drovers to move the animals to port in
order to meet the year's second rent payments in late
October.

I remember May Day bonfires and Midsummer's Night
revelry where everyone strained for the voice of the
cuckoo which would foretell a good corn harvest and
Halloween, the grandest of them all, for the potatoes were
up, the rent was paid and the whole countryside was alive
with banshees and fairies and ghosts and headless horsemen.

And then winter would come again.

*

Of all the things I remember of Ballyutogue, nothing
warms my heart more than an annual event that came
into being because of the famine. In those blue months
of midsummer when we waited for the first harvest, it was
quite possible to go hungry. After the famine Kilty Larkin
made a successful negotiation with the Hubbles for some
of the wrack rights in the lough.

The entire village—men, women and children—moved
down to the coast and set up primitive housing in an
abandoned fishing village along the shore.

Daddo Friel told us that before the famine the seaweed
harvesters would work naked, which was both practical
and comfortable. However, the good priests took over
blessing this enterprise and naturally we had to preserve
our morals, so the only thing bare any more was our feet.

As Conor and I grew older we were allowed to use the
knives, scythes and specially sharpened hoes. Yards upon

yards of coiled rope were readied on the shore. When low tide came we moved out in curraghs to the offshore kelp beds towing a raft behind every two boats.

As they had worked their fields side by side all their lives, Tomas and Fergus labored in adjoining curraghs to cut loose and pile kelp on the raft. Colm worked with Daddy, and Liam, Conor and me did a man-size job between the three of us alongside Tomas. Soon the rafts would be running back and forth to be beached. The piles of seaweed were tied, then dragged by hand over the soft sand to firmer ground where the cart wheels wouldn't sink under the weight. Carts and ass creels were loaded and the weed carried to a long stone wall to be shaken out and laid over to dry. Before Kilty became infirm, he was in charge of that part of the operation. Kilty and the older villagers rummaged through the drying kelp, picking out thousands of trapped cockles and mussels, and separated the seaweed by its variety and use.

At the same time my ma and Finola and Brigid went out into waist-deep water to harvest kelp that had been tossed up by the storms, cutting it loose and carrying it back and forth with all they could hold in their arms.

If low tide came during the night, everyone worked by lantern light. When the shoreside harvest was completed and the sea calm, we'd go out with our daddies as part of sixteen-curragh teams into the deeper water and cut loose an entire bed and drag it ashore like a waterlogged whale.

Part of the wrack rights included taking shellfish. Throughout the night, parties of boys and girls dug for clams and scallops and oysters and chipped mussels off the rocks. This was the part Conor and I liked best because we'd choose our girls weeks in advance. There was Alanna one year, she was the first I ever kissed, and Lissy . . . we did more than that. There was Brendt O'Malley, who did about everything, so I even shared her with Conor. Father Lynch and Father Cluny tried to watch the clam digs but we had perfected ingenious methods of decoying them up blind alleys. As they observed us, we observed them and had so refined our bird call signals, you couldn't tell most of us from a robin. The digs were the best part of the wracking but confessions went on afterward for weeks.

Separating the kelp was a great and messy chore. Some

of it was used for animal fodder, some for making iodine and some for fertilizer. There was edible seaweed that my ma mixed with potatoes and another type that could be jellied to thicken the milk and butter.

Oily fires smoked along the coast to burn the weed down and boil it for use in making soap and bleach, and yet other kelp was watered down to preserve the shellfish. Shells were crushed and made into whitewash. A few weeks after the wracking was done our cottages gleamed with new coats.

After clam digging with the girls the feasting was best. Those who had survived the famine still had the bitter taste of seaweed and shellfish in their mouths. Loathing famine food was traditional and remained with us all our lives but in the blue months it was the difference between a full or empty belly. Besides, not having lived through the famine, I wouldn't mind dying with the smell filling my nostrils that came from the great cauldrons of boiling cockles.

The kelp was slimy and the water dirty and sticky and the stink from the burning as bad as rotting flax. It was the lowest kind of croppy work, yet recalling the nights under the lanterns and sleeping on the sand with the girls, it was also our first step into the world of men and women in love.

We did so many things together in Ballyutogue. We prayed together and farmed together. The joy at birth, the tears of weddings and the wailings of anguish at death were all a communal affair. But nothing again in my life was as dear as the harvesting of the wrack.

I wrote a lot of this to my brother Ed. I know he had experienced it all when he was a kid, but seeing as he had been in America so long, he may have forgotten and I thought he might like to remember.

CHAPTER SEVEN: My brother Ed wrote he was very happy to receive my letter and proud I was getting an education. He said it was very important, particularly if I ever intended emigrating. Ed asked me for more letters and in the last paragraph offered to send me books from America. Well, that was like putting poteen before the village drunk because books were scarce as winter sun.

Conor and I discussed the matter heavily because receiving the kind of books we hungered after wouldn't be all that easy. As soon as a package arrived from America everyone in the village knew about it. It would take about ten minutes for Father Lynch to come nosing around. In my case he would demand to see the books, take them, burn them and preach a damnation on Sunday.

Conor and I, therefore, devised a desperate plan. Conor didn't exactly like the idea but decided to go along with me because the bait of books was too tempting.

He visited with Mr. Ingram regularly once a fortnight and had already read some of the early Irish writers like Edmund Burke on the French Revolution and Oliver Goldsmith and Jonathan Swift's *Gulliver's Travels*. In fact, Conor could just about outread anyone except Mr. Ingram.

We went to the school at a time we knew he would be there alone and sure enough he was in his office correcting papers. He smiled and said, "Hello, lads," and shoved his work aside. "What's the occasion?"

"An extremely important matter, sir," I answered, handing him the letter from Ed. "Concerning the last paragraph."

"Well, well, books from America. That is exciting. You'll be coming into great wealth, Seamus."

"Aye, and we'll be needing your help to suggest what he ought to send," I said.

"I'll be happy."

"However, there's a slight problem," I said. "If I get a package, Father Lynch will be knocking at the door no sooner than it arrives."

"There's almost nothing we're allowed to read," Conor said.

"I see. Well then, we'd better figure out a way to get around that," Mr. Ingram said, smiling, ". . . unless you've already thought of something."

Both of us shifted about, scratching our heads sincerely, trying to make the best of our limited abilities as liars. "Can't imagine how," I said.

"Well now, let me see. How about if Ed sends the books to me?"

Conor and I beamed on cue. "Oh, that's a grand idea,

why didn't I think of it?" I said. "But we wouldn't want you to get into any trouble," I added quickly.

"What kind of trouble could I get into?" he asked.

"Father Lynch will go into a fury if he ever finds out," Conor said.

"Seems I've alienated every Protestant minister in the district. I might as well make it unanimous," he said.

Conor was acting strange all the way down to the school and I had a feeling he was going to botch things up. "No, we can't do it," he said. "If Father Lynch finds out he'll never let another kid come to the school again and we can't be responsible for something like that."

"I have to disagree with you, Conor," Mr. Ingram answered. "If he does that it's his responsibility and not yours."

"Nae, it would be wrong," Conor said.

"The only thing wrong is submitting to tyranny. You've a right to inquire into anything you want to."

"No, I don't."

"You do. You were born with it, now don't surrender it that easily."

"There's another problem," Conor said. "If the Orange-men find out, they'll turn you out of here."

"Seems like we have an awful lot of problems," Andrew Ingram answered. "Fortunately they don't have the slightest idea of what exists inside of a book cover. I suspect you want books on Ireland."

Conor and I exchanged glances. "As a matter of fact . . ." I said, with my voice squealing clear off the track.

He just sort of leaned back in his chair, grinning. "You boys wouldn't be thinking in terms of a little insurrec-tionist literature?"

"Oh no, sir, no, sir, not at all, sir," I said.

"That's exactly what we want," Conor corrected.

"Done," Mr. Ingram said.

I guess we must have just stood there gawking. Mr. Ingram returned to correcting his papers, then looked up at us. "Is there anything else?" he asked.

We shook our heads.

"Then kindly draw the door to on your way out."

Entering into a dire conspiracy with us, Mr. Ingram personally wrote to Ed, and in late spring four treasured books arrived from America, including the autobiography of Theobald Wolfe Tone, as well as *The Rising of the Moon,* a volume of revolutionary songs and readings.

*

Tomas had had a small streak of bad luck with crops and several litters of pigs pinching the family finances so that Conor's job at the forge was all the more important. Nonetheless, his concern over Conor's drifting from the land and the home deepened. Liam was doing almost all of his chores now, so that between the forge and keeping his face in a book, breaking his eyes by candlelight, Conor was becoming like a stranger in the house. It was traditional that the youngest son (being Liam) go up into the mountains to shepherd during the summer while the oldest worked with the father. A problem was in the making and I was there the night Tomas reached his decision.

"I'm keeping Liam on the farm with me," he announced abruptly. "Conor, you're to go up to the booley house with the livestock."

Conor was stunned. "But why!"

"Because you've proved yourself less than useless around here."

"But, Daddy, what about my job at the forge!"

"I've spoken to Mr. Lambe. He'll take you back on a part-time basis provided you come down from the pasture remembering you're a farmer first. Otherwise, forget about being a blacksmith altogether."

Oh, Tomas was being hard like I'd never seen him. It was obvious that Conor was being sent to purgatory as punishment. There could be no doubt at all that his daddy's words were final. He just stood there pale, his world all crashed down on him with the threat of losing his job as well. Tomas had calculated it was frightening enough to snap him back into line.

"Is it all clear, Conor?"

"Aye," he said, pushing his way from the table and leaving the cottage.

I caught him down the road and spun him around. "Let me go," he snapped.

"Don't you see it!" I cried.

"I see it all right. I see what he's trying to do."

"Oh, Conor, my God, sometimes I think you're stupid

as an Orangeman. Look, man, here we are with four new
books plus the pickings of Mr. Ingram's entire library
and a whole summer up at the booley house by ourselves.
We can read our arses off with nobody to bother us and
no secret hiding places!"

"Oh, Jaysus, runt, I never thought about that!" He
flung his arms around me, nearly knocking my head to the
ground. "Let's get down to Mr. Ingram in the morning
and pick the rest of the books!"

We were the happiest two kids on Inishowen when we
packed the ass cart with provisions, pretending to be sad
and making certain our books were well hidden, for
Tomas would be seeing us up to the booley house.

Conor and Tomas rode the nags out of Ballyutogue,
droving the sheep and cows with the dogs scampering
about in a tight circle. I brought up the rear in the cart.
We moved inland, due west, past the thick belt of high
bogs in country that changed from rolling hills to
mountains. It would take us three days if all went well.

I don't believe Tomas and Conor exchanged a dozen
words till the third day when we skirted the foothills of
Crocknamaddy and began to rise toward the booley
house, which sat in a saddle between Slieve Sneigh and
Slieve Main at a height of fifteen hundred feet. Our party
climbed under the watchful escort of circling sparrow
hawks and golden eagles.

The booley house rested in the shade of a fine grove of
larch before a stream which found its way down from
Slieve Sneigh. It was a wee circular affair, about eighteen
feet in diameter, built in the beehive manner by stacking
corbeled stones without mortar and covered by a sod
roof. A souterrain adjoined the booley house for storage.

We chased out the nesting bats, then unloaded bedding,
pots and pans, a churn, tools, some traps and fishing gear,
candles, some sacks of potatoes, dried beans and oats.
There was always enough turf left from the previous year
to get a new fire started and keep it smoored until we
could clamp and dry another batch.

While Tomas made the fire, Conor and I paced off a
hundred and seventy-four paces parallel to the stream,
which led into a thick growth of gorse, and we shoveled to
uncover a cache of arms. All the weapons were found
clean and dry, well wrapped and greased. I selected a
shotgun and Conor, who was the better marksman, chose

a small-caliber rifle. We rewrapped the rest of the arms
with great care and set them back into the hiding place.
As it turned dark we hobbled the horses, cleaned up our
weapons, ate, and bedded down weary.

In the morning Tomas inspected the meadow with us.
The bent grass was thick and mixed with wildflowers.
Along the stream clumps of bracken, gorse and young
heather would be fine for feeding the sheep. A number of
still ponds which had been dug by hand and renewed each
year seemed to be running full with fish.

A dozen or more dilapidated buildings were interspersed about the meadow. When we were wee wanes
Daddo Friel told us these were homes of fairies who had
been angels once and were evicted from heaven for their
pranks. Later, when we were growing, he told us it was
most likely an encampment of Finn MacCool and later yet
he identified them as ruins from Viking invasions. More
than likely they were nothing but old booley houses of
our ancestors.

Our booley house was in fine condition, needing but a
few days' work, mostly sod scraws for the roof. Conor
and I went to a small surface bog nearby and examined
it. It was very soggy so we reckoned our first major chore
after repairing the booley house would be to clamp the
summer's turf for drying.

When we returned, Tomas had the horses tethered
behind the ass cart ready to return to Ballyutogue. As
we went to say good-by to him, we could see his face
straining in leashed anger. All our books, the four from
America and four from Mr. Ingram, were in plain sight
inside the cart. We stared at them in horror!

"Did you think that after fifty years as a farmer I
couldn't tell the weight of a sack of beans?" he said,
revealing their hiding place. The both of us were too
scared to defend our shattered world for the moment.

"Why did you try to do this behind my back?"

Conor became calm as he always did when the ground
got muddy. "I thought you wouldn't understand," he said.

"I understand that your head's out there in the stars
when there's enough troubles right down here."

"Maybe out there is the only place to find the answers,"
he said.

"Where do you think this road is going to carry you,
Conor? It never took any of us any place but to the

hanging tree. You're digging with the wrong foot, boy, and you're making yourself a hell on earth. You'd better spend your time up here thinking about a lot of things before you come back."

Tomas stepped up to the cart seat, slapped the donkey on the rump and it rolled. Conor dashed around and grabbed the bridle. "When you get home, you be sending Liam back here because I'll be gone!"

Tomas was down in an instant. The back of his hand slammed into Conor's face, knocking him sprawling to the ground. I ran to Conor and laid over him so he wouldn't be hit again with Tomas towering over us raging and Conor looking up, his mouth and nose spurting blood. I swear that one was just as fearful as the other. Tomas Larkin broke first. He walked back to the cart, stood a full three minutes, then reached in and threw the books out to the ground.

"Daddy!" Conor cried, running to his father and flinging his arms around him. Only this time it was Tomas who stood like stone, taking his son's arms away from him and getting into the cart.

"Make sure you've got a kill before you shoot. Don't use up all your ammunition the first week. I'll see you in the autumn."

And then he was gone.

CHAPTER EIGHT: After repairing the booley house and clamping turf, we set in our food supply. There would be a never ending supply of fresh milk from the herd, which we could sour or churn to mix with potatoes as well as a crude cheese made from sheep's milk. We foraged like stone age settlers, gathering sacks of mushrooms which grew wild in the damp earth beneath the conifer stands. Three or four different varieties of heath berries were worth eating when mixed with cream, and thousands of edible snails inhabited the edges of the ponds. After picking beans from the gorse pods, we tried the luck of the fish. Trout and roach were hitting up to two feet long. Our first catches were filleted and salted for the days when they wouldn't be biting and the bones and guts were left in the sun to draw maggots for bait.

Conor set snares for hare and red squirrel which we also hunted by gun with some luck. With the souterrain stocking up, we settled down with our books in the company of jackdaws, magpies and ravens happily scavenging the camp, keeping it clean and getting friendlier every day so's they'd soon be eating out of our hands.

At daybreak we'd rush to get our chores done so we could read. As it turned to summer the light stayed longer and longer. We'd nap here and there between hunting and fishing and milking, leaving time for talking during the dark hours in order to save on candles. I guess there wasn't much we didn't talk about that summer. The books had fired us to dreaming and longing, one minute fighting and dying as martyrs for Irish liberty and in the next we'd travel to mystical lands beyond Ballyutogue.

Occasionally, we'd get company from those ever migrating tinkers or other shepherds in the lower pastures. Stray fugitives on the run sought a day's respite now and again. None were the desperate sort and harboring was common. We were safe with our dogs and arms and rarely did a fugitive do anything harmful, for it would destroy an ancient custom of sanctuary. They'd always represent themselves as fighters for Irish liberty who had fallen from grace for a crime against the Crown, though God only knew what they were really wanted for. We'd feed them, let them rest the day, then move them along to the next set of safe booley houses at Crocknamaddy.

There was a major subject of growing interest concerning matters of a sexual nature. The one thing we would miss would be the wracking harvest this particular year as both of us had ideas of advancing our knowledge with Brendt O'Malley. There was so much we didn't know, we were pondering the notion of approaching Mr. Ingram for books on the subject. Conor reckoned he would be of an open mind on the matter.

It must have been around Midsummer's Night when he came because it was light nearly all the time and we were reading so much we spent half the day dozing at our fishing lines.

The dogs yapped, alerting us to strangers. We took observation positions and spotted two horsemen on the horizon trailing a pair of donkeys loaded with provisions.

As they came into closer view our hearts jumped with joy! Sure it was Andrew Ingram on one of the horses and we dashed out to greet him. To our utter astonishment the rider on the second horse was a lady.

We were introduced to Miss Enid Lockhart, who was a teacher herself in the national school in Muff. Quickly concealing our amazement, we shook her hand, pretending that her being there was nothing at all. Mr. Ingram said he was looking for a few days of good fishing. Was he ever in luck!

A booley house about a half mile from ours was in decent condition. We raced off to fix it up for him and his lady friend, which we did in short order. Then, as we helped them unpack, Mr. Ingram gave us the most magnificent surprise of our lives in the form of six more books. I will never forget them: *The Confederate Chieftains,* after the rising of 1641, and *The History of Ireland* by John Mitchel and *The History of the Irish Rebellion of 1798.* There was *The Life and Times of Daniel O'Connell* and *The Life of Lord Edward Fitzgerald* by Thomas Moore. The last book was really for Conor, for he trembled all over when he read the title. It was an English translation of the great Celtic epic, *The Cattle Raid of Cooley,* part of the Fenian tales of Finn MacCool, Queen Maeve and Cuchullain, a most pulsating drama also known as the Irish Odyssey, and the most magnificent words to have been born from Ulster.

"Well," said Mr. Ingram, seeing great white spots from our bulging eyes, "these ought to keep the old insurrection brewing. Seems that there is a full-blooded Fenian bookstore in Philadelphia which your brother Ed has discovered. *The Cattle Raid* is my own present from Dublin." We were still too shocked to speak as he turned his sack over, tumbling out two notebooks and a dozen pencils. "It might be a good idea to put some thoughts down as you go along. Miss Enid will be happy to show you how to make a proper outline."

I finally got around to thanking him but Conor remained in a euphoric stupor. He took my shotgun and said he would be back in a while, and took off over the meadow with the dogs. He returned after a time holding up a handsome-sized ring-necked pheasant. It was his special way of thanking Mr. Ingram.

"I knew she was there," Conor said excitedly. "I spotted the nest a time back and was waiting for a special occasion."

Miss Enid Lockhart turned out to be an extra fantastic cook, doing things the likes of which our mas had never heard. She stuffed the bird with meal made of this and that and mushrooms and snails, pouring rum, if you'd like, right on the dressing, and roasted it over a spit. We had some eggs copped from a golden eagle's nest and berries and cream and tea which was spiked with poteen that we had traded for with one of the passing tinkers. I mean they didn't even say a word about us drinking poteen.

Miss Enid Lockhart was a very pretty lady in a manner of speaking, if you like fragile Protestant types. She seemed just as open-minded as Mr. Ingram, because it was she who suggested that poteen would go well if we had any. Otherwise we'd have never taken the jug out in front of them. Anyhow, the way they were acting, it wasn't hard to fancy they were in a marrying mood.

I think Conor and I were most proud of the fact there was an unspoken bond between us all. Unmarried couples just didn't roam around the mountains together, even Protestants. If such a thing became known it would stir the sanctimonious ire of every preacher on Inishowen. The fact that they trusted us without even instructing us to that trust made us feel very close and I guess we both knew that Mr. Ingram had a special place in his heart for his two papists. He fired his pipe and gazed over the meadow, which was filling up with the low violet and purple colors of a softening sun, and we all groaned our contentment.

"Who plays the flute?" Miss Lockhart asked.

"I do. I learned it from my daddy, Fergus, who is the poet of our village."

"Would you?"

It was ever so still with but a wee breeze stirring the heather and naught but the sound of my flute mixed with occasional harmony from the animals and the dogs racing around wrestling and tumbling. I was sincerely impressed with the sounds I was making because they never sounded this grand before. When I was done Conor sang an old shepherd's air as peaceful and lovely as the land around us.

"That was just beautiful," she said, "both of you."

"I've always theorized," Mr. Ingram said, "that when we do get to heaven we'll find it a rather decent place. Our earthly wants and woes will be lifted forever. However, one must consider that, with all the billions of souls there, the administration of the place must be staggering."

"Sure I never thought of that," I said.

"For example, transporting the souls in and out of purgatory. Someone must register them all and keep track of them just to see if they are qualified to stay. I'm certain that everyone will be assigned to a job of sorts, one he or she likes, but the organization of the place has to be tremendous. After one is there for six or seven centuries all the contentment might get a little dull."

Obviously we hadn't heard this assessment of heaven from Father Lynch and had supposed that everything would be done up there by magic. Mr. Ingram's dissertation on the logistics of running heaven was certainly a revelation.

"To get to my point," he said, "it seems that we have to have moments of turmoil to contrast to moments of peace in order to truly understand and appreciate that peace. What we have captured this moment in this meadow is an instant of peace. Right here and now, this is paradise, do you agree?"

"Aye, it's paradise," Conor said.

"What we have confused is the belief that heaven and paradise are the same. So long as we are capable of moments of paradise here, we ought to cherish them, because we may not find paradise in heaven."

"Bravo," Miss Lockhart said.

"You're right," I said, "heaven can't be any better than this."

After that I played the flute again and we all sang some Scottish songs led by Mr. Ingram.

*

Conor stopped at stream edge and flipped a rock into the still pool on the opposite side. "You'll be finding good roach fishing there, especially now that it's clouding up."

Mr. Ingram rubbed his hands together, a man yet in paradise. "I'll show you how to fish, lad, the way a Scotsman does it."

"Well, have your go," Conor answered. "I've seen strange luck that defies reason at times."

"You'll mind your words later when you look into my creel."

"Well, try to get enough for one decent meal for the lot of us," he said. "I'll be getting on to my chores now. I'll see you later, sir."

"Conor!" he said sharply.

"Aye?"

"Don't you think we'd better have a talk?"

Conor sighed and nodded. "I guess so." He sidled down on the bank, letting his feet hang in the water. "My daddy told you where we were, didn't he?"

"He did," Mr. Ingram said, sitting alongside and pre-paring his fishing rod.

"What did he say to you?"

"A lot of things. Essentially that you're a farmer."

"I've been so happy at the forge and with my books. Why must I be made to feel guilty over it? And why in God's name should I be threatened that I'm going to lose both?"

"Don't you know the answer, Conor?"

"What did you say to my father, Mr. Ingram?"

"I told him that because a man is a farmer is no reason to shut out the light and beauty one can find through books. A farmer has the same right to enrich his mind as anyone."

"Did you meet my brother Liam?"

"I made it a point."

"He's a good lad, Liam. All he wants is the farm and to be a follower of my father. My daddy knows what Liam wants and he knows what I want. He could make us both happy by doing the obvious."

"Does he know?"

"Maybe he pretends not to. Why, Mr. Ingram?"

The teacher shook his head. "He considers books and ideas as a threat that will lure you away from Ballyu-togue. He's terrified of you wrapping yourself up in the cause for Irish freedom. To him it's a path to misery and death, nor does he want the Larkin dynasty to end. They've been strong men, one after the other, the kind of leaders Liam can never be."

"But can't I do that as a blacksmith?"

"No. He places infinite value on the land and, with the Irish peasant, it goes deeper than the breath of life. Conor, every parent I've ever spoken to has told me he loves all his children exactly the same. Most parents actually believe that. It's not true. Your father loves you more than the others. As you know, people leaving Ireland is the tragedy of Irish life. Seeing you with books, with a trade, he becomes desperate because passing the land is the only way he knows of closing the circle of his life."

"Mr. Ingram, I love my daddy but . . . but . . ."

The teacher's arm went about Conor's shoulder knowingly. "In most places most parents come to realize that their children are going to find their own way. They may not like the idea but in time they make peace with it."

"But my daddy never will, is that what you're saying?"

"He can't do it any more than he can give up breathing."

"What am I supposed to do?" Conor asked shakily.

"Well, you and I are both of Celtic stock. We know that our kind can go on for a hundred years without talking to one another. Eventually you're going to have to face him and make your decision clear."

"I can't, Mr. Ingram, I can't do that."

All right, lad, Andrew Ingram thought, go and keep it stuffed inside you for days and years. Sometime the breaking point must come and, when it does, it will be a day of terrible sorrow.

*

"Conor."

"Aye?"

"You sleeping?"

"Not since you just woke me up to ask."

"I made up my mind what I'm going to do with it."

"With what?"

"The notebook Mr. Ingram gave me. I'm going to write my version of the history of Ireland."

"That's grand. Go to sleep."

"What are you going to do with yours?"

"I've not made up my mind."

"Ah, you're lying to me, man. I saw you writing in it. What are you writing?"

Conor didn't answer so I asked him again.

"Poems," he said finally.

"Can I read them?"

"Maybe later. And don't you go poking around behind my back or I'll give you a bash in the melt. Now go to sleep with you, will you?"

"Conor."

"Aye."

"She's nice."

"Who?"

"Miss Enid Lockhart."

"Sure that's true enough," Conor agreed.

"Did you ever consider what it would be like to be a priest?" I asked.

"Jaysus, Seamus, Jaysus."

"My ma is always making sly suggestions at me. I think that's why she decided to let me go to the national school. After all, she says, what am I going to do with my life? Colm is getting the farm. And here am I knowing how to read and write 'just like a priest.' She says I would be the most important person in the village, nae, the entire parish, maybe the only person who can read and write. And, if I become a bishop it would be like having my own earldom. All I have to do is tell everybody what to do and they obey. After all, she says, what's the good of all the education?"

"My ma is going to make a priest out of Dary," Conor said.

"Oh, really. Won't your daddy be fierce?"

"He's got nothing to say about that wane."

"How can you tell?"

"By the way she's got Dary tied to her. He's two years old and he's already imitating her on her knees. He could pray before he could talk."

"I know what you mean," I said. "I liked to got my head broken for just yelling at Dary once."

"Ma doesn't let anyone look at him sideways. He even sleeps with them." Conor propped on an elbow. "I'd never make a priest. I'm going to enjoy fucking too much."

"There must be something good about fucking if it's so sinful," I agreed. "I was kind of hoping maybe we'd get to fuck Brendt O'Malley this year at the wrack."

"You'd be foolhardy to do that," Conor said.

"How come?"

"She's always confessing."

"Yeah, I guess you're right. I'll remember that," I

said, salvaging my manly intentions. "It's probably not that great anyhow. I never heard of anybody who enjoyed it after they got married. Well, certainly not after the first baby."

"My ma and daddy always did," Conor said.

"You're putting me on."

"Nae, it's true."

"How did you know?"

"Well, even with the door shut in the loft, there's cracks to look through. They always laughed a lot when they were doing it, and kissing and saying the dumbest kind of words."

"Surely!"

"Aye, they did. And they used to do it three and four times a week."

"Honest to God!"

"Aye. I could always tell at supper when they were getting in the mood. My daddy would hang around the fire slapping Ma's behind and pinching her and she'd giggle. Sure enough . . ."

"Wow!" I said. "It's certainly not like that at my house. I could hear Ma and Daddy from the byre and it was nothing like that, I can tell you. Daddy would make awful grunting noises, you know, like some of the farm animals, and Ma would complain about some aches and tell him to get it over with. I don't recall them ever having fun at it. Conor, did Tomas and Finola enjoy it through all the babies and everything?"

"Well, they haven't since Dary was born. You remember when I had to fetch Dr. Cruikshank."

"Do I ever remember that," I said. "All the women waiting around the cottage muttering that Finola was going to get away. I was so scared."

"I think something happened to her insides," Conor said, "because they don't do it any more. But once, before Dary was born, they were sending the same kind of secret messages to each other like Mr. Ingram and Miss Lockhart."

"Do you think they're doing it!" I said, astonished.

"Are you daft? Look at them."

That was too much for me to comprehend . . . fucking without sin. "Maybe Protestants are permitted to enjoy it for some reason we don't know."

"Everyone is," Conor said.

*

The summer fled too fast and our hearts died as the days' sunlight grew less and less. The time to go was on us. We had fattened the cattle and brought a dozen calves into the world without loss, and the sheep were bulging with wool like the great white clouds that passed above.

Liam was sent up with the cart and horses to fetch us. We stored our arms, took up our nets from the stream, broke camp and killed the fire, coming down from Slieve Main near to tears.

I had finished my notebook on Irish history and intended to give it to Mr. Ingram as a present. On our last night, Conor let me read one of his poems.

THE MAGIC MEADOW

I go high to a magic meadow
When it's light the full day round,
And I set me down in a fairy rath,
And wait for the banshee's sound.

The voice of Wolfe Tone from his cell
I hear quite clearly now,
Calling up all his sons and daughters
From the hearth and the byre and the plow,

And I gaze o'er the magic meadow,
Where the gorse is growing thick,
And there's nae a body there to see.
Is it all a fairy trick?

I come down from the magic meadow
When it's brown and the harvest's soon,
But the voice of Tone won't leave me alone
For a rising by the moon.

Conor Larkin, 1887, age 14

When we crossed the River Crana we took a last look back to that place where the world beyond opened and beckoned and where full cycle of our own Irish tragedy became known to us. It was also a place where time stood still in that moment we came to know as paradise.

CHAPTER NINE: The seasons came and passed, one after another. Nothing much changed except the deepening weariness of our people trudging that endless treadmill of struggle and futility. The step became slower and the prayer more fervent for the final sleep to overtake them. There was an ever growing number of "American wakes," as sons and daughters emigrated and relatives and neighbors gathered to mourn them as they mourned the dead, for once they left Ireland they left forever.

The marriage of Mr. Ingram to Miss Enid Lockhart came as no surprise at all. Conor and I were invited to the wedding and reception and did not attend for obvious reasons, but we did watch the ceremony from outside the church. A reception was held afterward at Hubble Manor where Mr. Ingram had become a great favorite of Lady Caroline. We watched everyone going in through the main gates. I must admit that Lady Caroline was the most beautiful woman I had ever seen. When they returned from their honeymoon in Scotland, Conor and I went to see him. Conor made the most beautiful set of wrought-iron bookends you'd ever hope to see, which he gave as a wedding present in both our names. I think Mr. Ingram was sincerely moved. He never asked us why we didn't come because he knew. There were a lot of things between us we never exactly put into words because they were understood.

"I should like to give you something too," he told us. "Miss Enid . . . Mrs. Ingram has a surplus of family Bibles so I should like you to have mine." Both Conor and I stared at it as he set it on his desk, for it was the most dangerous contraband imaginable for the likes of us.

"The farmers of Scotland are a very poor and hardworking lot," Mr. Ingram said. "Things were never as bad for them as they've been for you, but it's been no picnic, either."

He ran his hand over Conor's bookends and smiled, then walked to the window and put his hands behind him as I'd seen him do so many times in class. "No one knew how to read very well except for the holy book.

Every night before retiring was a time of special joy.
We'd gather around my father before the fire, four sons
and four daughters, and he would read from the Bible.
The tradition from his father was so deep that he and
most of the others could recite it by heart. It is the
wellspring of our language."

He turned from the window. "I've come to learn
that it's not quite as rich a language as yours, but it's
not so poor either . . . see, I even speak a bit like you
now. If I had my wish you'd be able to learn the Bible
in your own language. You see, lads, there is no more
beautiful way that words have been used and thoughts
expressed."

Conor nodded that he understood. I leaned in front
of him as he opened the cover. It was very, very old,
with each new son who inherited it placing down his
name. From Adair Ingram it was over two hundred
years to Andrew.

"We're very honored," I said, "but I think we don't
deserve it."

"I want you and Conor to have it in particular
because I believe you've a gift from the fairies with
your own words. Father Lynch notwithstanding, would
you accept it in the spirit of learning?"

*

Conor and I like to died from the pain of it when
Andrew Ingram and his darling wife left Ballyutogue.
On the nomination of Lady Caroline he was appointed
to run the largest school in Derry.

From the time we returned from the booley house
Conor and Tomas went into a silent spell. Conor was
allowed to return to Mr. Lambe's forge and he studied
as hard as ever but it was a soiled game they played.
Tomas continued to pretend that Conor would remain
in Ballyutogue and take up the farm and Conor never
came right out and said anything to the contrary.

Their silence was finally broken with the news that
Daddo Friel had gotten away. Daddo was a long ways
up the road but even so it came as a terrible sorrow.
Along with Mr. Ingram, he had been the important
teacher in our lives. We traveled up to his village of
Crockadaw to what was to be the last great wake on
Inishowen.

Kevin O'Garvey came from Derry and delivered a eulogy that would have made the old Fenian stand up in his grave. The night was filled with many stories of Daddo and the circle of his closest friends were weeping out loud in their poteen.

By the second dawn Kevin broke down and babbled his anguish over the political strife that had torn the fabric of the Irish Party. Charles Stewart Parnell had been driven from the leadership and Kevin, being among his own, spilled his overfull heart on our ears.

Parnell's enemies had long been a pack of jackals eternally on the prowl for the great man's throat. They had thrown him into that hall of Irish martyrs, Kilmainham Jail, years before when the Land League was declared illegal. The British ended up with their foot in their mouth over that one, redeclaring it legal.

Later, Parnell was accused of taking part in the political assassination of the British First Secretary in Dublin. Only in the courtroom under cross-examination did his accuser, Richard Piggot, break and admit the letter of accusation was a forgery. Piggot fled to Spain afterward and killed himself.

No sooner had Parnell weathered one political storm than the British were after him again. He was finally destroyed by the dragging up of an ancient affair. Early in his career, Captain W. H. O'Shea was a trusted associate. O'Shea had long been estranged from his wife, Kitty. She became Parnell's mistress and over the years bore him three children, one of whom died. It was not until after a decade of Parnell's life with Kitty O'Shea that her husband saw fit to sue for divorce and name Parnell as corespondent in an act of cold-blooded vengeance. After an uncontested decree, Parnell married his beloved, but the gates of wrath had opened.

At first the Irish Party and the people rallied to him but soon every Catholic pulpit in the land rained damnation on the adulterers with our own Father Lynch not being the least among them. As the bishops raged and the scandal deepened, Gladstone, that shining Liberal knight, demanded Parnell step down from leadership of the Irish Party as the price for introducing another Home Rule Bill.

The Irish Party members of Parliament convened in a room in Westminster. In the battle that ensued, Kevin

O'Garvey was with the twenty-six who remained loyal
to Parnell. Among the leaders of the opposition who
ousted him was the selfsame Michael Roche who had
once exhorted us from Celtic Hall in Derry.

Parnell returned to Ireland with Kevin O'Garvey
and made a futile attempt to regain control. On the
first night of Daddo Friel's wake Kevin confided to us
that Parnell was exhausted from fourteen years of
unabated warfare. Kevin was deeply concerned over the
man's health.

"He's half crippled with rheumatism and rancid over
his defeat. I begged him to rest himself but he wouldn't
listen."

Hearing such words was frightening. For Conor and
me, Parnell was like a god. Tomas fed the fires of
Kevin's bitterness, saying over and over that freedom
was a mirage and the only logical end was the hanging
tree. I knew, of course, those words were for Conor's
consumption.

Kevin was called away from the graveyard the instant
Daddo was put into the earth. The caller was a
messenger from the General Post Office carrying a
telegram, which often as not was a harbinger of death.
We went looking for Kevin frantically as soon as we
could get away, and found him on the edge of the
village, salted with tears, sobbing convulsively, unable
to speak. Conor took the message from his hand and I
saw the desire of life drain from him.

"Parnell is dead."

We were to discover that he had gone to his deathbed
during a short visit to England. Kitty was at his side.
His body was returned to Dublin where Irish leaders
are profaned in life but exalted in death. The outpouring
of genuine and hypocritical grief had never been duplicated as he was laid to rest near Daniel O'Connell. It
all took place in the year of eighteen and ninety-one.
Parnell left us at the age of forty-five.

The magnificent Irish Party he had forged, and which
became a menace to the British, now fragmented and
knuckled under to British demands. With Parnell gone,
much of the Irish aspiration went with him. What
seemed to go out of Conor and myself went out of the
Irish people. The great thrust for freedom came to a
sudden, confused halt. We were croppies again, standing

out in the cold and freezing with our noses pressed hungrily against the window . . . waiting . . . waiting . . . waiting . . .

CHAPTER TEN: "I came as quickly as I could," Roger said. "How is he?"

"He has cancer, Roger," Clara answered calmly, having called into play her full theatrical skills for the final ritual. "He's in and out of intense pain. At any rate, you have to know it is fatal."

"Why didn't you let me know sooner, for God's sake?"

"Arthur is good at pretending that what is real isn't real. It makes little difference now."

His father looked frightful. Roger feigned that it was reassuring to see him more fit than he had anticipated. Lord Arthur was propped up with pillows, sucking at a cigarette and holding a snifter of cognac in his other hand. Roger protested the excesses but his father answered it really didn't matter and he'd just as soon slip under with a decent taste in his mouth.

"Clara trimmed my hair up just for you. At least you haven't had to pay my barber bills on top of everything else."

"Father, I don't find that very amusing."

"You'll have to forgive my newly found sense of humor. It becomes downright diabolical at times."

"Now you listen to me, you're going to be all right."

"Roger, this blasted thing is awful, really awful. Let's both dispense with any pretense that I'll get out alive. Now tell me, how are Caroline and the boys?"

"Frightfully worried. She's on her way back from England now. She'll be down as soon as she can fetch the boys. Sir Frederick is sending his private car so we can take you back to the Manor."

"No, I shan't go. Only this time I mean I shan't."

"I have to insist, Father."

"If Caroline can have her sons on the kitchen table at Hubble Manor, I am entitled to die in Daars. Fear not, dear boy, you'll have the corpse soon enough for pomp and solemn occasion. But, Roger, no Orange bands, no matter how important it is to family interests. I shall not be en-

tombed in that family vault with the strains of 'The Old
Orange Flute' ringing in my ears. I should prefer something more dignified, the garrison band from Belfast
playing an old regimental requiem. Perhaps Caroline can
whip together a chamber orchestra. She's got such smashing taste, that girl, I'm putting it in her hands. . . ."

"Father, that's quite enough!"

"I told you about my sense of humor."

Roger gritted teeth and twitched face muscles, seeing
no object in argument and disliking the torrent of self-
abuse from his father.

"Roger, you and I have managed to tolerate each other
all these years. That shows good breeding." He gnashed
his own teeth and moaned, waving the cigarette. "Put this
bloody thing out."

"Is there anything that can be done about the pain?"

"No, I'm quite doped up. Clara has even slipped me
an opium pipe obtained from one of her old stage mates.
Helps a bit. The rumor is that you and Caroline do a bit of
that on the Continent. Smashing woman, Caroline. The
Chinese are terribly civilized. They put the ailing elders
off in a corner when they've got this thing and give them a
pipe and let them just drift away. How're the boys?"

Knocked out from the opening amenities, Lord Arthur
drifted for a time. His eyes opened hard, as though jar-
ringly frightened, from his trance. "One does a lot of
moralizing, lying here day after day. Know what I'd do
if I were you?"

"What, Father?"

"Sell everything and get out of Ireland. God knows
how many little Parnells have been spawned in the gutters
of Dublin. The quaint folk are all rested from the famine
by now and you can be sure their dirty little back rooms
are seething with rebellion. . . ."

After medication, Arthur wearied and spoke in semi-
coherent patches as his son took up the death watch. He
and Clara had tea without words, then she left to rest at
his insistence.

Arthur groaned to consciousness halfway through the
night.

"I'm here," Roger said.

"Roger?"

"Yes."

"Good of you to come. How are the boys?"

"They're fine, Father. On the way to Daars."

"Good. You know, Roger, I've been thinking a lot these days. The new century is bound to be ushered in with an insurrection by these people. You ought to get out of Ulster."

"It's our home," Roger whispered harshly.

"Is it? Has it ever really been?"

Roger walked to the foot of his father's bed and spoke, as though to himself. "In every game one has to consider if the rewards are worth the risk. I suppose colonization is a high-risk game, like shark fishing out of Kinsale here. Frankly, we should be the last to complain over the rewards."

"Hear, hear, well said. Rampart of the Empire and all that. I feel though . . . the Crown is about to abandon me . . . they won't care to follow where I'm going . . ."

"I don't want you to be frightened."

". . . and in the end . . . they may not choose to follow where Ulster leads them. . . ." Another scorching pain convulsed him. Roger took his father's emaciated hand, startled by the sweeping wetness and cold.

"I give you," Arthur rasped, "the legacy of colonists. After three hundred years of attachment to the homeland with all the feelings of inferiority that are aroused by looking back over the shoulder . . . sometimes wistfully . . . sometimes defiantly . . . but always . . . always as an outsider. We are as a stranger to those who sent us here. We are strangers to those whom we have usurped and exploited. And now . . . we are strangers to ourselves. . . ."

Roger pulled the service cord trembling. The door opened fast, knowingly. The end came mercifully swift.

After communicating arrangements for a proper funeral, Roger, Caroline and their sons set out to accompany the body back to Ulster.

"I'm frightfully sorry," Roger said to Clara, "but you'll have to say farewell to Father here."

"I quite understand. I was never comfortable at Hubble Manor. Daars was our home. At any rate, I'll be moving out in a week or so."

"No hurry, of course. Can I help you with any plans, Clara?"

She shrugged.

"Where are you going?"

"Wherever old whores go."

"Come now, none of that. There are a number of bequests in accordance with Father's wishes. I think you'll find everything . . . quite . . . generous."

"In payment for services rendered," she said acidly.

"I know how much the two of you loved each other and I've never for a single moment begrudged your relationship. Now, please . . ."

The impact of coming loneliness hit her, the bitterness of total abandonment, of being placed forever on the outside. She reared up like a monumental bitch. "Some of our most amusing hours were spent trying to figure out ways to torture you. From time to time, since Caroline, you seem almost human, but of course we all know better."

Roger's eyes turned dully expressionless.

"He often used to speak of who was the worst of the Hubbles, you, he, or his father. He loathed himself but, as you know, he was too weak to do anything about it. His own father was suddenly faced with a crisis not of his creation, the famine. He reacted viciously for his survival. But you, Roger, you are coldly, carefully planning what it's going to be like twenty years from now. You are the calculator, the creator of a new era of tragedy. Oh, Arthur envied your strength and your craft. He would say, 'The boy's a marvel, see how he contains all that cruelty behind a façade of English pleasantness.' "

"Yes," Roger answered blandly, "one can see how amusing you were with Father."

"Well, you and Ulster deserve each other," she hissed, "and I can think of no greater curse. Now get out and leave us to what time we have left."

Roger walked to the door and opened it.

"Roger! Oh, God . . . I'm sorry . . ."

"Well, one cannot deny an old whore her curtain speech. That would be poor form indeed," he said, and left.

The mourning Hubbles, armbanded in black, returned Lord Arthur's remains to the land of their ancestors. The principal public ceremony was held at Londonderry's Guild Hall, a quasi-Gothic symbol of the Crown's everlasting power and presence. It was London, clear to the four-faced clock, an imitation of Big Ben in her namesake mother city. The Queen sent high envoy to pay homage to one of her great earls of Ireland.

In a quiet but noted ceremony some time after the funeral, Roger Hubble was declared the Eleventh Earl of Foyle and his eldest son Jeremy was named the new Viscount Coleraine.

*

Two years after veto of the second Home Rule Bill by the House of Lords, there was another death of note. Lord Randolph Churchill, the would-be creator of a new kind of imperial conservatism, met his end. Having been the master orator who played the Orange card and masterminded the fall of a Gladstone government, he had been rewarded at first with high offices but his early instability degenerated into debility and then madness. He died, insane, at the age of forty-six of syphilis.

CHAPTER ELEVEN

1895

As I went into my twenty-first year the Larkins had settled into that all too familiar family pattern in which affection between parents was replaced by indifference. A devouring sense of possession by Finola for Dary stretched normalcy and reason. Finola had joined the majority of Ballyutogue mothers who had long lost any physical and esoteric sensations of love-making. Her home became like all the others in that her husband was a boarder and the sons treated as gentry.

Dary seemed more and more certain to fulfill Conor's prediction of priesthood. A woman living beyond the memory of carnal pleasure fails to understand why anyone else would crave or miss it. These women were more than willing to push a son into a life of celibacy, which was in the purest Irish tradition. Dary was his mother's precious child, smothered and fitted with blinders that would allow him to see only in the direction of the seminary. By eighteen and ninety-five at the age of ten, he was indulging in a full range of priestly behaviors. Finola did everything to encourage him short of addressing him as "Father."

Tomas lost the will to combat his wife's obsession and gave her a wide berth. He often burst into uncharacteristic flashes of hostility against Dary but remained too proud to apologize after.

Conor alone preserved a precarious balance within the family. He stepped into the vacuum left by Tomas to become a surrogate father to Dary. Ignoring Finola's entreaties, Conor took his brother hunting and fishing, and shared the long walks and philosophies that went with them. Often as not, fair day would be spent in great part with Dary riding on his big brother's shoulders. At the same time Conor understood Tomas' dilemma and kept his daddy from slipping under. Without him the Larkins would have fallen to the Irish curse of family warfare.

Dary remained fragile but despite his mother's pampering grew to be a lovable boy. He was a gentle one with sharp wit and a grand knack of persuasion that made him a leader over the bigger and stronger kids. He was the shanachie, the maker of tales, and everyone in the village shared Finola's delight that he was a special child.

Because of his size Dary came to certain understandings about himself. From the time he knew he would become a priest, he felt the first principle of being a good one was the ability to bear pain and mortifications as Christ had borne it. He was able to defeat larger enemies with the weapon of compassion. His ability to endure more punishment than anyone could invoke and to never show tears downright frightened would-be tormentors. Dary was truly the son of Tomas Larkin in more ways than Tomas realized.

*

Conor and I drifted into the "brotherhood" of drinking bachelors, a fixture in post-famine life. The older men, both married and single, who drank with us had largely given up on life.

Those of our own age were mostly marking time. A few would come into their parents' land. Others would emigrate or leave for the city . . . or give up on life also.

Lads with no possibility of inheriting land had no desire
to get involved with the girls nor were they particularly
attractive as prospective husbands. The burden of
marriage was looked upon as a fateful finality. Courting
and chasing with no intention of marriage was a sin, so
we courted little. Most of the girls would accept a
serious advance only with the idea of marriage. With
the normal pursuit of girls whacked out of our life by
the Church and economics of the land, we found our
respite in the "brotherhood" of drinkers.

Liam was a good plain lad who seemed to accept his
landless status without rancor. He had neither the charm,
wit nor strength of his older brother and father, and little
of the brain of his smaller brother. It was coming time for
Liam to make a decision as he neared his twentieth year,
to leave or to remain and wither. Liam, with his limited
capacities, became more and more torn. The lands unknown out there were frightening but the living example
of those who stayed behind was equally terrifying.

The weak of Ballyutogue who lacked the courage to
emigrate stood every chance of remaining lifelong
celibates. At best they might stumble into a late-in-life
marriage. We had a full complement of the old toothless
uncles and old maid aunts who never loved or married
but stayed on to live in the byre or hayloft on a dole of a
few pennies for helping around the farm. As our villages
filled up with this kind, and the strong departed, our
strain became weaker. Despite the plight of too many
people and too many landless people, Father Lynch
insisted on babies and insisted that we remain in the
poverty of Ireland rather than emigrate where we would
"live among heathen niggers and Chinamen."

Liam Larkin edged to his moment of truth a frightened
young man.

Brigid and the girls had the sorriest lot of us all, for
their choices were almost nil and their fate sealed. They
vied hard to get husbands even though marriage meant a
life sentence of servitude and perpetual pregnancy, for
what else was there? They could become the old maid
aunt, a dried-up potato, or they could join the convent
and become a nun. Emigration was far more difficult for a
girl. The chance of a full, rich life didn't seem to exist.
With the hammer of chastity pounding on them from

birth, fear of committing the most mortal sin circled them
like a vulture on death watch. Brigid and her girl friends
were denied the release of drinking, sports and roaming
that the lads were allowed. How long the days would be
for them between laughter, how long the nights without
pleasure.

Brigid Larkin was no beauty but the daughter of the
likes of Finola and Tomas could not be without certain
qualities of handsomeness. She seemed content to take
the course of finding herself a lad who would have land
and never leave Ballyutogue. The Larkin name would
mean a decent dowry, so her chances in the husband-
seeking competition were quite good.

Conor! There was a lad! He wasn't behind the door
when they passed out good looks. He grew strapping and
tall like his daddy and, although he could outdrink and
outfight anyone around, his true strength was in his
softness. You could hear the angels weep when that boy
sang, and there was music in his poems, which were seen
only by Dary and myself, for he was not a man to boast.

Mr. Lambe's blacksmith shop had a constant stream of
lassies seeking repairs on things which weren't broken.
Even the Protestant girls were after him. Conor never
got to nesting with a single bird, for his eye was always
out on the horizon. He became a master ironworker, the
peer of Mr. Lambe, and with the old blacksmith slowing
up considerably, he took on much of the responsibility of
the forge. Josiah Lambe had had the disaster befall him
of fathering four daughters, all of whom married farmers,
and gossip was strong that Conor would be coming into
the shop. The two of them had the special bond of men
who worked side by side creating out of iron.

We'd meet by night in the shebeen or the public house
with the bachelor brotherhood and gamble on cards or
dog races in town or anything there was to gamble on.
Coming from Armagh, the Larkins had brought the game
of road bowling with them, and after Tomas retired from
the sport, Conor became the undisputed champion of
slinging the two-pound iron ball on the course that ran
the road from the Upper Village to the Township. We'd
gamble on that, too, burning hungry invaders after
Conor's crown.

Conor Larkin was our leader. Everyone accepted that
he would take over when Tomas left but he never

committed himself to it. He was more like himself on
those pensive mountain walks with Dary and me, by
the stream, reading a new poem. It was eight years since
our summer in the booley house but our hearts never
left it. The awful battle of wills between Conor and Tomas
went on and on. Tomas slowed some but remained the
dominant figure among us as Kilty had before him. He
quit his heavy drinking after a time and settled to being the
boarder of Finola, who now hung onto her sons fiercely,
daring the lassies to come near those proudest possessions
of the Irish mother.

*

It was just after the corn harvest that the terrible letter
came from the president of the Baltimore Fire Fighters
Benevolent Association telling us that Ed had been killed
in the line of duty. Throughout the years we had grown to
a dear relationship and I'll never get over the fact I didn't
get to meet him again. Ed carried an insurance policy of
fifteen hundred American dollars which was left to me
on the condition that I use it for an education. His death
became my liberation.

My inheritance was the event of the year in Ballyutogue.
Can you imagine the advice I was getting? In came
Father Lynch with the face of a Lurgan spade and the
heart of a wet fortnight. Arguing with a tongue that could
curdle cream, he insisted that a liberal gift to the Church
(meaning himself) would win points with the Almighty.
The pressure became fearsome, with my ma encouraging
Father Lynch's intervention to push me into the seminary.

The money was more than enough to see me through
college, which I craved and thought I'd never live to see.
Conor demanded I stick to my guns and, thanks to God,
enough of the Larkin steel had rubbed off on me over the
years to enable me to make my stand. Things were still in
a state of monumental discussion the day Kevin O'Garvey
sent word that the money and papers had been received.
Enough heat was on to melt the skin off my back, but I
made the first defiance of my parents since the riot at
Bogside, coming to my entire height of five feet and four
inches and announcing, "I am going to Derry to consult
with Mr. Ingram."

It sounded more like a wake with the weeping and
wailing that followed.

"What on earth can you do with that education but become a priest!" my ma pleaded.

"I intend to become a teacher and perhaps a writer as well." There! I said it!

"But what of Father Lynch!"

"Father Lynch closes minds, I intend to open them."

Oh, my ma clamped her hands over her ears to hear no more of that and my daddy merely scratched his head till I thought he'd wear out his scalp. Even as I left for Derry they were both in St. Columba's praying for my immortal soul.

Mr. Ingram was headmaster of the largest school in all of Derry, and he and Miss Enid had two children of their own. I was never so proud as on entering his office and seeing the bookends we had given him right there on the shelf behind his desk.

The choice of schools was extremely limited. Trinity College in Dublin was an unobtainable dream. It had been an ascendancy institution for centuries and, even if a Catholic could get in, the bishops forbade it on pain of excommunication. Mr. Ingram advised me of a new Catholic college in Dublin run by Jesuits, but the curriculum was extremely limited for non-religious studies.

"It seems to narrow down to Queen's College in Belfast."

God, that sounded frightening. He put me through a series of tests that lasted almost a full day and after he evaluated them I went to his home. I could see by the worried expression both he and Miss Enid wore that the results were not good.

"You've kept up on your English and literature well enough but you're going to need quite a bit of private tutoring to make the entrance examinations. Knowing your capacity for work, I'd say you'll be ready after four or five months of penal labor."

Tutoring! My dreams went flying and the gravy ran out of me. "How much will all that tutoring cost?" I peeped.

"Do you still play the flute?" Miss Enid asked.

"Aye."

"How about two tunes a night?"

"I don't think I understand," I answered.

"I've had a hunger to teach since I've been stabled with the two children," she said. "We've a splendid attic room, grand for studying by day and daydreaming by night. We'll get you all plumped up and ready for Queen's, so go home and pack your things and let's get to work."

I bit my tongue and did everything I possibly could but I cried nevertheless and when I could talk again I said that I'd make them proud.

"You've done that many times already," Mr. Ingram answered.

* * *

The drinking brotherhood, virgins one and all except for Conor, who had done some fucking with Protestant girls, gathered for a last blow at Dooley McCluskey's. They told me not to break too many hearts in Derry and surely I would knock them dead when I got to Belfast. Me . . . Seamus O'Neill, the first college student in Ballyutogue's history. Make a million and buy the earldom from Lord Hubble . . .

. . . all except for Conor were done in with joy . . . he was hurting.

. . . my back was sore from all the slappings and my ears rang with huzzahs to beat the world. McCluskey sprang for a round of drinks, a rarity between wakes, then pointed to the clock. The stage to Derry would be due in the diamond soon . . .

. . . outside the pub and under the hanging tree we all fell all over each other one more time . . .

. . . then McCluskey himself held everyone back so's Conor and I could make the walk to the Township alone . . .

. . . and we did with no words between us and we waited in the diamond . . .

. . . and pretty soon, the stage came . . .

"Good-by, runt," he said, putting an affectionate head-lock on me, then slapped my bottom and pointed to the coach . . .

. . . am I ever to forget Conor Larkin standing there alone in the diamond as we clip-clopped away . . . just standing there . . . his hands shoved deep in his pockets . . . his cap on in its jaunty crooked way . . . looking out to that horizon where I was heading.

CHAPTER TWELVE: Liam entered the forge near quitting time. Conor waved to him, pulled a glowing metal from the fire, laid it over a hardie on the anvil and in a few moments had it beaten into the scooped-typed lazy bed digger preferred by most of the farmers of Ballyutogue. He ordered the apprentice boy to bank the fire and clean up the shop, untied his heavy leather apron and slapped Liam on the back.

Outside at the well, Conor dunked his face and assembled himself. Liam handed him a letter and watched his brother's face break into a grin as he ripped the envelope open.

"Aye, there's a lad," he said. "Seamus has passed all his tests for Queen's and has moved to Belfast to his Uncle Conan. I'll stop on the way home and read this to Fergus and Mairead." He folded it and shoved it into his pocket for rereading later. As he set to go, Liam seized his arm and held him in place.

"I was in Derry yesterday," Liam said with nervous speed. "I got the word from Kevin O'Garvey to come in and see him."

"About what?"

Liam plopped on the big rock by the wheelwright's hub band. He hung his head and nibbled at his lip.

"About what?" Conor repeated, sensing trouble.

"Do you remember when I went to Derry for the special wool marketing auction last year?"

"Aye."

"I went to see Kevin at the same time."

"About what?" Conor asked apprehensively.

"Suitable emigration. He's been looking into the matter for me."

Conor reacted like a snared rabbit with a jolt of fear shivering him and shutting his voice down. His eyes widened as Liam scooped up a handful of pebbles and pitched them out to the road one at a time. "I'll be leaving in a matter of days," he said.

"Why have you kept this a secret!" Conor snapped.

"It wasn't exactly no secret. Everyone knows I was up to emigrate. One minute I wanted it and one minute I didn't. I just didn't know how to make up my head on the matter, Conor. You know, I was just confused."

Even as Conor agonized he patted his brother's shoulder in understanding. The weight of it was like an anvil on his back and his mind continued muddled. "Where are you going, Liam?" he managed.

"New Zealand," Liam answered.

"New Zealand! You can't go there, man. It's too bloody far!"

"What difference does it make how far?"

"Oh no, you're daft, man," Conor said, seizing at the straw. "We've not the money to send you there, it's no good, no good at all." He paced and beat his hand into his fist, trying to find one more straw. "Call it off. Then we'll talk it over."

Liam shook his head, puzzled. "I can't. I've signed onto a scheme to work off my passage. They've large ranches in the southern half of the country and they need sheepmen, farmers and drovers. It will take two years to pay the fare but then I'll be in the clear. I hear tell there's land to be had, so in another two or three years after I work my passage, I might be able to buy some of my own."

"See there," Conor cried, "it's a bloody trick, like the famine ships. I'll not let you get into a scheme like that. Once they get you there you'll be working your passage for life ... that's it ... you can't go, Liam."

Still confused over his brother's seizure, he gestured to cut it off. "It's a legitimate plan. Kevin himself assures me of that. It was originated by a dozen Irish immigrants who've made it big and we're being supervised by the Church. Kevin has already sent three lads out of Derry and they're all starting to do well."

Conor knelt on a knee, deflated, and his eyes darted a bit wild. He knew he'd better calm down. There was only one way to go at it and none other. "New Zealand," he whispered.

"So much the better for my chances," Liam said.

"New Zealand," Conor repeated as though they were the heaviest words in the language. He looked up to Liam with deliberateness. "I'm putting something to you straight. I don't want you to go. I've my own trade and I'm earning almost as much as a carriage maker. Would you stay here if Daddy agrees to pass the farm to you?"

Liam shook his head. "Now it's you talking daft. You've got to know I've never felt ill of you because the land is rightly yours."

"But if Daddy were to agree."

"He won't, I know he won't."

"If he does,"· Conor insisted, "would you stay?"

"Aye," Liam answered as if in a sweet dream, "that's all I've ever wanted. Oh, holy Mother, I know every dear inch of every plot and every stone in every wall. Conor, I chill all over with fright when I think of going so far away. We never got to talking about it because I didn't want to get my hopes up, but there's a couple of lassies looking right good to me and I would be after courting one of them if only . . . oh, Conor, what the hell are we talking about? Tomas will never agree. Listen, you've got to know I hold no ill feeling to you."

Conor grabbed his brother's arms fiercely. "We're talking to Daddy, Liam, and we're going to make him see."

Liam backed away. "You'll have to do the talking. I could never face Daddy with it."

"I'll do it, I'll do it."

There·was a positive time Tomas entered his cottage and that was after the rosary was said and before supper was served. When Brigid, Dary and Finola got off their knees, the men came in. Supper was held in its usual silence.

"Are you going to make lace tonight, Brigid?" Conor asked as she cleared the table.

"I've no plans to."

"Go visit a girl friend . . . and take Dary with you."

"Oh, listen to himself," Brigid snipped back.

Brigid half jumped out of her skin as Conor's fist all but split the table. She'd never seen him act that way. As all their eyes interplayed, the sense of pending battle was obvious. "You'd best do what your brother says," Tomas said softly.

"Come along, Dary," Brigid said, "sounds like there's going to be a haymaker." She banged the door after herself deliberately. The three men sat in stone silence and Finola whined under her breath as she shuffled around the fire.

"Liam's leaving for New Zealand next week," Conor snapped.

"Oh, Mary save us!" Finola cried.

"Quiet, Ma," Conor commanded. He leaned over the table so that he was nose to nose with his father. "Daddy, I'm telling you to ask Liam to stay."

Tomas slurped at his tea.

"I'm an ironmaster and I'll not take the farm," Conor continued. "Now you tell Liam you want him to have it!"

Tomas drank again with deliberateness, set the cup down slowly, his eyes moving from one son to the other. "You'll not be making decisions that are mine to make," he said.

"And you'll not be making decisions that are mine to make!" Conor shouted.

"You're just saddened to see your brother leave. It's a part of our life none of us will really get used to no matter how many times it happens. How many nights I've lay awake crying to be able to keep the both of you. It's not the way in Ireland and it will never be so long as we're tenants in our own country."

"Tomas, be reasonable," Finola implored. "It's in your power to be reasonable. If you want both of your sons here you can keep them. Be reasonable, Tomas . . ."

"Reasonable! Who's unreasonable around here? The way you suffocate the air and hide the light from Dary."

"Dary's nothing to do with this!" Conor cried.

Tomas was up and shaking a fist at his wife. "He's fragile because you want him that way. Shut up, woman, or get out! This is between me and my sons!"

She shrank into a corner sobbing. Tomas heaved a sigh and went to Liam and patted his shoulder. "You understand how it's got to be, lad. I'll grieve for you."

Liam screamed and pounded on the table. "For me you'll grieve! That's a lie, Daddy! You love Conor! That's why I'm going to the farthest place on earth . . . because you love Conor! Liar! Liar!" He tore up the ladder and flung himself into the loft and Conor started up after him.

"Leave him be!" Tomas ordered.

Conor halted, then inched down the ladder and came to his father. His eyes looked up as the sound of his brother's anguished sobs reached them. In the loft great gobs of salt tears ran into Liam's mouth and down his chin.

Conor rose before his father. "I'll not have your fucking land!" he screamed.

Tomas reached for him but he jerked away. "I did it for you, Conor," Tomas begged. "You'll stay, lad, you'll stay . . . the devil you know is better than the devil you don't."

"And what about the devil Liam doesn't know!"

"It's his burden. He knows it. Ah, Conor, boy, you're the Larkin. You're the Larkin who's tall in every man's eyes."

"No, Daddy!" Conor rasped. "You've created a Conor who has never lived. I don't want to be that Conor! I'm me, goddammit, I'm me! I'm not Kilty or Tomas . . . I'm me and I've got to live!"

"Oh, listen, boy, I've done everything for the love of you."

Liam's sobs fell soft and weak now as his fingers clutched and released the hay. The two giants who cast their shadow over his life now spewed venom on each other.

On the same night, Conor Larkin left the cottage, never looking back over the crossroad. He stopped for a moment before Mr. Lambe's shop, fighting for control of his tortured mind.

"Conor!" wee Dary's voice called through the darkness. "Conor!"

He turned away quickly and continued down the road.

"Conor!" the voice pleaded again and again.

He stopped and listened as the tiny feet ran hard at him and the boy's arms wrapped desperately around his knees. Conor lifted him as he had done a thousand times over and he buried him in his mighty arms, then set him down gently and shook his head to say he was unable to speak and Dary nodded that he understood and Conor went on his way.

Dary entered the cottage. The look of him told Tomas and Finola everything.

"You'd better ask Liam not to leave," Finola said.

Tomas shook his head. "That would be so unfair to Liam," he said. "Liam knows he has to go. He's always known that. I can't ask him to stay because . . . when Conor comes back . . . everything must be ready . . . when Conor comes back . . ."

END OF PART THREE

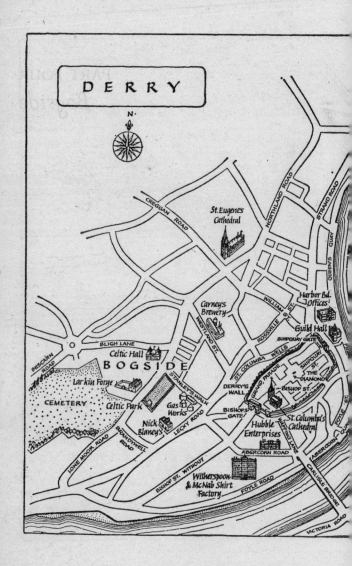

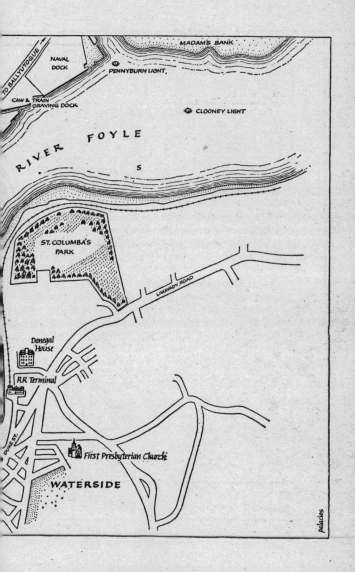

CHAPTER ONE: "Who's out there?" Kevin O'Garvey called from the second-story window.

"Conor, Conor Larkin."

In a moment Kevin opened the door of his fine new house on Creggan Road in Derry and held the lantern close. "Is that yourself? It's three in the morning, Conor Larkin, and you look the wrath of God."

A bleary-eyed, bearded wreckage followed Kevin into the parlor where he slumped, hung his head, drooped his arms between his legs and stared misty to the rug. Teresa O'Garvey followed her husband in a moment, buttoning up her dressing gown. She took one look at Conor and said, "Bring him to the kitchen."

The big stew pot was always at a simmer in the O'Garvey kitchen, for there was no telling who would come and when. She dished up a bowl and sliced him a half loaf of bread.

"Throw that across your chest," she said.

The heat of it burned deliciously all the way down. Conor coughed and slurped, trembling with hunger, and mumbled he'd not eaten in three, maybe four or five days. He'd been wandering aimlessly, sleeping in the fields. Three bowls later, the food took hold. Conor's story came out in bits and pieces at the kitchen table. Kevin eyed his wife in such a way as to tell her to leave them alone.

"Merciful God," she said as she left the kitchen.

Kevin paddled around getting tea together. "It had to happen," he said. "You've been brutalizing each other for years."

"I kept telling myself that Daddy would have to see it clearly sooner or later. I kept telling myself he'd change his mind and sit us down and talk it over and ask Liam to stay. As I was walking through the country, I tried to go back a thousand times and plead with him, but it would be no damned use. I've gotten better responses off a wall. Kevin, would you talk to him?"

O'Garvey took off his thick glasses and rubbed his eyes, then sugared his tea.

"You've got to do it before Liam's ship leaves, would you?" Conor repeated.

"I don't know," Kevin answered wisely. "Did you ever think things might be better for you away from Ballyutogue?"

Conor nodded, half ashamed that those were his thoughts indeed.

"It might solve things for Liam if he returned but it will never solve them for the Conor Larkin I know. It was never a matter of you leaving there, but only when."

"That's the worst of it," Conor said, "I know you're right. I know I can't go back."

"No, you can't. Liam's emigrating in a few days. Will you be following?"

"I'll not be driven out of Ireland," Conor answered.

"Look, you're done in, lad. Let's not think about it tonight. You know where the room is over the stable."

"Aye."

"I don't want you to rush. I'll be going to London for a session of Commons. Stay on and get your head cleared at least till I get back. Will you promise that?"

Conor said he would and, as he did, exhaustion flooded him so that his walk to the stable was uneven. He took the lantern and started up the ladder and whispered, "Thanks."

"For nothing," Kevin answered.

"I've hurt my daddy. I've hurt him bad."

From their bedroom window Teresa stood watching until the light from the stable quenched. "Poor lad," she said.

Kevin paced at the foot of the bed. "I ought to be used to watching them go by now. What an abortion of a people we are, sending away boys and girls like him by the thousands every year, leaving behind the weak, giving away our wealth. How many more can we afford to lose?"

"You're rambling, man," Teresa said. "The Larkins have always been too close to your heart."

"Aye, but it's what it's all about, Teresa. Parnell . . ." He quit as he choked on memory of the name. "Parnell and I would talk about it for hours. It all comes home to roost when you think of losing one like Conor."

"Perhaps we can keep him here somehow."

"We've got to. There's only so much we can keep giving up. Conor may make it. He'll not go down easy."

"Come to bed now."

He tucked the blanket about him but continued to stare up to the ceiling. Teresa reached over and took the glasses from his face and set them on the marble-topped stand.

"I wish Parnell were alive. There was always hope then. . . ."

*

Liam left the Harbour Board Office. Conor waited at the corner. He picked up Liam's battered wicker suitcase and they walked along for a bit. "Papers all in order?"

"Aye."

"Let's have a look." Conor opened the large envelope with documents covered with stamps, seals and ribbons. "Would you ever!" Conor said. "Rabat, Tunis, Alexandria, Suez Canal, Aden, Bombay, Ceylon, Jakarta, Perth, Melbourne and Wellington."

"Never heard of most of them," Liam said. "You have, haven't you, Conor?"

"In a manner of speaking. Seamus and I used to discuss them and we read a few books on the subject. Oh, they're exotic places and thinking you get to walk around in them and feel them and smell them and all. Man, you're in for a fantastic adventure."

"What do you know about New Zealand?" Liam asked with quivering voice.

"We never got much farther than Australia. However, I went to the library here. Actually, there wasn't too much on it. It seems to be a lovely land, from what I can tell. And the journey! You're a lucky one, Liam."

They turned the corner to Prince's Quay, then stopped in their tracks at sight of a rusty old tramp steamer, S.S. *Nova Scotia*. Liam got sick to his stomach, clutched it, went into a sweat, closed his eyes and turned and faced the wall.

His brother patted him but he was unfeeling of it. Conor looked desperately for hope beyond hope that Tomas would suddenly appear down the quay and call for them.

Oh, God, Daddy! Please!

"I'm so scared," Liam croaked.

"Only because it's new and unfamiliar. Ten minutes after you're under way, you'll be yourself again, and after two months aboard ship you'll be so ready to conquer New Zealand, there'll be no holding you back." He turned and spun into Conor's arms for the first time ever, shaking from head to toe as he did and sobbing incoherently. "Get ahold of yourself," Conor demanded. "You're not the first lad out of Ireland to walk up that plank."

He shook him, hard, then gentle, hard, then gentle. Liam turned loose and stared at the ship, wavering. He licked his lips, drew in a wobbly breath and began his walk into exile . . . over the quay as though floating. He showed his papers and was waved through. Teresa and Kevin were there as they had been there for many years at the dockside of weary ships. She packed a basket as she had packed it for many years with salted and dried foods to augment the ship's food on the journey. Their parting words were as uncomfortable as they had always been.

"I'm not mad at Daddy and I'm not mad at you," Liam said.

"God look after you, Liam," Conor said.

"And the same God look after you. I think I've come to know you may need him more than me," Liam said.

*

When Kevin left for Westminster, Conor began the search for a job.

"Your name?"

"Conor Larkin."

"I'll put you on the waiting list."

He went to the shipyard, the graving dock and the carriage makers, then walked the quays from Buncrana Road to the Letterkenny Road, the rail yard in Waterside over the bridge and stopped at every stable and shop with a forge.

"Your name?"

"Larkin."

"Sorry, the job has been filled."

"Look, I can see with my own two eyes your shop is short a man."

"Sorry, the job's filled."

Belief that his skill as a master would make itself apparent any place he found a job, Conor offered to start as an apprentice boy. He was advised that apprenticeships had to be purchased, the cost was high and, at any rate, none were available.

Within a fortnight the Derry system revealed itself ugly. Caw & Train Graving Dock was the major employer of blacksmiths and ironworkers. Its factory automatically won every municipal corporation bid and most private jobs without competition. This was the established order of things. Smaller forges were handed out subcontracts so long as they did what they were told. All of the shops from Caw & Train down to its smallest satellite were Protestant owned and manned. The only Catholic blacksmiths were tiny affairs in Catholic neighborhoods verging on subsistence level and never receiving Caw & Train subcontracts. The single major Catholic employer, a brewery, with its farrier and teamster work, kept the Catholic shops from sinking.

If a man's name was Catholic it automatically eliminated him from upper trade work. If the name wasn't obviously Catholic, a quick reference check of his church, school or Orange affiliation established his religion. Continuation of the Derry system was assured through the sale of apprenticeships which few Catholic families could afford and, if they could, the apprenticeship became unavailable.

After exhausting every possibility in his own trade, Conor searched for other work. Derry had a large complex of mills and shirt factories but nearly all of that was female and child labor.

The bottom line of the Derry system became unmistakably clear. The only work for Catholics was menial labor. Building trades had long waiting lists. Even those Catholic men with jobs had to have their entire families, wives and children, in the mills and factories to make existence.

What was left was janitoring, dustmen for garbage collection, sewer workers, servants, male nurses in workhouses and the insane asylum. Forty per cent of the Catholic men were unemployed. Fifty men pounced on every job opening. Odd jobs of a few days at the cattle pens on the dock and as navvies on the railroads did come

open but Conor refused to compete against men who had
families to feed.

This was the Derry system of Roger Hubble's conception.
Cheap female and child labor and a vast pool of unemployed so their product could compete with and undersell
England. As long as Ulster remained in the Crown's realm
and received beneficial trade concessions, it spelled a
windfall for her industry. Even though the labor pool was
depleted by emigration, Bishop Nugent and the dictates
of his Church saw to it that Derry retained the highest
birth rate in the British Isles and Europe. The stench
of the Derry system quickly led to human stagnation in
the Bogside, a succumbing to lethargy or the pain of emigration.

With each new day ending like the last, Conor walked
back to his room over the stable more and more slowly.
He sought the solace of the library but was unable to
concentrate and his frequent appearances there were met
with hostile vibrations. The library was no place to harbor
the idle and he was made to feel unwelcome.

A storm at sea damaged two ships which limped into
port in need of urgent repairs. For a fortnight Conor
was able to work at Caw & Train for sixteen hours a shift
and displayed a skill equal to all and superior to most of
the regular smiths. There were rumblings about the papist
in an all-Protestant stronghold but the size of him discouraged personal harassment and, besides, they reckoned,
the job was temporary.

Inside the yard, Conor saw the final vileness of the
Derry scheme. It was obvious that work was plentiful
and blacksmiths were in demand, but work was kept solely
for loyalists in payment for their loyalty and his employment came to an abrupt halt when half a dozen blacksmiths arrived on loan from the Weed Works in Belfast.

Conor's revulsion brought him close to the breaking
point only two months after his arrival. A mixed reaction
of relief and apprehension greeted Josiah Lambe on his
sudden appearance in Derry.

Josiah Lambe was a simplistic man who had worked
with and for Catholics. As a youth he divorced the populist notion that Ulster need be a battleground for the Reformation. Although his Presbyterian devoutness was rea-

sonable, his true religion was blacksmithing. He never wore an Orange sash.

By the time he was ready to wind down his labors it was rumored that Conor Larkin would come into the forge. This was bearable to the Protestants of Ballyutogue, for the Larkins, even as adversaries, had a certain eminence. There would be no objection from the single lassies about Conor's presence.

Josiah had meditated hard on the problem of Conor's sudden departure. He had hoped to retire with sufficient income from the shop to see out his remaining years, yet with Conor out of the picture he could not bring himself to sell to a stranger. Josiah traveled to Derry, found Conor, and got directly to the point, offering him the shop. He allowed as Conor could work off payment in a reasonable time and still earn a grand living. The deal was uncomplicated, for the old blacksmith was an uncomplicated man.

After the shattering experience of Derry, visions of the peaceful little forge below the crossroad among lifelong friends had crept heavily into Conor's thoughts. Yet even as he aired his confusion, he was held by an invisible grip that would not allow him to return.

"Why don't you seek some outside advice from someone you trust?" old Lambe suggested.

"Kevin is still in London. He wakes up every morning and goes to sleep every night with other people's problems. He doesn't need mine as well."

"I'm not suggesting O'Garvey, fine man that he is. He'll not be objectively inclined and even more so in your case."

"You're not telling me to go see a priest, are you?"

"Oh, nae, lad. A priest would be even worse. Conor, you've a bonny old friend in Derry who's a little hurt you've not seen fit to call on him."

Conor looked away guiltily.

"Well, are you afraid to speak to Andrew Ingram?"

"I've been tempted so many times. Back home the Larkins meant something, but here I'm just another jobless, faceless Bogside downer."

"You'd never be that in Andrew Ingram's eyes any more than you would be to me. Don't you think he doesn't know why you haven't called on him? Aren't you a bit ashamed?"

"Aye, I am."

"He said to me, 'Conor has to place more value on our friendship.'"

"You're right, Josiah, I am afraid. Afraid of being told the truth."

*

Enid Ingram hustled her children from Andrew's study, closing the door behind her. "They're great wanes," Conor said. "Seamus has written me about them many times."

"Just as Seamus has told them about you. You are a minor deity around here, you know."

"The lad is doing fine at Queen's," Conor said.

Mr. Ingram smiled and passed it off. "I think we all knew Seamus would cut a tidy niche for himself."

Conor's eyes became filled with pleading. "And me?"

Andrew Ingram stuffed his pipe with that certain deliberateness, showing a touch of sorrow as he did, and it seemed to outline telltale graying about his temples and the first deep lines of aging. He studied the brawny young man opposite him strangely, knowing so much about him.

"Certain of us are meant for certain things," he began. "I thank God I discovered at an early age and was able to make peace about myself within the narrow framework allowed to me. There's a book kept on all of us from the moment we're born. If only we could open it and really learn what's in store. The problem is it takes most of us most of our lives to understand what we should have known from the beginning."

"What's in store for me?" Conor asked.

"Well, you're not going back, Conor," he said with finality.

"I guess I know that now. But I'll not be driven out of this country, either."

"I'm painfully aware."

"Painfully, Mr. Ingram . . . just because I can't stomach the injustice?"

"Painfully, because you're going to spend your life trying to do something about it. There's nothing wrong with fighting injustice. It's only that, well, I'm trying to tell you what your father had tried to tell you."

"What . . ."

"So long as the voices ring in your ears you may never find peace."

Conor stood and waved his hands to say that was nonsense. "I don't know what book you thought you read on me, but you're mistaken."

"Am I?"

"But how can you know?"

"Conor, there's a certain moment in each man when he becomes completely alive. Alive like at no other time, when he lights the very sky with his vivacity. Of course some people lack that capacity and others don't seem to have it outside of the sex act. This fragment, this instant of electricity that strikes, is really you, your soul, your being. I sometimes feel it in me when I hear a magnificent actor reading Shakespeare. I become transformed, unique, complete. We're friends, Conor, I know I've seen that moment in you many times."

Conor paled. "Are you passing a sentence on me, Mr. Ingram?"

"No, but if you realize and accept, it may make it easier."

"Tell me what you read in the book, Mr. Ingram . . . tell me!"

"I read that Conor Larkin of Ballyutogue joined a small band of brothers because he had no real choice in the matter. They called any cot in any hidden peeling room their home. In the beginning he was fired up with slogans and an awesome sense of righteousness. Then, when blow after blow and disenchantment upon disenchantment rained down, the slogans became shadows without substance and, in the end, very little changed for all his efforts."

"Aw, you're daft, man, no such thing's been written for me!"

Andrew Ingram made no effort to reply for a time. His pipe soured and he set it down and his eyes moistened. "The day that Seamus left for Queen's, Enid and I talked the night through wondering whatever was to become of our two papist rebels. I marked a volume here that night and I said, 'Perhaps Conor will visit one day and ask me why things are as they are with him.' Would you like to see it, Conor?"

"The book of truth?" he whispered.

Ingram went to the shelves and withdrew one. A marker
was in it. He opened the page and spoke now, with a
voice rich from reading.

"Innumerable force of Spirits armed,
That durst dislike his reign, and, me preferring,
His utmost power with adverse power opposed
In dubious battle on the plains of Heaven,
And shook his throne. What though the field be lost?
And is not lost: the unconquerab'e will,
And a study of revenge, immortal hate,
And courage never to submit or yield,
And what is else, not to be overcome?"

He handed Conor the volume of *Paradise Lost* and Conor
opened it to the first page where it had been inscribed,
"For my beloved student, Conor Larkin, a soldier in dubious battle."

CHAPTER TWO: From the moment Liam and Conor
left, Finola's mind was ablaze, for the passing of the land
had to be seriously thought out. Tomas would not accept
that Conor wasn't going to return, but Finola knew it as
reality. In her eyes, both of her sons were gone and
should be considered gone forever. Dary was along his
way toward eventual priesthood, spending a great deal of
his time serving mass and otherwise in the vicinity of St.
Columba's.

This left Brigid to be considered as sole heiress. Plain,
religious, hard-working Brigid was toward her seventeenth
year and the object of many quiet discussions and subtle
plots by the circling hawks of mothers. There were a number of eligibles in Ballyutogue due to inherit land who
could do worse than marry the name and get the dowry
of a Larkin.

Putting two and two together, the answer always came
out to be Seamus' older brother Colm, who, in his late
twenties, was just the proper age among the younger
bachelors in line for a farm. It was completely logical to
Finola that the joining of Colm and Brigid and their two

farms should culminate a lifetime of neighborliness together. Total combined acreage would number over sixty and set them among the most prosperous Catholics in the district.

Yet it was a dicy subject, even between such close friends as Finola and Mairead. True to fashion, Mairead stood ready to claw out the eyes of any young thing who got too close to her Colm. If traditions were followed, Mairead would keep him a bachelor even if she became widowed in the event Fergus departed first. The idea of sharing her kitchen with another female was unthinkable. Nonetheless, Finola knew Mairead harbored deep and motherly feelings for her daughter and in the event of widowhood there would still be two cottages and things could be worked out so the women wouldn't get on top of each other. Finola inched into the matter gingerly. To her utmost joy she found her dear friend had been considering exactly the same matter on her own.

Fergus and Tomas knew the workings of their wives' heads. Besides, it took no particular genius to figure out what they were arranging. Both men gave tacit blessings to the matter. Tomas simply left the possibility of Conor's return unsaid.

Everything seemed to be proceeding in grand order except for a small detail. Brigid, a sweet and innocent lass, had no idea of the maneuverings and, never having been made a party to it, had germinated a few little seeds of her own.

For near on two years, what with Liam in the fields, Conor at the forge, and Dary being kept from menial tasks, Brigid had done the daily milking and carted it to the crossroad for collection. At the crossroad and under the hanging tree she met Myles McCracken, who was doing the same. The McCrackens had the smallest, poorest, stoniest, highest-in-the-heather farm in Ballyutogue. However, poverty did nothing to detract from Myles's good looks and in a way he reminded Brigid of her brother Conor.

Their eyes started seeking each other at the daily gathering and after a time they began to arrive at the crossroad earlier and earlier for, without truly saying it, they did so in order to be alone together. Conversation came haltingly, with neither of them relating their growing feelings. They always made certain the other would be attending a fair or ceilidhe and when an event such as a wake or wedding took place it meant they could spend hours together, however never relating their true and growing emotions.

Finola, ever on the alert, sniffed trouble over Brigid's anxiety to get to the crossroad each morning. One day she trailed her as far as St. Columba's where she slipped into the church and lit a few candles for her departed sons. From a vantage point alongside the confessional she was able to see the hanging tree and confirm her suspicions. They were mooning at one another like sick calves. Myles McCracken was the worst possible thing that could happen. The family was so poor they had to count the crumbs they threw to the birds. Myles was the middle of seven sons and wouldn't be inheriting so much as the skin off a potato.

"We'd better be having a talk with Brigid," Finola announced the very same evening to Tomas. "It's time we be thinking of making a suitable arrangement for her."

Tomas grunted a knowing breath. "I suppose you've given full consideration with whom such an arrangement should be made?"

"If your eyes could see farther than your pint, you'd know Colm O'Neill himself is seeking her favor."

"And I suppose you and Mairead have done all the preliminary groundwork?"

"And I suppose there is a better match to be had in Ballyutogue," she snapped.

"And I suppose you wouldn't be thinking of joining the farms, now would you?"

Finola knew she had to tread her ground carefully, for joining the farms meant acceptance of the fact that Conor wasn't coming back, something Tomas would never concede.

"No such thing," she said. "I'm considering the fact that they make a good couple and have known each other their entire lives. Well, are you for the match or not?"

Tomas flopped his arms. "Jaysus," he moaned, "I wish Colm weren't such a blister. He's a real bog swaddy. Does Brigid truly care for him?"

"What's that got to do with marriage?" she asked.

"It had something to do with us once," he answered.

Perhaps a twinge of memory stirred when he said that, but if it did she covered any feelings, pouring tea emotionlessly and pressing her case. "If you want to know who she likes, I'll tell you who she likes. She likes Myles McCracken."

"The tall streaker?"

"That's who indeed. There's a bad scant to the entire McCracken image. The whole family together has about as much meat on them as a pair of tongs."

Tomas didn't like that, either. He had been battling with devils of doubt since his sons left and wanted no more of another weighty decision. Myles McCracken did mean trouble.

*

Naïve as Brigid was, she could not help but pick up the vibrations around her. Visits on three consecutive nights by Colm unnerved her. He was an old friend, indeed, the oldest she had, but Colm could never be anything but a friend. Now he was making bumbling approaches so even their friendship was in jeopardy.

Brigid loved her brother Conor dearly but she knew in her heart he would never return and she began to harbor her own desires about the farm. Her initial caution became an unspoken determination. With the scent of conspiracy growing pungent, she vowed to take a stand on Colm O'Neill.

The young people of Ballyutogue plotted to get away from their parents and Father Lynch's eyes by covering each other's chores and acting as lookouts at the rendezvous points. The ruins of the old Norman keep had a perfect vista to all approaches and a single watchman could warn a dozen pairs of lovers with a simple bird call.

Myles waited at the footbridge just over the stream from the keep. She crossed to him and they held hands and kissed each other's cheeks, which was fairly minor among the sins, then disappeared into the ash grove.

"I've missed you, Brigid."

"And I've missed you."

"When your ma showed up at the crossroad with the

milk the last three days I knew she was getting suspicious."

"Nothing of the sort," Brigid lied. "I'm just doing some of the heavier work because she's had a bad back."

"Oh, that's good that she doesn't suspect," Myles said.

"Myles," she said sharply, "I want you to kiss me."

"Ah sure!" he answered, pecking her cheek.

"No. Kiss me on the lips."

"On the lips!"

"Aye, and hold me in your arms while you're doing it."

He held up his hands defensively and backed off. "My God, have you taken leave of your mind? It's very dangerous. We can get into all sorts of trouble."

"I checked with Abbey O'Malley. Her sister Brendt used to do it all the time before she married, even with Conor and Seamus."

"My God, suppose something happens?"

"Well, what could happen?"

"Well, you know."

"You can't get pregnant from kissing," she said.

"But it can lead to all sorts of things."

"Will you or won't you?"

"You're scaring the life out of me the way you're acting, Brigid Larkin."

She flung her arms about him, pressed her bosom close and kissed him fiercely on the mouth.

"Holy Mother!" He reeled back and sat open-mouthed on a large boulder.

"Didn't you like it, Myles?"

"Surely it's the grandest thing that ever happened."

"Then let's kiss some more."

In a relatively short time they got the gist of it. Myles's mind bent with excitement and his hands were touching her hair and her cheeks and her shoulders and even once or twice dared brush against her breasts. They felt sensations in their throats and stomachs and began emitting wild sounds and perspiring. It was Brigid who became fearful and broke it off and they stood gasping from it, so wonderfully confused.

"Are you furious with me, Brigid?"

"Oh no, no, no. I never knew anything could feel like this, even praying to the Virgin."

Myles waltzed around dizzily and stamped his feet. "We must be crazy."

"Do you think we went too far?" she asked.

"No, not that. I mean getting serious. We can't do that. There's just nothing I can do for you in this world."

"Myles McCracken, you listen to me. Maybe we ought not to get this aroused in the future, but I do want to keep seeing you."

"Whatever for? We're so bloody poor, I couldn't even give you the dirt off my neck, we'd need it for topsoil."

"Do you want to see me or not?" she demanded.

He hung his head. For an instant the life half drained from her. Then he lifted his eyes and sighed, "Aye."

Brigid ran over the footbridge, past the keep and never stopped till she reached the cottage out of breath.

"You're late," her mother greeted her. "The butter's not going to churn itself."

Brigid turned aside to conceal her gasping and blushing. "I'm sorry, I'll do it straightaway," she said, bee-lining for the byre.

"Brigid!" Tomas called.

She froze.

"Colm's to be calling on you tonight. He's meaning to take you on a ride in a hired sidecar after mass on Sunday."

There could be no mistaking what that meant! "I'm not feeling too well, Daddy. I'm coming down with the throat. I think I'd better be getting some rest."

"And I think you'd better be paying a little more mind to Mr. O'Neill," Finola said.

Brigid spun about and cracked out without thinking with the first defiant words against them in her life. "If you like Colm so much, you pay the attention to him." And then she became paralyzed at the sound of her own voice.

"You'll not talk to your mother that way," Tomas said.

"You might as well know," Finola said, "an arrange-ment is in the making."

"I'll have no part of it!" she cried, and fled into the byre.

Finola was up with a switch in her hand but Tomas blocked her way quickly. "It's that Myles McCracken!

He's never to set foot in this house! Tomas, you order her to break it off!"

A sense of fright over another disastrous interference with his children gripped him. Tomas released his wife and slumped down at the table.

"I'll not have that girl defying us! I'll put her in a convent first!" Finola shrilled.

Tomas shook his head. "No," he said softly.

"I'll see Father Lynch and I'll make them confess what they've been doing behind our backs!"

"No, you won't," he said softly. "She's to have her fling with the lad, it will do no harm."

"Are you mad!" His silence was becoming more confusing than words of anger. "Have you seen the number of girls who go to the altar every year with a baby in their belly?" she thumped. "Is that what you want!"

He looked up with a face filled with yesterday. "I want her to know the feeling of being in love," Tomas said, "if only once and if only for a little while. It might help later on to know that for one little time there was a boy desperate for her. She's got to have that much, woman, she's got to have that."

CHAPTER THREE: When Kevin O'Garvey was first elected to Commons he took a room at Midge Murphy's boardinghouse off Jamaica Road in one of London's "Irishtowns" close to the penetrating aromas and singing steel teamster wheels of the Surrey Commercial Docks and a short underground ride beneath the Thames to Parliament.

Little changed in his way of life during the first decade of Westminster. He graduated to the finest room in the Murphy house and was granted certain privileges that befitted his status. Midge was originally an Aran Island woman, slow in granting friendship, and ran a tight ship with life centering about the kitchen. Few were allowed to visit it except at mealtime, fewer still allowed to linger, and Kevin alone had "freedom of the kitchen." After supper he used an alcove by the larder as his office.

Otherwise, things were much the same. Kevin held

nightly court in a back booth at Clancy's Public House a few blocks away. The saloon was filled with the lust of Irish dockers where an endless line of countrymen sought his help. Since the death of Parnell, the Irish Party had become a watered-down affair bereft of its former sting, with O'Garvey one of the few remaining eminents in its ranks.

A Select Committee was voted into existence by Commons as the sludge of the Industrial Revolution filled the cesspool of abuses to overflowing. With the need of reform legislation growing urgent, the committee was charged to investigate labor conditions in the industrial areas. From the outset O'Garvey established himself as the dominant figure and placed Ulster on the investigation venue.

Their first hearings had been in the English Midlands in the Bradford-Leeds area. O'Garvey was chosen to write the draft report on their findings and rumor spread that it would be devastating. Apprehension in Ulster grew throughout the industrial community over their own pending investigation. Then came a shattering rumor that O'Garvey personally had chosen the Witherspoon & McNab Shirt Factory in Londonderry as his chief target.

Working late at night to complete the draft report, Kevin canceled his usual evening session at Clancy's Public House. A few days before the report was completed, one of the lads from Clancy's showed up in Midge Murphy's kitchen.

"There's a quare swell looking for you," he said, handing Kevin an envelope. It contained the calling card of Brigadier Maxwell Swan. He had fully anticipated a visit from the tensing Ulster industrialists and Swan was their likely agent. Swan would be particularly interested in keeping the committee away from Witherspoon & McNab because he was dividing his time these days between Belfast and Derry, setting up a labor spy system in the Hubble enterprises as he had done for Sir Frederick Weed.

Kevin gathered up his work, put it away in his room, refreshed himself at the basin, then put on his tattered jacket and walked to Clancy's. The Brigadier's carriage was at curbside.

As he entered, the tone was unusually subdued, with

obvious curiosity over the bald man with the military bearing waiting in Kevin's personal booth. Everyone pressed forward at the bar in order to get a glimpse in the back-bar mirror.

Swan indicated that a confidential discussion might be better held elsewhere and in a moment they drove off, coming to a halt at nearby Southwark Park, then, taking to foot, strolled along the park's edge in the damp and fogging night air. They came to a stop at a park bench and sat.

"We appear to be out of earshot of our mutual informers," Kevin said.

Swan rested both hands on the knob of his cane and looked blandly out to the mounting, eternal fog. "We have to remind ourselves from time to time that Lord Roger is one of your constituents and has the same right to petition you and express his view as anyone else."

"That's a fact," Kevin answered, "but I usually don't meet my constituents on park benches."

Swan smiled steelily and touched the cane to his hat in a salute. "Obviously, we are concerned with the Select Committee's pending visit to Ulster." He proceeded to build an articulate case. Industrial Ulster had invested heavily and wagered everything on the linen power loom. With America fully recovered from the Civil War, cotton was again in direct competition with linen. Linen was a squirrelly market at best, and anything that endangered it undermined Ulster itself. An investigation of the Witherspoon & McNab Shirt Factory, now the largest in the United Kingdom, could set up a fatal shock effect over the entire linen industry. "We think it is in Ulster's interest if the Select Committee keep out of Belfast and Londonderry and away from linen."

"You're talking hogwash, Swan. You're afraid of exposure of your very filthy operations, nothing more."

Swan had suspected O'Garvey's intransigence in the argument. "Let me make a few practical points," he said, changing course. "Point number one," he said, still looking off into space, "Witherspoon & McNab employs over a thousand Catholic women. It is the largest single employer in Londonderry. Along with the other shirt factories, it is the backbone of the economy."

"Point number one is correct," Kevin said.

"Point two," Swan continued. "That factory is Lord Roger's largest single profit maker. We are in a headlong race to make our gamble in power looms pay off. Any investigation and subsequent legislation that would bring profits down to a marginal operation would lead us to close down. The economy of Londonderry would collapse and a depression would follow."

Kevin O'Garvey shook his head in disbelief and laughed. "Sure I don't believe what I'm hearing. You know we investigated six factories in Bradford-Leeds and all six factory owners told us the same damned thing. Either let them bleed the workers or they'll shut down. Take your blackmail elsewhere, man. So long as there's a ha'penny in it, you'll operate."

"Suppose I can show you figures to prove we can't stand heavy capital expenditures and stay in business."

"Then close down. You've no call to operate on the premise you've a right to take it out of your employees' guts. Conditions in Bradford-Leeds are filthy enough but they don't start to compare to those slimy, tubercular, deafening, rheumatic linen mills, and what really terrifies me is the Witherspoon & McNab building. It's no more or less than a seven-story unlighted bomb. You've no right to make your shirts monogrammed in human blood, no right at all."

Maxwell Swan remained utterly impassive. "Well now," he said, "we've both stated our points of view. Let's examine some practical aspects."

Kevin knew he was dealing with an icy number who hadn't begun to shoot his ammunition. Swan's surgery in breaking up union organizing threats had been hangman efficient. As he studied Swan he throbbed to bring his own anger under control.

"Now then," Swan went on, "the Select Committee comes to Londonderry and conducts its investigation. A scathing report is issued with recommendations for corrective legislation. What do you suspect we are going to be doing in the interim?"

"Threaten to close down until that bluff is called, then threaten the workers against testifying."

"Yes, more or less. We'll fight you every inch of the way. Any new bills you manage to get through Commons will come after one, two, three years of arduous and bitter battle. In such situations it will come through as a watered-down compromise and in the end it will be the kind of law we can easily circumvent. In other words, count on us to go the limit to protect our properties."

"Oh, Lord," Kevin said, "the dirty scheme Hubble and Weed have laid out for Derry. Everything on two distinct levels. The top level supplies enough good jobs to hold a loyal population in your sacred city. The bottom level is a manipulation of human beings as so many head of cattle. Instead of putting new industry into a place where thousands are jobless, you deliberately keep it impoverished and leave us scrambling like famished dogs so we literally beg to slave in your death traps for pennies."

"That's a way of looking at it, rather extreme, O'Garvey. There is an order of things, a system long established. The inheritors of that system aren't just going to chuck it all away. Do you really believe Bogside won't be Bogside fifty years from now? Do you really believe that a few piddly little laws are really going to change things?"

"That's what you people said about the Land League," Kevin retorted. "I've not spent my life in vain because we've bloody well changed the system on the land and we'll change it in your dirty factories as well."

"In your lifetime?" Swan asked.

"That doesn't matter."

Swan flipped his cigar on the walkway and poked it out with the tip of his cane. "Suppose you had an opportunity to change things in Bogside right now?"

Kevin tensed.

"Shall I go on?"

"I'm not on the make if that's what you're fishing around for."

"Good Lord, I wouldn't be foolish enough to try to bribe you."

"And why not? Your people have tried to bribe every man in the Irish Party and not without some notable success."

Swan managed a smile. "Shall I go on?" he repeated.

"Yes, but I very well might get up and leave."

"You, Frank Carney and Father Patrick McShane formed a Bogside Association a few years back in an attempt to finance small business and things of that nature. It fell flat."

"Because you fought us out of fear of Catholic competition."

"Whatever. Suppose the association were refinanced and a private accord made so that several new enterprises could be sponsored in the Catholic community. Further, suppose you could buy, say, fifty apprenticeships a year and it was guaranteed to you the apprenticeships were available. What kind of effect would it have in Bogside? What is your most desperate need? Pride? Dignity? Male labor?"

Kevin O'Garvey was stunned. He had expected almost anything to keep the committee out of Londonderry but not this. Bogside, the mother of desperation where men wallowed without hope and nothing ever really was done to dent the poverty or create self-esteem. What Maxwell Swan had diabolically concocted was a crumb of hope. Yet how urgently was that crumb needed?

What was the alternative? Kevin knew that he would be in for years of trench warfare in which he would pit himself and his diluted party against an all-powerful system operating in their own halls of justice. If he did take up the battle for industrial reform the outcome was beyond his lifetime.

Was it a bribe or was it not a bribe to take money in order to give hope where no hope lived? What was the price? He knew that abominations like Witherspoon & McNab would go on regardless. His fight in the Land League was an ancient one that had kept Ireland in a blood bath for centuries. How dearly they had paid for the successes. The war for industrial reform would be even more bitter. Indeed, could one man do much more than give a ray of hope to his desperate people?

Swan had all the answers, all right. After clearing the Bogside Association debts there would be money coming under the table for several years to support small businesses and buy apprenticeships. Why in the name of God couldn't this support come from simple human need? Why in the name of God did the price tag keep women and children in sweatshop labor? Why? Because that was where the profits were. Why? Because that was the Derry scheme, the Ulster scheme, and any hint of assistance to Catholics was not permitted. It had to be kept secret at all costs.

Kevin O'Garvey agonized for three weeks, alternately torn by visions of the putridity of the mills and the bedlam aspects of the shirt factory. These visions struggled with visions of despair in the eyes of his Bogsiders, tormented eyes that tore at his soul every day of his own life. Whose voice wailed louder? Hope . . . now! Hope now! HOPE NOW!

The House of Commons Select Committee on Industrial Relations traveled to Ulster on the recommendation of Kevin O'Garvey of the Irish Party. They visited neither Belfast nor Londonderry but the mill town of Ballyomalley, an advanced experimental town established by Quaker interests. There they found the best working and living conditions in the province and Ballomalley was eventually cited as a shining example of Ulster's progressiveness.

CHAPTER FOUR: An oasis in the forlorn morass of Bogside was Celtic Hall, the activities emanating from it and the nearby recreation grounds. The Gaelic Athletic Association, reviving the old Celtic sports and, with them, a touch of national pride, spread over Ireland beyond expectations. Bogside, in particular, had been a place of poor little Irish vainglory. Hurling and Gaelic football drew packed crowds on the dusty playing grounds each Sunday after mass.

Several years after the GAA, an urban and sophisticated counterpart, the Gaelic League, came into being, spearheading a renaissance of the ancient language and culture.

The organizations were legal but everyone knew the GAA and the Gaelic League fronted borderline republican activities in the climate of discontent. Their glorification of Irish history and Irish dissenters ran counter to the centuries-old British attempt to Anglicize the colony. These scents of Irish nationalism were considered dangerous by the Crown as a spawning ground for future Fenian agitators and their activities and more vocal members were kept under scrutiny.

Small wonder that Conor's frequent appearance at the

League's sparse library was greeted at first with suspicion.
A brawny stranger like himself could well be a member
of one of the special squads in the Constabulary or Dublin Castle assigned to infiltrate their ranks. One had to be
constantly wary of informers, the lepers of Irish life.

Conor had exhausted every possibility for a job and
wanted to move on. Teresa O'Garvey sensed it and communicated with her husband in London and he, in turn,
wrote Conor reminding him of his promise to remain till
he returned from Commons. While he waited, Conor
drifted to those places where idle men congregated to
make idle talk. They were men like himself, now down to
the last ha'penny, so that even the small comfort of a brew
was a luxury.

After his daily trip to the Gaelic League library he'd
hang around the playing fields watching practice. The
regularity of his presence brought about the usual protective inquiries and it was only then discovered he lived
with Kevin O'Garvey. Once safe credentials were established he was accepted with nods of recognition.

* * *

"Hey, you, big fellow."

"Me?" Conor asked.

"Aye, we're short a man for practice. Would you be
after standing in as mid-fielder?"

"Afraid I don't know very much about the game."

"Have you played it before?"

"A few times only."

"You'll do for practice."

Conor had played some soccer football, which the Scots
introduced to Ulster, and a few games of Gaelic as well. He
was strong enough for sure and a hard runner. A pivotal
part of the Gaelic game required brute strength within a
pack of men where one had to leap higher, grab the ball
and be able to hold onto it with surety. It is said the game
was old as Patrick and the patron saint may well have had
Conor in mind as a mid-fielder. Like most farm lads, he
could leap stone walls like a deer as soon as he was able
to walk, and with blacksmith's hands for grip and over-all
might of body, his raw material at six foot and two inches
and two hundred and fifteen pounds was formidable.

No sooner had Conor stepped out on the field than a

blue-shirted regular sprinted upfield directly at him with the ball. The forward stopped, threw out a cunning hip and leg fake, then tried to dance past. Conor was twisted off balance by the maneuver but managed to grab ahold of his blue shirt, snatch him off his feet and bounce him to the ground thumpingly in a most effective, if unscientific, tackle. The runner went one way and the ball went the other as he crawled around on hands and knees gasping for air. He staggered to his feet and walked up to Conor shaking his fist.

"You stupid bastard!" he screamed. "It's only practice!"

"I'm sorry. Did I do something wrong?"

"You like to killed me, that's what, you dumb shit." The man reeled off, still shaky, then stopped and returned. "Hey, I'm sorry, man," he said, holding out his hand. "Just a bit stunned, you know. The name's Pat, Pat McShane."

"I'm Conor Larkin. Didn't mean to be so hard."

"Not at all. I'll buy you a brew at Nick Blaney's after practice."

Cooey Quinn, coach and manager of the Bogsiders, observed the Larkin lad keenly as he seemed to pick up the game by the minute. Cooey had been in the GAA from the beginning, one of Derry's greatest Gaelic footballers, a bandy-legged speedster. After quitting as a player he had built the Bogsiders into a regional power. His years in the sport did little to line his pockets, for it was an amateur sport played for pride with overtones of nationalism. He made for Conor the instant practice was called.

"Hello, big fellow, I'm Cooey Quinn."

"Sure I've heard of you," Conor said, introducing himself.

"How much have you played?"

"Three or four games at most. We mainly played association football up on Inishowen with the Protestant teams."

"You in Derry for a while?"

"Aye."

"I think you'd make a hell of a mid-fielder. If you come out for practice I'll see to it personal that you get some coaching on the finer points."

"That's grand of you but I'm hunting for a job."

"You'll not find one here, so you might as well get some training." Cooey studied Conor's size hungrily, then edged close and spoke in confidence. "Frankly, there's a bob or two to be made on the side."

"How?"

"Some of the swells around put down wagers on us and if we win . . . well, you know . . ."

"That's sure not the way I figured on earning a living," Conor replied.

"Unless you got something better to do, why not give it a go?"

Conor shrugged. "Why not?"

"Good, come on over to Nick Blaney's and meet the lads."

The establishment of Nick Blaney was Bogside's finest, all done up proper with tile floors and highly polished mahogany and a mirrored backbar lettered with a show of local chauvinism, CARNEY'S DERRYALE, a pretender to the throne of Guinness. Nick was of the sporting crowd, a boxer who had once been number three middleweight in the entire United Kingdom. Except for getting caught cold by a lucky punch, Nick explained constantly, he'd have gotten a shot at the championship. There were a lot of regulars at Blaney's, men with jobs and small businesses. The athletes were their alter egos and they were always willing to fill up a player's glass.

"Look at the size of you," Mick McGrath said, looking every inch the star of the Bogsiders, oaken built and sure of himself. He stuck out a strong hand of greeting. "How much do you weigh, Larkin?"

"I don't know for sure. I think maybe over fifteen stone."

"By Jaysus, that's just what we need," Mick said.

"I can vouch for the fact he hits like a runaway beer wagon," Pat McShane said from the fringe of the gathering. Conor looked over to him. He turned crimson. Pat McShane wore a Roman collar.

"Mary save me," Conor mumbled, "I've gone and busted up a priest."

With introductions done, Conor got over to Father McShane, still chagrined. The priest rather enjoyed his embarrassment and broke into a smile revealing a pair of missing teeth that indicated someone had gotten to him long before Conor.

"I don't understand this, Father," Conor said.

"I've studied all the holy Scriptures and nowhere could I find a single word forbidding a priest to play Gaelic football."

"But Bishop Nugent. Doesn't he get furious?"

"Only when Bogside loses."

Never having met such a priest, Conor continued to stare puzzled but Pat McShane had seen them come from the country before. The father was cut out of another mold than the indifferent and middling fodder that filled the seminaries. He had come from new wealth in the south and was schooled at Cambridge for two years before his decision to enter the Church.

In the next days the comradeship between them became instantaneous, for the two were both strangers of sorts to the world of Bogside. They quickly found that there were poetry and literature to bind them. If Bogside priests were of another breed than the dogmatics Conor had known, Father Pat was different, even among them. On the secret, he was the guiding light of the Gaelic League and when Conor was invited to a meeting it spelled his happiest day in Derry.

*

Lookouts were posted at every approach to the abandoned stable on Lone Moor Road. Only when an all clear was given did small groups of twos and threes filter in. They were young, poor and shabby and to Conor's surprise nearly half were girls from the mills and shirt factories. Once in the stable, they made up the ladder to the loft where heavy burlap shut the light to the outside. The dimness inside made one barely visible. They spoke in low, controlled tones, yet there was an air of excitement and defiance.

Conor had come with Mick McGrath and Cooey Quinn and was greeted with silent handshakes and nods of the head as he was introduced around.

Maud Tully, a snip of a lass with great brown eyes, called for attention. "Gather in close," she said, "so's I don't have to talk so loud." The thirty-odd who packed the loft formed a sitting circle around her. "Father

Pat just sent word he was called to the bedside of a
critically sick parishioner."

A groan of disappointment went up.

"He said he'd get here as soon as possible. In the meantime I'm suggesting we start a discussion about the subject
for tonight, Theobald Wolfe Tone."

They looked disappointedly to one another. Conor had
brought along his autobiography of Wolfe Tone when
Father McShane told him about the lecture. He held his
peace.

"Doesn't anyone know enough about Wolfe Tone to
begin?" Maud said.

As she was again met with a rumble of dejection, Conor
raised his hand tentatively.

"It seems we have a crack of luck," Maud said. "Our
new brother, Conor Larkin, has volunteered. Why don't
you come up here, Conor?"

He got up from the floor and moved through them
over a buzz of curiosity. His bigness was all the more
apparent in the closeness of the loft. Maud pointed to the
box to sit on and as he did they gathered in tightly. In
that magic instant, he saw them all as Conor and Seamus
sitting brightly at the feet of Daddo, eager, hungry to
learn.

"I hope you don't think I'm presumptuous," he began.
"I could never give a talk the likes of a learned man such
as Father Pat." He reached in his pocket and took out the
small volume entitled, *The Life and Adventures of Theobald Wolfe Tone written by himself and extracted from his
journals. Edited by his son, William Theobald Wolfe Tone.*

"To begin with," Conor started, "we've a history in
our republican aspirations of a number of patriots who
came from the Protestant ascendancy. It is a tradition
from Robert Emmet, Napper Tandy, Henry Joy Mc-
Cracken, Thomas Davis, Isaac Butt, as well as the very
founder of this Gaelic League, Douglas Hyde. Two of
these Protestants were as important to Catholic emancipation and Irish longing for freedom as the liberator,
Daniel O'Connell, himself. I refer to Charles Stewart Parnell, whose loss has never been recovered, and tonight I
will speak to you of the father of all Irish republicans,
Theobald Wolfe Tone."

The room had been struck to a hush.

"Wolfe Tone was born in Dublin on the twentieth of June in the year of seventeen and sixty-three," he continued with a voice not quite comfortable in its task. Yet Conor felt the instantaneous communication from those arrayed at his feet. From uneasiness he moved to a strange sensation of power, for their eyes and ears were riveted to him and he was quickly gaining their minds. Suddenly all of his years of listening to the tales of Daddo and his conversations with Andrew Ingram and all the books he had read in the fields and under the candle began to weave that unique Irish magic into his words and he drifted into touches of fantasy and spice and humor. Conor was in the sudden moment the shanachie and the story came from him as though he had been there himself.

By line, verse and chapter he traced the turbulent career of the first of the great patriots: the vow at Belfast to unite Ireland, the flight to America, the influence of the French Revolution, the intrigues in Paris to gain support, the storm at sea that destroyed the French fleet, the second futile invasion try in Lough Foyle, capture, condemnation, the death sentence . . . suicide.

The eyes of Conor's galvanized audience were misted and their cheeks wet, to a person.

Dead silence followed for a long time.

"Bravo!"

Everyone turned to see Father McShane, who had come up unnoticed and witnessed the last of the mesmerizing performance.

*

"One last round, gentlemen, if you please," Nick Blaney said.

Conor wanted to talk the night through with Father Pat but Cooey Quinn and Mick McGrath were slapping his back, introducing him around and blowing hot air like a tread bellows. "Aye, it was a night," Cooey repeated for the umpteenth time, "everyone is in high spirit. Now if youse can learn to play football the way youse got the gift of gab you'll be the unofficial mayor of Bogside, Conor Larkin."

"That is definitely so," Mick agreed.

"I hope not, it's a curse in my family," Conor said.

"Gentlemen, gentlemen," Nick Blaney pleaded.

From the mustiness of Derryale the four stepped out into the odors and sounds of poverty that lingered like an incurable rash. Father Pat stopped suddenly as though he were afraid to walk through it one more time. The stray drunk urinated at the base of the sacred walls, the vile sound of domestic rancor stung the air, bringing on a discordant cry of an infant who was more than likely hungry as well as frightened. They made babies in the dark, more babies for their numbers than any place in the kingdom. Babies to eat pork scraps and work the shirt factory, babies to pitch ha'pennies against the wall, babies to grow old and wait to die in bare monklike cubicles.

Father Pat gripped Conor's arm for an instant to steady himself. "If there was only something we could do," he whispered.

"I'm breaking out of here one day," Mick said.

Conor nodded.

"Sure," Cooey said, "that's what youse all say."

"Mind my words, I am."

"Going our way, Father?" Conor asked.

"I've got to check on my parishioner. I'm afraid he'll get away tonight."

Conor and Mick watched Cooey and Father Pat disappear down the muddy street of doll-size row houses as a choir of starving cats shrieked their discontent, then turned up their collars against the chill and made up Lecky Road. The wall of Derry hovered above them, bearing its omnipresent column and statue of the Reverend George Walker with finger pointed into the half-moon, the constant guardian who scorned the dregs down in Bogside.

"Cooey thinks I'm going to rot here, he's crazy. Only trouble is there's just about nothing I can do."

"No skills at all, Mick?"

"I was a butcher's apprentice once, nothing much other than that. I waited four years for an opening in the building trades but it came to naught . . . but you mark my words, I'm not going down in this place."

Mick jerked his head to steal a glance over his shoulder.

"Shit, Conor," he whispered, "we've been followed from Blaney's."

Conor looked back. A pair of constables behind them slowed down, then inched up toward them.

"Somebody's put the finger on you already," Mick said.

"What for?"

"The talk you gave tonight. I bet they figure you're an agitator from Dublin. Now listen, we hit the end of the block, split up and run for it."

"Can't," Conor said. A second pair in plain clothes holding batons in their hands approached from their front so they were boxed in. Mick took off his belt from his trousers and wrapped it around his fist, leaving the big brass buckle dangling loose as a flail, and at the same time bent down and snatched up a stray paving stone. He nudged Conor and in unison they turned around and ran straight at the two pursuers, catching them off guard.

Conor blocked the baton with his forearm as Mick sent the buckle splaying into the policeman's face. He screamed, clutching the rip that ran from eye to mouth, and dropped to his knees. Mick put him down and away with the paving stone.

The second constable jumped Mick and caught him two, three times with his baton and he dropped and, as he stood above him, Conor slammed him between the eyes. Conor tried to extricate Mick from the tangle of bodies but before he was able the second pair reached them and he was pounded to the ground by hissing batons.

"Fenian bastards!"

As Mick struggled to his feet a boot slammed into his stomach, choking off his breath. He gagged and vomited. Conor reeled up, struggling back to ward off the rain of blows, half of which found his face and ribs. He sagged away but as they turned on the fallen Mick McGrath a rage welled up and he returned, driving his fist into an attacker's belly so hard it lifted the man off his feet. He pulled Mick to his feet. The lad's front was covered with blood and vomit. Conor held one arm about him and the other fist stuck out warningly at the remaining constable, who looked at his three semiconscious mates, started as if to attack, then turned and fled as Conor dropped Mick and squared off to face him.

Lights and shouts went up and in an instant the Bogside was alive with police whistles.

The Constabulary attempted to hush the matter as they

did with all matters concerning Gaelic League suspects, but the hospitalization of three constables was the talk of Bogside. The assortment of broken noses, cracked ribs, stitches and missing teeth in the three-minute encounter was awesome. A face-saving story was leaked that the policemen had been jumped by a gang of a dozen ruffians.

So far as the authorities were concerned, the incident was officially closed, but it did not die among the Bogsiders, who knew what had really taken place.

CHAPTER FIVE: For several months after Kevin O'Garvey returned there was a flourish of new businesses financed with loans from a suddenly revitalized Bogside Association. A bakery, two pubs, a draying service, a ropemaking plant, a print shop and a cottage industries retail store were all launched with ceremonial fanfare.

In addition, a dozen new apprenticeships were strangely available at the shipyard, the fishery, and in the rail roundhouse. These were sold for the first time to Catholics and financed by the Bogside Association. A sliver of light had penetrated the gloom, and since as far back as one could remember, a few men walked about with an air of briskness.

Frank Carney, the flamboyant member of the association's three-man board, gloried in his role as benefactor. He was Derry's most successful Catholic, owner of the brewery and a wheel in municipal politics. He displayed his success visibly with brocaded vests, waxed grooming and gold wherever possible on watch and chain, cuff links, rings, teeth. Carney's self-esteem was bottomless, for he had come up the hard way through Bogside. Although many of his dealings were questionable, he maintained loyalty to his own and devotion to his Church.

Father Pat McShane, the youngest and second member of the board, merely blessed the new Bogside enterprises and sent them on their holy way, leaving the showmanship up to Carney.

The Bogside's most ardent champion had been Kevin O'Garvey, just as he had been the most tireless worker for the Land League. Yet Kevin seemed to get little joy

from the burst of activity. Conor noticed right off that
during his absence something had changed in Kevin's
very essence, from outgoing to suddenly withdrawn. He
and Father Pat talked about it and concluded that the
years of turmoil were taking a toll and perhaps Kevin
was aging, a thing they didn't want to believe. Conor was
not so sure of the real cause, but he knew that his friend
was not himself.

When Conor was summoned to the Bogside Association
Board in Celtic Hall and told to work up a set of figures
to finance a blacksmith shop, it was a crack of a miracle,
for he had been prepared to move on. After his astonishment at the sudden turn of events abated he dived into
the matter and found the abandoned stable on Lone Moor
Road suitable and cheap to house a forge and reckoned
he could save greatly by making most of his own tools.

Yet there was a problem. Conor wanted a loan several
times higher than had been granted to the other new
shops. There had long been need for a first-class forge in
Bogside and he envisioned something more than just another smithy. He wanted not only a place capable of doing
ordinary work and turning out a line of hardware, but
also to go after his calling in the field of decorative
wrought iron.

Father McShane and Kevin O'Garvey agreed after only
minor balking and budget trimming. It was Frank Carney
who blew through as the enthusiast. He had long been
chief sponsor of the football and hurling teams and, after
all, Conor Larkin was a rising sporting figure. The forge
should become the Bogside Association's showpiece, he
reckoned. Some deep breaths were held but the loan
went through.

Business was reasonable from the start. Mick McGrath
and two other lads from the team were given the first
real jobs of their lives as apprentices. Conor was eager to
get going on his hardware but was hampered because his
men were novices and there was a complete shortage
of skilled Catholic ironworkers. He reached across the
River Foyle and hired a Protestant, Tippy Hay, as his
foreman to run things and train the apprentices while he
turned full time to develop product.

Tippy was an excellent craftsman, too old and slow

to go full time for the Caw & Train Graving Dock where he had labored for thirty years. He was given enough work to keep alive in peak seasons but had otherwise come to lean times and had gone heavily to the bottle. The man proved so grateful for the second chance, he moderated his tippling enough to carry out a decent day's work and proved to be an excellent teacher.

Tippy was called back to Caw & Train on one of the periodic emergencies from a ship disaster and told Roy Bardwick, the dock director, to stuff it.

A few weeks later he was found unconscious in the street and was hospitalized. The first rumor had it that the devil's brew had finally gotten to him but physical evidence of a severe beating changed that story to say it was the work of an avenging gang of Catholic thugs. Tippy refused to name his assailants. It was not until several months later he blurted out in a drunken stupor that his old mates at Caw & Train and lodge brothers in the Orange Society had warned him to quit Larkin's shop. When he refused, an example of his disloyalty was required. Notice was posted that Conor Larkin would be tolerated only so long as he kept his proper place.

Unable to find a suitable replacement, Conor doubled his own workload to some eighteen hours a day and eventually put out a line of wares: claw hammers, files, knives, axes, adzes, augers, bits, reamers, hinges, nails, scissors, latches, bolts, doorknobs, weather vanes, wagon and tack hardware, shovels, tongs, cranes and what the women used in their kitchens. The quality was the best in Derry and the price lower, but Conor was unable to place his goods in the better retail stores outside the Bogside. He sold on the premises and, despite a tacit boycott, Protestants began to trickle in, for saving money was nonsectarian and an old Scottish trait.

"Try at Larkin's, you might find it there."

"Larkin will make anything up for you special and the price will be right."

Sheer excellence expanded his reputation so the trickle became a steady stream. There were growls of wariness over the same Conor Larkin who had been involved in a known Fenian activity and perhaps a scuffle with the Constabulary, yet his success grew moderately.

At the end of his first year, Mick McGrath and the other
two apprentices had moved up several notches to take on
responsibility for some of the less skilled aspects of the
trade. Of the other two blacksmiths operating in the Bogside, one died and the second, old Clarence Feeny, sat
down with Conor and figured he could make out better as
the Larkin foreman than on his own. When he came in
Conor inherited all of Frank Carney's brewery work, which
encompassed the stable, teamster wagons and considerable
barrel making. Clarence Feeny's son became one of two
new apprentices and soon a dozen men were employed,
including a salesman and a draying service.

With old Clarence there to move along the day-to-day
work, Conor was free to pursue his longed-for goal in the
wrought-iron field.

Frank Carney opened the way by commissioning a
grille and gate for the private chapel he endowed in St.
Eugene's Cathedral. The work proved so lovely that
Bishop Nugent himself ordered a wrought-iron pulpit,
the first in that part of Ireland. Following Bishop Nugent's
lead, a series of commissions followed from churches as
far east as Limavady and as far west as Ballyshannon.
Conor didn't particularly like the church work, for he
envisioned a lot of Father Lynches taking it out of the egg
money of the parishioners, but there was no way he could
turn it down.

Entering his second year, the forge had made a small
but definite inroad. This was even more apparent as a
number of the Bogside Association's other businesses had
folded.

Life was tolerable in Derry if one were Conor Larkin.
He entered a small, select, non-sectarian circle of intellectuals based around Andrew Ingram, Father Patrick
McShane and the faculty at Magee College. A reasonably
decent cultural life was imported under the sponsorship
of the Countess of Foyle, Lady Caroline Hubble.

In the Bogside, Conor had become a well-known figure
in the Gaelic League and on the GAA playing grounds.
From crude technique, Cooey Quinn and Mick McGrath
brought him up to a savagely effective player and the
possessor of a never empty glass of Derryale at Nick
Blaney's. With Conor Larkin in the middle of the pack

and the ball floating down toward him, his hands were
iron sure and the power of his body was intimidating.
Once an opposing runner was in his grasp he had to expect punishment. The sporting crowd bet on him heavily
and a small but steady source of income came back to him
along with the free drink.

Conor worried about this, too, as he had worried
about his church commissions, but Pat McShane assured
him that his presence among the derelicts as their alter
ego was more than a fair bargain. In the mire of Bogside,
men gambled and drank to blur reality. They wagered
with money. They wagered without money. Gambling
was a way of life just as losing was a way of life and
the loan shark was a way of life. Evasion of the rent
and rate collector was a way of life as the old woman
working was a way of life. Men lost their pride and
languished in foggy dreams. Conor Larkin and Mick
McGrath were heroes in a hero-starved landscape.

For the moment he seemed at peace and even cast
his eye about for a permanent relationship. There was
Maud Tully in the Gaelic League, who had the keenest
mind of any female he had ever met, and Gillian Peabody, a Protestant schoolteacher with all the polish and
charm of a high-bred lady. One or the other was his
usual escort to the cultural affairs. There were others,
all possibilities. For the moment, Conor Larkin had lulled
himself to believe that he had beaten the Bogside and
the Derry scheme.

*

Andrew Ingram's own success ran parallel to Conor's
when he was appointed district superintendent of the
national schools from Strabane to the south and as far
east as Dungiven.

On opening night of a ten-day Shakespearean Festival,
Enid Ingram greeted Conor at the door of their home on
Academy Road with a look of despair. "I'm afraid you're
stuck with an old married hen tonight," she said, "Andrew is clear up to here in paperwork."

"Ah, that's a pity. Well, they'll be repeating *King Lear*
at the end of the festival."

"I hope he's finished by then. I sometimes wonder why

he took the new appointment. By the by, when I heard you were coming by yourself, I gave Andrew's ticket to Gillian Peabody. I hope you don't mind."

Conor grunted and smiled at her slyly. "Not up to any skulduggery, are you now?"

"Of course not. Besides, you could do a lot worse," she said, rapping on the door of her husband's study and entering.

The burden of the new position was visible in his face. He greeted them, scoffing over the demands of administrative work. "The annual budget and contract bids," he said, slapping the thick ream of paper on his desk. "A fine way for a scholar to spend his dying days."

The doorbell sounded. "That must be Gillian." Enid said, leaving Andrew and Conor to exchange knowing glances.

"Enid's a woman. The sight of a happy bachelor bends her female blood. She's backing her own horse in the Conor derby," Andrew said.

"Gillian's a nice girl," Conor said, "but I've already seen her this week. Not to worry, we'll have a grand time."

"Take your time, Conor. You're in a position to choose your own potion. Of course you could do worse."

The jibbering of the ladies reached their ears from the foyer.

"Conor, before they come up."

"Aye?"

Andrew took off his specs and rubbed his eyes with the heels of his hands and nodded to the stack of contract bids. "Would you drop in after the play? I'll still be working. There's something I want to discuss with you."

*

Andrew Ingram raised his eyes from deep thought as Conor opened the door to his study. It was past midnight. He nodded for Conor to shut them in and make himself comfortable. As Conor slipped his jacket over the back of the chair, a bottle of scotch whisky and two glasses appeared from the desk.

"I want you to look at this," Andrew said, shoving forward a set of bound papers.

"What is it?"

"Ironwork for the district schools and recreation

grounds for the next two years. Desk repairs, fences, hardware, flagpoles, new railings. As district superintendent I am also a member of the Londonderry Corporation Council. This second booklet here is the city's iron bid, light poles, benches, wrought-iron work. Includes the municipal and Constabulary stable." He paused and sipped at his whisky.

"I have a feeling if I touch these I may be married to them," Conor said.

"I want you to look at something else." A third booklet was handed Conor. "This is the bid entered two years ago by Caw & Train for approximately the same amount of work as in the present contract."

Their eyes rested long and hard on one another before Conor looked to the old bid. Andrew Ingram shoved his desk lamp nearer and raised the light, casting a shadow of Conor off the back wall of the office. He opened the cover and glanced down the first page for a few seconds, then set it down.

"Well?"

"It was a bit high," Conor said.

"A bit?"

"What do you want to know, Andrew?"

"How high?"

"They're stealing you blind," he said, leaving the chair and walking to the window, shoving the lace curtain aside and staring down at a passing carriage.

"How much?"

"If the rest of the figures are the same as on that page, they're overcharging by more than fifty per cent."

"Want to read the rest?"

Conor shook his head no.

"Caw & Train has been in operation since 1855. They've done this work for the city as well as for all the school districts in the western half of the county without a single challenge to their bid in forty years."

"Let me try to guess what you're thinking," Conor said softly.

"What kind of shape is your forge in?"

Conor shrugged.

"Can you handle it or not?"

Conor turned from the window. "That's not the question and you know it. They subcontract more than half the work to the little shops around the Waterside. Anyone can do that. Is this closet worth opening? I'm doing just fine as it is."

"Let me put it to you this way. I can open a new school in Dunnamanagh with what we can save on this contract. They've been waiting there on promises for eight years. They've an enlightened priest and he's promised me a starting class of forty students."

"Look, I'm in debt up to my eyes to the Bogside Association. I could never do this without discussing it with Kevin O'Garvey, and he's in London."

"How convenient."

"I've got a dozen men and their families to feed. You're close to Lady Caroline. Why don't you ask her to intercede for your new school?"

Andrew's face grew taut and he leaned over his desk, pointing a ruler like a teacher. "Because education is not a Hubble charity. Moreover, no new school should be the object of a conspiracy. This whole place reeks with deals made behind closed doors."

"For God's sake, I'm just getting on my feet, Andrew."

"Sorry I brought the whole thing up."

"Mind you, I'm not a coward."

"You don't have to explain, Conor. It's one thing to dream of insurrection in the lofty mountain air of a booley house. You're getting to be a big man here."

"And yourself, Andrew. They'll snuff out your whole career like that."

Ingram rested back in his chair and shrugged. "This is my career, Conor. All I know is that every child in this county could have been educated on what they've stolen to create a false prosperity in order to pay off and hold onto loyal subjects in Londonderry. That's Ulsterism, Conor Larkin. Of course I'm not an idealist of the Gaelic League or an Irish alehouse revolutionary like yourself. I'm just a plain old schoolteacher."

"You've no right to talk to me like that!"

"No, I guess I don't. I suppose a year of comforts can water down one's rage over injustice."

Conor snatched up his glass and downed its contents and glared at the stubborn, needling, hurting man opposite him. He poured another shot and did that one in as well, then hung his head, standing in the center of the floor, and tried twice, three times to argue but no words came out. He edged back to the desk, sat and turned the booklets around and took a pencil from the holder. "Mary help us," Conor said.

CHAPTER SIX: From the moment Conor entered his bid, he kept a watch on the forge by rotating a guard among the four apprentices. A simple but effective alarm was rigged up to set off a steam whistle if the doors and windows were tampered with. It could be heard at Celtic Hall and the recreation grounds where the small army of loiterers was always about.

The whistle went off for the first time in the middle of the night several hours after the Londonderry Corporation Council opened the sealed bids. Frank Carney had tried to slip into the forge and was in a boil. When calm was restored, Frank made up the ladder to the loft where Conor lived.

"Why didn't nobody tell me about that goddamned whistle!" he demanded.

"I'd have gladly disconnected it if I'd have known you were going to make a two o'clock visit."

Frank roared about in the quarters cluttered with books. His gold and lacquer didn't shout out, but drooped just as Carney was disheveled and irate.

"Jeese, I thought you were a smart kid. Well, you've gone and done it. I've been talking myself blue in the face to the Caw & Train people and the Corporation Council for four solid hours. What the fuck were you thinking of!"

"The only sin I'm guilty of is catching a thief in the act," Conor answered.

"Come on, you're talking to me, Frank Carney. We've got to live with those people, boy. This shit's got to get undone. You've got to cancel the bid."

"I don't see why."

"You dumb son of a bitch, where have you been for the past year? You've broken all the rules."

"They're not my rules and I don't intend to live by them."

"Oh, you don't, huh?"

"No, I don't."

"Then stuff this in your craw, Conor. You're in debt to the Bogside Association and you ain't making no goddam bids like this without our approval. We'll put you out of business just like we put you in."

"Hold on, Frank," Conor said softly. "If I had known there were deals attached to the loan, I'd never have taken it. If you're saying that you made deals about this forge behind my back, then close me down, man."

"I swear I don't believe you! All of life in Bogside is one big deal. How the hell do you think I operate my brewery? Do you think I own seven public houses on the Protestant side of the river because they like my Irish wit and charm? You don't have to spell these fucking things out. It's a way of life, man, and only a smart boy can make his way through it."

"I've never been accused of being smart," Conor answered.

"Bullshit! You want to be a hero with all your smart lectures at the Gaelic League and you want to be a fucking hero now with this bid!" Carney grabbed at his pulsating heart and slumped to a chair gasping for breath. "Get this straight, Larkin," he gasped, "I ain't getting closed down on account of you. I ain't going back after how far I've come."

"Why don't you pat a couple orphans on the head and give the Bishop a pair of golden candlesticks and tell everybody what a good Catholic you are?"

"You goddamned son of a bitch!" Carney screamed, lunging at Conor. His blows were warded off harmlessly, then Conor grabbed him by the lapels and exerted just enough strength to get the message across and Carney went limp.

"You're out of shape, Frank, you shouldn't exert yourself."

Carney reeled back grunting, then clutched at his roaring stomach. "They're looking to me to straighten out this mess," he snarled. "I'm talking to the Caw & Train people in the morning and you'd better not cross me up. You either get in line or I'm closing you down."

"Be careful going down the ladder, Frank, don't fall. It would be a great loss."

*

Conor Larkin walked the night out skirting the sacred bastions, then went along the strand of the River Foyle. He stopped for a moment as he always did at the customs station and remembered the day his frightened brother emigrated, and he wondered more heavily than ever if it was not the bottom line for them all. Past Magee College the way opened up, the old road to home. Dawn found him at Madam's Bank between Pennyburn Light and Crook Lighthouse at the last bend of the river. Derry looked so peaceful from here in its rolling rhythm of chimney-potted slate roofs.

The four-faced clock on the Guild Hall tower was heard faintly tolling the noon hour as he continued to look out aimlessly from a bench on the city gardens bordering Madam's Bank.

"Morning."

Conor peeked over his shoulder to see Father Mc-Shane take up the opposite end of the bench. "I found you here once so I figured you might be here again. We all have our favorite meditation places."

"Looks so peaceful from here," Conor said. "How's Frank?"

"Oh, he did a monumental amount of bloodletting. The vote of the board of the Bogside Association stands tied as of the moment. One in favor and one against C. Larkin's ill-advised bid. Frank realizes that Kevin will go along with me, so he's been with the Caw & Train people all morning trying to salvage his ass."

"I should have known all along he was buying his way into heaven."

"Frank's the ultimate corruption of the system. Natives taking jobs from the colonizers is against the primary dogma of Ulsterism and all civilized rules, old chap. Obviously, you knew what you were doing when you did it and Frank isn't going to get his throat cut following you."

"How do you feel about it, Father?"

"I voted with you."

"That's not what I asked."

His boyish face looked away with a certain longing as he pondered. "My first reaction was one of resigned sorrow. Aren't things bad enough without taking this on? But that moment passed. It had to come to this sooner or later and somehow I always figured you were going to be the one to pull the switch on them."

They got up and walked along the rose path. "Andrew Ingram, there's a lad," the priest said. "Are you worried about him?"

"Him? No. He's figured it all out a long time ago. He's like my daddy, quiet. I've been thinking about my daddy most of the night. He didn't do it once, he did it a hundred times. I remember him walking alone across the diamond in Ballyutogue to cast the first vote in our lifetimes. Tomas did it without singing his own praises. He lives revolution in his own way on a day-by-day basis. I'm worried about Conor Larkin. All my life I've prepared for a certain moment and said to myself, if there was only something I could do. The moment came and I choked with fear. I said to Andrew, 'Go crawling to Lady Caroline, do anything, but don't get me involved, a contract bid isn't the kind of insurrection I fancy.' He saw right through me, Father Pat; I'm a public house patriot, one of Ireland's vast number."

"I told you I groaned inside when I heard about the bid," the priest answered. "It's the same thing as you felt. We all lose sight of who we are and why we're here. Sometimes after a few brutal scenes down in the Bogside I limp back up to my room and look down on that dirty place and I think of how I'd like to be an ordinary man seeking ordinary pleasures."

"You're just buttering me up, Father Pat."

"To hell I am. I'm no image of Christ, only a tin replica. Do you think the idea of a woman has never passed through my mind?"

Conor was suddenly seized with the reality of the human hells the man bore and the strangeness of it awed him.

"It's neither sin nor failure to break in a moment of anxiety," he continued. "The only failure is not to recognize what you've done and let it slide by. Frank Carney has arranged a meeting between you and Roy Bardwick, the director of Caw & Train. Will you see him?"

"I've got to know if anybody on the board made any kind of deal about my forge."

"I didn't. That leaves two. Chances are Kevin didn't. That leaves one."

"It will do no good to meet with him," Conor said.

"Nor will it do any harm. You're his peer now and I don't think you should start off by doing to them what they've done to us."

•

Roy Bardwick seemed uncomfortable spirited to and hidden in Frank Carney's chapel in the cathedral. The room was filled with dull-eyed ornate statues of Roman paganism. Father Pat opened the gate in the grille, letting Conor in, then left. They studied one another. Bardwick was a big man, almost Conor's size, and would have been if his seventy years had not stooped him a trifle. His head was thatched in white but his grip was firm as they shook hands. For a moment the scene reminded Conor of his own daddy meeting with Luke Hanna to bargain, to maneuver for a little air to breathe for his people. Roy Bardwick was old but infinitely calm and certain of himself.

"I know you, Larkin. I've seen you before."

"I worked at the graving dock over a year ago for a few weeks during an emergency."

"That's it, when the two Canadian sail steamers hobbled in from a storm. I never forget a face. Let's get down to cases. Frank Carney has convinced me, at least, he was in the dark about your bid."

"Frank's telling the truth."

"It was you and Ingram, then."

"Maybe. As long as we're opening on a note of candor, what about Tippy Hay?"

"It wasn't my doing, Larkin. I personally like old Tippy. On such matters things are understood. You don't have to issue written orders."

"On the other hand," Conor said, "you did nothing to prevent it."

"Why should I?" Bardwick said, his toughness becoming apparent.

"Who are you speaking for?" Conor asked.

"Everybody, including myself. While I was sitting here waiting for you I was after thinking, How do I go about this? No use making threats because if you were the kind

of man who yielded to them you'd never have made the
bid in the first place. I'm thinking we'd better talk
straight."

"Go on."

"I know what you're after, I know what Ingram's after.
Now let me tell you what I'm after personally. I'm seventy
and I retire on full pension in two years. I've put in over
forty years at the dock, from the day it was built. If I
let that work get away, it could jeopardize everything. I
ain't talking about the money, only the principles. Do you
see my point?"

"Aye."

"As for Ingram, the Corporation Council is willing to
re-evaluate its budget in regards to new school development. He'll get his school in Dunnamanagh next year."

"That leaves me and Caw & Train," Conor said.

"Taking Carney at his word that this was your doing and
you're being obstinate, we all sat down and figured a reasonable approach. Some of the lads wanted all-out war.
I didn't. Maybe there's a new scheme of things coming
but we ain't ready for it. My people get very jumpy over
this matter. Going on the premise that war ain't going to
do any of us any good, we're making a proposal. We
want you to either withdraw your bid or don't contest it
when it's declared null and void. The Corporation Council
will find a technical reason, lack of facilities or something
like that. The Caw & Train bid will stand. As you know,
most of this work is subcontracted. All the small forges
around Waterside have depended on this income for thirty
years and we have to take care of these people."

"And my cut?"

"Out of the remaining work which is done at the dock,
I am willing to subcontract twenty per cent of it to your
forge."

Conor glanced at a bloodied Christ in the marble
arms of a doe-eyed Virgin. His hand traced over the
sarcophagus. The escape was there! He could come into
a windfall without a bloody nose. The rationale of live
and let live was almost palatable and by any accounting
it would have to be considered as a victory and a break-
through. Yet in the end the inflated bid would stand. Who
would pay for it if not his own people by substandard
lives? It would be another conspiracy made in a dark

place and, although an inch had been given grudgingly, the system would remain in all its foulness.

Bardwick unfurled a handkerchief and blew his nose vigorously. "As I said, Larkin, I'm not going to try to intimidate you but you'd be a fool to think you're home free if you turn it down. Go along with this for a while until my people get used to the idea of competition."

"For two years, when you're out of it?"

"I don't give a shit what happens after I'm retired."

"When I was a boy," Conor said, "we had an old squire in our district. Family had held the seat in Commons for generations. Can you imagine the threats and breast beating that went on when a Land Leaguer challenged him? 'Give us time to get used to it,' they cried along with their intimidations. But the time had come for a change and the Land Leaguer won and life went on. Sorry, Mr. Bardwick."

The old man, who had looked into the face of many challenges, did so again without a show of anger or menace. Time had told him what he had to do. He had tried to avoid it, but he knew he would go through with it. "I'm sorry too," he said.

*

As the bids were published and the contract awarded, Conor kept careful watch. Weeks turned into months with work fully launched on the school and city iron needs. Most of the Protestant forges in Waterside received the same work they had previously done under the old Caw & Train subcontract and their fears were quelled. Only at the graving dock itself and affiliated Orange Lodges did the rancor continue, and long memory was the most integral item of Ulster life.

St. Sinell had a particular identity in Derry's Bogside. On St. Sinell's Day there was always a huge pilgrimage to Lough Erne in County Fermanagh to honor one of Ireland's twelve apostles. It happened to come on the same day that the Bogsiders' Gaelic football team traveled to Enniskillen for the season's big traditional game. Because the two events were in the same general locale, a special train was chartered that all but emptied out the Bogside.

Clarence Feeny's oldest boy, Ahern, was the appren-

tice scheduled to stand watch at the forge that day. The
foreman had noted his son's unhappiness during the week.
Clarence had fallen behind schedule on a commission
church work as well, and on Friday told Ahern the good
news that he could travel with the team and Clarence
would stand watch.

The fire was concise. Conor Larkin's forge burned to
the ground minutes after it erupted. The alarm bell never
sounded. An imported arson expert from Belfast failed to
note anything that hinted of foul play, although evidences
to the contrary were abundant. In sifting through the
ashes, hundreds of small tools which would not burn were
missing. Most of the larger tools had been destroyed by
something other than fire. The coroner's report stated
that Clarence Feeny most likely had dozed after setting
the fire accidentally and was caught in it. The inference
was that he was a heavy drinker and more than likely
intoxicated at the time. Although the corpse was nearly
destroyed, the report failed to mention the skull was
found bashed in in four places.

A week later all remaining work under contract to the
Londonderry Corporation Council and the national school
district was transferred to the Caw & Train Graving Dock.

CHAPTER SEVEN: A year of penance had done little
to heal Kevin O'Garvey's wound. Whispers about had it
that he had never really gotten over Parnell's death. Whatever brought on the change remained a secret and at
times only Father Pat and Conor were able to get close
to him.

Kevin deplored the deal he had made with Maxwell
Swan almost from the moment he made it. His walks
through the Bogside by night always brought him before
the Witherspoon & McNab Shirt Factory, where the acid
of guilt eroded his innards. His file of complaints and
appeals for relief from the workers grew larger and went
unanswered, for he had sealed their avenues of protest.

The price had shown him making a bad bargain, for
few of the Bogside Association enterprises prospered and
many faded. The apprenticeships they purchased made no

impact in Bogside's chronic unemployment ailment or economic betterment.

Kevin entered the Georgian mansion on Abercorn Road that housed the headquarters of the Earl of Foyle's enterprises. His step was visibly slower. He stopped, as always, for a damning look down the street to the seven stories of lightlessness, airlessness, filth and danger, an aboveground dungeon that housed the shirt factory, and the stone in his chest became heavy again.

Ground floor of the mansion contained a bland collection of white-shirted, green-eyeshaded male clerks and long-skirted women, all in rows and rows. An assistant whisked him upstairs to the dour office where Brigadier Maxwell Swan occupied a cracking leather chair. They exchanged minor amenities. Kevin stared from the window to the view of the river. Like so many things in Donegal, it was picturesque from a distance, a hillside fairy town on a winding waterway. From this vantage the perspective changed, for the rot was everywhere and the flaws showed like an old whore without her cosmetics. He turned back into the office, wiping his specs and seating himself wearily opposite Swan.

The Brigadier had harbored many hours of second thoughts over his compact with O'Garvey. Few men had been able to intimidate him, neither tough labor leaders, Fenians nor colonial rebels. He had cut men down and he, Swan, was the only one who could stand nose to nose with Frederick Weed. Yet O'Garvey annoyed him. Perhaps he had made a bad judgment, a miscalculation. O'Garvey's record showed the full anathema in his life of threats, physical beatings, imprisonment, excommunication from his church. Nothing had deviated the man's will or changed his direction . . . except that bribe.

Maxwell Swan thought himself extremely clever in detecting a flaw in O'Garvey, who spilled great salt tears over the men in the Bogside, and Swan had exploited that by throwing a few crumbs to the Bogside Association. Had he made a mistake? Although there had been no repercussions and O'Garvey had kept the Select Committee investigation out of Derry, he could not help but feel he hadn't come out of it cleanly. Obviously, a cloud of conscience continued to hover over his co-conspirator. The torment of O'Garvey showed in deepened crow's feet

about the eyes and a sallow, pinched face. Maxwell Swan
was rightfully disturbed by what he saw.

"Who did it, Swan?" Kevin said. "The leader of one of
your more proficient goon squads out of Belfast was seen
across the river two days before the fire."

"I didn't realize you were a detective along with everything else," he answered.

"You have to be when you have coroners and so-
called arson experts from the Royal Irish Constabulary
on your payroll."

Swan took up his military best, his deep voice rolling
out words with surety and his blue eyes of a caliber to
slice steel. "What's the difference? You know damned well
we're not going to allow a precedent to be established
in Londonderry like a contract leaving Caw & Train.
You've got to share the blame, O'Garvey. You should
have told your people what the rules were when you gave
them loans."

"Oh, most of them knew that, all right. That's why
their businesses failed."

"I can't take the blame if your people are incapable of
operating a simple shop or two."

"Of course they're incapable! They've been made incapable by generations of subjugation! I lied to those
men. I said, 'Here's a few quid, set yourself up.' But they
never had a chance when you couple their ignorance with
the fact you cut their windpipes by eliminating competition. And I lied even worse to those women across the
street in your abominable sweatshop and I've wept with
shame every time I've walked through the Bogside. I
should have screamed in protest when it was in my power."

Swan cleared his throat. "I can't be responsible for
your morbid philosophies and, in the end, nothing will
really change here."

"Perhaps not, but I've got the power to take you down
to hell with me."

"I think you'd better be careful."

"What for? Letting my life's work end up in a deal
with an animal like you?"

Swan managed to conceal his reaction but, never having known a raw clutch of fear before, the feel of it was
pure terror. He was stricken with the same kind of dry-

ness he had inflicted on a thousand men before. He
wanted water but he knew if he reached for it he would
reveal a trembling hand. He shrugged at last. "Do what you
damned please."

"I intend to," Kevin answered, coming to his feet.

"Let's talk," Swan uttered, amazed by his own sudden
failing.

"Our little scheme, yours and mine," Kevin said, "has
succeeded in giving a few men dignity. Now that they've
tasted it, no matter how infinitely small, you're not going
to crush them. We break your strangle hold, here and
now. You went at the one man, Larkin, who has said,
'Look, lads, be proud of yourselves,' and you set out to
destroy him. But you're going to rebuild his forge and
you're going to return his contract."

"Or what?"

"Oh yes, conspirators always have little things hidden
in their pockets." Kevin threw down an envelope containing the story of his deal to accept a bribe in exchange for
keeping the Select Committee away from the shirt factory. "Would you like a half hour to read this?"

"Never mind," Swan answered, "I know what it says."

"And you know where the original copy of it is?"

"With some journalist in London, I suspect, with instructions on when and why to open his copy."

"It's good to work with a man like yourself. It saves
so much time in explanations."

Swan weighed it feverishly. He was reasonably certain that O'Garvey was ready to face prison for his role
in it. How much damage could the Hubbles and Weeds
sustain? Nothing between himself, Lord Roger and Sir
Frederick was in writing over the deal. If it were exposed, Swan knew he would have to shoulder the entire
blame in order to save his bosses. He would be finished
if he tried to turn on them. Moreover, he had carried out
far too many covert duties not to know what Weed would
do to him if he turned rat.

The brilliantly honed veneer of Maxwell Swan splintered
and the iron beneath that collapsed to dust. He had faced
other fanatics before who were ready to go to the wall
but never one who carried such a counterthreat. O'Garvey seemed only too delighted with the prospect of his
own self-destruction in order to purge his soul.

What queer stroke had taken him to O'Garvey in the first place? In the end he might save the shirt factory and some of the industrial filth but at the same time he was opening Londonderry to economic competition.

If it blew open, the scandal that would follow the revelations would sweep into Parliament and bring about just the very legislation he attempted to block. Certainly Witherspoon & McNab would be targeted at once for investigation.

He should not have played with O'Garvey because men like him enjoyed getting strung up for their dirty little causes. Swan, the manipulator, had manipulated himself into a noose.

"The Larkin forge will be reopened and the contract returned. I want all copies of this masterpiece returned to me and your assurance you'll not author another."

"It's a pleasure to do business with you, Brigadier Swan." Kevin put on his hat.

Swan welled in an unprecedented surge of rage. "You know what happens to men who go back on their word!"

"Yes, I rather suspect I do."

"You know if you cross me it will mean your life."

"I know."

"You seem only too anxious to throw it away, so if you go back on this, I promise you, Larkin and a few of your other friends will never see the end of the day."

"I know," Kevin whispered.

"And from now on, keep your people in the Bogside where they belong!"

"I'm afraid they might not listen to me. Good day, sir."

Swan fell into his chair with the violence plunging as quickly as it rose. "O'Garvey," his voice trembled. "Why?"

"Why?" Kevin said. "My father whom I never knew followed Daniel O'Connell, our liberator. He followed him with the same adoration I followed Parnell. O'Connell and Parnell were men of peace and decency without a violent bone in their bodies. Their reward was a trail of betrayals, and final destruction by your filthy lying Parliament. You see, Brigadier, I've come to realize it's a fixed game I've played all my life because I've played it in your court by your rules. Oh, you bend a little here and there when the going gets hot but at the bottom of it there

is always British deceit. In the end there will have to be
an uprising. I've only now come to realize that it will be
the only way to throw your fucking asses out of Ireland."

CHAPTER EIGHT

1897

When the villagers of Ballyutogue exhaled, they did
so wailing with grief. However, when they inhaled, they
sighed silently with relief. Blessed Father Lynch had fall-
en to a sudden and fatal heart attack. Their outward
display reached sorrowful proportions as Reverend Bishop
Nugent, rigid with age himself, tolled the final mass.
After their priest of four decades was put under, a big
dark cloud lifted from the parish and floated over Lough
Foyle toward Scotland.

Father Cluny, who was elevated from curate, was an
infinitely gentler man and, without Father Lynch about
to prod him into petty tyranny, a blissful peace prevailed.

Brigid Larkin approached her twentieth birthday, which
meant her twenty-first was not far behind and that was a
time of uneasiness for most unwed girls. Once a lass
crossed that line, spinsterhood loomed large and the number of spinsters in the village was growing. She would no
longer be the object of all those plots and schemes. Her
battle of wills with Finola took on aspects that marked the
Larkin stubbornness and the ugly trait of living together
in silence. Her affair with Myles McCracken stagnated
from sorrowful encounter to sorrowful encounter. They
continued to meet secretly, hold hands, lament in circles of
despair and then depart unfulfilled and morose.

Every so often Myles had his fill of it and would
tighten up with anger and refuse to rendezvous or threat-
en to leave Ballyutogue and Brigid became swept up with
fear. The only way she knew to pacify him was to permit
a few uncontrolled moments of passion which were shut

off abruptly when they reached the threshold of the most mortal of sins. Each such scene was followed by days of gnawing frustration.

Brigid grew increasingly nervous, short-tempered, and was given to sudden spells of semihysteria. Finola said that it was the work of the fairies, that Brigid was being invaded by them. After a time Brigid began to believe it and question her own sanity.

So long as Father Lynch was alive, she was too terrified to confess the sins she had committed with Myles. This added to her unhappiness and she was among those who inhaled the most deeply with relief when the old priest died. At last, she thought, she could go to Father Cluny.

She picked the day of her confession with deliberateness and marched to St. Columba's. Once through the door, with no turning back, she trembled at the gravity of having withheld her sins. She prayed that she had not truly gone mad as her mother suggested, and that some miracle might intercede for her and Myles. At the end of a long shopping list of favors, she also prayed for the strength to resist having sex with Myles until they could be married.

"O Blessed Virgin Mary, Mother of God, my dear guardian angel, and all you blessed angels and saints in heaven, pray for me, that I may make a good confession and from now on lead a good life, so I may join you in heaven to praise our dear Lord, forever and ever."

Consumed with tears, she recited an act of contrition twice for having offended God. She prayed herself into a trance and, thus mesmerized, entered the confessional and knocked weakly.

The little door opened.

"Forgive me, Father, for I have sinned. Father, please forgive me, for I have been sinning for three years."

Father Cluny's high-pitched voice could not be mistaken. "This is a grave thing you are saying. What is your sin, my child?"

After a desperate period of silence during which ideas of escape flitted through her mind, she cleared her throat and leaned ever so close to the little door and whispered. "Please understand, Father, I have confessed all my other sins regularly, all that I could think of except for the sins in this particular matter."

"I understand, my child."

"Father," she croaked, "Father . . ."

"Yes, my child."

"Oh, Father," she blurted, "for three years I have engaged in giving impure looks and touches to a boy. I have . . . kissed . . . and embraced."

"I see," the voice answered grimly. "With just one boy?"

"Of course only one boy!"

"Now how many times have you done this with this boy?"

"Before coming here today I made my best effort to recall. I must have met him on one hundred occasions. Half of these were in secret places. To the best of my recollection, I kissed him at least twenty times at each secret meeting."

"Let me see, my child. That would be a thousand kisses, more or less."

"At least," Brigid concurred, taking Father Cluny's word.

"Tell me, my child, were they of a deeply passionate nature?"

"Oh yes, very passionate. And I had been giving him impure looks for two years before I kissed him."

"Is that the full extent of your sins?"

"Oh dear." Her voice quivered. "He touched me a few times . . . not more than twenty or thirty . . . and only for very short periods . . . and . . . and . . . I touched him . . . once . . . well, two or three times."

"Is that it?"

"I have thought unchaste thoughts so many times, I am unable to count that high."

"When was the last unchaste thought you had about this boy?"

"To be honest, just before I came here to confess."

In the ensuing half hour Brigid made full disclosures, which included rolling in the grass and hay with him, pressing her body to his deliberately and enjoying it to the point of allowing further liberties on her breasts and three times between her legs, however with clothing in between.

Since the death of Father Lynch, Father Cluny had been receiving a great number of retroactive confessions. Some were more serious than this, some were better. He was thinking in terms of declaring a general amnesty rather than have half the parish serve penance. Their crops might rot, what with all that praying.

Only two days earlier Father Cluny had heard the confession of a young man who clearly matched up to the one he had just listened to and allowed as he had heard from Myles McCracken and Brigid Larkin. It was becoming a great sport for him during meditation to match up confessions. At any rate, things would not be dull in the parish confessional for some time to come.

*

Tomas Larkin was alone in his home and dependent on Brigid for a heavy share of the labor. A new century was coming into focus and, with it, new hope of sorts, but that concerned him little. His sons were gone and one by one friends were being laid down in the St. Columba graveyard. So many of the young men had left and so many of the old had become world weary. Death reached beyond the mere taking of people. The scent of it filtered through the entire village and onto the land itself, for the land was as old and worn as they.

During a day Tomas looked over his shoulder a hundred times out in the fields as though he were expecting Conor, or even Liam, to be coming up the path. He lived on memories of Conor's hand in his own and Conor's intent eyes fixed on him joyously and filled with love and awe. And his step slowed. More and more time was spent in the sweat house to drive off the rheumatic demons that had stiffened his hands and kept his back in constant pain.

One day a whisper spread over the bog as it would with the presence of an intruder. Although Father Cluny was hardly an intruder, the only time he was seen in the bogs was during an emergency. He wended his way down the cut until he found Tomas, who unbent himself, set his slane aside and walked with the priest to a patch of scrub oak out of earshot.

"Thank you for coming, Father Cluny."

"I think the appropriate observation is something about the mountain coming to Mohammed."

Tomas laughed. The priest had blossomed into his own man since Father Lynch took leave and was rather an enjoyable fellow. "My presence here with you has started all sort of gossip and I'm more than a little curious myself, Tomas."

"Aye," Tomas said. "Meaning no disrespect, I don't think it would be entirely in order for me to enter St. Columba's and it is a grand day for a walk."

"The ground appears to be quite neutral," the priest agreed.

"Now mind you, Father, I just want to chat. I'm not confessing but I need counsel and I find you a piously adequate man."

Father Cluny nodded with inward delight, noting that this was a giant step for Tomas Larkin and reminding himself not to appear sanctimonious.

"It's like this, Father. I've made a bloody mess of things." Tomas licked his lips and sighed Irish. "I'm after making amends before, well, before my time comes."

"What kind of amends, Tomas?"

His eyes moistened. "I guess even I know that Conor isn't coming back. The time is past for me to keep on fooling myself. There are amends to make. You see, I took the lives of my sons into my hands and the results were ruinous. What I have to tell you now must be kept in great confidence."

"You have that confidence."

"I've been having dizzy spells and spells where I almost go blind. I've managed to keep it from Finola and Fergus O'Neill as well."

"Don't you think you'd best go down to see Dr. Cruikshank?"

"Ah, that's not so important. What will be with me will be. What is important is to set things right. I want Liam to come home and I want him to have the land. Would you write a letter for me?"

Father Cluny got to his feet awkwardly, for he was a hefty man with little grace or muscle. He watched over Tomas, whose face remained downcast. "What about Brigid?" the priest asked.

"I'm doing all this for her sake as well," Tomas answered. "It is a certainty Finola will survive me and she will never accept the McCracken boy. However, when Liam returns and takes over the farm, Brigid will have to give up her ambitions for it. Now, I've a few quid saved and Conor's doing well in Derry. Between the two of us we could raise passage for Brigid and her lad so the two of them can marry and get away from here."

Father Cluny tried to follow the reasoning. It sounded simple, but yet . . . "I don't know, Tomas. It's a dicy plan. So many things can go wrong."

"What else can I do, Father?"

Not the most inventive of men, the priest could come up with nothing better. "I'll write the letter to Liam for you. It will do no harm and it may just work."

"Now, that's a good man you are. I only wish I could be there in New Zealand when his priest reads it to him. He'll be one happy lad."

Tomas got to his feet unevenly and in that moment Father Cluny realized the deterioration that had taken place. Tomas Larkin seemed to be aging before his eyes. He looked wearily up the path to the bog and the ever waiting spade. He had told himself over and over he would keep going somehow until Liam got home. Then perhaps he'd rest a bit.

"I want to try to make friends with Dary, too," Tomas said. "You see much more of him than I do. He's a good lad, you see, despite certain problems in his raising. I've come to realize he's going to make a fine priest, a fine priest."

This sudden acknowledgment to the Church puzzled Father Cluny, who studied Tomas with suspicion. Tomas had more to say but balked, and the two men remained awkwardly silent. Just then Tomas crossed the line with his decision. "There is one more matter," he said. "Speaking just now of Dary happened to remind me of it. I don't know how to put this to you, Father, but if anything should happen to me, well, let me put it another way. Finola has had to share my life and, although things have not been entirely right for us for a long time, we once had something wild and grand. The least I could do for the woman who has shared my bed is to seek absolution. I'll do it for her sake. So you know that if I fall sick you can go right ahead with it."

"Tomas Larkin, you're not telling me the truth, man."

"No, no, it's the entire truth," he insisted.

"No other reasons to seek absolution?"

"Well, I'd like to rest next to Kilty."

"Sorry, Tomas, I'll make no deal like that."

"Come now, Father, you're the priest. It's your duty to give me absolution."

"I'll give it to you but you'll take it here and now and you'll be coming to church for the rest of your days."

"Ah, Father Cluny. You're all alike. Now don't go trying to make an example out of me."

"You know I wouldn't do that."

"So why don't you give it to me just before last rites?"

"In the first place, you're not telling me the complete truth of why you want absolution. In the second place, I'll not have Conor raging at me the way you raged at Father Lynch at Kilty's funeral."

Tomas scratched his jaw and grumbled. "I do see your point."

"Very well then. You will be seen regularly at mass. I'll not have the parish whispering behind my back that I coerced you on your deathbed."

"Aye, aye. I see your point. Let me give the matter further consideration."

"Surely, there's no hurry. Now, if you'll come to my house tonight we'll get on with the letter to Liam."

CHAPTER NINE: Conor was unconscious by the time he slammed into the ground. Cooey Quinn charged onto the field with a squad of stretcher-bearers as excitement from the spectators reached an epidemic high. Conor was lifted by five puffing bearers, slung awry on the stretcher, which promptly ripped from age, and he crashed to the ground. Under Cooey's frantic directions, each of the other five grabbed a dangling arm or leg and dragged him to the sideline.

Mick McGrath, the second party to the collision, crawled on his hands and knees moaning. He was fetched beneath the armpits by a pair of teammates and slid off the field and plopped alongside Conor. Mick tried to rise but went down face in the mud.

"Resume play!" the umpire shouted over the uproar.

"Holy Mother of God!" Cooey cried, waving smelling

salts alternately under the noses of his stars. "Ah, wake
up, lads! Wake up for Cooey, would youse! Goddammit,
stand back, everybody, and give them room!"

Mick unglued his eyes and waved his head around
and was just getting in tune with the ringing in his ears
when Cooey slapped his face. "Who am I!" Cooey demanded.

"Shiiiiiiuuuut!" Mick wailed. "Shiiiiiiuuuut!"

Thundering feet rumbled the earth as play swung peril-
ously close to the fallen warriors. Cooey stepped before
them, waving them back lest his lads get trampled. They
rumbled the other way.

Mick came about slowly, glazed-eyed. He swished
about to gather up all the loose blood floating in his
mouth, spat it out and, with it, a tooth, then studied
Conor and began to approximate events.

In another moment Conor responded to smelling salts
and propped up on his elbows. Both of them were greeted
with buckets of water to the face. Cooey leaped back and
forth over the sideline shaking a fist at the officials, yelling
to his faltering team, swearing at the opposition, then
back to Conor and Mick, imploring.

In another moment Conor successfully gained his feet
and pulled Mick up by the jersey just in time to see the
Strabane Eagles score on the Bogsiders with a clean goal
to take the lead.

Dr. Aloysius Malone was convoyed through the throng,
stood on tiptoes and peered into Conor's eyes, then Mick's.
He asked a number of questions; for instance, who were
they playing, what were the names of their brothers and
sisters, their teammates, and several catechisms. As he did,
the knot on Conor's head grew egg-size and, as it went up,
his eye went down to a slit.

Strabane grew fierce in the absence of the Bogsider
stars.

"Hey, Mick," Conor said, "what you say?"

Mick smiled and blood squirted from his mouth. The
pair of them trotted back onto the field of play and the
stands like to tore apart. Cooey cried for joy at the same
time he screamed to them to be careful. The inspired
Bogsiders rallied, but the game ended in a tie.

Nick Blaney's bar looked more like a slaughterhouse
than a pub, as sportsmen and players of good cheer

gathered to congratulate each other before the GAA banquet to celebrate the all-Derry finals.

Cooey Quinn elbowed into Conor and Mick, bringing a dandy with him, looking as grim as if he had been visited by a banshee. "This here's Derek Crawford," he said with obvious unhappiness. "He wants to talk to youse both."

The dandy was a big man and his hands were knobby and his face busted up to indicate he had been a warrior of some sort in the past. "Can we go some place private?" he asked.

They worked their way out of Nick Blaney's slowly, backslap by backslap, then down the road to Conor's newly rebuilt forge. He dismissed the guard and gave some attention to Mick's swollen mouth. Derek Crawford looked the place over and propped his foot up on a low anvil. "Great game," he said. "Did Cooey tell you who I am?"

"No."

"Derek manages the East Belfast Boilermakers," Cooey said.

The mention of Ulster's most prestigious rugby team received the desired effect. It was the club of the Weed Ship & Iron Works, the only professional team in Ireland, and nearly as illustrious as the national team itself.

"I'll get right to the point, lads," Derek Crawford said. "I've been touring the province scouting out new talent. We've signed on three lads from the national team, the same team that won Ireland the triple crown by whipping Scotland, England and Wales in a single season. Needless to say, the Amateur Union is hollering and screaming over that and just as needless to say what kind of a team we'll be fielding next season. I'm hereby inviting you two gentlemen to Belfast for a tryout and I'm wagering you both can make the club."

"Holy Mother," Mick garbled through puffed lips.

"We're not rugby players," Conor said.

"Anyone who can play Gaelic, we call it garlic"—he paused and waited for the laugh—"can learn league rugby. We've a junior club, more or less amateur, but you've every chance to be on the Boilermaker squad before the end of a season."

"Holy Mother," Mick repeated.

Derek Crawford painted an exotic picture. There

would be a guaranteed job at the shipyard for a quid a week minimum and they would be paid ten bob a game (under the table) while they played on the junior club. Later, when they made the big team, the pay was a quid a game and bonuses for winning.

Mick, whose head hadn't been exactly right since the crash, almost fainted at the size of the offer. Crawford went on with his non-stop pitch, glorifying Sir Frederick Weed's determination to have the greatest club in the world and dabbing in the final strokes with a dramatization of the annual team tour of the English Midlands . . . *in a private car of the Red Hand Express train.* Conor said nothing. Cooey was fearfully uneasy.

"Oh, it's a powerful offer," Mick said.

"Yeah, what about Catholics in the shipyard?" Cooey snapped.

"When it comes to the Boilermakers, we've only got one religion, winning. Almost half our lads are Catholic. I got no personal use for the sectarian shit and so long as you're on the team you'll have a decent job and have no problems at the yard. What's more, if you give us a few good years, your bread will be baked. Sir Frederick always retires his lads in style."

Conor grabbed Mick's sleeve before he could agree. "We've got to talk it over with Cooey," he said.

"Sure, lads. I'm at the Donegal House till tomorrow morning. Don't, for God's sake, allow this golden opportunity to pass. You'd be making a dreadful mistake."

*

At the banquet in the social room of Celtic Hall, two lads from the Strabane Eagles and Mick and Conor of the Bogsiders were named to the County Derry team to carry their banner into the all-Ireland playoffs. By a flip of the coin, Cooey Quinn was chosen as manager, with the loser as his assistant. While brotherhood waxed supreme as befitting a celebration of County Derry's co-champions, Mick and Cooey sat through it as though they had lost their favorite sisters. They maintained morose silence and ugly glares until the call for the late train to Strabane emptied the room, leaving behind a minor shambles.

Conor nodded to Father Pat, who closed the door after

the final reveler had departed. Mick made an attempt to slip out but his way was blocked.

"I ain't staying here and talking as long as Cooey makes me feel like a shagging traitor."

"Well, that's what you are," Cooey retorted. "Maybe you didn't hear the speeches tonight or Father Pat's very own words on the subject of the meaning of our games. Look around the room, Mick McGrath, at them pictures on the wall, if you will. That's the meaning of it, man, us playing our own games in our own country and not going off and playing fucking British games . . . excuse my words, Father, but I'm like to breaking inside."

"Bullshit," Mick retorted.

"Bullshit, is it? Insulting the ideals on which the GAA was founded ain't bad enough, but what about running out on your mates when we've a crack at the Irish championship? It's a sellout and you know it."

"I'll bust your head in, that's what!" Mick blabbered through bloated lips.

"Hold it, hold it," Father Pat said. "You're getting a bit thick, Cooey."

"Oh, is it now? You should have heard that sweet-talking Derek Crawford. He took those two lads from the Strabane Eagles as well and God knows how many more from the county team. He doesn't give a shit, excuse me, Father, about us. I asked him to hold his trials till after our playoffs, but do you think he'd do it? He's pumping a lot of hot air about jobs you'll never see."

"I've checked into his claims, Cooey," Father Pat said. "It's a professional team and they can't hold trials during the winter, that's obvious. He wouldn't give Mick a round-trip ticket to Belfast unless he was serious."

"Them tickets don't cost him nothing. His boss owns the railroad."

"Shut up, Cooey!" Father Pat demanded. "What do you think, Conor?"

"It doesn't concern me, I can't leave Derry," Conor said.

"Thank God someone around here has some loyalty," Cooey retorted.

"It's nothing to do with loyalty," Conor said. "I've got a business. I can't go."

"What about me?" Mick pleaded.

Conor shrugged.

"Well, answer him, Conor," the priest said.

"In a year or two I was envisioning Mick becoming foreman of the forge but if the talk was between the two of us alone, I'd tell him to get the hell out of this place. I think you ought to go, Mick. The welcome mat will be out for you here if you don't make the Boilermakers."

The blood drained from Cooey Quinn's cheeks. Squat, bandy-legged Cooey was thirty-seven, beyond dreams. At his best no one would have offered him a shot at the Boilermakers. Gaelic football? A poor boy's game played in weed-covered stony fields for the collection of ha'pennies. A pub full of yesterday's heroes hustling drinks. Cooey would go on driving a draying wagon and his wife and kids would work at the shirt factory till they emigrated or died. Yet the Bogsiders were the pride of his life. Nae, the only thing in his life. It was he, Cooey Quinn, who had discovered and made players of Mick and Conor. It was he who had given them their Irish identity that they seemed so quick to dump at the first offer from bloody strangers.

"Why is it, Father Pat," Cooey snarled, "every time we have a man of substance in Derry, he's got to up and go!"

"Because in Derry all a man can hope for is to reach the upper level of stagnation."

Cooey seemed crushed and Mick McGrath began to cry. It was partly comic because of his bloated mouth. Then the tears became doubly sad because they gurgled from a tough stocky kid who had spilled very few of them in his life. Conor tried to comfort him but he pushed away and stood with his face to the wall and beat his fist against it.

"See what you've gone and done, Cooey," Conor snapped.

Mick spun around. "Goddammit! Look at me! I'm nearly thirty and all I ever worked was for two years until Conor opened his forge. Jesus, at least I've got to try. You got no right making me feel like a shagging traitor."

"Cooey Quinn," Father Pat said, "dreams in this place are bashed around enough. You can't stop a man with a fighting chance to see one day in the sun."

"What about my dreams, Father?" Cooey said.

Cooey looked around the thready walls at the photographs of ragged teams. In a passing flash he was able to envision himself for a single instant as he did so many times alone with his own thoughts on the delivery wagon. There he was, his photograph on the wall, larger than the rest, and alongside that a framed account of his prowess. COOEY QUINN, the Belfast *Telegraph* headline sang out, STAR LEFT WING OF THE BOILERMAKERS AFTER THREE SCORES IN A SINGLEHANDED DEFEAT OF THE BRIGHOUSE RANGERS. IRELAND'S MOST FAMOUS RUGGER ON A TEAR! COOEY QUINN, CHEERED BY THOUSANDS! COOEY QUINN, A NAME THAT WILL LIVE IN THE ANNALS!

He walked up behind Mick and jabbed him in the ribs. "Like Conor says, you're always welcome back. Come on, Mick, let's go down to the Donegal House and see that Crawford fellow."

Father Pat and Conor braced against the nip in the air as they made automatically in the direction of Nick Blaney's.

"And you, Conor?"

"I don't know, Father. It can't end here, can it?"

"The Bogside gets to us all, sooner or later, but it's part of Ireland, maybe it is Ireland."

One by one they left, all the lads who had an iota of spunk, unwilling to settle for the upper level of stagnation. Letters from Seamus O'Neill had been a conduit to the outside world, taunting him. He tried to keep the peace he had found, but the life pattern warned him off. Those rows of half-tumbled shacks, the muddy streets, the desperation to avoid sinking, the despair that sapped any zest for life. He had become defeated by his own success and each new evidence of that success added weight to the millstone.

Mick would have his go and perhaps return with enough reflected glory to fill him for a lifetime. Was Derry all of Ireland in reality? Was it the end of the line?

He stopped for a moment and stared at the forge, all rebuilt in brick with a full load of work.

"Is that you, Conor?" the apprentice boy on guard called.

"Aye."

"Ah, good you're here."

As he entered, his sister ran into his arms and seized him. "It's Daddy!" she cried.

CHAPTER TEN: It was not only the smallness of Ballyutogue but the peeling off of all vestiges of past beauty. She had turned white-haired overnight, shoddy with age. Even the Protestant Township and their grand farms showed signs of erosion.

Conor Larkin walked up from the diamond along his childhood path, hurt by the deceit of his memory. The national school was shuttered. Mr. Lambe's smithy was a third the size of his own and filled with cumbersome work and operated by a stranger who had come from over the water. The hanging tree was dying. Dooley McCluskey had aged so, he questioned Conor for several moments before recognizing him.

Brigid had warned Conor to see Father Cluny before coming to their cottage and the priest told him to prepare for a drastic change in his father, then fetched a letter.

"This came in response to a letter I wrote for Tomas last year. As you can see, it's taken several months for the round trip. A few days after I read this to him, he just collapsed in the fields."

As Conor opened it, Father Cluny left the room.

Christchurch, New Zealand
May 3, 1898

Daddy,

It has taken a measure of time to answer your letter which arrived a number of months back because my nearest priest is in Christchurch a long ways from where I am. The priest writing this is Father Gionelli, who is Italian but Catholic and begs to apologize about his English which isn't perfect.

I worked my passage on a big ranch near Dunedin. I thought I would be there for two years but Conor has been sending me money so I was able to pay my passage off early. I started saving right away. Things are different here because the government is after having good farmers and they are making good land available at low prices with loans. I've told you it's different than at home. You don't believe it, do you? We not only have no landlords or estate agents, but no one has even heard of gombeen men except the Irish immigrants. People here are mostly British but they don't act like it because they are really nice. Them and the natives who are dark-colored people even get along all right.

At the end of last season I was able to make a payment on some land and get a loan for the rest. I don't know if you'll believe this but the government even loaned me money to stock sheep. I know you won't believe this, but I've got six hundred acres and almost a thousand head. I've been able to build a small homestead, keep up with my payments, and I'll own my farm in just another eight years.

Sometimes the land reminds me of Inishowen because it is so green, but the soil is better and there aren't so many people. There is a Catholic family about fifteen miles away. They are English, but good Catholics, and they've this one daughter named Mildred. I've been courting and I've spoken to her family. We are going to marry as soon as sheep shearing season is over. It's queer because even though it is May we're starting winter because things are upside down. Mildred was educated by a convent in Auckland and when we marry she will write letters for me more oftener.

I like to cried when I got your letter. I'm so thankful you wanted to give me the farm but I don't want to ever leave New Zealand.

Tell Ma I say the rosary every night and also the angelus and when me and Mildred marry we'll have a Catholic home and she shouldn't worry after that. Say hello to all my old friends. Say a special hello to Brigid and Dary. I paid Conor back some of the money and will send him more after shearing season. Here is some money for you. You can change it for Irish money at the post office.

Your son,
Liam

Tomas was in a deep sleep. Even preparing for the worst, Conor was shocked by what he saw. He embraced his father softly.

Finola's old bachelor cousin, Rinty Doyle, had been taken on as a hired hand and slept in the byre. Rinty said little, stayed out of everyone's way and seemed to echo a house about to fall. He saddled a horse for Conor, who rode off to the Township seeking Dr. Cruikshank.

Diabetes, the doctor told him. The laboratory results were conclusively grim. The condition was apparently terminal, for no known medication could change the chemical balance that had been destroying his body. From what Ian Cruikshank could piece together, Tomas had contracted the disease at least a year before and it was a miracle the man had not already fallen into a lethal coma.

Tomas could be kept comfortable and alive, perhaps for years, but it would require sending him to a hospital in Derry and keeping him under close regimen. Thank God, Conor thought, there would be enough money between himself and Liam to see it through.

"You have to know," Cruikshank said, "this disease is virtually incurable and the victim is wide open to infections his body is unable to combat. So far he's been adamant about leaving his home."

"What will happen?" Conor asked.

"The alternatives could be blindness, loss of limbs, heart and kidney disease. That is no way for Tomas Larkin to go. Get him to come to Derry."

"I'll do what I can," Conor promised.

*

Rinty Doyle fixed a pot of tea while Conor sat by his father. Rinty was a peaceful little man willing to work for bed and board. He was in his fifties and still able to turn in a decent day's work, enough to keep things going with Brigid and Finola. Fergus and the other villagers saw to it that Tomas' fields were kept up. As Tomas stirred, Rinty slipped off.

Tomas mumbled in his sleep. Conor turned his cover back as his father broke into a sweat. His arms were filled with boils and a rash and thinned for the loss of appetite, and his breath smelled of telltale acetone.

"Conor?"

"Aye, Daddy."

"Is it truly you or am I in another of my fantasies?"

"I'm here, Daddy."

"My eyes are poorly. Give me your hand."

The grip that was once all power was fragile. He ran his fingers over Conor's face. "How are things in Derry?"

"I'm faring well."

"Did you ever hear about that letter I got from Liam?"

"Aye."

"Six hundred acres that boy has. Why, that's a barony. Isn't that something to sing a song about? And what a good brother you are helping him out. . . . I'm always so thirsty. Would you be so kind?"

He propped his father up. Tomas gagged from his attack on the water. "It's the sickness. My insides are fairly rusted from all this water I'm drinking." Tomas rallied minute by minute, forcing his eyes to see, and a smile returned to him again and again. "I guess you know Finola took in Rinty Doyle."

"Aye."

"He's a fair enough old crack but I never could figure for the life of me what manner of man would be content taking orders from a woman and sleep for the rest of his days in a byre. Ah, I should talk. Look at me. Living through the great hunger just to give in to a woman's sickness."

"On with you. They'll be making hay in the new century and you'll be here to watch them."

His eyes said to his son, "If I want to." After another drink he fought for his thoughts.

"I saw something awful happening on the land before I was done in by this sickness. I saw a steam machine down in Ballyutogue being tested out by his lordship's people. Can you imagine a steam machine plowing fields? It was doing the work of twenty men and they say it will be able to do other things as well."

"You'll never see the day a machine can dig a lazy bed," Conor comforted.

"Aye, but a machine doing men's work. Maybe I'll be leaving this world in the nick of time. What does it really mean?"

"Surely, I don't know the answer to that," Conor lied, for he and Andrew Ingram had talked of it by the hour.

"I think I know," Tomas whispered. "It will be the end of us in time."

"How can a man say that?"

"How can a man say otherwise?" Tomas answered. "If a machine does the work of twenty, then nineteen must give up their farms and move into the city. Those who move to the city will not be making their own cloth as we do or building their own homes or growing their own food. They will have to buy everything, and in order to do so they will have to work in factories on other machines which make the things they have to buy. It's mind-bending, Conor, but machines on the land are our death knell. Everything we fought for out here will be gone. The machine will do what the famine and the British together weren't able to do. And the cities will grow bigger and uglier and dirtier."

"You're talking too much, Daddy. You'll weary yourself."

"I've been waiting to talk for three years and if I wait much longer it will have to take place in heaven. Conor, I've something very important to tell you."

"What, Daddy?"

"Father Cluny is a credibly pious man and spiritually adequate. He's become my best friend next to Fergus. Conor . . . Conor . . . I've taken absolution."

"Are you sure, Daddy? Are you really sure?"

"Aye. You see things differently at this end of the path."

Conor stared about the wee bedroom of his birth and the birth of his brothers and sister. It was edged in growing darkness. He opened the window for a flight of air and the new lace curtains Finola had put up danced into the room.

"Why, Daddy?"

"I've not exactly told Father Cluny the truth," Tomas said. "He has to remain after me and I didn't want to add to his own burdens."

"Why, Daddy?"

"I owe it to my neighbors. We came into the world together and we lived together. There was some joy, but for those who remained we went from despair to despair. They're dying off, all of them. If I can show them now that I've seen God, then I'll leave them a legacy, something to hang onto. It might make things just a little easier for them to get through to the end. . . . I can't leave them all alone without hope. . . ."

"I understand, Daddy, but look, man, you're not getting out of here so quick. I swear to that."

"Ian Cruikshank is a fine man, a fine man indeed, but he doesn't lie so well. And while we're at it, I'll not go to any hospital in Derry, thank you."

"You've got to go."

"I'll not go to any hospital in Derry, thank you."

Conor gripped him. "I don't know what Cruikshank told you. You're not as sick as you think. You're sicker."

"Jesus, lad, don't you think I know how sick I am?"

"Then stop making so much fuss about it. I'll be in Derry with you and I'll see you every day."

"That part of it's tempting, indeed."

"Then you'll go?"

"Ah, Conor, how could you wish your daddy to a dark hospital ward? I can't leave my land or my friends."

"No, dammit, listen to me. If you don't come to Derry, do you know how it's going to end? You'll go in pieces, your eyes, your toes, your fingers, your heart. Is that what you want?" Conor trembled to choking as his voice gave way. "I'll not see that!"

Tomas reached for him and smiled once more. "Look at us going around like a chicken who just laid an egg. You know I can't leave. You know that, don't you, lad?"

"Aye," Conor wept, "I know."

"Now then, that's settled. Will you be able to stay for a time?"

"Yes, Daddy."

Tomas said no more. He was at peace. He knew by strict orders of Dr. Cruikshank it would be fatal for him to drink alcohol. He would go into a coma from which there would be no mortal return. Tomas had kept a pint of poteen hidden under his mattress for such a possibility. He pondered about receiving absolution, then deliberately poisoning himself, for suicide was a grave sin. He reckoned he would be in purgatory for a long time and once there he could sort things out and argue his case. But he need not concern himself with that just now, for Conor was with him and would stay.

*

The days passed with Conor and Dary standing watch over Tomas and during those long hours Conor related to

his brother the full story of their daddy and Kilty as well.
Dary had long ago figured out why there had been a re-
moteness between himself and his father but he loved
Tomas nonetheless and had always held himself account-
able. For the moment there was a resurgence of the love
and family strength that had once made the Larkins
unique.

At first Conor was distressed by Tomas' absolution.
Then it softened. He had made the most intimate friendship with Father Pat and come to know other kinds of
priests, Bogside priests, priests engaged in secret activities
of the Gaelic League. A great deal of his resentment
against the Church had modified. Father Cluny, in constant attendance and comfort to Tomas, added to the
air of compromise. In the end, Conor accepted his father's wishes but likewise vowed it would never be for him.

He was quick to grasp the undercurrent of struggle
between Brigid and his mother, for the change in Finola
had been nearly as dramatic as that in Tomas. She had
completely given in to fears that the fairies had invaded
Brigid's mind and were plotting day and night to steal
her land and cast her out in the cold.

During Tomas' waking hours he never failed to bring
up the matter of getting Brigid and Myles McCracken
out of Ballyutogue in order to settle his account for the
misery he had brought on his children. Conor broached
the subject with Father Cluny but the priest seemed vague,
fearing he was in violation of confessional information
and fearing a wrong decision, as well.

Of a morning a fortnight after he arrived, Conor
watched Brigid leave in the direction of the Norman keep,
a rendezvous place over the bridge well known to him
from his boyhood. He turned the watch over to Dary
and made after her. Brigid was pacing nervously, awaiting the arrival of Myles, when Conor slipped across the
bridge and made an unexpected appearance.

"It's all right," he said.

She looked about, a frightened deer, poised to break
and run, and edged toward the bridge speeding her steps.
Conor caught ahold of her midway over.

"Calm yourself, girl. I want to help you. I want to help
you and Myles together."

"You can't just barge in once in three years and take over running everyone's life," she retorted.

"We're still a family and you don't count time as minutes on a clock or miles of an ocean." Brigid tried to shove past him but he held fast.

She wrung her hands, then sagged. "I'm daft. Haven't you heard, I'm daft. The fairies have me."

"It's Ma who's gone daft. She's trying to make you think you are. The reason you're so nervous and jumpy is because you've been denying yourself perfectly normal desires."

"They're not normal!" she cried. "They're sinful and I'm being punished."

Conor's modification of bitterness toward the Church reversed again to anger and outrage. He uttered a string of oaths, smashing his fist into an open hand, then grabbed his sobbing sister and shook her. "You're a normal, decent, wholesome human being with normal, decent, wholesome desires of any girl of twenty. You want to make love to your lad. You want to sleep beside him. There's nothing sinful about it!"

"I can't listen to that!"

Even weeping in the strong arms of her brother and wanting to believe in his words was unable to dent two decades of building the holy fortress that locks out reason and locks in guilt. At last her weeping subsided. "You don't think I'm mad, do you, Conor?"

"I do not and you are not."

She became tranquil, took his hand and they walked back over the bridge to the big rock she had shared so many times with Myles.

"Darling, you've got to stop playing this game with Ma. The way she is now, she wouldn't trade a thick penny for a thin one. You'll destroy yourself if you keep it up. For God's sake, is it Colm O'Neill who you want?"

"I can't even stand the sight of Colm any more."

"And why should you? You've a strong, handsome lad who loves you, Brigid, and that's worth more than a thousand acres of this rock pile. I want to bring the both of you down to Derry. I'll teach Myles blacksmithing."

Brigid got away from her brother and shook her head no.

"Why, why? What's to lose but a dirty game with an old woman who's gone daft?"

"I hate Derry," she said. "The sun there has no warmth to it. It does not kiss you like the sun of Ballyutogue. When it's hot it burns the skin off your back and melts the gravy from you. The rain gives no after sweetness. You swog around like your feet are anchored in clay and the air hangs thick over Bogside like breathing in clouds of a dust storm. I'm afraid of Derry. I'm afraid of the bonfires and the drums over in Waterside and of the ugly brawling and men and women screaming at each other and their children covered with sores and the eternal sadness of it. Ah, you're meaning well enough, Conor, but that day will come when there will be no work for you or Myles and he'll stand against the wall and pitch pennies while I go up to the shirt factory or muck someone's toilet and the honor and manhood will fade from Myles's eyes."

Conor flopped his arms. Oh, Lord, he cried to himself, oh, Lord, she is so right. He came up behind her, took her shoulders once more. "If it's land you must have, lass, there's all you want in New Zealand and Liam there to start the two of you out. But go from here while there's still a chance."

"Nae, Conor. This farm might not have been good enough for the likes of you but it was good enough for three generations of Larkins and, by the holy Virgin, I'm as much a Larkin as any of us."

He turned her around, cupped her face in his hands. "Would it be worth losing your lad?"

"Why can't you understand that everyone in the world isn't like you, unafraid to go marching off into the dark unknown? I've not your head for learning, your charm for wooing or your strength. I'm a simple old thing. I love every corner of our cottage. It is my place. The world beyond Ballyutogue frightens me. I want to pull our cottage about me every night and wrap myself in it."

Conor touched his sister's cheek with his lips, held her hard for a moment, then turned and went back to the village alone.

In a moment Myles appeared and they stood questioning each other silently.

"I heard," Myles said.

"So you did," she whispered.

"Maybe Conor is right. If I could go to Derry and work for a few years and save and learn a trade, then I could come back as someone."

"Nae," she answered, "no one ever returns to Ballyutogue."

"Oh, Jesus," Myles said, "our situation at home is desperate. I'm next in line to emigrate. My brothers in America have sent my passage. I can't stay any longer. Brigid, my only choice is to become like Rinty Doyle. I know I'm not strong like Conor, either, but I'll not become anyone's hired man. Don't you see, lass, I've got to leave!"

She became lightheaded and half crumbled to the rock, her face contorted as the look of madness crept its way back in.

"I'm after talking to Conor," Myles said. "I'm after going to Derry with him and learn. If I'm in Derry I won't have to go over the water . . . I'll be able to see you from time to time."

"Oh, Myles," she wept, "Myles, Myles, Myles . . ."

"You'll see. We'll beat this thing. In a year or two some land will come open here and I'll have the money to buy it. You'll see."

*

When Conor left the cottage Tomas was asleep. Shortly after, he awakened. His sight was reduced to vague shadows and his left foot throbbed with excruciating pain.

"Gonor?"

"Conor is away for a time," Dary said, "I'm here with you, Daddy."

"Is it you, wee Dary?"

"Aye, Daddy, can't you see me?"

"Oh, surely I can," Tomas lied, "it's the sand in my eyes." The pain tore through his leg as though a white poker had branded him. "Dary," he groaned, "would you ever run and fetch Father Cluny. I want to talk to him."

"Aye, Daddy."

As the boy dashed off, Tomas Larkin summoned the last of his strength and dug about under the mattress for the bottle of poteen.

*

Conor arrived at the cottage the same moment Dr.
Cruikshank dismounted. The aging villagers inched in
closer in hushed fear, for if Tomas Larkin truly got
away it marked their own time with terrible clarity. In
the best room all were on their knees in low prayer.

Finola, Dary and Father Cluny clustered around the
bed. Conor and Dr. Cruikshank spotted the empty bottle
at the same instant. The doctor snatched it up as the two
exchanged terse glances. When the doctor cleared the
room, Conor reeled out to the byre.

Ian Cruikshank came to Conor in a few moments,
tapped his shoulder and the two walked away from the
cottage until they reached the stream beyond the village.

"How long?" Conor asked.

"Hours, perhaps a day or two."

"What happened?"

"He knew it would be fatal to take a drink. I warned
him of that some time ago and I repeated the warning.
But I suspected he kept a bottle."

"Why didn't you try to find it?" Conor demanded.

"I think I know Tomas."

"So you let him kill himself," Conor raged suddenly.

"Can you take it, boy?" the doctor said.

Conor backed off trembling.

"Your father went blind this morning. I'm going to
have to go back in there now and amputate his foot."

"I'm sorry, Dr. Cruikshank," Conor moaned.

"Don't worry, lad. I'll make it as painless as possible."

Conor wavered until Dr. Cruikshank disappeared, then
staggered aimlessly, aimlessly, and fell to his knees and
doubled over with grief and vomited on the path. "Daddy!" he screamed his torment. "Daddy!"

*

For sixteen days Tomas Larkin, the son of Kilty, lay
in a coma. Inishowen itself shuddered. The villagers and
Fergus O'Neill were sick with fright at facing life without
Tomas Larkin. His powerful heart refused to give as if
to repudiate what he had done to himself.

On the seventeenth day, the giant fell.

CHAPTER ELEVEN: Caroline Hubble seemed to grow more lovely with the years. Stylishly exquisite in her late thirties, she had been entrenched as cultural partroness of western Ulster for a decade with Hubble Manor the centerpoint. The Hubbles never ceased to be the object of gossip, with the social humanization of Roger her subtle masterpiece, and the taming of Caroline his. It was said they were a kind of magic couple of one mind working in two bodies in total and constant communication.

There was no lack of tittering innuendoes in the narrow confines of Irish society about their long visits to exotic places, whispers of opium parties and other excesses away from Ulster's puritanical reaches. The whispers spilled over about their hunting lodge in the Urris Hills, said to be done up as an erotic fantasy, and whispers about a mirrored, tented, hidden apartment in the Manor. Their public life remained picture perfect, their private life tantalizing in its mystique.

Roger was entrenched as western Ulster's political major-domo. Within the enterprises he pressed on relentlessly to reduce unwanted land and to convert to cattle and flax and what was necessary to feed raw material into the manufacturing complex. A series of interfamily arrangements with Weed solidified holdings so it became difficult to tell where Hubble began and Weed ended and vice versa. Their moves were concisely calculated to that master plan that would hack Ulster away from the other three provinces of Ireland, should the Irish demands for liberation become imminent.

The marriage produced two male heirs, Jeremy, who became Viscount Coleraine upon Roger's accession, and Christopher, who followed a year later. They were different and complementary, an answer to their grandfather's dreams. Jeremy, the apple of Sir Frederick's eye, was cut of the old cloth, a boy's boy who would become a man's man. Christopher showed Roger's studious mind from the beginning, so their contrast would make a perfect combination to direct the family empire.

With the question of heirs solved, Sir Frederick's cavernous appetite for expansion slowed. From here on out it would be consolidation of holdings, direction of the Ulster scheme and training of the grandsons. Sir Frederick embarked on his own campaign to achieve peerage. A program was devised to support the proper charities, attend the proper conferences, serve on the proper committees, give the proper public service.

He envisioned himself as the Baron of Holywood, perhaps even Viscount Holywood. The latter was not out of range. A well-deserved seat in the House of Lords, just deserts, homage. Oh yes, Weed growled, contented. Caroline had done well by him and she had made her marriage work brilliantly and Roger was like his own son.

*

Renewal of Hubble Manor had taken almost six years, creating an acclaimed home at a cost reputed to have run over three hundred thousand pounds.

Yet there remained a single ogre, the wrought-iron screen in the Long Hall. As it remained uncompleted, it became a bone of contention and a hovering challenge. On two separate occasions Caroline imported ironmasters from Italy and Germany. The Italian succumbed to the mystery of the screen and gave up after several months into the ordeal with frenzied bravado. When he stormed from Ulster, leaving a trail of curses, Caroline found Joachim Schmidt, who held the reputation as Europe's greatest in restorations. The screen refused to give up its secrets and mocked his methodical attacks of historical logic. When Schmidt left, beaten and shaking his head, Caroline was tempted to remove it and replace it with a wood-carved screen. This would have inferred defeat, and dogged stubbornness inherited from her father demanded otherwise.

*

Gary Eagan, the new apprentice boy, stuck his head into Conor's office wide-eyed, then made a jerking gesture toward the shop with his thumb.

"Talk up, Gary," Conor said.

"There's a swell lady outside. Came in a carriage with

a driver and footman, she did, and she's asking after you."

"Well, show her in."

The forge skidded to a gawking halt as Lady Caroline raised her skirts off the blackened floor and whisked through. "Mr. Larkin?" she asked from the doorway.

"Aye," he answered, coming to his feet. He looked about his cluttered space. "Gary, go up to my room and get the lady a chair, a clean one." He extended his hand, then withdrew it rather than dirty her.

The chair arrived in Gary's hands as he was assisted by a pair of blacksmiths, but the office held no room for it. Conor looked about chagrined. "Would you mind terribly if we went over the way to Nick Blaney's? I'm half crowded into the street."

"Not at all."

As he led her through the forge, work ceased again. He stopped at the door. "It's not O'Connell's birthday!" he barked.

Conor ordered a pint of Derryale and a sherry for the lady.

"I'd like to talk to you about some work," she said. "First, let me introduce myself."

"Only the village idiot doesn't know who you are. As a matter of fact, I met you personally on one occasion but I don't think you met me."

"Really. Where?"

"The Shakespearean Festival of a year ago. My shop was one of the small patrons as it is for the concerts and opera season as well."

"How delightful. And do you attend regularly?"

"Aye, I do. I wouldn't miss a one. And by the look of you, you're wondering what a blacksmith would be doing at the concert hall, right? It's a well-known fact that St. Patrick was a Roman living in England and was spirited off to Ireland as a slave by our coastal raiders. Not so well known, but equally as true, is the fact that Shakespeare likewise made a secret voyage to Ireland before he embarked on his career in order to learn proper use of the English language. From the time the shanachie told me that authentic story, my interest in Shakespeare was aroused."

"Go on with you, Larkin," Caroline laughed, "you're awful."

"The question is not how I know you, Countess, but how do you know of me?"

"I saw the balcony you made for Andrew Ingram as a birthday present and he led me to some other work you've done."

"Ah, Andrew, I should have known. So now you want me to come up to Hubble Manor and see if there is anything I can do about the screen in the Long Hall?"

Caroline smiled, shook her head and wiggled her finger at him.

"Well, Countess, you are public property of a sort and, being in ironwork, stories of the screen somehow got back to me. I was wondering when you were going to get down to the bottom of the barrel and see me."

Caroline smarted. It was one thing to be friendly with artisans but another thing to have them forget their place and this young man was obviously delighting in her dilemma. "Tell me, Mr. Larkin," she said with deliberate curtness, "are you always so brash?"

"Only when I've got something a customer wants badly enough. You know, I wouldn't be human if I didn't glory that you finally had to look right here in Derry, right in the Bogside, for what has evaded you all over Europe."

Caroline toyed with the notion of setting him down and leaving. On the other hand, she had dealt with artisans long enough to know they insisted on artistic dues. She had never truly considered an Irish Catholic to be in that category. The damned screen had been haunting her for years. She didn't really believe this Larkin was capable where a Joachim Schmidt had failed, but at that point she had to give it a last try.

"May I expect you at Hubble Manor tomorrow before noon?" she said.

"Sorry, Countess, the shop is backed up with work. I'll not be able to get out until next week." Now why the hell did I go and say that? Conor wondered. He knew, of course, there was pleasure in one of the earldom's croppies giving a bit of comeuppance to the Countess of Foyle but was it also because she was a beautiful woman? Or both?

Caroline lifted her sherry glass with studied coldness.
Conor knew she had been waiting for a decade and had
come to him as a last resort and she wondered, Was he
establishing male ego, artisan ego or some basis of future
equality? He was a handsome chap, and he probably
knew it well enough. There was that intriguing business
with his unlikely cultural pursuits. All right, little boy, she
thought, have your sport.

"Next week will be just fine," she said.

*

The mighty bronze doors to the Long Hall gave way.
Conor walked over the vestibule toward the screen with
the reverence of an impoverished monk approaching the
Pope. He asked Lady Caroline if more light could be allowed in and if any of the original sketches of the
screen existed.

"I'm afraid the drawings were destroyed in some war
or another," she said. "I do have the architectural plans
of the recent restoration of the hall and some renderings
by Joachim Schmidt and Tustini before him."

"Yes, I could use them all. What I should like is a tall
ladder and an hour or so to study this. I hope I can talk
to you sensibly then."

After Caroline withdrew, Conor came before what,
illuminated, was a delicate concerto in iron. Each welded
joint was covered by leaves and scrolls, a classic of re-
pousée decoration. What was left of the screen was perhaps a third of the original. In full glory it had soared to
forty feet in height and was just as broad. It might have
been among the three or four most magnificent ever
executed, he thought.

"Oh my," Conor Larkin whispered, "my, my, my."

*

Lady Caroline returned in two hours with a tea-
bearing servant. The plans she had sent earlier were spread
out on a heavy oaken-slabbed refectory table which
Conor had moved directly in front of the screen. His own
sketches were mixed with the others. He was steeped in
them as she peeked over his shoulder curiously.

Feeling her presence, he looked up, dropped his pencil
and made an expression to relate that just seeing this

work was in the nature of a religious experience. His
eyes continued to linger on it as a lover viewing his
naked lady in adoration.

"Tijou," Conor said, "Jean Tijou."

In that instant Caroline deflated. She had hoped he
would be able to live up to her hidden expectations. He
had been so cocksure. It was obvious that he was unable
to determine between an ultimate master and a very good
imitator. Yet one had to be gracious at this point. It
would have been poor form to downgrade a Catholic
workman.

"Yes, I know," she said. "Everyone believed it to be a
Tijou. Schmidt thought so too at first. I'm afraid it's not
Tijou."

"It's Tijou," Conor repeated quietly.

Caroline's patience was ruffled. She did not want to
get into a long discussion over the matter. "It's not possible," she said. "We have researched the matter with an
Oxford historian among others."

"What is your understanding of it?" Conor asked.

"That Jean Tijou was a French Protestant who took
refuge in Holland, in Orange. We know he came to England around 1690 with King Billy and was patronized
by the court of William and Mary. His work was done
between 1690 and 1710. There is no record of his ever
having come to Ulster."

"But he did come to Ulster," Conor interrupted.

"Mr. Larkin, we have letters proving that this screen
was built some sixty years before Tijou's time and these
letters are irrefutable."

"That's not correct," Conor said bluntly. "You've
pieced together wrong information."

As she arched her back, Conor stood before the screen
in a semidetached euphoria.

"Mr. Larkin, I'd like to know what you're talking
about."

Conor returned to the table, sipped at the tea, thanking her for her consideration. He checked the sketches
and doodled for a moment and as something unlocked in
the screen's secret he smiled, then set his pencil down.
"Daddo Friel probably knew as much about this castle
as most of the earls who lived here."

"Would you mind telling me who Daddo Friel is?"

"Was," Conor corrected. "He was a shanachie, a master storyteller. My best friend and I were two of his favorites. He could go on with us for hours, even days."

"And did he tell you that coastal raiders spirited Tijou out of England?"

Conor laughed. "Ah, I don't blame you at all for that," he said. "Seriously, Daddo's history has proved unerringly accurate when it came to the local sieges and risings."

Caroline had a feeling that a bit of Irish charm was being worked on her but she was too intrigued to halt the discussion and too mystified about Larkin himself; he seemed so positive of his ground.

"During the Peasants' Rising of sixteen and forty-one," Conor began, "the Earl of Foyle led Cromwell's counter-insurrectionist forces, as you know. At one stage he rounded up five hundred croppies and put them into the Long Hall and locked them behind the screen. I need not go into the subsequent torture, starvation and massacre of these prisoners."

"I've not heard of such an event," she challenged.

"I have a two-volume work on the insurrection in western Ulster by the British historian, Wycliff, published a year ago by Oxford University. His accounts are amazingly close to Daddo Friel's."

"Continue," she said tersely.

"The point is that the screen became a hated symbol. It is still part of the language in my village of a mother trying to frighten her child . . . 'I'll put you behind the Earl's screen.' "

Caroline managed a small smile, warning herself at the same time not to be drawn in too completely.

"During the siege of Derry in sixteen and ninety, Hubble Manor was attacked by the forces of James, whose first target was the screen. It was completely destroyed, as was most of the Long Hall and the original castle."

Folklore as history was doing well up to this point, Caroline thought.

"In gratitude to the Earl of Foyle for his service to the Crown, King Billy personally dispatched Jean Tijou to Hubble Manor to replace the destroyed screen."

Caroline's complacency faded. She was puzzled. It was

logical that the original was destroyed. The time period
and events indicated the screen was newer than she had
believed and might be a Tijou. Yet so much Irish fantasy
was woven into it and one knew the shanachies could be
frightful liars.

"There was a short local rising in seventeen and twenty-
two," Conor went on. "The Long Hall was again razed and
when the roof collapsed two thirds of the Tijou screen
was destroyed. The balance is what we are looking at
right now."

"Mr. Larkin, are you telling me that your village
shanachie actually heard of Jean Tijou?"

"Not by name but I'd heard of 'The Frenchman' time
and again in tales of the rising of the era. My village is a
particularly proud one and it has been traditional that the
priest keep a record of the day-to-day history of the
parish. After you visited me last week I went up to my
village and borrowed the volume of that era. The reference is in Gaelic but there is mention of thirty of our
men traveling to Castle Hubble, as it was called then, and
working on the restoration of the Long Hall where a
magnificent wrought-iron screen was being built under
the direction of a Frenchman."

Caroline Hubble was abashed into silence.

"I agree with your skepticism, Countess," Conor went
on. "The bits and pieces fit but the final, conclusive
evidence is right here," he said, pointing to the screen.
"Every artisan leaves his own brush strokes and Tijou is
all over this screen. I can see it as clearly as you can see
an Impressionist painter. This screen could not have been
executed sixty years before Tijou's time. The work in
those days was too ponderous, too tight. He alone was
the one who made lace out of iron and let leaves float
as though they were bubbling down a stream."

Conor shuffled through the recent restoration plans,
found what he was looking for and spread it out. They
were the architectural details for reinforcement of the
beams and foundation of the Long Hall required to hold
the screen securely. "This footnote is in French."

"Yes, the recent restoration on the hall was done by
Frenchmen of the Le Duc school."

"Aye. I can't read it exactly but wouldn't it say that
anchor bolts and other attachments were found every

three feet that were totally unrelated to the present screen?"

She turned the plans around, held her pince-nez to her eyes, then stared at him in astonishment. "Yes, it says that."

"Wouldn't you conclude that those bolts must have held an earlier screen in place?"

"The one destroyed during the Cromwell wars?" she said excitedly. "So that, in fact, Tijou did make one later on."

"That's my conclusion," Conor said.

"Mr. Larkin, I believe I owe you an apology. I've been very skeptical. As you know, this has been the object of tremendous research."

"Well, they didn't have Daddo. The question is, what to do now?"

"Do you think you can build a full restoration from this?"

Conor shook his head no. "Come here, Countess, let me show you something."

They stood as close as their eyes could focus and he traced his fingers over a sweeping curled bar that wove into a narrowing circle, ultimately sprouting iron vegetation in a recurring design. "At this point here you can see with your own eyes where Tijou ends and the German master, Schmidt, begins. Not only are the tools and castings a different size but the composition of the iron itself becomes different. Like oils or marble of different texture, certain irons take on their own unique character. However, the most important difference is that one master cannot get into another master's mind. Schmidt is great but could Cézanne make a perfect imitation of Renoir?"

"I see your point," she said, enthralled.

"Tijou must have known he was creating a masterpiece in the class of his fountain screen at Hampton Court. He set up traps to make certain this could never be duplicated. Copied, yes, but never duplicated. Look at these corner scrolls, would you? Surely Tijou brought in a left-handed blacksmith to execute these. And as for the Italian restoration on the upper section, it's the difference between Verdi and Wagner."

Caroline had shown or told him nothing to indicate an Italian had worked on it but it was obvious he could read

the screen like a book and she was not about to question
his mastery any further. She was flushed with elation that
it was truly a Tijou, truly an immortal work of its kind.

"What should I do, Larkin?" she asked, but even as she
uttered the words a tinge of suspicion lingered that he
might be trying to oil his way into her confidence and
strike out for a commission to establish a nationwide
reputation. "What would you recommend?"

"If it were mine there would be no choice," Conor
answered. "Jean Tijou means as much to me as Da Vinci
means to you. One third of a Tijou is worth a hundred
Conor Larkins. I'd leave it alone." As Conor's eyes played
over the screen, Caroline closed the book on ever questioning his motives again. "There is some careful restoration that should be done and those counterfeit German
and Italian sections ought to be removed."

"Will you undertake it?"

"I'd like to give it a go."

An arrangement was made whereby Conor could come
to the Manor once a week to do the job on site.

"I'm curious to know where you were trained."

"Oh, that. Well, in a number of unlikely places. In a wee
shop in my village with a very fine master, and under a
tree . . ."

"Under a tree?"

"That's where I do most of my reading. Then, there
is a stonemason's yard, a good old stony in Derry who's
a right fair hand at sculpture. I suppose stonecutting is
one of the oldest professions in the world. It predates
writing, even ironwork, by thousands of years so they
must know something. When I asked him the secret of
carving he told me to study the leaves. 'Conor,' he said,
'no two leaves are alike.' "

"So Tijou is Tijou and Schmidt is Schmidt."

"Aye, something like that."

Caroline left him to make some further sketches and
retreated to her boudoir. She was drawn to the window by
sounds of the boys playing outside. Jeremy and Christopher and a number of visitors from England were in a
rugby game on the vast lawn below. Her attention shifted
to Larkin as he emerged from the Long Hall.

He was a finely put together man, the kind of body she
had once frothed over in fighters and other brawnies, yet

his brawn was modified by the stack of drawings under his arm. He was so utterly Irish with his cocked cap and sweet talk but so terrifyingly knowledgeable. Suddenly the ball sailed in his direction and he nimbly brought it to a stop with his feet, picked it up and booted it away. It arched heavenward and seemed to fly forever. After the lads finished gaping they rushed to him and implored him into twenty minutes of play.

*

Roger always brought any late paperwork to Caroline's boudoir, where they set up face-to-face desks in order to work their evenings together. Midway through a stack of correspondence she signaled that it was talking time.

"I think we may finally get something resolved on the screen."

Roger set his work aside and braced for the announcement that a Hungarian ironmaster had been unearthed and would soon be screaming around the Manor corridors.

She related the story with great detail that King Billy had possibly commissioned a screen as a gift to replace the one destroyed. Roger dug about in memory but could add nothing.

"I rather like the idea of restoring and keeping the old screen," he said.

"So do I," she said.

"That chap must have a remarkable background to dig up all that history."

"I should tell you right off he's a Catholic and from Londonderry."

"Really, you're joshing."

"True enough, darling. He'll be the highest of his class we've had about so I thought I'd better brace you to brace everyone else."

"I think we can bear it. Show of democracy and all that. What did you say his name was?"

"Conor Larkin."

"Larkin? Is he a blacksmith? In Londonderry?"

"That's right."

"Larkin? Family has been around for years. Fenians, I believe. Swan had quite a piece of nasty business a year or so ago. Something to do with Caw & Train."

"You're not going to cancel out on me, are you?"

"Of course not," he said. "Frankly I don't remember all the details. Well, never mind. Be sure to check him out to see if he's honest and reliable. You know how bloody feckless they are."

"I have the feeling he'll be quite all right," Caroline answered.

CHAPTER TWELVE: Father Cluny arrived at the Larkin cottage overcome with excitement, for he had received a letter from Liam containing twenty quid to erect the most beautiful tombstone possible for Tomas.

Conor had his stonecutter friend in Derry create a fitting monument and added money of his own for a more appropriate stone for Kilty. When these were done he brought them up to Ballyutogue along with a wrought-iron fence to encompass the Larkin plot.

The Larkin graves had always been beautifully kept with devotion from Brigid, Dary and Finola. Now they had the added distinction of fine tombstones from sons who had done well on the outside and remembered.

The letter from Liam also told that he had married the English girl, Mildred, and she was pregnant. As a new Larkin was preparing to enter this life halfway around the world, another Larkin of Ballyutogue prepared to make his departure. As Dary reached his fourteenth year, it was time for him to go off to the diocesan seminary. Although it had been planned for many years, that moment of leaving was a moment of sorrow.

Once again Finola packed the few belongings that each of her sons had taken in some beaten-up piece of luggage purchased from peddlers years ago at some forgotten fair. She fussed over him for the last time, giving all sorts of advice and restraining her tears somehow.

As Father Cluny came she held Dary's hand and they trudged down the path with all the cottage doors open to impart the oft-imparted words of farewell.

"God watch over you, Dary."

"And may the same God watch over you."

The family led a trail of black-scarfed women into St.

Columba's for the lighting of candles and prayers, then Dary went alone to the graveyard and said good-by to the daddy he had never really known. The lad stopped at the crossroad and took the suitcase from his sister. "I'll go the rest of the way alone," he said, repeating a Ballyutogue adieu. Finola seized, then released him.

"Good-by, Dary," Brigid said.

The wee one smiled and walked away.

"He's so tiny," Finola wept, "so tiny and frail."

For that instant Brigid felt given to comforting her mother but stopped short at the point of touching her. Father Cluny studied the two women and felt done in by the pity of it. The priest was filled with his own urge to command Brigid to leave. Myles McCracken had gone to Derry to work for Conor and the Larkin cottage would become a mausoleum, but Father Cluny held his tongue. Long before, he had learned to share the never ending sorrows of his parishioners in silence.

A ghastly emptiness encased the Larkin house as each went to a separate cell, Finola to her bedroom where she once had slept with Tomas and where her children had come into the world, Brigid to the loft she had shared with her brothers, Rinty Doyle to the byre to make himself as inconspicuous as possible. As if each had taken a monastic vow of silence, they moved about in their chores with but the barest bones of conversation.

With Myles McCracken out of the way, some of Finola's fears subsided. Any breaking of the silence generally came in short, terse tirades admonishing Brigid to marry Colm O'Neill. Brigid kept her tongue until she could bear it no longer, then countered with verbal violence so fearsome that Finola became wary of pushing her further. Even the matter of Colm joined the other matters of silence.

Brigid had always been plain but managed a touch of loveliness as long as Myles was around. She turned drab. She hated herself for entertaining a persistent nagging thought of how much better life would be if her mother died. She confessed this over and over. After each confession the rancor toward Finola deepened.

The cycle of wanting her mother's death, guilt, confession and penance became her treadmill of existence. After a time she began to forget what Myles looked like.

She forgot the sweetness and pain of the sensations that
had surged through her when she ran over the bridge into
his arms. It all dimmed as though Myles had never really
existed. Then, as he faded, hatred for her mother faded
too.

Brigid Larkin became totally resigned to spinsterhood,
being able neither to love nor to hate any longer with any
great fervor.

*

Eight miles out of Derry where the bridge crossed the
River Burntollet, a side road wound up onto a wooded
crest to the walled confines of the Sacred Heart Seminary
of the Holy Order of the Fathers of St. Columba.

Dary Larkin was among eight novices passing through
the forbidding gates. For the most part they were smooth
of cheek and soft of hand, indicating they had been
lorded over by adoring mothers. Some had come eagerly,
like Dary, and some at the prodding of an overburdened
family. For some, the journey would be of short duration, a washout. The others would continue to travel it
for twelve years into priesthood.

Dary gave up his possessions save his rosary beads,
and was assigned to an eight-by-eleven-foot cell in the
isolated building which housed twenty other novices. It
would be his home for the next four years; simple,
roughhewn, stone-floored and dingy, with only the crucifix
on the wall and a faded picture of the sacred heart as
company.

On their first day they met the consecrated brothers
who were teachers from the Christian Brothers Order.
Afterward they were issued a terse command to genuflect
as the Monsignor entered the assembly room. A wizened
old Monsignor recited why they were there and what
would be expected of them in uninspired monotone, never
really seeing the faces that held an august glow or were
frozen with apprehension. Dogmas of poverty, chastity
and obedience were imparted, equally devoid of passion,
and the rules, a chronicle of long hours and complete
devotion, were tolled.

The machinery that moved the seminary operated on
few spoken words and these were imparted in whispers.

The nod and the beckon gave all movement in the place a sense of flotation.

The rosary was said with fervent ejaculations, the menu varied by the season, always bad, the hours of classical education, an endurance battle, and humility, total. God was beseeched in states of barefooted prostration with limitless prayer and tasks and duties of chamberpot-cleaning variety.

Brother Dary seemed at ease, although there were quiet, hidden tears among many of the others who fell to fright or loneliness. In that first instant Dary was singled out as a strong one, for he had obviously prepared himself since earliest memory.

*

Myles McCracken and Conor became the closest of friends. Myles eagerly plunged into blacksmithing, an opportunity he had never believed existed for him.

Away from the forge, Conor and Cooey Quinn brought him up to a fair level in Gaelic football and he took to hurling as well. Myles was a welcome addition not only to the GAA but to the Gaelic League, where he strove to find his Irish roots.

The crunch was on from the girls, for Myles had the greatest of all qualifications for marriage, steady work. He was nearly as big and handsome as Conor, could sing a ballad even more sweetly, and his smile could charm a worm away from a mother robin. Having lived his life stone poor and unwanted, the sudden rush of attention was a thing to revel in. He would remain faithful to Brigid, of course, learn his trade and then return to her as a man of substance and demand what he could not demand before. That was the plan. He could not bring himself to visit Brigid until then, for the pain would be too much to bear. Ah, but once he was a man of substance, that would be different!

In the beginning, Myles slept in a nook of the forge, then later moved upstairs with Conor. The passage money which he did not use was given to the next brother in line to emigrate so that three McCracken boys were left in Ballyutogue. The eldest was to inherit the land and those who had emigrated or left Ballyutogue sent

back money for the two remaining for their passage. A
good part of Myles's salary went for that. Yet there were
a few coppers jingling in his pocket, a fact he could not
comprehend at first. With his first raise in pay, Myles
took his own room, the first of his life.

Conor became a bit wary. Although Myles never deviated from his intentions toward Brigid, he just wasn't all
that adept at holding the girls at bay.

"You listen to me good, Myles," Conor warned. "Traps
are being set for you. You'd better keep your pants buttoned or you're going to end up another Bogside swaddy."

"On with you, Conor," Myles insisted, "I'm true to
Brigid."

"Maybe in your heart, but that rod between your legs
has no heart and less conscience. The word came back
that you're quite the lover."

"For Christ sake, man, I'm just playing around a little.
You know, just playing around."

"That's what all those poor bastards said."

"Not to worry. I'll not be trapped."

Myles's words did not match his deeds. Being in the
big city away from communal discipline and poverty and
being sought after was too irresistible. Conor's concern
deepened.

"If you've got to get laid, for God's sake, don't stick
your pen in any Catholic inkwells. Between all the Hail
Marys and the weeping and the guilt, there's not great
joy in it. Besides, their intentions are deadly."

Again Myles sloughed it off.

"I know some fine little Prod girls in Claudy and
Dungiven as well. They'll give you the roll of your life
with no strings attached. So don't go fucking any Catholic
girls!"

Despite Conor's advice and good intentions, Myles
McCracken's eye roved from lass to lass until it came to
rest on Maud Tully. There had been talk of Maud and
Conor as a twosome but that was more than a year back.
When she pressed her seriousness, Conor had backed off.
He enjoyed her well enough, particularly as a date for
cultural affairs, but her intentions carried overt finality.
Besides that, he rather leaned toward Gillian Peabody.

Maud Tully was a clever, bony, vivacious little thing of
nineteen who had worked at the Witherspoon & McNab

Shirt Factory from the age of ten. She was one of eleven children, eight of whom survived infancy. None of her five brothers ever held a regular job. Her father had been unemployed, except for brief periods, for thirty years. As his sons emigrated, Henry Tully became a gentle drunk, wizened and toothless, seeming twenty years older than his years and never fully out of an alcoholic haze. Maud's mother and two sisters labored in the shirt factory as piecework operatives, averaging about fourpence an hour.

Maud Tully was passionately singular in her determination to avoid the Bogside fate. She found a first crack of hope in the Gaelic League and its lure of Irishism. She was fierce in her drive to learn to read and write and she studied the old language and held a headful of thoughts about politics and poetry and nationalism and human desires.

A woman of her sort was non-existent in Ballyutogue and totally fascinated the likes of Myles McCracken. When they walked together of a Sunday along the riverbank beyond the town, Myles would break into song, often as not, for no reason at all. They'd find a tree and she would read to him from books and they would talk about things a man could never get to know in Ballyutogue unless he was smart like Conor or Seamus O'Neill. Myles had no intention of comparing Maud to his true love, Brigid, yet he could not help but realize the difference. When he had been with Brigid, it was always in a state of sadness and frenzy. Maud made him laugh.

*

The August night was so sweltering that heat blistered the dust from the stones of Derry's walls. Conor was stripped to the waist and heavy with perspiration as he worked on some sketches for a new ornate commission of massive candleholders for the church in Buncrana.

Myles appeared suddenly, looking the color of death. Conor glanced up from his work and was alarmed that Myles had fallen sick, for he stood there grunting and gasping.

"What's wrong with you, man!"

Myles wrung his hands. Great tears streaked down a tortured face. "It's Maud Tully," he blurted, "she's going to have a baby."

Conor's fist boomed into Myles's mouth, careening him backward till he came to a halt falling back over an anvil. He sat there numb, his head swarming. He blinked his eyes dumbly as Conor hovered over him, then ran the back of his hand over his mouth and tugged out his shirttail to sop up the blood.

Conor unclenched his fists, returned to his office, slumped behind his desk and covered his face. Myles got to all fours, staggered to his feet and swayed for the front door, his face already taking on a deep color.

"Don't leave," Conor croaked.

Myles turned, still uneven on his feet, unable to speak, and they stood opposite one another for what seemed an infinity.

"I'm sorry," Conor whispered.

"Nae, you've every right to kill me."

"Nae, Myles, I've no right at all."

"You can't know how bad I feel after all you've done for me, Conor, and all out of the love of your sister."

"Shut up, man. We're all too butchered up from other people running our lives. I've no call to run yours."

Conor patted Myles's shoulder tenderly, which only made him feel worse. "Do you hate me?"

"I don't hate you," Conor said. "Do you love Maud?"

"Aye, I do. I don't know when the change came, but I do, I love her."

"We'd better go to see Father Pat right away."

*

Maud Tully wasn't the first Bogside girl to go to the altar pregnant, so the shame of it would be short-lived. The celebration afterward at Celtic Hall was particularly filled with joy and hope, for this one girl would make it out of Bogside if anyone did.

Conor reckoned it would take Myles two years to be a complete ironsmith, one able to strike out on his own. There were two choices open: to emigrate, for there was always blacksmith work anywhere in the world, or to take over a smithy somewhere in the area. Maud wanted Ireland but the other prospect was palatable. Her determination to get Myles on his feet was strong and bottomless. A lot of girls had made the vow on their wedding day but

those who knew Maud knew she would succeed where the
others had failed.

She made Myles give up his room and move into the
family hovel in order to save rent. The place was perpetually overcrowded and they had to settle for an alcove
in the kitchen which they made private at night by hanging up a blanket. She would continue to work at the shirt
factory right up to the minute of the baby's birth and
every last penny would be banked.

The initial awe and fright of marriage faded for Myles
with that snip of a lass at his side. He swore to match her
sacrifice for sacrifice, with longer hours at the forge, and
to cut out every luxury and pleasure, for he knew that
what he had won in life was grand. Two years would be
nothing at all; it would go by quickly and when it was
over they could walk in the sun for the rest of their lives.

CHAPTER THIRTEEN: Each Tuesday Conor set out
from Derry by horseback before daylight and would be
at the Manor's forge and scaffold before the house was in
motion. Lady Caroline's interest in the work was intense. She instructed her personal secretary that she was
not available for outside activities on that day. After
breakfast she showed up at the Long Hall where Conor
went over the plans for the day and returned each evening
with a light tea to inspect the progress.

After erection of the scaffold, Conor cleaned off two
centuries of scum, rust and soot from the fires with acids,
wire brushing and emory cloth, and bit by bit unlocked
Tijou's secrets. The master had built the screen in sections
and set it in place by block and tackle. Afterward he had
covered each seam and weld in such a manner that only
another master would be able to detect them.

Age and neglect were only part of the problem. The
screen had been twisted and weakened by bombardments,
fires and falling roof at one time or another, demanding
an inch-by-inch decision on what to replace, how to
strengthen and what he could match with the old filigrees,
leaves and vegetation.

As one week fell behind another, the work began to take on an aura of elegance. Conor had deep-seated misgivings about working in Hubble Manor, just as Caroline realized he was a special case. He forced himself to set aside generations-old inbred hatred. The screen as pure art required his professional best and, moreover, he knew he was into an ultimate experience working on something the likes of which he would never see again, and was headily devoured by it.

Conor remained away from the mainstream of Manor life, gracefully warding off the aspirations of an entire flock of female domestics. In fair weather he ate alone outside on the lawn under a tree and when it was foul he remained in the Long Hall.

The single friendship that blossomed was with Jeremy, the Viscount Coleraine, who seemed far more interested in hanging upside down from tree branches and spitting farther than anyone else than in his aristocracy and title. Jeremy was bound to show up under "Conor's tree" with football in hand and a dozen comrades in the wings and a plea for a short game. When the weather was bad he hung around the Long Hall, a privilege not even accorded Lady Caroline, and made himself helpful by fetching tools and ultimately doing apprentice work.

As his own prejudices of Larkin for Hubble tempered, he admitted to himself he liked the way Lady Caroline held her arms out wide to her family as well as her relationship with her husband. Gossip was a sea on which all the great manor houses floated and he could not help but overhear the clucking about the Countess' stand against her husband and father to keep her sons in Ulster instead of transporting them to England for their education.

Conor became eager for Tuesdays for something other than the screen and it annoyed him to the point of distracting his concentration on the work and set him to snapping at Jeremy and sending him off. As the rift widened in his own mind, he deliberately set distance between himself and the Hubble family.

Caroline watched it evolve with annoyance of her own. Jeremy, obviously in a state of hero-worship, would not be put off. She was in her boudoir of a given Tuesday and caught a glimpse of Conor reading under the tree when Jeremy stormed toward him with football in hand.

"I've no time for you today," Conor snapped.

"Come on, Conor, please."

Conor stood up irate, snatched the ball from the boy and booted it away. "Now go get yourself lost and don't bother me!"

Jeremy simply stood there and stared up, then sobbed as he ran off for the ball. Conor watched him, disgusted with his own performance, and stomped off.

Should she speak to him or just let it pass? Would that be extending too much familiarity on a personal matter with a hireling? Or did Larkin's special status command it? As she pondered, she saw that he had left his book beneath the tree and decided to take it to him. With the volume in her hand an overwhelming sense of curiosity overrode the indiscretion of peeking into Conor's sanctum and she returned with it to her quarters.

She curled up on the chaise longue. Her eyebrows knitted in puzzlement at the title. *The Kalevala* by Elias Lönnrot. Pages within held the epic Finnish poem, a rambling folk legend not unlike a Celtic tale. There were several sheets of loose paper tucked away in the center of the book. Some held drawings, obviously for the screen, but others were filled with random scribblings in his hand, a series of small verses. She hesitated a final instant, then plunged.

THE BISHOPS RAINED
DAMNATION
PARLIAMENT RUED
TEMPTATION
THEY DEEMED TO KILL HIM THRICE
SICK MORALS SPEWED FROM VENAL LIPS
DEMANDING SACRIFICE

PARNELL IS DEAD
PARNELL IS DEAD
AND ERIN'S SOUL IS IN HIS GRAVE

I loathe the swill 'neath Derry's walls,
This pigsty Bogside place I'd flee,
But if so prodded could I find peace
As an immigrant whore on a foreign shore?

Once out there I'd ne'er again
Be bruised by sight of Derry's walls.
Where is it, man? Is it out there?
Or stay a swaddy in my tired land?

No ceilidhe or fair or pleasure I seek,
Could match the sheer joy of wracking week,
With the salt of the sea in your mouth
And you actin' as free as the loon
With the girls all wet from the harvest of kelp
And their breasts showing fullness of bloom.

FATHER LYNCH
BOW, KNEEL, PROSTRATE,
ACT OF CONTRITION
SHAKE WITH SUBMISSION

GUILT, FEAR, PENANCE,
FOLLOW THE BLIND,
OF EMPTY MIND

CONFESS, REPENT, ABSOLUTION
LIFE IS BLED,
SAFE IS DEAD.

A Walk to Derry

Tumbled homes,
Famine walls,
Mouths gone green from eatin' grass.
Are we horses or cows feeding?

Swollen bellies,
Fever wards,
Death ships wait with stinking holds,
Are we horses or cows being transported?
Corpses piled,
Communal pyres,
God save our noble queen . . .

There was more, a long, unfinished, mystic sonnet to
his father and half-coherent scribblings about the thrill

of football and a friend named Seamus O'Neill and a hedgerow teacher.

Caroline closed the book pale and quickly retraced her steps down to the lawn. Conor had returned, looking for his book. She handed it to him.

"I'm afraid I'm guilty of shameful prying," she said.

"Not to worry," Conor answered softly. "We're all alike, you know. I suppose the one thing Ireland doesn't need is another bad poet."

"Mr. Larkin, would you tell me right off if you've misgivings about working here?"

Conor studied his hands. The black of the forge was never fully out of them, like a coal miner's lungs. "I've a personal liking for yourself," he said in his best evasive Irishness. "As for Lord Hubble, I've been treated fairly and I've a sincere liking for young Jeremy and Christopher as well."

"You've avoided my question with consummate skill," she said.

"Aye, I've had mixed emotions."

"Are you going to finish the screen?"

"I made a bargain."

"But you don't want to," she pressed.

"I want to finish it for two reasons," he said. "It would be a criminal act to know you can do something about a work like that and leave it undone. I've enough conceit to believe you'll not find another like me."

"I agree," she said, "and reason number two?"

"Perhaps when we see or hear of each other again in future times it may not be so pleasant. It's been an unusual and lovely relationship. I'd like it if you and Jeremy always kept some kind thoughts of me. I don't know why it's suddenly so important, but it is."

"Thank you for that," Caroline said.

*

As the end drew near, Caroline Hubble toyed with the idea of creating a commission that would keep Larkin on, but she abandoned the notion. It was filled with things that had best be left alone.

One day the screen was done and he said good-by.

One of the strengths of the Hubble marriage was an un-

derstanding that two people could love each other with
complete devotion but still hold normal admirations, love
and even physical desire for someone else. So long as
Caroline and Roger freed one another to hold such
thoughts and so long as the two of them talked about it
openly it had never become necessary to act out their
desires in secret. It took no special insight on Roger's part
to realize his wife was taken by the Larkin chap, probably in all sort of ways. Caroline had never abandoned
her adulation of muscled, sweaty workmen and Larkin certainly had his share of both. When Caroline or
Roger had such passing pulsations in the past it was cause
for playful and dirty conversation. What was annoying to
Roger about Larkin was that Caroline never mentioned
him. It was as though she was cheating for the first time
by wanting to keep this particular fantasy to herself.
Yet when one shares the freedom and trust they held, it
would have been poor form on his part to throw up Larkin like a jealous bull. However, he could not help but feel
a sense of relief when the screen was done.

On the evening Conor departed, Roger came down to
dinner disturbed. "You'd better see to Jeremy," he told
Caroline. "He's up in his room crying." Later, Roger
broke an evening-long silence during their billiard game.
"Damned place acts in mourning. Did Larkin get to many
of our girls?"

"I'd be the last to be informed of that."

"Did you get to know him really well?" Roger asked.

"No, he kept a distance."

"Well, he certainly made a mark on Jeremy."

"Rugby, that sort of thing."

Should I or shouldn't I? Roger inquired of himself
as he lined up a shot. He did. "Did you find him terribly
attractive?"

"I suppose so," Caroline answered.

"You might have mentioned it."

"I found him distressingly attractive, soberingly so. He
is a strong, keen man and I've a feeling we've not heard
the last of him. I don't mean him alone, I mean all of
them. He gave me an opportunity to have an insight into
our enemies. It makes you shiver a bit to think there is a
country here filled with his sort."

"Yes," Roger agreed, "Father grumbled about that on

his deathbed. Well, so long as Brigadier Swan is watching
the store, things will be in good order during the rest of
our days."

"And Jeremy's and Christopher's?"

Roger laughed at the serious turn, replaced his cue
stick in the rack and embraced his wife. "The screen is
absolutely smashing," he said. "I'm glad it's solved, once
and for all."

*

After six months Dary was allowed a Sunday visitor
and permission to leave the seminary grounds. Over the
Burntollet Bridge there was a lovely wooded stand called
the Ness, which included a stunner of a waterfall, Shane's
Leap, named after a legendary Robin Hood of Derry who
was said to have made an escape by jumping it.

Dary and Conor picnicked and soon the red squirrels
and birds were chattering and scampering about looking
for handouts. Conor smiled at his brother. It was so much
like Dary with the little beasties eating from his hand,
sensing no fear. Dary had been the object of Conor's
pity, a beautiful small and delicate creature seeming hardly geared to take on the sorrows of life. Yet there he
sat in total command of himself and in a full bloom of
inner peace.

Dary knew his brother was bubbling up for an explosion. He had read Conor's anxieties in the words of his
new poems and throughout the day Conor nibbled around
the edges of his frustration. There was always the matter
of his disapproval of the priesthood and he made the
usual pecks at Dary's loss of freedom.

"See here," Dary said abruptly. "I'm happy. There's
no lock on the seminary gate. Someone always thinks it's
a tragedy when a brother goes into the priesthood."

Perhaps you're right, Dary, Conor thought, if you end
up being a priest like Pat McShane. But I have seen the
spirit drain from Father Pat's eyes as well, and yes,
I've seen those fleeting instances of human longing. You'll
suffer, too, and you'll hunger.

"There hasn't been a priest who hasn't battled with
temptation," Dary said, reading his brother's mind. "I
don't suppose I'll be the first."

"You're too bloody smart for a kid," Conor snapped.

"You're ready to burst, Conor. For God's sake, tell me what's going on with you."

Released from his self-imposed bond of silence, Conor mused. "I don't know, Dary. Maybe it was the bloody screen at the Manor. It was a queer situation. Here I was giving my heart in a place and to a thing that is a total symbol of injustice. I liked their kids and I liked that woman. I suppose, more than I can admit. It was like a dream working on that screen. I couldn't wait for Tuesday to come. I'm lonely without it and I'm disgusted with myself."

"You've had some fires stoked you'd rather have left cooled. You didn't want to see anything decent in people you've been born to hate. You didn't want to like them. You wanted them to be evil clear through to confirm your hatred," Dary said.

"Damn you, Dary! You're scary the way you see through people!"

"You're my brother, Conor. It's not the Hubbles that ail you and it's not the screen . . ."

"Oh, you'll make some bloody priest, you will," Conor said, stripped of his rationalized defenses.

"Then what is it, Conor?"

"If you want to know, wee Dary, come walk with me through the Bogside. Look at the pleading eyes of the little wanes all scrawny and old, old men of ten and eleven, and the glazed expressions of their beaten daddies and look, if you will, at all the tough young micks huddled against the cold drizzle with their hands shoved deep in their pockets wasting another day and another and another until they chase the final fantasy to America. And the gangs of factory girls dragging home too weary for singing or love-making or knowing joy, only to have their bellies filled till they waddle and become even more drained of life. And the puke in the gutters and the fist fights and shrill screaming, venting frustrations on each other like animals. And them up in Hubble Manor seeing to it the Irish monkeys are kept unfit for anything but mucking their sewers. I've betrayed Conor Larkin, that's what! There's a roll of fat growing around my gut from endless money to buy endless pints and I'm so fucking pleased with myself I can't hear the sounds of their weeping any longer. I don't hear it because I don't want to hear it. I want peace but there can be no peace. Do you know why? There's a curse on me as there's a curse on the Larkin name. The curse comes back, again and again, to taunt me! Ronan! Kilty! Tomas! And now me! What are the Irish among men? Are we lepers? Are we a blight? Will there ever be an end to our tears?"

They could hear the angelus toll, a signal that their day together had come to an end. Dary tossed the last of the crumbs to the little beggars. They returned over the bridge, up the path to the seminary, and halted before the gate knowing it would be a long time before another visit.

"Not that it will do much good, but squeeze in a prayer for me now and again," Conor said.

"I always have."

"Sure I know that, runt. I've watched you pray since you could walk. Of course you were always mighty quiet about it. Tell me, Dary, what is it you say for me?"

"What's the difference?"

"Nae, tell me. I think I need to know."

"I pray that my brother Conor won't be shot down by British guns."

CHAPTER FOURTEEN: No one knew for certain that it was half four in the morning but when that hour arrived movement began by rote. The single-bedroom row house of eighteenth-century vintage on Sparrow Lane was less crowded these days with only two daughters of the eight Tully children remaining. Henry and his wife Bessie occupied the bedroom. Peg, the oldest sister, her husband and their four children slept in the parlor.

For the privilege of their privacy in a curtained-off alcove in the kitchen, Maud and Myles had to be first up. They spent the night wound around each other and held on till the last instant with the baby kicking up a fury as Maud ended her seventh month. Maud sat up on the mattress looking only half her size, thin arms and small breasts understated by the hugeness of her belly.

They dressed in silence with long-practiced movements of people who lived in crowded quarters and awakened to darkness.

Myles rolled the bedding up off the floor and tucked it beneath the staircase as she made to the back yard to lead the parade to the privy and water pump in the pre-dawn chill.

Breakfast of minced pork scraps and potatoes was eaten by Bessie, Peg and Peg's daughter, Deirdre, who had started working at the factory. Their meal was taken in red-eyed drowsiness, a morning stupor orchestrated by Henry Tully sleeping off his perennial drunk with a bombardment of snores. Peg's husband stayed in bed also with their three remaining children cuddled on a single mattress.

When they finished, Maud and Myles got the table and took their breakfast with an egg, one of the two they spoiled themselves with weekly. Lunch of a pork sausage, a potato, an apple and tea was packed into her small net shopping bag. She lit her lantern and stepped into the darkness, the chill of it frosting her breath. Myles always walked his wife to the factory although the forge wouldn't be open for almost two hours. He spent the time doing extra work if any was to be had, or in Conor's office studying Gaelic or reading from the extensive collection of books on wrought iron.

Up and down the side streets, lanterns glowed as the women wended their way to Witherspoon & McNab and the other factories and mills for the six o'clock starting hour in a dirgelike procession. Maud's niece, Deirdre, had just turned eleven and joined the sorrowful parade along with hundreds of other Bogside children to disappear from childhood in the black jaws of the Londonderry workshops.

Myles put his arm about his wife to ward off the sting of cold. It would be a particularly hard day because the factory had no heat except from the presser's stoves on the third floor and she would be working too far from it to reap much benefit. Winter added to the cruelty, for Maud would rarely see daylight except on Sunday, awakening and returning from work in darkness like a miner above the Arctic Circle.

She was frightfully tired but refused to submit. Summer would come and there would be light. A year and a half would fly by and they would leave the Bogside forever. They came to a stop across the street from the factory and stared as it swallowed up its human fodder. As banks of gaslights were turned on inside, their faint glow penetrated unwashed windows, casting a dim yellowish illumination. Maud climbed to the sixth floor more slowly each day, yielding reluctantly to the burden in her stomach.

"I hate that place for taking you away and for what it does to you," Myles snarled. "I'll work my hands raw to make it up to you."

"Sometimes," she whispered, "I loathe myself for wanting you so badly at any price and I'm ashamed of using you to get me out of Derry."

"It's only your condition making you talk this way. I'll hear no more of it. This will pass, Maudie, like a bad dream. Look what's coming up, would you? We've a League meeting tonight with a lecture by Father Pat and Sunday we take the train to Convoy after mass and look over the forge that's up for sale."

"Do you really think he'll wait until you're ready?"

"He promised he would and what if he doesn't? There will be others to buy."

She girded herself for entry. Myles seized her shoulders. "I've never had anything in my twenty-three years except your love, Maudie. Without you, I'm nothing. With you, I'm everything."

"On with you, lad," she said, pinching his cheek and forcing a small smile. "It's not so bad up there; I get to think of you all day."

The girls tittered on their way in as Myles and Maud McCracken stood there holding each other and kissing as they did almost every morning. One would think they were still courting instead of herself nearly eight months' pregnant. Myles could scarcely bear the sight of her disappearing into that dark place; he turned quickly and left, with the darkness consuming him immediately. Deirdre ran beside her aunt. Maud looked up to the sixth floor and sighed, "Come on, love, let's give his lordship his pound of flesh."

*

The Londonderry Corporation Council fathers thought
Angus Witherspoon and Simon McNab slightly mad when
they unveiled plans to erect a shirt factory on Abercorn
Road. The year was 1870 and the two immigrant Scots-
men had prospered famously. Shirts were made through
a complex of small shops and piecework done largely in
homes as a "cottage industry." Before the reform laws,
that wily pair utilized labor of the orphanages, workhouses, prisons and borstals. In 1870 linen never looked
so good. The world cotton market had bottomed and
busted because of the American Civil War and linen was
on a binge.

Their idea of unifying all the small, scattered elements
into one large modern building conceived for mass production was a staggering idea. Even more staggering was
the building itself. What pierced the Londonderry sky in
1873 was a seven-story monolith, the mightiest architectural achievement ever in that part of Ireland. The
structure was made possible by the use of huge, hollow-
tubed cast iron pillars. Each of the seven floors was designed as a segment of a unique master plan to make
shirts on an assembly line basis.

The ground floor on Abercorn Road housed the company offices and directly behind them on the left side of
the building stood the receiving department where the
linen was disbursed. On the right side of the ground floor
the finished shirt came down for shipment so the rear of
the building held a bustle of horse-drawn draying wagons
and a large stable.

Bolts of white and dyed linen moved to the seventh
story on the left-hand side by a huge rope-and-pulley
hand-operated elevator. The top of the building held the
cutting room where natural light could be best utilized.
Simon McNab, production genius of the partnership, designed mammoth cutting tables and the sixteen-inch
bladed "McNab shears" capable of slicing through seven
thicknesses of linen and thus making seven pieces at a
single cutting.

Cutters were male. Although linen was more difficult to
work with than cotton, pure brawn was needed to cut the
magic number of seven. With seven sets of sleeves, pockets, fronts and backs cut from the pattern, the cutter
bundled and tagged it by color, size and style.

"Runner!" he called. "Bundle, bundle!"

Girls ranging from nine to fourteen kept a constant stream to and from the cutting tables, holding a bundle under each arm, totaling fourteen unsewn shirts. Moving down a matching elevator on the right side of the building, they got off at the sixth, fifth and fourth floors. Each of these contained a battery of two hundred foot-treadle sewing machines and a much lesser number of buttonholers. A bundle was dispensed at one of the six hundred machines requiring it and the apprentice girl returned to the cutting room by the left elevator in what was a never ending cycle of movement.

Sewing machine operatives, all females, pulled their special tags off the bundle. One tag per shirt, one penny per shirt, and proceeded to stitch them together at a rate of three to five shirts an hour.

The buttonholers on each of these three floors then applied their craft, hand-sewing the buttons and attaching collar bands. These were the elite workers on a flat salary of one pound, two shillings a week.

The finished shirt continued down to the third floor, the sweatbox, to the pressers. Twenty-five coal-burning stoves were interspersed about the block-square room near ironing tables. Intricate pleats and tucks required a woman's hand at the iron. These were girls of fifteen and sixteen graduated from being runners. Five apprentice boys, future cutters, kept the coal stoves roaring. The third floor of Witherspoon & McNab was a prelude of hell where human endurance was at a breaking point, winter and summer. The pressers remained at their trade for a year or two until a sewing machine became open on one of the upper floors.

Continuing ever downward, the second floor was for labeling, packaging and boxing by older women no longer able to do ten hours at the machines. They were allowed to finish out their years with no further body or mind damage but at half the former pay, eleven shillings a week.

On the ground floor the finished product, some thirty thousand shirts a day, went to shipping docks and were moved to warehouses, to city stores, to the rail station for disbursement about Ireland, or to the waterfront for Britain and the world market.

When Simon McNab conceived and executed his fac-

tory he took everything into consideration except the fact
that the eleven hundred women, three hundred men and
two hundred children laboring therein were human beings.

Within weeks, he had the movement of his production
line refined. But no regular maintenance was kept except
for the ground floor, which housed executives, bookkeep-
ers, salesmen and designers. Up in the factory it was
expected that every man and woman would keep his or
her own area clean, which was an impossibility. Layers of
filth grew gummy on the floors, grimed the pillars and
blackened the windows.

Cutters had the best of it, for theirs were the only
windows cleaned, for use of natural light sped production. The balance of the factory's windows could not be
seen through. There was a single toilet stool on each
floor for use by some two hundred workers, both male
and female. These, likewise, were not cleaned and the
sink faucets clogged in a few years so there was no
running water. Odors of urine and feces grew so powerful they penetrated into the working areas and men
and women held their bowels and bladders for hours rather than enter that place.

McNab's design never smoothly regulated the inflow of
raw material so that a backlog of linen bolts was stacked
on the stairs, landings and aisles, impeding passageways
and adding to the universal clutter.

Within a year the windows were stuck shut from filth
so that there was no circulation of air whatsoever and
lint and linen dust were inhaled into the lungs with
every breath.

The workrooms were lit by banks of gas mantles never
fully turned up so as to save expense, so there existed a
grayish light insufficient for close work. Competition
among foremen on the three floors of piecework was vicious. The high man was rewarded, the bottom man under
brutal pressure so the operatives were pushed and kept at
their limits.

Human wreckage set in in a matter of a few years.
Ten hours a day, six days a week at the foot-treadle machine put unnatural stresses on the body and few women
escaped severe back and neck ailments and their eyes
were mercilessly overtaxed. The lungs fell to coughing fits
from lack of fresh air and inpour of dust. Tuberculosis

scourged the Bogside. Rheumatic swelling of joints crippled in those long damp winters without heat.

The summers were the worst. Heat from the stoves and irons on the third floor raised the temperature of that room to over a hundred and fifteen degrees and was transmitted up the cast iron pillars to the upper floors, turning the entire plant into a furnace.

Noise from the machines, which had damaged the hearing of every operative, came to a halt only twenty-five minutes a day, during the lunch period. Congestion in the stairways made it impossible to leave the plant so meals were eaten at the machines.

Even so, things were better than in the old days before the reform laws, when most of the labor came from public sources, prisons and orphanages, some from cottage labor. Wages then ran about sixpence a day. When girls were needed from the outside, they were compelled to live in dormitories on the premises with only Sunday to visit their families. Things, indeed, had gotten better.

*

Maud reached the sixth-floor landing straining for every step and hung onto the railing gasping until the furious thumping in her chest slowed. Peg put her arm about her shoulder, steadied her, then pulled her out of earshot behind a stack of linen bolts.

"I'm all right, Peg."

"The devil you are. Look at you, you're skin and bones. It's your first baby and you should be taking better care of yourself." She felt her sister's clammy forehead. "I'm talking to Myles tonight."

"No, I won't have it, Peg."

"For God's sake, your husband's making a living."

"We need the money if we're to get out of here."

"It will do you no good at all if you kill yourself in the process."

"Don't talk to Myles."

"I am."

"I promise I'll quit in a few weeks." She pushed past her sister and entered the workroom. It was out of focus and whirling. Two hundred girls . . . two hundred machines. The gaslight turned up grudgingly. She made her way unevenly toward the chair before that machine as she had gone to it two thousand times over . . . only a few more times till after the baby comes . . . The foreman strutted up and down the aisle in his pre-work blathering. The sixth floor had fallen behind the other two in production for a week now. Changes would be made if they didn't get on it proper! Maud buttoned her sweater up against the cold. There would be some heat coming through the pillars on the third floor soon. Thank God she worked near the pillar. If only she didn't have to work near it in summer as well. The fingers had been cut out of her woolen gloves so she could keep her hands warm and still operate the machine. A bundle of seven waited on her machine. She snipped the cord, pulled her tags and placed them in her apron pocket. Seven pence for seven shirts. Seven pence for freedom. Seven pence for the blacksmith shop in Convoy. It wasn't too bad on the sixth floor except for the walk up the steps. Winter's cold was more than compensated for by the fact that the heat from the third floor didn't reach them in full fury during the summer. Peg was at the machine beside her and Deirdre would be running to their floor from the cutting room.

Poor Deirdre. In a few months she would put in her terrible year or two at the irons on the third floor. After that, a penny a shirt. Her niece, Deirdre, and her ma, Bessie; the old and the young of it. Bessie was a ravaged old woman of forty-four now, doing the last of her days in packing on the second floor.

Deirdre came between Maud and Peg and gave a bundle to her ma. "The dawn just came up," she said. "It looks like it may be a nice day. Maybe we can go to the roof for lunch."

With that lovely thought in their heads, the six o'clock whistle shrieked the room into bombastic action.

After an hour of the aches and discomfort of the treadle, the hunching over, the baby, the cold, the noise and turmoil, she became oblivious to it all. Maud was in Donegal, in Convoy, where the hills rolled lovely, and she was standing in the doorway of Myles's shop with a wee wane in her arms and another hanging onto her apron and Myles looked up from the anvil all muscled and sooty and smiled and wiped the sweat from his forehead and washed his face and hands before kissing her and they walked with their arms about each other as they always did to the big tree between the shop and their cottage where she had spread their lunch ...

*

Angus Witherspoon, the business half of the partnership, sensed a nibbling around the edges of the linen market as cotton made its return. He and Simon McNab were old, without suitable heirs, and with more money than they could spend in a lifetime. When a serious buyer appeared in the form of the Earl of Foyle, it was time to unload.

MacAdam Rankin, representing Lord Arthur Hubble, brought in a respected firm of architects to examine the physical property and they came up with a list of staggering flaws. With this in hand, Rankin had a bargaining tool. He argued that a minimum of two hundred thousand quid would be needed to set the factory straight. Countering their claim that the building was fireproof, the architects maintained that if the cast iron pillars ever became overheated in a fire and were hit with water they would crack. This could cause the entire building to collapse.

In addition to introducing steel framing to get rid of some of the beams, a sprinkler system and fire escapes would be required. Moreover, an additional warehouse had to be built to end the practice of cluttering passageways with material. Finally, a head-to-toe renovation was needed, from replacement of most windows to ventilation and heating systems to redesigning the women's chairs, all in order to obtain maximum production.

MacAdam Rankin used this cleverly during negotiations to depress the price of the business. Once Witherspoon and McNab sold out, the architects' recommendations were filed away and never acted upon. The old building rattled along as grimly as before, aging garishly, growing filthier and more dangerous by the year.

When Rankin passed from the scene and Lord Roger took over, linen was again in a bull market and the factory was in full production. He made a single inspection of the building and never again went above the ground floor. With his control of flax lands and mills, the shirt factory profits were staggering, some half million quid a year, and this money largely financed Lord Roger's plunge into railroads, ships and other acquisitions. There was talk now and again about doing something with the building but this proved idle patter. No renovations were made on the excuse and rationale that linen might collapse again. It became a prime and basic policy of Foyle Enterprises that the shirt factory was going to be milked dry.

With concern shifted away from renovating the old building or putting up a new one, the major problem was to keep union organizers out. Maxwell Swan had long shown his mettle in that area at the Weed Works in Belfast. After personally setting up a spy system in the factory, he detached his first assistant Kermit Devine to remain in Londonderry with Lord Hubble. Although Devine was a Catholic, he had been a loyal servant of the Crown for three decades when Swan bought him out of Dublin Castle.

Devine's spy system was not only the peer of that in the Weed Works, he developed a special action squad of fanatical loyalty to the Earl. They were constantly at hand ready to apply their union-smashing skills at any level, on any assignment, at any time. Despite them, labor peace at Witherspoon & McNab remained tentative. The factory was almost totally Catholic, not the brand of loyal workers Sir Frederick had in his Belfast domain, and alertness against anarchy was an around-the-clock business.

*

Lord Roger arrived at Foyle Enterprises headquarters at precisely nine o'clock. The Georgian mansion on Abercorn Road stood about a block away from the shirt factory and could be seen from some of its upper windows. Coming to the office was jolly fun these days, for his father-in-law had a bright new toy to play with.

For a number of years a quandary had existed on the home island concerning the telephone. The national company was privately owned and deemed a threat to the government-monopolized telegraph system which was operated by the General Post Office. While Parliament argued the issue and select committees investigated, the telephone's growth remained stunted. New lines in the cities were wanting everywhere but stringing wires from house to house was unsightly and unmanageable and the government was reluctant to grant underground leave-

ways. Applications were also declined on the long-distance
intercity rights-of-way.

Sir Frederick became enamored of the telephone from
the beginning and bought heavily into an Ulster subsidiary
of the national company which established the first switchboard in Belfast for local subscribers. It was easier to
manipulate things away from the mother island and, after
years of hassle, Sir Frederick was able to obtain a leave-
way from Belfast to Londonderry by using the route of
his trans-Ulster railway.

The long-distance system in Ulster began at a switchboard at the Weed Works and terminated at Foyle Enterprises, another coup of the dynamic Sir Frederick.

Lord Roger came to his office twice weekly, on Monday and Friday, to open and close the week's business. He
deplored that absenteeism during his father's reign that
put everything into the hands of underlings and made
their holdings deteriorate accordingly.

Along with his personal assistant, Ralph Hastings, Kermit Devine was constantly at Roger's side and served as
a daily courier to and from the Manor. Devine never
achieved Swan's status but he was heavily into the under-
cover side of things as the unions attempted to infringe.
A nondescript man of total loyalty in his late fifties, Devine's squad carried on the seamy affairs of beatings, kid-
nappings or whatever was required to maintain labor
peace.

After the morning round of meetings with his factory
and mill directors, rail and shipping people and solicitors,
the toy would be put into play. Lord Roger chatted with
Sir Frederick in great detail twice a week, usually during
the noon hour. In addition to old business and new
schemes, Caroline and the boys came into Londonderry
one day for the titillation of their grandfather. It was
gossamer, pure gossamer, this telephone!

On this Friday it was ten minutes to twelve when Lord
Roger rang through, precisely the time the fire started.

*

Terry Devlin had just turned sixteen, completing a full
five years of apprenticeship on the third floor. He was at
the top of his wage scale, nine shillings a week, and next
in line to move up to the cutting room. That would be a

glorious day, a signal to manhood. He would have a job, that illusive Bogside rarity, and could begin drinking in the pubs, what with a bob or two in his pocket. Terry worked among the blooming girls, pressers of about his age. He had held secret longings for a number of them but was in no position to blurt out his feelings. Before he could get truly friendly, it seemed, they always moved upstairs to become sewing machine operatives. Becoming a cutter meant he could start courting, if he so desired.

It had been a long and cruel go and during the summer months he thought he'd not outlive the heat, but it would all be worth it now, with his promotion. The third-floor routine before noon was to clean the ash and cinders from the stoves which heated the irons and run them down to the bins outside. Terry Devlin knelt successively before the stoves in his care, opened the door below the grate and shoveled the overflow into a pair of buckets. When these were full up he grunted under their weight, carrying them out of the workroom.

He quickly adjusted his eyes to the sudden plunge into darkness, for the gaslight in the hall was always blocked by stacks of incoming shirts. Today's backlog ran to two thousand, leaving almost no walking room. He sucked in a breath of fear. In the darkness it was difficult to pinpoint the elevator shaft, which was neither gated nor guarded. Over the years a number of people had fallen to their deaths, including his best friend. Others had been crippled by being trapped and crushed between the shaft opening and the descending elevator.

He tiptoed gingerly but suddenly left his feet, tripping over an unseen bundle of shirts, and both buckets of ashes spilled over. He sprang up in a frenzy with first thoughts of dirtying the shirts. What to do? Try to brush up the ashes and sneak down unnoticed? Try to get some light on the matter? No, someone might see him then. It was too dark to work . . . maybe open the workroom doors . . . no . . . no . . . they'd see him. If his clumsiness were revealed it could cost him his life's dream of becoming a cutter.

He stood trembling and whimpering and biting at his finger. His eyes widened suddenly on sight of a hot cinder from his bucket eating through a stack of shirts. The red

ring in the material widened and deepened and little curls
of smoke rose from them. Terry plunged his way through
the mass of garments to a shelf near the lavatory where a
bucket of water was stored and grabbed it down and
flung it! It was empty, the bottom rotted out! The boy
became hopelessly confused at that moment and, as he
whirled about looking for respite, the shirts closed on him
like the tentacles of a soft octopus. He threw his hands up
to knock them off, backing up as he did, and his feet
slipped over the edge of the elevator shaft. Terry Devlin
plunged down screaming but it went unheard, for the
noon whistle drowned it.

*

Peg and Maud left their machines quickly at the sound
of the whistle and were immediately joined by Deirdre. If
all were in luck, if things were not too crowded on the
stairs, it would take four minutes to get up to the roof
and four minutes to return. That would leave seventeen
full minutes up there.

The cutters on the top floor let the girls have the roof
on good days. They had the advantage of working in
natural light and ventilation. So many girls would be
attempting to get up the four iron ladders through the
trap door it would be unfair to add to the congestion
. . . unless one were courting and it was a chance to
spend a few minutes together. Besides the gallantry, one
could get a peek up a skirt, invited or otherwise, by
helping them up and down the ladders.

Each woman in turn groaned for joy as she reached
the burst of light and air and soon the roof held sixty or
seventy, chomping away at their lunches and looking out
to the ever splendid view of the river at its bend.

Maud McCracken alone looked down on the Bogside.
From here she could almost make out the forge on
Lone Moor Road. Thank God the week was nearly over.
Sunday they would take the train to Convoy and see the
forge. She toyed with the notion of quitting. This week
had been particularly agonizing and it wasn't going to get
better. She had barely made it up the steps today and by
noon she was on the brink of passing out. Peg was right.
She ought to stop. It would do nothing but create worry

for Myles if she collapsed and had to be carried out. It would be grand if she could wake up Monday and not have to return till after the baby.

"Peg," she said impulsively, "I think, maybe, tomorrow will be my last day."

Her sister smiled and patted her hand.

*

For the last fifteen minutes of his call to Belfast, Lord Roger was constantly interrupted by one commotion or another outside. It began with the noon whistle. His office was in the rear so he was unable to see what was going on. The long-distance line faded more than usual, adding to his annoyance. By twenty-five after twelve any notion of continuing the conversation was killed by the sound of the fire brigade charging up Abercorn Road. He shouted to Sir Frederick that he would try to replace the call later when things had quieted down and he rang off.

At that moment Kermit Devine flung his door open. "What the devil's going on out there, Mr. Devine?"

"There's a fire at the factory," Devine said, opening the double doors into the adjoining conference room which afforded a view down Abercorn Road to the Witherspoon & McNab building. The two men watched the scene of workers pouring from both sides of the building, emptying into the streets in a half-carnival atmosphere.

Horse-drawn hose reel and chemical wagons came in from different directions followed in a moment by the hook and ladder and steam fire engines pulled by troikas of beating hoofs. A Constabulary van emptied its police, who cleared out operating room and set up a line.

"Doesn't appear too bad," Roger mumbled, pointing to a thin spiral of smoke out of the third floor.

"On the roof, m'lord, look!"

"My God," Roger whispered, gripping the curtains. He felt faint, then quickly gained control. There were women up there, shouting. If anything went wrong, it could be a calamity. He told himself to think. Think! Think! Think! No time to lose one's head.

"Mr. Devine, we'd best have our wits about us."

"I agree to that."

"Are your men at hand?"

"They are, sir."

"Good. We may have to come up with some special assignments if this isn't brought under control at once." Roger paced and shoveled at his hair, glancing back and forth at the growing commotion in the street. "You are fully aware of the past unpleasantness we've had with Kevin O'Garvey over that building."

"I am, sir. Fortunately, he's in London at the moment."

"Well, thank God for that. I want you to get down there, speak to the fire commander and get as accurate and complete a picture as possible. On your way out have the switchboard put me through to Sir Frederick. Keep a line open until he's located."

Devine nodded and was on his way. Roger watched the column of smoke from the third floor thicken as more people continued to evacuate the place. As he looked to the roof, the person of Kevin O'Garvey loomed more and more ominous. If there were deaths, O'Garvey would blow the lid and this time the results could be utterly ruinous. He cursed himself for not taking Swan's advice to get rid of O'Garvey when there was a chance. Well, too late for hindsight. It all became jewel-clear. Unless O'Garvey was intercepted and disposed of the old deal would be illuminated. Otherwise, there was even the possibility of manslaughter charges. With the reformists running Parliament the scandal would be shattering . . . dragging them all up to the dock. . . . As the first flames blew out of the side of the factory, Roger returned to his office and snatched up the phone.

"Where the devil is my call to Sir Frederick?"

"Sorry, sir, bit of confusion here."

*

Old Ben Haggarty, the ancient foreman of the cutters, came through the trap door with a number of men as the first whiffs of smoke danced around the roof.

"Ladies! Ladies! If you please!" he shouted, and held up his hands to ward off the barrage of questions. "If you'll kindly quiet down!" They gathered in close. "There seems to be a small fire on the third floor," he said. "The lads from the fire brigade are at hand and it should be under control in a matter of minutes. There is no danger whatsoever."

A massive intonation of relief followed and he waved their jabbering to a halt once more.

"We are going to make an orderly evacuation. I want no pushing or shoving. At all costs, no one is to panic. My boys will lead you down, we've lanterns, and you should be out on the street in ten minutes. One at a time, one at a time."

As Ben Haggarty spoke, Maud alone was able to pierce through his calm and detect pending disaster.

Perhaps she was dreaming it up, but somehow, at that instant, she knew she was going to die. As Ben spoke she maneuvered Deirdre close to the escape route. Deirdre, poor little ragamuffin, was an image of herself eight years ago. Maud looked at the girl who had never felt a single true flush of joy and she made her decision. Maud had had her moment or two, that spark of hope that came with the Gaelic League, a few wild times with a few wild lads, a touch of laughter here and there. With Myles there had been nights of complete magic both with him and with the dream they shared.

Deirdre had had nothing.

Ben Haggarty had done much to keep things orderly and with the help of his lads they began down the ladder. Maud shoved her niece to it.

"You go on down, love," she said. "I'll wait a bit. I'd just hold things up with this stomach of mine."

"I'll wait with you, Aunt Maud," the girl answered.

Maud slapped her over the face, hard. "Do as I tell you!" she commanded.

"You heard your Aunt Maud," her mother said. "Go down, I'll wait with her."

"Why did you slap me!"

"Go down!"

Peg gripped her sister's hand hard as the girl, still very hurt, swung over the top and out of sight. The noise below increased as a wind shift off the river blew a funnel of smoke over the roof.

*

Roger paced a mad route between the conference room and his office as he watched the flames move up the building with steady and unabated speed. He picked up the phone innumerable times. The screaming outside heightened as something went on beyond his line of vision. At last Kermit Devine gasped his way back.

"Afraid it doesn't look too good."

"All right, tell me."

"As much as we can gather, it started on a lower floor and is being carried up through the elevator shafts and stair wells."

"What about the women on the roof? How many are there?"

"We don't know, sir. Two of them panicked and leaped off. The firemen got their hand nets beneath them all right, but they went right on through to the pavement."

"Oh, dear God! Is that bloody chief an incompetent or something? Why the hell don't they get their ladders up?"

"They'll only go as high as the fourth floor."

Roger pulled himself together as best he could. As the two men exchanged knowing looks, Roger's assistant, Ralph Hastings, made an appearance.

"Not meaning to unsettle you, m'lord, but it has been suggested we evacuate here. I spoke to the fire officer myself and he says there's no danger of it reaching us but best not to take any chances."

"Yes, yes, Hastings. All right. Move everyone along. I shan't be coming for a few moments."

"Sir, I must insist . . ."

"Get the hell out, Hastings!" Roger shouted, pushing the man and slamming the door behind him. He returned to his desk in complete calm. "What are your thoughts, Mr. Devine?"

"My lads are standing by waiting for your instructions. I've sent one to the area commander requesting troops move up to Hubble Manor for the Countess and your sons."

Roger nodded.

"I also made a request that the balance of the garrisons of Londonderry and Donegal be alerted to move in to seal off the Bogside, in the event of a civil disorder. The main question is O'Garvey. If he were here, my men would do the job."

"We're going to have to keep news of the fire from leaving Londonderry until I can get through to Sir Frederick," Roger said. "I want the telegraph lines cut from

the General Post Office and stop all train movement.
Can you manage it, Mr. Devine?"

"Yes, sir."

"Good man."

As Kermit Devine sped out, Roger returned to the conference room in time to see the factory explode into
flame!

*

Deirdre scrambled back onto the roof screaming for
her mother and aunt. Half the women were on their knees
weeping out prayers and the others ran around screaming
hysterically. As billows of smoke blackened the sky, the
heat of encroaching flames slowly turned the roof into a
griddle.

Maud threw her arms about her niece, who babbled a
semi-coherent story that some of them got through but
the stairs collapsed, driving the rest back up. Mayhem and
frenzy took over as the first of the flames licked their way
over the cornice onto the roof and began to move them
into a corner. Peg shrieked and ran aimlessly, beating at
the fire, staggering back in total mania. A finger of fire
spurted onto her skirt and in a final last horror she threw
herself off the building. Maud had Deirdre mercifully covered from the sight.

"Hail, Mary," she said, going to her knees, "blessed art
thou among women. . . . Pray for us now and at the hour
of our death."

*

Roger hacked as smoke reached his nostrils. He shouted
into the phone to no avail. Now the heat could be felt
creeping in. He fought his way out of his jacket and
loosened his collar. For an agonized instant he hovered
on the notion of abandoning the call but realized it
could mean the end of them all.

"Hello! Hello!" a dim but blessed voice bellowed as
though it were trying to shout over the breadth of Ulster.

"Freddie, thank God. Who's on the switchboard?"

"Me, sir, Devine."

"Good of you to call back, Roger . . ."

"This is a grave emergency. Listen with extreme care."

"Go on."

"The shirt factory is afire. Did you hear that?"

"Yes . . . go on."

"We are going to have a number of deaths. You know what kind of reaction there's going to be."

"See here, Roger! I want you to get Caroline and the boys out of there at once."

"No, no, no, no. We are in no personal danger. A military unit will be on hand at the Manor within the hour. What concerns me is Kevin O'Garvey. Do you fully understand me, Freddie?"

"My God . . . that's right. . . ."

"Exactly. He almost broke silence on us once. He's bound to put us under with this. Hello, Freddie . . . hello . . . hello. Freddie, he's in London now."

"I understand you completely, Roger. We're in luck. The Brigadier is there also. But, Roger, even if it all goes well at this end, it will take a few hours to get ahold of Swan. News of the fire will be all over by then."

The line faded as a blast of thermal air shattered the windows and, behind it, a rush of smoke. Roger was half blinded and he was drenched in sweat and broke into a fit of coughing.

"Hello, Roger, hello, hello."

"Yes, you're back on, Freddie. All telegraph and telephone lines and trains from Londonderry are out of order. We'll probably have until morning to play with in the confusion."

"I'm already cracking on it. I suggest you get Caroline and the boys to the hunting . . ."

As the line went dead, Roger held the phone, wavering in stupor. Hastings returned. "My lord, you must get out!" He grabbed Roger and led him from the office.

As they reached the landing Roger screamed for Devine to abandon the switchboard and cut the lines and the three of them reeled into the street.

Witherspoon & McNab was entirely out of control, a mad holocaust, an all-consuming pyre!

Conor Larkin and Myles McCracken reached the police line as a rain of bodies hurled from the roof.

At that instant the water from fire hoses which had reached the third floor powered into the cast iron pillars. One after the other they shattered. Rumbling slowly at first in a death rattle, the building twisted and trembled, then the floors cracked open, splitting like an earthquake, and one story emptied down on the other in an avalanche.

CHAPTER FIFTEEN: Brigadier Maxwell Swan kept active files on enemies, potential enemies, anarchists and competitors as a workaday way of life. It was his past years in counterinsurgency that had made him so totally valuable to Sir Frederick. Daily movements, habits and peculiarities of someone as important as Kevin O'Garvey were catalogued in Swan's head.

When Sir Frederick first reached him it looked good, a stroke of luck that both he and O'Garvey were in London and that Lord Roger had shown the presence of mind to block the news out of Londonderry.

Swan had a number of people in London he could call upon for ready assistance. Some of them were former officers and informers. Others were Irish Catholics who had worked for him in covert operations in Dublin Castle, made their passage, and situated well in England. These men were in his debt. He went to work instantly to find suitable henchmen.

Six hours to the minute after Sir Frederick relayed the information, Swan arrived at his London address, the Colonial Club, where Chief Steward Tompkins greeted him in the foyer.

"Evening, Brigadier," Tompkins said in the prevailing whisper that ruled the club as he relieved Swan of his cape, cane and top hat. "Heard the news, sir?"

"No, I've been tied up."

"Terrible fire in Londonderry. Many deaths feared. If I'm not mistaken, one of Lord Hubble's factories."

"That's ghastly," Swan said.

"Sir Frederick tried to reach you by long-distance cablephone forty minutes ago. I took the liberty of checking the time of your dinner reservation and booked a call for about that time."

"Ah, good man, Tompkins. I'll take my sherry in the Command Officers' Lounge and wait for the call there."

"Very good, sir."

A loner in his own circle of officers, Swan scootched off to his usual lounge chair tucked away behind a pillar and buried his face in the day's papers until the call came through.

"Hello, Freddie, Max here."

"Anything new in London?" Weed asked.

"Some news of a fire in Londonderry. First reports came in about a half hour ago. Was it serious?" Swan asked.

"Very. Several dozen dead, I fear. They won't know the full extent for a day or two."

"Ghastly."

"Were you able to keep your appointment, Max?"

"Yes, it all went extremely well. Negotiations came through without a hitch. The deal is closed and sealed. I attended to the final signing personally."

"Splendid. How's the theater this season?"

*

NOTED IRISH PARTY MP DISAPPEARS
London, December 5, 1899 (Reuters)

Scotland Yard reports that Mr. Kevin O'Garvey, M.P. (Irish Party-East Donegal), has been missing for four days from his London address on Jamaica Road, Southwark. Answering a call for assistance from Mrs. Midge Murphy, owner of his rooming house, a routine investigation of known relatives, usual haunts and his residence in Londonderry, failed to turn up either clues or motivation for the disappearance.

O'Garvey was last seen Friday evening at Clancy's Public House, Neptune Road, Southwark, where the patrons consist largely of Irish dockers, seasonal workers and immigrants. Mr. O'Garvey was well known in the establishment, visiting it several times weekly to assist Irish constituents. Mr. Enda Clancy, proprietor of the establishment, saw O'Garvey leave the premises at approximately 6:00 P.M. in the presence of a young man who had sought him out there. This person was unknown at the establishment but, from speech and manner, Mr. Clancy and others concluded he was of Irish origin. However, he was in and out of the place so quickly, an accurate description was not possible.

In answering questions by Inspector Arnold Sheperd of Scotland Yard, Clancy saw nothing unusual about the situation. "Kevin O'Garvey was almost like a priest or doctor," he said. "He was always answering emergency calls." This was confirmed by Mrs. Murphy, who testified to O'Garvey's frequent comings and goings on behalf of petitioners.

When questioned about O'Garvey's recent health and behavior, "nothing out of the ordinary was noted," Inspector Sheperd said. O'Garvey was extremely methodical in his habits and movements, generally crossing Southwark Park to and from the public house and his lodgings. "A thorough inspection of the park turned up nothing," Sheperd reported.

O'Garvey was first elected to Commons a decade and a half ago in the Parnell landslide and has been known for Irish "republican" activities. "His long history of Fenian activities is public record," Sheperd added, "and he was bound to pick up innumerable enemies. He was easily accessible to his constituents so foul play cannot be ruled out."

*

Lord Roger and Sir Frederick put their forces into play massively. They wanted a quick conclusive investigation underplayed as much as possible, although the British press had swarmed into Londonderry. Rumors abounded that the fire was either the work of anarchists or Fenians, a thesis latched onto promptly by the journalists.

Opening smally but with proper pomp and solemnity, the commission of inquiry reviewed the fire, safety and work laws which were almost nil. It was immediately ascertained that no law had been broken. A window-dressing parade of "experts" testified that the building could not have possibly burned unless it was the work of arsonists, which heightened the anarchist/Fenian theory for the eager press. Furthermore, most of the dead were on the roof, which was in violation of a company safety regulation. None of the experts were cross-examined to a meaningful degree and the people who worked there were not considered authorities or qualified on fire matters and were not permitted to testify to conditions which were ruled irrelevant. No one said why women were driven to the roof if indeed anyone ever knew there was a rule against it. The conclusion on the end of the first day was that the building was absolutely safe and fireproof and under normal conditions on the day of the holocaust.

At the beginning of the second day of inquiry, the commission was stunned by the chief of Constabulary, who asked permission to interrupt the proceedings and commenced to read a signed confession of arson.

One Martin Mulligan, "a known Fenian and republican," had signed an admission to setting the building afire before three witnesses in his cell in the Londonderry bridewell. Unfortunately, the chief concluded, Mulligan's body had just been found. He had apparently committed suicide by hanging himself by his belt in his cell immediately after the confession.

Displaying stunning efficiency, the confession was followed in minutes by a battery of witnesses who established that Mulligan had once worked at Witherspoon & McNab as a stable hand for a short period but had been fired for drunkenness on the job. Thereafter, he had been overheard at numerous public houses repeating a threat that he was going to burn the building down. He had likewise boasted publicly of innumerable Fenian and republican exploits of an illegal nature.

What went untold was that Martin Mulligan was known as a harmless old sot who hadn't drawn a sober breath for years and who often as not turned himself in to the Constabulary for a night or two's free lodging in jail before returning to his true occupation of vagrancy. No one on the panel of witnesses was there to testify that Marty boasted of countless other fantasies, all the babblings of a mindless alcoholic. No one said they saw him in the vicinity on the day of the fire or tried to explain why the arson wasn't accomplished during the night hours. No one testified to the fact that he didn't even own a belt but wore braces and that the suicide itself was highly questionable.

Yet with all this flimsiness there was no one around to set matters straight. Kevin O'Garvey, the Bogside's champion, was missing. Had he been there, the farce would have been halted, for he had too much evidence against the building and too much mileage in proceedings of this kind to permit such a travesty. But Kevin O'Garvey was gone.

The coup was delivered in the form of three men who witnessed and swore to Martin Mulligan's confession. Two who heard it were the Constabulary chief and a Hubble solicitor who was also a Londonderry Corporation Councilman. Although those two gentlemen and their motives might be suspect, it was the third who closed the book on the matter, for he was among the most respected Catholics in Londonderry.

Frank Carney swore he had heard Martin Mulligan's words.

The confession was accepted and the investigation officially closed before Christmas.

CHAPTER SIXTEEN: A macabre reign of horror followed. When the fire was finally cooled down they dug through the rubble, then sifted through the ashes and as the toll mounted it hammered numbness on numbness. Those with missing loved ones hung onto foolish hope that a saint had interceded with a miracle in their case but none did. The missing were dead and that was that.

Most of the forty who leaped from the roof were bashed beyond recognition and lay in a ghoulish line, twisted and mangled, in the morgue where screams pierced that awful place as the parade of terrified family recognized a piece of clothing or a ring or shoes. The corpses dug out of the collapsed rubble were in worse condition. The charred bodies of most of those who had burned were beyond recognition. The death count topped a hundred, and another hundred lay badly burned in the hospital.

The bulk of the dead were seventy-two women who broke a company rule by seeking seventeen minutes of sunlight on the roof. Two dozen of this number carried unborn babies.

Ten cutters, most of whom had stayed to help evacuate the women, were crushed or suffocated when the building collapsed, as were five firemen when the pillars split.

The rest were children, eighteen in all, from nine to fifteen years.

The Tully family lost three women. Others lost as many or more. There was no compensation or medical money for those who had been burned and a single mass grave took the unidentified blackened waste.

During this time an investigation had been conducted and closed and Christmas made a sordid appearance. The

twentieth century came into being, a symbol of hope celebrated elsewhere in the world.

For weeks the Bogside was incoherent in its grief. The
already weakened muscles and sinews were further ripped
and shattered. Whitewash of the fire investigation came as
no surprise, for no one's memory went back so far as to
remember justice. Commissions of the Crown had done
this before in Derry, they would do it again. Passion to lash
back at their oppressors and tormentors was sapped.
Bursts of pain and rage at the time of the funerals were
wept out at graveside and prayed out by half-maddened
survivors. When this blood was spent, the old lethargy,
the old acceptance of tragedy drove them deeper, deeper, deeper into the mumbo-jumbo of Jesus and Mary and
escape in drink and drug. Bogside was Bogside was Bogside.

Four months passed before anything resembling normalcy returned to Bogside's speech and movement when
a touch of the pain began to subside. During that time
people were too dazed to comprehend that Kevin O'Garvey was no longer with them. No trace was found. When
the agony of Black Friday tempered, a new agony, realization of their champion's demise, crashed down with delayed impact.

In those months the night of Conor Larkin was without end. He was strong and they were weak, yet he was
wan and dull of mind and red of eye. The might ebbed
from his powerful body and the poem from his heart and
the song from his lips. He backslid into becoming all of
his drunken Bogside brothers, falling into a few moments
of tormented rest when the brain was soaked full with
deadening gin. He dragged about the Bogside grungier
each day, barely nodding to those who worshiped him,
despising them for that worship. I have no magic answers,
he pleaded silently to their hungry stares, I have no answers.

The only thing that seemed to keep him from crossing
the line was a desperation to keep Myles McCracken
from going under. He took him in, listened to the endless
wail of despair, choked on Myles's tears, dressed him,
fed him, talked him through night after night. Deeply as
the wound was driven, somehow the answer seemed simpler for Myles. It was clear that he was finding it in the

endless bottle. He drank from morbidity to silliness to
stupor in a cycle that never started or ended. Conor
thought it was no time to take the man off his drug, for
without it Myles slid immediately into breast-beating tan-
trums of agony. For the moment he needed drink as he
needed air. Perhaps, Conor prayed, when the shock had
lessened it would be time enough to grab Myles by the
shoulders and shake him and slap him back into manhood. Not now. No lectures, only to watch and wait for
the healing process to start, to be there, to help. Conor
prayed there might be a coming back for Myles, but for
now he was dust.

Away from Myles McCracken, Conor's own depression
was a miracle of all Bogside. Confusion raided the brain
until thoughts lost value and one had no desire to wake
up after a sleep but only to sleep again. But even sleep
brought no rest, for sleep meant that bedlam of pus-filled
sores and human fire bombs hurling into Derry's walls and
at the top of those walls great cauldrons of boiling oil
pouring down, drowning old beggars, and bony cats
scratching out children's eyes and thumping drums leading endless lines of blacksuited men marching at funeral
cadence with orange crosses in their hands and fields run
white with the mush of rotted potatoes and hundreds of
women trapped as a fire raged, unable to break past the
wrought-iron screen.

Bogside was devouring the will from him. Bogside was
gutting him alive. Bogside was winning.

*

Bishop Nugent passed on in his eightieth year, an
uninspired prince of the Church whose three-decade reign
over the diocese was marked by mediocrity. An ordinary
Derry priest with a good line of gab and a grasp of
church politics, he ran a pragmatic office keynoted by
vacillation until he was certain to be on the safe side of
every issue. Bogside's rot and ruin stirred nothing more in
the man than platitudinous prayer.

In his final decade, his old fence sitting degenerated
further into an inability to make any clear-cut judgment
and the diocese hung in a kind of theological limbo. Stern
church disciplinarians surrounded the Bishop, sealed him

off and set plans for an era of heavy-handed ecclesiastical power.

Bogside had always been a bone of contention. Ignoble circumstances there gave rise to liberal priests who took a free hand and even freer view of church law. As Bishop Nugent's mind began to stray, a small band of young turks led by Father Patrick McShane pressed their ideas and stretched rules to suit their needs and the needs of their beleaguered flocks. These priests plunged into the Gaelic League to revive the Irish language and culture, a position contrary to both the Church and the British overlords.

While Nugent gasped out death rattles, his palace guard closed ranks, formed a unified front, and placed in nomination Charles Donoghue to the Cardinal in Armagh as Nugent's successor. Donoghue was chosen.

Hardly any power in Ireland was more total than that of an autocratic Bishop in the good graces of the British. The new Bishop Donoghue asserted immediate authority with a series of swift dicta aimed at reduction of the young turks in Bogside. Doctrine was an unbending adherence to the harshest interpretation of Catholicism. Humility by priest and laymen became the new order. Bogside liberalism was done.

In the weeks after Black Friday a rash of labor organizers, reformers and republicans descended on Derry and the young turks identified with them. This was intolerable to the full skein of the establishment, be it Orange, Protestant, British, the Earl or the new Bishop Donoghue. He used the moment to rearrange things, thumpingly.

*

Father Pat entered the forge just as the delivery wagon was made ready to leave, with Conor up on the driver's bench. The priest was pleased to see him shaved, cleanly dressed and reasonably clear-eyed. He got up alongside as Conor released the brakes and they rode off without conversation up into the walled city where the delivery was made. The father nodded to a direction of privacy and the horse was hitched along the Grand Parade where the two continued on foot to the wall.

From here the Bogside below didn't appear all that
bad. There was a certain odd beauty in the rows of perfectly matched slate rooftops rising and falling in symmetry and the chimney pots all sending up thin streams
of peat smoke. The smell of that was always grand. They
found a nook where they would not be annoyed.

Father Pat as well as Andrew Ingram had given up
haranguing Conor over his months-long depressed binge,
knowing that the man would start to come up when he
could sink no further. Obviously, that return had started.

"It's beginning to show touches of life again down
there," Father Pat said, "and so are you."

"I'm going to live because I don't want to die," Conor
said, "but that place is dead. It was dead before Black
Friday and before Kevin O'Garvey disappeared. It will
never get its face out of the muck, now. It's Myles that
I'm worried over. I can't seem to do anything with him,
Father Pat."

"It's time you cut him loose, Conor, or he'll start to
drag you down."

"I can't bring myself to it, I just can't."

"Myles McCracken was born a loser," the priest said.
"Twice in his life he's dared to love and each time it's
ended up in a disaster. He'll never give his heart again.
He'd be too terrified."

"But to get up and live, Father Pat . . . he's got to do
that."

"Some men can overcome tragedy, even attain great-
ness because of it. Most men can't and the Bogside is
full of those."

"I know what you're saying because it's been going
through my mind as well . . . what's to become of him?"

"He's too scared to go back and even more scared to
go forward. So he'll stay put. The Bogside will swallow
him up and in time he'll become a harmless old drunk
who keeps himself in a state of alcoholic bliss as a shield
against his nightmare."

Conor knew the pronouncement was cruel but correct,
the words he had tried not to say, himself. So that was it.
The weak remain and wither as they always did in Ireland.

"I'm leaving, Conor," Father Pat said suddenly.

Conor jolted, closed his eyes and made no effort to

hold back his tears. The sickness of the past months crawled all over him again. He faced his friend bleeding of heart.

"It appears that Father Eveny, Father Keenan, Father Mallory and myself have overextended our ration of sin," he said, trying to be casual.

"Jesus, Father! Not this on top of everything else!" Conor exploded.

"Aye, man, it's so. You don't make any deals with God in this business."

"God my ass. God's not sending you away. It's that bastard of a Bishop!"

"I'd rather not indulge in a Jesuit dialogue with you over who is doing what and why. I'm transferred, I'm going, it's that simple."

"Where! When!"

"I'm to be jugged for a few weeks of meditation at the seminary to cleanse and rededicate myself. I'll be able to see Dary. Then, what the devil, I've always wanted to get out of Bogside."

"Where, Father?"

The gaslights rose on cue, breaking into the imminent darkness. Father Pat shrugged boyishly but was unable to ward off Conor's persistence.

"Oh, there's a grand old priest by the name of Father Clare who is no longer able to cover his parish. The parish is too poor for him to have made enough to retire and, as you know, our order makes no provisions to take care of older priests."

"I said where!"

"To the farthest reaches of Bishop Donoghue's domain. Everything north of Carrigart on the Rosguill Peninsula."

"No, dammit! I'll not see you a curate whistling litanies to the wind in half-empty churches of dying Celtic mystics."

"I'm sorry, Conor, but they're entitled to a priest, too." He gripped Conor's arms. "It's either there or emigrate to America, and I'll not be driven out of Ireland any more than you. Besides," he laughed, "that's just what America needs, one more Irish priest."

Conor quelled his revulsion and Father Pat released him, then went into a long hesitation of his own.

"I need to confess," the priest whispered.

"I don't understand you."

"I said I need to confess. Will you hear me, Conor?"

Father Pat walked a few feet along the wall, far enough to see the gutted shell of Witherspoon & McNab. Then the light gave out. "Frank Carney and myself joined in a conspiracy, a conspiracy of silence. About the time you came into Derry, the Bogside Association was dead broke, virtually defunct. Then it suddenly came into great funds through Kevin O'Garvey. Your own shop was financed by it. Frank and I never asked where the money came from because we really didn't want to know. We always suspected Kevin took soiled money from Lord Hubble in exchange for an agreement not to investigate that factory."

"Oh, my God! I don't want to hear any more of this!"

"You're going to have to, boy."

"Nae, Kevin wouldn't do a thing like that, nae, dammit, no, no, no, no!" Then he stopped. He started to ask . . . did he? Did he really? And he pleaded with his eyes to not have to be made to believe it.

"No real proof," Father Pat said. "Only a guess. He confided in me not once but a hundred times his hatred of the factory and finally once that he was going to investigate it. Suddenly he didn't. But all of us in Bogside have made our deals with the Devil. Frank did before the commission of inquiry over the fire. It takes no genius to figure out who got to him and why he testified the way he did. I've made deals. So did Kevin."

"No!"

"Only to be able to see some poor soul smile once in his life. You can't damn a man for that, Conor. I've been so dragged down by despair I've thought of leaving the priesthood. I've even thought of taking my own life. Well, Kevin O'Garvey did it for others. And never forget he did it for you."

"Aye," Conor whispered, knowing. "I'd be hard put not to do the same for him."

"So you see, we're only men. The Hubbles and the British own us so completely they are not only responsible for our sorrows but they dole out our little bits of joy. That's what Kevin bought, a moment of joy for a few people. They even have the power to ration and control our hopes."

Conor's face tightened with a sudden notion. "Do you think they killed him?"

"No, not really. Bogside killed him. Perhaps he heard of the fire, perhaps not. Either way, he'd not have lived long after it."

"Christ, I'm sick, Father Pat. My soul is drained. I'm sick," Conor moaned.

"That's a luxury you cannot afford any longer. They'll be leaning on you down there, more and more."

"Nae," Conor groaned, "nae." Outlined by lamplight, he cast a shadow and his hands shoved into his pockets as he scanned the sky sightlessly, then moved to his friend. "I am not their Father Pat. I am not their Frank Carney. I cannot bargain with my enemies. Nor can I walk among those lost souls and do my praying in silence. I cannot turn my other cheek. I cannot do what I cannot do or be what I cannot be. I must find my way, Father. I'm leaving too."

"Where will you go, Conor?"

"There's talk of the Brotherhood organizing again in Belfast and Dublin."

"You know I won't give my blessing to that."

"I'm not asking for it."

"I suppose it's impossible to convince you that it's the wrong way."

"Take a look down there, Father. Can you tell me your way or Kevin's way has been any better? In one fleeting moment Kevin looked at me and said, 'In the end we're going to have to have a rising, there's no other way.' It's the twentieth century, Father. Some light has got to shine on this land. We cannot walk in the darkness any longer."

*

Conor climbed down the ladder from his room and shook his head at Father Pat. Myles was up there, unconscious, in a terrible state.

"I'll try to do something with him tomorrow," Conor said. "He'll have to go to the hospital if he doesn't stop." He walked around the shop looking at this work and that and turned down the lantern in his office, all filled with plans and drawings. "Funny, I just made the last payment on my loan. I own the fucking place now."

The two men moved about with bowed heads and hands jammed into pockets along the ways of misery of Bligh Lane, into Stanley's Walk barely hearing the trails of "Evening to you, Father Pat, evening, Conor." Conor waited outside while the priest made his last call, then they doubled back to Nick Blaney's. As they approached they heard a voice singing. There had been no song in Bogside for so very long. It was not the sweet voice of a Myles McCracken, but it was song, nonetheless.

"Oh, Danny boy, the pipes, the pipes are callin'
From glen to glen, and round the mountainside."

Their entry usually brought a hale burst of welcomes but the sour mood of the pair was being worn on their sleeves and everyone parted quietly to make room for them at the far end of the bar.

"But come ye back, when summer's in the meadow,
Or when the valley's hushed and white with
snow. . . ."

Three shots of paddy each met swift ends braced with chasers of Derryale. Both Conor and Father Pat pointed to their respective glasses.

"Then I'll be here, in sunshine or in shadow.
Oh, Danny boy, oh, Danny boy, I love you so."

Blaney's wept to a man, it was that lovely.
"Are you Conor Larkin, himself?" a dandy asked.
"Aye."
"Sammy Meehan talking to you from Cleveland in O-Hi-O. I'm visiting the old sod of my father and his father before him. Could I be shaking your hand and buying you and the good father a drink?" The man backed off, frightened at the sight of tears streaming down Conor's cheeks. Conor reached out with his mighty hands, seized Sammy Meehan under his arms and lifted him to sitting on the bar as though he were weightless.
"I'm after giving our Yank friend a little song of insurrection!" Conor cried. His voice was off key and cracked in the hush of the room.

"Oh, then tell me, Sean O'Farrell, where the gathering is to be?
In the old spot by the river, right well known to you and me;
One more word for signal token, whistle up the marchin' tune,
With your pike upon your shoulder, BY THE RISIN' OF THE MOON."

Conor gulped another paddy down. "Am I to sing alone!" he cried, smashing his glass against the wall.

The silence remained awkward and frightened as Nick set up a new shot glass and filled it. Father Pat nodded to the fluter and the accordionist, placed his hand on Conor's shoulder and added his wanting voice.

"Out from many a mud wall cabin, eyes were watching through that night,
Many a manly heart was throbbing for the blessed warning light,
Murmurs passed along the valleys, like the banshee's lonely croon,
And a thousand blades were flashing AT THE RISIN' OF THE MOON."

One by one, the voices joined in, beaten, proud, hopeless, defiant.

"Well they fought for poor old Ireland, and full bitter was their fate,
Oh, what glorious pride and sorrow, fills a name of ninety-eight!
Yet, thank God e'en still are beating hearts in manhood's burning noon.
Who would follow in their footsteps, AT THE RISIN' OF THE MOON!"

END OF PART FOUR

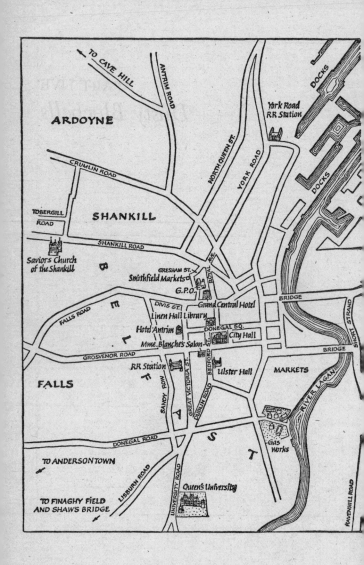

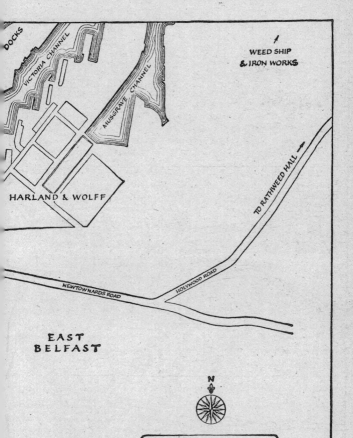

CHAPTER ONE: I was born short and never grew much taller, neither carrying the day nor losing the game at Queen's College. Numerous O'Neills were scattered about Belfast, enough to furnish me a bed and keep me in scroggins. Queen's College carried its usual token number of Catholics but I did find the liberal sanctuaries one might expect of a campus. As a mirror of the restlessness of the society and often its soothsayer, I came to know that one day Queen's would be a wellspring of republican aspirations.

I think the motto of the Hubble family best described the political atmosphere that prevailed at the end of the nineteenth century. It was embedded in stained glass over the family crest in the library at Hubble Manor and, translated from the Latin, read, ONE MORE CHARGE FOR THE GLORY OF THE CROWN. The old lady Victoria in Buckingham Palace was pressing eighty with her name already stamped on the era as the zenith of imperial adventure. A return to power of her Conservative ministers happened just in time for the celebration of her diamond jubilee as monarch.

For the Irish the jubilee was repugnant. All the banalities of empire were magnified by the event, a reminder that we were a subject people, the first to be colonized and reduced to servitude citizenship. Throughout this great celebration many Irish served faint notice that the old bitterness had not diminished and that our long republican hibernation was soon to come to an end.

Spearheaded by the Gaelic Athletic Association and the Gaelic League, nationalistic spirits were on the rise and the Celtic revival at full gallop. Dr. Douglas Hyde, founder of the League, like Emmet, Wolfe Tone and Parnell, was an ascendancy Protestant but no less a Celtophile and republican.

Victoria's diamond jubilee was marred in its London celebration by a boycott of the Irish Party and in Ireland

by an outbreak of riots and the kind of rhetoric that left
no doubt but that another chapter in the "Irish question"
was in the writing.

For thirty-five years the old Queen mourned the loss of
her husband, continuing to sleep beneath a photograph
of him in his coffin and each morning had the servants lay
out his clothing. Ireland was not entirely unlike Albert's
corpse. Any republican recovery we had made from the
famine and aborted Fenian rising was demolished by the
death of Parnell, but as the Empire now girded for
"One more charge for the glory of the Crown," we were
arising from the dead and contemplating "ONE MORE
CHARGE FOR IRELAND."

*

No great rush of job offers greeted me upon graduation
after the turn of the century. I joined that small handful
of educated Catholics who were not entirely accepted by
the Anglos and was looked upon with raised brows by my
own people because of my liberal Protestant schooling.
Body and soul were kept intact as a journalist for a small
and obviously impoverished Catholic Belfast newspaper
and some odds and ends in private tutoring. I also wrote
a little—some poetry, some plays, some essays. Neither
the British nor the Irish quaked under the might of my
pen but I satisfied my Celtic appetites.

*

The vainglory that trumpeted in during the jubilee had
saturated imperial-minded arrogants into a state of
euphoria. Britannic appetite to acquire was bottomless and
the opiate of conquest deafened her to those whiffs of
discontent and subversion cropping up among all her
subject peoples.

Headiness of the jubilee spilled over into yet another
imperial thrust, but one destined to become an epic
turning point in history. Predicated on old greed, a
bumbling and costly adventure opened the first cracks in
Britain's boundless domain. Cecil Rhodes, the epitome of
Empire man, was not content merely to control the
cornucopia of diamonds, gold and other riches pouring
out of the Cape Colony and other South African holdings.

He lusted for the Transvaal and engineered a crude, raw display of power by annexation of the neighbor state into one large British "union."

The Transvaal had been colonized mostly by Boers, a tough breed of Dutch origin. When war was imposed on them, they shocked the British by guerrilla-oriented tactics of swift movement and ambush. With their traditional massiveness and archaic maneuvering, plus the Boers' unexpected furiousness and finesse, was inflicted a series of ignoble defeats on the British forces.

The War Office awoke to the startling fact that in their march to empire the British had not engaged a modern, white, well-armed force for decades. They reacted by pouring upward of a half million troops into the fray from units throughout the Empire. Ireland chipped in with the Royal Irish Fusiliers, the Ulster Rifles, the Inniskillings and the Hubble home regiment, the Coleraine Rifles. We were once again playing out an ancient fate of proving our fighting ability in uniforms other than Irish and on battlefields far from home in a war of someone else's making.

Wherever the British fought, some sort of Irish token force would generally show up to fight on the other side. The Boer War proved no exception. A few soldiers of fortune, mostly Irish-Americans, a few Fenian relics and a few new republicans seeking direction, formed an Irish Brigade to fight alongside the Boers. Although they never numbered more than a few hundred, their presence was telling in propaganda value. In Baltimore, Boston, Philadelphia and New York there was such a stirring of Irish conscience as had not been stirred since the famine. In Dublin, a Transvaal Committee opened in the heart of the city and was manned by the new republicans and fed on the growing fires of the Celtic revival.

Enter my good self.

I operated a small but boisterous branch of the Transvaal Committee in Belfast with a fever in my pen. In mid-1901 I was contacted by a syndicate of Irish-American newspapers to go to South Africa as their correspondent.

By the time I arrived in the Transvaal most of the heavy fighting was done. British massiveness had simply worn down the Boer capacity for tenacity and valor. They continued to resist in small sporadic operations but these were splintered and without the earlier impact.

Yet something else was taking place when I arrived, something shocking and repugnant, and this was turning the British annexation into a pyrrhic victory. A hundred thousand or more Boers, men, women and children, were rounded up and put into what the British referred to as "concentration camps." Another thirty thousand Boer soldiers were in prisoner-of-war camps. Their lands were confiscated, their homes and fields burned to the ground.

As the British Parliament imposed another patented "Act of Union" (as they had a century before on the Irish), thousands of Boers perished behind barbed wire. The death toll ran to thirty thousand in their concentration camps with over twenty thousand of these being children.

I bribed my way in and out of the most notorious of these camps at Bloemfontein and wrote a series of twenty dispatches on conditions. My stories were to reach far beyond the small group of contracted newspapers I was writing for, being picked up not only in Ireland but throughout continental Europe and in England itself. A number of other journalists and the Quaker lady, Emily Hobhouse, collaborated with me in unmasking the British horror.

While her generals seethed, the English public that had been hysterical with conquest during the jubilee suddenly sobered at the revelations. A half century earlier the Irish potato famine had failed to move them. Now they were revolted by their behavior toward the Boers.

I believe a seed was planted in the Transvaal and the fruits of the matured tree would spread discontent throughout their imperial scheme and all future imperial schemes. Something magnificently human was challenging man's ancient rites of conquest and enslavement. Something was going to happen in the twentieth century to overturn the age-old order.

I knew somehow that Ireland and the Irish people would be among the first to make that challenge.

*

My daddy Fergus O'Neill died during my stay in the Transvaal. I had last seen him at the wake of Tomas

Larkin and I knew from the tragedy in his soul he would
be getting away soon. They had worked their fields
together through the joys and sufferings of a half century.
It could not be otherwise. Fergus had followed Tomas all
his life and would have to follow to St. Columba's.

The old women were left, Finola and my ma, Mairead,
along with the weakest of our strain, Brigid and Colm.

*

I won no popularity contest with the British for my
Bloemfontein concentration camp articles but on certain
matters they are honorably fair. There was no way they
could prosecute a legitimate journalist for doing his job.
My return to Ireland found me well established on certain
Dublin Castle enemy lists but a minor hero in the
budding republican movement.

Dublin pulsated. Words poured from Irish pens by
the millions, all filled with ancient hopes. A national
theater had been founded. Writers were turning it into a
latter-day Athens. I settled in grandly.

My inquiries after Conor Larkin led nowhere. He
had vanished from Derry shortly after the fire at the
shirt factory and Kevin O'Garvey's disappearance.
Some had seen Conor wandering about Ireland like a
soul in purgatory. Then he was gone. I didn't know
where but my heart was broken. The one thing Ireland
didn't need was another playwright, but the only way
I could work out my sorrow was to take up my pen
seriously and write about our youth in Ballyutogue.
I wrote a play about our summer in the booley house
and each line I penned was like a cry in the darkness
to him.

One day my prayer was answered. A letter came
from Liam in New Zealand. He had received a cable
from Conor from Shanghai. Conor was aboard ship
and on his way to Christchurch.

CHAPTER TWO: The bells of Belfast rang out and
the gospel-singing city on the River Lagan glided into motion for the Lord's Day and all that holiness. In the

Shankill, along Sandy Row, in East Belfast and the other strongholds of Calvin, Luther and Knox, the pubs were shut sourly and the doors of the Lord's houses sourly flung open.

From this vast armada of churches, these capital ships of the Reformation, dirgelike cantatas emerged sounding like the funeral movement of a tragic symphony. Work-hardened hands held tattered hymnals and voices went their own way, above, below and against the struggling choir.

> *"Come, ye sinners, poor and needy,*
> *Weak and wounded, sick and sore,*
> *Jesus ready stands to save you,*
> *Full of pity, love and power,*
> *He is able, He is willing,*
> *Doubt no more."*

Over in Andersontown, along the Falls and in Bally-murphy, the Catholics disposed of their business with God and Mary in rapidly intoned low masses in forty-minute shifts.

Protestantism in Belfast was a far more serious matter among the Anglos and their Scottish brethren, for this was the entrenched, unyielding front line of the "as-saulted" faith and nowhere were He and His son so gloriously and zealously proclaimed.

Lucy MacLeod awakened trembling. The counting of weeks had given way to days and soon it would be only hours. One Sunday more and she could reach over in bed when the bells tolled and feel her Robin beside her again all warm and drowsy and lovey.

His twelve-week tour of the Northern Rugby League in the English Midlands would be over and he would be home again. She had dreaded his annual departure since he made the team six years before, but never a com-plaint left her lips. Her man was a member of the East Belfast Boilermakers, a status of high achievement, and the income from it kept her out of the factories.

As Lucy went through the motions of dressing, she felt and admired what was female of her body. It was not dainty or pale but good solid stuff that Robin adored.

Large breasts with big rosy buds that had lost none of their firmness. She sat before the mirror pretending as she did that she was sitting before Robin. Him with his back propped up on the bed, his eyes glowing to watering. She rehearsed precisely what she'd wear, how she'd smell, what nicies she'd surprise him with.

Lucy's reverie was broken by a relentless ticking of the clock. She covered herself reluctantly. Once all tightly corseted, she buttoned a flowery print down her hourglass figure and complimented herself as still lovely and crowned herself with a large-brimmed hat, bowed, plumed, flowered and veiled.

"Matthew," she called for her son.

He trudged in, all ten years of him, a condemned little man. She inspected him and declared him fit for church.

"What time is Daddy's boat coming?"

"You know just as well as I do," she answered. "Friday at noon."

"Can I quit school, Ma?"

She twisted his ear, gently but with a hint of firmness.

Their wee house on Tobergill Street was exactly like the one next door belonging to Grandfather Morgan and Grandma Nell and they marched to it as they had done for Sundays eternal, exchanging Lord's Day greetings and expressing joy that Robin would be returning to them in a few days.

Grandfather Morgan was an awesome figure. He was noble as the photographs of royalty in his finely cut gray frock coat, silk top hat and his roughhewn hands disguised under white gloves. He tugged out the gold pocket watch from his vest and snapped it open. Morgan MacLeod had gone to work at the Weed Ship & Iron Works on the very day it had opened in 1878, and in the next two and a half decades had never missed a day to illness. It was said of him he'd be working on the day of his funeral. Every man looked up to Morgan. He was known from one end of the Shankill to the other and in many other parts of Belfast. Church deacon, Grand Master of his Orange Lodge, foreman of the shipwrights on the "Big Mabel" dry dock.

The only thing out of kilter in this otherwise perfect setting of piety was Matthew's Aunt Shelley. Auntie Shel-

ley alone successfully resisted Grandfather Morgan, all
the reverends (and there were many), all the neighbors'
snickers (and these had died), and anyone who infringed
on her unprecedented independence.

In her own way she was just as big a MacLeod as his
daddy and Granddaddy, a wonderment. Even Robin faltered before Morgan. Auntie Shelley made no secret of the
fact she occasionally smoked cigarettes, read forbidden books and disappeared for long weekends without
bothering to explain to anyone where she went or in
whose company. To Matt she was beautiful, even more
so than his mom. Grandfather Morgan seemed resigned
but still played out a little game that perhaps some of the
godliness about would eventually rub off on his daughter.

Morgan patted Matt's head as he did each Sunday and
often during the week. However, the Sunday pat carried
special inference. Once more the watch was out, a show
of impatience for Grandma Nell. They were all gathered
as Nell came down the stairs as flowery and stiff-laced
as her daughter-in-law.

The MacLeods then stepped into the street and joined
the ethereal march of the holy. It was as though Belfast
had been drained of blood for its Sunday embalming.
Holiness permeated everything, their clothing, Grandfather's beard, and his own squeaking patent leather shoes.
They nodded rigidly and in unison as they passed promenading neighbors who nodded back rigidly and in equal
unison. The burden of their religion hung as the heavy
albatross and wedged deeply into wrinkled, unsmiling
faces.

> *"There is a fountain filled with blood,*
> *Drawn from Immanuel's veins;*
> *And sinners plunged beneath that flood*
> *Lose all their guilty stains.*
>
> *I do believe, I will believe,*
> *That Jesus died for me,*
> *That on the Cross He shed His blood,*
> *From sin to set me free."*

The Reverend Mr. Bannerman acquitted himself
reasonably. His flock listened variously. Even the verbal

richness of the gospel was delivered in the unvarying manner of a man having no other personality than automatic righteousness. Considering the mediocrity of the Reverend Mr. Bannerman and a small army of his fellow preachers, the faithful thronged and filled the church and droned through hymns and dozed through the sermons as captives in a place out of fear of being someplace else.

Matthew MacLeod was trapped in a grim cell of dark varnished wood. His backside ached through the thinly padded pea-green velvet seat, a color that would revolt him for the rest of his life. Just above him there was an ocean of flowered hats, lacquered white collars and waxed mustaches.

"Be not among the winebibbers," the preacher extolled without enthusiasm, "look thou not upon the wine when it is red . . ." He cleared his throat in the manner of a man desiring to expectorate but daring not to. "At last it biteth like a serpent and stingeth like an adder."

Matthew counted the flowers on the hats, then the curlicues on the wooden pillars, then made out faces in the wood grain of the seat back in front of him. There was the face, of a fox, a clown and perhaps a lady's hat if one stretched imagination that far.

The Reverend Mr. Bannerman had warmed up to temperate, his outer limit of wrath, and denounced the nontemperance folk, wherever they might be.

Matt leaned forward ever so cautiously, peeking down the long row past great bosoms and great beards. Near the end of the pew a little head all filled with ribbons likewise, peered out. Matt wiggled his finger and she wiggled hers, then he made a face and she made one, then he stuck out his tongue and she stuck hers out. At that time a heavy hand of authority addressed the back of his neck and towed him into line.

> *"Precious, precious blood of Jesus,*
> *Shed on Calvary;*
> *Shed for rebels, shed for sinners,*
> *Shed for thee!"*

On and on and on they groaned down the verses, the steam propelling their lungs losing vigor with each new verse. Outside, Matthew could hear the muted sounds of children singing "Dusty Bluebells."

A recitation ensued of those to be remembered, of bazaars, of bees, of collections, of special services, of potlucks, of men's clubs, of ladies' auxiliaries, of the sick to be visited, of Orange events.

The organ playeth! A horrendous solo ensued by the wife of the largest donor, a hodgepodge homage to Christ in which the lyrics defiled the tune of "Londonderry Air." He scratched one elbow . . . carefully . . . then the other and, as though electric currents were running up and down his spine, he began to wiggle. He wiggled and wiggled and wiggled. Grandfather Morgan glowered and he froze.

"The drunkard shall come to poverty; and drowsiness shall clothe a man with rags . . . every man shall receive according to his own labor."

Variation on the Ulster theme of themes, the goodness of work. Even at the age of ten, Matthew MacLeod knew that Protestants were more industrious than Catholics, and Presbyterians more industrious than Anglicans or Baptists. The Bible was a veritable catalogue of the exalted status of industriousness and likewise filled with the sin and corruption of sloth, a well-known affliction of the Catholics along with their drinking. There could be little doubt who was on God's side and whose side God was on.

Deep into the second hour, Matthew was abruptly elbowed from his doze and sprang to his feet automatically.

"What can wash away my stain?
  Nothing but the blood of Jesus!
What can make me whole again?
  Nothing but the blood of Jesus!
Oh, precious is the flow,
That makes me white as snow!"

Socializing in the vestibule was far more than perfunctory, for Morgan MacLeod was a man of high esteem. Today the talk was over the return of his famous son, Robin. With Grandfather's hand tightly locked around his own, Matthew was subjected to several more pats on the head, pinches on the cheek and "he looks just like Robin, that one."

A half dozen times Morgan would be pulled off to the side out of general earshot as he was petitioned to save this job at the yard or put in the good word for that promotion. As an Orange Grand Master, Morgan inherited that special power in the Belfast scheme.

Sunlight! At last, sunlight!

Matthew, still locked in firmly, looked with longing as the heathen children played "kick the can" and "Ulster flag" and skipped rope to "Dusty Bluebells."

So that they would not forget the message of the Reverend Mr. Bannerman's sermon, Morgan analyzed and reiterated the preacher's words over Sunday dinner.

By now, nothing tasted good to the boy. He was admonished for not eating and warned not to get dirty, for much still remained of the day.

The next round with God was the subject of a long discussion between Grandfather and Grandma Nell. For evening services she preferred attending the great, shiny new Savior's Church of the Shankill and hearing the Reverend Oliver Cromwell MacIvor. At least, Matt thought, he wouldn't be bored. On the other hand, the Reverend Mr. MacIvor frightened him. When he got a full mouth of lather going, people were known to faint all over the church, others stand up and scream and writhe, and others fling themselves at the foot of his pulpit.

Grandfather expressed grave doubts about MacIvor and on this Sunday he won out. Their horse was stabled two streets away and Matthew went with him to hitch it to the brake. With the boy firmly wedged in between his mother and grandmother and all those corsets they went for a ride along the river to the outskirts of town where a full-blown flurry of late religious frenzy ensued in evangelical tents with no-nonsense thunder and damnation fundamentalist gospel.

Tent preachers came and went on various holy tides. Any man with a gift of gab and a few shillings could get himself a degree in short order and go into business. The game was to shop around to find the new up-and-comers in the everlasting revival.

After a final Bible reading from Grandfather Morgan, Matthew went to his house next door with his mom. His daddy would be home soon and next Sunday would be different. There was a church for everything in Belfast and his daddy chose one that specialized in short sweet services. It was remarkably well attended. After that they would spend the rest of the day having fun.

Then, of course, his daddy would go on tour with the team again. Matthew MacLeod prayed at bedside in earnest for the first time that day. He prayed he could go to jail on Sundays when his daddy was in England and escape all that goodness.

CHAPTER THREE

CHRISTCHURCH, NEW ZEALAND, 1904

The train slowed as it crossed the river on the northern approach to Christchurch and swung around the Botanical Gardens of that garden city. Conor saw them on the platform, the Larkins of New Zealand. Liam, trying to look well dressed to no avail, a rather dumpy lady with the widest of smiles, she being his wife Mildred, and four wanes, two boys and two girls who held bouquets. All of them seemed scared stiff.

The awkward handshake melted to an embrace, then the tension fled as Conor swooped his nieces up in his arms and offered to let them search his pockets. Necklaces from Hong Kong of semiprecious stones and real pocket watches for the lads. It was a jabbering, happy lot that made into the station to wait for the inland train.

Liam spotted the flecks of gray in his brother's temples. "You've been traveling hard," he said, "you'll stop and rest awhile."

"Aye," Conor whispered, "that will be grand."

*

Ballyutogue, the farm of Mildred and Liam Larkin, was some fifty miles inland, halfway across the narrow waist of the island. At Kowi Bush they continued by rig to a place in the foothills of the Southern Alps where the Waimakariri River plunged down for the sea. The land ran a gamut

of green from iridescent to ultramarine. It was no sodded
cottage that greeted him but a two-story frame house
finer than that of any Protestant farm on Inishowen. Liam
Larkin was like a squire himself with a thousand acres of
rich meadow and cropland with topsoil running deep and
no less than two full-time hired hands.

For a week the wanes, Spring and Madge and Tomas
and wee Rory, heard glorious tales of the sea and the
singing of chanteys. Mildred and the spinster girls from
the surrounding ranches and the men as well had the
spots dazzled off them.

Conor and his brother talked the nights half through.
They seemed to talk of everything. Except Ballyutogue,
except Kevin O'Garvey, except Finola, except Ireland. A
lot was spoken but nothing was said. In the end Liam
knew very little other than that Conor had spent fifteen
months in Australia and the rest at sea.

*

Liam plopped at the round oak table. Mildred brought
him a cuppa and one of her own, doffed her apron and
both of them stirred in unison.

"Did you talk to him?" she asked.

"Nae, not yet."

"He's been here a fortnight, luv."

Liam studied the checks of the tablecloth and ran his
finger over a tiny tear. His wife patted his hand and they
sipped from their cups with matching slurps.

"Don't let it go any longer," Mildred said determinedly.
"It's three hundred acres of the best land around and the
Smiths are almost willing to give it away. You know,
luv, we could finance him ourselves."

"That's not the half of it, Millie."

"On with you. Why that look in his eyes when he
searches over the hills? I know when a man is hungering
for land."

"We all looked that way when we first came," Liam
said. "It reminds us of home."

"Are you telling me it's natural for a fine person like
Conor to just pick up and roam for five years, disappearing from his home, leaving word to no one?"

"It's natural enough for my brother," he answered. "He's
a different sort, Millie, with strange sides to him no one

ever gets to know. When I first heard he was coming, I was scared. All my life I had lived under his shadow. But seeing his pain, it's me who's sorry for him. I don't know if he'll ever find what we have here."

Mildred paddled to the wood-burning stove, stoked it, then oversaw the brewing pot, stirring all within to her satisfaction. They were brothers but they were not brothers. Conor had given off sunshine to them but as he did he betrayed a darkness in himself. Five years of smoldering. What sort of man would do that? She returned to the table. Liam wore an apologetic expression to say that Conor was beyond his reach.

"Maybe after he's here for a time," Mildred said, more hopeful than practical and with female calculation. "The loveliness of this place will come to him as it did to you and all the other Irish boys."

Liam shook his head. "Don't go making plans."

A week passed and another. One night Conor announced he would be going into Christchurch to inquire about finding a berth on an incoming ship. There was always a shortage of blacksmiths afloat, so something suitable would not be long in coming. Gloom fell on the house.

*

Liam rode his horse up a florid hillside to a place crowned with a giant spreading oak. He had gone there five hundred times, when he got his first parcel, when he wooed Mildred, with his children. He had whiled his time beneath it fishing the stream but never daring to dream that nearly everything in view would be his one day. He hitched up his horse and examined Conor's creel. It was empty.

"You're not giving it much of a go," Liam said.

"I think the fish here are a little smarter than back home," Conor answered.

"You'll not find another trout stream like this, even in Ireland. Let's see," he said, examining the flies. "This here Taihape Tickler never fails to do the job this time of day." Liam rolled up his Wellington boots and within minutes hooked a rainbow, and in New Zealand fashion worked the fish to the bank, set his toe under it and flipped it ashore.

"Well done."

Liam laughed, content, and the two settled against the tree trunk. "Put this in your jug and jiggle it," he said, passing a bottle to Conor.

Liam was the portrait of a happy man. Conor smiled for it. "I can say things to you now that choked on their way out before," Liam said. "I envied you going off with Daddy or Seamus O'Neill sitting under trees like this. Having a tree of my own on a stream of my own, I know how comforting it can be. We've changed places in a way, you and me."

"Aye, it's good to see you like this, Liam."

"We don't want you to leave, Conor," Liam said abruptly. "Any feeling of jealousy I've had for you is gone. I want you to have the happiness I've got. I want you to stay."

"I don't think it's for me," Conor whispered.

"What's to go back to?"

Conor didn't answer but his silence was loud.

"I owe this land everything," Liam said. "Sure, my wife is English and my wanes are New Zealanders. Sure, I celebrate the King's birthday but so what? I love this place. Funny, everybody loves the Irish outside of Ireland and England."

"That's the story of our people," Conor said.

"If you ask me, I say fuck Ireland. What has it ever given either of us but pain?"

A flash of anger came and went over Conor. He was speaking rightly for Liam and for all those who had left. It hadn't worked for him. Five years of trying to purge Ireland from him had made no difference. Conor came to his feet very weary. Liam gaped, sorry and a bit frightened for his brother. "I didn't mean all of it," he said.

"It's the story of our people," Conor repeated.

"Conor, don't go down, not just yet. I've something weighty on my mind. I've done a bad thing. Over the years I've heard from Seamus O'Neill, who's been searching the world for you. I promised if you ever came here I'd let him know. This letter arrived before you did. After seeing you, after seeing how you needed rest and peace, me and Mildred decided to hold it in case it said something

to bring you sorrow again. We kept on holding it in the
hopes you would agree to stay. Well, now that you're
going in to look for a ship . . ." He handed the envelope over. "I'm sorry."

Conor stared without opening it. As though he knew
what the words would read, Liam slowly unhitched the
horse and left his brother alone.

> . . . each day Dublin grows more alive with the spirit.
> Theater and meetings and associations and pamphlets.
> It's a swelling wave you can now see with the naked eye.
> I'm in the middle of it and so many brilliant and dedi-
> cated people are coming forth. I can say for the first time
> in my life I am proud to be Irish in Ireland. . . .
>   . . . it's coming, Conor. It may take a few years, per-
> haps even a decade but nothing can stop the tide now. . . .
>   . . . I remember the booley house and all the trillions
> of hours we talked about the moment. Oh, the moment,
> the moment, the moment. Can you be gone when it
> arrives?
>   . . . the Brotherhood is born again. Sure, it's small and
> weak but it's on the rise. Can you repeat the very words,
> the Irish Republican Brotherhood, without a chill?
>   . . . for God's sake, Conor . . . come home. . . .

CHAPTER FOUR: The night had been talked through
but Conor had only given off hints of his odyssey. We
paused for a moment, catching the first light as it
broke over the flat roofs of Georgian Dublin.

My digs on Cornmarket High Street had been
institutionalized as a writers' and actors' quarter
situated between the infamous Dublin Castle and the
St. James Gate Brewery of Guinness renown and
fringing the Liberties, which had been one of Europe's
most ghastly slums. The Liberties was a long-standing
womb of insurrection. Within my triangle there was the
omnipresence of the Crown, the wellspring of revolution,
and endless kegs of brew. I was immaculately situated
for any eventuality.

Conor let the curtain fall across the window. I had waited patiently for him to let it pour out. A day and a night of drink and groping had brought him once again to the brink. With the dawn he had grown lucid and less cautious of hearing the sound of his own ordeal.

"After the fire, when Father Pat McShane told me of the deal Kevin O'Garvey probably made, it wasn't possible to remain in Derry. All his life Kevin had tried to play the game by their rules, in their courts, in their Parliament, the same as Parnell and O'Connell. In the end he was cheated by the British the same as all of us have been cheated. Oh, they're lofty-worded, high-minded cheaters, they are, but cheaters nonetheless. It exploded before me with utter clarity that the O'Garveys and the Parnells can only take us so far along the road. Armed insurrection and only armed insurrection is the only reality the British will understand. I left Derry for that somewhere in Ireland where the Republican Brotherhood still lived.

"For a solid year I walked the roads from Donegal to Cork, from Galway to Dublin, from Belfast to Kerry, from Wexford to Sligo. There was no Irish Republican Brotherhood.

"Even as it had stripped us of our manhood, destroyed our dreams and dispersed our seed, fear of the famine lingered on like a mighty black cloud into a second generation. I saw the Irish people broken, shorn of the will to protest, obedient, subjected, semi-comics. I wanted to grab them by the thropple and shake them and scream for them to be men but they were dogs. They played dogs' games, yapping false courage, courage they did not possess. Dogs content to scrounge their fields for scraps and send their children off to the city as beggars. Don't educate, don't strive, don't anger. Live in foggy visions.

"Aye, Seamus, there was no Brotherhood, no ability to rage. I became so broken with frustration I did what I swore would never happen. I was driven out of Ireland. Ah, not by the British but by the apathy of our own people."

Conor had sunk to the edge of my cot, his shoulders hunched over, staring down at the floor. For

a moment he lifted his head and searched the room as
though he were still seeking that miracle. I lowered
the gaslight and let in the gray light of day.

"All of Ireland was one large Bogside. I could no
longer shout from empty mountaintops to unhearing
ears, so I had to leave. You understand that, don't
you, I had to leave?"

"Aye."

"And I found our people again ... out there. ...
The sewer keepers of the world, fighting other men's
wars, eternal wanderers of the universe, tucked away
in little Bogsides all over mother earth, the quaint
folk, a breed of cursed men and women, so dear, so
gentle, so precious, yet so weary and so broken.

"I saw Bogside after Bogside of the colonizer's
creation. Black Bogsides in Africa, red Bogsides in the
Caribbean, yellow Bogsides in Asia, brown Bogsides
in India. We were them and they were us. How long
could we be held in the bloody grip of British
arrogance? And I would run back to sea with a fever
in my brain.

"I lit for a time in Australia. It's a decent enough
place. Yet wherever I felt a measure of comfort and
peace I began to smell turf fires and hear singing from
Dooley McCluskey's and I'd end up in a sweat in the
middle of the night. I tried, Seamus, I tried, but the
world was not large enough to dim the vision of Ireland
or purge the curse of it from my soul. I had become a
traitor to myself and I fled back to sea.

"When I was out there on the late watch I could be
alone at last. I could suddenly feel the sensation of
myself standing still and looking inward and I could
see the world beyond the horizon going mad."

He walked back to the window, drew the curtain
aside and blinked. I shuffled about to fix breakfast.
"I can't say that I don't hate this place in many ways
but I can say I'll never leave again."

"The Brotherhood is so small you can barely see
it but they are men whose feelings run as deeply as
your own. It may take years but I swear to you, Conor,
that we are mounting up on the wings of a golden
phoenix."

*

Barrymore was there from County Cork. Butler was there from Clare. O'Bourne and Nolan were Dubliners and Gannon came from Kerry. Madigan was there from County Kildare and Larkin and me from Ulster. We had been painfully hand-picked and assembled in a room above the bakery on Marrowbone Lane in the heart of the Liberties. The room was starkly revolutionary.

The man who stood before us had once been a giant, a minor folk hero and a relic of the Fenian Rising. In '67 he had been captured in a raid on a Constabulary station. He was only sixteen at the time but he was a big kid and despite his age he was jailed in Brixton in England. After escape and recapture he took up residence in half a dozen prisons as guest of the Crown and for the next two decades underwent every sort of humiliation they could impose. As a student at Queen's, I remember seeing drawings of him being forced to eat on his hands and knees like a dog with his arms shackled behind him.

After release and exile he showed up from time to time where two, three or five old Fenians would listen in Canada, Australia, England and finally in America with its two million Irish-born.

He was a full-blown revolutionary. He was a man rebuffed the passion of women, if any had ever reached in that close. He would not touch liquor, for he wanted a clear mind to handle men, explosives and decisions. Realities of prison cells and rooms "on the run" like this one had made him acid to slogans and banalities. Yet a crucifix dangled above the headboard of his bed as some ancient reminder from boyhood not to break the final thread with a church that had denounced and disowned him. He was reality in revolution and his entry into the scene in Dublin marked the serious attempt to resurrect the Irish Republican Brotherhood.

His name was Long Dan Sweeney.

No man among us had not been raised on the blood he sacrificed.

Long Dan's hair was completely white by his twenty-fifth birthday. His skin had an unhealthy reddish pallor as one who had been denied sunlight. His face was in

crags and slits. Time and the British had knocked him up
to a point where he often doted on cynical eccentricities.
But we listened, for he was revolution that was.

"I hope you're not in a hurry," he said with a voice
almost devoid of quality. "Just because Brother Seamus
O'Neill over there and some of his fellow writers and the
politicians are blowing out words like an Aran storm
doesn't mean the Irish people are going to run out into
the streets and rise. The Irish people," he said with
unmistakable disdain, "are almost as much our enemy as
the British. They have been subjugated for too long.
When you leave this room, leave it knowing that most
of them will hate you and everything you try to do. The
British are supreme masters at manipulating Irish against
Irish."

He reached beneath the pillow of his bed, pulled out a
Webley revolver and waved it so each of us would get a
whiff of the muzzle. "Informers are the bane of our
existence. Take a good look at one another and trust no
one else."

Click, click went the pistol as he cocked and aimed it.
"Informers will be destroyed without mercy." We all
winced and ducked as he pulled the trigger. It was empty.
He threw it on the table with a thud. "Without mercy," he
repeated.

"We are a people of notorious barroom courage. Them,
across the water, fancy themselves Irish by decking
themselves in green on St. Patrick's Day and marching
boastfully up and down the world's boulevards. We are
without peer in passing out unmitigated shit about our
longing for the old sod. But they really don't care. Ask
yourselves, you with brothers over the water . . . do they
really care beyond that yearly token tear? We are alone, you
and me, alone. Alone here. Alone over there."

Long Dan Sweeney blew neither hot nor cold, bitter
nor enthusiastic. He was merely telling it.

"We do have some support out of America, a handful
of loyal who will pay our way. Without them, we'd be
lost. With them, there are some goals we can accomplish.
What we must do is build some kind of organization and
have some kind of contingency plans ready for that day
when the Irish people decide they've had enough. Some of
you may live to see the day we rise but don't count on it.

And don't fart higher than your ass. We are, of now, a totally ineffective group representing a totally ineffective people. No one is as disorganized as the Irish. You'll tear your hair out trying to execute a simple plan.

"So, you're asking yourselves, what are we wasting our time for? What have we got to go on? After all, we're a weak, subject, disorganized, informing people. I'll tell you what we've got. We've got British hatred. They fear us no less than they hate us. Why? Because, so long as a single Fenian continues to be restless, as long as three men like us meet in rooms like this, their Empire is never entirely secure. The British know that the Irish will be the first to rise against them and therefore must be the first to be stopped. We, you and I and the Irish Republican Brotherhood, are the tip of a poison arrow and if we break the British skin, our struggle and our ideas will spread to their colonies around the world. That's what we've got."

As we reeled on his powerful thoughts, he rubbed his hands together. These, too, were as wrinkled with premature age as his white hair but they still had their legendary size, measuring almost ten inches from the heel of the fist to the tip of the middle finger.

"The enemy sits in mahogany rooms and makes up rules. By their rules they declare their legality to colonize people who don't want to be colonized, rules to conduct warfare by, rules to legally starve people to death, rules to carry out whatever they want to carry out. They say, with enormous pride, these rules come from the mother of Parliaments so obviously they must be right and anyone who goes against these rules must be wrong. We are expected, as a subject people, to live by their rules, fight by their rules, and obey their rules. But we don't have an army or arms and cannot fight by their rules and as this struggle develops we will have to make up our own rules. Now, according to their rules, we are depraved . . . killers, fanatics, anarchists, gunmen, or whatever scum they so designate, and therefore fit to be destroyed by their self-declared legality.

"Not only do they own the rule book, they own the press and the journalists to expose us to the world and denounce us as lunatics and we have no voice to argue back. We must be prepared to accept the denunciation and wrath not only of our own people but also the world at large. Their press will hound us vehemently and viciously. They will scream that we aren't playing by their rules."

He leaned over the table, his fists rapping it with his first show of emotion. "If you remember nothing else, remember this. No crime a man commits in behalf of his freedom can be as great as the crimes committed by those who deny his freedom. We will not starve English bodies in a famine, we'll not scatter their seed around the earth, we'll not deny them ownership of English land. Our armies will not patrol the streets of London. Our courts will not hang them.

"We engage in a fight vulnerable to scathing propaganda, unloved by most of our own people, but God and God alone will eventually decide which side was just in its aspirations and which side was evil.

"Sure, we'll never see the day we can meet them in open warfare and match them gun for gun, so they'll denounce our tactics as cowardly. But we are not without weapons of our own. Remember that the British have nothing in their entire arsenal or imperial might to counter a single man who refuses to be broken. Irish words, Irish self-sacrifice and, ultimately, Irish martyrdom are our weapons. We must have the ability to endure pain to such an extent that they lose the ability to inflict it. This and this alone will break them in the end. Martyrdom."

I know he was sizing us up. Who might break, who might inform, who would boast without delivering. Who had the tools of martyrdom.

He jolted us with a crack of a smile and took a seat behind the table. "That's your first and last lecture," he said. "Now I know you're eager to learn about that rumored cache of weapons stashed away in England. It's true."

Long Dan went on to tell the story of the ships returning from the Boer War, most of them landing in Liverpool. One, in particular, carried a cargo of small arms and rifles and landed during a dockmen's strike. An army unit was called in to unload it onto waiting freight cars. In a typical bureaucratic mess-up, Irish Fusiliers were used as longshoremen and some of them tipped off the Brotherhood in England.

The train left Liverpool lightly guarded for an inland arsenal. It was cleanly derailed in the countryside, the engineer, crew and guards disposed of and the cars looted onto waiting teamster wagons. When the train had been picked clean it was dynamited to make it appear that it had been an accident. The arms haul was dumped into an abandoned mine and later moved to other defunct colliery pits. Publicity was kept to a minimum to cover the War Office's embarrassment. The train had been so totally destroyed it was never learned if the British knew of the missing guns or not.

"It was one of those rare occasions," Dan Sweeney said with that misshapen contortion of a smile, "we ever pulled anything off without entirely fucking it up.

"Our most urgent mission is to get those guns out of England, into Ireland, and dump them. Three or four years from now when the Brotherhood has grown into operational units the British will be on the alert for gunrunning. At this moment, their guard is down. Now is the time to move the guns over and get them hidden on Irish soil. I want each of you to study your own local situation and come up with some kind of plan."

Long Dan picked up the pistol once more. "And don't ever forget what I told you about informers."

CHAPTER FIVE: We had no way to match British arms on a battlefield. Our weapons were the weapons of the conquered; a dogged ability to endure and preserve our culture, a sense of humor and, most of all, words. Never at a loss for words, we Irish laid down a barrage in the euphoria of the Gaelic revival.

This was the moment Dublin poured forth from Connolly's "Workers' Republic" to Arthur Griffith's *United Irishman,* named after the insurrection of a century before. Arthur Griffith had been in the Transvaal and returned with visions of glory. A legendary beauty of ascendancy stock, Maud Gonne, formed the Daughters of Ireland and tramped the countryside championing the peasants' cause as well as that of the slum dwellers. Young Irish Societies and Wolfe Tone Clubs spread like brush fires. In America, the Clan of the Gaels ended its hibernation.

On the political front the issue of Home Rule had been kept dormant for over a decade during the last charge of the Conservatives. John Redmond, inheritor of Parnell's Irish Party, had floundered. Sick of the ineptness, Arthur Griffith founded a new party, Sinn Fein, "Ourselves Alone."

At the moment, Sinn Fein was as weak as the fledgling Brotherhood, but many of the best brains were being drawn to it and it was becoming the central spokesman for republicanism. I had no doubt but that Sinn Fein was destined to carry out the war of words just as the Brotherhood would ultimately carry out the war of bullets.

In those throbbing days the inner core of the revival was declared in a manifesto above the signatures of William Butler Yeats, Lady Gregory and a man named Edward Martyn.

> "We propose to have performed in Dublin, in the spring of every year, certain Celtic and Irish plays, which, whatever be their degree of excellence, will be written with high ambition and so build up a Celtic and Irish school of dramatic literature. . . . We will show that Ireland is not the home of buffoonery and of easy sentiment, as it has been represented, but the home of an ancient idealism. We are confident of the support of all Irish people, who are weary of misrepresentation, in carrying out a work that is outside all the political questions that divide us."

And so our national theater was born, Irishmen doing what was best in them, giving us a prideful and powerful spokesman. The playwright against the Crown, the actor against the Crown's artillery and bayonets.

In the spring of 1905 my play, *The Booley House*, was presented in the Mechanics' Institute Theater on Abbey Street. It was respectfully received. Later the theater became known as the Abbey Theater, the national theater of Ireland, our finest achievement as a people.

The night after the opening, Conor Larkin was assigned by the Irish Republican Brotherhood to Belfast, the darkest corner of the country. He was ordered to live normally and steer clear of outward republican activities. He was to look things over, work up a comprehensive physical layout of the city, scour the bars, listen. Later he would contact a few solid old-line Fenians and search carefully for new ones, find safe houses and escape routes.

Most urgently, Conor was to see if Belfast offered a possible route to smuggle our guns in from England.

*

From my own years at Queen's College I came to know Belfast as a queer city on the Irish landscape. If there was a revival in the south, little of the impact reached that place. There was some weak activity on the labor front, and some publications such as the *Shan Van Vocht* (*The Old Woman of Ireland*), but for the most part there were few takers and the republican cause was engineered from hole-in-the-wall offices with little funds or resources.

For this was the heartland of the Protestant settlement. Counties Down and Antrim never did figure greatly in native Catholic habitation. When the Presbyterians settled as planters in 1600, Belfast was born from a swamp. Nearly all the early population came from Presbyterian farms in the two adjoining counties. Communal living and work sharing, an agrarian tradition brought into Belfast, tended to give the city more of a look of linked villages.

Landlordism moved into the city from the countryside and Lord Donegal became one of the great urban renters in the British Isles, fathering the future slums and setting the tone of red brick monotony. In the end he received his deserts by destituting himself on gambling debts.

By 1800 Belfast had entered the Industrial Revolution a half century late with a textile industry that vanguarded the most wretched squalor in the realm. The stink of Belfast's poor districts flowed in open sewers and erupted from piles of dunghills, tanner shops, home breweries and the ammoniated urine against walls of courtyards entered by six-foot-wide alleyways. Once inside, the defilement was locked in and air and light shut out. Families of a dozen or more huddled in abysmal hovels without water or sanitation. A few public bathhouses were inadequate to cope with the crush of filth. Open sores, matted hair and warped growth were part of the costume of the poor.

The looms boomed on with shattering relentlessness,

first cotton, then linen, with labor supplied by women and children, for, like Derry, it was a city of female workers. As linen rose and fell in cycles of recession, boom and depression, the few pence a week was uncertain and thousands of spinners and weavers made off to America.

*

For the first two centuries there was no significant Catholic population in Belfast. When they first came, the liberal Scottish Presbyterians lived humanely with them. Catholics began to arrive in massive gulps on the heels of land evictions, rural unemployment, and in the wake of the famine, and attitudes changed forever.

Catholics settled in their own small "villages" around the heartbeat of a church. Their large numbers were neither welcome nor wanted. They arrived into an established order in which they shared no involvement and little voice. They were strangers in Belfast, invaders. As their numbers grew, Catholic "villages" linked up in the western part of the city and in other places became isolated enclaves. What was originally a series of communal settlements in Belfast matured into tribal pales of two hostile clans.

*

As the steam power loom exploded industrial growth the girth of Lough Belfast and the towns to the immediate south, hundreds of looms sprang up along the avenues of running water. With the collapse of cotton during the American Civil War, Belfast rocketed as the linen capital of the world.

By 1878 Frederick Weed had begun his monolithic shipyard along with others and for the first time thousands of men were put to work. They were Protestant nearly to a man, mostly from East Belfast and the Shankill, which became his personal fortresses.

The Belfast complex multiplied into industries of heavy machinery, armaments, ropemaking, distilling, tobacco, flour milling, graving docks and a major shipping center.

Nothing then or ever again would keep the pall of industrial filth from putrefying the air around the lough. By 1870 the horror of it brought on commissions of inquiry which expressed grave concern that Belfast's air and water pollution were having a debilitating effect on the people. These alarms went unheeded, for nothing could stop the loom, the steam hammer and the riveter.

Protestant slums and the waterfront were bilges of crime and inhumanity. Catholic slums festered within whose bounds the law or even the clergy rarely cared to tread. Most vestiges of a Western civilization ceased. These slums were the frequent hosts to onslaughts of cholera and typhoid and had an incidence of tuberculosis hundreds of percentages greater than the rest of the kingdom. Uneducated, scurvy-ridden, social lepers and physical wrecks were left to wallow in squalor where morality had fled. Beggars, fever carts, workhouses, whores, pimps, stabbing, theft, starvation, madness, dope, alcohol were workaday. When there was no dogfight or cockfight to wager the last farthing on, mothers threw their scrawny sons into the pit to battle themselves bloody.

Beyond the ghettos, great blocklike uninspired Victorian edifices threw up a façade of grandeur to hide the putridity. Buildings for commerce, industry and government continued to bulk and along the sea fronts rose the manor houses of the world's newest gold coast.

*

Belfast's golden age of riots entered on the damnations of fire-breathing evangelists who kept the Protestant poor on razor's edge. Mammoth open-air meetings by the Reverend Messrs. Drew, Cooke, Hanna and their ilk burst into savage rioting in 1813, 1832, 1835, 1843, 1852, 1864, 1872, 1880, 1884, 1886 and 1898. Bloodletting in Belfast was no twentieth-century phenomenon. It was the poor being harangued to fight the poor, the tribal units of Protestants in Sandy Row, the Shankill and East Belfast bashing heads with the Catholic tribal units in the Falls, the Pound and Divis.

The structure of rule was an interlaced alliance of the Union Preservation Party, the Orange Order, and elements of the Protestant clergy. The purpose of rule, a continued manipulation of division of the laboring class with police and government apparatus entirely in their control.

*

Oliver Cromwell MacIvor, preceded by Drew, Cooke and Hanna, fit into this scheme as the most feared and fearsome preacher of them all. Now enshrined in his magnificent Savior's Church of the Shankill, he held enormous sway and power.

Heavily endowed by Frederick Weed, MacIvor keynoted the temper at the turn of the century. On his word, the Shankill could plunge into frenzy or despair or its feet could be set into a tempo of crusadelike marching. He was the man to communicate from ruler to masses and his mission was clear. MacIvor was the keeper of the myth, the satirist on Christianity, for nowhere in the world did a two-hundred-year-old political deity, William of Orange, retain such infinite power. MacIvor was his spokesman beyond death.

To back up the Reverend Mr. MacIvor's spiritual might, Weed and Weed's cronies endowed him with practical might. As one of Belfast's leading Orangemen, MacIvor had hiring rights at the Weed Works and a number of factories and mills. Word from him could get a man a job or make him a social outcast. In his good hands, Sir Frederick kept things under remarkable control in the Shankill. Between Maxwell Swan and the Savior's Church of the Shankill, the ambition of men was dulled in the seeking of liberation from their industrial bondage. MacIvor and his eternal "Reformation" shut out culture and beauty and freedom of thought. The Savior's Church of the Shankill was the symbol and epitome of Ulsterism.

*

With the advent of the twentieth century, Belfast was a major factor in the British scheme, an industrial giant, a revenue maker which paid off for the loyal, the perfect colony which policed its own dissidents, with marginal prosperity for some and a windfall for the elite. Her trade and economy were tied to the fact she was a British city and any question of Irish Home Rule or republicanism brought reactions of fear and rage.

Belfast ran with her clock over two centuries behind time, a feudally contrived vessel in which the "disloyal" natives continued to be punished with a minuscule portion of wealth, work and power.

Separation of the working class was the principal canon
in insuring the flow of wealth to the gentry and locking out
progress and liberal thought.

Colonizers in Derry had established a walled fortress in
an outpost surrounded by and in constant siege by hostile
Catholics. Belfast was different. Belfast was deliberate.
Belfast was born as the mongoloid child of British
imperialism.

*

Conor Larkin had been told by his friend Andrew
Ingram and again by Long Dan Sweeney he was destined
to be a soldier in dubious battle. As he arrived in that
gross identity of red brick, no place was more a battle
site in dubious battle.

CHAPTER SIX: The Ardoyne was one of those small
areas cut off from the main Catholic settlement in West
Belfast surrounded by Protestant Woodvale, Cliftonville
and the Shankill.

Conor left his digs, a room on Flax Street, and made
down the Crumlin Road arterial. It was Saturday, pub
night before the Lord's Day. Muscled numbers from the
shipyards and others engaged in hard labor lined up deep
at the bars, bulling down Guinness and talking in swift,
clipped Belfastese. The language was tough. The humor
was tough. Toughness was their trade mark, their badge of
honor, their constant boast. Tough men sense and respect
tough men and Conor walked the Crumlin line peacefully.

The New Lodge, a bit removed, held another Catholic
enclave. Conor passed a Constabulary station girded for
Saturday night warfare both on the borders and within
the tribal pales, turned into Shandon Lane, stopping midway down a dingy line of oversized dollhouses wearing
eyebrows of white brick above the doors and windows. He
knocked. He was let in without greeting into the room
where Long Dan Sweeney looked up from a small, square
wooden table. Long Dan raised the level of the lamplight
as they spoke over a map of the city. Nothing much seemed
to be happening, a drifting about the Catholic areas from

pub to pub, church to church, a few quiet questions about an old "Brother" or known former sympathizer. Conor and his counterparts were like tiny cells floating about without definite shape, groping for points to solidify.

It was all buried in the minds of a few men. While the agitation and pressure of words made or missed their marks, those ultimate leaders in the Brotherhood glided about in the shadows. Conor had already learned that patience was the elixir of revolution. No prose could force a man with a full belly into the streets to rise, nor could any law stop a hungry man from taking to the streets. Long Dan Sweeney was in no hurry. Fiery miracles and self-deception had fled him long ago. He planned like a surgeon.

Catholic Belfast would ultimately become involved in some kind of street warfare. The Boer tactics were studied closely, for it would call for small mobile forces using the support of the Catholic population to tie up large numbers of conventional troops. Perhaps it wasn't in keeping with the mahogany-room rules but it was designed to equalize the odds and taunt and frustrate and wear thin the patience of a cumbersome military power.

How long? Two more elections, three, and maybe the Conservatives would be gone from power in England. There would be talk once more of a Home Rule Bill but faith in John Redmond and the Irish Party was low. Redmond would try. Redmond would fail. The people would start flocking to Arthur Griffith's Sinn Fein Party. One more crop failure, one more depression, one more deception by the British and men would start seeking out the Brotherhood. The Brotherhood would be ready, small but organized into concise units with concise plans.

Belfast was a mind bender. Long Dan grunted that the city was always a step away from madness. He knew things were difficult for Larkin. Everywhere else, in Cork, Dublin, Galway, out on the land, the population was overwhelmingly Catholic. The Brotherhood could always find someone sympathetic in a key position, and in a showdown most of the people would back them. Everything in Belfast was Protestant-controlled and ultra-British, the government, docks, transport, Constabulary, everything. By the time of a rising the Brotherhood would have developed some good fighting units from the festering Catholic slums but otherwise the population would be loyal to the Crown. The Brotherhood would be sorely put to find anyone in authority to play along.

Long Dan folded the map along with the other information Conor had gathered without compliment or comment.

"I've a notion about smuggling the guns," Conor said.

Dan nodded.

"I'm after trying for a job in the Weed Works."

Long Dan frowned, puzzled. "There are less than two hundred Catholics inside the yard out of a work force of ten thousand men, so you've got about as much of a chance as a bottle of gin in a Tipperary pub. But even if you get in, what good will it do?"

"Private docks," Conor answered.

"Go on."

"I don't know how well the ports are guarded elsewhere in Ireland but here in Belfast it's tight. They've a heavy customs operation, almost Protestant to a man."

"It's like that everywhere," Sweeney said.

"The Weed Works has a private sort of setup. There's a constant flow of material and ships to and from England almost daily. There's almost no security and the few old-timers in customs aren't checking much of anything. What I'm thinking is that the yard might be an unguarded back door. I don't know how, what, where, when or why, but I'd like to get inside and look around."

Long Dan's single frailty was an indulgence in tobacco. His face contorted with thought as it became engulfed in smoke. What an idea! Slipping guns right through the most powerful Protestant stronghold in all of Ireland, the Weed Ship & Iron Works. It was madness, yet with such sweet simplicity.

"It will do no harm to try," he said. "Of course you've figured out how you're going to get a job in there."

"Aye, I've a notion on that," Conor answered.

Sweeney's cynicism faded. "How's that?"

"An old friendship or two."

The mind of the ancient rebel chewed on it. He nodded. "Give it a go."

"Aye."

*

The season had been arduous for the East Belfast Boilermakers, heading in the general direction of disaster. After successive losses to Batley, the Rochdale Hornets and Wigan, manager Derek Crawford subsisted heavily on charcoal biscuits, Lavalle's Gout Mixture and a variety of patent medicines to contain chronic colitis. With more than a half dozen games yet to play in Belfast before the English Midlands tour, unhappy growls could be heard from Rathweed Hall clear down to the fans in the pubs.

In his office beneath Boilermaker Stadium Crawford cracked his knuckles vociferously as he studied the rosters of all the amateur clubs in the surrounding counties. Relief, it appeared, was not in sight.

"Come in," he growled to a knock on his door.

Conor entered his oversized cubbyhole and approached the rolltop desk. "You probably don't remember me. We had a drink in Derry a few years back. You invited me to try out for the club. Larkin, Conor Larkin."

Crawford squinted in non-recognition.

"Bogside," Conor clued.

"Jesus, it must have been a century ago."

"Yeah, was a long time. I'm off ship and considering a move to Belfast so I'm looking for a job and a team."

"Bogside? You played garlic football, didn't you?"

"That's right but I played some Northern League rugby in Australia a couple seasons back. The Melbourne Outbacks."

Crawford studied the gray flecks in his temples and the seaman's weathered face. "How old are you, Larkin?"

"Thirty-one."

The coach grimaced from a sharp gas pain. He shook his head. "Well, we ain't the half-assed Outbacks. I had three men go downhill on me just like that this year, all younger than you. Too tough a game for old men."

"I'm tough enough," Conor asserted softly.

Crawford liked swagger in a man. He fished about into the vagueness of the past and recalled somewhat that Larkin had impressed him with his strength. Crawford's eyes went up, then down. Nothing in Larkin's appearance indicated he had grown weak. On the other hand, twenty-five years as coach and player told him there was no such

thing as a guy showing up off a ship and making a club.
"What position?"

"Front row, loose head prop."

Jesus Christ, Crawford thought, one of his glaring weak
spots. Bart Wilson had held the position for nine years,
then suddenly thinned out. The team had been unable to
control the scrums for the lack of sheer strength in the
front row. On the other hand . . . a front-row prop just
doesn't walk in off a ship.

"Really think you can cut it, man?"

Conor shrugged. "I'm here. At this point in the season,
we've got nothing to lose by giving me a tryout."

"All right, Larkin, I'll give you a try," he said with an
air of magnanimity, "but don't get your fucking hopes up
. . . eh?"

"There's a job that goes with it, right?"

"If you make the club."

"I'm a blacksmith."

"So you are," Crawford said. "Doxie!"

His summons was answered by a squat beer-bellied
man looking off horse in rugby shorts. His moon-shaped
ruddy Irish face held an off-center flattened nose and
other mementos of service to the sport. "Doxie O'Brien,
coach of the junior squad and my assistant. This here's
Conor Larkin, one of your people from Londonderry. He
wants a tryout. Played garlic and the Northern League
game in Australia . . . the Sydney Outhouses or something. Look him over."

While Conor was told to wait outside, Crawford opened
his desk drawer and unfurled a bottle of paddy.

"You shouldn't be hitting the stuff the way your stomach is tore." Crawford ignored Doxie's advice and passed
the bottle.

"I genuinely and sincerely like his spirit," Derek said in
answer to Doxie's quizzical stare. "I clearly remember
him. Strong as boilerplate."

"Shit. The way the season's going, you're casting lingering looks at every outsized docker and iceman. It's one
thing to run over a bunch of skinny micks and another to
play Northern League. What the fuck we got here, a
nursery?"

"What about the Australian Outcasts . . ."

"What do they know about the game down there?"

"Enough so Sir Frederick is considering a tour down under, that's what. Give him a tryout."

"For Christ sake . . ."

"Bugger off, Doxie."

●

Boilermaker Stadium, an eighteen-thousand-seat gem and one of the first of steel structure, was another of Frederick Weed's personal plums. He had been a rugby great at Cambridge, a scrum half who was long remembered. After Cambridge he won eight caps in international play as a member of the Scottish National Team and another two for the Irish National Team after moving to Ulster.

Shortly after he opened his yard, the East Belfast Boilermakers became his creation, alter ego, and a monument to his past prowess. He coached them and played in the company of shipfitters and riveters until the demands of his growing empire and his growing girth dictated he quit as an active player, but his interest in the sport never dimmed. Weed built a club that was the pride of Ulster, the scourge of Ireland and one which gained mindful respect over the water. He stocked it with players to whom he gave special consideration, jobs and favoritism. This brought him and the Boilermakers smack into the great rugby confrontation over professionalism.

The amateur game was winked at not only by Sir Frederick but in the English industrial Midlands, where the players were miners and factory hands and money was passed to them freely. Confronted with breaking up their clubs, they bolted the parent Rugby Union and formed the professional Northern Rugby League. The Boilermakers joined and became the first and only professional Irish team.

In addition to salary, a paid-for home in Bangor, and use of a hunting lodge in Scotland, the new Boilermaker stadium finally lured Derek Crawford away from the Brighouse Rangers in which he held a part ownership. The stadium adjoined the yard, all set in deep Ulster green and backdropped by jetties, slipways, dry and wet docks and the four great smokestacks of the steel mill. Beyond that, the azure expanse of Lough Belfast. Sir Frederick's personal box and lounge on the roof was unique, a showplace of trophies, a viewing place of unparalleled luxury containing its own bar and dining room.

Also unique were the players' facilities below the stadium, with personal spaces for each man and showers with soap and towels provided by the club. It held the only players' lounge in the United Kingdom with leather chairs, a billiard table, darts and a bar with a bottomless Guinness dispenser.

Small wonder that every growing boy in Belfast envisioned himself a member of the Boilermakers, for it meant a top job, local fame, a tour of the English Midlands and a chance to earn double a normal salary.

*

Conor and Doxie O'Brien walked out of the tunnelway onto the grounds as the yard whistle screamed, followed by a massive march of workers along King William Channel. Lunch buckets in hand and dirt of the day lingering on their faces, they slowed and some stopped to catch a glimpse of the heroes at practice.

"Don't get your hopes up," Doxie said through his teeth.

"I've already heard that once today."

"Look, man, Sir Frederick and Crawford got nothing against you and me being Catholic if you're good enough to make the club. However, we're carrying one more R.C. than usual and before they take another you'd better be half again as good."

"I am," Conor said.

As the players entered the grounds and moved down to the tunnel they looked Conor over with respectful hatred. He knew he was being sized up and in the next hour, day and week he would be battered and bashed and otherwise have to prove himself worthy of their company. A few cold greetings, no handshakes.

"By the way," Conor said, "there was a lad out of Derry named Mick McGrath who tried out about eight years back. I was looking over some of the team photographs. I couldn't spot him."

"McGrath out of Derry? An R.C.?"

"Aye."

"I vaguely remember. He never got past the juniors. Took an injury, then later went to work at the yard.

Seems I remember hearing he left. Talk to enough priests around Belfast, maybe you can find him."

"Conor! Conor Larkin!" a voice called.

"Well, what do you know. Jeremy Hubble himself! How are you, runt?"

Lord Coleraine was neither man nor boy, something in between at nineteen, a sprouting weed.

"Now let's be having a look at you, Jeremy. How close are you standing to your razor these days?"

"Conor, it's smashing to see you!"

"And the same back to you. How's your lovely mother?"

"Fine. She'll be absolutely delighted to know I've run into you."

"And your brother Christopher?"

"Oh, he's off in London studying at the School of Economics and the Inns of Court. Law and business and the like."

"And are you working here for your grandfather?"

Jeremy's smile flashed of his mother. "I'm studying to be the black sheep. I'll be going to Trinity in Dublin at the end of the year but Grandfather and I are in a conspiracy to let me make the tour with the team. I'm a full member of the juniors, you know." Jeremy stopped short, realizing Conor was wearing a practice uniform, and his handsome face broadened. "Are you going to play for the Boilermakers?"

"It's highly likely," Conor said, putting his hand on the lad's shoulder. "I certainly want no advantages because of past friendships, but in the event I make the club I'll be working in the yard. Maybe, just maybe, you might put in a word with your good mother . . ."

"What, Conor?"

"Oh, it's a bit silly."

"No, tell me, I insist."

"I've had a yen to work around trains since I was a youngster of your age. It would be the thrill of my entire life if I could blacksmith around the locomotive shop."

Jeremy flashed another smile, winked and dashed off down the tunnel to change. Conor flushed at the surge of luck. Things were going his way. If he could only hold up his end and make the bloody club, Jeremy would get him right into the middle of the yard.

*

Several days after Conor's debut he was still being asked back to practice. He had been grudgingly named "The Blacksmith" and attempts to keep him off the club were proving costly.

Within minutes of the first scrummages Conor always found himself in possession of the ball and forced to run with it. The ball would be tossed to him slowly and badly in order to give the pack a chance to converge. The instant his hands were on it, bodies crunched in audible impact along with assorted trippings, groin kicks, butts, forearm blows, shin blasts and kneeings.

Conor chose not to respond in kind but played rugby. He ran over the smaller backs and rendered a number of the bigger ones senseless. Their desire to devour him was steadily tempered by the demands of self-preservation.

Once Conor established his ability to survive, the other qualities of his game came to the fore. He was a thunderous kicker and sure-handed in passing and receiving. His tackling was intelligent in use of lanes and angles to cut off swifter backs. Once he got his hands on a runner, the runner went down. The brightest aspect was an ability to carry the ball in close to the opponent's goal line where he bulled his way through tacklers with terrifying power.

Despite the surprising show Conor was far from a polished player and could be badly burned by his mistakes. What seemed logical to both Derek Crawford and Doxie O'Brien was to put him on the juniors and hope he would develop faster than he aged.

*

A summons to Sir Frederick's office never failed to upset the delicate balance in Derek Crawford's stomach. He approached the building as though it were at the end of a long plank, heading overboard. The coach was surprised to see the usual scowl absent from Sir Frederick's face and more surprised to see Lady Caroline pacing the office.

"Derek," Sir Frederick said, getting right to it, "Lady Caroline has a personal interest in the Larkin chap."

"Yes, sir." Crawford sighed at the reprieve. "I gathered that from Lord Jeremy. He worked at Hubble Manor a time back?"

"Yes, that's right," Caroline said.

"How's he shaping up?" Sir Frederick asked.

Crawford scratched his jaw. "He's got the makings, all right. Strong as a fucking . . . sorry, m'lady, strong as a bull. Fine pair of hands, boots the ball well, but you know this *is* the Boilermakers and the man is over thirty. I just can't tell how he'll hold up in the week-after-week grind. Then, there's the fine points of the game. Takes time and experience to learn."

"Larkin is an extremely intelligent man," Caroline said with oversimplification of the problem. "He'll grasp things quickly."

"Perhaps he will, but I don't want to go losing any more games just to advance his schooling."

Sir Frederick rattled his fingers on the desk and exchanged glances with his daughter. "Derek, what would you say if we carry him as an alternate?"

Up till now Weed had been rather gentle and undemanding. Crawford realized that the "request" had bite to it. "If I could force-feed him, push him along."

"What will you require, Derek?"

Crawford fidgeted. "Well, let's say we gave him some highly special tutoring. In my mind, Robin MacLeod has the best rugby mind of us all. If Sir Frederick isn't averse to letting MacLeod off work early and putting him with Larkin say two or three hours a day before regular practice . . ."

"Fine with me. Go on and arrange it."

Crawford heaved a sigh as the tummy sputtered up. "There's one more slight problem. We've got six R.C.s on the club. We've never carried seven. If Larkin makes it he'd be replacing Bart Wilson. Bart's, well, you know, an old-timer and it might be unpopular. I mean, Bart's large in the Orange Order. It will have a bad scant all over East Belfast what with him being replaced by a Catholic in midseason."

"Oh, horseshit," Weed grumbled. He chewed on his cigar end, bit it off and twirled it between his lips in meditation. "I'll call Bart in myself and suggest he resign for the good of the club. There'll be a foremanship open for him so he'll suffer no loss in salary."

"In that case," Crawford said, "you'll find him totally loyal for the good of the team. Bart will personally, himself, keep all the rumbles quiet." He arose and left in obvious relief.

Weed threw up his hands to signify "capitulation" to his daughter's desires and she pinched his cheek and told him he was a dear.

"By the way," she said, "Larkin's going to work at the farrier shop."

"Hummmm, yes, I guess so, he's a blacksmith or something."

"Hardly, Freddie. You saw the work he did at the Manor. I don't think it's quite fitting to have an ironmaster shoeing horses. Just by chance, Jeremy mentioned something about Larkin having a preference for the forge near the locomotive shop."

"See here, Caroline, those chaps down there take their seniority seriously. . . . I can't go about buggering up the whole yard."

"Do you know what occurred to me? It would be absolutely smashing if Larkin executed something which you could present as a gift to the new City Hall. You see, if he's on a special commission, then there won't be all that bother about seniority and petty jealousies."

"Good Lord, you've thought of everything. All right. That's more than I bargained for, but I'll do it. Now, for your half of the bargain. Jeremy is to take the tour with the team."

"Freddie, I made no such deal."

"Oh yes, you did and I have just given you the shirt off my back."

"Freddie, that boy has you wrapped around his little finger. He's got to have special tutoring if he's to get into Trinity. He just can't go trotting off to the Midlands."

"Oh yes, he can."

"Christopher is a year younger than Jeremy and is halfway through a most difficult course of studies."

"Quid pro quo, my darling Caroline, quid pro quo. I've disrupted my entire operation for this Larkin chap and you will keep your end of the bargain."

"You are a bastard. Roger will be insane with anger."

He roared out a laugh. "Roger is your domain, darling; besides, you've a powerful selling point with that paddy of yours on the team."

"I don't understand."

"Well, what better chaperon for Jeremy than the Larkin chap? Good old friends and all that."

Caroline looked into his impish grin, knowing he was going to get his way. "Very well," she sighed, "but let me break it to Roger in my own good time."

CHAPTER SEVEN: Matthew MacLeod and a gang of his pals pressed against the kitchen window. Inside, his daddy and Conor Larkin all but filled the tiny room.

"That's him!" Matt cried. "Conor Larkin!"

"Aw, look at the size of him, would ye. With them feet of his, he'd keep right on standing a long time after they shot him."

"My daddy says he could run through a brick wall. Yesterday in practice he scored a try with three men hanging all over him."

The side-by-side MacLeod houses on Tobergill were landmarks of some note. Morgan, the patriarch, was a foreman of the "Big Mabel" dry dock, a stalwart of the Orange Order and church. His son Robin was one of the best rugby players in Belfast. Whenever Robin brought a teammate home it was always a neighborhood event.

Robin MacLeod liked the cut of Conor Larkin the instant the two bashed heads on the playing field. As for Conor, Robin reminded him of Mick McGrath in many ways. He was built a bit like Mick, solid, quick and game with strong good looks and sporting a head of sandy curls. Robin was the on-the-field brains and spark of the Boilermakers and when Conor was assigned to team up with him for schooling they hit it off right away.

Matt had been shuttled outside but Lucy fluttered back and forth with a number of unscheduled appearances. Just as they settled in for some serious study, Morgan made his entry.

" 'Tis a rare pleasure, indeed," Morgan said, pumping Conor's hand, and after amenities Nell followed, and then a number of neighbor men who wished a word to the wise with the new Boilermaker so they could report their findings at the pub. Loose head prop was a non-sectarian position. It was the team that counted. Conor was accepted as one of the more outstanding examples of his religion, a man with a trade like themselves.

"For Chrissake keep them lugs out of here so we can work!" Robin shouted to Lucy after one more interruption.

"Would it be better if we did this at my digs?" Conor asked.

"Naw, they'll settle down in a few days and leave us be."

Robin had laid out a program so Conor would know the team plays, the opposition club by club, fine points and the rules. He was greatly impressed by Conor's intellectual attack on the game. This season the only thing the Boilermakers were setting on fire was Derek Crawford's stomach. Robin was determined to deliver a player polished enough to make the team and the Midlands tour.

Within the week everyone in a two-pub radius of Tobergill Road had paid their respects. Everyone except Shelley MacLeod. Conor was made to feel at ease with them but was given to understand that Robin's sister was a bit of an off horse, somewhat uppity.

With the knowledge her brother was teaching another new player, Shelley avoided his house studiously. She was a Shankill lass indeed and from time to time could be drawn into the Saturday night Guinness scene but she was also aloof for long periods and much of a stranger to her kind. Robin's mates, decent as they were, were a dull rough lot with primate range and desires. Another player held little allure.

Despite Shelley's aversion, the special aura of Conor Larkin's seemingly appearances failed to dull. The family seemed taken with him. There was the vibration that one could feel between the two houses that made it an event when he appeared. After a fortnight of careful evasion, her healthy curiosity needed to be satisfied.

She announced that she would join them for a Saturday dinner to which Conor Larkin had been invited. He was an impressive sight, she thought, if one merely took physical appearance into consideration, for he stood a half head over Robin and, when they were introduced, a full head over herself. She found herself mumbling an awkward hello as he continued to hold onto her hand and silently study her. His eyes went only from the long red hair to stop at her incredible green eyes. He was filled with a strange kind of hunger, not lust, but the hunger of a searcher who had suddenly struck onto something. They simply stood and stared until the trance was snapped when Matthew was plucked off the street, giving her a chance to break it off and march him away for a howling scrubbing.

Morgan dropped his temperance posture for the event by snitching a drink with the lads, then returned to full-blown pomp as he placed himself ceremoniously at the head of the table. He adjusted his glasses, which needed no adjusting, for he always read the Bible from memory. After opening the five-generation heirloom he cleared his throat as a signal for heads to bow.

" 'These are the things that ye shall do: Speak ye every man the truth to his neighbour; execute the judgment of truth and peace in your gates; and let none of you imagine evil in your hearts against his neighbour; and love no false oath: for all these things that I hate, saith the Lord.' "

Having intoned his acceptance of Conor Larkin, he closed the book and bowed his own head. As he did, he caught a glimpse of his daughter and Conor staring at one another point-blank over Matthew's head and he knew from his years that the oldest of ignitions was taking place in his home. He had never seen his daughter so swiftly stunned or even realized she had the capacity for it. Shelley was always in control of Shelley.

"Thank ye, Lord, for Thy bountiful gifts and for the presence of a new friend who has graced our home." Morgan looked up with the expectation Conor might want to cross himself or add a word. Getting no response, he said, "Amen."

After dinner they adjourned to the parlor about the reflector stove purring in family warmth. Lucy perched uncomfortably at the piano stool when Morgan's unabashed and thunderous voice forced them all into a songfest. By the fourth round, uneasiness toward one another vanished and Conor galvanized the moment with a voice that no one expected with a Donegal ballad of ages and ages. There was a brief moment of blanching when Matt called for a rousing Orange number. It was pounced over quickly by a haymaker of "Coming Through the Rye."

Matthew dozed, Robin carried him home and everyone seemed to fade, leaving Conor and Shelley quite alone. The uneasiness of the first instant of their meeting returned.

"It's been a grand evening," Conor said. He took his cap from the rack and left.

*

A long week later Shelley knocked on Lucy's kitchen door and entered. Conor was by himself, assembling loose-leaf notes at the table.

He looked up. "I think Lucy and Matt have turned in. Robin's down at the pub getting us a few pints."

"I know," she said. "I waited for him to go." She seemed stuck to the floor in obvious anger with herself for following the urge to come to him, then telling him so.

"I've been looking out for you every night," Conor said. "I'm glad you decided not to wait any longer."

Shelley had warded off Shankill toughs all her life with little more than a sharp look. She wanted to cut him down but found herself unable to strike at him. His observation was simple truth. She had avoided him; he waited. She seemed no longer able to avoid him. The lure during the week had become irresistible and wholly uncomfortable.

"Well?" Conor asked.

"Well indeed," Shelley answered, still puzzled by her own behavior.

"Shall we be seeing each other, Shelley?" he said straight on.

"Is tomorrow night soon enough?" she answered.

CHAPTER EIGHT: Sir Frederick enthusiastically endorsed Caroline's proposal that something in wrought iron be executed at the yard and given in the Weed name to

the new City Hall on Donegal Square. Larkin was dispatched to examine the building, which was nearing com-
pletion, and return with an appropriate suggestion. One
might have thought that the ponderous structure was
headquartering the capital of Ireland or at least a province, instead of a mere city of four hundred thousand
inhabitants.

On the site of the old Linen Hall, its dimensions were
enormous and all of it was capped with a dome which
soared a hundred and seventy-five feet above Belfast, an
ode to her industrial prowess.

Conor quenched his own hatred of the project, for it
had established him exactly where he wanted to be within
the Weed compound. He decided on a pair of gates from
the foyer into the Great Hall, which occupied the entire
east front of the quadrangular building.

On the premise that Belfast was the heartland of that
thick, pious Ulster mentality, Conor realized something
in the nature of the airy lace of Tijou or the Italian
school was out of the question. He set out to design, instead, a quasi-German Baroque that reeked of "Reformation." Its heaviness of style allowed him to fill the gates
with all sorts of heraldic shields and symbols of progress
to stir Ulster blood.

Conor realized Sir Frederick was an art collector and a
man of great taste and had to take care not to offend
him. At the same time the gates had to be kept in harmony with both the building and the theme of the land
and people it ruled. He walked a thin line that hovered
between a very subtle joke and grandeur.

The detailed rendering was submitted personally after a
month. Sir Frederick lit the customary cigar, spread the
drawings and proceeded to be deliciously puzzled. It was
there, yet it wasn't there. The good strokes were brilliant.
The bad taste seemed to be exquisitely managed. Weed
studied Larkin as well as the drawings, both amused and
suddenly respectful. He knew the man was completely
deliberate in what he was doing.

"See here, Larkin, are you pulling my leg?"

"Have you seen the inside of the building?"

"Humm, not recently."

"Perhaps you'd better have a look."

"Well, it does say Ulster, all right, I'll give you that."

"Could I suggest you show it to the city fathers concerned and get the benefit of their reactions?" Conor suggested.

Weed did exactly that. They raved to a man. Larkin had hit the mark and the plans were approved.

*

Rumbles could always be expected when a Catholic infringed on the all-Protestant domains within the Weed Works. They were kept to a minimum when Bart Wilson, whom Conor had replaced on the Boilermakers, was elevated to foreman of a plating shop to quell any rippling waters. He personally introduced Conor around, which led to tacit acceptance. Members of Sir Frederick's rugby team had special status. Moreover, Larkin didn't appear to be a job threat in that he was on a personal commission for Sir Frederick. Mutual coolness and staying out of one another's way prevailed.

The locomotive works at the complex expanded along the south side of King William Channel opposite the shipyard, sprawling from under the shadows of the steel mill. A line of support shops adjoined the main assembly plant where Conor was established in one of the forges. He was as welcome as a leper but was left largely on his own.

Afforded the freedom to move about at will, he dissected the gigantic complex. Somewhere in the vastness there would be that blind spot, that back door into Ulster, through which to bring over the guns from England. Yet, as he took it on, area by area, the key remained tauntingly elusive. One promising prospect after another led to dead ends. What seemed to be a loose operation from the outside was far tighter than he had expected. All material, cargo and movement was under strict control. Even if one managed to get guns over from England to Weed's private docks, what then? How could they be unloaded in the yard and transported beyond the yard? It began to look impossible. Yet he was on the inside and somewhere, somehow . . . the back door was there.

He moved about from iron mill to slipways to docks, mapping inch by inch in his mind, later to translate it to paper. His eye became an instant calculator. He searched until he became suspicious of his own freedom of movement. If he were seen four or five times in the same

area, just observing, sooner or later it would be bound to
draw an inquiry.

In the beginning he wanted to be near the locomotive
works because it was the most central place in the
complex. For reasons not known to himself, he sensed
something about it. It was just a bit down the line from
his forge and he could easily go in and out several times
a day, for he had befriended Duffy O'Hurley, driver of
Sir Frederick's private train.

*

The driver who was at the throttle of the Red Hand
Express which broke the hundred-mile-an-hour barrier was
Duffy O'Hurley out of County Tipperary with his brother-
in-law, Calhoun Hanly, as fireman. Duffy had survived all
of the early perils of railroading including numerous brake
and coupling failures, derailings and one monumental
crash. He was a "pounder" whose black-smoke tactics and
consumption of coal and water spelled speed. The team of
O'Hurley and Hanly were a tad more legendary in a profession that created legends. Despite the fact they were
Catholics, Sir Frederick hired them out of sheer frustration.
When Duffy and Calhoun came down that Newtownabbey
straightaway at one hundred and six miles an hour on the
first crack out of the box, Sir Frederick rewarded them
with lifelong tenure as the crew of his private engine.
Nothing could dissuade Weed's loyalty, even the constant
grousing of his daughter over O'Hurley's heavy-handed
driving.

Part of the lasting allure of the Red Hand was the
continued modification of the superb basic design and Sir
Frederick's personal effort to keep it in the public eye.
An annual promotion was made in England tied to the
Boilermakers' tour of the Midlands.

Each year the newest model led the private train with
renewed fanfare. In industrial England, its arrival was
looked forward to and welcomed as a county fair. Engine, tender and private cars were painted in Ulster colors,
buntinged, flagged and decorated to the stack. Sir Frederick
personally partied prospective buyers and the press with
elaborate day rides and champagne picnics. There were
rides for the school kiddies with contest winners in each
town getting to sit up front with O'Hurley himself. Photo-

graphs of Sir Frederick's latest pride never failed to make the British press. A number of persons close to royal sources rumored that his antics all but cost him an elevation to peerage. Yet this was in the finest tradition of those flamboyant builders of the era who were also its supersalesmen.

Duffy O'Hurley fitted into the scheme famously, a stage Irishman who gloried in the role, a colorful addition with an everlasting joke to impart, an everlasting bet to wager, everlasting gregariousness and an everlasting drink in his hand.

When he wasn't on the road with Sir Frederick's private train, he stationed himself at the Works in the locomotive assembly plant like an expectant father chaperoning the construction of the coming model. With ultimate responsibility for the engine's performance, he fawned over it, supervising every last detail.

When he wasn't at the locomotive works he was at Boilermaker Stadium, for surely if he hadn't become Ireland's greatest driver he would have been her greatest rugby player. A big, gruff man of total nerve, he was accepted as an equal by the players and alone had the privilege of their lounge. His position and intimacy with the team gave him hero's status in every bar he deigned to grace.

It was a small matter for Conor and Duffy O'Hurley to become quick friends. Larkin's forge stood a short way from the locomotive plant and generated Duffy's curiosity. Larkin was a man of substance, like himself, an artisan as he was an artist in locomotive driving, both were fellow R.C.s (and at times it got lonely in the yard) and both were members of the Boilermakers, so to speak.

Conor immediately sensed O'Hurley as a potential ally and returned the visits, where he was shown the inner workings of the Red Hand engine. Duffy was more than pleased to endlessly explain anything and everything. Conor took care to keep the friendship on an easy level and did no probing of the man's sympathies, habits or past.

It wasn't the engine itself that began to catch his fancy but the coal and water tender and the movements of the train throughout the year.

Of a day after practice, Duffy was at his usual station

at barside in the players' lounge gushing with excitement, for he'd be testing his new engine within a week.

"What happens to the engine when the tour is done?" Conor asked.

"It stays in the private service of Sir Frederick for a year, till the next model."

"Travel much?"

"Oh, not too much for a bachelor, mostly to Derry and back. A run or two to their summer place in Kinsale, in and out of Dublin, and over to England maybe four times a year. But it's first class all the way."

"Aye, that's good. Now what happens to the old engine after you put the new one on?"

"Could you ever believe there's a waiting list a mile long to buy it? Every pipsqueak maharajah and every gold mine owner in South Africa wants that personal engine, even used. We got four South American generals on the waiting list. Are you thinking of buying it, Conor?"

"Maybe," Conor answered softly. The back door into Ulster had just opened a crack.

CHAPTER NINE: Markets, a wee Catholic enclave, lay at the River Lagan wedged between the gas works and a conglomeration of warehouses and factories. It consisted of a stand of eighteenth-century dwellings decayed beyond mere dilapidation. Slimy cobblestones held a veneer of unwashed filth. Conor trod so softly an egg would not have broken under his feet. He found the opening to a dead-end court. The street sign had long been unreadable. Four little girls skipping rope blocked his way.

"In and out go the dusty bluebells,
In and out go the dusty bluebells,
In and out go the dusty bluebells,
I'll be your master.

"Follow me to Londonderry,
Follow me to Cork and Kerry,
Follow me so light and airy,
For I'll be your master.

"Tipper-ipper-rapper on the left-hand shoulder,
Tipper-ipper-rapper on the left-hand shoulder,
Tipper-ipper-rapper on the left-hand shoulder,
I'll be your master."

"Good morning, darlings," Conor said when the skip rope stopped swinging. "I'm looking for Cyril's Close."

"This is it here, mister."

"Would you be knowing where Mick McGrath lives?"

They immediately fell silent, a conditioning of constant flight from bill collectors. Conor smiled. "Don't you be worrying, I'm not a tick man. I'm an old friend of his from Derry."

They looked at one another, verging on flight, then the smallest stepped forward and took Conor's hand and led him to the end of the court and pointed. Then she fled.

Conor sucked in a sigh as he looked over the surroundings. The immense gas works storage tank hovered directly above the court, blocking any possibility of sunlight. His knock was greeted by the sounds of darting movement inside. He knocked again, louder. From the corner of his eye he spotted someone giving him a glimpse from the crack of a drawn window shade.

Conor pounded. "Open up. It's a friend!"

A baby's cry inside gave it away. Conor repeated his pounding and the door opened slightly. Mick McGrath blinked his eyes at the onslaught of daylight. He didn't look himself, he'd gone that rotten. "Who is it?" he rasped.

"Conor Larkin from Derry."

The door dared open a crack further, revealing the wreckage of Mick McGrath. Reluctant memory brought an expression of remembrance. "Well, bless me," Mick said, "so it is."

Conor shoved it open wide and was greeted with a foul smell of mold and an unclean stench of human odors.

"Hey, sorry about not answering the knock sooner," Mick said. "The tick men have been on me. No heart at all so long as they get their bloody rents."

Conor stepped into the room. In the peeling grayness he saw an old granny rocking and mumbling to herself, obviously not in her own mind.

A skinny, stone-eyed woman sat awry on a cot, her back propped against the wall.

"My wife, Elva, she's been feeling poorly."

The baby shrieked. The woman reached for it in a robot manner and shoved a flat breast into its mouth. She coughed over and over from the pressure of the baby's sucking until it wracked her and she shoved it away, spat and reached for a bottle of poteen. The baby resumed screaming.

"I . . . I've got one of my heads this morning . . . the bloody thing's opening," Mick said.

Conor backed to the door. "Get yourself together," he said. "I'll meet you at the pub on the corner of Little May Street."

As he closed the door behind him, the four little girls who had been singing "Dusty Bluebells" were standing and gawking and all around the court he could feel the glare of hidden eyes. "Get on with you," he said, brushing past them.

He was heavily involved with straight shots of paddy and Guinness chasers when Mick finally arrived and sidled up next to him. Conor slid the bottle over without looking. Mick did a couple in quickly, hands trembling and spilling from the need of it.

"How'd you find me?"

"Who knows? You ask and you ask again."

"Why didn't you mind your own fucking business?"

"Sorry," Conor said, getting off the stool. "Help yourself to the bottle."

Mick grabbed his arm. "Don't go."

They sat without words through half the bottle. "I made the junior team all right," he said. "I was on my way, Conor, on my way. They was looking me over real close to move me up to the big club. Things was never so grand. I was making over a quid in the yard's farrier shop, my pockets jingling and on the way up to the big club. Oh, shit, what's the use."

Conor's hand felt warm on his shoulder and the memory of the two of them playing for the Bogsiders and the glory of it filled his mind. He turned his eyes from the back-bar mirror to avoid sight of himself.

"I was rooming with Elva and her old widow mom.

That's the granny you saw there. Fourth game, maybe it was the fifth. I don't remember. I . . . I recall Doxie O'Brien watching my every move because they were going to move me up."

"What happened?" Conor said.

"Knee. You could hear it pop all over the stadium. The pain was so brutal I was screaming like a baby all the way to the hospital. They cut me up something fierce. I got myself into a real head beetler laying there day and night knowing I'd never play again and then I got the idea they was going to take my leg off. It was because of the fucking pain, you see, my head was playing tricks. So I jumped the hospital."

"You must have been behind the door when God passed out brains," Conor grunted.

"It was the pain. Elva and her old mom were wonderful to me. They was dead poor but they saw to it I was liquored up so I could bear it. After a time some of the pain went . . . I always got some of it, you know, but . . . it's pretty butchered up down there. Yourself, Conor?"

"I've been around."

"Aye, there was a rumor that you'd left Derry."

"Aye."

"Still a football man?"

"Aye, I'm in Belfast for a time. I'm working out with the Boilermakers."

"Then you've met Doxie O'Brien?"

"I have."

"Being a Catholic like us, I went to see him about getting my job back in the farrier shop. He done me a good turn, that Doxie. It's okay to work over there so long's you're on the club but Mary save your balls if you're not. Even becoming a cripple playing for their bloody team didn't make no difference. You know what it can be like working in a forge filled with hot metal if they don't like you."

Mick rolled up his sleeve, showing a ghastly burn scar. "Got one on my back, too. White-hot rivet was dropped on me from a drydock scaffold."

"For God's sake, Mick, there are hundreds of blacksmith shops in Belfast."

Tears welled in Mick's eyes and he shook so badly

Conor had to pour his drink. "I know. I was fired from half of them. I never got off this shit. When Elva's mom got her first stroke, I felt I had to take care of them."

"What's wrong with your wife?" Conor asked.

"She's been a hackler in the linen mills since she was twelve years old. You ought to see these fucking mills here. Some of them are half as big as Bogside. The windows are all hot with steam from the engine shutting out the light and they work barefoot on the wet floors twelve hours at a crack. . . . First the noise gets them, softens their minds and they never hear so well again. Then the damp creeps into their joints and gnarls them. And after a time the lungs are shot from flax dust. Two of her sisters were hacklers before her. They were done in before they reached thirty. All the hacklers stay drunk in order to keep working."

Conor called for another bottle and tapped his fist on the bar in broken rhythm. "Can you bring yourself around, Mick? I'll help you."

Conor's offer did little to stir him. It was all gone. "If I burned you for a fool," he said, "I'd have wise ashes. You saw us. We'll not last long enough to grow a decent beard." Then Mick broke into a fit of laughter that pleaded for Conor not to pursue bottomed-out hopes any further. "Tell me, Conor Larkin, how is your rugby game?"

"Good enough for a few seasons."

"Juniors, is it?"

"I'll be with the big club by the time of the Midlands tour."

For the first time, Mick's face opened brightly. "The tour!" he said, as though he had just seen the Virgin Mary. "Oh, I hear it's grand! Get to wear a team jacket, eh, and Sir Frederick puts you up in first-rate digs and there's a baron of beef at the table every night and all the paddy and Guinness you can swizzle, and I hear himself comes over, and you get to travel in a private car and himself always puts down twenty with a bookmaker for the team to split if they win. By Jaysus, the tour itself! That's the one thing I regret. I'd have given it all for one season of the tour."

"Yeah," Conor whispered, and slipped from the stool.

Mick held up his hand, refusing the desperately needed money. "Don't look me up any more, Conor," he said, "just don't look me up. I've a job delivering coal for a relative of Elva's. It doesn't pay much, but, on the other hand, we don't need much."

"So long, Mick," Conor said.

"So long, Conor."

CHAPTER TEN: Their Sunday trip up Belfast Lough ended lovely in the hushed elegance of the Old Inn in Crawfordsburn, a generations-old, low-roofed beam and brick pub. They sipped aperitifs on the veranda by a garden wild with the full bloom of Ulster roses as he placed the dinner order.

The little maître d' nodded with approval or consulted with concern over each course, then bowed. "Thank you, sir, very good, sir. Your table should be ready in a few moments, sir."

Shelley MacLeod was stunning. She worked for a haute couture establishment and knew how to make the best of it. She had emerged from the tiny dressing room down at the beach in the best Cinderella tradition. Matching greens of silk to the delicacy of her own complexion and with just the proper décolletage and cleavage. The two of them, side by side, had all but silenced the place when they entered. Conor found himself staring at her as he had done all day and a number of times before that, as well.

"Sure, you're spoiling the devil out of me, Conor Larkin," she said.

"Sure you can't spoil diamonds," he answered.

Shelley had lapsed now and again into long, uncomfortable silences during the day, unlike the other times. Now she was downright nervous and wanted to light a cigarette but kept her hands in her lap. A renewal of the fire just inside the veranda set her profile aflickering. Another grand day of it. The lovely instant when she flung open the door, picnic basket in hand, and change of clothes in a suitcase beside her, faces all beaming, sighing with relief at the sight of each other, the festive train ride up to Helen's Bay, the choppy sail on that choppy lough, the band concert at Bangor and now the glorious topper and a slow tired trip back to Belfast. There had been a rush of such days, yet something was dreadfully missing. They were getting in close to each other, so comfortable, so filled with endless talk. Lord knew she didn't want to run him off but if there was a dark side to him she was going to find out before it went any further.

Conor sensed her unmistakable vibrations and went into a silence of his own. They pecked at their drinks until she set hers down with deliberation.

"Conor," she said abruptly.

"Aye."

"There's something wrong between us. It's showing up more strongly each time."

"Like what?"

"Like hugs and kisses and rolling in the grass. Obviously, I'm terribly taken with you. We've been out together fifteen times or more in a month but I don't understand this subtle brushing up against each other and your long hungry looks. Why haven't you tried to make love to me, man?"

"I have tried, at least within myself. I can't say for sure what's holding me back. Maybe I don't want to be just another Shankill tough."

"You know damned well there's a difference," she answered.

"Let me tell you something; you're an awesome woman. For one thing, you're the most beautiful thing I've ever laid eyes on."

"Come now, Conor, I can't believe that . . . of all the places you've been and all the things you've done and all the women you must have loved."

He held his glass up in the direction of the waiter, who fetched it for a refill. "Don't let my good looks deceive you," he laughed with a touch of self-debasement. "We're a backward lot, you know. Some of the men in my village didn't marry until they were over fifty. Some never married. Some never loved. We've a different set of priorities imposed on us, I guess. I'm a strange Irishman, all right, because I do prefer women to drink. On the other hand, enough of the old traditions have rubbed off on me."

She didn't have to ask him if he'd ever been in love; she knew, and she knew lads like him, no matter what their outward manliness, they froze up in the face of it.

Conor was so damned beautiful, she thought, as he went into that hidden part of his mind to find some scrapings to throw out. He lifted his head a bit sadly. "When I was a young lad I saw a beautiful lady one day. She was a Countess and I wanted to hate her for who she was but it was quite impossible. I'd see her from time to time, always looking through the hedge. One day I became her friend. She was my secret idea of what was perfect in a woman. So, wherever I roamed and whenever I looked into a woman's eyes, I had to compare and I'd never let anyone hold a candle to the Countess. Shelley, the Countess can't hold a candle to you and I don't quite know what to do about it or if I can even handle it."

"I'm not porcelain, Conor," she whispered, "under this silk I'm just a Belfast girl."

As they studied each other, Conor Larkin found himself backing away from a woman for the first time in his life. Having his defenses cracked, he was in disarray.

"I swear to God I think I'm scared, Shelley. If I take you, it's going to be different. I'm afraid we can't stop on the surface. I'm afraid I'll want to reach inside you and devour you. I've avoided that so goddam long, I'm not sure . . ."

"As far as you and I are concerned," she said bluntly, "you're fighting no one except yourself."

"Look, lass," he said in sudden defense, "there are things you don't know about me."

"And there are things you don't know about me," she retorted. Shelley dropped the game. There was no fear, no pride, no poking sentiment. Her green eyes all but blazed as she leaned close and put her hand on his. "You told me you sailed around the world seeking. Did you seek something alive and breathing or was it only a game locked up in your mind?"

Conor shook his head. "I told you our priorities are scrambled," he said shakily. "Can you believe that all that searching out there never included a woman?"

"Reach for me, Conor," she said.

"I want to."

"Let me put it to you straight and simple. I've had too many bad times in my life. I've not been face to face with a man like you and I don't intend to let it slip away

by being coy. I want to grab and hold on, only to see if
there's something different in this world and if there's a
little of it for us."

Conor lifted her hand to his lips and brushed her
fingertips. They straightened up as the maître d' returned
and nodded. He slipped Shelley's dolman over her shoulder. They followed into the paneled hunting room, rich
in pewter.

*

The train back to Belfast was excruciating, for there
had been born a physical desire over which Conor was no
longer master. He had been rudely jolted from his aloofness in that high and exalted place where he placed himself over the games played by the weak and the mealy. He
had been too strong for such nonsense. When a man believes that in himself and is rudely shown otherwise, the
impact of it is so much more devastating.

His arm was about Shelley as she lay against him all
sleepy and cuddly and her fingers gently played with his
shirt. So many others had tried but the man had always
been in control of himself.

The feel of her skin was overwhelming and the passion
in her eyes flushed him with sensations. He shut his own
eyes and laid his head against the cool window, allowing
the jerky movement of the train to tap it. Outwardly, they
seemed to be sweetly tired and still but her deepening
breath was returned by his own until the unison of their
rise and fall fell into lovers' rhythm. They tightened their
closeness to one another. He fingered her downy hair,
did a feathery tracing of her neck, felt the prints of his
fingers on her eyelashes.

The train slowed. They separated and corrected their
dress. He looked through the window and was hit with a
chill of countering confusion as it passed the Weed Ship
& Iron Works slowly.

"Belfast! Belfast! Queen's Quay Station! End of the
line!"

Weary picnickers debarked.

The hansom cab made up a deadened Shankill Road.
Their breasts pounded. It turned into the wee streets of attached houses where a few late lovers lingered in doorways. All else was gone.

Shelley trembled the door open, seized his hand and drew him into the vestibule. They exploded into one another's arms. It was there! Fast, wild, total.

"Conor," she managed, "take me somewhere."

He was halfway through the door with her in tow when an awful reality battered its way through their euphoria. The hour was deadly late and the only place was his own room, which was strewn with diagrams, maps and papers of the shipyard and locomotive works.

He got hold of himself, taking her in his arms tightly. "God, I almost forgot. I've a pal up from Dublin crashing at my digs. We'll have to wait till tomorrow."

"Tomorrow," she gasped, "will it be tomorrow?"

"Aye, tomorrow."

*

Something had been happening in pieces since he'd met Shelley, now it crashed down. He didn't like the moment he left her. He didn't like the walk from Tobergill Road to the Ardoyne. He reached his room, taking the stairs very slowly. Loneliness had never bothered him. A book and later a book and a bottle were all he had ever needed. His own thoughts kept him company best. Tonight, loneliness had become an enemy. He stared at the bed. It was empty. Conor craved her.

The power of his fall had been swift, consuming and total.

He had allowed Shelley to invade his thoughts for days, take his mind away from his work. She inundated those hidden domains now. He tugged off his jacket, rolled up his sleeves and tapped the once endless reservoir of will power and discipline. At his desk he spread his maps and plans and concentrated with all his ability.

What would Shelley's body look like?

He shoved the papers back angrily and paced, ending up at the kitchenette cabinet, and pulled the plug from a bottle of paddy.

How would her breasts feel? How would they react to his kiss?

Conor flung himself on the bed. In a moment he was writhing uncomfortably. His mind drifted to other beds in other places. He felt a tinge of kinship for all the women who had lain down beside him who had loved him without

his true return of that love. How many times had he
feigned false sympathy over their tears and wished all
along they'd get up and go home? When did it start? Almost from the first day. On the mornings he awoke knowing he would see her, it was a day of flight.

"Shit!"

He spun off the bed and returned to his desk with renewed determination. That blurred vision of the Countess
Caroline came to him. It was always blurred, for she was,
in truth, the fairy princess, the illusion of convenience. He
had deliberately designated the unattainable as his ideal.
If I ever find a woman like that, then I'll go for her. That
was the game. That was the fraud. He knew he never would
find her so he was safe. Now Shelley MacLeod had obliterated his ancient defense and had reduced him to just a
man like all other men with the same bloody weaknesses
he deplored.

*Tomorrow she will be naked on that bed. I'll explore
her, I'll know her, I'll mouth her and fondle every inch
of her. I'll cover her.*

As if his own disgust with himself were not enough, the
stupidity of it made it worse. He was in the Brotherhood,
he belonged to the Brotherhood, and that kind of oil and
water could not mix.

Shelley, lying there, looking to him . . . those eyes . . .

He'd thought of making love to women, of course.
There had been long voyages without port. He even
needed a woman from time to time. A romance was nice
if that was in store but he'd settle for less if it wasn't.
There was never an affair he hadn't controlled or walked
away from with a second thought. He had never thought
of one particular woman, much less longed for her. He
could hurt her badly. Funny, he never thought much
about hurting the others. He had been brutal in asking
them to do combat with his unattainable ghost.

Shelley, Shelley, what loveliness, too lovely to hurt . . .

He was annoyed by the sudden introduction to his own
human frailties, wracked by the conflict of the Brotherhood, unnerved to realize he might need the strength of
another person. Playing a game that it might happen to
him someday, he never really thought it would. And now
his thoughts returned to her and to downright lust. As the
hours of night passed, one thing emerged for certain:

nothing would keep him from his rendezvous with her the next day.

Once that thought settled in as truth, he began to like the idea and he began to enjoy, rather than resist, the strange range of sensations. Dawn found Conor exhausted but blissful. His capitulation to her now found him counting the hours until he would bring her here.

He continued to poke through his drawings and papers. Long Dan would be in Belfast soon and Conor wanted very much to have an answer for him. Suddenly he found himself riveted to a diagram of the tender car which he had looked at a thousand times before. Something was different! In a golden instant he saw the answer to the puzzle with total clarity. He glared, bleary-eyed, and gasped in disbelief. It was so simple! So bloody simple! Perhaps it was his foggy state of mind. He ran to the sink, pumped it with water and soaked his head to clear it, then dug out every drawing with the tender car in it. Yes, it was true!

"God, that's it!" he cried. "That's it! I've found it! I've found it! I've found it!"

CHAPTER ELEVEN: The slits behind which Long Dan Sweeney's eyes lived were horrendously magnified by glasses of ancient vintage. He squinted close to Conor's drawings and calculations. Most were views and cross sections of the tender car.

"All right, explain very slowly what I'm looking at," he said.

"Actually, it's quite easy," Conor said, leaning over Dan's shoulder and using a pencil as a pointer. "The tender holds six tons of coal and three thousand gallons of water. The coal bin is in the front and its floor is tilted at a forty-five-degree angle to keep the coal sliding forward by force of gravity."

"Yes, I see that."

"The balance of the tender is a water tank in a U shape, running along both sides of the coal bin and across the rear of the car. It's like a thick horseshoe wrapped around the coal bin on three sides."

"I've got it."

"The water tank is the hiding place. It's filled through a manhole located on the rear top of the tender. My idea is to cut out two trap doors, carefully concealed, and large enough to lower two waterproof metal boxes down into the tank, one box on either side."

"So the boxes will ride right down in the water?"

"That's it. The guns would be in them. In order to load and unload all we'd have to do is lower the water level, open the trap doors and send a man down to open the boxes."

Sweeney puckered at the simplicity. "Two boxes of guns would displace quite an amount of water, wouldn't it?"

"It won't matter for several reasons," Conor said. "Duffy O'Hurley is known in train circles as a pounder, a black smoke man. He uses half again the fuel a conservative driver would use. He's fueling up all the time. No one counts the lumps of coal going into Sir Frederick's private engine. Our position is not to get greedy and keep the boxes small enough so the water loss won't be a factor."

"How many guns?"

"I made my calculations on the British Army Boer War standard, the Lee-Enfield rifle."

"That's the most of them," Dan said.

"Considering their size and weight, we could go fifty rifles a box or one hundred for each round trip."

The tea whistle caused Long Dan to withdraw his glasses. He rubbed his prison-tortured eyes, steeped the stuff and poured it into two unwashed glasses.

"The beauty of the plan is that the train makes five round trips to England a year. It comes and goes on a train ferry owned by one of the Weed shipping lines and docks right at the Ship & Iron Works. The train itself never undergoes a customs inspection. The rifles can sit in the yard or ride around Ireland until the train deadheads."

"Deadheads?"

"Rides empty, with just the driver and fireman. It makes innumerable runs to Derry and Dublin and Cork, as well. Potentially it can deliver the guns anywhere along these routes. A few minutes' stop at night alongside a country crossroad could effect a swift transfer."

The old Fenian had trained himself never to show emotion or reaction. It was difficult as he returned for a second and third look. Without the guns in Ireland nothing else could really move, no units could be formed, no real training. When he took on the responsibility of getting them over, he wanted a number of different plans so if one failed he could still use the others without giving away the entire operation. Larkin's idea was brilliant but how long could it hold? Five hundred rifles a year if all went well. As yet there were no acceptable alternatives.

"What will you need?" Sweeney asked.

"Two things. First, can you move the rifles from their dump in England to Liverpool? The train always arrives and leaves from there."

Dan nodded that it was possible.

"Secondly, I'll need a shop, preferably in Liverpool, to convert the tender and build the boxes."

"We've a good man there. Give me a list of materials. How long will it take?"

"Several hours at most. I'll cut those trap doors so they'll be impossible to detect with the naked eye."

"Well, with my eyes, anyhow," Dan said. Larkin's covered it all, Sweeney thought. He wanted to show a gesture of appreciation but merely gave off one pat on the shoulder and took up a pace. He liked Larkin and looked forward to his visits to Belfast. He enjoyed visiting with Larkin. The man always had something positive to report. So far, he showed qualities to become a top commander. Yet years of self-discipline disdained intimacy. All the men he had really ever cared for were dead. It was a mistake to get to like people who would die on you. He returned to thoughts of the plan.

"It all boils down to the driver and fireman," Sweeney said. "What about them?"

Conor shrugged. "I don't know too much. O'Hurley is in complete charge of the Red Hand. He can take it on trial runs, into the shop for repairs and modifications, complete freedom."

"Got any hunches about them?"

"O'Hurley blows Irish all right. He's a bachelor and about what you'd expect out of the train fraternity. Big, rough, likable. The fireman, Hanly, seems to be a follower. He's married to O'Hurley's sister. Stiff as a board when he's not shoveling coal. My guess is that he'd go along with

O'Hurley. They're both out of Tipperary, been on Weed's payroll a decade, drink like fish but always show up sober for the job and glory in it. My own relationship with them is perfect."

"Just keep a normal friendship going," Sweeney said. "Don't probe. If you pick up some leads in a natural way, so much the better. You're not to take any chances by talking to him about the guns. If he reacts wrong, it would mean your neck. We've some contacts at Dublin Castle and we'll get a background on them. Do you need the drawings any longer?"

"No, it's all in my head."

"Burn them."

"Aye."

"I've got to talk this over with a few people. As soon as we get the information on O'Hurley and Hanly I'll be back up. You'll be contacted in the usual way. I may have to go to another location next time. This one is sprouting eyes."

Conor gathered up the papers and put on his cap. "Single me out in your prayers, Dan. I'm playing my first game as a Boilermaker Saturday evening. Pray I don't break a leg and get left behind."

"You'll do all right, Larkin."

They shook hands briefly. Sweeney was already back at the table studying another matter before Conor reached the door. He looked up.

"Conor."

"Aye."

"Good work."

"Thanks, Dan, thanks a lot."

CHAPTER TWELVE: It would be a few hours before Shelley got off work. Conor rode into Gresham Street aboard Belfast's new pride, the first of her electric tram lines, and debarked into high carnival-like spirit. The street was filled with hokeypokey men who hawked refrigerated, flavored iced milk and sparks flew out of the knife grinder's wheel, the barrel organ played to a few comers and a pair of sandwich-board men lolled past the shops of saddlers and shoemakers and tailors. Conor waded through the crowd to the row of pet shops just beyond the open-stalled Smithfield market. Homing pigeons were all the back-yard sport these days and a birthday was coming up for Matthew MacLeod.

"What can I do for ye, mister?"

"I'll be needing a pair of very, very fine homers."

The shopkeeper sized Conor up as a gentleman of some means, dressed as he was in a fine covert coat and cashmere trousers. He wiggled his forefinger and led him secretively to the rear of the store, then slowly, lovingly drew back the cover on a cage holding a beautiful set of white doves. "Tumblers," the shopkeeper said, "never had a luvlier pair."

After terse bargaining, he paid the man and made arrangements for delivery on Matthew's birthday and returned into the hubbub, browsing along the lane of secondhand bookstalls. The air was punctured by the beating of drums on the corner.

"Drink is ruination, the handmaiden of Satan and the destroyer of Christian families!" cried an intemperate temperance preacher holding aloft a bottle of alcohol with a large chunk of meat floating in it. "Do ye want yer liver lookin' like this!"

Conor drifted onto Royal Street, a fine broad way leading into the newly finished City Hall. He never failed to wince. The presentation of his gates was scheduled to take place just before the tour. The Linen Hall Library which once occupied that exalted ground had been moved over the way. He buried his face in newspapers and periodicals from about the world, checked the card catalogue and put his name on the waiting list for some of the newer titles.

With time left to kill, he retraced his steps into the Grand Central Hotel, through the lobby and in a half jog made down the marble stairs to the barbershop. Good, an empty chair. "Shave and friction; I've got but twenty minutes."

The barber looked his customer over, then to the wall filled with rows of personal shaving mugs, some of which were kept there by traveling salesmen. "I don't have one here," Conor said as the apprentice boy relieved him of jacket, collar and cuffs, then returned with the first of the

hot towels. As Conor was stretched, the barber threw out
the usual inquiries. Traveling? Visiting? On business?
From where? To where? He stropped the razor and inspected Conor's beard, stropped and inspected. "And how
would youse like yer shave?"

"In silence," Conor answered.

*

The day started off on tenterhooks for Shelley Mac-
Leod. She had awakened in Conor's arms as she had for
several nights, remembering the cold decision, now determined to go through with it. Conor got her home with
the dawn and continued on his way to Weed Ship & Iron.
She arrived at Madam Blanche's Salon on Bedford Street
in a noticeable state.

Blanche Hemming served in the dual capacity of best
friend as well as employer. One look at Shelley and she
was whisked through the sewing room to her office. Shelley
insisted she was not ill.

"Did you see David? Was there a fight?" Blanche
pressed.

"David doesn't fight, you know that. I wish to God he
would, sometimes."

Blanche nodded knowingly. "You certainly gave him
enough messages in the past few weeks. He should have
stood on his hind legs and roared."

"That's not his style," Shelley said. "I'm going through
with it, Blanche."

"Are you sure about Conor Larkin?"

"I don't know. How can you know? It's been so sudden.
Oh, it's mad and it's wild but I don't know if it's for a day
or a year. I do know Shelley has had a good look at
Shelley. I can't play this game with David." She studied
herself in the mirror uncomfortably. "I look a wreck."

"Just stay here and get yourself together."

"I've a fitting for Lady Dryden in ten minutes."

"I'll take it," Blanche said.

Shelley stared at the telephone for a full five minutes before lifting the receiver and cranking for the central exchange. "I'd like 492," she said.

"Government House, Department of Ulster."

"Put me through to Mr. David Kimberley, please."

"Kimberley here."

"David, it's Shelley."

He looked about his office quickly as he always did when she initiated the call as if to see that the door was locked and there were no eavesdroppers. His voice trailed down to just above a whisper. "Yes, what is it?"

"I'd like to see you this evening before you get away to Dublin."

"That's going to be rather difficult," he answered.

"I'm afraid it's important," she insisted.

He knew it must be urgent, for she hardly ever made the demand of him. He whipped his engagement calendar out and scanned it, marking off the late afternoon appointments.

"Will four be all right?"

"Yes, that will be fine."

It was nine o'clock now. Seven hours. Shelley braced herself for an agonizing passage of time.

At his end of the line, David Kimberley paled. She had called off a number of visits in the past weeks. It was rather obvious she had been seeing someone. It had happened before. He had a dread of Shelley coming to that day. Her note of solemnity set his mind treadmilling.

*

In the days that followed her first meetings with Conor Larkin, Shelley found her placid existence upheaved. He was an entirely new sort of person, neither Shankill nor gentry. Actually, he fell into no category except his own. At first there was confusion at being invited to a poetry reading and a rather grim prospect of two hours of it. That was when the first light of him came through. Before they entered the hall he had gone over it with her, explained the hidden meanings, nuances, seemingly confused passages, the poet's own torments. As the words poured from the lectern, suddenly there was something where there had always been nothing. The rest of it, theater, concerts, lectures, opened her mind gloriously.

It was those late parts of the evenings when the easiest rapport she had ever known with a man plunged them past midnight and time fleeted unaware. Shelley found herself intensely desiring to absorb his thoughts, but it was more . . . an unexplained outcropping of silliness that came on waves of sheer gaiety. She delighted when he was

happy, for she sensed that laughter had not come easily
and she discovered ways to make him laugh. While they
seemed to be unlocking each other rapidly, the presence
of someone and the anticipation of meeting someone took
on new meaning. Both reached out, trying desperately to
touch one another over a vast, dark empty space.

Then came that Sunday, and the night after and nights
after that. She believed that making love to him would take
her beyond any place she had been. She had not known a
man could be so gentle, thoughtful and tender, yet so commanding. He was the wildest of men with exquisite control and he could arouse her with words and looks as well
as with touch. He could arouse her by just staring off into
space. It was a moon trip from the beginning and it never
came down.

*

Shelley MacLeod was among a tiny number of women
who had successfully escaped the predestined doom of
Belfast's working class with its limited choices of the
mills or, at best, marriage to a man with a steady job.
There were a few lady schoolteachers, clerks, nurses,
almoners and the like, but choices were severely limited.

She had been different since childhood, a strange withdrawn little girl portrayed by great, sad green eyes. Her
waking hours were spent in lonely pursuit of the illusion
that she was a fine lady who had flown the Shankill.

As she grew older, she taught herself painstakingly to
speak without trace of the confusing Belfast accent and
to carry herself erect and display proper manners. The
illusion was the fortress moat against the reality of borderline poverty which always hovered about and of the
ugliness imposed by a neurotic mother who darkened every life she touched. Hatred spewing like poison bile from
fanatic preachers worked its way into every fiber of her
mother and mildewed her home and pained her husband
and children. Shelley clung to her brother Robin as her
only close friend during her growing years, and pitied her
father, who was helpless in contending with a growing
madwoman. Being one of the Belfast poor had destroyed
her mother early in life.

When Robin ran off to sea, Shelley could no longer bear
it and fled to England, lied about her age of fifteen, and

wormed her way into employment as a maid in a manor house in Essex. The job granted little personal freedom, so the illusion was carried on once again by observing the finery of life about her, and she dreamed of it desperately in her closet-sized quarters. Shelley was driven further into herself when she discovered she was a commodity who would be afforded poor little dignity because of her low status. A pair of extremely unpleasant experiences, one with a head butler and another with one of the master's sons, could well have spoiled a lesser determination. Part of the retrenchment that followed was raw determination to break clear of the institutionalized class system.

When her mother died, Morgan came begging her to return to Belfast. The man was mired in guilt over the life he had given her, and Shelley came home. After a proper mourning period, Morgan began his courtship of Nell MacGuire, a fortyish spinster and a stalwart member of his church. Nell held an enviable position as governess to the three children of the Baron and Baroness of Ballyfall, Lord and Lady Temple-Wythe.

When she accepted Morgan's proposal of marriage, Nell urged Lady Temple-Wythe to give Shelley a try at her position and, although the girl was not yet twenty, her years of self-training caused her to succeed famously. She became rather close to her ladyship and when Lord Temple-Wythe passed away from a stroke, she was the widow's comrade and confidante. Shelley raised the children with a steady, loving hand.

Remarriage for Lady Temple-Wythe meant a move to England. Although Shelley and the Baroness and her children were close, the idea of aging as a governess was not in her making. She had seen her benefactor through a difficult period and taken her own step into self-sufficiency. It was time to move on. Despite the Baroness' implorations, she remained in Belfast.

Haute couture establishments in Belfast could be numbered on a single hand with two fingers to spare. Those who could afford it generally refrocked during the London season or on a trip to Paris. A few posh establishments existed for the gentry and the new rich of the gold coast. Over the years, Lady Temple-Wythe had dropped a few thousand in Blanche Hemmings' Salon. The favor was returned by giving Shelley a position.

Shelley MacLeod fitted in easily. She had charm but retained a trace of champagne snobbery and handled her
clientele delicately without being solicitous. No one would
have believed her from the Shankill. Independence was
her foremost trait.

As she befriended Blanche Hemmings, she was guided
through the discreet game of charming those gentlemen
most likely to open their pocketbooks. The most vulnerable and highest spenders proved to be those playing
the mistress game. There was an annual buying trip to London, her blessed independence and a small group of friends
in the fashion business and a social life outside the Shankill.

But Shelley rediscovered what she had already learned
as an upstairs maid in England. The gentry prowled for
females with no less vigor and much more cunning than
the Shankill lads. She had frightened off prospective
suitors in her own neighborhood and this had good and
bad results. She would not have to spend her Saturday
nights wrestling out of unwanted clutches or find herself
bored in that man's sporting world. Yet there were fine
lads about, many whose very earthiness was attractive.
She would not get serious with them because she could
not accept the Shankill life as the end. There was much
sheer joy in Shankill life which her father and brother
thrived on. For them the neighborhood was the joy of
life itself.

She was disallowed into the world of the gentry, except
as a commodity. Even in her intimacy with Lady Temple-
Wythe there had never been a trace of equality.

At Madam Blanche's she realized she was a lady in
limbo between opposite ends of the cultural and social
spectrum. For the gentlemen patrons of the Salon, Shelley
was a lady to be propositioned but never to be taken
seriously.

The game was always on with offers consisting of long
weekends at a hunting lodge or in the manor house while
the madam was off on a continental spree, or as the
occupant of that little nest in town or up along the
coast. At best, a cruise or holiday. Most girls of her background and station considered it an ultimate honor to be
selected as a mistress. Shelley demurred. At least the men
were honest in their lust in the Shankill. Moreover, the
gentry spilled over with bores.

A few times she chanced an affair out of sheer loneliness. They were always with attractive and rather decent chaps but she wouldn't play the mistress game. She retained total independence, accepted no prizes, made no demands, created no scenes. She made love because that was what she wanted to do and she counseled herself to get the best that each brief encounter had to offer.

It didn't work. There was always a sobering dawn, frustration, and a deeper plunge into herself, alone. She wanted to have Blanche Hemmings' frivolous cynicism at times but she couldn't play.

Her station was fixed as though by mathematical law and after a few brief burnings she became more and more of a recluse in the only place she had known warmth, the home of her father, and with her brother close at hand.

One day the Kimberleys came into the Salon. David was a different sort, an extremely gentle man with an overpowering need for compassion. She went into it because she was weary of the game and needed warmth herself. She breached the unwritten law of becoming serious with a married man and they established a sanctuary where they could find respite against the daily battering and the damning hells of loneliness.

Shelley knew his position was impossible from the outset. He was the scion of a banking family, fully married and deeply into his caste. The marriage had been loveless from the beginning, he and his wife remaining strangers under the same roof but keeping up a decade-long public façade.

David followed the family tradition of a tour of government service in Dublin Castle as an administrator in Ulster affairs, with half his time spent in Belfast. His wife almost always remained in Dublin or was in London.

Morgan MacLeod could never accept Shelley's conceptions of morality. Yet the clashes were faint stuff, for he realized his daughter was as much her own woman as he was his own man. He swallowed his own sense of righteousness and sorrowed that his daughter would have only half a life at best. Shelley needed her place within his walls, particularly on that day when the affair should find its inevitable end.

Morgan's own marriage to Nell MacGuire became a

cementing force of what was right about family. A saint-like woman, she made up for most of the unhappiness his children had suffered in growing. The houses, side by side on Tobergill Road, became the visible monument of his life's achievement.

All that was prayed for now was for Shelley to grow out of David Kimberley. For Shelley it was better to have those hours with David than surrender at some point along the middling path for security and accompanying dullness.

*

The flat in Stranmillis Gardens held almost five years of memories, a sharing of the best one could give the other under the circumstances. There had been warm evenings, tender nights, relief from the pain outside. It all seemed so somber and sterile now.

David Kimberley looked paler, more helpless, hand-somer than ever as he sat like a condemned man, arms limply in lap and head bowed. He uttered a long, half-mumbled soliloquy of remorse, an outpouring of guilt, an epic of confusion, self-condemnation and self-pity. He had treated her rottenly, he wept, spent her youth, kept her working as a shopgirl, been too gutless to face up to his family and wife.

Shelley listened as she always listened to David, with consummate patience, then sat at his feet and put her head on his lap and kissed his hands. When he had spoken himself out of words, she arose and took that determined stance of hers.

"It's not been like that at all. No one forced me and I haven't a single regret. I've wanted to be with you every time we've been together."

"You see, that's the trouble," he lamented, "you've been too decent. You've never made demands. Perhaps I could have coped with the family better if you had made demands."

"David, David. We both needed a safe harbor. We've had that. I want to sail beyond the harbor now."

A sense of desperation swelled in him as he cast about for something to cling to. "Do you love me?"

"Everything I've ever known or felt as a woman has been with you, here, in this room. But we've had our go and it's passed. What I needed is past for me. You've got to tell me it's right for me to go and that you want me to go . . ."

"Did you ever love me?"

"David, don't ask."

"But I am. How much did I really mean except as some sort of buffer?"

"All we've ever shared," she said, "is a room, a bed and a little time. We've never shared the sunlight or the wind or the feel of rain. When we were together it was always so temporary we never had time to be ourselves. Love can't mature in one room. It has to come out of the full sharing of everything: joys, aspirations, downfalls, all of it. That's the only real path to love."

He trembled to his feet, frightened by her cool and rational approach. "What happened?"

She smiled smally. "One night," she said, "I found myself laughing. I laughed and laughed until I had tears and pains in my side. Nothing like that had ever happened to me before. The next morning I awoke feeling quite strange. I went to the Salon and I talked to Blanche and I told her about all the peculiar sensations I was going through and I asked her what was wrong with me. She said, 'My God, Shelley, you're just happy, that's all.' "

The defeat of David Kimberley was on him now. Lord, it was true. He had never really made her happy. He had given her pleasure from time to time, but what they had really shared was flight from mutual disenchantment. Within their relationship they had found some carnal desperation but never happiness.

"Strange," Shelley said, "feeling happiness for the first time in your life and not even knowing what it is."

"This . . . this chap. Are you in love with him?"

"I want to be. We may or we may not. I just know I have to make a try. I can't let it go by."

"I'll wait. Have your go. I'll wait," he said.

"No, David. I've got to stop one thing before I start another. It would be indecent to all of us," she said firmly.

"Does he know about me?"

"Yes."

"I see. Has he made love to you?" his voice cracked out unevenly.

Shelley didn't answer.

"I said, has he made love to you?"

"There's no purpose in torturing yourself."

"I demand to know!"

"All right, we've slept together."

He slapped her face. Shelley accepted the blow with no other reaction than that of pity. David Kimberley sobbed and fell to his knees and held onto her.

"I didn't mean it. I'm sorry. Please forgive me."

"I know it must be awful for you," she said.

A hundred waves of desperation spent themselves. No outburst, no implorations, no promises would save it. The time had come. Perhaps it would even be a relief because the guilt would be finished. She had been so fair about it all, given him so much. He begged himself to act like a man, got to his feet, flopped his arms about, then turned to her.

"I hope your happiness continues and grows. God knows you deserve it," he rasped.

"And I hope you find some for yourself."

He shook his head. "I'm afraid I don't have your courage to make the break or make the plunge. Well, anyhow, among other beautiful things, you've always spared me scenes. I'm sorry I couldn't spare you one. I thank you for everything. I mean that. Come to me as a friend if you ever need me."

She brushed his cheek. "I'm sorry for this pain and I'll weep for you, man."

*

Conor studied the barber's work in the mirror, complimented and paid the man, then made up to the hotel lobby.

Shelley entered the hotel breathlessly, looked about with a sudden touch of desperation at not seeing Conor right off. They spotted each other over a vast lobby and came together ... happy.

CHAPTER THIRTEEN: Conor and Shelley counted the steps in unison as they climbed upward through the glen to a shimmering hazel grove a thousand feet over the lough. They walked along the flank of Cave Hill, slowing to catch their breath from the climb, and found a place of privacy removed from the promenading Belfasters and their running, shouting kids. It was a shaded vista back down on the city and, although it was Sunday, the week's smoke and haze clung on.

He was pensive. His right eye was a broken rainbow of awful colors, slitted near closed from yesterday's game. He had played extremely hard to prove they'd made no mistake on him and, largely because of it, the Boilermakers turned in their first victory of the season.

Shelley ran her finger over the battered eye, trying to heal it with a magic touch. The Saturday game had always been a MacLeod family affair. Shelley attended from time to time out of duty to her brother but otherwise thought it a rough, dirty sport. It never really affected her until she saw Conor crumble to the ground and lie terribly still.

She fled from her seat, hid beneath the stands, and wept as a flush of fright came on without warning or ability to control. Until that moment the Midlands tour had meant little except her sympathy for Matthew and Lucy. Now it struck down that Conor would be gone for twelve terrible weeks.

Shelley lay back lovely on the grass, her red hair all floating in and out of deep green blades and the sun making her skin whiten to near translucence. Conor propped on an elbow and kissed her cheek and forehead and the tip of her nose and her eyes. "Did I ever tell you how glad I am to have made your acquaintance, lady?"

"Oh no, never," she answered.

"Well, let me tell you then. I've walked through crowds of crowds all my life. I've seen the faces of the women in the church and heard the listless priest intone. I've seen the men come down from the fields and be felled to their knees at the angelus. I've seen the hard cities. And all the time I looked past sterile eyes into sterile hearts. Then one time I looked and it was different than all the other times and I told myself I'd have to be the worst kind of fool to recognize something had happened and not do something about it."

Tears moistened in her eye. "Of all the luck," she whispered, "finding myself a bard. You people have a way with words."

"Aye, we're a canny and clever lot, for words is all we've had. But they're only your own thoughts coming back to you. You make me say things I no longer care to hide and I have no fear of hearing my own voice saying them."

Shelley rolled away from him, sat and shook the grass from her hair and dress, then lay her cheek on her knees and hummed softly.

" 'Dusty Bluebells,' " Conor said.

"Aye. I sang it to myself when I was a little girl skipping rope or just to myself alone. I dreamed a lot," she said.

"What does your family think about us? Do they think you've gone from the pan into the fire?"

"I don't believe so. They see how happy I am. I think as long as they know that, then all the rest will take care of itself. At the bottom of things, behind their holy façade, there's a great deal of love in them. Besides, Conor, it wouldn't matter what they thought."

"You say that but it's not true. The MacLeods have a fierceness for one another you don't even realize yourself. You're into each other's lives very deeply."

A burst of warmth flowed over her as the sun came from behind a cloud. She lay back on the grass again and stretched and moaned out her contentment.

"Talk smutty to me, Conor. I go wild when you say filthy things into my ear."

He laughed and scratched his head and gazed down on her. "Well, let me tell you right off that you're a reasonable fuck for a Protestant."

"On with you. I hear the Catholic girls have ground-up glass between their legs."

"Don't go kidding yourself about that, lass. There's a lot of wild Catholic mares in heat out in the pasture who haven't heard a word the priest said. Besides, I didn't have that particular comparison in mind. I was thinking more of some of the girls I ran across during my sailing days."

"Like whom," she snapped.

"Well, for instance, the ones in Bali. Ah, yes, the ones in Bali."

"And what's so bloody great about them?"

"Well, first there's the hospitality. And the attitude. And the dress, or lack of it. And the brown skin. It's a quality of satin one doesn't find beyond those islands. They've been raised in the service of man and that is how it should be. From girlhood on they've developed a sensuousness, a delicacy, a mood, a way of fondling that entirely escapes the Western female. Oh, I tell you it bends my mind just thinking about it. Fantastic! Utterly fantastic. And no shyness, you know. When two or more are involved, especially sisters . . ."

She leaped on him and he fell to his back and she tickled him in his vulnerable spots.

"Come on now," he begged, "you're much too strong for me."

Shelley sighed and shook her hair. "You know what's so great?"

"I can't imagine."

"When we start. Those times you close in and roll me over on my tummy and play those subtle games all over my body. Your touch is so delicate, it's maddening, and you make the transitions from softness to firmness and back to softness and you find every single little spot to perfection."

"All I'm doing is following the messages you send. It's you who's telling me what to do."

"Really?" she said earnestly.

"That's a fact."

"Isn't that a miracle. Oh, look at me, man. I'm turning into a wild woman. I walk down the street and I say to myself, I'm a wild woman, and when lads look me over I think, You'd lose your mind, boy, if you knew how wild I am. You know, and I may blush saying it, I spend the day long thinking about what I'm going to do with you that night. I adore doing them!"

"You're absolutely disgusting."

"I know, isn't it wonderful? Do you think it will ever stop getting better every time?"

"Not for a few days, anyhow."

"Man, it was dull before I met you. Here I thought

I was the greatest lover in the world. How did I survive? Conor, do you know what's a pity?"

"I haven't the slightest notion at this point."

"You'll never know what it's like to be loved by you. That's a terrible shame. You'll never know what it's like to have all that power pouring into you."

They held their cheeks together. "I was lying," he whispered, "you're better than any girl in Bali."

"Oh, man, wherever did you learn to make love?"

He dwelt in her eyes. "There's making love and there's making love to Shelley. It's two entirely different things. I learned it from you."

They sat and held hands and just that suddenly Conor seemed to drift. It came back to him. It always came back. It was always there, when making love, playing rugby, at the forge. It was always hovering. Sooner or later he would have to tell her the meaning behind those years at sea. Sooner or later his search for the Brotherhood would have to come out. For now, he wanted desperately to have more of her and to shove the rest into a corner. There was too much rapture to stop the carrousel but it always came back to Long Dan Sweeney and tender cars and guns.

"Hey there," she said.

"What?"

"You left me."

"Just thinking of the tour and going off."

Shelley stood suddenly and walked to the brink of the hill to where it dropped abruptly down to the shrouded city, then spun around as she sensed him coming up behind her. Her look and her voice stiffened to someone who was not quite Shelley.

"Do you know what happened here on Cave Hill?" she said.

"They say they're the lairs of the ancient Celtic king, MacArt . . ."

"No, not that. What happened might have happened on this very spot. Theobald Wolfe Tone stood here before his journey to America in 1795 with his United Irishmen around him and he vowed to return to liberate Ireland."

Conor was unnerved. "What made you say that!"

"You don't have exclusive rights to Irish history."

"What made you say it, Shelley?"

"I'm not a fool any more than you are. Don't you think I know where your mind wanders? Don't you think I've some notions about the work you're in? I just don't want it to come between us any more than I would let my family come between us."

"It won't," he said. He took her and held her. "It won't." They began down the path. "We've reached that place, you and I," he said.

"We were there the first night we met. It's taken this time to decide to go after it. You gave me poetry and music and Conor. I'm ready, man, and I mean to give it all."

He stopped and his great hand purred over her hair and the fierceness of her look ran clear through him. Until that moment he had never returned such a look.

"We've a week's holiday at the end of the tour," he said. "Let's find a place in England or Scotland. A wild, lonely, brooding place with the light of a fire at night."

"I'll be there," she answered.

He put his hands beneath her arms and lifted her off her feet so they were eye to eye, with him holding her in mid-air. He wrapped her inside his arms and kissed her.

"I love you, lass," he said, "I love you."

CHAPTER FOURTEEN: The location had changed as Sweeney had predicted. It had changed but in fact it was very much the same as the room on Shandon Lane and the one in Dublin. Deep in the Catholic Ballymurphy District, he would be harder to find.

"We still haven't got a hell of a lot to go on with O'Hurley and Hanly," Long Dan said, gangling about. "There was always a lot of Fenian activity in their home town and between Tipperary and Limerick, but we can find nothing to connect them directly with republican sentiments. They were simply remembered as a wild railroading team until Sir Frederick Weed took them north. Have you picked up any information?"

"Nothing really," Conor said.

"Speaking in generalities, Catholics like them who are well situated usually steer clear of republican involvements. Most of them are downright loyal to the Crown."

Conor nodded that it was his understanding also. As Sweeney had said, men with full bellies don't run into the streets and rebel, and the fuller the belly, the less the inclination.

Sweeney indulged in a cigarette. He rarely failed to apologize for this weakness but rationalized that one could hardly be a revolutionary without them.

"We've a theory to tinker with," Sweeney continued. "O'Hurley farts higher than his ass. He's a big spender and is always running late at his bank, a notable Irish trait. A man like him might be bought."

"Isn't that dicy?" Conor asked.

"Yes and no." Sweeney shrugged. "Everything's dicy in this business. The main thing is, we all like your plan. Sometimes it's better to have a man in your debt. Once you've got something over his head he can find a sudden sense of patriotism he never knew he had."

"Who puts the bell around the cat's neck?" Conor said.

"You stay out of it. Somewhere along the tour someone is going to approach O'Hurley. When do you play in Bradford?"

Conor closed his eyes to draw up a mental image of the nineteen-game schedule. "Bradford? Right near the end. One of the last two or three games."

"Good. By the time you reach Bradford you'll know if O'Hurley is in or not."

"Why Bradford?" Conor asked.

"Does the name Brendan Barrett mean anything to you?"

"Brendan Sean Barrett?"

Long Dan nodded.

Brendan Sean Barrett was another of those minor Fenian heroes and poets known to any young lad who had been brought up in a republican house. Barrett, like Long Dan, had firsthand knowledge of British prisons. He had been a schoolteacher and went on to be the writer, idealist and lecturer of the slumbering movement, remaining in America for years in the equally dormant Clan of the Gaels. His greatest claim to fame was that he became the first republican to try a hunger strike in prison. "Silent defiance," they termed it, a new kind of weapon of self-imposed martyrdom. Barrett won his demands after twenty-four days of starving himself. Songs had been written about it.

"Brendan is our man in England," Sweeney said. "He's the conduit for our funds from the Clan in America and he's the keeper of the arms cache."

Conor feigned a nod of quiet understanding in the best Sweeney tradition, trying to hide the jumping of his heart.

"You'll make contact with him in Bradford and he'll advise you if O'Hurley is with us or not. If it's go, Brendan will give you further instructions on where and how to convert the tender car. You'll go to Callaghan's Funeral Parlor, Wild Boar Road, Wapping District, Bradford. Callaghan will set up a meeting. Brendan's got a heavy price on his head, so make the contact with extreme care. Use your judgment. If you feel you've been followed, wait until the tour is over, then return to Bradford."

"Aye, I've got it all."

"One more thing. Brendan will be handing you a packet of money, a lot of it. Three thousand quid. Don't lose it."

"I'll try not to. Anything else?"

"Yes. You've a week's holiday at the conclusion of the tour. I want you to use it to make some further contacts in London and Manchester."

Conor froze and paled, unable to cover his reaction this time. "Dan, listen. Between scouting the yard, working the districts by night, the rugby and my regular job, I've been going like twenty hours a day. After nineteen games in twelve weeks on tour I'll be done in. I've made plans for a holiday."

"Change them," Sweeney retorted.

Conor sucked in a breath and clenched his teeth a moment. "I don't think I will," he said.

The two men locked stares over the rickety table. "A woman?"

"Maybe."

"Call it off," Sweeney commanded softly.

"No."

Long Dan's chair squealed back. He got up, shoved his hands into his pockets and turned his back to Conor for a long, long time. He showed his face again only after his own mind was clear. "The plan is off. You're out of the Brotherhood. Get out."

"I don't want out!" Conor cried, alarmed at the sudden sharp burst of his own words.

"I said you're out and you're lucky to get out now. It's early enough in the game and I don't take you for an informer so you'll shut up about what you've learned. If it were any later, you know what would happen to you, don't you?"

"I've an idea," Conor said harshly.

Sweeney returned to his seat and breathed out foul breath and tapped his monstrous fist on the table as he nodded toward the door.

"Can't you change your mind, Dan? I'll see the girl and call it off."

"All right, this time. Your soul may belong to the Virgin but your ass belongs to the Brotherhood. Yea or nae?"

"Yea," Conor said, shaken.

"Who's the girl?" he demanded.

Conor sagged at the first real beating of his life. "The sister of a teammate."

"Catholic?"

"No."

"You'd better give her up."

"Now look, Dan. I said I'd give up the holiday, but there's no rule against having a woman."

"I'm the rule book as far as your life is concerned, Larkin. I've seen a lot of smart lads who think they can handle both things but they were all fucking fools, all of them, every last one. If you really care for this girl you'd better consider what you're going to do with her life. Hell, you'll give her hell. Hell with every tick of the clock. Is he coming back from this one or are his brains scattered over half the street?"

Conor reeled over the room and came to a stop leaning hard against the wall. "I'm thirty-one," he said harshly. "I've waited so long, Dan. I'm in love, man. Just because you've never felt it yourself, you can't condemn me for it and you can't purge me of it. You've no bloody feelings!"

Sweeney's surge was abruptly halted as he turned ashen.

"You're right enough about that—I was sixteen when they put me away."

"I'm sorry," Conor said, "I shouldn't have said that . . . I'm sorry. . . ."

"No man is sorry for me!" the old man cried. "If you want to know, Larkin, I felt it once but it was so long ago I can't remember what she looked like and her name has become a totally meaningless word . . . Aileen . . . Aileen . . . O'Dunne." Long Dan's shoulders slumped. "Don't you think I don't know you, boy!" he groaned. "Don't you know that Dan Sweeney was named after Daniel O'Connell and don't you think he didn't write poetry in his father's booley house? Don't you think I didn't weep at Parnell's grave and run off to sea? Don't you think I didn't crawl back to Ireland hating myself for returning!"

Conor held his face in his hands. When he looked up, he looked into the old man's face and he shuddered as he saw himself horribly aged in a mirror of time.

"Take your girl and go on holiday," Dan said.

"You'd better not let me, Dan. I'm liable not to come back."

Sweeney grunted in old wisdom. "You'll come back," he said. "Dumb bastards like us always come back. So go have your fucking fling. When your own time comes perhaps the memory of her might lighten up your prison cell brighter than was the case in mine."

Conor held out his hand an instant, then withdrew it and sagged off for the door.

"In the future," Sweeney said, returning to Sweeney, "you'll not disobey an order. It's a fucked-up little army but make no mistake about our discipline. I'll not hesitate to put a bullet through your kneecap any more than you will when you've got to do the same. I'll pray for the success of your mission . . . and for yourself as well. Now, get the hell out."

CHAPTER FIFTEEN: The entourage consisting of the Earl and Countess of Foyle, Viscount Coleraine, Sir Frederick Weed, staff and various servants and aides disgorged from a line of carriages at Weed Ship & Iron Pier Number Three where the overnight train steamer to Liverpool lay in waiting.

On the dock, Derek Crawford, Doxie O'Brien and the Boilermakers stood at a semblance of attention before several hundred workers gathered on the lunch break along with a combined band from four Orange Lodges. Opposite the team and its proprietors stood a row of municipal and other dignitaries all bloated up to impart their farewells.

Sir Frederick promised smashing victories. Captain Robin MacLeod vowed redemption of Ulster's honor. The dignitaries spewed accolades. The band whipped it up and partisans shouted hurrahs as the team boarded.

On the steamer deck there was a rush of excitement and backslapping, for there was a glimmer of hope for salvaging the disastrous season. Conor Larkin's sudden large presence plus acquisition of two "gentlemen players" pumped in new hope. The gentlemen players were high-standing amateurs who had done meritorious college and national team service. Sir Frederick lured them to the professional game in exchange for a few bright pennies and for the "good of Ulster."

Robin and Conor lingered at the rail observing the spectacle at dockside which peaked with the arrival of the Red Hand Express decked out for royalty. The throngs cheered. Duffy O'Hurley and Calhoun Hanly fielded the honors with Shakespearean aplomb and O'Hurley rolled her aboard. Conor's eye never left the coal tender.

Who would reach Duffy? Where and when would it happen? How would they react? He'd know when he got to Bradford. . . . Calm down, it's three months off. Calm down. . . .

"Shelley told Lucy and me about it last night."

"Uh, what?" Conor said.

"Shelley told us about it. You know, her coming over after the tour. I want you to know we're happy for you. Hey, Conor, you might have thought your pet dog died the way you're acting."

"Sorry. I'm glad you both approve. It's just that it's a long time off yet."

"Mind you, it'll go quick."

After the Red Hand was aboard, a shuttle engine rolled

on Sir Frederick's private cars. There were four in all, one
for the masters, one for the team, one for the staff and
one for the guests. Lady Caroline's personal assistant, a bliz-
zard-faced Germanic woman, directed the line of trunks
to the various cabins. Jeremy Hubble wedged in between
Robin and Conor, the band played "Auld Lang Syne" and
the boat divorced itself from its land ties.

"Mr. Larkin?"

Conor turned and was handed an envelope by one of
the servants containing a handwritten note.

Dear Mr. Larkin,
I should like the pleasure of your company after
dinner. If the weather is decent I shall meet you on
deck. Otherwise, please come to our cabin.
                                    Caroline Hubble

Roger Hubble looked on the annual trek of the Boilermakers with something other than delight, but a necessary
appeasement of Freddie and his wife. His own schedule
was overloaded, demands on his time ponderous. Roger
had risen in Ulster life to be one of its most prominent
figures, the single most powerful Unionist in the west. He
attended to his seat in the House of Lords faithfully as
well as having a total involvement in the Hubble-Weed
combine. For three years he had served Dublin Castle
as a special adviser on Ulster development, an additional
burden, but one that gave him a great deal of say over
the province's future.

Except for Caroline's demands for play time he would
have grown into a consummate public and corporate
figure. This year she insisted to a point of intimidation
that he slow down, at least long enough to enjoy the
London season.

Roger was scratching away at omnipresent paperwork
on a small ship's desk when she came from the adjoining
cabin in a lounging robe and stroked away at his hair.
She adored it now, it had grayed handsomely. She leaned
over from behind, making certain his neck came into contact with her bosom and his nostrils got the full scent of
her perfume. As the message became quite clear, Roger
doffed his glasses, just a tad annoyed at being seduced
at this particular moment. When Caroline required atten-

tion, she got it. He set the pen down and responded to the overture.

Caroline filled a sherry glass and, with him fully in tow, rubbed the back of his neck until he succumbed with a resonant growl. "You are to enjoy London and even try to enjoy a few of the rugby games."

"Not going to be all that easy. For the next three months I'm not going to get a lick of work out of Freddie. Do you know what that man has gone and done? He's hired a personal photographer and someone full time to do nothing but put out releases to the press. He's like a child on the tour."

"Bother, bother," she said, "you'll not change him now."

"Besides," Roger continued, "I rather believe you like this rugby insanity as much as he does."

"The story goes that Freddie went up to the Mourne Mountains and wept for a month when he found out his first-born was a female. I made it a point to love it."

Roger slipped out of his smoking jacket and liberated various attachments to his shirt, then dunked his face into the water bowl, emitting large "ahs," and neatened himself in the mirror. "I see how you light up every year."

"I'm off on that ugly little right wing three quarter," she said. "He's got halitosis, pimples, yellow teeth and yards of hair. But, let's face it, his tight little ass is absolutely beautiful under those silk shorts. I've had my eye out for him for weeks."

"You are dreary, Caroline."

She sat cross-legged on the bed. "What is really sexy, really, really sexy, is seeing them at the end of the game all sweaty and bloody and matted and stinking to heaven."

"Good God, woman, you grow more ill with age."

"I hear the whispers, Roger. They still think I'm good-looking, they does." Roger responded to that by going up her leg and helping himself to a half bite, half kiss on the backside. Caroline had succeeded, for the twinkle was on between them. As he returned to dressing, buttoning into a stiff shirt, she nibbled at her lip, sparring around to find an opening.

"Darling," she ventured.

Roger had already picked up the signal and sat beside her curiously.

"It's about Jeremy," she said.

"What about our monster child?"

"Freddie and the boy will be absolutely crushed if he doesn't stay for the tour. Jeremy's been dreaming of it for two years."

Roger's gameful mood changed noticeably.

"Roger, don't be a prig," she implored. Then she sagged, seeing his total immobility. He simply glared, that dirty Roger Hubble glare. "Well, say something, dammit."

"I'm full up to here," he said, holding his hand up to eye level, "at this conspiracy. Thank God we've one son who has decided to forgo this aspect of his enlightenment."

Caroline recoiled. "And I am just as delighted, no, utterly overjoyed, that Jeremy Hubble is going to become a big, hairy, smelly player instead of a senior clerk."

Roger grunted disdain and returned to dressing before the mirror. "It's been difficult enough to accept the fact, thanks to his mother, that he is going to that monstrosity of a college in Dublin instead of a proper school. It borders on tragedy that you and he have conspired to ignore his studies so that even getting into Trinity has become a monumental achievement. If and when he does begin his studies I have no objection if he plays rugby for that provincial outhouse down there, but I'll be damned if he's going to spend half his adult life letting blood for the East Belfast Boilermakers."

Caroline silenced under the assault. Her deflation reached him. He patted her and turned completely serious. "We've a problem with Jeremy. I'm not going to compare him with Christopher. No, I won't do that. Nor will I appeal to you on the grounds that I am looking forward to the boys coming into the business. It's Jeremy's mind, his lackadaisical attitude, his world-is-an-oyster playground mentality. He's got tremendous responsibilities up the road and he's got to get on with them."

"He's sweet, he's charming and he's got the devil in him," she said. "And I know one man who never stopped resenting the fact his father rushed him into all those responsibilities before he was ready."

Roger dropped his hairbrush at that. "Not the same thing, at all. I'm not Arthur and Jeremy is not Roger. My father did it to pursue his pleasures. I don't think you can say that about me."

"I didn't mean to bring up anything unpleasant but the boy is nineteen and has all his life to serve God, country, Ulster and the enterprises. Let him cut loose. If we restrain him at this moment, we're liable to pay for it later on with a confused, perhaps hostile son. A few bloody years aren't going to make that much difference."

Roger threw up his hands. "Yes, madam, I quite agree. Please take my order for ten—no, make that an even dozen Red Hand Express engines. I've never run into a salesman of your caliber."

"Roger, tell him he can take the tour."

"No, you tell him. It's your present, yours and Freddie's. He'll be Freddie's responsibility, totally."

The victory bell tolled hollow. Caroline uncrossed her legs and scooted off the bed. "Do you remember a chap named Conor Larkin?"

"Yes, quite well."

"He's with the club now."

"I know."

"Jeremy adores him. Larkin is a good, sensitive man. Twelve weeks under his wing might be the best thing in the world for the boy. There's a whole universe of things he can open up for Jeremy."

"Are you saying that this Larkin person is better suited to take care of our own son than his own grandfather?"

"I'm saying that when there's a problem like this an outside force can be the best possible influence. At this moment in Jeremy's life, he'll respond to a big brother."

So that was it, the full extent of the conspiracy, Roger thought. He walked off to the adjoining parlor cabin; Caroline left him alone to collect his thoughts.

When Roger first saw the drawings of the gift doors to the Belfast City Hall on Freddie's desk, he had been alarmed over the return of Larkin. That man and Kevin O'Garvey had been thick as flies. O'Garvey reneged on their deal in order to have Larkin's forge restored.

Roger had been uneasy since the shirt factory fire. Anything that remotely hinted of it aroused his suspicions. For over a year certain journalists had continued to snoop in an attempt to discredit the commission's report. Follow-up stories about conditions in the building had been embarrassing. Fortunately, Frank Carney never broke in his story that he had heard the arsonist's confession. Carney had held them up for plenty.

Roger related his fears to Freddie about Larkin's return and only then discovered that Jeremy and Caroline had interceded in his behalf. For two months Larkin was kept under surveillance by Swan's people. Nothing suspicious showed up. Books, concerts, pub crawling and then a woman, the team captain's sister. Larkin was cleared.

Well, all right, what now? Roger knew that if he reacted violently to Caroline's request it could backfire. Caroline's initial reaction would be that her husband was jealous, a thing that had never crept into their marriage. Otherwise, an assault on Larkin could just possibly stir up Larkin's own thoughts about the fire and O'Garvey. It would be far better to concede and outwardly show that there was no resentment of Larkin whatsoever.

What of the rest of it?

How many times in his own life had he longed for communication with that weak scoundrel of a father of his? Wasn't that really why he had plunged himself into a singlehanded conquest of western Ulster? And Caroline . . . Caroline who opened the door to all those lovely rooms in life that he would never have known otherwise. Caroline who was his best friend, his big brother, his mistress, as well as his wife. Caroline had fought a hard battle against the English system which pawned off responsibility by the cold and impersonal exile of the sons to boarding schools, the Army, the government service. His own father had done that to him. Christopher wanted some of it on his own. That was all right. But Jeremy was rebelling.

Roger stopped in the doorway. "You want this very much, don't you?" he said.

"I swear I believe it's the right thing."

"Has Larkin agreed to take Jeremy on?"

"No."

"It might be best if you spoke to him, rather than I," Roger said.

"Yes, it might be," she agreed.

*

The crossing, exceptionally calm this night, afforded an occasion for artificial comradery. Those rawboned lads of the club were on their gentlemen's best at the communal feasting table. Those gentlemen players recently acquired and the peers made every attempt to be ordinary folk. In that upheaval of the established social order almost everyone was ill at ease.

There were notable exceptions, all being keenly observed by Roger Hubble this night. His father-in-law was entirely at home. He had supped at skull crackers' tables before. His wife, who had done garret duty with wine-drinking artists, never lost her common touch. His son Jeremy reveled in the friendship of those rough, sinewy men . . . and Conor Larkin, who had a classlessness about himself. He'd be at home anywhere, Roger thought. The family power play had won.

As for Lord Roger, he was as uncomfortable as if he had been caught in original sin, as were the men, who were equally awkward in his company.

The uneasiness of imposed solidarity modified as the bar was thrown open. Roger retreated quickly to his quarters. In a moment Sir Frederick and his gentlemen players were in a deep strategy session with Derek Crawford and Robin MacLeod. Jeremy wove in and out of the drinkers rubbing elbows. The off-the-field leader of the club, Duffy O'Hurley, organized a songfest while his fireman, Calhoun Hanly, planked out in a corner table. Doxie O'Brien played as much piano as his broken knuckles would allow and songs, neither Orange nor republican, neutrally followed in a show of non-sectarian brotherhood.

The crossing was particularly calm. Caroline settled in a deck chair, covered her lap with a robe and listened to the voices in harmony of sorts as it reached that mellow shank of the night.

Conor came on deck, looked about, saw her and took the edge of the chair next to her. "How's the screen in the Long Hall holding?"

"It should be good for a few hundred years, barring insurrection," she said. "You've been away for a long time. What and where?"

"Just having a poet's go at the world. Nothing much of value was learned except that Ireland's not such a bad old place after all."

"Lucky for Ireland," she said. "Is there a lady as lucky?"

Conor smiled. "I can't say how lucky she is."

"I'm glad for you."

"It took me long enough. You're looking fit enough to play fullback," he said, shifting the subject. "You said you wanted to see me. It's about Jeremy, isn't it?"

Caroline nodded.

"I figured as much."

The moon brought them to the rail. "What with me getting all that special attention when I tried for the club and then having my own forge in the yard and a commission . . ."

"Just a deserved gesture to an old friend," she said. "And nothing, I might add, you wouldn't have made without my help."

"Jeremy's at practice every day," Conor said. "The two of us have always had a good, open rapport. I think I've got the gist of what's going on."

"He has a lot of wild oats to sow, like myself and my father. At nineteen we shouldn't be in all that much of a hurry to get him regimented."

"Aye, and you're a good mum to know that. If you're lucky enough to fall in love, that's one thing. Otherwise, all that was ever truly beautiful to me was my boyhood. It's the meal we sup on for the rest of our lives. Love puts the icing on life. But if you don't find it . . . you must call on your childhood memories over and over till you do. In Jeremy's case, these next years are very necessary as a place to build."

"The boy adores you, you know that."

"Oh, little wanes always make heroes out of big lugs until they find them lying in the gutter drunk one morning."

"Will you take him under your wing?"

"Can I be blunt with you?"

"Of course."

"It's not that we go whoring and drinking till six every morning but the lad will cramp the team's style. I don't care about that too much, I'm pretty much alone and I could keep his nose clean on that score, but we don't exactly come from the same neighborhood. I'd be a fair crack of a freak toting a Viscount around through the Irishtowns of some pretty ugly cities."

"Don't you think that would be good for him if he's going to become the Earl of Foyle?"

"You're a wise lady indeed. There's a possibility of Jeremy collecting a few republican fleas."

"I'd risk that if the boy would pick up a few other things from Conor Larkin."

He laughed. "Who's pulling the Irish blarney on whom?"

"You'll take him on then?"

"You ought to have your bottom paddled just once in your life," he said. "You always get everything you want."

"Not always, Mr. Larkin," she said, meeting his eyes right on.

Conor was confused. He held himself to keep his mouth shut and gripped the railing to stop himself from making a move at her. Caroline held her place, making no effort to either retract her words or remove herself.

"You walked the deck of a ship for years, I understand. Did you ever think about me?" she asked.

"When you're out there alone, night after night, you think about everything, sooner or later."

"That's not what I asked."

"Aye, I thought about you."

"And what did you think?"

Conor smiled softly. "It would do no good to tell you. No one could live up to those thoughts."

"Well, just because you walked the deck of a ship doesn't give you the exclusive rights to daydreaming. I've had a few thoughts of my own about you."

"Oh . . ."

"But it would do no good to tell you about them, either. Not even Conor Larkin could live up to my fantasies."

"Well," he stammered, "I think it's time for a nightcap, myself."

"Just a minute, Conor," she said firmly. "Allow me to say you are one of the loveliest men I've ever met in my life. Nothing is ever going to come of it. Yet I feel no wrong in sharing Jeremy's feelings toward you. Good night, Conor."

"Lady Caroline."

"Yes?" she said, turning.

"I'll take good care of the lad."

"I know." And she was gone.

He watched the sea for a time and, as he did, the growing sense of distaste in himself mounted. He had played on his friendship with her and with Jeremy to perfection. He had lured the boy to help intrigue him into the tour and a close companionship. Before that he had used them both to get into the yard, onto the team and in a position to have freedom of movement. Now he had an ultimate cover, a British aristocrat as his ward. It was bound to keep any possible suspicion from his activities. Affection for one's enemies was not part of Dan Sweeney's lexicon. Sweeney would loathe to see him have feelings for those people.

Conor found himself drawn down the ladder to where the Red Hand Express was choked down, rising and falling on the movement of the steamer. He stood at the side of the tender car, then touched it.

"Hey there!"

Conor turned, startled. Duffy O'Hurley, who always limped a bit when swacked, swaggered up to him. "What's doing, Conor!"

"Just walking round and round to clear my head from the excitement."

"Yeah, that's right. Your very first tour. Ahhh," he groaned, "just look at this darling. The best Red Hand of them all. Excuse the overburdening sentimentality of it, Conor, but I always come down to say good night to my engine."

O'Hurley was a back thumper with power to spare. Twice Conor had seen Calhoun Hanly's false teeth fly out of his mouth after a backslap. He took the affection from O'Hurley with only a slight wince. What would the answer be when the question was asked? Conor wondered. How many days till Bradford and Brendan Sean Barrett?

CHAPTER SIXTEEN: Of the Larkin brothers, only Dary had come up from Maynooth Seminary. Conor was in England and, of course, Liam too far away.

Brigid stood before the Larkin cottage for what seemed an eternity. The long wait was done. The cairn was over her mother's grave, the last prayer intoned. This cottage was hers now as the land was hers. Ever so slowly to the door. She shoved it open tentatively as though she were entering for the first time. It was exactly the same but all so very different. Her eyes played over the room. The seat nearest the fire would be her own and all the great cook pots would be scrubbed to a shine they had never had before. The creepies and benches and crane and churn and weaver's light holders . . . everything she saw was her own. Tomorrow she'd walk through the fields counting up all that was hers.

She made from room to room, fondling all her possessions, patting the down quilts just so, brushing off specks of gathering dust, mentalizing how she would clean so there would not be another cottage like it.

She came to the bedroom door. She stood at the foot of the bed of the birth of herself and her brothers. The bed of Tomas and Finola. She edged onto the side of it as she had done while attending them sick, then stretched and buried herself in this softness and she closed her eyes as tears filled them.

Back in the best room she smoored the fire as only the woman of the house would do and laid on new turf, then cooked her first meal, setting the table for herself and Rinty Doyle. First, she took Finola's seat for her own, then changed her mind and placed her setting where Tomas had been the head of the house.

"Rinty!" she called to the byre. She poked her head in. "Rinty, where are you?" He was nowhere to be seen. She threw her shawl over her shoulders in a fit of pique and marched steadfastly down the path to the crossroad and burst into McCluskey's public house.

The gentlemen at the bar took off their caps in unison in respect and remembrance of her sainted mother. Old McCluskey squinted, for he was half blind with age and couldn't hear much better. Wee shriveled Rinty was curled up alone deep in the deepest corner enjoying the life out of a glass of Derryale.

"There you are!" Brigid snipped. "And just who gave you leave to get yourself jarred!"

"Jarred? Woman, I'm sober as Father Cluny. I'm having

a farewell drop in memory of your blessed mother, Mary save her soul."

"God rest her," Billy O'Kane said from the bar.

"God bless all here," Rinty encored, lifting his glass.

"You'll march home this instant or there'll be no tea for you tonight."

Rinty looked at the gentlemen at the bar mortified. They cowered en masse. He smacked his lips, hungering for that last swallow, but capitulated, shuffling to the door and out to the road after her.

"She's got two tusks hanging down over her lip, that one," McCluskey said.

"I wouldn't like even the half of it."

"Jaysus, you'd think they was married."

Back at the cottage Brigid slammed the door and arched her back angrily, wilting the man with the mere look of her. "I'm not against a man having his pint now and again but I'll not be slaving over that fire and you not here for your meals. From now on, if it's McCluskey's or the shebeen you're after, you'll be asking me first. Is that clear?"

"Aye," he whimpered.

"Let's get on with the rosary."

Rinty scratched his head, trying to puff himself up with enough courage to protest. "Can I have a civil word with you?"

"Speak!"

"What I mean to say is there's only the two of us here, each being individual people. If, for example, the party of the first part, myself, finds solace in an evening pint, then why couldn't the party of the first part have that pint while the party of the second part says the rosary? In that manner, both parties will have fulfilled their urgent needs."

"God have mercy on you, Rinty Doyle."

"I'm a man and I have me rights."

"You've been allowed to stray from God because my poor mother was too sick in the past year to contend with a heathen inside her own walls."

"I've me rights, you know, I've me rights."

"So long as you're under this roof you will say the rosary and you will go to mass. I was going to permit you to move to the hayloft but you'll stay in the byre until you give our Lord Jesus Christ his due. Now, on your knees, Rinty Doyle."

Rinty looked heavenward but relief was not on the way. He flopped his arms and grunted down to the floor, kneeling alongside Brigid.

*

The two of them went on living as though Brigid were running a large estate over which she was a baroness. The prayer never started or ended, merely continued. No cottage in the Upper Village was cleaned so ruthlessly, so manicured and so orderly. Every speck was an intruder to be banished, every plate polished to gleam, every doily precisely in place. Dirty boots, tobacco ashes and other manly droppings and their droppers met swift retribution.

The pity of it was that Brigid did not keep herself as well as her home or fields. She grew heavy and what loveliness of youth she had owned vanished as she stood on the threshold of her thirtieth year. Good looks were never so important as land in Ballyutogue, and the Larkin farm was still the best. The bachelors in their early forties and upward sniffed about but they were a sorry lot, indeed, and she all but ran them off with a pitchfork. The drinking brotherhood soon gave her a wide berth.

In the months that followed, Brigid Larkin impressed one and all with her shrewd management of affairs. After nearly working poor Rinty to his own grave she brought in another distant cousin as the second hired hand. She organized a cottage industry, the linen work, marketing for a better price than the individual piecework, and made it otherwise evident she had a touch of Larkin power and intelligence.

Liam and Conor sent the money for Finola's tombstone. The younger son who had prospered greatly in New Zealand also sent money for slates for the roof of the cottage. Liam was also the first of Ballyutogue's sons to commission a stained glass memorial window in the church.

*

After imposing final prayers of the day, Brigid checked out her barony and any unleft business before retiring and each night she opened the drawer of the highboy and took out that faded letter that had come so long ago from Conor. It was the letter that said that Myles McCracken would never return to Ballyutogue. There were only a few words she was able to make out herself but she knew it by memory and it was worn from folding and unfolding.

Due to various circumstances Myles is taking a wife in Derry.

"What are various circumstances?" she had asked Father Cluny when he first read it to her.

The priest said he didn't know but it was useless because he was a married man and she should not see him again.

Her heart cried out for Myles when she learned of the fire and she went to the priest again after a time and asked him to write to Conor. Perhaps she might visit Myles when a year had passed. But Conor had left Derry and no one knew where. Father Cluny dutifully made the trek to Derry in her behalf. He returned with the sorrowful news that Myles had been committed to the insane asylum.

The ritual of the letter was as regular as the recitation of the rosary. She'd return it to the drawer, turn down the lantern and cover herself in the bed she had craved all her life.

"You were a fool, Myles. If you'd of only waited eight more years you'd be lying beside me now."

Her eyes would flutter from weariness of running the farm and so much praying.

Due to various circumstances Myles is taking a wife in Derry. . . .

CHAPTER SEVENTEEN: The tour!

No royal visit could have caused greater tension and festive air than the rugby fever. The East Belfast Boilermakers were among the few of consequence to come to

that black industrial necklace of Lancashire and Yorkshire. There was a mystique about the team being filled
with wild Irish rovers.

WELCOME BOILERMAKERS, the banner at city hall declared. Dignitaries and bands greeted, bookmakers sized
up, local press of destitute journalistic stature devoured.
There was always front-page coverage and usually a hint
of non-existent wagering scandal or rumor of a predawn
sexual foray. The pubs were opened wide and those ladies
who indulged placed themselves in evidence.

Sir Frederick's spout erupted endlessly and in full glory
as he confided that his latest Red Hand with Duffy O'Hurley at the throttle could turn a hundred and ten miles
per. He and Duffy and Calhoun Hanly doted over the
lines of school kiddies waiting to glimpse through the fa-
bled private cars, and he addressed civic groups and private clubs on matters of Ulster's industrial might, rugby,
his charities, Unionist politics. He threw lavish champagne
and caviar parties for clients and prospective buyers in a
second decade of replaying everybody's childhood dream.

In the days and weeks that followed, Conor often
wished Mick McGrath had gotten his taste of the tour,
for he wouldn't have spent his life hungering for it. The
grand tour was the grand illusion.

Aside from the larger cities, Bradford, Leeds, Hull and
the cling of Liverpool suburbs, the rest were of fifty to a
hundred thousand population in a tightly clustered textile
belt spawned ugly with monotonously matched odors,
colors and grime and all belching out the same debilitating
waste as Belfast. Those barons of beef in Mick McGrath's
fantasy were stringy, salty and overdone and the fancy
digs turned out to be a series of creaky, dark, soot-stained
rooms in the lesser railroad station hotels. Boredom and
homesickness were the constant companions of postgame
pain.

Game day!

Out they trotted in their green, orange and white uniforms with the flag of Ulster over their backs and the
Red Hand of Ulster on their chests. The stands rumbled
under the ovation. Playing fields of Batley, Halifax, Swin-
ton and the rest were set in rare patches of green where
dilapidated wooden stands held from ten to thirty thou-

sand exalted, swilled-to-the-gunnel fans in a state of semi-levitation. Bookmakers auctioned odds and little boys cried from the outside, "Hey, mister, boost me over the fence, please, mister, boost me over the fence."

GOD SAVE THE KING.

Mayhem commenced on the field as well as in the stands.

The professional game was wide open. A blur of rushing men, a meeting of bodies, a tangle of limbs, one remains stretched and still, then writhes as he slowly, slowly regains awareness, then writhes again as the awareness of pain stabs in, the ball floats high and drifts downward into a pack, two walls smash together in the scrum, a brutal tackle twists the neck of the running back in demi-decapitation but he staggers to his feet and wobbles back in, elbows and fists powder in close, a power runner sheds and drags tacklers who grimace in frustration.

The agony of Derek Crawford never varies except when the cap of the well blows off in his stomach. Doxie O'Brien is forever on the gallop up and down the touch lines shouting plays, cursing umpires, jeering back at the crowd.

Inventory takes place in high-ceilinged changing rooms under the stands where accumulated filth is a constant morbid gray. Splintery wooden benches sag and sway under the weight, and the smell of a generation of supercharged sweat has permeated forever. The fountain spouts cold-water showers and stamp-size towels amass soggy on the floor. Doxie O'Brien passes among them counting lost teeth, gashes requiring stitches, sprains, flattened noses, bruised ribs, gimpy knees, fearful-appearing discolorations.

"Good game, lads," Sir Frederick says, pounding into the morgue-like place.

A guinea or two guineas a man has been earned and another twelve bob per player after splitting up the pool from Sir Frederick's wager. Damned good team owner. None like him.

And ah! The comradery afterward. Having given their best to make one another into human wreckage, the opponents fall into one another's arms for the long night of drink. Drink to waylay the descending mantle of pain.

And ah! The girls! To swagger off with a dainty lady
before rigor mortis sets in and cancels out the final performance of the day.

With the "Blacksmith," Conor Larkin, learning his craft
in the front line and those two "gentlemen players" showing their national team caliber, the East Belfast Boilermakers regain some of their legendary esteem in Lancashire,
running over Leigh, Oldham, Salford and Runcorn in a
fortnight. On to Wigan for a pivotal game.

Wigan, one of the smallest towns in the Northern
Rugby League, was nonetheless a perennial powerhouse.
When cherry and white bashed green, orange and white,
the result was standstill for nearly eighty minutes in one
of the most bruising games in memory.

In the waning moments stamina told the tale. With the
Wigan lads doing a regular day's work, one would think
that the Boilermakers would be in better physical condition. However, the Boilermakers' long days of practice
and heavy schedule were further burdened by long nights
of indulgence and inordinate quantities of Guinness. Their
edge was nullified. The Blacksmith alone had enough
strength to score a try with his patented power plunge.

The flag of Ulster flew high over Lancashire. Yorkshire
held its breath and quivered.

Argyle Dixon, an uncaged wild boar of a man at tight-
head prop, shared the "police" work with the Blacksmith
in keeping thuggery out of the opponents' hearts. Rough-
ing a Boilermaker back unnecessarily brought an instant
reprisal. The message got out about the league that Argyle Dixon had a helper and to tread softly. By the time
they reached Hull the team had pulled the win and loss
record even with six games left. Derek Crawford was redeemed and Sir Frederick in ecstasy.

*

The Hubble party splintered after a few games. Lord
Roger acquitted himself rapidly of family duty and departed. After a time Caroline plunged onto the London
scene. While Roger was more or less content to remain
in London, Caroline found herself continually on a north-
bound train to catch the Saturday play.

During this time Jeremy made a mighty attempt to
walk in Larkin's footsteps. Conor treated his charge as an

eaglet, brooking no serious straying from the nest. Conor roomed with Robin MacLeod but kept Jeremy within whistling distance. A bit of boozing was allowed the boy but he was kept strictly off the seamier side of the night prowling. This permitted Jeremy to place a foot on the bar rail and talk bawdy with the men but gingerly steered him from trouble. Between talk of women, drink and rugby, he was being given an illusion of tough manhood and he gloried in it.

Conor did a work of art on the boy, subtly applying doses of his own love of the written word and the heady thought. Jeremy worshipped Conor to such an extent that it was rationalized that if Conor truly loved something such as books, then books must be good. Time was a plentiful commodity and there were long talks over little beer and a guiding into plays and concerts. Jeremy was enticed by Conor's descriptions of the beauty and joy of Dublin, building an excitement over the boy's coming seasons at Trinity College. Lady Caroline marveled over the small but rich changes coming over her son. It was Jeremy Hubble's summer in the booley house.

Huddersfield fell to the thundering Boilermakers as did Brighouse, Derek's old team and always a satisfying victory.

*

Suddenly a cold damp dawn arose despite the late summer. It was that kind of morning when one could see one's piercing breath. The private train oozed over the brown gooey River Ayre and into the Leeds City Station without fanfare because of the small hour. The team filed out, bent-shouldered, half asleep, for the short walk over the square to the hotel.

Conor's eyes moistened in the cutting fog. He was numb, but not from cold. For ten weeks he had tried to divorce himself of thoughts of Bradford. Each time it invaded his mind, he counted the weeks as eight weeks off, seven, four and, after all, four was a month. Now it was down to a fortnight.

The next stop, Bradford.

Brendan Sean Barrett would be in Bradford. Barrett would tell him what had been done about Duffy O'Hurley. In how many pubs had he joked with the driver, always

wondering as he did. How many times had he boarded
the train and stared at the tender?

Something strange had been taking place within his
own reaches. Exhilaration over the gunrunning scheme had
begun to dim. He would not admit it to himself but he
had reached that point where he secretly hoped the plan
would be aborted. Maybe O'Hurley had rejected it when
the approach was made? Maybe he would get to Bradford
and Barrett would be on the run, unable to make contact. Maybe Barrett would just send him off. Everything
would be solved then.

Everything solved? What did he want solved?

All those summers of dreaming of joining the battle,
of patriots and liberation and all those tormented nights
of walking the decks of wayward ships, would be coming
to fruition in Bradford. The moment he shook hands with
Brendan Sean Barrett was the moment of life's commitment, the first stir of the rising. Why was this slipping from
his longings?

Leeds . . . then Bradford. It was no longer Mother Ireland that flooded Conor Larkin's mind. It was Shelley
MacLeod.

CHAPTER EIGHTEEN: It rained.

Conor came into the hotel room, shook off the wet and
opened the adjoining door and peered in. "Where's Jeremy?"

"With his grandfather," Robin said, looking up from his
new James Grant novel, *Letty Hyde's Lovers.*

"He didn't tell me he was going out."

"You hover over that kid like he was a mental."

Conor flopped into an overstuffed chair sprung with age,
swinging a leg over the chair arm and fiddling for his
place in his own book.

"You'll have to keep a tight watch on Alfie Newton,"
Robin said of Conor's counterpart on the Leeds Loiners.

"Yeah, I know, I know."

"Bloody monster, that. He's the only man in the league
Argyle can't handle by himself. Can't be stopped even
with a judo arm tackle."

"Argyle gave me a lecture on him, Doxie gave me a lecture on him, Derek gave me a lecture on him. Everybody's been Alfie Newtoning me to death for a week." Conor popped up restlessly, studied himself in a small mirror over the basin. He ran his finger over the scar healing on his cheek.

"Don't let Alfie Newton see that," Robin said on cue.

Conor grunted and took a look out of the window as though some miracle might make it stop raining. Even the rain seemed black. It spattered oilylike over the cobblestones below, blending into the listless shining wet rows of red brick and slate roofs. Everything outside moved about huddled and miserable. He settled and returned to his book but quickly picked up scents of Robin's edginess. Conor peered over the edge of the page. Robin wore a patented expression of guilt and he knew what his mate was building up to.

"I need you to cover for me tonight," Robin blurted.

"Sure. Her place or here?"

"Here. She's married."

"What time?"

"About half eight." Robin tossed his book to the stand. "You think I'm a bastard, don't you?"

"No," Conor replied.

Robin paced the confining room, caged. "You've got to know, man, I love Lucy and I don't fuck around at home but after ten weeks of this shit . . ."

"Shut up. This isn't a confessional booth."

"Look, I got to explain it to you. You're like family and I don't want you to have any wrong ideas about me."

"You've got nothing to explain," Conor said.

"It's getting to me."

"What?"

"Me being married and acting like this and seeing you behaving yourself, just waiting for Shelley. Playing it foursquare with her, right down the line. It makes me feel bad."

"Don't kick yourself. We've all got different requirements. I know you love your wife and kid."

"You're all right, Conor. Jeese, I like to shit when I heard I would be rooming with, you know, an R.C. and a single one at that. See, I've always teamed up with married lads and, with one covering for the other, a man can reason his way out of what he's doing. You know what I mean. Anyhow, that's what I like about you, you're all right."

"Not to worry, Robin."

Robin took up a post at the window. "Fucking rain."

"Yeah."

"The guys are getting edgy. I can smell it. Ten weeks out and the fucking rain. You can bet there'll be a couple fights before the week's out. Jeese, you're calm."

"Maybe," Conor said. You don't know the half of it, Robin, he thought.

"You think about Shelley much?"

"She's not hard to think about."

"Yeah," Robin said. "I guess that next to Lucy and Matt I think about her most. You're a lucky scut. Shelley's someone, she is." Robin stretched on the saggy bed, hands tucked behind his head, and treated himself to memory. "You'd never believe a beautiful woman would ever come from such a funny-looking kid." He lit a cigarette and blew a ring to the ceiling. "You know, I ran off and did time at sea myself."

"Shelley told me."

"Oh, it was desperate. When you're poor in Belfast, man, you're poor."

"Sure we've no monopoly on poverty," Conor said. "But growing up on a farm can help dim some of the ugliness of poverty. I learned that when I went to Derry. Back home we always had neighbors and centuries of helping each other. There's always something to grow, and if that goes bad there's always something to hunt. In the city it closes in on you in a different way, a feeling of total helplessness."

"That's it entirely," Robin said. "You can't eat the pavement." His eyes were speaking now in that ruggedly handsome face and a touch of light from the outside played up his strong features. "If a man doesn't have green fields, he invents them."

"And fields of dusty bluebells . . ."

"Of course, Shelley told you. Ah, she'd sing that song by the hour. When me and Shelley was old enough, maybe nine or ten, we'd take off, adventuring. We'd get on the tram at a crowded corner and slip past the fare collector pretending our parents had already been through and paid our way. At the end of the line in Malone we'd beg a ride on a horse cart out to the country. It was green out there, truly green. We'd yell for joy just at the sight of it. Our favorite place was Shaw's Bridge, a small stone crossing over the Lagan set in the widest and greenest field you'd ever hope to see. It was our place, Shelley's and mine, and our initials are still on the bridge rail."

He swung up to sitting. "Jeese, I'm spouting."

"I like to hear things about Shelley," Conor said.

Robin smiled. "Me and Shelley," he said, "well, we'd dive from the bridge into the river in our underwear. It was dangerous but in those days before the pollution the water was clean and fresh and deep. And pretty soon a barge would happen along. For a penny I would ride the lead donkey on shore and pull the barge and Shelley would steer the tiller, giving the bargeman a half hour to nap. They always had something to eat and if we stared at them hard enough they'd share it.

"On a good day we'd collect four or five pennies and begin the long trip home. The instant we reached the Shankill we'd race to the fruit merchant at the end of our street and show him our money and we'd be allowed to pick as many as fifteen or twenty pieces of bruised fruit from the damaged barrel and we'd off to a secret shed and fill ourselves till we was in pain. Queer, ain't it, how your most vivid recollections are of food?"

Robin's face contorted suddenly. "One day," he said, "Shelley like to drowned when we was jumping from Shaw's Bridge. Only by God's grace did I save her. I can still see her lying there on the bank, wet hair down her face, so still. She was in a fearful chill when we brought her around and we had to take her to the hospital. You know Morgan. He's as good as he is large but when he's angry few men would touch him with a pitchfork. When a doctor brought her home he grabbed me by the thropple and gave me such a hiding I thought I'd never live to grow a beard. Shelley ever tell you why I ran to sea?"

"Aye."

"Why did you, Conor?"

He did not answer.

"Shagging Belfast," Robin said. "We were always Shankill people and shipyard workers. Morgan was there at

Weed Ship & Iron on opening day and his father worked the smaller yards before that. When there was work, life could be tolerable except for those awful Sundays and all that holy blather. When there was no work the desperation became terrifying. The fear in men's eyes and the pain of having to face their families empty-handed warped their minds and turned them on their neighbors. We're so bloody desperate for our jobs, they're held at our throats like the point of a dagger. That's half of what's wrong between your people and mine."

Robin MacLeod remembered his mother as a woman with the severity of her religion etched as deeply in her soul as the lines of her face. She was never given to laughter, only screeching prayer.

"Oh, she had the face of a winter's night and a heart to match. If she wasn't cross, it wasn't day yet. During the hard times, she'd blame our dire straits as the Lord's punishment for the evil ways of me and Shelley.

"Morgan's immense pride would never submit to allowing Shelley or me to work in the mills. The quarrels got so fierce during a big layoff that I ran to sea and Shelley fled to England.

"Mercifully, my mother was relieved of earthly misery early, praying and singing hallelujah up to the last gasp. Morgan married dear Nell later, as saintly a woman as ever graced the Shankill. He pleaded for the two of us to come back because he said if we weren't a family we were nothing. I guess a lot of Belfasters are like that. It's better to live in those little pillboxes than scatter around the world and die off."

Liam gone, me gone, Dary gone. Our seed is scattered ... our strain grows weaker ...

The door burst open to the enthusiastic entrance of Jeremy Hubble, who dripped into the middle of the room. Conor looked at his watch. It was a bit past seven.

"Dry yourself up and let's go have some scroggins," Conor said to the boy.

"The training table's not set for an hour," Jeremy said.

"I'm after some decent food tonight. And afterward! *The Siege of Ladysmith*, no less, adorns the stage of the local playhouse."

"Super! You coming, Robin?"

"I've got to go over plans for the Leeds game with Doxie and Derek."

Jeremy glanced from one to the other. "I wish you wouldn't always treat me like a kid," he said.

*

Victory over the Leeds Loiners was sweet nectar and mud done before twenty-six thousand soaked spectators. No sooner had play gotten under way than the fearsome Alfie Newton (and a human rhino he was) took dead aim at the cut on Conor's cheek from a blind side. Argyle Dixon trailed closely and got a warning off in time. Conor turned, lowered his head and caught the rampaging Alfie directly between the eyes with his own forehead, doing in a nose that had been done in many times before.

Alfie was able to come around during the time out for injury but was never quite himself thereafter. Argyle and Conor took turns in shadowing him like a second set of skin, giving him no room to breathe at all. Before half time, Alfie retired from his first game in ten years. The Boilermakers owned the scrums after that and the final score, East Belfast 24 and Leeds 3. It was the highlight of the season.

At game's end, Conor sat long and hard holding a wet cloth to his knotted forehead which had dealt the blow to Alfie Newton. It was not the pain of it that sickened him, it was the realization that time had run out. Bradford and Brendan Sean Barrett waited up the road.

One by one his mates all patted his back and left the changing room for serious celebration until only Jeremy and Robin remained.

"On with you both," Conor insisted. "I'll catch up."

They left, too, and what light remained turned that sickening gray-black. He continued to sit with his face in his hands staring at nothing. The aged changing-room keeper picked up towels, groaning, and cursed the mess and swabbed a floor which was as bent and creaking as himself.

Conor wove to the tubs and swabbed himself off in cold water.

The old man continued to complain that his work was never done and now there was yet another mess to clean, then he caught sight of Conor's forehead.

"Oh, matey," he said, "that's a nasty bash you got. Say, you're the Blacksmith, are you not?"

"I'm the Blacksmith," Conor whispered.

*

Conor caught up with the festivities at the Old India House and for a moment he allowed himself to be swallowed up by adulation and drinks. The pub was flooded with songs, Leeds songs, Belfast songs, smutty music hall songs, mining songs, sentimental Irish songs.

Then, as always, the Catholic lads filtered off to their own, those little Irishtowns that existed in the inner core of destitution. The Chapel Town and Quarry Hill pubs were opened for their heroes.

Jeremy Hubble protested all the way back to the hotel to no avail and Conor continued on to Tooley's public house to accept the accolades of his countrymen. The Blacksmith had come to visit, an occasion that would be long remembered and re-remembered to ease the sordidness of their existence.

Duffy O'Hurley, Doxie O'Brien and Calhoun Hanly held court in a corner of the pub. Duffy was strangely subdued, not his boisterous self, of this night. Conor's eyes met his over the din. Ever so slowly Duffy nodded yes and lifted his pint in a salute.

CHAPTER NINETEEN

BRADFORD

Robin groped in the darkness, located the lamp and turned it on. Conor stood near the door buttoning up his pea coat. Robin propped up on an elbow, shook his head to erase the sleep and sighted in on his watch.

"I need some air," Conor said.

"Jeese, man, it's past eleven. We've got a bloody game to play tomorrow."

"I know. I'll not be long."

Robin bolted awake, throwing off the covers and sitting

on the bed edge. "Hey, Conor, what's eating you? You've been a real slooter for the past three days."

"Just roll over and go back to sleep."

"Anything wrong in that letter from Shelley today?"

"Nothing!" Conor snapped.

"Jeese . . ."

"Sorry . . . I'm just a little tense."

"Well, don't be late. We've a hard game."

A final hansom cab stood at the hotel entrance, both driver and horse sleeping at the ready. Conor nudged the man. The horse snorted.

"Where to, sir?"

"Up in the Wapping."

"Any place in particular?"

"No, just find a pub along the lower part of Boulton Road."

As they pulled away, Robin watched from three stories above. He let the curtain fall and shook his head curiously. What the hell, none of his business. Didn't seem likely he was fucking around on Shelley. The R.C.s were all funny about getting off by themselves. He crawled back into bed, doused the lamp and pulled the covers over him.

Conor dismissed the cab at the cathedral where Boulton Road joined Cheapside and continued by foot into the heartland of the Irishtown. They had fled the famine to Bradford in droves, going from nowhere to nowhere, the charwomen, washerwomen, hawkers, peddlers, miners, paupers, wool combers, navvies. Squalor begat degradation. It reeked.

A bobby came in his direction. "Excuse me. How do I find Wild Boar Road?"

"Five blocks up and on the right."

"Thank you." Conor walked into growing quiet until he was alone with the street lamps and little more. He came to the short street, sucked in a breath and wavered, looking behind him for the tenth time. There was activity up the block, a light and some people moving about. He braced himself, walked for it, then stopped directly across from Callaghan's Funeral Parlor. A traffic of black-kerchiefed female mourners and capped workingmen moved in and out past the curtained window front.

Conor crossed the street and stepped inside.

They were on their knees praying around the earthly

remains of Vincent O'Cooney, late of County Cork, God rest his soul. Vincent O'Cooney, killed in a mine shaft at thirty-two, leaving his widow, Mary, and nine kids.

The room was afloat in candle shadows casting off the stony faces of the kneeled worshipers. A timeworn priest granted uninspired sympathy. There was little weeping or wailing. They were too weary.

"Are you a friend of the deceased?"

"I only knew him slightly," Conor said. He looked about trying to spot the one who might be Callaghan, then slipped to his knees and joined the rosary. His eyes continued to search the faces. As the prayer came to an end, the rear door opened as if on signal and a man emerged. His vicuña morning coat was frayed and his pinstriped trousers shabbily in keeping with the neighborhood.

Almost everyone filed out into the night, leaving the widow to continue the waking. With the room nearly empty, Conor got to his feet, wiped a rush of perspiration from his face and walked to the mortician.

"Mr. Callaghan?" he said at last.

The man nodded. "You're a stranger here," he said.

"I, uh, was a friend of the deceased a time ago. This all came as a shock. I was just passing through Bradford and . . . uh . . . I heard about it at a pub . . ."

"Would you care to come into the back room and rest? You look done in," Callaghan said.

His lips went dry. For the first time in his life he felt faint, as though he would go down. Everything began to swim . . . Callaghan had his arm and led him toward the back.

Conor stopped. He turned and left the place at a half run.

CHAPTER TWENTY: A large number of Welshmen played on various teams in the Northern Rugby Union but had no professional teams of their own. After the regular season Sir Frederick arranged a pair of exhibition games between the Boilermakers and the rest of the Welsh players on an "all-star" club. Advertised as Ireland versus Wales, the matches took place in Swansea and Cardiff before overflow and delirious crowds. Although the Welshmen were superior on a man-to-man basis, the Boilermakers had played as a cohesive unit for years and won out handily in a pair of wild games.

The season had turned triumphant. Sir Frederick plunged into plans for professional tours to Australia, New Zealand and France, and argued in his convincing manner that Wales should join the Northern Rugby League with teams of its own.

With the tour done and a week's holiday coming up, Sir Frederick arranged a final bash. The celebration in league with fellow Welshmen took place in a posh hostelry in an area known as the Mumbles located midway between Thistleboon and Oystermouth on Swansea Bay. Conor left the festivities early in order to get a head start in the morning for the train to Liverpool to meet Shelley's boat. His ward, Lord Jeremy, was placed in Robin MacLeod's good hands.

At five in the morning Conor responded to a hammering on the door, staggering over the room in a state of grogginess. He opened it, saw his mate and his eyes widened. Robin MacLeod was a mess. Conor whisked him into the room and locked the door behind them.

"A slight altercation," Robin managed through puffed lips throwing off the pungent smells of overindulgence.

Conor marched him to the water stand, sponged him off and examined the severity of the damage.

"All right, what happened?"

"Well now, let me see now. I suppose you left the Lord Pembroke Hotel around the stroke of twelve, did you not . . . eh . . ."

"I did, indeed."

"Well now, let me see, now. There was a little something extra special laid on in one of the better houses of course . . . right in Thistleboon, if you please. So a number of us arrived with a number of the Welsh laddies. There was myself and Argyle and Big Brett and O'Rourke and Clarke . . . Oh, we was having a grand time. Everything was in a most dignified social manner . . ."

"Yeah, I'll bet."

"Anyhow, Brett latches onto this one, a real looker with tits like yeaaaaa and you know . . . well then . . . we all know how Brett behaves sometimes when he gets

on the stuff . . . so after a time we all feel Big Brett
should ought to be passing her round. And those Welsh
lads can be particularly nasty. All of a sudden, dirty,
rank nationalism creeps into an otherwise dignified assembly. And even though Big Brett is a loathesome son
of a bitch, we have to defend him as a matter of Irish
honor . . ." Robin said, collapsing on a chair.

Robin winced and gave off a cry as Conor cleaned out a
deep cut.

"So there was a brawl," Conor said.

"Tore the fucking place apart. It was a donnybrook
of monumental scope. Bodies flying, furniture smashing,
the girls screaming. One of the most beautiful evenings
I ever spent in my life. Anyhow . . . I was fortunate to
make a successful exit just as the police arrived. I slipped
back here undetected. I am afraid the others are being
slightly detained," he groaned.

"That's Sir Frederick's problem."

Robin heaved a sigh of the ages and bowed his head.
"I've got something important to tell you," he said.

"What else?"

"Well, let me see if I can explain it . . . you see . . .
well now . . . there was someone else with us . . ."

Conor threw open the adjoining door. Jeremy was gone!

"You son of a bitch!"

"Now, now, Conor, lad. Now, now."

"You son of a bitch!"

"Let me say, with all the fervor I have in my breast,
the lad did us proud. Punched one of those Welshmen
silly. He was doing just fine, he was, all cuddled up with
this here big blonde, happy as a hog in shit . . ."

"I'll kill you, Robin!"

"Now, Conor, I'm your mate. We are practically blood
brothers. Just mind the temper, mind the temper."

"Where is he!"

"If you'll just put me down and calm yerself . . ."

*

"Viscount Coleraine nabbed in brothel brawl," Caroline
read, trembling with rage. She flung the newspaper to the
carpet and picked up another off the stack on the tea
table. "His lordship's night on the town. Earl of Foyle heir

loses teeth in predawn romp with ladies." Then another. "Lord Jeremy delivers knockout punch for mates."

Sir Frederick was unusually docile, slouched in an over-sized chair at the far end of the parlor of the hotel suite attempting to make himself as inconspicuous as possible, but to no avail, as Caroline waved a paper in his face.

"Look at this trash! Every cheap scandal sheet in the British Isles is full of it!"

"Yes, filthy business," Weed mumbled, "terrible, terrible journalism."

"Freddie, I am addressing you on your grandson's disgusting behavior!" Caroline said in something resembling a shriek.

"Storm in a teacup," Sir Frederick defended weakly.

She spun around to Jeremy, who stood on the sizzling carpet. "You are to tell me one more time exactly what happened and I want the truth. Your father has probably arrived and will be here directly. The truth, Jeremy, the truth!"

As Jeremy opened his mouth Caroline grimaced at the two missing teeth all nicely matched up with cut lip, black eye . . . to say nothing of bite and scratch marks she had found all over the boy's back and neck.

"The truth!" she snapped as he cleared his throat.

"Well, Mother, we were all dining together at the Lord Pembroke, just celebrating, good fellowship and all that, when the word passed about that some . . . well . . . some . . . company had been arranged . . ."

"You mean whores," his mother said.

"Yes, uh, rather, one might say that. As the dinner broke up, Conor, Mr. Larkin, said, 'Come on, runt . . .' "

"He calls you runt?"

"A nickname, Mother. Said with affection. 'Runt,' Mr. Larkin says, 'time to shove off.' "

"Continue," Caroline snapped.

"Well, I told him I'd be right along with . . . with another member of the team . . ."

"Who?"

"Don't ask me to tattle."

"I said . . . who!"

"The captain, Mr. MacLeod."

"So Robin MacLeod took you to this party, is that it?"

"More or less. I found out where the party was to be and went back to our hotel, stuck my head in Conor's room, said good night, then slipped out and joined them."

"And you were subsequently dragged off in a police van like a common criminal at four in the morning . . . without trousers . . . bloody from head to foot. At least you could have gotten away when that disgusting brawl started."

"Well, Mother, one doesn't just run out on the team, does one?"

Caroline whipped around to Freddie, who was cowed in his chair. "He's lying in order not to implicate Mr. Conor Larkin."

"Mother, I'm not lying. Conor wouldn't stand for that sort of thing."

"It now also comes to my attention that Conor Larkin allowed you to consort with a prostitute in Hull, even transport her to Halifax. True or not true?"

"Well, not exactly, more or less, one might say," Sir Frederick mumbled.

"Did Conor Larkin allow you to consort with a whore for a period of several weeks?"

"It is true," Weed said. "Larkin came to me and told me Jeremy was wrapped up in a childish romance and was taking it seriously. We discussed the matter and decided to let it run its course. If we'd broken it up, there would have been all sorts of trouble with the boy."

"Grandfather is right," Jeremy said. "I thought I was in love. Conor, Mr. Larkin, let me show myself what a fool I was."

"Well . . . this was a grand tour, indeed," Caroline said. "And did he or did he not also allow you to drink your way through every public house in England?"

"Mother, I simply can't feel that Conor was responsible. I had two pints a night, no more. And he certainly can't be held responsible for me sneaking out on him . . . which was usually what I did."

"Send Mr. Larkin in!"

Conor answered the summons by going directly to Jeremy and examining the boy's wounds. Jeremy lowered his eyes in shame.

"Tsk, tsk, tsk, shame, Jeremy," Conor sighed.

"Is this how you take the responsibility for a minor

child?" Lady Caroline said with a voice quivering with anger.

Conor shrugged.

"Now just a moment, Caroline," Sir Frederick intervened. "It's obvious that Larkin had nothing to do with this incident."

"Oh, I see. All the stout chaps hanging in there together."

"If truth be known," he continued, "I was the one who arranged the late . . . er . . . celebrations."

"Freddie! You are despicable! And as for you, Mr. Larkin, you've a thing or two to answer for."

"Well, don't expect straight answers. As you well know, we are all psychopathic liars. If you'll excuse me."

"No," she commanded. "You are not excused." She marched to him, raised her hand and swung it. Conor reached up before the slap could connect, seized her wrist and gripped it hard enough to tell her she should go no further along that route.

"If you do that again," he said, "I'm going to paddle your backside right in front of your son and your father."

"Bravo, Larkin," Sir Frederick said.

He released a very astonished lady. The mask of rage dropped and she suddenly broke into uncontrolled laughter. "Oh, you're beautiful, Larkin!" she laughed, and then Sir Frederick darted out of his chair and joined the laughter. Slowly and awkwardly Jeremy shifted weight from foot to foot, flashed his teeth minus two and laughed and Conor laughed.

Caroline threw her arms about her son and wept.

"It's quite all right, Mother," Jeremy said, "and you'd be delighted at the way I bashed that one chap about. Conor taught me how to throw short punches behind my body."

At that instant Roger Hubble appeared on the scene. One by one the laughter stopped as he stood in controlled disgust at the door. He looked from one to the other, imparting scorn to each in turn. As icily as he had entered, so he turned to leave.

"Father!" Jeremy cried. The boy raced across the room and blocked the door. "Father," he whispered again, "Father."

Roger slapped him across the face and left.

"Jeremy!" his mother cried.

"Shouldn't have done that," Sir Frederick said harshly.

It was Conor Larkin the boy raced to for solace. He was embraced and comforted. "It's all right, runt, it's all right."

CHAPTER TWENTY-ONE: Blackpool was hauntingly devoid of life, leaving Shelley and Conor virtually alone on the long promenade with the sand and the sea and only the shrill cry of the gulls and the thump of the breakers. All of the uncertainties that had built up during the separation disappeared the instant they came together.

What had begun in Belfast took wing, ethereal wing, in the gray brooding place. They were neither alive nor dead, but suspended, out in infinity, a vast timeless space. They realized at once that this journey could go on forever, they could explore it together and never need to retrace their steps, for what was always ahead was endless love-making, each time new, each time completely different. Perhaps they were doing much of the same thing over with their bodies but that was not how their minds read it.

They stood before a cave, its entrance blocked by a huge boulder which gave way. They entered together, for that was the only way in, in pairs. Eternities were opened as they knew they had come into the unique gift of constant and complete regeneration. A floating kind of thing that went on and on. It was awesome to comprehend that they had discovered nirvana.

For Conor Larkin loving Shelley MacLeod was a time of reckoning. He had edged himself to the brink that ruled out this kind of love but backed down in the final instant. He had fled from Callaghan's Funeral Parlor. He had to find Shelley first, see her once more before that final commitment, see if this thing he felt was really true or if it were some kind of poet's illusion.

From the very beginning, Shelley had crept in and brought on doubts over the course in which he was directing his life. She got him to wondering if his longings had always really been for the love of a woman. Perhaps he never understood it until she came. In her warmth he had found peace for the first time in his manhood and that peace was limitless. She was the giver of peace. His self-doubts turned into a war. He knew he could not make that final step into that back room until Shelley.

Each night and during the days as well, they walked into the cave to fly and were shortly in a place of tens of trillions of galaxies, exploring in a web of miracle. When they knew they had reached the final nirvana, they found another even more thrilling . . . again and again.

As the hours of Blackpool ticked off, Brendan Sean Barrett, Long Dan Sweeney, the Brotherhood, tender cars, guns, grew dimmer.

The hotel was deserted except for a few stragglers. A sudden late storm swooped in, setting off a wild surf and filling the sky violently with heat lightning. They went out on their porch and watched it, enthralled by the spectacular flashes which lit up the maddened whitecaps.

The decision came that quickly, that clearly. He gripped her shoulders from behind. "I want to take you away," he said, "will you come?"

"My bags have been packed all my life," she answered. Conor stared at the woman outlined against the storm. "I know how you've been pondering this in the past twelve weeks. It may be penny plain, Conor, but are you sure? Are you absolutely certain?"

"I can make it with you, Shelley, I can make it with you."

*

There was little sleep that night, for there was something even more wild for them to discover. When they fell to rest it was a time for holding on profoundly, for touching, for reiterating the decision to go. By morning the storm was spent and the two lovers were as exhausted and peaceful as the sea.

Conor was babbling now, soft, blissful. . . . "The more I'm thinking, it's Australia. We can do anything we want down there as long as I've got these," holding his hands up.

"Any place," she purred.

He covered her back with kisses and touched her in a way that never failed to stir her, even in a state of utter weariness.

"I feel so good," he said. "We'll do the marrying business before we ship out and we'll land in Australia as mister and missus."

Shelley wept her happiness. He reached to the night stand for a handkerchief for her eyes and to blow her nose. As he propped up against the headboard she wiggled as close as she could and watched him thinking furiously.

"We'll go on an early ship, right from England. I'll run down to London and see after passage and to get our papers fixed. You skip back to Belfast, pack our things and close my account."

"Won't you come?"

"I don't want to go back to Ireland," he whispered. "I don't want to go back," he repeated, "I've nothing much there . . ."

She put her fingers to his lips to silence him. "Don't say any more, Conor, except how much you love me."

"Love you? Are you daft? Your breasts are too small, you sing off key, you walk flat-footed, you can't drink worth a damn and, worse, you pray standing up."

They passed the day walking on the promenade, reassuring and reassuring, never leaving touch of one another. Over dinner their eyes made love in a prelude for the new venture of that night.

Conor lit a fire and as she cuddled on the chesterfield and warmed they repeated their plans. Then he sat down at the desk and started letters to Robin, Seamus O'Neill and Jeremy. He was interrupted by a knock on the door. It was Mr. Thornton, the proprietor.

"Sorry to disturb you," the innkeeper said, "but there's a gentleman downstairs to see you."

"Me?"

"He asked for Conor Larkin."

Conor shrugged, thinking it must be one of the locals who knew him as a rugby man, and said so to quell Shelley's inquisitive stare. "It must be, no one else knows we're here." He slipped on his jacket, kissed her. "I'll only be a few minutes, love," he said.

Mr. Thornton pointed down the long veranda beyond the

lobby which faced the sea. "He's waiting for you out there, Mr. Larkin."

Conor stepped outside, braced against the chill, and looked about. A bright three-quarter moon silvered above a much calmed sea. At the far end of the porch stood a small man caught up in the machinations of the waves. Conor approached his rear.

"You asked to see me?"

The man turned. Conor was dumbstruck! At first he thought it was . . . no, it couldn't be. He stepped closer, thinking the moonlight was playing tricks off the man's face. He was quite old and bent but the similarity . . . Conor shook his head in confusion . . . could it be?

"Kevin O'Garvey?" he said hoarsely.

"Aye, it's me," Kevin answered. There was no mistaking that voice!

"This must be some kind of madness!"

"No, it's myself all right. I know this must come as a terrible shock to you. I'm sorry I was unable to give you advance warning."

"Wait a minute," Conor said. "I don't believe this."

"I've changed, I know, but take a good look and try to get ahold of yourself and I'll explain."

Conor remained rigid, his mind became cloudy as he attempted to rapidly piece together the sequence of events around Kevin's disappearance. It was difficult because he had been in a funk himself, at the time. "Jesus, my head's all fucked up."

"I know you feel biffed. Can we sit down and talk?"

Conor nodded and half fell into a rocker while Kevin pulled up one opposite him. "Where to start? Well, let me see. For reasons you'll learn in a few minutes I've contacted no one in Derry since my disappearance except for Father Pat and I held him to an oath of secrecy. Father Pat wrote to me after he was transferred from Bogside, telling me he had to inform you of his suspicion that I had probably made some kind of deal with the Hubbles not to investigate the shirt factory."

Conor nodded tentatively, still trying to unfog his mind.

"I suppose you took the news very hard."

Conor nodded again.

"You must try to realize what it did to me when I

learned of the fire. I was as much responsible for those hundred deaths as if I had set the place ablaze with my own hand. The horror of it all but crushed me. In addition, my whole life was a failure. Oh, I considered the possibility of coming back to Derry and facing it but I couldn't, I didn't have the strength, Conor. And more, I was in a state of shock, deep depressed shock. Do you understand?"

"So was I," Conor answered. "The pain of it eventually drove me from Derry. I can't even begin to imagine what it did to you."

"I ran," Kevin said.

Conor bolted from the rocking chair, leaving it swinging empty. "I don't believe what I'm hearing. It's all a crazy fantasy. If I'm not dreaming, then how could you possibly know I was here? No one knows I'm in Blackpool, much less the ghost of Kevin O'Garvey."

"Brendan Sean Barrett told me."

"I've never met the man. He's no way of knowing."

"For God's sake, Conor, they're not idiots in the Brotherhood. The minute you stepped ashore in England you were singled out. Brotherhood men have been watching you on every city of your tour. Callaghan was in the railroad station when you stepped off the train in Bradford. . . . You still look as though you doubt me. Well then, did you or did you not go into Callaghan's Funeral Parlor on Wild Boar Road two weeks ago and did you not leave the establishment without making contact?"

Conor stared a bit wild-eyed. If it was a ghost, it was a well-informed ghost indeed. He studied the pinched face worn to near emaciation by sorrow but it was unmistakably Kevin O'Garvey before him.

"Then it's true," Conor said.

"Aye, it's true," he answered.

"How did you know I was in Blackpool?"

"You seem to have forgotten I've been a member of the Brotherhood since Fenian days. I've always been in contact, all during their dormant years. The instant I was elected to Parliament I helped get things re-established in London."

"Go on," Conor whispered.

"Brendan Sean Barrett received a letter from Dan Sweeney just as you arrived on the tour. He advised us to keep a close watch on you." Kevin jerked a thumb toward the hotel proper. "A woman, I believe. We checked your rail tickets and hotel reservations when you left Swansea."

"I see," Conor said, totally deflated, "so I am under suspicion by the Brotherhood."

"You yourself told Sweeney you were serious about the woman. He was only taking studious precaution."

"He was right," Conor said. "So you've been hiding in England all these years."

"Not exactly. After the Witherspoon & McNab fire and my decision to flee, the lads found a safe country for me. A place where a lawyer can practice and make a living with no questions asked."

"Where did you go?"

"Paraguay. It took me three years to return to a semblance of normalcy. Of course I was never out of contact with the Brotherhood. Using Paraguay as a base, I began traveling for them. Their passport got me in and out of America as well as England."

"And all this time you never let any of us know you're alive!"

"Just Father Pat. He's a priest and he could tell me about my friends and about Ireland. I could have brought nothing but pain and sorrow by letting anyone else know."

"What about your wife, man!"

"I've wept tears over that, you can believe me. But Teresa knew I was a Fenian the day she married me. She's always understood there were things more important than the two of us. You see, Conor, I was remembered as a Land Leaguer, a lawyer who fought for his people. I was a respected man, perhaps even loved. I could have accomplished nothing by letting them know except to destroy that image."

Conor stopped his pacing and braced himself. . . . "Why have you come here?"

"I came to England bringing money from the Clan in America. Three thousand quid. I gave it to Brendan Sean Barrett to be passed to you. When the lads assessed that you were acting strangely after you bolted from Callaghan's we had a meeting. I convinced them that you'd give it to me straight, being as we were old, old friends."

"I'll give it to you straight," Conor said. "Tell Barrett

I'm through. You know enough about me to vouch for my integrity. I hope you trust me enough to believe me when I tell you no one knows anything about the Brotherhood from me."

"Mind you, Conor, no one took you for an informer because of your behavior. We all knew about the woman."

"All right then, Kevin. It's a clean break with no one owing the other anything."

"Sure. So, you're really through. The woman?"

"Aye, the woman."

"You love her that much?"

"Aye."

Kevin nodded sadly. "It was much different with Teresa. She was one of our own, a Catholic girl. She knew I was a Fenian and would never give it up. You see, the Brotherhood could never come between us."

"It's not her," Conor said. "It's me making the choice. She'd do whatever I asked but I've found something I love more than the agony of Ireland."

"You have that right, indeed. The Brotherhood will be sorry. All the old-timers thought a lot of you."

"I love my woman," Conor said firmly, "I love her . . . in a way you wouldn't understand."

"You must, indeed."

"What the hell, Kevin, look what love of Ireland has done to you."

"Yes, yes, it has. I've reached the age of spending a great deal of time in reflection over it. Actually I've made two great mistakes in my life. The first was to try to make a pact with the Devil in form of Roger Hubble. The second was to run. I should have returned to Derry and faced up to what I had done, even if it meant the rest of my days in jail and losing the love of my people. I've lived in limbo, Conor. Limbo is no place for a man to exist. It's living death, worse than death, praying for death."

"The place I'm going to is not limbo," Conor snapped.

Kevin stopped the rocker and stood up wearily. "Sure," he said, "I know you've got it all figured out."

Conor grabbed his arm. "You think I'm a bloody traitor, don't you?"

"How can I think that? I held you in my arms when you were a baby. I watched every step of your life. The son of Tomas a traitor? Never. You can't betray us. It's not in your scant. But you can betray yourself and, worse, you can betray that woman. Australia, is it?"

"How did you know!"

Kevin shrugged. "You were there for a year. It's the farthest point from Ireland. I hope it's far enough. I hope you never hear the name of Ireland again as I have. Memories, smells, passing faces, hearing the words . . . it can destroy you in time. I hope you don't hear about it when the rising comes. That will surely kill you. But . . . I told Brendan Sean Barrett that coming to see you would be of little avail. I told him that Conor Larkin was a man of his own mind. Not to worry. We'll get those guns over there somehow. Well, I've outstayed my welcome. God be with you, Conor."

Conor stuffed his hands into his pockets and merely nodded, showing no desire for an affectionate farewell, but only for Kevin to understand his resolve and to leave him in peace. Kevin nodded and turned down the long veranda. Instead of making into the lobby he went down the steps to the beach. His feet dragged through the sand as though they were suction cups. He moved toward the water.

"Wait!" Conor called. "Wait! You're going in the wrong direction!"

Kevin did not seem to hear and Conor thought him blind, as well. He continued over the strand to the breaker's edge where the sand became hard and then he continued directly into the water.

"Wait!" Conor called, running after him, down the steps. Suddenly he was unable to move! The sand entrapped him and held him motionless. He stood struggling futilely to free himself, terrified as Kevin moved into the water!

"Wait! Wait!"

Kevin O'Garvey continued out steadily, waist high, to the chest, then the water passed over his face and his entire self disappeared. . . .

"Wait! Wait! Wait!"

"Conor, wake up! Conor! Conor!"

He lifted his head from the pillow as though it were a stone. Daylight flooded into the room and the curtain blew on waves of a gentle warmish breeze. Both his fists were wrapped hard around the tortured sheet, then he felt the desperation of her body pressed against him, her fingers kneading the back of his neck. "Conor!" Shelley cried.

His head dropped back on the pillow and he lay there gasping, waiting for his heart to quit pounding, then worked his way from the bed daring but a peek at her disturbed stare.

Two letters sat on the desk. A third was half written. He had stopped writing when Shelley came to him. They had made love and fallen asleep.

He said nothing, dressed quietly, pecked at breakfast, then excused himself for a solitary walk on the strand.

*

He returned in a bit over an hour with the strong edge of the nightmare flushed out of his system. As he passed through the lobby, he started. Shelley's suitcases were by the reception desk! He dashed up the stairs and flung the door open. She sat stiffly on the edge of a chair dressed to travel.

"What the devil!"

"There's a train leaving for Liverpool in about an hour," she said. "It will arrive in time to make connections with the Belfast steamer."

"But you weren't to leave till tomorrow. Of course, if you want to get back early, we'll be on our way that much sooner."

Her lack of response told him all he needed to know and only then did he see her eyes, red-rimmed. He was too frightened to speak at first. "Don't make too much of it," he said, "it was only a bad dream."

"The first of many, I fear," she answered.

"Shelley, listen to me, darling. Just now out there I thought it through and I know what matters. Two people matter and the rest of it is nothing. What have you won in the end if you don't have the love of a woman? The only thing that can keep the stink and the pain of the world away are two people with the ability to create a sanctuary of one another."

"We can't live our life in a sanctuary," she said softly. "Those who try become sterile."

"Shelley . . ."

"Let me finish. A man must do what he must do. And

a woman must do what she must do as well. What must be done must be done, no matter what agony it entails. Only then have you earned the privilege of finding a sanctuary in one another to get through the dark hours. Because, my love, when the time comes around again, you've got to go out and face it all, with all the stink and all the pain."

"No," Conor said. "I'll not do that to you. In the end it would have to be me against your family. I'll be the enemy of your father and brother. If I take you back to Ireland, you'll wither."

"And if we run, you will wither."

"Shelley, what we have is new, for we thought we'd never have it. Reaching out now, taking it, cutting the past is frightening but we've the power and the love between us."

Shelley MacLeod remained immaculately calm. Her serenity in the midst of a volcano made her all the more beautiful. "Don't you know, Larkin, I can cope with anything but an Irishman's dream? It will come pounding after us no matter where we try to hide. What we have discovered here will turn sour and, as you grow bitter, it will turn violently against us. How long can we hold it off, Conor? How long can we pretend? A year, two, three. Sooner or later it will overtake us and we will have squandered the ability to fight it. What then?"

"Shelley, I don't want to go back to Belfast! I don't want to live for this fucking thing any more. It's a bloody curse. Shelley, come with me . . ."

"And watch you die, man? Like your father, in pieces? Do you think I love you that little?"

"Shelley, I'm begging you!"

She spun out of his grasp and backed away. "Who is Kevin O'Garvey?" she cried.

Conor stiffened in his tracks.

"Who is Brendan Sean Barrett? Oh, Conor, for a few lovely days I deceived myself into believing we could do it. But all the while, under the fierceness of the lovemaking, I sensed the boiling inside you. Oh, man, I love you so . . . almost enough to run. . . ."

Like the giant of his father before him, he stood helpless against the forces that brought him to this moment.

The hurt of it made him paw helplessly at the air . . . defenseless against screaming out . . . too stricken to weep . . .

"I'll be in Belfast," she groaned, "and so will you. You'll do what you've got to do. If things get very bad, if you're alone, if you're frightened, I'll come to you. I'll always come to you. If I were married, I'd leave my husband's bed to come to you."

Conor reeled out to the porch and held the post, trembling, every inch of him. He heard her footsteps . . . and then . . . the sound of the door close. He turned slowly. Shelley was gone.

END OF PART FIVE

PART SIX
Sixmilecross

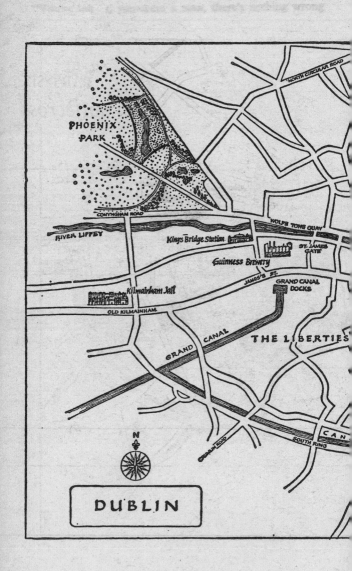

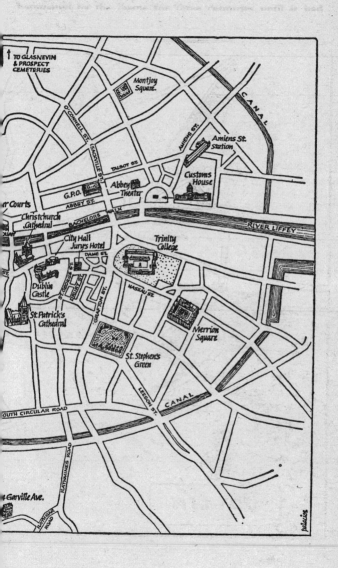

CHAPTER ONE

1905

Dudley Callaghan the mortician made contact with Conor in the Goit Side District of Bradford. The two of them waited for nightfall, then made by foot to Braddock's Coal Yard on Pool Alley. The door to the small adjoining house was opened by a severe, tight-lipped, fat old woman who led them down a short dark corridor into a bland musty room. Callaghan leaned against the wall staring like a blind man. Conor seated himself on one of the room's two chairs, which creaked under his weight. They waited. An hour passed with no word between them.

A noise out in the yard caused them to lift their eyes and catch a glimpse of a shadowed figure hastily crossing the black piles into the house. The door opened and Brendan Sean Barrett entered, looked to Callaghan and nodded for him to leave.

He was a smallish man, sallow of color, with eyes that must have been in a constant state of redness. His dress was that of a proper teacher's, but ten years old and hardly pressed since. Both man and suit were seedy with age. His nerves seemed fairly well shot, attested by heavy telltale nicotine stains on the fingers of his right hand. He was the poet whose dreams had fled.

He was deliberately unpleasant, for that was his nature, the unfulfilled intellectual who continued to hold his audience in small regard. He reeked of disdain and suspicion. He disliked almost everyone, including the new young men who would be taking over the movement. He placed himself before the table as though it were a governor's desk, the ever present cigarette held in a just-so curl of his hand.

"Callaghan reported that you came into his establishment on Wild Boar Road and left without making contact," he said, immediately going to the attack.

"Aye."

"Why?"

Conor braced himself to do business with a man who was pressing, immediately making him feel uncomfortable.

"Dan Sweeney warned me to be careful. I had feelings I might have been followed."

"What made you think so?"

"I had been followed by Weed's men for the first two months I worked at the shipyard in Belfast. I'm playing on Weed's club. There was a brawl in Swansea and some hard feelings. Besides, I didn't like making contact with Callaghan with a room full of people. Anyone could have been there doing something besides praying for the dead."

"Anything else?"

"I had some personal problems. You might know about them, you might not. They've been solved."

"What?"

"A woman. It's done with."

Brendan Sean Barrett gazed at him with his set expression of disregard, then opened the button of his jacket and untied a money belt from about his waist and slid it across the table. "Hand this over to Dan Sweeney personally."

Conor took it, lifted his shirt and tied it about his own waist.

"There's three thousand. I think you'd better count it first."

"No need for that," Conor said. "We're trusting each other with a lot more than money."

The corners of Barrett's lips turned up slightly. "We are going forward with the guns. O'Hurley and Hanly have been contacted. They are in."

Conor seized up for an instant, a feeling of weak swooning came and went and he returned to Barrett's unyielding glare. "How much did we have to pay them?"

"What makes you think that?"

"What makes you think I'm a fool? I don't know too much about them but I do know there isn't a drop of republican blood in their bodies. They're too comfortable and they like their status."

Barrett lit a cigarette with the butt of the old one and

scratched the back of a hand always on the verge of bleeding from the itch. "You're right, of course. We had to buy them. One quid per rifle, one hundred for each delivery."

Conor's fist cracked the table. "Fucking thieves. It's half the cost of the guns themselves!"

"Well, we got them for a steal, one might say. Maybe next time we'll find a bargain-rate revolution for you to follow. Listen to me, then repeat. Proceed to Liverpool tonight. Take a room at the Moorfields Hotel opposite the Exchange Rail Terminal at Pall Mall and Titheborn . . ."

"I know the place."

"Good. Do not leave your room. You will be contacted by either Owen O'Sullivan or one of his sons, Brian or Barry. The one making contact will identify himself by handing you a copy of my pamphlet, 'The Ultimate Tyranny.' You will identify yourself by saying the words, 'Oh, that's the one he wrote in Strangeways Prison.' Beyond that, they know who you are and you will know who they are. They can be completely trusted."

"Does Duffy O'Hurley know that I'm the one?"

"No, not yet. It could abort. There's a touchy question of getting the train into O'Sullivan's foundry. If it's still clear when you reach Liverpool, you will be taken to O'Sullivan's works at Waterloo Road and Boundary Street, six o'clock tomorrow. There's a rail siding directly into their factory. The rifles, and all the necessary materials you requested to make the conversion, will be ready."

Conor repeated it to Brendan Sean Barrett's satisfaction, then he rose.

Conor wanted to ask more details. Beyond that he wanted to know something about the man opposite him. He wanted to know about Barrett's early heroic stands, his writings, his hunger strike, but the man before him was a waste, a shadow making no move to be civilized, much less friendly.

"You might as well know, Larkin, I've poor little faith in the plan."

"Why?"

"Everything we attempt of this nature goes wrong. There might be more harm in it than good if the price of those rifles means exposing people like Sweeney. But then again, Dan Sweeney is the chief of staff of our non-existent army and he sees things one way. I see them another. However, I'm only one vote on the Supreme Council." Brendan Sean Barrett extended his hand with all the warmth of a disinterested bishop about to have his ring kissed. "I'll leave. Wait ten minutes before your own departure."

Conor watched him slither through the coal yard into the night. Dudley Callaghan returned.

"Is he always that pleasant?" Conor asked.

"He's gutted. I've worked on corpses with more life. Everything's dead in him except his mind. It refuses to stop working. He was a man you could love once. Be honored to just sit at his feet and listen to him expound."

They waited the designated time, each departing in a different direction. Dudley Callaghan went immediately to retrieve the first hundred rifles from their dump and ready them for shipment to Liverpool. Conor left for that city on the late train.

●

Coffins bound for Ireland were not uncommon on the Liverpool docks. More than half of Callaghan's clients were returned to the old country for burial and the same held true in all the "little Irelands" in the English cities.

On the late express of that same night two coffins, each containing twenty Lee-Enfield Mark I rifles, arrived at the freight depot of the Exchange Terminal. Three more arrived on the morning mail, all consigned to the O. O'Sullivan Foundry for decorative work and transshipment to Ireland. The large number of coffins had been decided upon so the weight of each was kept close to that of an average corpse, thus avoiding suspicion. In the future, when this route was firmly established, coffins from Callaghan would arrive at frequent intervals to be stored in Liverpool and held in readiness.

Brian and Barry O'Sullivan, lads in their mid-twenties, arrived at the freight docks with two flat-bed wagons, received the coffins and made to the foundry, a short distance away.

●

The hours of Conor Larkin ticked off agonizingly. This was the dirty end of the business, the loneliness in the empty room. The torn curtain, the sagging bed, the life in semishadow. From here on out loneliness and waiting would be his brother and his sister. The limit of his discipline was called upon to close off thoughts of her or hunger for her. To linger in those kinds of memories would devastate him. Years of this were up ahead . . . he had to learn. He was now the disciple of Sweeney and Barrett. The rock was back in place before the entrance of the cave and he would never enter it again.

Nor would pacing the room and looking out to the street every few minutes or watching the clock be of much help. Discipline. Alone. Wait.

He picked up the pamphlet, "The Ultimate Tyranny," which he had found at a secondhand stall. It was crumpled with age. Brendan Sean Barrett was too arrogant to ask if he'd read it but still had enough life in him to say, "Read this, boy, I was once something myself in my own right." BY BRENDAN SEAN BARRETT from his cell in Strangeways Prison, Manchester, 1880.

The British subjugation of Ireland constitutes the most abhorrent of all occupations. In ways it is even more cruel than the Spanish occupation of the Hispaniola Group (Cuba, Puerto Rico, Santo Domingo and Haiti). The Spaniards systematically destroyed two million native Indians and replaced them with imported black slaves, thus erasing their culture in a single stroke. Similarly, the Spaniards destroyed the three original American cultures, the Mayan, the Aztec and the Incan.

British conquest in areas such as India, the West Indies and the like shows a different pattern of intent. The British governed in these places by compacts with the local rulers, maharajahs, tribal alliances which declared loyalty to the Crown. Although much of British law, education, language and government was adopted by the native, the Crown kept an aloofness from them and each pursued his own unique culture.

The conquest of Ireland shows a throwback to the Spanish occupations in which the old was destroyed. The Spaniards simply murdered and replaced the old with the new. The British attempted to superimpose the new upon the old, allowing the native to survive or die on economic considerations.

British intent was not only to occupy, govern and exploit Ireland but to eradicate the Celtic culture and superimpose an Anglican culture upon a people totally alien to it. By guile, gun, coercion and quasi-legal manipulation, the British have attempted to divest the native Irishman of his language, his religion, his lore, his literature, his traditions and his customs. The ultimate goal, therefore, to first sterilize the Irish people, then rebuild them into Anglicans. . . .

The Town Hall clock rang the hour in unison with a knock on the door. Conor opened it and faced a young man of good Irish looks.

"Larkin?"

"Aye."

"Barry O'Sullivan."

"Come in, Barry."

"I brought you a copy of 'The Ultimate Tyranny' but I see you have one."

"Yes, that's the one written by himself when he was in Strangeways Prison."

At that the two shook hands warmly. Conor's bags were packed, for they had not really been unpacked. Barry took one as Conor tightened the strap about the other, looked around the room briefly, and they left.

As they turned on the waterfront at New Quay, Conor began to calculate in terms of distances and potential obstacles. They were at the Prince's Dock, which held the Riverside Rail Station and the trains for the Belfast steamer. The Red Hand Express was always housed there when it was in Liverpool. Tracks continued to parallel Bath Street, which became Waterloo Road after a few blocks. They came to a halt at Boundary Street. O. O'SULLIVAN AND SONS, the sign read, BELL FOUNDRY AND REPAIR YARD. The rails led directly into a fenced enclosure, then into a large building.

Two men awaited them by the door.

"My brother Brian, my father Owen. Conor Larkin."

Brian seemed the twin of Barry in looks though a few years younger. The elder O'Sullivan was a Kerryman with a ready smile and the air of one who had been nothing but a republican all his life. The main shop of the foundry was impressive, a complete line of molds for rail bells, ship bells and other marine fittings as well as molds for tower bells. The shop did a potpourri of repairs, mostly on the small shuttle engines that worked the dock area. There was a complete forge as well and overhead block and tackle hoists.

"Quite a place you've got here, Owen. When is our train due?"

"Half eight."

"Come along, Larkin, let me show you what we've done."

As they passed out to the yard, Owen O'Sullivan told of his devotion to the cause, boasted he was a self-made man and otherwise advanced his own image to the newcomer. He was, indeed, one of the thousands of the dormant in the "little Irelands" of England and in Ireland itself who would be tapped somewhere along the line. Conor had learned that strongly during the tour.

A large storage shed was unlocked and they entered. The yards of oilcloth and buckets of grease Conor had asked for were waiting, as was the steel plate he needed to cover and conceal the cut he'd have to make on the water tender. Two boxes to hold the weapons were completed, cast in thin bronze and absolutely watertight.

"By God, Owen, they're works of art. I didn't expect anything this fancy. They're fit for a king's coffin."

"Aw, what the devil," he answered, "it's for the Brotherhood. Good-lookin' boxes, you think? I done the molds myself and me and the boys made the plate by night after the rest of the crew quit work." He walked to the far end of the shed and pointed to five coffins resting on the floor. "There's the bodies."

"From Callaghan?"

"From Callaghan. Dear departed souls for their final rest in Ireland. Barry, fetch me a crowbar."

The lid squealed open under his prying. There lay the guns. The four of them stared, just stared.

"We should say something profound," Owen said.

Conor reached down and took one up. He studied the piece from muzzle to butt, worked the bolt, snapped the trigger, opened the sights, aimed, then handed it to Owen O'Sullivan.

Conor rubbed coal dust on his fingers and grunted. He gathered they had been dumped in colliery pits around Bradford. "They're in terrible condition. I have no idea of where they're going to be dumped in Ireland or how much time we'll have to get them cleaned. We'd best get them protected as well as possible here. I saw you've steam in your shop."

"I do."

"Put your boys on the chore. Pull the bolts and we'll need a vat of hot soapy water, a vat of fresh water, then steam. We'll paint them up afterward with grease and wrap the lot in oilcloths."

"Got that, Barry?" his father asked.

"Yes, sir."

The bronze boxes, the covering plate and the guns were taken to the main shop. By half eight the gun cleaning was on at full gallop. Brian went outside to watch for the train. Nothing in sight. It would be hard to bring it in precisely on the minute. With the gun cleaning moving along well, Conor told the boy to stay out on watch.

Nine o'clock. Nothing.

As the minutes ticked off the tension began to rise. The guns were cleaned and ready. The first of the bronze boxes was attached to a block and tackle ready to swing into the tender car.

Half nine.

"What do you think we ought to do?" Owen said, showing the first tinge of nerves.

"Give it another ten minutes, then we'd better get the guns out of here in case the wrong people have found out. Do you have a dump, Owen?"

"We've made provisions."

"Ten minutes," Conor said. "We load up, dump them and I'll go snooping around for O'Hurley. Come on now, Owen, don't look so grim."

"I didn't figure on this. Callaghan said the train was arranged."

"Probably a simple explanation."

Five minutes went by, then ten. Just as Conor was to call for the guns to be removed, Brian rushed in.

"It's coming."

The doors were cracked apart. The Red Hand Express was inched in. Duffy O'Hurley was alone in the car and climbed down unevenly. His eyes were bleary and his breath a blend of rare Irish whiskeys. Conor came before him.

"So it's you, Conor," O'Hurley said. "I thought maybe it was you . . ."

"Where in the hell have you been!"

O'Hurley grumbled uneasily and burped out a story that Sir Frederick had sent him on a last-minute trip. He was unable to contact O'Sullivan and inform him. Conor knew what had really taken place . . . last-minute fear. He had to decide on whether to buy the story or abort the plan. O'Hurley was tanked up on dutch courage and even at a hundred pounds a trip it might be a bad bargain.

"Where's Calhoun?" Conor snapped.

"I . . . I . . . I . . . didn't think he'd be needed at all. I left him off at a pub . . ."

"We're shorthanded and we've lost time. Where is he?"

O'Hurley scratched his head and tried to remember. It was useless. "What are you going to do with my baby?" he wailed.

Conor looked back and forth from the silent men to the guns to the tender. He made his judgment. "Brian, get this bastard some coffee. You get yourself sobered up!"

"But you said yourself it was too late . . ." O'Hurley mumbled.

Conor snatched him by the shirt with a strength he had never known before. "You're in and you're not getting out. You got it, Duffy?"

O'Hurley whined weakly.

"Now get a grip on yourself," Conor snarled. He climbed up on the tender and threw back the manhole cover to the water tank. "The fucking thing is full and so is the coal bin. Goddammit, Duffy, didn't anybody tell you to bring this in empty?"

"Jesus . . . I . . . I'm sorry . . . I got confused."

"Take the train outside to the yard and dump the water, then go find that goddam fireman of yours. Brian, you and Barry better start shoveling some of this coal out."

"What are you going to do with my baby?"

"Shut up, drive that train outside and dump that water. We've got time to make up."

As the train was eased outside, Owen placed a hand on Conor's shoulder. "We'll make it on time," he said softly. "The man's scared. You've seen men scared before. Only this one happens to drive a train we need and we can't replace him."

"I'm still thinking of calling it off."

"Conor, we've waited too damned long. What's more, we'll be dealing with a lot more frightened men before we're through. You better get him calmed down."

"I want to spit on him, Owen, that's what. A hundred quid." Then he looked to the older man. He knew at that instant O'Sullivan was a leader. He steadied everyone in an instant while Conor had hovered on anger and indecision.

"I'm thinking," Owen said, "as we get into this deeper some of our best men might have rotten motives and fits of fear. It's best not to stand in judgment now, just get the job done."

"Sometimes I'm too much of a bloody loner," Conor whispered.

With the tender emptied, Conor and Owen O'Sullivan used their torches like surgical instruments. With the top of the tank cut away, the bronze boxes were lowered and bolted into place, then filled with rifles. With this done, the thin steel plate was put back into place to cover the scars and then the tanker was refilled.

O'Hurley's fears subsided throughout the night as he saw the precision of their work. Unless one knew and was looking hard, it would be impossible to detect.

An hour before daylight the Red Hand Express rolled out of the O'Sullivan Foundry onto Sir Frederick's rail steamer at the Prince's Dock. Destination Belfast.

The Boilermakers had gathered for their triumphant return to Ulster, although without the Hubble family. Lord Jeremy had been banished to Trinity College in Dublin and the Earl of Foyle had once and for all time divested himself of further pretense about that team.

For a week the train remained in its shed at the Weed Ship & Iron Works. On the eighth day after their return, Duffy O'Hurley, now a portrait of calm, sought out Conor at his forge and informed him a trip had been scheduled.

The train picked up Lord Roger in Derry and continued down to Dublin for his regular monthly economic conference at the Castle. While Roger remained in Dublin, the train deadheaded back to Belfast. En route it pulled to a siding near Drogheda where a covered motor van and four members of the Brotherhood lay in wait. The coal was shoveled away from the top, the water level lowered, the covering plate removed and the bronze boxes emptied of their treasure within a half hour.

The Irish Republican Brotherhood had received its first arms of the twentieth century.

CHAPTER TWO

1906

Gloom at the Union Preservation Party headquarters was stifling. After a night filled with concerned telephone calls, the telegraph tape from London petered out, having related the full devastating news. The Conservative Party with their Ulster allies, the Unionists, had been crushed in the election. A decade and a half of imperial-minded rule was done.

Sir Frederick and Lord Roger emerged from the inner council room through the gathering of the shattered loyal. Weed intoned a few words to the effect that Ulster would continue to fight Home Rule despite the Liberal landslide. He was greeted with feeble applause.

Outside, a brisk dawn air greeted the two smack on. As they turned down Great Victoria Street in graylight, only the tapping of their canes and the clip-clop of their carriage trailing them punctuated the silence. Reaching the Hotel Antrim, they retreated at once to Sir Frederick's apartment and were joined shortly by Brigadier Swan to assess the damage.

It was not as though the country were in any sudden new grip of republican outcry but the Home Rule issue would be on the rise again. How much would the nationalistic new Sinn Fein Party benefit?

Home Rule talk always shivered the Ulster industrial establishment. Her competitive position depended largely on keeping the province a decade behind England in wages and workers' conditions. Swan, Hubble and Weed needed no amplification of the threat.

Yet there was a queer bit of luck in the election. In the past the Liberals had depended upon the Irish Party to form a coalition government. In return for their support the Irish had always extracted a promise of Home Rule. This time the Liberal victory was so overwhelming, they held a majority without the Irish and really didn't need them. On their own and without Irish pressure, the Liberals had shown they were not in any rush to give Home Rule. Of course the bottom line of protection for the Unionists was, as always, a veto of Home Rule in the House of Lords.

Roger was pensive, speaking little. "I say, you're being funereal," Weed said.

"What it boils down to is that, eventually, we are going to have to play the entire Orange card over. Perhaps again and again."

That grim message settled in as the butler appeared. "Beg pardon, Sir Frederick. The Reverend MacIvor is in the lobby and wishes to see you."

"Oh, horseshit," Weed grumbled, "he's the last person I want to see today. Tell him I'm indisposed."

"No, wait a minute," Roger said, "let's hear what the enlightened one has on his mind."

Oliver Cromwell MacIvor had flourished through the years far beyond the generosities of his benefactor. With his Savior's Church of the Shankill filled to overflowing and no longer in need of Sir Frederick's charity, he heightened his sights and ambitions. By singular decree he proclaimed a new sect, the Universal Presbyterian Church, establishing a Protestant version of a quasi-papal state.

To back up "his" new church, the Universal Presbyterian Missionary and Theological Center was established adjoining his Lord's house in the Shankill. Churches of the new faith sprang up in Londonderry, Larne, East Belfast and Dungannon, with a dozen more in the planning. A publishing house spewed out MacIvor's mass-oriented fundamentalist gospel with the right hand and a damnation of Rome with the left.

As his power over the masses expanded, he dived into the Orange Order, attaining high rank, and sniffed on the perimeter of the Unionist Party. Throughout his rise, MacIvor's excessive language and occasional incitement to riot were tolerated by the authorities, for they blended with the over-all Ulster scheme. Roger had warned Sir Frederick time and time again that MacIvor's growing independence was a threat but Weed reckoned the day would never come when he could not bring the man under control.

Oliver Cromwell MacIvor was shown into the parlor. The man was never out of touch with his personal magnetism. The offer of tea was expected and accepted.

"We are all exhausted," the little preacher said, "from two nights of vigil and prayer. This is a tragic day for Christians." His thin lips suckled at the teacup, causing Weed to wince.

"Obviously we're all a bit down," Sir Frederick said, "but on the whole we do not anticipate any drastic upheavals. We are firmly of the opinion that Home Rule legislation is still years off and surely Lords will support us with a veto when that time does come."

MacIvor set the cup down and emitted the kind of holier-than-thou glare that turned his flock into the jibers, although it had little effect in this room. "Ulster has entered the valley of the shadow. It is no time to play word games with the Protestant folk of this province whose very existence is in jeopardy."

Roger astutely set himself on the man. It seemed obvious to him that MacIvor was sniffing about to find his head in some sort of power play. Just what position did he believe himself to be in? What was his card?

"I dare say, Reverend," Sir Frederick continued the dialogue, "overreaction at this stage could very well boomerang on us. I'm in touch with many of these Liberal chaps. It's one thing to promise Irish Home Rule during a political campaign, it's another thing to come through with that promise. I really don't think we ought to run up a hurricane warning. Let's wait and see what their intentions are. My guess is that the Home Rule issue will just sit and rot."

This brought MacIvor to his feet deliberately. "I cannot see how you fail to read the writing on the wall. I cannot see how you choose to remain inert with a dagger now poised at our throats."

Well, of course, Sir Frederick reckoned, the man's

penchant for evangelical powerglory, pending disaster and forecasts of doom were all part of the fuel that stoked his ovens. Yet his tone and manner were changed. He seemed, at the moment, transformed from beholden to beholder. The pretense of spontaneity was a game he played on his flock but Weed knew the man was never spontaneous, but an infinite calculator. Just how long had he been awaiting a political disaster? The sting of the election had not yet been felt and something new seemed in the making in the way things were in Ulster.

"You may continue to procrastinate," MacIvor said, "but I am prepared to answer the disaster that has befallen us by inspired divine revelation. I am going to call for a province-wide crusade in which we will organize every Christian man, woman and child to defend his freedom and British heritage."

Swan and Roger exchanged glances as they watched Sir Frederick contain his urge to boil. Weed unearthed a cigar with deliberate severity and, without asking MacIvor's leave, lit it up. "I suggest you tread softly," he said in what was obviously an order.

"And I suggest I am not seeking your advice in the matter," MacIvor responded.

So that was it! A cutting of the umbilical cord. Snip! Just like that.

"The problem," MacIvor continued, "is your complacency. You've failed time and again to recognize the growing dangers. You've answered these satanic papist schemes with pacification. In the past three years you've stood by idly while the Crown has bought up tens of thousands of acres of Protestant land and turned around and all but given it away to the very people who have vowed to destroy us."

Weed's patience narrowed. "See here," he snapped, "the Land Act has done nothing more than take over encumbered, useless acreage from indebted estate owners."

"And given it to the papists!"

"Gentlemen," Swan said quickly, "we are all shaken by the election. I think we should allow the moment to settle and then we should all sit down when our thoughts are clear and reorganize our strategy."

"Perhaps your interests and the interests of the common folk of this province have grown irreparably apart," MacIvor answered.

"Am I to understand this to mean a disassociation between ourselves, Reverend?" Weed said bluntly.

"You may take it to mean, sir, that I am no longer bound to your advice or decisions. You may soon see a groundswell of little people from the Shankill to Londonderry who aren't so content to allow their freedom to be robbed and will seek new directions in their leadership."

"You've thought this out for a long time, haven't you?" Sir Frederick said softly. "For fifteen years you've been breeding on adversity and waiting for the Conservatives to fall from power. Good day, Reverend MacIvor."

Before the preacher could launch a tirade, Swan had him by the arm and walked him out the door. Oddly, Sir Frederick did not explode in the face of the affront. He was shaken.

"What do you make of it, Roger?"

"Obviously, we've been handed a bill of divorce," Roger said.

"Horseshit! I still employ half of Belfast. If they don't know out there where their bread is buttered, they'll soon find out."

"How? It won't be that easy. Would you care to go to the reverend's church and debate with him from the pulpit? You see, Freddie, it's the same bloody thing that happened four decades ago in England. Gladstone came up with all that reform and campaigned outside of his constituency. He caught the ear of the masses and for the first time in English history the people rejected the wisdom of the ruling class and the gentry and changed it for populist reform and populist politicians close to their own breed."

Sir Frederick knew Roger was right. Ulster had been deliberately kept behind England. While Gladstone's Liberals pushed through reform, Ireland and Ulster were locked in a struggle of nationalism. One party fought for Home Rule, the other party struggled against it. Ireland continued to lag in social reform and thus created a vacuum. With the defeat of the Conservatives, Ulster was serving notice that it, too, was rejecting the age-old rule of the gentry and seeking out its own populist voices.

"We can no longer count on the people here to follow us automatically and blindly," Roger said.

Sir Frederick slowly chilled to ashen with the truth of his calculation.

"MacIvor has figured that he is strong enough to rush in and fill the empty space. He will summon up that old breed of Ulstermen and try to lead them politically."

"I'll break his balls if it's my last act on this earth," Weed menaced.

Roger Hubble, ever the pragmatist, seemed skeptical. "Our problem is that we deliberately set up MacIvor and a lot of little MacIvors as our spokesmen to the masses. They've been conditioned to listen to him. We've created a monster and we've no real way to communicate to the Shankill except through that monster."

Ashes dripped from Weed's cigar. He brushed off his trousers aimlessly. "You told me time and again this sort of thing would happen."

"I had always hoped that somewhere along the line we could abandon MacIvor and his ilk. Yet we've been so consumed with this Home Rule fight we've had to keep him. I personally have worked with the Irish in Dublin Castle long enough to realize that by and large they are decent people. Sometimes I believed we could compromise and work things out with them. But always there is this big Orange ogre of our own creation between us. I suppose that the English and Irish always manage to bring out what is worst in ourselves and each other."

"So that dirty little bastard thinks he can replace the ruling class of Ireland. Well, thank God the Crown doesn't see it that way. In a showdown I think even the Liberals will stand with us."

"Today they will. Once Ulster's balance sheet shows red ink, England will bail out."

"Do you really believe that, Roger? Deep down, do you really believe it?"

"We are here to show a profit, you and I. What happens when we're no longer profitable?"

"How are we to combat Mr. MacIvor?"

"Do nothing for the time being. After a time he'll come to realize he can't go it alone and he'll come back to make an accord with us."

"I'll never deal with that scum, never!"

"Oh, it might not be all that bad, Freddie. There may be a shift in power but MacIvor's still really fronting our cause. Could you imagine for an instant how ruinous it would be if MacIvor were a Gladstone? If suddenly we were confronted with a voice appealing to the masses who was bent on social and labor reforms? We can be grateful that he's done his job keeping the good Ulster folks' minds on the Reformation. He's a dog with only one trick. He'll keep the Catholic and Protestant mobs separated and fighting one another. He'll buy us time."

CHAPTER THREE: Ordination Sunday.

The great day arrived for Dary Larkin several years ahead of time due to his sizable inheritance of family brains. He had been moved up in his studies a number of times and was to be among the youngest priests ever ordained out of St. Patrick's College at Maynooth.

Ireland exported most things in modest quantity, save emigrants, Guinness, Donegal tweed, Waterford crystal and . . . priests. Priests to tend Irish exiles about the world and priests as missionaries who went to places only an Irish priest would go. Dary Larkin chose a missionary order.

His final advancement had come quickly, once he declared for the order. A new course had been inaugurated at the church-run University College in Dublin in African languages to which a small select group of priests had been nominated. When Dary was accepted to these classes, his Bishop obtained approval for ordination by papal petition.

Priesthood was a great event in the life of an Irish family. Despite the personal leanings of Conor and myself we had dealt with too many free-spirited Wolfe Tone republicans in the priesthood and the excitement of the day rubbed off on us as well.

The night before the event I met Conor at the station in Dublin, setting eyes on him for the first time in many months. He was a sorely changed man, for all vestiges of youth had flown. He had not seen his woman, Shelley

MacLeod, since his return to Belfast and the sorrow of it was plain enough for me to see. Although Conor had come to terms with it, my own feeling was that he would never truly get over her. Continuing to live in Belfast and only a few minutes' walk from her house must have caused him daily pain but, Conor being Conor, I expected he would make little mention of her to me.

I am certain that Conor wanted to leave Belfast at this point but one might say he was a victim of his own success. Because of his rugby prowess he remained a favorite of Sir Frederick and continued a relationship with Jeremy Hubble as a sort of big brother.

Although Conor was assigned to a particular blacksmith shop in the yard, he had complete freedom and worked mostly on special projects and commissions. Some of the time found him doing wrought iron jobs at Rathweed Hall, Sir Frederick's home.

For our purposes, his situation was absolutely perfect.

My second play was running at the Abbey. Conor promised to remain in Dublin for a few days after Dary's ordination and see the work. Well, don't you know, any day I get to talk the night through with that lad was a grand one. I had looked forward to it for weeks. Yet when the moment came I found him terribly inward.

I waited patiently for that explosion that usually came halfway down the bottle but this time he only grew more somber. We spoke mostly of the continued success of the Brotherhood and the gunrunning operation. Sir Frederick Weed's lovely private train had made four lovely trips to England since the rugby tour and had returned with two hundred rifles, a hundred carbines and ten thousand rounds of ammunition. The whole operation had been a masterpiece of silk. Conor's main concern was the erratic behavior of Duffy O'Hurley, who blew hot and cold.

Conor had come up with a second scheme on dumping the guns around the country. The Brotherhood knew sympathetic priests in Belfast, Dublin, Cork, Derry, Newry, Waterford and Mallow, which were along the route most traveled by Weed's train. Once dropped, the guns were placed in coffins and the "bodies" buried in churchyards with the aid of the priests. Tombstones bearing the names of either Carrick, Cassidy, Conroy, Coughlin, Concannon or Considine marked where the guns

lay. The first name of Elva, 1879–1904, and the
engraving, *A True Daughter of Erin,* held one of the
stashes of weapons.

*

Early the next morning Conor and I returned to the
Amiens Street Station for Brigid's arrival. She debarked
greeting us awkwardly, for it was by far the longest
journey to the biggest city in her life.

Now, a man couldn't precisely say she'd aged lovely.
For the occasion Brigid had garbed herself in store-
bought clothes from Derry that might never come out of
the closet again. And what she was wearing were
strangers giving one another no comfort at all. She limped
as well from the pinch of her new shoes. Appearances
aside, greetings were long and warm for this momentous
occasion.

We transferred to the Westland Row Station for the
short ride to Maynooth in County Kildare where St.
Patrick's College stood in a setting of magnificent
serenity on the site of an ancient Fitzgerald castle.

By noon the gathering of families from all over the
country milled about on the green before the Chapel. Half
of them seemed equally out of place as Brigid. The
Chapel left nothing undone as a showpiece, a Gothic
wonderment thirty years in the building and crafted
literally by hand in marble, wood and mosaic. Why, the
choir stalls alone held half a thousand men. The sense of
tension and exhilaration built as we entered that
awesomely high-ceilinged domain.

Concelebration commenced with the lavabo, a ritual
of cleansing of hands and feet by the candidates, who then
entered the nave fanfared by a thundering of the mighty
Stahluhut organ. They moved majestically down the aisle
all white aflow in their albs, amices, chasubles, gemials,
cinctures and stoles.

And there was wee Dary still the smallest of the lot and
half again as smart. We all exchanged smiles as he spotted
us and Brigid joined the brigade of sniffling women.

The Bishop arrived between a pair of priests and
enthroned himself.

"Let those who are to be ordained priests come
forward," the deacon summoned. "Martin MacRannall."

"I am ready and willing."

"Edwin O'Meagher."

"I am ready and willing."

"Dary Larkin."

"I am ready and willing."

"Pearse MacSheehy . . ." until all twenty candidates had been tolled.

"Do you know if they are worthy?" the Bishop inquired when they had all arrayed themselves before his seat, looking like a pile of white sheep shearings.

"I testify that upon inquiry among the people of God, and upon recommendation of those concerned with their training, they have been found worthy."

The Bishop droned from memory as to their coming life and duties and questioned them on their worthiness and rendered an oath of obedience and then they prostrated themselves before him on the marble floor, becoming a candent cloud.

Having been presented, elected, instructed, examined, vowed and invited to prayer, the concelebration reached the Litany of the Saints.

Lord have mercy	Lord have mercy
Christ have mercy	Christ have mercy
Lord have mercy	Lord have mercy
Holy Mary, Mother of God	Pray for us
Saint Michael	Pray for us
All you holy angels	Pray for us
Saint Joseph	Pray for us
Saint John the Baptist	Pray for us
Saints Peter and Paul	Pray for us
Saint Andrew	Pray for us
Saint John	Pray for us
Saint Mary Magdalen	Pray for us
Saint Stephen	Pray for us
Saint Laurence	Pray for us
Saint Ignatius of Antioch	Pray for us
Saint Agnes	Pray for us
Saints Perpetua and Felicity	Pray for us
Saint Gregory	Pray for us
Saint Augustine	Pray for us
Saint Athanasius	Pray for us
Saint Basil	Pray for us

Saint Martin	*Pray for us*
Saint Benedict	*Pray for us*
Saints Francis and Dominic	*Pray for us*
Saint Francis Xavier	*Pray for us*
Saint John Vianney	*Pray for us*
Saint Theresa	*Pray for us*
Saint Catherine	*Pray for us*

It was a staggering ritual and Conor and I loved Dary enough to set aside our own bitterness toward the religion and share his glory.

Yet, as they droned into the Irish saints, all two hundred and seventeen of them from Abben to Our Lady of Youghal, that old queasy feeling crawled into my stomach. I had not said the rosary since I'd left Ballyutogue.

Halfway through all the Irish saints, all the Irish saints in Scotland, all the Irish saints in England and all the Irish saints in Europe I was having a job keeping my peace.

Only a few weeks earlier I had written an essay on the premise that if two hundred and seventeen saints acting as demigods wasn't paganism, what was? Our people fall on their knees to dull-eyed idols in a saint worship we would condemn as paganism by a black man in an African tribe.

Was it not paganism to ask a statue for fertility of field and fertility of womb, for rain when it's dry and sun when it's mildew? To throw away crutches at shrines filled with saints, to ask a saint to win at sports, smite the enemy, cause warts to disappear, find gold, keep the butter from spoiling?

How much light, how much truth, have we shut out by blind obedience? Or could we have borne the truth of our poverty and servitude? Did we require the false hopes to ease the pain of living?

In all this awesome splendor I wondered about this hold . . . this terrible mysterious hold on an otherwise enlightened people. Is there an inherent weakness in most people that requires a mystery to keep them going?

Saint Turninus	*Pray for us*
Saint Tutilo	*Pray for us*

Saint Craik Ultan   *Pray for us*
Saint Fosses Ultan   *Pray for us*
Saint Ursinus   *Pray for us*
Saint Aosta Ursus   *Pray for us*
Saints Wiro and Plechelm   *Pray for us*
Our Lady of Youghal!   *Pray for us*
      OUR LADY OF YOUGHAL! I made it!
All men and women, saints of God Pray for us
Lord, spare us   *Lord, deliver us*
From all evil   *Lord, deliver us*
From all sin   *Lord, deliver us*
From everlasting death   *Lord, deliver us*
From the mystery of your incarnation
                                   Lord, deliver us
By your death and resurrection   *Lord, deliver us*
By the sending of the Holy Spirit *Lord, deliver us*
Be merciful to us sinners   We ask you, hear our prayer
Guide and protect your holy church
                       We ask you, hear our prayer
Keep our Pope and all the clergy faithful in religion
                       We ask you, hear our prayer
Grant peace and unity to all nations
                       We ask you, hear our prayer
Strengthen and keep us in your service
                       We ask you, hear our prayer
Bless these chosen ones   We ask you, hear our prayer
Bless these chosen ones and make them holy
                       We ask you, hear our prayer
Bless these chosen ones, make them holy and set
them apart for sacred duties
                       We ask you, hear our prayer
Jesus, Son of the living God, Christ, hear us,
                                   Christ, hear us

As the soft inspirational light bathed the mighty hall
and the moment pressed ever closer, the Bishop prayed
long, hard and ancient, then touched their hands and
heads, attired himself holy, fed them ceremonially and
planted upon them the kiss of peace.

Outside on the lawn in the burst of relief and flow of
tears, photographers plied a thriving business before the
stupendous tower for that photograph that hung in fifty
thousand Irish homes and cottages. Over and over and over

the gathered tested out that revered word, "Father."
"Father Dary," Brigid wept, "Father Dary."

CHAPTER FOUR: My play, *The Night of the Pilgrim*,
was neither stop nor go. It had a few sparkling moments
including a stirring soliloquy near the final curtain, a
speech from the dock, no less, that never failed to mist up
every Irish eye that saw it.

If there was a saving grace in *The Night of the Pilgrim*
it was Atty Fitzpatrick, who played the leading role. When
she agreed to do the part, they say you could hear my
heart sing clear to Tralee.

Dublin in particular was a man's world, with its pubs
and sporting scene. Our good Catholic girls learned their
catechisms, bore their children and remained docile on
worldly matters. Yet the revival was giving birth to a
number of extraordinary ladies cut of different cloth. This
breed, Anglo-ascendants for the most part, had been
moved to outrage over the centuries of British misrule.
None was more beautiful, more volatile than Atty
Fitzpatrick, a sort of Irish Joan of Arc. Long Dan
Sweeney himself characterized her as the best fighter in
the Brotherhood and sometimes the only one with balls
on the Supreme Council.

She was born into this world as the daughter of Lord
and Lady Royce-Moore, a landowning institution out of
County Galway. By the time Atty Royce-Moore reached
her twenties she had had her seasons of social graces and
schooling in London and on the Continent. She had also
been fatally bitten by the plight of the peasants and before
her twenty-first birthday renounced her own class.

The first that Ireland was to know of Atty was when she
became sole inheritor of the family holdings. She
immediately broke up the estate by selling parcels for
pittances to the peasants who had farmed it since time
eternal. The move shocked the gentry and British down
to their imperial roots but also endeared her to the
people.

Atty was ever on the gallop. If a rent and rate strike
was going on in Wexford or Waterford or an epidemic

struck the Liberties in Dublin or if evictions grew heavy in
the west, she was at the head of the protest. She had been
jailed twice for her activities and boasted that it was her
intention to be guest of the Crown in every bridewell in
Ireland before she was through. And a mere woman at
that.

Well, not exactly. She was a lithe, statuesque beauty,
standing taller than most men and casting an image only
slightly less than that of Mother Ireland herself.

Her marriage to Desmond Fitzpatrick seemed as natural
as heather in the mountains. Fitzpatrick was the scion of
an old Norman Catholic family of that number who had
originally conquered Ireland for the English in the twelfth
century. After a time the Normans integrated so
completely they became "more Irish than the Irish." The
old families, the Morrises, Fitzgeralds, Barrys, Roches,
Burkes, Plunketts, Joyces, Fitzgibbons and Fitzhughs,
fared better than the croppies down through the ages.
Before their integration they were the mighty "Earls of
Ireland." As the Catholics emerged from their dark age,
our non-Anglo middle and upper class was largely of
Norman background.

Young Desmond Fitzpatrick was an early follower of
Parnell, a barrister who fought the peasants' cause in the
courts with stunning success. When they married and
moved to Dublin, they plunged into the Gaelic revival
with unabated fervor. Atty converted to Catholicism and
in between bearing three children carried on her own
work relentlessly. They were patrons of the fledgling
national theater where she found time to participate as an
actress, mostly to help new playwrights.

The Fitzpatricks immediately identified with Arthur
Griffith when he formed the Sinn Fein political party and
were among the first secret members of the reviving Irish
Republican Brotherhood.

Desmond Fitzpatrick dropped dead in the Four Courts
defending a croppy at the age of thirty-eight. I was there
when it happened.

We who loved her watched her closely for what seemed
to be a crushing tragedy. Instead of the expected retrenchment, Atty battled her way out of her grief by fanatical
devotion to the movement. Desmond Fitzpatrick had
become among the first of our new martyrs and his widow

venerated him with brilliance. Yet I was sometimes given to ponder just how deeply love ran between them. I came to the conclusion that the real power of their union had been based on a foundation of republicanism and that that was more important to them in their marriage than being man and woman.

All of this is to say that my play was smiled upon when she accepted the role several months after widowhood. I was nervous as a prostitute in the Vatican when Conor came to see *The Night of the Pilgrim* and redeemed by a bear hug of approval at the final curtain.

We went backstage to meet Atty and set up a late go in the pub at Jury's Hotel, a watering hole for the theatrical and newspaper crowd.

Neither came as a stranger to the other. Everyone knew of Atty Fitzpatrick. Being as she was the only woman on the Brotherhood Council, she was completely aware that Conor was the author of the gunrunning scheme, an artisan of note and a man of prowess on the sporting field. At the instant of their introduction, I knew it was on between them. Conor had been without a real woman for a long time and obviously liked what he saw. She had been a widow long enough to have precisely the same thoughts.

In that my small presence was not required, I suddenly remembered a news story I had to cover, and told them I'd catch up with them later at Jury's.

*

When Atty Fitzpatrick entered a room it was seldom unnoticed. She and Conor settled in the lounge and she received the usual homage. They nibbled at their drinks until Seamus O'Neill's absence became conspicuous.

"I wonder what became of him?" she said.

"I think the lad's gracious enough to think I'd like to talk to you alone," Conor said.

Atty liked that, right off. Most men either tried to brag to build themselves up to her presence or shriveled at her imposing stature. "Do you want to?" she asked.

"I'm not completely certain," he said. "I've been going through some of the same loneliness you've been going through. I can't say it's as severe as suffering the loss of one's husband but I can't say it's not very painful, either.

When is the right moment to start coming out of it? I
suppose it's natural to think in those terms when you meet
someone like yourself."

Atty weighed the words, the man and the situation. No
one really knew how terrible the loss of Desmond had
been. Some said she was brave Atty. She knew others felt
her callous. She had been around men, in their world,
most of her life. She was unusual in that it had been on
her terms. Seldom had there been a relationship she
couldn't handle at the outset or later manipulate to her
own liking. The big fellow was intriguing and refresh-
ing and quite devoid of nonsense. He was also more than a
little intimidating.

"I'm lonesome, Atty," Conor said, speaking directly
into the big brown eyes which had melted half of Dublin.

Her hand came slowly over the top of his. "So am I,"
she said.

*

The next night the theater was dark and she invited him
to her home in the suburb village of Rathgar, a short tram
ride south of Dublin. Atty Fitzpatrick's house was an attached, flat-fronted, three-and-a-half-story Georgian affair
at 34 Garville Avenue, sporting a wild-colored door and
brass polished to a fare thee well.

Atty's proletariat leanings stopped at the entrance. It
was an immaculately run home with a selection of lovely
graces. Her children seemed delightful and trained to accept the comings and goings of strangers as well as long absences of their parents on behalf of the movement. After a
dinner during which Conor made himself deliberately
popular with the kids, they seemed to disappear on cue, as
if knowing that Mum and the stranger had republican
business.

"Come along," she said, forgoing the formal parlor.
She led him to the top floor and opened the door into the
front room. It was a combination intimate parlor, library
and office, and had been the private retreat with her late
husband adjoining their bedroom. It was now a memory
room filled with all his writings, lawbooks, photographs
and other vestiges of the life they had lived for the movement. For the first two months after Desmond's death she

had barely left the room. Once she did, she had not re-entered till this moment.

In the small grate below a marble mantel, Conor fixed a turf fire with a farm boy's expertise, and he was taken back the instant he smelled it. They talked about the situation of the peasants in the west and the Land League and wrought iron screens and jails. They talked about the vitality of life these days in Dublin and of lands beyond Ireland. They talked about guns and the Brotherhood and they talked of the evasive republican dream.

The time came round when Conor could no longer stay on without awkwardness. "It's gotten late on us, Atty," he said, "I'd best be taking leave."

"It seems like we've just started," she answered. "Oh, I'm a well-known talker. I talk at speeches and Council meetings like an obsessed banshee. Dan Sweeney has out and out told me to shut up on more than one occasion. But I never really get to talk to one person. Sometimes Seamus and I do but it seems like we're either getting our backs slapped in a pub or we're rushing through dinner to get to a meeting or catch a curtain. Des and I would talk here sometimes through the night and be absolutely astonished to see daylight come up on us. You know?"

"Aye," Conor said. "When your lover is also your best friend, that's all the world in that room, the two of you."

"Oh, Lord," she said, "I'm doing the lonely widow thing and I detest pity."

"Not to worry, but I do think the last tram to Dublin is about due."

"Conor," she said, "put another brick on the fire. If you miss the tram there's a bed downstairs next to the children's room. Between having this as a safe house and all-night meetings, the children are quite used to finding strangers there in the morning."

"All right," he said. He poured another drop of cognac. "You're a hell of a woman, Atty, and you'll have the worst of your sorrow behind you in no time."

"What makes you say that?"

"Because the thing you love in this world most is your own strength. I don't know if anything could break you."

She mulled over whether it was a compliment or a put-down. "And you?"

"I find I'm having a terrible time going it alone. I never minded being alone until Shelley came. With her gone, I hate every moment of being alone." He sat on the floor and stared into the glowing turf and she did likewise, both of them content to go their separate ways for a time. Then she found herself engrossed in Conor. He was a frightening man. Unlike almost every man she had ever known, he had no fear of his own frailties and made little attempt to hide them and no attempt to spout his masculinity. With him here in this room there seemed little choice but to compare him with Desmond.

Larkin ran deep and quiet. Seamus had told her he went into monumental poet's rages now and again, but it often took years of stuffing it inside him to come to it. There was certainly none of Desmond's bravado and flamboyance. Des loved himself, loved his courtroom antics, loved the sound of his voice at a speech, loved what he was doing for Ireland in particular, for it reflected back to him in self-glory.

The room was warm and sensuous as it had always been but its sensuality was not because of Des and Atty. It was sensuous for the movement. Wasn't that what she and Des really wanted? Riding on this thing they were achieving together had become their heartbeat. She'd pondered it for long hours after his death. Strange, but in this room they'd never let go for one another. Was the movement their mutual crutch to shield them from themselves? Didn't they know that they were not capable of giving and receiving the kind of love to each other they had poured into the movement?

Everything she knew of Conor Larkin indicated he was no less devoted to the cause. Yet he also had the ability to turn inward to his woman. Des had given her the independence she had demanded within the marriage. His needs from her had been nominal, for he was happy in his own ego. Conor Larkin would possess his woman and he alone would shine in her eyes. Atty knew that.

Could she handle something like that? How many women had sensed that intensity in Larkin and fled from him? How many others longed to taste it and failed? Could a man like that be had in a casual relationship? Or would he be so strong as to make her change her whole psyche to hold him?

He was frightening but so terribly tempting. What would it be like having the first man able to take her over? Atty shivered.

"I want to see you again," she said abruptly. "The play closes in a few weeks. Why don't I come up to Belfast for a visit?" She'd said that before to men she wanted, yet . . .

"I'm flattered," Conor answered. "I'm afraid your fame would precede you and you'd stand out like the lovely statue you are. Frankly, Dan Sweeney and the Council would rightly object to us cavorting about in public, particularly in Belfast."

"I didn't think of that. Would you come down to Dublin?"

"I'm not able to get away very often and, if the truth be known, I don't feel too much at ease among all these high-sounding intellectuals. Sure I love Seamus but I can't get to feel really at home."

"Most of it's blather, all talk. Everyone chatters, chatters, chatters. Arthur Griffith, Yeats, Seamus O'Neill, Atty Fitzpatrick," she said.

"Words are our bullets, Atty."

"Don't think so poorly of yourself. When all the talkers have shot up their verbal ammunition, the Brotherhood is going to have to depend on a handful of men like yourself to get the job done. And besides, you're not so bad with words, yourself. I've read some of your poems."

"Seamus shouldn't go showing that junk. I've not written in a long time."

"You ought to."

"Well, Dan tells me I'll have a world of time once I reach prison."

A second wave of awkwardness was on them.

"Funny," Atty said softly. "I've prided myself on my desirability and my ability to reject. This is rather difficult for me, Conor. I've never asked a man to take me to bed before."

Conor stood and pulled her to her feet. He embraced her fully and held a great deal of woman in his arms as he did so. Then he stood her off. "I think we'd better let it settle for a time."

Atty paled and tears of obvious hurt wanted to show. "I've made a damned fool of myself."

"You're lonely, you want a man, there's nothing wrong with that. You're also a great woman, Atty, and I don't want to do the disservice of taking you on lightly."

She managed a stage laugh. "This is a new experience for me."

"I'm not rejecting you, lass. Surely I was thinking about it the instant we met. Only I realize how unfair it would be to make love to you because I'm still weeping inside for my Shelley. Can you understand?"

She knew all right if she hadn't known it before. She knew the price of playing with this one would endanger her barriers, smash up the self-containment and self-contentment that she had managed to retain through a successful marriage and three children. He would take her to places inside herself she had never been with herself. For a crazy instant she longed to lead him into the next room and keep it dark and tell him to pretend if he so wished or to cry aloud in her breasts. But she was afraid, for she had never given anything like that to a man.

CHAPTER FIVE: In the months following the election, Oliver Cromwell MacIvor seized upon the panic of another Home Rule threat, unfolding plans which had become his blood, light and air during fifteen agonized years of waiting. Using his own churches as the sounding boards across the province, he rode on the waves of ancient Ulster fears.

"When the Lord thy God shall bring thee into the land whither thou goest to possess it and when the Lord thy God shall deliver them before thee; thou shalt smite them, and utterly destroy them; thou shalt make no covenant with them, nor show mercy unto them . . . for thou art an holy people unto the Lord thy God; the Lord thy God hath chosen thee to be a special people unto himself, above all people. . . ."

Roger Hubble had been right in that his interests would continue to be served by MacIvor despite the split between them. The preacher added little new in a place screaming for social change, warming up the same old stew and serving it. The Protestants of Ulster had been hammered by the theme for three centuries until it had become an integral part of their mentality from birth. They were one side of the Irish trinity along with the British masters and the natives, and they continued to be manipulated away from the real issue of betterment of human life for the common people.

One more time it was dragged up by telling them they were the same as the ancient Hebrews in pursuit of their promised land and privileged people in God's eyes. All that was new was the first step in shedding an age-old automatic tradition of politically following the gentry. All that was really happening was a subtle change of the guard. Yet MacIvor hypnotized the throngs and he in turn became more and more steeped in his own vision of his messianic power. Tent revival meetings overflowed where there was no church. Massive outdoor assemblies followed where there was no tent.

A decade earlier he had formed the Knights of Christ, an elitist group, an inner circle of the ultrarighteous. Their true purpose, the core of a mob, had been held in check for the propitious moment.

As his evangelic wildfire burned over Ulster, he subtly converted the Knights of Christ into a vanguard "for the defense of the Protestant faith from assault by satanists, papists and turncoats." As though the Orange Order were not already in business for precisely the same purpose, MacIvor's scheme required a private army. Using former military officers and numerous off-duty Constabulary as group leaders, the Knights were drilled in roughhouse tactics. Although he was skating on thin legal ice, the authorities vacillated and remained inert. Within a period of months a body had been created to bully local situations, create havoc on signal, and disrupt certain gatherings of dissident preachers, for no other gospel was true gospel but Oliver Cromwell MacIvor's.

New Universal Presbyterian churches shot up, seemingly overnight, in Armagh, Lisburn, Carrickfergus, Coleraine, Bangor and Lurgan. These were stocked with clergy rushed through his "theological" school on a four-month course and ordained by the Moderator himself.

As the year of 1907 came into being, a riot was instigated by the Knights of Christ in the Catholic area of Downpatrick over the hiring of three Catholic teachers in a new public school. Coming off the incident with success served as a forewarning of larger things to come in Belfast and Derry later in the year.

With his troops in place and his institutions established over the breadth of the province, Oliver Cromwell MacIvor pulled his coup. Traveling to London to get the greatest coverage, he called a press conference and announced the formation of the Loyalist Party.

"We have followed the old order obediently and have been led down the primrose path for our efforts. The plain Christian folk of Ulster whose lives are the most affected now intend to make the decisions concerning themselves and the future of their province. This is a party of the people. The era of subjugation to the old ruling class has come to an end." After which he unloaded the party's slogan, OUR ONLY CRIME IS LOYALTY.

There it was, the grand scheme unfurled, Oliver Cromwell MacIvor's Universal Presbyterian Church, Oliver Cromwell MacIvor's Knights of Christ, and Oliver Cromwell MacIvor's Loyalist Party, the father, the son and the holy ghost . . . an unholy trinity.

*

Nineteen-seven came in restlessly. A great deal of reform had taken place on the land and, with it, a period of relative well-being. The focus of poverty was squarely on the cities. These were in a state of squalor. In Dublin alone nearly half the population lived in dwellings of one family to a room. Half of these lived six persons to a room. Human degradation was rampant and there was little in the way of British industrial investment to alleviate it except in the loyal counties of Antrim and Down.

As the labor movement was heard and made inroads, the Protestant working class of Ulster examined its own situation and found it not to be all that exalted. It began to penetrate to the Protestant worker that his class had been used. It was a situation that could only be corrected by unity with the Catholic working class.

Strikes erupted and a dialogue between Catholic and Protestant worker took place for the first time in Belfast's sordid history.

The Unionist, Orange establishment counterattacked in full blast. Oliver Cromwell MacIvor, who had no true program of his own other than that of a vulture feeding on a diseased carcass, outdid them all in the battle to keep the working classes divided. Once again Roger Hubble proved correct in his prediction that the preacher would continue to work inadvertently in their behalf.

Despite, the universal unrest and mounting labor problems, Sir Frederick Weed went about the business of being humanitarian and benefactor on his own terms. His newest project was to give the province an Ulster Rail & Marine Museum, to be erected near Boilermaker Stadium.

After the tour, Conor Larkin had been assigned to the project for the purpose of repairing locomotives collected for its permanent exhibition. In the interim, the Red Hand Express had made two more trips to England, to convey Lord Roger to and from the House of Lords and to take Sir Frederick on an extended business foray. On both occasions O'Hurley got the train into the O'Sullivan foundry and picked up a load of weapons.

With the gunrunning continuing smoothly, Conor began considering ways of raising the haul by hiding additional carriers in the private cars and engine, as well as the tender. There were innumerable ingenious possibilities for making sliding panels and false floors and even attaching boxes to the undercarriages.

With the latest Red Hand model off the drawing board and about to go into production, Conor formalized his own thoughts and was ready to approach Duffy O'Hurley with his ideas and carry out some of the conversion right at the yard while the engine and tender were being built.

It had been a devastatingly long and lonely time without a glimpse of Shelley MacLeod. More than one night he prayed that Dan Sweeney would transfer him away from Belfast, but he knew in reality it was impossible, so long as gunrunning continued through the yard. He longed for the, day Sweeney would tell him to start to piece together some small Brotherhood units so at least he would have a working relationship with other men thinking and talking about the same thing.

"Too early to start forming units," Dan said, "far too early. Patience, is the elixir of revolution."

Conor lost his appetite for the theater and all those things that had once consumed a bottomless curiosity. On

one occasion he traveled to Dublin deliberately to visit
Atty Fitzpatrick, but it was no good, for Shelley Mac-
Leod would not set him free.

In the beginning, thought of spring rugby practice was
welcome. He'd be out in the open, rubbing elbows with
old mates, working off some of the pent-up frustration. As
he walked out to the grounds the reality of thirty bruising
games up ahead came to roost. He was approaching his
middle thirties now. Toward the end of the last season it
had taken him a few more seconds to lift himself off the
ground after a jarring contact and a half day longer for
the stiffness to leave his body after a game. Last year
there had been the excitement of Shelley, a close comradery with Robin and the pure pleasure of the exuberant
Jeremy Hubble. All of that would be gone now.

Jeremy kept up a weekly correspondence with Conor,
one filled with the excitement of a young man on the rise.
He had managed to acquit himself well in his first terms at
Trinity College and he wrote that he had gained a stone in
weight and ought to be right at the top of the Trinity
team. He aspired to play for the national team as had his
grandfather, but alas, further travel with the Boilermakers
was out.

•

Conor and Robin had nodded to one another when they
passed in the yard but exchanged no words. On the first
day of spring practice it was Robin who sought Conor
out.

"I think we'd best have a few words," Robin said and
they went out of sight behind the stands.

"I know it's awkward as hell for both of us," Robin
began, "but we've got to be in close contact for half a year.
It'll be best for us and the team as well if we're on decent
terms with each other."

"Those are my feelings as well," Conor said.

"Good, I thought you'd understand."

"And how're Lucy and Matt and your dad and Nell?"

"We couldn't be better, man. Matt's grown like a weed
and he misses you like blazes. If you must know, so have
I."

"Robin, I don't know what Shelley ever told you but
none of our problems had anything to do with the family."

Robin shook his curly head slowly. "She's not said a word about it or hardly a word about anything else as well."

"How is she?" Conor whispered.

"Sorely, man."

"Did she ever take up with the Kimberley chap again?"

Robin shook his head no. "Bleeding Jesus, I don't know what happened but, from the looks of it, it's killing the both of you."

"Certain things couldn't work. We'd have been foolish to try."

"Has it got anything to do with . . ." Robin cut himself short. "Never mind, it's none of my business. Look, Conor, I don't want you to take this personal but under the circumstances I talked to Derek and told him it would be best if we weren't roommates this year."

"Sure I understand," Conor answered.

"Well, let's go up and get our glorious welcome."

The first team meeting always took place in Sir Frederick's private lounge on the roof of the stands. Amid trophies to past eminence, a veritable gold and silver mine, the annual dissertation flowed thick and gooey. After introducing the prospective new players who were being sized up to have their brains knocked in, the personalized history of the team and one man's vision was told without so much as a blush. The manager then said dead on that they had a clear shot at the championship and his assistant said the juniors had never looked so good. It appeared the three converted Irishmen, Weed, Crawford and O'Brien, had cornered the market on blarney. Saving the best till last, Sir Frederick held out bait of an Australian tour now in tentative negotiation . . . if the team came through.

When they adjourned to the players' lounge, Duffy O'Hurley was at his station before the Guinness tap. Conor had not seen him in several weeks during which he had pinpointed his plans to expand the gunrunning capacity.

"Ah, the squad looks bang up this year, fit and raring to go," Duffy extolled. "Mind you, Doxie told me we're making a run at the championship and I quite agree. We'll not have the early season losses as last year."

"Aye," Conor said. "We'll be tough."

"And I hear there's talk about Australia. By God, I

can see myself opening the throttle on those vast stretches."

"Not with me aboard, I hope. Say, Duffy, lad, it's been a long time between drinks."

"I've been on the go, running the wheels off the train. Haven't set down in Belfast for more than an overnight for a month."

"How about us getting together for dinner and a few rounds tonight?" Conor said.

"Sure, Conor, sure. That sounds grand."

*

Duffy O'Hurley was comfortably situated in the Hotel Balmoral on the Lisburn Road arterial in what was benevolently referred to as a mixed neighborhood. As a man whose status transcended sectarian lines, Duffy reveled in his own image. He was but a short walk from the homes of his sister and brother-in-law, Calhoun Hanly, and his best friend, Doxie O'Brien.

Conor was disturbed the instant Duffy let him into his apartment. The big driver wore his midnight eyes and it was only seven in the evening. The bottle on the table was half emptied for supporting courage, as he was in obvious and nervous need to unload.

"I've been meaning to talk to you but, as you know, Sir Frederick's been running my ass off. He's in constant touch with the Castle over these labor strikes."

"What's on your mind, Duffy?"

"First, I don't want nobody in the Brotherhood getting mad at me. I've done everything you asked. Me and Calhoun's talked about it, what with a new train and a new tour coming up. We want out. One year of this shit is enough."

"Anything gone wrong?"

"It's nothing in particular, I've just had it."

"It's a bad time to pull out. The scheme's moving beautifully and we still have lots of weapons to bring over."

"At the rate we're going, it'll take ten years and something's got to muck it up along the line sooner or later."

"Need more money?" Conor said softly.

"Not really. All I do is drink it up or gamble it away. Man, it's the fucking tension. I spend half my days, and nights as well, thinking up excuses to get the train here, get the train there. Sometimes when I think I'm deadheading they'll stick on servants or some goddamn minor executives. And this shit of getting into Owen's foundry every time we're in Liverpool is wearing me out. Then sometimes I'm riding around Ireland for two weeks with them fucking guns in the tender. It's wrecking my health, Conor."

"You've got to give it one more season," Conor said bluntly. "I've worked out plans to increase the capacity of each run to just about a thousand rifles."

"Oh, shit," O'Hurley moaned. "I had a fucking notion you was going to slice all the cars apart. I had the notion almost like a vision in a miracle the minute I heard Sir Frederick was putting a new private car on the drawing board. I said to Calhoun, and these is my words, 'When Conor hears about it he'll turn the train into a rolling arsenal.' Man, I want out before the new engine gets on the tracks. If you got any notion of reworking these cars inside the yard, forget it. It'll be our necks for sure."

Duffy was at the bottle, hard. Conor evaluated a man in a fit of nerves. No use turning the screws on him now. In his state of mind and with his temperament, he could make a real blunder or blurt it out drunk.

Conor poured himself a short drink, watching the driver fight to control his heaving chest, then dab up the rush of perspiration.

Conor downed the shot and got up. "I've got to talk this over with some people," he said.

"Now, for God's sake don't get any ideas I'd do anything against the Brotherhood. Once them boxes is out of the tender, my lips are sealed and you've got to tell them that."

"Calm down, man, just calm down."

Duffy gulped and half fell into a deep chair once the ordeal of getting it off his mind was done.

"I want to know one thing, straight on, no shit," Conor said.

Duffy lifted his eyes, again filled with fright.

"Does anybody know about this other than you and Calhoun Hanly?"

At that instant Duffy gave it away with a rather wild telltale hesitation. His eyes darted away from Conor's, then he knew he'd better control himself. "No," he snapped too quickly.

"I mean anyone, including your sister?"

"What makes you think that?"

"Because when you're scared you drink, and when you drink you talk. Doxie O'Brien is your best friend and you talk a lot to him. Does Doxie know?"

"On my mother's grave, he doesn't know."

"I hope it's a true statement for Doxie as well as for yourself."

"You've got to believe that, Conor."

"I'm not sure. I'll get back to you in a few days."

* * *

Oliver Cromwell MacIvor continued to raise the stakes, press his audacity and openly scorn his former masters. If there was a center point of his hatred it was the fact that the gentry loathed him, never accepted him as an equal, never granted him the respect he craved. He intended to make them pay dearly for the lifelong snub.

A decision was required when an off-year election was called to fill a vacancy on the Belfast Corporation Council, a Shankill seat held by a Unionist crony of Weed until his death created an opening.

MacIvor's first thought was to run for the Council himself but the gamble was too great. If he lost it would be a terrible blow for his infant Loyalist Party. He chose instead the one man among his followers who had achieved a bit of status and stood a notch above the masses and was an answer to the gentry's snobbery.

The first candidate to represent the Loyalist Party was to be Lieutenant Colonel Howard Huntly Harrison, a retired army officer and titular "commander" of MacIvor's troops. HHH, as he was universally called, was a dull, bitter baggage who never ceased grousing at being passed over for higher rank in the military and knighthood. He found his cup of vengeance playing soldier at the head of MacIvor's corps.

The by-election for the Shankill seat became a focal point. MacIvor sensed that Weed's position had become vulnerable as a general strike rocked Belfast and crossed sectarian bounds with Catholic and Protestant workers joining hands. Brigadier Maxwell Swan had his hands full these days with the labor situation, so to make things more difficult for him, MacIvor's people openly campaigned for HHH in the yard. As this went unchallenged the Knights of Christ within the complex began holding prayer meetings during the lunch hour, bullying workers to attend. The tactic was simple. What quicker path to power than to challenge and disrupt Weed inside his own kingdom? Swan's special units now had the additional mission of keeping close eye on the Moderator's activities.

With the marching season at hand and Lambeg drums uncoiled before Orange halls across the province, the million flags bloomed like wildflowers. Weed Ship & Iron took on the scant of an unexploded bomb.

*

"O'Hurley's running scared," Conor said. "He's not too smart and his fireman's twice as dumb. I've no proof but it's my belief he's gone and blurted it to Doxie O'Brien."

Long Dan had lived a life of walls caving in on him but he'd never gotten totally immune to it. The Brotherhood was desperate for the weapons. "Typical," he grunted. "I don't see as we have much choice but to close down the operation."

"Not quite," Conor countered. "I've got to have one more crack at it. The plans are worked out. If the train sits still in the yard for just a few weeks I know I can make the conversions. Weed is making a last trip to England just before they sell off the old engine. In payment for letting O'Hurley and Hanly out of the deal, I say we make them carry one last load."

"How many?"

"Up to a thousand Lee-Enfields, maybe even more."

"What the hell am I supposed to say, Conor? You know what it means to us and you know the risk as well."

"I say give it a try. That will be the bargain. One trip, one thousand guns, then the operation is over."

Dan's fist beat a tattoo on the table. "I'm not backing away from the responsibility but it's got to be your choice, your decision alone."

"Go," Conor said.

Long Dan nodded. "I want you out of the Weed yard as soon as you make the conversion. We've got better use for you than playing rugby in England."

"Aye, if truth be known, I'm ready. It's getting ugly in there, Dan, bloody ugly. Prayer meetings and vigils, talks of riots. It's a nasty place."

"Huh," Dan laughed, "it's Belfast, it's always been Belfast."

＊

Conor's final plan called for two more bronze boxes in the water tank and one in the coal bin, two smaller ones in the engine and a series of plates at various places along the undercarriage of the cars, creating a series of false bottoms. The goal, one thousand rifles.

＊

"That's it, lads," Conor said, looking first to Duffy O'Hurley, then to Calhoun Hanly. "I want no conversation about it unless we run into technical difficulties. Otherwise you carry the guns in or take the consequences." The fireman nodded that he understood.

"Duffy?"

"Aye, but you swear it's the last run, you swear that."

"You've my word."

"Aye," O'Hurley said.

"We start converting as much as we can in the yard. The rest will be done in Liverpool."

Conor stood and threw a packet of money on the table. "Here's half in advance. Our show of good faith. The Brotherhood intends to keep its word in all matters. You understand, all matters."

CHAPTER SIX: It was the Fourth of July, American Independence Day. Just as Ulstermen likened themselves to the ancient Hebrews coming to the promised land of Ulster, they identified as strongly with their Scotch-Irish emigration to America.

Besides, any reason to break out the band was a good one. The marching season approached full blaze. Weed Ship & Iron floated on an ocean of red, white and blue Union Jacks and a bibliography of Orange slogans.

It was also rumor time. Annual rumors rolled from

lilting tongues punctuated by the bang of the Lambeg. Rumor of a sellout by the British Parliament, rumor of a papal plot, rumor of a Catholic conspiracy to gain equality in Ulster through the labor strikes, rumor of a deepening depression.

During the noon hour there was to be the annual gathering at the "Big Mabel" dry dock where massed Orange bands would play and oration would commemorate the American holiday. With the by-election coming up, the Loyalist Party demanded that Lieutenant Colonel Howard Huntly Harrison be allowed to address the throng just as the Unionist candidate was scheduled to do. When this was denied, the rumor was on that the Knights of Christ were going to make trouble.

Conor divided half his time between the locomotive works and restoration work at the half-completed Rail & Marine Museum at the far end of the complex. On this day he was at the museum building piecing together a vintage 1850 South Eastern Railway "Folkstone" engine. As it neared noon he was alone, for everyone drifted down to Big Mabel and the celebrations. He looked up from the scattered parts to see Robin MacLeod enter the building breathing heavily as though he had been running.

"Hello," he said curiously. When he caught Robin's expression of panic his first thought was that something had happened to Shelley.

Robin looked about to see there were no listeners. "I got to tell you something," he gasped shakily. "I been looking all over for you . . ."

"What is it?"

"Look, man, don't ask no questions but don't go back into the yard."

The strains of "Dixie" could be heard drifting from the concert a quarter mile away at Big Mabel. Conor sensed it at once. Riot! Almost all of the yard's two hundred Catholics, including the lads on the club, worked in the copper plant near the locomotive works. For some odd reason it was the one craft not brought over from Scotland. Whenever trouble hit the yard, the copper shop got it first. And then Conor clutched! Duffy O'Hurley and Calhoun Hanly were in the locomotive plant today!

"There's going to be a riot, isn't there?"

"Don't ask no questions, just get out."

"MacIvor's people, those Knights . . ."

"Look, man, will you just leave!"

"Are you certain of it?"

"Aye, I'm certain. Morgan heard it at the church."

"Some bloody church," Conor spat. "Have you warned the other lads?"

"I can't, Conor, I can't. I don't care for myself, but it would be too easy to figure out who did it and it could mean Morgan's ass."

"They're your mates!"

"It's them or my dad. The lads on the club will be able to fend for themselves. But . . . but . . . but . . . I had to come and warn you, no matter."

"Get out of my way," Conor said.

"I won't let you go back there, Conor. I don't care about the others but you're like a brother to me."

"I'm not your brother! I puked inside every time I walked in your home and saw your bloody fucking Orange sash hanging there! Now stand aside, boy!"

Robin backed up, fingers darting out at Conor's chest. "I can't let you."

As Conor tried to push him out of the way Robin uncorked a pair of punches to his face but they only dented and did not stop the larger man's momentum. Conor's blacksmith hands gripped Robin and flung him to the concrete floor like a sack. As he rushed past, Robin crawled quickly to his knees and brought Conor down from the rear with a brutal tackle. They thrashed on the ground clawing and hacking for a hold and as it grew wild, knees and elbows whacked and thudded.

I wish I was in Dixie, hooray hooray.

Conor reached his feet first with Robin all over him. Again his great hands pried himself free and they stood nose to nose slugging until Robin faltered and backed up wobbling under the blows. He lurched blindly, half dazed. Conor put a vicious bear hug on him until he wheezed for breath and, as it deflated him, his face purpled and his eyes rolled back. He fainted. Conor released him and he crumpled to the ground.

He flung the door open. The quickest route was to cut

diagonally across the playing pitch, down the channel road and over the high bridge to the steel mill side.

Somehow Robin MacLeod got up and came at him from behind. Whap, in the back of the neck, whap, whap, whap. Conor reeled and as Robin gathered strength for a last surge he was met with a backhand followed by an awesome blast to the stomach. As Robin sank to his knees, Conor booted him in the jaw, lifted him up and sent home the blow that laid him unconscious.

When Johnny comes marching home again, hurrah, hurrah.

The noon whistle shrieked!

The grass under Conor's feet melted and the grandstands blurred. Down King William Channel to the bridge. He climbed the steps and stopped for an instant in the middle.

"Oh, God!"

Several hundred men moved as a mob in his direction, wielding clubs with spiked ends, crowbars, wrenches and rivets. He shot over and down the stairs to the row of small support shops and tore into the copper plant.

"Riot! Riot! Catholics out of the east gate! Riot! Riot! Catholics out!"

As a melee flooded past him to escape through the rear, he returned to the entrance and caught sight of them pouring over the bridge. He looked behind him. Catholics were fleeing for safety with but an iota to spare.

"Locomotive shop," he gasped, "locomotive shop." He inched along hugging the buildings and came to an end, then girded himself for a dash over open ground just as the mob reached the copper shop and blasted in flailing.

"Papist pigs!"

"Death to the Taigs!"

"Kill them!"

"Fuck the Pope!"

"Traitors!"

Conor made his move.

"There's one!"

Weaving through the locomotive assembly with exquisitely gained knowledge of the place, he found Duffy

and Calhoun loafing in the foreman's office unaware of
the chaos outside. He seized them both and dragged them
from the office.

"You gone crazy?"

"There's a riot on!"

"Oh, mercy, Jesus!"

Conor looked about desperately for an escape route.
There was none. Blurred images of the rioters formed up
on the frosted windows outside, encircling the building.

"Up on the engine, quick," Conor commanded. "Hide
inside the boiler."

"Get up here with us," Duffy cried.

"No, they know I'm in here. They'll tear the place to
pieces looking for me and they'll find you as well. Go,
go, go!"

As they disappeared to tentative safety, Conor allowed
himself a few steadying breaths, then walked directly at
the main door at the same instant it was breached. Seeing
him standing calm and unarmed, the mob screeched to a
halt.

Vessey Bain, a Catholic hater of demented proportions
and most noble of the Knights within the yard, hissed
rage but even so he knew an attack on Larkin would be
no easy out.

"Out of the way, Larkin," Vessey snarled, "there's
Taigs here and we're getting them."

Conor held fast.

"You fucking papist son of a bitch! You're no privileged
character!"

"Weed's ass licker, that's what!"

"Aye! Kill the fucker!"

Before Vessey could make a decision a half dozen
rivets were hurled out of the pack. Conor crashed in
blackness as one found its mark on the side of his head.

He regained consciousness after a dousing and
strained but found himself held in place, lashed, spread-
eagled to the spokes of an engine wheel.

Left empty-handed of Catholic blood due to Larkin's
alarm, they aimed to make him pay. Vessey Bain spat in
his face and kicked at his shins maniacally, sweating and
half choked with rage. With the others screaming for
him to be done in, that strange glimmer of self-preservation prevailed. "Killing's too good for him," Vessey

grunted. "Let's put him into dry dock for good. Let Joey Hooker have a go!"

Hooker had once been a half-decent middleweight boxer until his mind got knocked soggy. Sir Frederick took him in as a charity case. Without too many independent thoughts of his own, Vessey Bain had talked him into becoming a Knight of Christ for the benefit of the man's punch.

He laughed silly-like at the man tied up before him. Pop, pop, pop, went Hooker's jab into Conor's face, pop, pop, pop. A right into the stomach, vooooom!

Joey Hooker snorted through his broken nose from the exertion of each punch.

AS THE CHEERS SWELLED UP AROUND HIM HE WAS IN THE RING AGAIN DEFENDING THE MIDDLEWEIGHT CHAMPIONSHIP OF ULSTER. HIS OWN EYE WAS GASHED AND AS HE STAGGERED HE COWERED AGAINST THE ROPES, THEN CAME OFF SWINGING, PLODDING, THROWING . . . "PUNCH, JOEY, PUNCH!" HIS MANAGER SCREAMED AND THE CROWD TORE THE PLACE APART IN DELIRIUM AS HE RALLIED. "PUNCH! PUNCH! KILL HIM, JOEY, KILL HIM . . . YOU'VE GOT HIM, JOEY . . . PUNCH . . . punch . . . punch . . ."

CHAPTER SEVEN: Calhoun Hanly propped Conor against the wall as Duffy O'Hurley fished through his pockets and found his key. As the door opened Conor attempted to make it alone. He stumbled into the vestibule but crumpled at the foot of the stairs.

The two brawnies lifted him to his feet, gathered his arms about their necks and dragged him up the steps. He doubled up screaming as a violent pain ripped through his body. They labored, one step after the other, making the landing at last. As Duffy turned to unlock the door of the flat, Conor slipped to his knees, then gripped the railing, pulled himself up, lurched inside the room and stood wavering, fell again and crawled to the bed grabbing at the sheets to pull himself up, but rolled over on his back, sending the coverings down on him.

Calhoun struck a match, found the gas mantle and the light rose softly. They rushed to help him.

Shelley stepped into the open, went to him and saw it.
Both eyes were bloated to slits and violent colors and his
mouth was too split to speak. She did not scream but
clung to him as life itself, fighting off her own tears and
nausea.

"Get him up on the bed and help me get him undressed." At last she turned her eyes away as Hanly
pulled off his shirt and trousers. His body had been beaten
yellow and purple from thighs to shoulders.

She hid her face in her hands as Duffy put his arm
about her shoulder to steady her.

"How bad?"

"He's pretty busted up. Stitches inside his mouth, half
his ribs are cracked and a couple small fractures in his
cheek. His face and head got little stitches all over. The
doctor took a picture of his head. Thank God there's no
damage there."

"Why didn't you keep him in the hospital?"

"The mob's still prowling around. He came around long
enough to demand to leave. I called someone for him in
Dublin. There are some armed lads on the way . . . don't
ask no more."

"I'll take care of him."

"Aye, come here, lass."

Duffy unrolled a packet of drugs which included a
vial of morphine and syringe. He went over the doctor's
instructions, then the three of them got him arranged in
the bed and shot in a dose of the drug.

"Thanks," Shelley said.

"Thanks for nothing. I might be dead if it wasn't for
him. Keep on the watch, will you?"

"We'll be all right," she said.

She bolted the door behind them, went quickly to the
place he had fixed beneath the sink, found his pistol, then
took up vigil at his bedside with the gun in her lap.

*

Twenty hours later a drowsed Shelley allowed some
light into the room. She drew the curtains, lifted the
shade and looked down to the sidewalk where a pair of
lads leaned against the walls, hands in pockets, loafing.
One nudged the other and as they looked up one of them

tipped his cap and nodded to tell her the place was guarded.

Conor blinked his eyes and forced the slits apart, then groaned terribly at the awareness of pain. He steadied himself to work his mind backward and recall events. His hand slowly left the covers and he felt his mouth and the bandages about his head and ears. The agony stemming from his body made movement almost impossible and each breath a shock.

"Shelley . . ."

"I'm here."

"Shelley . . ."

"Don't talk, love. You've had a terrible ordeal. The doctor has come and gone. He said someone else might have been crippled, even dead. It will take a few weeks to get on your feet and a few months for the pain to subside but you're going to come out of it all right."

"Water . . ."

She got her weight beneath him to help him upright. Half the water spilled down his chin and neck, for he was unable to control it.

"Robin ran all the way home, then to Blanche's, and told me you'd gone back into that riot. I came here and waited. The two trainmen brought you back. Conor . . . I'll not leave you again."

As she laid him back on the bed tears fell from the corners of his eyes.

"Shhh, shhhh. It's been no good this way, man. I'd rather be dead than go through another nine months of it."

The gurgle of him crying made her weep as well.

"It will do no good to throw me out because, every time you do, I'll just come back," she said. He groped about until she gave him her hand. "It doesn't matter what you're doing, Conor. It makes no difference to me. I'm not asking for the world. All I want out of life is whatever time we have together. That's all I want, man."

"Shelley . . . I'll ruin your life . . ."

"Sure, you've done that already. Being apart is the most terrible ruination I can endure. Listen to me. This is the one thing I'm completely sure of. When you go out of that door I'll never question you about where you're

going or what you're doing. I'll never demand a minute
of your time you cannot freely give. But when your day
is done, where your bed is, that's where I'll be from now
on. . . ."

CHAPTER EIGHT: Frederick Murdoch Weed's and
Brigadier Maxwell Swan's reply to the riot was breathlessly swift! As the mob milled at the King William Channel
on the second morning, fighting flared when the Catholics arrived to work. Not having had their full cup of
blood on the first day, the Knights of Christ wanted
more. One Catholic was killed and another seriously injured.

Swan's special squad personnel pinpointed the leaders
and during the day warrants were issued. That same evening Vessey Bain, Joey Hooker and twenty other Knights
were rounded up, arraigned and locked up in the Crumlin
Road Jail without bail, for inciting a riot, extensive property damage at the yard and the murder of the Catholic
worker.

They were advised they were all under suspicion at
work until such time as their innocence was proved. Further "prayer" meetings and Knights of Christ assemblies
within the yard were forbidden on pain of instant dismissal.

The Reverend Mr. MacIvor, who had been in Cookstown, returned immediately to Belfast and announced an
open-air protest rally on the steps of the City Hall. He
called Lieutenant Colonel Harrison and the top cadre of
the Knights together to draw up rally plans, which called
for a march on the Crumlin Road Jail afterward. The
meeting was interrupted by the sudden appearance of a
representative of the Attorney General's office who informed them that a requested permit for the rally had
been rejected, that the gathering would be illegal and the
consequences apt to be severe if they defied the order.

As battle lines shaped up by the minute the word came
back to MacIvor that the military barracks at Holywood,
Lisburn and Bainbridge were on the alert with supportive

Constabulary units to converge on Belfast if MacIvor cared to test the ban.

In the past such niceties as permits to hold open-air meetings were only loosely sought and enforced. Subsequent riots had always been of an anti-Catholic nature, and deemed as fair sport to alleviate the tension and fears of the Protestant workers. After such a riot, if it had been a severe one, a commission of inquiry generally condemned the behavior but rarely was anyone called to account.

This time the riot had been against Frederick Murdoch Weed and this time the meeting and march would be directed against a penal institution of the Crown. That made it a different game. Oliver Cromwell MacIvor might have caught the attention of the masses but the Hubble/Weed combine was one of generations-standing with Dublin Castle, personal friends of the military commanders, and closely allied with the judicial and legal systems.

In the following hours the Moderator and his people had to consider the difference between bullying one's way through an almost defenseless Catholic enclave and taking on the Crown. He inched away from the showdown, citing divine revelation as his reason for avoiding further bloodshed.

The height of the marching season had always been a traditionally slow time at Weed Ship & Iron. Many of the workers wanted time off between mid-July and mid-August to partake in the plethora of Orange activities. The tone was set on the glorious Twelfth of July with a massing of lodges and bands from all over Ireland, the march through Belfast and the rally at Finaghy Field. This was followed by another immense gathering a day later at Scarva Castle for an annual re-enactment of the Battle of the Boyne. Those Orange feet stayed in motion for a solid month, culminating in Londonderry for Apprentice Boys Day.

During this time of year it also became more and more popular to have workers' holidays. Travel agencies, an institution that had been operating in England for several decades, were making inroads in Ulster and arranging specially priced group tours of England and southern Ireland.

To accommodate all this the work force had been

rotated, leaving half on and half away. This year came
the blunt announcement that, beginning July 10, Weed
Ship & Iron would close down completely and remain
closed down until further notice. In that move, Sir Frederick went directly to the heart and gonads of the situation. However thinly veiled, it was an economic lockout
with the finger pointing directly at Oliver Cromwell Mac-
Ivor as the instigator.

On July 8, two days before the yard was scheduled to
close down, all of Belfast was awakened at three in the
morning by a bombastic explosion from the Shankill
which shattered windows in a half-mile radius and lit the
night blindingly. When the dust had settled the Universal
Presbyterian Missionary and Theological Center and its
adjoining publishing facility no longer existed.

Although the bombing was labeled as the work of labor
agitators, seditionists and papists, most people had other
thoughts. The short war all seemed to boil down to a single issue and that was the upcoming by-election for the
vacant Shankill seat. If Lieutenant Colonel Howard Huntly Harrison won, it would spell the success of a populist
candidate and a warning that the new order was here to
stay despite the establishment's harsh countermeasures.

Of course, if Weed's Unionist candidate prevailed, the
Moderator's long dream would suffer an awesome setback.

*

Doxie O'Brien's large comfy house was located near
Queen's University and the Botanic Gardens in a lovely
Belfast area where affluent Catholics were welcome.
Closeness to the university gave off airs of both liberalism
and aloofness from all that Belfast sectarianism. The
Catholic teachers, lawyers, doctors and Doxie O'Brien's
who lived there were pretentiously aware of their elitist
difference.

Doxie's best friend Duffy O'Hurley resided just a few
blocks away as did the Hanlys. It was a nice place to raise
children.

A month after the shipyard riot Conor was able to get
about stiffly, his ribs still heavily taped but the assortment
of wounds within palatable bounds.

Doxie puffed up and boasted as he showed Conor

about his home, introduced him to endless children, one of whom was named after the late Queen and another after Frederick Weed. They settled in Doxie's personal glory hole, a heavily photoed den. Doxie cracked the whiskey bottle. As he did with home, furnishings and well-dressed children, so did he boast about the quality of his liquor, Bushmills, black label.

"What's on, Doxie?"

"As you know, even though the yard is closed, Sir Frederick has kept the lads on the club on salary and most of them are working out quietly up at Rathweed Hall."

"I heard as much."

"He has confidentially informed us, Derek and myself, that he intends to make the tour this year. It would be a pity to cancel. I think we have a shot at the championship. Well, anyhow, I took the liberty of checking with the doctor, who is of the medical opinion you'd be fit for play in about another six weeks."

Conor didn't say anything. Doxie had been a good player and a decent enough coach but wasn't much at hiding his intentions. Doxie had at his Bushmills and paddled about the den with deep concern. "As you also probably know, none of the Catholic lads have returned to practice."

So that was it. Conor wondered why Frederick Weed had chosen Doxie as an emissary. He had a good rapport with the man, himself. The only possible reason was the Catholic issue and certainly the two of them could have discussed it better than he and Doxie. It occurred to Conor what he already knew and that was that the British had learned almost nothing about the Irish after centuries of dealing with them.

"Small wonder they haven't come back," Conor said. "They stood a good chance of ending up like I did."

"That's surely the case," Doxie agreed. "Anyways, I've talked to them on an individual basis. You know, all of us being of the same faith. Well, Sir Frederick has given me the responsibility of getting the family back together, so to speak. He's put a high priority on the matter and it means a lot to me, personal. There's the Australian tour to consider, likewise."

Conor's failure to respond irritated Doxie. "Well, here

it is, Conor. If you was to call a meeting of the Catholic lads and give them the word, they'd return to practice. Sir Frederick told me to tell you you're wanted with the club even if you are unable to play."

"I'll let you know," Conor said, getting up to leave.

"Some goddamn way for you to act!" Doxie burst out with a tinge of desperation. He needed an answer. "You owe some loyalty to Sir Frederick."

"For what?"

"For what, Jesus, man! Didn't he throw Vessey Bain and Hooker into jail? And what about you and Robin's sister getting a two-week holiday in Bantry Bay? Didn't the entire family, Jeremy and Lady Caroline herself, render personal apologies? Where's your fucking loyalty, man?"

"The next day after I got mine they came back and murdered Nappy Flynn. He was bashed in so bad his wife and eight kids didn't even recognize him. And Dick Talbot, twenty years at the yard and now in a wheel chair for life. Not one bloody fucking quid!"

"Sir Frederick can't be paying off every goddamn widow and cripple in Belfast. The precedent would be dangerous. The man's got to take care of his own, no more, no less."

"Sure, he's good to his pet monkeys but don't get the idea they threw Hooker and Bain into prison for me. And as far as Larkin and Weed are concerned it's all even up. Value given, value received, so spare me the loyalty bullshit."

Doxie wrung his hands. What he couldn't say was that he had to have the tour to Australia. Weed and Crawford had promised to resettle him down under as coach and manager of the new Sydney team. He had to deliver the Catholic boys.

"You got it all wrong, Conor. It's all the agitation from all the radicals and anarchists that makes the Prods go crazy and turn to rioting. Weed built his yard with his own two hands."

"Sure, Doxie. It's good that some of the R.C.s like yourself understand that so well."

Doxie crimsoned, then began to sniffle. "You can rap me about my loyalty. I was an over-the-hill mick, one foot in the gutter and the other in the grave, when him and Derek picked me up. You're fucking right I'm loyal and I think it's time the other Catholics on the team he's treating so decent give him the same consideration. He told me personal that he wants this championship more than he ever wanted anything in the world. It's up to us to give it to him."

"Christ, Doxie, when do you get your bowler and Orange sash?"

"Fuck you, Larkin! I know what the fuck you're up to!"

As quickly as he said it, he choked on it and his eyes widened.

"What am I up to?" Conor asked softly.

"I didn't mean nothing."

"What am I up to!"

"Nothing, nothing. I . . . I . . . I only meant . . . I can't stand no disloyalty to Sir Frederick."

Conor placed a hand on Doxie's shoulder. "Don't do anything foolish, man."

CHAPTER NINE: "The train left for England last night," Conor said to Dan Sweeney. "Funny pair of ducks, Duffy and Calhoun. They came to me like two kids still in my debt for saving them. They've their own bedrooms on the second car with their own keys and locks. They're willing to fill them with guns and at no extra cost. They sure blow hot and cold."

"Good luck, that. What will the haul be?"

"With the extra boxes Owen is making and what I've fitted myself at the yard and now with the use of their bedrooms, I'm thinking in terms of two thousand rifles and twenty thousand rounds."

Sweeney flipped his pencil down, whistled, jammed his hands into his pockets, paced, lit a cigarette and smoked it down in a half dozen puffs. "Two thousand," he whispered as though he opened the lid of a pirate's treasure. "It's mind-boggling."

Conor had never seen him excited before. Sweeney allowed himself a moment of it, then returned to his grim groove.

"You're sure O'Brien knows?"

"Duffy says no but I think so."

"Will he keep his mouth shut?"

"Time will tell."

"Two thousand rifles. The line of making a judgment is so thin, Conor. I have to say again, you are the one dealing with these people and it will have to be your decision."

"If Doxie knows he also knows it will be the last gun run. He knows I suspect him. He knows I've called the Catholics together on the team and given him his chance at the Australian job. All told, if he knows, he should hold still. On the other hand, I may be all wet."

"Go or no go, Conor?"

"For two thousand rifles, we've got to gamble."

Dan nodded. "I'll contact Owen O'Sullivan and advise him it's on. He will return a cable to Seamus when the guns are loaded. How long will Weed be in England?"

"No more than a few more days. He's due in Derry for Apprentice Boys Day." Conor grunted from a jolt of pain in his back.

"How's the healing coming?"

"Slower than I figured."

Sweeney treated himself to a one-snort laugh. "There's a rumor out that Bain and Hooker are going to get off scot free. Want to do something about it?"

Conor glanced suspiciously and shook his head no.

It was the kind of question Long Dan asked when he was fishing. Dan had posed it deliberately. He had had Larkin on his mind excessively. Larkin would be pulling out of Belfast soon. Up to now he had looked like a leader. Dan was ready to move him to the Council but there were things he had to be sure of. Could Larkin pull the trigger, even on the ones who had beaten him half to death? Was Conor's lack of desire for vengeance good judgment or a weakness?

"I remember once when me and Brendan Sean Barrett was in Strangeways Prison and Brendan was acting up. They was hell on Fenians. He was fed dog and cat guts for a solid month. That son of a bitch, all he would do was look at them and smile. Like to drove them crazy. Eventually he went on a hunger strike, confused the hell out of them and made them back down. We ran into the prison governor in America years later. He'd retired there. Brendan had him cold."

"And?"

"He just kept smiling."

Dan stretched his long frame and the eternal flame lit the eternal cigarette. "I had the same sort of experience. There'd been a fight in the yard, a man was killed and I was one of those charged with the murder and moved into the death cell. From there I could see my scaffold being built. When it was completed there was this one warder, Harold Barr was his name . . . Harold Barr . . ." The old man's eyes still angered with the memory of it. "Harold Barr marched me out to the scaffold every night, tied me by the legs and dropped me head first through the trap door. The length of the rope was such that my head came within an inch of bashing on the stone floor. Mr. Barr would release me only after I sang him an Irish ditty or passed out first."

"And?"

"We met by chance. He was on holiday doing some pike fishing around Lough Derg on the River Shannon."

"Did you smile?"

"I broke his neck with my bare hands and dumped him in the lake."

"What ancient parable are you about to impart, Dan?"

"You're getting out of Belfast, as you know. I'm not sure where you're going. I'd like you on the Council and I know what jobs I'd have in mind."

"What is that?"

"It would require a lot of moving around."

"And making decisions to break the neck instead of smile?"

"Something like that," Sweeney answered. "If I move you into the work I have in mind it could put you on the run."

"Talk plain to me, Dan."

"I was glad when you returned from England last year. For a moment I thought we were going to lose you. What I'm telling you now is words from a wise old man. I was sorry to see you go back to that woman. If you're moved up in the ranks as I wish to do it would be an absolute disaster course to continue living with her. Make the break, Conor."

"No," Conor whispered. He stood slowly, jerked the table from the floor by its legs, wheeled about and smashed it into the wall, shattering it.

"Do you know what I mean, Dan!"

There had been moments like this, of course. Moments when he as commander had been issued a challenge. Larkin confused the hell out of him. So daring on some things, so smart . . . yet so full of human frailties. Indeed, would he pull the trigger on his worst enemy? Indeed, was he cut from the cloth of a man ready to make the ultimate personal sacrifices required? Indeed, was he too much of a loner like Brendan Sean Barrett? Sweeney teetered on the brink of accepting the challenge, then suddenly shoved his hands into his pockets, turned his eyes down from the frozen, fierce man before him.

"I know what you mean," Dan whispered, "I'll not mention her name again."

CHAPTER TEN: The crisis which had begun for Frederick Weed with the fall of the Conservative government was over. The labor unrest, general strike, and the threat of trade unions collapsed. In the end, because the workers had been so downtrodden for so long and there was so much disunity between the Catholics and Protestants, they simply didn't have the stamina for victory.

In his personal war with Oliver Cromwell MacIvor, the results were becoming equally conclusive. The immediate jailing of Vessey Bain and the troublemakers in the yard, the lockout and the bombing of the Moderator's seminary jarred the Shankill and East Belfast. The wind went out of their marching season and the tone of the rhetoric fell from vitriolic to moderate. As the marching season drew to a close the main concern was whether or not Weed would reopen the yard.

Weed's crowning victory came in the Shankill by-election in which the Unionist candidate crushed Lieutenant Colonel Howard Huntly Harrison and the Loyalist Party with eighty per cent of the vote. The people might have become disenchanted with the gentry but they were unwilling to cast their fate either to MacIvor or to liberal ideas that would lead to Home Rule.

Oliver Cromwell MacIvor licked his wounds, swallowed his pride and, in order to salvage a fast-waning prestige, petitioned for a meeting with Sir Frederick.

Weed kept MacIvor waiting for a week, then summoned him to Oxford were he was delivering a series of summer lectures at Magdalen College to a high gathering of industrialists and executives.

When they came face to face in his rooms overlooking the Cherwell River it was a highly different kettle of fish than their last encounter. Sir Frederick blasted him with forbidden tobacco smoke and belted down forbidden whiskey.

The Moderator reckoned that there had been a grave misunderstanding. Forsaking any responsibility for the riot, he blamed it on overzealousness of a few disparate Knights of Christ, who, out of Christian charity, should be forgiven. As for his Loyalist Party, he said there never had been an intention to challenge the Unionists but merely a wish to have a closer identification with the people in local issues. Finally, he wondered how long Sir Frederick intended keeping the yard closed, as a restless fear was creeping over the Shankill and East Belfast. Was there a possibility of mending things, a show of the old unity to shore up flagging spirits among the people?

Weed glared coldly during MacIvor's dissertation. "You made a stupid blunder," he began. "You tried to seize power and you fell on your ass."

"I don't know what led you to that conclusion," MacIvor begged.

"Let's stop the horseshit," Frederick Weed snapped. The preacher paled. There was no fury, for he held no cards. "Perhaps fifty years from now some of this populist Gladstonian shit may reach the Ulster masses, and, God help them, they will follow a man like you. As for the here and now, decisions will remain in the hands of the men most competent to contend with them. Am I quite clear?"

"I have come here in the spirit of conciliation," MacIvor said.

"You came here because you've been routed." He stood and clasped his hands behind him and walked to the tall window and stared at the lovely wending stream outside. His back remained turned to MacIvor as he spoke. "Unfortunately we still have a number of common interests and there are difficult years ahead. With all your loathsomeness and despite my desire to divest myself of you, you still have a necessary function. I trust that from here on out you will fulfill this without making a nuisance of yourself."

For the first time in his life, Oliver Cromwell MacIvor had nothing to say. He felt lightheaded and drained of energy, yet as Weed's words came through to him he was thankful for his reprieve. "I think we have found the basis of a new understanding," he capitulated.

"Good. Go to Liverpool and wait for me. I'll be there in a few days. We shall proceed together to Londonderry for Apprentice Boys Day, on which occasion you will make it clear that you support the Unionist principles completely in matters of national policy. I shall appear at your church a few Sundays hence, at which time you will announce from the pulpit that through my generosity that theological thing of yours can start rebuilding. When all of this has been done to my satisfaction I will announce the reopening of the yard, but not a moment before. And keep your fucking Knights of Christ out of my business."

He returned to the desk, blew a long thin deliberate stream of smoke in the preacher's face. "You may take your leave."

MacIvor beat a hasty retreat. As his hand touched the doorknob Weed came to his feet and his fist thumped the desk.

"MacIvor!"

The preacher froze.

"What gave you the idea that a phony little evangelical adventurer could overturn three hundred years of imperial experience and usurp the Frederick Murdoch Weeds of Ulster?"

*

On August 8, Seamus O'Neill received the following cable from Owen O'Sullivan in Liverpool. HAPPY BIRTH-

DAY. MAY YOU LIVE TO BE TWO THOUSAND YEARS OLD. ALL OUR LOVE. THE FAMILY.

A day later Conor met Duffy O'Hurley for lunch at the Grand Central Hotel. He seemed calm enough as they spoke in tones below the quiet of the room.

"How's the train look?"

"Fucking arsenal, that's what. I'll be glad when it's over."

"As will I," Conor said. "I take it everything went smoothly with O'Sullivan?"

"He's an artist. Everything's well concealed. On the other hand, I wouldn't want to be riding around with it too long."

The waiter interrupted.

"How are you feeling, now?"

"Getting better. I kicked a few footballs yesterday. Mostly for the team's morale."

"Think you'll play this season?"

"Maybe, maybe not. I've been asked to travel with the club. The lads are still shaken from the riot."

They looked up and placed their order. The waiter left.

"I'll be moving out of Belfast tomorrow," Duffy said. "I'll be leaving Sir Frederick and party at Derry for the celebrations. At the moment there's a good chance I'll be deadheading down to Dublin on the Great Northern route."

"Let's see . . . Strabane . . . Omagh . . . Portadown . . . Newry . . ."

"That's it."

"We've never dumped in that area before. I'll see if I can get things organized on a contingency basis. When will you know for certain?"

"When we get to Derry I'll ask Sir Frederick what plans are for the train. We should arrive in the late afternoon."

"I'll wait for a telephone call from you from five o'clock onward at the General Post Office. That will give me the rest of today and half of tomorrow to get something organized."

"For Christ sake, get them bloody crates off my baby."

"I'll do my best. We're both of the same persuasion on that account."

"Conor."

"Aye?"

"I know I did it for money but after what you done for me and Calhoun I'm glad I did it."

*

AUGUST 10, 1907

Conor patiently read his magazine, glancing up to the big wall clock from time to time in the telegraph section of the General Post Office on Royal Avenue and Berry Street. It bonged the hour of eight.

"Mr. Larkin."

He closed the magazine and approached the desk.

"Your call from Londonderry finally came through, sir. You can take it in stall number four."

"Hello."

"Hello, it's me. I had a pleasant trip. Sorry I couldn't get to a telephone earlier."

"That's all right. What's the word?"

"I'll be leaving here tomorrow night around nine or ten o'clock along the route we discussed."

"We'll be ready for you."

Conor could hear a sigh of relief.

"We'll be watching out for you, say, from half ten onward. The signal will be somewhere between Beragh and Pomeroy. You know the lay-by I mean?"

"Near Sixmilecross?"

"Aye, Sixmilecross."

CHAPTER ELEVEN: The passing of old Rinty Doyle was ever so sad. He had been barely making the public house and the shebeen, much less the fields to work, and jawed a constant complaint of aches from gutted teeth to swollen joints. After he came down with pneumonia and the fever got him, it settled right in his head. Of a night before the full moon he crept down from the loft and ran from the cottage in his nightshirt up to the fields in a delirium.

It was not until the following morning that he was discovered by the men on their way up to work. Old Rinty was standing there, shirttail flowing and a club in his hands, blocking the gate to the communal pasture.

"Get off my land!" he screeched, brandishing his shillelagh. "Get off my land!"

Those who knew Rinty knew he had never owned much more than a pair of shoelaces, much less his own land, and recognized at once that he had gone daft.

They fetched Brigid, who like to got her head knocked off when she approached him. As the men closed in after him he ran up higher, throwing rocks down at them and continuing to scream, "Get off my land!"

Not wanting to harm the old dear by taking him by force, they summoned Father Cluny. He, likewise, was not recognized by Rinty. After a long discussion they sent a party into the township and returned with Dr. Cruikshank himself. By that time Rinty had hidden himself in the caves up in the heather. An all-day search proved futile and darkness forced them to call a halt till morning. During the night they all heard him again and saw him as well, by the full moon, running around above the cottages, his voice pitched like a departed spirit: "Get off my land!"

Of the next morning he was found mercifully deceased. Although she had been hard on the old scut, Brigid was likewise kindly to him, keeping him on long after he was capable of a day's work and seeing to it he got a decent meal and enough of a dole to allow him the comfort of his nightly pint. Actually she thought so much of old Rinty that she allowed him to be buried in the Larkin plot despite the fact he was quite a distant relative. All who knew the Larkin graves knew they were the most beautifully kept on Inishowen and allowing Rinty to rest there was high honor indeed for such a person of little consequence.

Need of a good strong field hand was long overdue and, after seeing Rinty into purgatory, Brigid set out to find one, when queer and unaccountable fate intervened in the matter.

Mairead O'Neill likewise got away one night from the burden of too many years, leaving her son Colm a man in great necessity. When Colm's mother died, Brigid's heart softened.

She and Colm had lived side by side for a lifetime, during which she saw little of note in him. He was locked in the closet when good looks were passed out, with a personality to match.

Living with ghosts and memories had become her second nature. She remembered young handsome Myles McCracken, whose image grew in stature with every passing year. She remembered her epic stand against Tomas and Finola (God rest their souls) when they attempted to foist Colm on her. And that's to say nothing of her equally epic stand for her rights to the land. She was the custodian of the family ashes.

On the other hand, Colm didn't hold many thoughts about anything. From his cradle to his mother's death, the precious son had not lifted a finger within the house on his own behalf. With Mairead around, he never so much as learned to butter his bread properly.

Mind you, it was not that Colm had suddenly grown attractive in middle age, only not quite so unattractive. Their homes being side by side, as well as their farms, brought them into numerous discussions of mutual interest about horse trading, marketing, working their fields and the like. With the passing of his mother and in his state of despairing helplessness, she could do little else than extend Christian mercy. Colm hung around the Larkin kitchen as much as the traffic would bear and Brigid predictably swept around his feet and complained about inheriting a non-paying star boarder.

Of an evening or two, now and then, she'd allow Colm to have the comfort of her fire. Actually, he was harmless enough, content to puff away at his pipe, and of course they had their farms in common to discuss.

It was not that Brigid was totally and completely without suitors and they did indeed sniff around on occasion. But these were men twenty years or more older than herself who got a glint in their eyes only after seeing her fine cottage and prosperous fields. It was a sorry and washed-out lot, the best among them being widowers with large broods and in search of a house slave.

Come a ceilidhe or wedding or fair or wake, it seemed natural enough, being as they had lifelong adjoining cottages and fields, that they attend together . . . but certainly not as an intended couple.

Her years of built-up disdain for Colm tempered to toleration. There were some decent points about him. He was a good farmer and trader. He paid his rents and debts on time. His drinking was within bearable bounds. Moreover, he said the rosary every day of his life with his blessed mother and never failed to attend mass.

As one month led to another and these into seasons and years, Colm O'Neill became accepted by her as a reasonable human being, his good traits admired and his bad ones not as bad as once feared. It occurred to her, in their daily dealings, Colm was not exactly what one would call a hard man. He'd never bang on tables as had her father and brother. He'd do what he was told so long as he was fed, his fire smoored and his cows milked. He'd never raise his voice, much less lay a hand on her in anger. All of this was highly commendable.

There was another side to it. The bed. It was so empty. Yet thought of sharing it with Colm continued to be utterly disgusting. He was less than better than nothing. It was the bed that seized her up with apprehension. She was awkward and inexperienced and it would be difficult at best. With Colm it would be impossible.

If, however, it was her decision to marry him she could not go into God's church and make sacred vows while lying in her heart. Every man had his marriage rights and every woman her sacred duty to produce children. Could she bring herself to do it?

A long visit with Father Cluny provided some of the answers. The priest intimated that Brigid would not be alone among the women of Ballyutogue who found the sexual experience with their husbands a sacrificial part of life. God, the priest said, had never intended that the sexual union be a pleasurable aspect of marriage. Carnal delights in themselves were terrible sins and any good Catholic wife had to come to understand that these should play no part in the marriage.

The point was, Father Cluny impressed, that Brigid loved Jesus and Mary more than she abhorred the idea of performing her Christian function as wife and mother.

Once she realized love of God was what prevailed, she could accept the discomfort of sex.

Father Cluny was a wise man indeed and gave Brigid much to consider. Yes, she concluded, after much meditation and prayer, she loved God enough to bear the revulsion. After all, wasn't that what most of the women of Ballyutogue felt?

*

The harvest was in and it had been a fine one. Days and nights became long and idle this time of year and Colm found himself spending more and more time in her cottage. Despite her love of God, she never quite got onto the idea of sleeping with the man.

... so there he was of a winter's night sitting by her fire like his lordship at the manor, playing glink with his crony, Muggins Malone ...

... what was forthcoming did not take long to come forth ...

"I'll thank you not to be dragging in half the mud of the town and tracking it through my house ..."

... at which Muggins slipped off quietly to Dooley McCluskey's ...

... leaving Colm scratching his head and looking about for telltale footprints. "There's no mud here at all," he said. "Sure we left our boots in the byre before coming in."

"Well, maybe you did this time," she snipped, "but it seems I spend half my waking hours cleaning up after you and attending to Your Worship's needs."

Colm scratched his head some more, then mumbled his way to the byre door, plopped on his prat and tugged on his Wellingtons.

"And where do you think you're going, Colm O'Neill?"

"Home."

"Or Dooley McCluskey's?"

Now you've got to realize that Colm was a docile sort, and not too quick in receiving heady thoughts either. This one was quite clear. He grunted to his feet. "Indeed I can go there if I want to," he said, "we're not married, you know."

It was true she had ministered to a number of his needs

since the departure of his beloved mother but she was making inroads into his freedom as well. It was a freedom guaranteed by Mairead since his birth and had negated any desire for the burden of a wife. Brigid Larkin now displayed the evils of matrimony. Why shouldn't he drink at Dooley McCluskey's? The crops were in. The rents were paid. Why the hell shouldn't he?

Just as clearly some new thoughts dawned on Brigid. There were damned fool concessions men demanded and she'd have to be wise enough to accept this if she intended to attain him as a husband.

"Aw, come now, Colm," she cooed. "I've the kettle on and tea will be but a minute."

"I don't want no tea," he pouted. "I want a hardy go."

She pacified him by producing a bottle of poteen, then oozed about saying as how she was constantly concerned over his well-being since his saintly mother had departed. This was followed by a practical discussion over the terrible waste of cottages, two fields and two of everything. The money that could be saved was in staggering amounts.

Colm half heard it and half didn't, for he was after testing his newly discovered authority and polished off several slugs of poteen in rapid order, which upped the level of his courage as he did. He wobbled to his feet, inhaled and burped the belch of true manhood. "I have seen the way you treated Rinty Doyle. Why, the old dear groveled about like a mongrel. And speaking of dogs, I'll come here no more until mine is welcome to share the fire with me. Why, woman, you keep this place like an institution. The cows are even afraid to shit in your byre!"

"Blessed Mother, hold your tongue, Colm."

"Why?" he asked, wavering. "Shit in the byre, SHIT IN THE BYRE!"

"You can take your leave!"

"Aye, I will. I wouldn't have the half of it"—he snapped his fingers—"not the half of it."

"And don't you be crawling back!"

"Nae, I won't, not until my pals and my dog are welcome, and I'll tell you as well that Fanny O'Doherty doesn't find me all that disgusting . . ."

"Indeed!"

Brigid found herself weeping pitifully when she was alone. She was down to herself and no one else. It was so bad even Colm O'Neill didn't want her.

For a week he did no calling. Each night she walked from room to room studying the sterilized world of her creation. Thank God there was no slob about to muck things up. It could be that way for her up to the end . . . if she wanted it. . . .

*

There was not much of a celebration when Colm and Brigid were married. The aged bachelors and those married men waterlogged with children all shook their heads with certain knowledge. Colm had won some concessions for now but how long until she began her fumigation again?

With her wedding day accomplished, she began to flirt with the idea of the glory of motherhood. Yet in all her anxieties about herself she had little anxiety for Colm. He was nearly as inexperienced as herself, as shy, and with poor little capability to adapt to the new situation.

Night followed night in which they undressed separately, one getting beneath the covers quickly so the other would not see, and they lay still, back to back, unspeaking and untouching, neither having the wherewithal to do anything about it.

After a time the day's work and the evening's drink took its toll and Colm would break the tension by announcing sleep had come with a thunderous snore.

In a few months certain things did not matter to Brigid, such as Colm and his mongrel dog leaving their fire for Dooley McCluskey's. It was a relief, truth be known, when he left, for she would be able to prepare herself for bed without the usual embarrassment.

As various times of the year came and went without Brigid announcing pregnancy, the wise old hens of Ballyutogue clucked that the Larkin legacy had come to an end.

CHAPTER TWELVE: Shelley read the unsaid messages. She knew from past experience that Conor would soon be going into that mysterious world she could not share. The first hint was his arranging time off. The yard was still closed but he had been traveling to Rathweed Hall daily to work out with the club. He set up a three-day absence for himself, the longest he had taken.

That day and evening he avoided liquor, an indication he wanted nothing to cloud his mind. He always abstained before taking off alone.

The final clue was the way he made love to her that night. It was devoid of fierceness, a lingering state of not being awake and not being asleep, the softest kind of statement, an attempt to stretch minutes into timelessness.

The alarm jolted them into reality and they continued to loll until several minutes past their deadline, then pensively set the day into motion.

Despite Shelley's outward show of placidness, they were totally into each other's minds, knowing the other's apprehensions. Conor sensed her rising fear as she waited for some kind of word.

Shelley had told him nothing of the anonymous hate letters. There had been three of them, each spewing venom and depicting her as the lowest kind of harlot for living with a Catholic. Each threatened her life for her unutterable crime.

Before that it had been the trauma of the break with the family. Apparently it had been palatable for her to carry on a years-long clandestine affair with a married man but living in the open with an R.C. was too much to bear. Morgan commanded the family not to see her and never to mention her name within his walls. Robin alone defied his father in continuing a rather mournful relationship with his sister. The others obeyed. She and Conor had moved out of his Flax Street flat to a more receptive area near the Cavehill Road but no place was far enough away within Belfast.

"I want you to stay with Blanche," Conor said over breakfast. She said that she would. "It's very important this time. I'll be away for several days. It could be a bit dicy, so let Robin know you are at Blanche's and if anything goes wrong you might have to leave Belfast in a hurry. Robin better know. Get to Dublin and go to Seamus or Atty Fitzpatrick."

She waited until he left the table to allow herself to

shudder. He had never given such instructions before. Obviously, there would be great danger. Conor returned with the pistol and set it down.

"Take this thing," he said.

"Shouldn't you be carrying it?"

"Either I make it or I don't. This will make no difference."

Shelley stared at the weapon and shook her head. "You know I could never use it."

"You were certainly ready to shoot when you were sitting at my bedside guarding me," he said.

"That was different," Shelley said.

Conor shrugged and strapped on his shoulder holster. "That's the trouble with both of us, lass. I'm not sure I could pull the trigger either. My commander is fully aware of that possibility."

"I think I like you better this way," she said.

Conor looked at his watch and grimaced. "We'll most likely be leaving Belfast for good after I return from this trip. I'll be glad about it myself. Every time I come back here I have the feeling I've entered a madhouse."

Shelley had said nothing of her own recurring dream. She was all alone and all the streets were completely dark and she walked endlessly down rows and rows of red brick houses, through mazes, into dead ends without sight of human life. She would awaken knowing it was a vision of death.

Conor gulped his tea down, put on his jacket and cap and allowed himself a last lingering look. It would be good to get out of Belfast. It was no place for a Catholic man and a Protestant woman.

The Sandy Row toughs had an outstanding score to settle over the imprisonment of Vessey Bain and Joey Hooker. Talk of it never flagged at certain pubs and Orange Halls. They were no more apt to forget than they would forget the Battle of the Boyne or Derry's walls.

And Oliver Cromwell MacIvor's ladies seethed with a score of their own to settle with Shelley for the shame she had brought on her fine and pious family.

Conor and Shelley touched cheeks.

"No matter what happens, it's been all I've wanted," she said.

"No matter what," Conor said, and he was gone.

*

Long Dan Sweeney came to Belfast the instant the cable was received from Owen O'Sullivan that the guns were on the way. When Conor reported the train route, Sweeney sent for Kelly Malloy out of Dungannon.

Kelly was a rose grower by profession, a breeder of varieties of the magnificent Ulster roses that gave him a measure of note throughout the eastern part of the province. He was titular head of the Dungannon Clubs which had sprung up in the area with the Gaelic revival. They were first cousins of the Wolfe Tone Societies and other republican-oriented groups in the north.

He was also a member of the Irish Republican Brotherhood.

His business required a number of wagons as well as an intimate standing with the hill farmers in the area where he constantly tested soils, water conditions and fertilizers and used some of their acreage for growing export bushes.

Kelly reckoned he could organize the gun drop in the thirty-odd hours allotted him. It would mean rounding up enough sympathizers and finding a good temporary dump. The hills around Omagh were filled with abandoned booley houses, souterrains and mine shafts. Sixmilecross was pinpointed as the best siding in a cover of forest.

When Kelly left, Dan Sweeney found Conor in a snit.

"What's wrong, Conor?" he demanded right off.

"You ought to know. Up till five minutes before Kelly arrived I told you there was an element of risk beyond normal risk. You know damned well we may be flirting with an informer. He should have been told. I'm willing to take the chance but at least I know it exists."

Long Dan studied Conor, his own continuing notions about the man being compounded. Every time he wanted to promote Conor to the Council doubts crept in to qualify it. Larkin continued to evade him as a man and it could be too late to find out in a crisis situation.

"It's incumbent upon a commander to inform his men," Conor snapped. "Do you think a British officer wouldn't explain it to a patrol?"

"I told you once, Conor, we can't play by British rules. As you may have noted from our conversations, we have four members of the Brotherhood between Dungannon and Omagh. Four men, mind you. That's it, the total

number. Before this war is over you're going to have to
order good men into death a dozen times without their
knowledge of it . . . if you have the ability to do it . . ."

"Maybe I don't."

"Maybe you don't, indeed," Dan answered. "There is
only one decision to be made here, and the rest of it is
useless rhetoric . . . those rifles are more important than
Kelly Malloy, the men he recruits and Conor Larkin, as
well."

*

Conor debarked from the passenger train in late afternoon at Sixmilecross, examined the area, liked it. Beyond
the one-street town, it was completely inconspicuous and
held an obscure siding surrounded by trees as Kelly Malloy had promised. The crossroad led directly into the hills
toward Ballygawley and the spray of booley houses and
abandoned mines.

He continued by foot toward Carrickmore, inquiring
after and finding the farm of Sterling McDade.

Throughout the early evening wagons arrived one at a
time from Kelly Malloy's nursery in Dungannon, from
Coalisland, Pomeroy and Ballygawley. By seven at night
they had all assembled. There were the four brothers and
six other sympathizers in all, including Kelly and Conor,
and six wagons. Crude maps were passed around pinpoint-
ing the dump locations. Sterling McDade, the ugliest of
Irishmen, was the most intimate with the area, having
trekked the hills for over fifty summers of his life. Specific assignments and routes to them were given over
lamplight. Conor reckoned that, with the unbolting of
plates and various other problems, the transfer of the
weapons would take two hours. Provided the train reached
the crossing no later than midnight, Sterling reckoned
the dump could be accomplished before daylight.

As the planning went on Conor studied them. They
were the faces of Ballyutogue, the crust and wrinkle and
leather skin of men who really needed no explanation of
what they were doing or why. They were the Kilty and
Tomas Larkins and Fergus O'Neills of their own villages
who had lived in privation in the shadow of Orange hysteria and British arrogance. Craggy specimens, the lot.
They were the Irish.

By half eight, each man in turn had recited his specific duty to Conor's satisfaction. McDade's wife, a lovely contrast to himself, and the daughters set out a spread of scroggins, a stomach-warming stew and soda bread.

They puffed their pipes and stared into the fire as the minutes to rendezvous came close. Kelly Malloy left and returned at half nine with word that the Omagh stationmaster had been telegraphed that the special Red Hand Express would be passing through around eleven. Estimated arrival at Sixmilecross, a quarter past midnight. Although the message was entirely expected, it came as a shocker. Conor allowed a few minutes for each of them to look inward by themselves and to themselves, then it was time to move out.

"Well, lads, a wee drop before facing the night," Sterling McDade said.

"No liquor," Conor snapped, then laughed. "We'd best all have a clear head. We'll do our celebrating for sure tomorrow morning."

At a quarter past ten the teams began moving from McDade's farm to an area just out of Sixmilecross at intervals of several minutes. Conor arrived first and scoured the area. It was clear. As they came in, one at a time, their wagons were moved to prearranged places of cover and the men assembled down close to the track. At ten minutes to midnight everything was in place. The horses were given oat bags to feed and assure their silence.

Midnight. Conor studied the sky, grateful that cloud cover had blotted the moon and further darkened the area. He nodded to Sterling McDade, who lit a lantern and moved down the track to signal the train.

Two minutes past midnight. Two drunks from the public house in town wove to the crossing and decided to sit and rest for a spell, then went into their repertory of song.

Conor looked desperately down the track to McDade's position, then turned to the others.

"Who knows them?"

"I do," Adam Sharkey said.

"Get your wagon, fetch them and get them out of here."

"How about my load?"

"We'll have to make do with one less. Each of you put on a hundred more pieces and two or three boxes of ammunition. Do you have it?"

"Aye," they whispered as Sharkey emerged from cover. He took the feedbags off his horses, climbed up on his rig, loosened the brake and pulled out to the road and stopped before the midnight revelers. "Evening to youse, Jerry Hayes, and to yourself as well, George Gleeson."

"I do believe it's Adam Sharkey or a facsimile of his ghost, and what be you doin' wandering around in the middle of the night?"

"Me and me old lady had a fierce go. She's been wearing the smile of last year's rhubarb on her face. Could I be takin' youse home and layin' myself down in your byre tonight, Jerry?" he said, going down after them and pulling them to their feet. As the two headed in opposite directions with great uncertainty, Adam Sharkey steered them hard to the wagon.

The light of McDade's lantern signaled down the track!

"In with youse, lads, just pile in and grab a nap . . . in with youse . . ."

The sound of four faint whistles reached Sixmilecross the instant Adam Sharkey moved the wagon out with the rear occupants breaking into song.

Ellen O'Connor, Ellen aroon!
Say youse love me, say youse come back soon,
The angels in their mercy to guide you o'er the spray,
To keep youse from all harm, till youse return some-
day. . . .

"Steady, lads," Kelly Malloy whispered.

In a moment Sterling McDade's lantern swung back and forth, back and forth. The sound of the train was now clearly within earshot. It slowed under a braking. The eight at the crossing tensed. As it rounded a slight bend into sight Conor ordered the men to their wagons. The train grew larger and larger. The brake screeched and it hissed to almost stopping. McDade ran alongside, threw the siding switch, and it inched into the lay-by.

"Let's go!" Conor commanded.

The wagons moved alongside in a line, the horses protesting the abrupt halt to their reverie and the strange duty.

"Lower the water tank!" Conor yelled up to the car. "Darren and Carberry, get them out of the tank!" he repeated their orders. "Kelly, grab your wrenches, let's get these underplates removed."

As Kelly Malloy slipped between the wheels under the car and lay on the ties, he lit his lantern. Conor jumped up to the engine for a quick exchange with the drivers.

They wore different faces!

"Scatter!" Conor screamed, leaping from the side. "Ambush!"

At that instant the thunder of two hundred pair of boots erupted as soldiers spilled out of the cars.

"You're all under arrest!"

Conor rolled below the undercarriage to Kelly Malloy. He caught a glimpse of the crossroad where a second force was converging by motor van.

"Attention! Attention!" the commander shouted over a megaphone. "There is no possibility of escape! You are under arrest! Anyone caught moving will be shot!"

"Mother of God!"

"Ambush!"

"Attention! Attention! Do not resist! Raise your hands and gather by the engine!"

The emptied train quickly threw a cordon around the smuggling party. The troops had all come out of the left-hand side to the wagons. Conor elbowed Kelly and pointed and Kelly nodded. They rolled down the bed of the un-guarded right side, crouched and drifted toward the end of the train and looked to a covering growth of under-brush a few yards away.

"There goes two of them!"

"Halt!"

"Halt, do you hear, halt!"

"Open fire!"

Just as they reached the brush the night was shattered with gunfire. Kelly Malloy screamed and pitched forward. Conor buckled . . . a queer sensation flooded him . . . his legs went awry . . . he dived for cover. . . .

* * *

Shelley sat up and shrieked, her heart thumping and her face soaked with sweat. The door was flung open. Blanche Hemming rushed in, lit the room and threw her arms about her friend.

"Conor! Conor!"

"Get hold of yourself! It was only a dream!"

"Blanche! I saw it! He's all bloody!"

"Shhh . . . please . . . please . . . Shelley . . ."

"Get Robin," she gasped, "Blanche, get Robin . . . I've got to get out of Belfast . . . now. . . ."

CHAPTER THIRTEEN: We waited, half out of our minds, for some kind of word from the disaster at Sixmilecross. First Shelley MacLeod arrived with her brother and I got her to a safe house at once.

Then we heard.

Kelly Malloy was dead. Conor Larkin had been seriously wounded. Sterling McDade and the hill farmers Carberry, Darren, McGovern, Gorman, Gilroy and McAulay were in Mountjoy Prison. Over the water Owen O'Sullivan and his sons Barry and Brian and Dudley Callaghan were interned in Brixton. One of the farmers, it appeared, had somehow escaped capture. It was a shambles, an utter catastrophe for the Brotherhood.

When we read the papers a day later we could not believe our eyes. In their heady zeal, the British had made a horrendous blunder. The Crown information office boasted that they had "smashed a well-organized ring of gunrunners of the Irish Republican Brotherhood which had been operating a smuggling route for months." The story went on to give a full account of how Sir Frederick Weed's private train had been used in the plot.

For years Dublin Castle had refused to acknowledge existence of any Irish Republican Brotherhood. It had been stated on occasion after occasion that there was no such organization except in the minds of a few feeble old Fenians. Well now, just how could such a nonexistent nonentity smuggle guns into Ireland? What the British had admitted in their haste to blow their own horn was that their years of customized propaganda had been a lie. Suddenly the disaster of Sixmilecross took on a different dimension. The audacity of the scheme was the kind of lunacy to capture Irish hearts and was greeted with humor that we understood and the British never would. The country erupted in one long loud laugh. Dublin Castle realized too late what they had done and their faces reddened with humiliation. By admission of our existence they had achieved a notoriety for us that we had been unable to achieve for ourselves.

So the Irish dog refused to lie still and the Brotherhood was alive. As quandary replaced arrogance (and the information officer was replaced as well) news of our revival reached into every corner of the land. Dublin Castle became our greatest recruiter as Sixmilecross changed from a defeat to a bizarre kind of victory. We'd lost the guns but we'd gained the ear of the nation and, perhaps, thousands of willing men.

*

Robert Emmet McAloon, a rumpled old legal wizard who had been an intimate of Desmond Fitzpatrick, inherited the full responsibility of republican matters after the latter's demise. He jumped into the breach but ran into a stone wall.

The governor of Mountjoy Prison advised him he was under orders to keep the Sixmilecross prisoners isolated and allowed no visitors, even legal counsel. The whereabouts of Conor Larkin was kept secret. All that we knew was that he was alive and the only information we were allowed to get to him was that Shelley was safely out of Belfast.

Robert Emmet McAloon was a tactician of rare acumen and had struggled too long in the backwaters of anti-Irish law to be dismayed. For three weeks no action was taken on his petitions to the court. As he pressed the word came down from the Four Courts, the home of British justice in Ireland, that habeas corpus had been suspended in the case. The court cited several of the more than one hundred coercion acts they had enacted against the Irish during the nineteenth century.

Robert Emmet McAloon then switched to a different tactic. The British were still smarting over the incident and wanted to regain their dignity. Brotherhood Council members also held high positions in the legally accepted Sinn Fein Party and moved forward with plans to use Sinn Fein as a front to unleash a plethora of orators to beat the drums, boil the pot, raise funds, gain national attention, indignation and sympathy for the Sixmilecross men. As a street corner speaker, Atty Fitzpatrick had few peers and she was tuned up and ready.

Shortly after Sinn Fein announced a series of public protest rallies, Sir Lucian Bolt arrived from England bearing the title of special prosecutor for the Attorney General's office. Bolt was no friend of the Irish, having authored some of the most repressive legislation against us during his time in Commons. He was to be feared in republican circles. McAloon reckoned that the government had finally worked out a policy in the matter and Sir Lucian Bolt would soon be getting into contact. . . . He was right, as usual.

*

Brendan Sean Barrett was slipped back into Ireland where we felt he would be safer, and along with Dan Sweeney, Atty and myself, we became the Brotherhood's liaison to McAloon on Sixmilecross. After Bobby's first meeting with Sir Lucian we convened in the elegant library of a safe house in Ballsbridge. Robert Emmet was never far out of the courtroom in spirit and paced before us as though we were a jury on the make.

"I have agreed for the moment," he began, "to call off the public protest meetings."

Atty groaned discontent.

"Sir Lucian is obviously fishing about for a deal. On the way here I was allowed to visit the seven in Mountjoy unofficially. Small wonder they didn't want us to see them earlier. They've been brutally tortured."

Brendan Sean Barrett and Long Dan showed no emotion at the revelation. It was an old story to them.

"They've been hooded, forced to stand at attention against the wall, spread-eagled, for periods of up to twenty hours without food, water or toilet facilities. The Gorman chap sported some nasty cigarette burns. Gilroy had been urinated on several times and McDade had been forced to run barefooted through a corridor of broken glass. The lot of them reported being fed something which caused vomiting and hallucinations."

"Old but reliable methods," Sweeney said.

"Of course they were played off one against the other. They had nothing to give in the way of information except the name of the one man who seems to have gotten away. They knew nothing except that Kelly Malloy recruited them for the job and Kelly is dead."

McAloon plopped his seventy-year-old frame into an overstuffed leather chair and went into instant disarray.

"What about Conor Larkin?" I asked.

"Apparently he's not at Mountjoy. They promised to let me see him in due course. I'm telling you this because I have agreed for the moment that your pen will remain silent, Seamus, as well as your lungs, Atty."

"What do you reckon the government is up to?" Dan asked.

Robert Emmet McAloon leaned forward in the chair and pinched at the flab on his neck, then held his forefinger aloft. "I make it that the British want to quiet this down and avoid public inflammation on three counts. Point number one," he said, grabbing his forefinger and wiggling it. "Nothing will benefit the Brotherhood so much as a bitter court trial and a long prison sentence. Agreed?"

We did.

"Point two," Bobby continued, adding his middle finger. "The situation in Europe. Wouldn't you think so, Brendan?"

He nodded. "A land war in Europe is inevitable," Brendan Sean Barret continued. "Britain has just concluded the triple entente with Russia and France to counter the alliance of Germany and Austria-Hungary. As we know, one of Britain's ancient justifications for the occupation of Ireland is that we straddle their sea lanes, they are an island and our geographic location makes us necessary to their defense."

"Precisely," McAloon interrupted. "It can be a phobia with them. They envision, no doubt, an enlarged Irish Republican Brotherhood flirting with the Germans to obtain arms."

"What's the difference?" Barrett mused. "We'll go to the Germans when the time is ripe whether they wish it or not."

Bobby threw his arms out wide. "Well, they're sitting around a long mahogany table playing these little games, refusing to accept the inevitability of the situation and figuring out how to delay it as long as possible."

"Point number three?" Atty asked.

"Point number three," the barrister continued, "and

this might be the most practical point of all. As we know,
the Protestants in Ulster have been arming for years. Obviously, this is the basket the British want to put their
eggs into. The defense of this vulnerable British flank
should be in the hands of loyal subjects, right? On the
surface they can't publicly approve Ulster gunrunning
without giving the same consideration to the south. It's a
tacit approval, one in which they turn their backs, close
their eyes and cover their ears. They want Protestant
Ulster armed as a hedge against Home Rule crisis and a
war in Europe. For the moment they want to play a game
of acting evenhanded. If they give the Sixmilecross
people severe prison sentences they will be faced with
counter-demands to do the same to the gunrunners in
Ulster."

"In other words," Atty said, "slap us down and hound
us in our smuggling efforts but allow it to slip through
up north."

"That's it," Robert Emmet McAloon said, "that's it
precisely." He stretched his legs to their limit on the
floor, tucked his hands behind his neck and stared at the
ceiling as though it held an audience. "It is my considered
opinion that Sir Lucian Bolt is prepared to go for mild
sentences, say a few years, in exchange for our keeping
quiet over the condition of the prisoners and halting
public meetings."

A long silence of digestion ensued. Atty would be
deprived of her public stage, her thing of glory. As for me,
I was plainly selfish in wanting to spare Conor twenty
years behind bars. The brunt of it fell on Dan Sweeney,
who was faced with the organizational task of the
Brotherhood. On the surface it seemed that he would
want public protests and to harvest a rush of new
recruits. Yet it was Sweeney made the strongest case of all
for restraint. Heavy recruitment at this stage of the
Brotherhood's development would leave it terribly
vulnerable. Staffs, commands and units had not yet been
formed. There were no procedures established to screen
applicants. It would be too simple a matter for the
British to load up our ranks with informers.

What could we do with several thousand men at this
stage? We had no weapons to train them with or even
enough safe places to carry out such training. Dan was

convincing. We would lay ourselves wide open by taking in too many people before we had set up proper foundation.

"We've got to build slowly, man by man," Dan said. "Every new recruit at this time must be a reliable piece of personnel. When we get ten good men in Cork, ten in Derry, ten in Galway, then we can branch out to units. I have to go along with Bobby and have him strike a bargain with Lucian Bolt."

With Atty, Dan and myself in accord, we turned to Brendan Sean Barrett, who had remained quiet during much of the discussion. He was sour, perhaps beyond his time and purposefulness, and I can't say as I felt a tad of human warmth from the man.

"Obviously, I'm outvoted," he said sarcastically.

"What's on your mind, Brendan?" Dan growled.

"This country is destitute. The labor strikes collapsed because we're too beaten and downtrodden to make a stand. There's a desperate need for consciences to be stirred. We have the moment in our hands. If we don't grasp it, it may take a long time coming again, if ever."

"And I still think it's premature," Dan retorted. "Open our ranks now and the British will infiltrate and crush us in a month."

Brendan Sean Barrett held up his hands in surrender as we nodded to McAloon to make a deal with Sir Lucian Bolt. Barrett's life had been a defeat, so one more wouldn't matter. He got up first, made toward the door, then turned.

"Tell me, Bobby, and you, Dan, when did you learn it?"

"What?" They asked in unison.

"That an Irishman can sit down and negotiate an agreement with the British and not get fucked."

CHAPTER FOURTEEN: As Robert Emmet
McAloon went into conference with Sir Lucian Bolt I became immersed in trying to piece together the events that had led up to the ambush at Sixmilecross. I was not kept waiting long.

Terry O'Rourke, a teammate of Conor's on the

Boilermakers, showed up looking for me at my newspaper one morning. Terry was from a republican family of long standing and knew of my friendship with Conor.

Conor was the admired leader among the Catholic lads on the club and after Sixmilecross they got together to try to figure out what had happened. When they did Terry was sent as an emissary to me. My republican leanings were no secret. Without putting it into words, Terry felt that I would get the story to the Brotherhood.

Doxie O'Brien, as well as Duffy, had been the informers. Duffy O'Hurley had blurted out what had been doing during one of his regular drunks. Doxie as well as another Catholic on the team heard it. On another occasion Terry himself overheard Duffy and Doxie arguing over his continued participation.

Doxie had a chance of a lifetime; fame and fortune went with the Sydney rugby job. It hung in the balance, depending largely on how well the Boilermakers played and if they went through with an Australian tour. Doxie was desperate to get the position, which depended greatly on the whim of his sponsor, Sir Frederick Weed. It was so tempting Doxie was willing to do anything to curry Sir Frederick's favor and "prove" himself.

Apparently Doxie had traveled to Derry and delivered Duffy an ultimatum. In the end Duffy was convinced he had to go to Sir Frederick and tell him everything in return for special consideration.

All of this seemed to add up, for Doxie was under heavy protection and his family already moved to Australia. Part of the accord between McAloon and Sir Lucian Bolt was a provision restraining the Brotherhood from seeking vengeance.

While the rest of the Sixmilecross people waited in jail, Duffy and Calhoun had entered guilty pleas and received sentences of under a year. It seemed obvious that they would also be resettled in a remote place.

The final agreement shaped up along the lines that Bobby had figured. Excluding Conor, who had not been contacted yet, the Sixmilecross men would plead guilty and receive one- to two-year sentences under less stringent articles of one of the coercion acts. In exchange, the Brotherhood would not pursue public sympathy, not avenge the informers, and this included a pledge from me not to write about it.

In a manner of speaking it was a backhanded compliment to myself. The British had never forgiven me for my Boer War concentration camp articles. No one knew for certain if I was a member of the Brotherhood but there was no mistaking my sympathies. They had enough respect for my pen to keep it silent. Of course, Conor was being held hostage to assure that silence.

For the moment, both sides seemed satisfied. The existence of the Brotherhood was public knowledge and both parties got the time they vied for. Brendan Sean Barrett was right about one thing. We would deal with the Germans for arms when we were ready and the British had lulled themselves into believing the Irish problem would disappear as they had believed it in the past.

We were called together again by Bobby and when we convened we found him in a quandary. He had been given permission and made the attempt to see Conor Larkin but Conor refused to speak to him. A wrench had been thrown into the agreement and no one knew exactly why.

Dan was angry and spilled out sorely over his doubts about Conor.

"Sure, he's been a good man," Sweeney argued, "but he's too much of a loner and if truth be known he's got other failings I've been worrying about as well."

"Just a minute, Dan," I said. "If there's something going on inside him, you can bet he's thought it out with great care."

"The Brotherhood has sent him a lawyer and he's refused to see him. That's disobedience of an order. He's no right to take decisions like this on his own. I want to know what the hell's going on."

Brendan Sean Barrett's face wore a look of wisdom. "We all have a suspicion what's in his mind, don't we, Dan?" he taunted.

"I've a notion and he'll screw us up royally if he tries to pull off something on his own. Don't give me none of your studious shit, Barrett, this is an organization with a code and discipline and he's going to obey."

"Now we've a problem," I interrupted. "It was you,

Dan, who told us something we've longed to hear and wanted to believe since we were kids. You spread on the horseshit as thick as Conor's ma spread butter on my bread. 'Don't be afraid of the butter,' she'd say. Well, Dan, are you getting afraid of the horseshit you spread ... you know ... one man's ability to endure is worth an entire army? You know, Dan, the martyrdom soliloquy. Quote Long Dan Sweeney our idol, 'The British have nothing in their entire arsenal or imperial might to counter a single man who refuses to be broken, et cetera, et cetera, et cetera.'"

"I hear you, Seamus, I hear you. You know fucking well that I have to wear more than one hat in this organization. At times when I'm standing before new men I have to make an attempt to inspire them. But day in and day out I'm the pragmatic organizer of a secret army. Our rolls will be filled with martyrs soon enough. At this moment we're not in a position to start up a fight."

"Sure, I don't know about that," the caustic Brendan Sean Barrett retorted before I could speak. "Dan, you're telling us it will start when you've got your units organized, trained and armed and your plans on the board. Dan presses his magic little button and says those immortal words ... 'Lads, commence the rising.' That's not how the Fenian Rising started, was it, Dan?"

"I know how it started and I know how it ended for the two of us."

"What makes you think it will be different this time? With all our dreaming and scheming and secret meetings and gun smuggling, we'll only be able to put a few thousand men out on the street. We're not going to do it without the weapon that a single man carries in his heart. That's what we're facing with Larkin and that's what we're afraid of. I'll tell you when it's going to start, Dan, not sooner, not later. It will start when one man alone has decided he's had enough."

We consumed this, trembling. Sweeney brushed at his white hair in uncharacteristic nervousness and all we could hear was Robert Emmet McAloon tapping his eyeglasses against his teeth, waiting for our decision.

"Atty?" Dan asked.

"It seems to me the British have made themselves a good bargain by silencing us. I agree with Brendan that we ought to stand up and scream while we have the opportunity and while the people are eager to listen."

Dan uncorked an audible sigh, looking from one to the other, completely outvoted. He closed his eyes and rubbed them with the heels of his hands as he spoke. "I appreciate your views. As chief of staff, I cannot take a position contrary to what I consider to be the safety of the organization. My decision is to instruct Bobby to see if the British will allow Seamus to visit Conor in the role of an old friend. Seamus is to convey the message that Larkin is to enter a plea of guilty along with the rest of the men. If he refuses, the Brotherhood is no longer bound or responsible to him." He looked up. "Is it your intention to overrule my decision?"

We swallowed hard, then accepted his ultimatum uncontested.

"All right, Bobby. Tell Sir Lucian we agree. An attempt will be made to convince Larkin. If he doesn't go along he is outside the accord."

*

A military staff car drove me out of Dublin into County Kildare to the secret place of Conor's incarceration. In a little over an hour we passed through the guard post of the British military camp at the Curragh. After a personal shakedown I was placed in an empty room in the disciplinary barrack and waited. It had been seven weeks since Sixmilecross.

As the door gave way and Conor was prodded into the room my heart waged war between tears of relief and tears of sorrow. He was manacled about the neck, waist, wrists and ankles.

"Hello runt," he rasped, sliding along the floor with a limp from one of the bullets. His left arm and shoulder were still heavily bandaged and in a sling from the other bullets which had entered his back. His eyes had sunk to ringed sockets, his beard and hair were caked and matted and the bones of his cheeks protruded. A ton of flesh had wasted from his body.

I put my arms about him and sobbed out of control. He turned away, dropped to the bench along the wall and looked questioningly to the guard detail where the young officer in charge sniffed his nostrils like a rabbit.

"I'll call you if I require room service," Conor said.

The officer grunted in contempt and left, locking and bolting us in.

"Has the room got ears?" I asked.

"God, no," Conor answered. "They may beat your brains out but they're far too proper to resort to anything as low as eavesdropping. How's Shelley?"

I nodded. "Fine, beautiful. As for yourself, I think we grew better-looking potatoes during the famine."

"I'll not be up for rugby this year," he said, lifting his shirt. I closed my eyes at the sight of his welted body thumped terrible shades of purple. I pulled my stool close, set my mouth near his ear and brought him up to date on everything. It was the first he'd heard that Kelly Malloy was dead and that Callaghan and the O'Sullivans had been taken as well.

I went on to explain the rest of it. The treachery of Doxie O'Brien, which he already suspected, and the secret negotiations with the British. I stated my personal happiness at the thought of him getting off with a light sentence.

"I understand the Brotherhood's problems," Conor whispered. "But I understand my own problem even more clearly. I understand it all, the days and nights of reading, the wandering and the pondering. All the years of groping. I understand it."

"What are you going to do!" I cried, frightened.

"I'm not completely sure. I am sure of what I'm not going to do. You see, runt, you can't just wait until the stars are in their right orbit to make your move in life, whether it's marriage or planting crops or having babies ... or staging a rising. Oh, we can fool ourselves and say we'll wait till things are right but, believe me, they can outwait us. We can negotiate but they'll outnegotiate us. After three hundred years of our faces in the mud and three hundred years of talking in circles, we've got to draw the line and test our mettle as a people. You see, we may not even prove ourselves worthy of freedom. We may not have what it takes. But we've got to find out. Maybe I'm not a good man for the Brotherhood because I can't still the anger in me any longer, no matter what my orders are."

"Look, you're not yourself. They've beaten you daft. Trust in me enough for guidance this once, Conor."

His black stare went right through me. "Look at me, man, look at me and tell me I don't know what I'm about. I'm Conor Larkin. I'm an Irishman and I've had enough."

I was so terribly ashamed. In my desperation to save him I'd forgotten so much. I was almost willing to throw away the very principles of my existence. He knew what he was doing, all right. I also knew at that moment that somehow I'd have to find a way to break my own vow of silence. . . .

CHAPTER FIFTEEN: The knocking on my door persisted me out of a heavy slumber. I staggered and groped, muttering that I was on my way, lighting the room and poking into my bathrobe. The air held a predawn chill so I allowed as it must have been Brotherhood business.

What a pleasant surprise to open the door and see the doorway filled with the tall and shapely person of Atty Fitzpatrick.

"Get dressed," she commanded, "I've a motorcar downstairs."

Volunteering no further information, I asked no questions. It was half four in the morning. Atty put on the kettle as I got myself together. We sipped a cup of tea and the stale remains of my bachelor cupboard, then made out to a stinging hoarfrost.

The driver was a Brotherhood lad of mechanical aptitude allowing Atty and me to bundle up in the back seat. Chugging into motion, we maneuvered southward through the empty streets.

"I got a call from Robert Emmet McAloon about an hour ago," Atty said. "The British are arraigning Conor and the other lads later this morning."

"It's five o'clock in the morning and it's Sunday. Where the hell are we going?"

"I'm not completely certain. Seems they've set up a courtroom someplace in the Wicklow Mountains."

"Oh, that's dirty business," I said.

My understanding of the agreement was that the British would hold the arraignment on the assize circuit in a small inconspicuous town where the proceedings would receive little note and be over with before protests could form. It seemed they were twisting the agreement to trickery. This hour of a Sunday morning in a secret place smelled like an *in camera* session.

Atty went on to say that Bobby had agreed only after the British consented to allow Atty and myself as observers. Once again they had made a good deal, for we were the pair bound to silence.

"I don't like the half of it," I mumbled, discontented.

*

Past the last suburb of Dundrum we continued south, soon rising in the foothills of the Wicklow Mountains through silent sleeping Enniskerry, demesne of Powerscourt, a great stately home of Wicklow granite razed and risen time and again in the wars and ultimately ceded to a loyal servant of the Crown, Richard Wingfield. Its tens of thousands of acres equaled the grants of the Hubbles and when you add on a hundred more baronies and earldoms you can get an idea of who owned what in Ireland.

The location, however, did serve as gateway to alpine wonderment. Although our drive was ominous and cold, I still could not help but quicken at sight of the night curtain rising on the forests, the falls and the streams in a land of wee folk and woodkerns. Atty and I were smitten by the rush of beauties beyond Great Sugar Loaf, up past Roundtree and the high reservoir of the Dublin waterworks.

We followed the River Avonmore to where it crossed the River Glenmacnass at the Vale of Clara, but a fairy's leap from the mystical ancient Celtic monastic ruins of Glendalough, which had been the fiefdom of St. Kevin.

A half mile beyond, Atty instructed the driver to turn onto an old military road that bisected the mountaintops east to west. It had been built by the British after the Wolfe Tone rising to deny future generations of rebels the cover of the high forests. In short order we halted before a barricade.

A British captain, eminently polite, requested identification, after which we were searched. The car and driver were ordered to remain as Atty and I continued on in a troop lorry up the twists and winds into the shadow of Lugnaquilla, the highest mountain in all of Ireland. We came to a halt where the River Ow plunged down past Aghavannagh.

We had arrived at a century-old barrack, a huge three-storied rectangular affair that still housed a contingent of troops to patrol the area. By queer coincidence, Charles Stewart Parnell once kept a shooting house at Aghavannagh which was still used by John Redmond, the present Irish Party leader. Otherwise we could not have been more removed and remote.

The barrack was ringed with troops at combat ready, requiring another identification and search before we gained entry. A Major Westcott finally escorted us into an abandoned armory hall which had been converted into a makeshift courtroom.

Atty and I sat alone for two hours under the surveillance of Major Westcott and a squad of his men. A bit before noon they began to filter in. First came Robert Emmet McAloon, dowdier than ever after a sleepless night. He threw his bundles on the counsel table, nodded to us and exchanged a few whispered greetings.

Then came Sir Lucian Bolt. He was an icy number indeed, a hedgerow stone with eyes.

The prisoners, save Conor, clanged and rattled into the hall manacled and chained to one another under escort of a dozen bayoneted riflemen, and were placed on a long single bench at the side of the room.

It was a sad-looking lot, hill farmers from up in the heather, yet they seemed unintimidated. Born into an eternal struggle, they had committed the crime of continuing the strife as their fathers had done. Fighting the British caused no moral quandary, for it was a way of life that everyone in the little Sixmilecrosses around Ireland lived by rote. Never a grand-looking group in the best of times, prison and special abuse accorded republicans made them appear like a dangerous pack of animals.

I looked up to see Conor enter, bearded, limping and drawn. He gave us a crack of a smile. From the look in

Atty's eyes I knew right then that any love she was capable of belonged to him. She reached for my hand in need of someone to touch and it was wet and trembling. Conor was separated from the others, locked to thick wall rings as though there were a mob outside ready to break in and free him. By the hush of the movements around him and the queer stare from Sir Lucian Bolt it was obvious the British respected the strength of this one unrepentant man.

The stone room, the chained prisoners, the preponderance of soldiers made the place seem more like something out of the post-Revolution era in France than a British court. All that was missing was the rabble in the gallery and the guillotine outside.

"All rise."

Sir Arnold Scowcroft, robed fit for a king's coronation, swept in with his entourage and seated himself at the head table. It was all over in a matter of minutes. Charges were read, some fifteen counts from stealing government property and illegally transporting it to membership in an illegal organization and violation of various articles of various coercion acts. By prearrangement Robert Emmet McAloon entered guilty pleas on two of the counts which were accepted by the prosecution. Thirteen counts were dropped by consent and the prisoners remanded to an unnamed penal institution to be sentenced at a later date and they were paraded out.

"We have the separate matter of defendant Larkin to dispose of, your lordship," Sir Lucian said.

"Bring the prisoner to the dock," the judge ordered, then broke into laughter. "I see we have no dock. Well, bring him before the bench."

Conor was unlocked and manhandled forward. Even in chains and rags he was imposing and more so because of his defiance. I was so afraid.

"Mr. McAloon, am I to understand that the prisoner has refused counsel?"

"That is the situation, your lordship."

Scowcroft studied Conor with the contempt only an English lord could impart to a croppy. "Read the charges."

The counts tolled off against him, building a case of treason of the highest order. After a further contemplation of Conor, the judge became menacing in his undertone. "You are aware, are you not, of the consequences of continuing this charade without counsel?"

Conor looked around the room slowly. "I am certainly aware a charade is taking place," he said. The room jolted to utter silence.

"How do you plead?" the judge asked at last.

Conor remained silent.

"Enter a plea of not guilty," Scowcroft directed.

"That is not my plea," Conor said.

"Perhaps you'd like to explain that to the court?"

"Yes," Conor said. "I do not recognize the existence, much less the legality, of this court."

Bobby looked to us puzzled but very interested. After a moment of digestion, Arnold Scowcroft became relaxed. He decided that, with all the travel to reach this secluded place and with all the other business dispensed of so quickly, he might enjoy a bit of sport. He leaned back in his chair, nodded and dared Conor to elucidate. "The court is interested in ascertaining how prisoner Larkin reached that conclusion."

"This court is illegal because your presence on Irish soil is illegal," Conor answered.

"And on what does the prisoner base that assumption?"

"On English common law."

Well, I'll tell you, you could have heard Charles Stewart Parnell and Daniel O'Connell stir in their graves if you listened hard enough.

"Take him away," Scowcroft said with a wave of the hand.

Bobby was on his feet! "The prisoner has the right to speak in his own defense," he said, citing one of the cornerstones of British justice. "Unless, of course, the court is satisfied to have the record bear out that he was silenced."

Sir Lucian Bolt came to the judge's rescue. "The Crown has no objection."

"I am prepared to allow prisoner Larkin to speak," the judge said, "but I advise him in advance that this is a court of law and his arguments will be restricted to issues and issues alone. You may go on, Larkin."

Conor took a few steps toward the bench and looked constantly from Sir Lucian Bolt to Sir Arnold Scowcroft.

"There are thousands of precedents in English common law of cases where a strong neighbor has used force by one means or another to impose his will on a weaker neighbor and such use of force as a method has always been deemed illegal in English courts. Without use of a proper legal library to support my argument, I will, nonetheless, attempt to cite a dozen or so landmark cases with which I am certain you are quite familiar."

Conor then went into the most magnificent extemporaneous dissertation I or anyone else within earshot had ever heard. At first, no one could believe the language coming from a man in rags and chains, then we all became totally swept up. He cited cases known to all lawyers of quarrels where force was declared illegal between neighbors in a close situation in cities, between farmers, between large estate holders, between municipalities, between counties and between British provinces on the mother island, Wales vs. England, Scotland vs. England. He went on to recite another dozen decisions, mostly made by colonial courts in the settlement of disputes between warring tribes and clans or provinces within a colony. His last set of citations dealt with international disputes in which the British had acted as arbitrator and, consistent with English common law, declared the use of force by a stronger neighbor on a weaker neighbor as no legal basis on which to settle a dispute.

"What you are saying through English common law is that you are desirous of existing with your neighbors in a country and a world where force is not permitted in the settlement of disputes because force by itself does not constitute right. As we know, by any definition, Ireland is the neighbor of England."

The place stood in awe. What I think astonished Sir Lucian Bolt, Sir Arnold Scowcroft and the other British who heard Conor's words was that such a profound theory emanated from a man representing a race which they truly believed to be inferior. I had the feeling that the legalists sensed they were hearing no idle rambling doomed to die in this room, but a statement which would be seized upon by every occupied people in the world who longed for their liberation. If English common law was an extension of God's supreme law, they were indeed in trouble in explaining their empire.

"If England had taken the position that we're going to have Ireland because we're stronger and we want it for exploitation, perhaps your presence here would be more understandable. However, the English went to enormous lengths to establish a legal basis for the entry into Ireland. Obviously they wanted to say to future generations, 'This is the reason we have come here.' What was the instrument of English legality for the invasion of Ireland? It was a papal bull issued in the year of 1154 granting you my country. Who gave you Ireland? The document was issued by an English Pope on the request of an English King . . . for the purpose of amassing kingdoms for his sons. . . . You hold up this document and say in this year of 1908, 'This is our right to Ireland.' Was it legal even then? Did the Pope own Ireland? Didn't an armed invasion negate the legality of the papal bull, according to English common law?"

"Your lordship," Sir Lucian said, rising, "I don't see why the court has to be subjected to what has degenerated into a Fenian tirade."

"I see nothing the prisoner has said to be outside the guidelines laid down by the court," McAloon snapped.

Scowcroft drummed his fingers on the table top. It had gotten to a point where he was afraid he would have to make a ruling on Larkin's thesis and he was a legalist of extreme pride.

"I wish to hear the rest of what Larkin has to say."

Conor drew a breath and took a step toward the judge, pointing his finger.

"On the assumption that England's presence in Ireland was gained on shaky legal grounds, subsequent actions of a quasi-legal nature have no legal foundation in fact. Again, without the facility of a law library I am able to cite some four hundred pieces of legislation enacted against the Irish people to aid, abet and expand British presence in which a deliberate attempt was made to destroy an ancient civilization by laws repugnant to every concept of God and democracy and laws in contradiction to your own public vows to bring civilization to the Irish savage."

He stopped, swallowed a number of times to erase the dryness in his mouth, coughing a bit.

"Laws," Conor cried, "were enacted to destroy the Celtic concept of Catholicism which was the light and the flower of Western civilization at a time when England and the European continent writhed in the dark ages. When your attempt to impose the Reformation failed you then enacted laws and shamefully bribed the Irish bishops into replacing Celtic Catholicism with Anglo-Catholicism totally alien to the Irish character. Laws were enacted in exactly the same measure to eradicate our language, an advanced system of government by the people, our economy, our customs, our heritage. Your legal basis of justification has come through convincing yourselves that we are an inferior race unfit to share an equitable life, even in our own land, and if we wished to continue to live in it we must become Englishmen. You have attempted to show the world and your own people that we are inferior and this gives you leave to treat us like animals. Nae, animals are fed, only Irishmen are deliberately starved in Ireland. Through the precedent of establishing the Irishman as a savage and the mission to rescue him from himself you have gone on to establish an empire in which you are also saving black, yellow and brown savages from themselves."

Now he paced with his chains clanging but no one was of a mood to stop him.

"These decades, generations and centuries of comic perversion of law and God, these self-serving acts of coercion, these instant laws that flip-flop or are enacted on a moment's notice according to your need of the day, these farcical unions imposed on unwilling people have always been carried out with total contempt for the savage. No Englishman really asks the savage how he would like to be ruled, for that is apparently the God-given right of your fine, advanced, Western culture and your mother of parliaments.

"The men who lead your government this minute are the same men who sat in the back bench of Parliament a few years ago expressing public horror and revulsion over your treatment of the Boers. But now that these fine gentlemen have gained power, their pity and their sense of decency have strangely fled as they always have when it comes to the Irish."

"Must this continue?" Sir Lucian cried out.

"Yes!" McAloon snapped. "Yes, yes, yes."

"I stand here in a world filled with rising and angry voices which will no longer tolerate their lives being manipulated by the perverse whims of greedy men. Before this twentieth century is out it will see you packing your kits and being drummed out of every corner of the world in scorn. You're a bunch of damned hypocrites holding yourselves up to the world as the successors of the ancient democracies while your hands are soaked in blood and your Parliament hosts this mockery. All you're really in it for is the money!"

"Silence! Silence!" Scowcroft burst from crimson cheeks as his mesmerism vanished.

Conor threw his head back and laughed as the guards closed in on him. "But, my lord," he roared, "even the lowest Irishman is allowed his speech from the dock."

"Silence the prisoner!"

"What are you afraid of? No one will hear me. You've made certain of that."

As Conor was seized Major Westcott bowed to the judge. "Does his lordship wish the prisoner gagged?"

"Aye, do that!" Conor shouted. "Let's stop the pretense that I'll get justice from the same lovely people who enacted the penal laws."

Sir Arnold studied himself back into control and waved Major Westcott away. "This court has been overly generous. No further presentation of the prisoner is required."

"Court?" Conor mocked. "I see no court. I see a hidden room buried in the Wicklow Mountains. There are no lawbooks, no journalists, no probing eyes or impartial minds. Are you inferring, sir, that this is a British courtroom?"

The judge was paralyzed with shock.

"Are you telling me you brought me to this place to dispense justice or are you saying that this is the justice you really have in mind for the Irish?"

Conor turned around, rattling his chains, and his eyes reached every man in the room and they backed off

from his glare. "Court? This is a star chamber, a day out
of the dark ages, a diabolical notion of justice, a reversion
to the Inquisition. Are you serious about this?" Conor
shuffled to the judge's table and leaned over, looking
the man in his eyes, and the man blinked.

"You are a stranger in my land, mister. In the end, your
fake legality will be exposed and you'll crawl out of
Ireland, reviled."

Silence followed, long, terrible silence.

"The prisoner," the judge said shakily, "is remanded to
solitary confinement while the court takes the matter
under advisement." As Scowcroft bolted from the room
his tipstaff snapped up.

"All rise," he said.

CHAPTER SIXTEEN: When it was revealed that Sir
Frederick Weed's personal train had been used by the
Irish Republican Brotherhood to run guns, he underwent
a period of grave personal mortification. Anger grew to
rage when he discovered that the Sixmilecross men were
to come off with light sentences. Gathering in Lord Roger
and the Unionist counsel, he pressed a demand for no-
nonsense legislation aimed at stopping the Irish Republican Brotherhood.

The key man was necessarily Alan Birmingham, Whip
of the ruling Liberal Party. At the moment Birmingham
was content to play the Irish question cozy. The Liberals
had won overwhelmingly, did not need the Irish Party in a
coalition and had no intention of pressing the Home Rule
issue. Birmingham realized that a great number of his
people resented their periodic shotgun wedding to the
Irish and spiritually sided with the Ulster Unionists.

What convinced Birmingham that a stiff new law was
in order was the wave of anti-Irish sentiment that erupted
following the Sixmilecross incident. "Little Ireland" ghettos around the country came under attack and the old
hue and cry was up to "deport all the feckless Fenian
bastards." The temper of the times plus his confidential
knowledge of the details of Conor Larkin's outburst made

him amenable to sitting down with the opposition to discuss legislation.

A conference was arranged to take place at Rathweed Hall. Sir Frederick and Lord Roger were there for the Unionists. Birmingham came over for the Liberals. Sir Philip Huston, Whip of the Conservatives, attended for his party and Sir Lucian Bolt came to observe and advise for the Cabinet.

It was an all-powerful group of cool calculation meeting cool calculation. Presence of Alan Birmingham showed that he wasn't going to be the one to drag his feet on anti-Irish legislation. He'd seen anti-Irish sentiment cause the fall of a government in the past and the others present knew he would play.

Sir Frederick pointed his cigar down the polished mahogany table, voice quivering with emotion. "My personal humiliation I can bear. What I will not bear is permitting an army of traitors to be built on this soil with the intention of tearing us away from the home island by force."

"Hear, hear," Sir Philip Huston concurred. He was inclined to doze and dodder from time to time but his mind was keen. He had canvassed the Conservatives and almost to a man they were prepared to support severe measures to preserve the Union. "We have our nose count. You know how the Unionists and Conservatives stand. Obviously, it's up to you chaps," he said to Birmingham.

Alan Birmingham had to measure the long term as well as the short term. The off-again, on-again affair with the Irish Party had been largely a self-serving device. At the moment the coalition wasn't needed and things were rather cooled. Yet Birmingham knew he could not lose Liberal rapport with the Irish, for things could be quite different in the future.

"I shan't go into, shall we say, corrective legislation as an official Liberal position. However, I am here because the necessity and urgency are quite obvious. What I am prepared to do is take off my hat as Whip of the party and set it aside. I will say to my people, 'See here, chaps, this is a matter of personal conscience to me and I am supporting this bill. You do likewise, each one of you according to his own dictates in the matter.' Do you see what I mean, gentlemen?"

They all understood quite well.

"Tell me, Alan, what do you think we can pick up from your people?" Sir Philip inquired.

"Oh, I'd say a hundred votes. Combined with your strength, it will give you a comfortable majority."

Sir Frederick smiled. Birmingham was shrewd enough. He'd support the law with his right hand and keep it out of an interparty fight with the left.

"Sir Lucian," Weed said, turning to the Crown's special man, "has the Prime Minister re-evaluated his position in regard to continuing this soft approach with the IRB?"

Lucian Bolt was an Irish baiter of long standing with near psychopathic hatred of them. The cabinet decision to tread lightly ran against his grain. He was practical enough to realize the Irish Republican Brotherhood would recruit the strength it required sooner or later and they'd court the Germans for arms. Why give them the time? It could only delay a showdown that had to come a few years hence. Apply pressure here and now, make them struggle every inch of the way. It was the only solution.

The only thing that restrained him was the need to protect the Protestant community of Ulster. They had to have guns. The new legislation was conceived to create "selective options." It would be a matter of judgment as to who should be prosecuted and who would not. It would allow the Attorney General to go after the Irish Republican Brotherhood but at the same time allow the Protestants to continue to arm.

"I am quite prepared to try these Sixmilecross people under the new legislation the minute it is passed and mete them out the kind of punishment they deserve."

Weed cracked his fist on the table in approval. "Bully!"

"Isn't there some kind of agreement in effect with Robert Emmet McAloon?" Birmingham probed.

"Considering Larkin's tirade, I don't see that it's valid any longer," Lucian Bolt answered.

"Let me get this quite clear," Birmingham pressed. "Wasn't Larkin placed outside of the agreement?"

"It is my belief," Sir Lucian answered, "that McAloon put Larkin up to it."

"Do you really think so?" Sir Philip Huston said. "It was my understanding McAloon was quite upset by Larkin's refusal to go along."

"That's just a bloody act," Sir Lucian answered. "All one has to do is examine the facts. This Larkin is a hill farmer, no education, a merchant seaman who never achieved anything more than being a blacksmith. Obviously he couldn't develop those kinds of theories unless McAloon put him up to it."

"I suppose you're right when you come down to it," Sir Philip mumbled. "I say, the transcripts were terribly interesting. All sorts of discussion about it among my people. You were there, Sir Lucian, how did he impress you?"

"He was amusing, I suppose. You know how those people can be. Just enough lunacy involved to have appeal to the Dublin rabble and that's just what it was intended for. Old Scowcroft did let him ramble on a bit too much." Sir Lucian stood and in best courtroom manner addressed the others while standing to emphasize his reasoning. "Let's get this all clear. We went into an arrangement with McAloon because the thinking of the moment was to avoid a public outcry. Our position is now advanced to a different plateau. We are about to enact legislation and subsequently try these men and give them the punishment they deserve. There will obviously be an outcry from the Irish so the deal we had with them is no longer valid. The purpose has changed from the time we made the accord."

Both Sir Philip and Alan Birmingham stared questioningly at being witness to an obvious double cross.

Lucian Bolt cleared his throat emphatically. "Besides, I insist it was McAloon who broke the arrangement by putting Larkin up to it."

"I'm curious, Freddie," Sir Philip prattled on to everyone's discomfort. "You had dealings with the Larkin chap. What sort is he?"

"I'll answer that," Roger Hubble interceded. "He's a despicable Irish devil. The sort that represents everything evil in his race. He's a liar, a conniver, a man who would cut the throat of his best friend. He all but hypnotized young Jeremy with his athletic heroics and led the boy into brothels, drunks and a disgusting brawl." Sir Frederick lowered his eyes and wished he could plug his ears. "By total deceit in representing himself as an ironmaster, he wormed his way into my wife's confidence and we all know, of course, how he used the friendship of three members of my family to carry out this scheme with the guns. He's clever, too damned clever." Roger cut himself short, realizing they were all glaring at him and he was rising up to a rage. "He's . . . brought a great deal of suffering to us all. . . ."

"Hell of a rugby player," Sir Philip sputtered absently. "Saw him score two tries within five minutes against Old-ham. Damned near broke my heart."

"I don't have an ounce of vengeance in my makeup," Sir Frederick said, "but I am trusting Sir Lucian to see to it that he's put into dry dock for good."

"That is my intention."

"Shall we continue, gentlemen?" Sir Frederick said, rapping the table for Philip Huston's attention. "Well then, we are in accord thus far. I hope we all take Sir Lucian's word that there is no agreement between the Attorney General and the so-called Irish Republican Brotherhood and Sir Lucian is free to prosecute the Six-milecross matter vigorously under the new legislation."

Alan Birmingham and Sir Philip nodded a bit reluctantly, but nodded nonetheless.

"The Unionist Party does not wish to introduce the bill because that could be interpreted as an act of vengeance and God knows it's the farthest thing from my mind," Weed said. "I have prevailed upon Sir Philip to have the Conservatives present the legislation. Finally, we have your tacit support on a non-official basis then, Alan?"

"That's the bundle," the Liberal Whip said.

"We in Ulster are obviously most concerned and closest to the situation," Roger Hubble said. "I have prevailed on all parties to let us go forward with the first draft of the act." Copies were passed around by Roger, who remained standing. "For sake of identification I shall refer to it as the Detention and Emergency Powers Act and, if you'll follow along with me, I'll read the preamble."

There was a mass adjusting of eyeglasses and fingering of the papers. " 'Certain crimes,' " Roger read, " 'of an extraordinary nature involving sedition have occurred which are not sufficiently covered by existing statutes and ordinary judicial procedures. The Attorney General alone is herein empowered to identify such crimes when they are committed and classify them into a category to be tried under the provisions of the bill.' It is the sole responsibility of the Attorney General to choose," Roger said, looking up from the paper. "Selection is his and his alone."

When the fine points had been ironed out several hours later Sir Frederick was ecstatic during the round of handshakes. "Well," he gloated, "we've made a new set of rules to play by."

Sir Philip had half dozed, stretched and commented that if one had to put in long hours at a stretch it was pleasurable to work in such surroundings. His hand ran over the polished grains of the table. "I'd say it was khaya mahogany, Nigerian, if I didn't know better," he boasted of his years as a colonial officer.

"You're quite right, Sir Philip," Weed said. "Caroline ran into the stuff years ago. Quintana Roo."

"Quintana Roo?"

"Yes, a remote province in Mexico. Most beautiful mahogany in the world, what? I had to send in a personal expedition to get it."

Four days after the Rathweed Hall conference the Detention and Emergency Powers Act was overwhelmingly passed by the British House of Commons.

CHAPTER SEVENTEEN: Two days after passage of the Detention and Emergency Powers Act, Conor was removed from his cell at the Arbor Hill Barracks in Dublin, locked into familiar shackles, hooded and moved by night to another dungeonlike room in the basement of Dublin Castle.

He was seated, tied to the chair and set before a long table with the hood remaining over his head. Observed from the outside through a peephole, he remained thus for several hours without food, water or use of toilet facilities.

At an hour unknown to him the hood was removed and four men paraded into the room. Three of them, army officers, arrayed themselves opposite him at the table. The fourth was Sir Lucian Bolt, who sat at a smaller table. The senior officer, Colonel Hibbert, cleared a passage for his words through his large brush mustache.

"Prisoner Larkin, you are now before a tribunal as provided for by the Detention and Emergency Powers Act. Sir Lucian Bolt is here in the capacity of special prosecutor for the Attorney General's office and will explain to you the rules of the game, so to speak."

"Why don't we cut out this nonsense?" Conor replied. "Give me my sentence, let me go to the toilet and get some sleep."

Major Disher on the right and Major Young on the left studied the dangerous Fenian. They'd heard he was rather wild. He was a grungy personage, indeed, and God forbid he should be unchained.

"This will be done properly," the Colonel said. "I'd advise you to cooperate."

"Colonel, you look like a fairly decent fellow. How'd they talk you into this silly business? Duty and all that? Hell, at least the last place they called a courtroom had a flag in it."

"I'm asking you for the last time to cooperate."

"Well now, I am trembling with joy at the notion that I'm about to receive the King's justice . . ."

"Guard!"

The door burst open and a quartet of pistol-drawn soldiers charged in. "Gag the prisoner," the Colonel commanded.

Conor's mouth was tied to the bleeding point. He rolled the chair and himself over on the floor and struggled so his back would be turned to them. The Colonel ordered it straightened up and for the guard to hold him by the hair so he had to look at the tribunal.

"You may proceed, Sir Lucian."

Lucian Bolt adjusted his glasses and rose, holding the new law in front of him, and ticked off the main articles.

The Attorney General alone could determine who could be placed on trial.

No further legal requirement was necessary.

Any person deemed suspect could be arrested and searched without warrant.

Any person deemed suspect could be held indefinitely without charges or bail.

Any person deemed suspect was not entitled to legal counsel.

Any person deemed suspect could be brought before a three-man military tribunal on request of the Attorney General.

At such tribunal all formal legal procedures and rules of evidence were suspended.

No legal counsel would be present other than that representing the Attorney General.

No records were to be kept of the proceedings; only a summary of the tribunal was required.

No witnesses could be called by the defendant, but only by the tribunal.

The tribunal was empowered to pass sentence from acquittal to any length of imprisonment or to impose the death sentence.

No appeal was permitted. Only the death sentence would be reviewed by higher authority.

Sir Lucian asked the three officers if all of this was clear and told them that such measures, while repugnant to English law, were the only means to combat sedition of this nature. The three officers agreed fully. Sir Lucian went on to read the charges and a summary of the events, then rested the Crown's case.

"In the interest of fair play," Colonel Hibbert said, "I am going to ask the guard to remove the prisoner's gag and allow him to speak in his own behalf. I warn in advance that no foolishness will be tolerated."

Conor tried to spit. Neither moist nor large but something managed to reach Colonel Hibbert's face. He wiped it slowly, never taking eye off his victim. The three of them adjourned with Sir Lucian and returned in three minutes.

"His Britannic Majesty's tribunal as empowered by the provisions of the Detention and Emergency Powers Act finds the aforenamed Conor Larkin guilty of all charges. He is to be remanded to a penal institution to be named at a future time to serve sentence for a period of fifty years. The tribunal further notes the hostile, provocative and uncooperative attitude displayed by the prisoner and sentences him to receive corrective punishment in the form of twenty lashes. The tribunal is hereby adjourned for a period of one hour at which time it will reconvene to pursue the matter of the other defendants in the so-called Sixmilecross incident. Thank you, gentlemen, for doing your duty, thank you, Sir Lucian. God save the King."

CHAPTER EIGHTEEN: "Let not thine heart decline to her ways, go not astray in her paths. . . . Her house is the way to hell, going down to the chambers of death!"

"Know ye not that the unrighteous shall not inherit the kingdom of God? Be not deceived: neither fornicators . . . nor adulterers . . . nor thieves . . . nor revilers . . . shall inherit the kingdom of God."

For Wednesday after Wednesday after Sixmilecross the sisters of the Ladies' Auxiliary of the Knights of Christ were harangued over the harlotry of Shelly MacLeod. It was an object lesson too horrendous and too clear to allow it to be forgotten and the Moderator was determined to brand it into the brain of every woman in his church.

At the end of the ladies' Wednesday meeting, MacIvor would make his appearance in the social hall for a final prayer and a word of wisdom.

"Even as Sodom and Gomorrah, and the cities about them in like manner, giving themselves over to fornications and going after strange flesh, are set forth for an example, suffering and vengeance of eternal fire. Likewise also these filthy dreamers defile the flesh, despise dominion and speak evil . . ."

He stood at prayer, hands open, thin lips quivering, teary-eyed. "Sisters! Christian ladies, mothers, daughters, wives. You have been debased. The harlot has fled but the harlot has not escaped either the eyes or the vengeance of the Lord. What mother among you does not tremble with horror and rage at the thought of your own virgin daughter lying flesh to flesh with a papist traitor! We must never cease our vigil in seeking the whore who has brought this shame to her people. You must never forget this terrible lesson in your march to purity and righteous womanhood. . . ."

The mark of Cain had been invisibly drawn on the MacLeod homes of Tobergill Road. Silence, the cruelest form of neighborly torture, had been imposed and this was broken by fits of wrath. For weeks not a word was spoken to Morgan or his son. Lucy had been spat upon, pelted with vegetables, doused with a hose. Matt was beaten up so many times he was removed to a private boarding school. Even dear Nell had garbage thrown in her face.

For a time, Morgan and Nell continued to march defiantly into the Savior's Church of the Shankill, cutting through the ice field of what had once been their neighbors. During such times MacIvor mouthed side-of-the-mouth remarks of hate, setting a keynote for the behavior of the others.

Many of their friends outside their neighborhood didn't think it their fault. Lodge brothers split on the issue. Although Morgan and Robin could not be blamed for "her" actions, it was a certainty that neither would ever again attain a high post in the order.

It was the same at the yard. Many old cronies came over to extend their sympathy. A few of the neighbors dared the same, not many though, for fear of getting the same treatment.

The infectious atmosphere of hate that never varied in Ulster made Shelley MacLeod unforgettable to the Knights of Christ and their ladies. MacIvor allowed them to know that all of it was far worse for the women because this had been a female transgression and perhaps Shelley MacLeod reflected hidden female desires, so they all had to share in some of the guilt.

The dignity of Morgan MacLeod and his family and their refusal to get up and run brought about a standoff. They had briefly discussed leaving but they were not of the ilk who filled emigrant ships and they were not going to be driven from their niche.

One day at the yard Morgan was seized by a terrible pain in his chest, unable to breathe, and he staggered helplessly and toppled from the scaffold, falling twenty feet to the pavement and breaking his back.

Overnight, Oliver Cromwell MacIvor became enlightened

with Christian charity. On the next Sunday he said that the Lord had received full retribution for the sins of their wayward daughter and now we must begin to forgive.

Steeped in shame over their behavior, a round-the-clock prayer vigil began as Morgan MacLeod hovered between life and eternal darkness.

*

The packet was empty. Robin crushed it and tossed it into the waste bin. He came in from the platform to the stationmaster's window.

"Dublin train on time?"

"Aye, right on."

Robin had been jumpy enough to draw the station-master's attention with forty minutes of caged-like pacing, mumbling beneath his breath, sitting and wringing his hands and chain smoking. The old man knew that a lot of unfamiliar people came down to Lisburn to meet people they didn't want to be seen with in Belfast. Good-looking chap, nicely dressed, so he must be meeting a lady friend behind his wife's back.

Robin checked the time. Ten minutes. He made to the kiosk. "Twenty pack of Player's navy cut." He returned to the platform drinking in smoke and staring down the track.

Robin was not sure he had done the right thing. The first month after Sixmilecross had been a nightmare. He told himself he could bear the pressure for himself but even the team was divided against one another. First, all the R.C.s were taken off and when they returned they stood around glowering in their own little groups, not drinking together, and worse, not playing for each other. It was so bad Sir Frederick called off the Australian tour.

All during the time Shelley and Conor were living to-gether Morgan had imposed a silence, ordering that Shel-ley's name never be mentioned in the house again. Yet it was wasting him, eating his innards, sapping his life. Mor-gan knew Robin saw Shelley on the sly but said nothing, asked nothing, gave no regards, no blessings, nothing. But Robin knew his father sat alone in her room for hours when he thought no one was around. His grief was con-summate.

Then came Sixmilecross and the full sting of neighborhood ostracism inspired by his father's church. If his sister was a whore, then the Virgin Mary was also a whore because Shelley was the most beautiful, decent woman who ever lived. Decent as Lucy. Decent as Nell. Never hurt a single body, never had a bad word against anyone.

Morgan tried to draw them all together after Sixmilecross but he was wasting before their eyes. Each night he'd read the Bible, hunting those passages which called for repentance and trying to reach out to let in the light of love.

"How much less in them that dwell in houses of clay, whose foundation is in the dust, which are crushed before the moth? They are destroyed from morning to evening; they perish forever without any regarding it . . . they die, even without wisdom."

Fuck the neighbors, Morgan, Robin wanted to scream. Don't bother to either excuse them or curse them. . . .

Then Morgan began to read about death, always death. The night before his heart gave way he spoke of death in a voice bent with weariness. It was the last time he ever read to them. . . .

"Give glory to the Lord your God, before he cause darkness, and before your feet stumble upon the dark mountains, and, while ye look for light, he turn it into the shadow of death, and make it gross darkness. But if ye will not hear it, my soul shall weep in secret places for your pride; and mine eye shall weep sore and run down with tears. . . ."

"Robin, it's your dad! He's fallen off the 'Big Mabel' dry dock!"

Rock of Ages, cleft for me,
Let me hide myself in Thee;
Let the water and the blood,
From Thy riven side which flowed,
By the sin of double cure,
Cleanse me from its guilt and power. . . .

Bloody hypocrites crowding around the house and wailing and praying. You killed him, you bloody hypocrites!

I never meant no harm, Robin . . .
He's in our prayers . . .

Would you ever shake my hand, Robin MacLeod ...
It's been too long, Robin ...
Would you and Lucy be coming to dinner ...
Hypocrites! HYPOCRITES! BLOODY FUCKING
HYPOCRITES!

Robin was startled as the whistle shrieked down the
track. He snuffed the cigarette end and put it back into the
packet, an automatic gesture of frugality from years at
the yard, and pulled himself together as the train slowed
to a halt at the platform.

Shelley and Robin clung to one another as the late
travelers glanced and faded into the night and the train
continued on to Belfast. By the fervor of their embrace,
the stationmaster knew he had been right. Those two, he
thought, were very much in love.

Robin led her to a bench.

"How is he?"

"I'll tell you about that in a bit."

"Can we get on into Belfast and see him?"

"Not tonight."

"Have you booked a room for me?"

"Look, you remember old Cappy O'Dwyer? He's ... uh
. . . a Catholic fellow. Used to play for the club just
when I was coming up out of the juniors. We was close
mates then. He taught me a lot. Anyhow, old Cappy's
made it big since he left the team. I think he's got a
monopoly on the poteen stills up in the Mourne Mountains.
Anyhow, he's a big lovely house here on the outskirts of
Lisburn. Even got a guesthouse if you can imagine. You'll
be safe there."

*

Cappy O'Dwyer's guesthouse had three uses: for various poteen runners, republican lads on the run and mates
with lady friends other than their wives. The kitchen was
warmly alive with ham and chicken soup boiling in a big
copper pot with other dishes of boiled crubeens, rabbit
stew and visitor's triffle. Cappy was proud of his cooking
ability.

"Now, I'll leave youse," he said. "Your good sister can
dish it up at yer own good time."

Shelley pinched his cheek and thanked him.

"There's an electric button over there and one at yer bedside as well and all youse have to do is press it and I'll come over from the main house. Make yerself to home and stay as long as y'like."

"Thanks for everything, Cappy," Robin said.

"Fer nothin'," he answered, looking at Shelley with an expression that said that Conor Larkin's lady was no less welcome than a saint.

They made a pretense of going after the feast but gave it up. Each was holding onto words and not letting them go, then Shelley turned from the stove abruptly.

"Straight on," she said, "how is he?"

"Morgan is dying," Robin answered. "He don't want to live no more. He's wishing himself to death."

"I see," she whispered, slumping by the table. "I suppose he hates me for real since . . ."

"It's how much he loves you. He started to die the day you left the house, but he didn't know how to come to you. Thought of seeing you is all that keeps him alive. He's calling for you day after day. I wouldn't have asked you to come otherwise."

She tousled his hair and he tried a smile without success. His face was pale with exhaustion and his eyes all veined up from drinking. For all his fearsomeness on the rugby field, she knew her brother was a weak man and that her father was his tower and light. Robin, above everyone, would be crushed if Morgan died.

"It seems I've brought a lot of suffering to you all," she said.

Robin shook his head. "It's this fucking Belfast!" he cried. "Why can't they let people alone! What business is it of theirs who you love?" He quieted.

"Nobody in the family blames you, Shelley. When I got you out of Belfast after Sixmilecross I admit I cursed the day you were born. I cursed you because of what happened to Matt and Lucy and Nell. But Morgan brought us back again. Morgan wouldn't let us be consumed by the same kind of hatred that had consumed our neighbors. He made me ashamed . . . because . . . for a little time . . . I had stopped loving you."

"That city is insane, demented with its sickness," Shelley

said. "Oh, Robin, take Lucy and Matt and get out. Just go somewhere else."

Robin lit up a cigarette, trembling, then found whiskey in the cupboard. "That's the sheer and utter hell of it," he moaned. "Even as they spit on his house, Morgan was forgiving them. You see . . . they are our neighbors. . . . Shelley, I was scared when I was at sea. I'm scared every year when I travel to England. I'm even scared when I'm out of the Shankill of a Sunday. You see . . . in the yard and on the rugby pitch and around the Shankill, I'm somebody. When I leave Belfast, I'm nobody. Morgan taught me that. God . . . I was never so proud as the day Morgan passed me his bowler and I was inducted into his lodge and I could march side by side with him while they were playing 'Dolly's Brae.' I never meant to hurt the Catholics. I never listened to those preachers preaching hate on them. Conor said he puked when he saw my Orange sash but the only reason I wore it was to be with my father, and him and me the king and the prince of the Shankill. That's the bloody hell of it. Even after what they've done, I can't leave. Lucy herself gets so scared when we go off on holiday, she's too tense to make love. All we know is our little houses there. That's our place, you know, our place where we're comfortable."

After a pair of hard drinks, Robin's face glistened with sweat. "How've you been, lass?"

"Lonely," she whispered. "Lonely for him. Lonely for you."

"Matt asked for you and Lucy as well." Robin straightened up and summoned what was left of his courage, but was unable to control the faltering of his voice. "How's Conor?"

They stared at one another, then he grabbed her hand desperately. "I never had nothing against Conor because he was a Catholic. Jesus Christ, I don't even understand why we're fighting each other! Shelley, ask the lads on the team! Ask Cappy O'Dwyer! Ring the bell and tell him to come over here and ask him if he ever so much as heard a bad word from me about Catholics! I don't know why Conor beat me up and called me names when I was only trying to save him. He hit me because I wore an Orange sash! Shelley . . . Shelley . . . you got to let him know I love him like a brother!"

Shelley came to him and held his head against her breast and rocked him as though he were a little boy. . . .

CHAPTER NINETEEN: Heather Tweedey was a different old scut in the neighborhood. She and her old mom had lived in the same house on Malvern Street for forty years. When the older woman became invalided, Heather took up her mom's work of custom-making ladies' hats and fancy lampshades. She later added on a house-calling route selling custom-fitted corsets.

There had been a gentleman suitor once, some thirty years earlier, a widower from the yard with four little wanes. Just as their courtship reached a serious stage, Heather's mom was smitten with a terrible attack that required Heather's round-the-clock attention. After the suitor left for more fertile grounds, Heather never had another one of any importance. Other than work and taking care of the old love upstairs, her life revolved around the church and the gospel. The male sex was her adversary, for they carried that frightening and evil instrument between their legs. Like her mom before her, Heather Tweedey became a surly and pinched-up number.

God bless the day, two decades back, that Oliver Cromwell MacIvor came into Belfast like a savior, a true disciple of Jesus all clean and pure and bathed in goodness. She loved him from the very beginning, his sweet shining sensuous face, his soft gentle hands, the holiness of his beautiful mind. Heather kept all of this to herself. So did the other ladies in the church of the same leanings.

The preacher knew full well he represented a dramatic contrast to the roughhewn bunch from the yard. He was the baby Jesus, the object of bringing out their deepest motherly instincts and their sexual longings as well. He plied it with sly references to passages from the holy book that spoke heavily of pleasures of the flesh. In one of his most famous sermons, MacIvor described Jesus as one describes a lover in an excursion into sexual fantasy thinly veiled to the untutored but titillated flock. . . .

". . . no Rose of Sharon is as lily white and snow driven as He . . . He is the scent of myrrh . . . His lips, thick and sensuous, drip with honey . . . His flesh has tones of golden fields . . . His kisses cause weakness and shivering."

Heather Tweedey was a stalwart of his church from the beginning, the most devoted lady in the flock, the most unstinting worker. Visitor of the sick, Sunday school teacher, leader of the social and fund-raising events. For her work she was perennially rewarded with the post of chairwoman of the Ladies' Auxiliary of the Knights of Christ.

Heather had harbored dreams of MacIvor for years, the kinds of thoughts she dared not share with a living soul and would hardly admit to herself. These were deep swirling secrets of the flesh. Not the crude grunting she could hear through the paper-thin walls, not of the ugly male instrument. These pleasures were lofty and lovely and drifting in cloudlike settings with harps and angels. Dreams of immaculate sensations. Dreams in which . . . her lover . . . was . . . Christ in the form of Oliver Cromwell MacIvor. In the hours over her sewing bench she began to let the dreams enter into full daylight and often arose with strange wetness between her legs.

Oliver! Precious savior!

As chairwoman of the Auxiliary, there was a weekly committee meeting held each Saturday evening at her house. In that small intimate group there was never ending talk about Oliver. She loved Saturdays. The others would glorify and revere her secret lover and she knew she would go to sleep that night and have a return of those forbidden sensations.

The ladies were a dedicated lot, fanatical in their life work. Heather could not realize that they belonged to the Auxiliary for much the same reason as she did because they were married ladies. How could Oliver mean that much to them? But he did.

Heather could hardly contain herself as the Saturday meeting time rolled around. Their old men had gone to the pubs and they had come to her house. When the six of them on the committee had gathered and her mom was tucked in for the night, tea was served. Bursting with excitement, Heather dropped the news.

"I've seen the harlot," she gushed. "Shelley MacLeod herself sneaking about the Victoria Hospital."

When the shock settled she assured them that her eyes were not playing tricks.

"I was sitting up with Arabelle Forbes last night. Being as the end was near for old Lawrence and being as I am so close to Arabelle, the nurses let me stay past visiting hours. It was eleven o'clock when I left and as I was going down the hall I stopped for a minute at the door of Moran MacLeod to pray. It was open a crack and there she was as big as life sitting at his bedside, holding his hand, painted and scarlet as she was."

"What do you think we ought to do?" Ade MacDougall said.

"We ought to go immediately to the police."

"No, the dirty bitch has done no civil crime."

"Then let's see Reverend MacIvor for advice," Mae Duncan said.

"No," Heather snapped. "No, we must protect him. Now listen, I have always marked every passage he has ever spoken. I marked the passages in red concerning Shelley MacLeod." She opened her Bible. "If we read together closely, the message becomes very, very clear."

*

The cell door opened. Warder Hugh Dalton entered and stopped before Conor's bed, leaned down and shook him from his sleep. "It's your time, Larkin," he said.

Conor rolled over and stretched. "What a pity to awaken to your face, Dalton. I was having a sweet dream. What'd you say?"

"You're to come with me."

Conor saw the quintet of warders arced around the cell door.

"I see. The royal escort. Good day, gentlemen. Is my carriage waiting? Where to? To the Hotel Russell on St. Stephen's Green for dinner with the Archbishop? Or maybe to the Tower to chop off me head."

"It's the flogging frame," Hugh Dalton said.

"Oh yes, the frame. I did book that one a time ago. I was beginning to think my appointment would never come through."

"Are you going to give us trouble?" the warder asked.

"How the hell do I know? I've never been flogged before."

Dalton nodded to the guards. "Better put the bracelets
on him." They clamped wrists already worn red by man-
acles. Hugh Dalton was a big man turned gray and
blubbery by his years of working in cells. He was one of
the few Catholic warders at Portlaoise Prison, a valuable
man who was able to keep the R.C.s under control with
real or false sympathy. He slipped a piece of hard rubber
into Conor's hand. "Put this in your mouth and clamp
down. It will help some."

As he was marched past cells of other men vaguely
convicted of republican crimes, they beat on their doors
and set up a crescendo of encouragement for Conor and
curses for the Crown.

The convoy disappeared down to the basement with
republican slogans ringing in their ears. Governor Greenleaf, Chief Warder Hyde, Prison Dr. Fraiser and Warder
Inch, who applied the whippings, were in waiting. Conor
was stripped to the waist.

The chief warder read the official document authorizing
the punishment. Warder Inch selected and tested a whip.
Beyond the handle, the whip held nine braided leather
thongs three feet in length, the tips leaded to keep them
from unraveling.

Conor was shoved forward to a timber flogging frame
with horizontal niches cut out at the waist and chest.
He was laid into it on an angle, chained at ankles and
hands and strapped around his middle. A leather collar
was placed around his neck to keep it from being broken.

"Twenty lashes. Keep the count, Mr. Dalton. You may
commence, Mr. Inch."

"One."

Fingers of pink suddenly appeared over the breadth of
Conor's back.

"Two."

The color deepened.

"Three . . . four . . . five . . ."

When the lash struck, the leaded tips were rolled by
whipper Inch in such a manner that they curled beneath
Conor's exposed armpit and ripped away his flesh like
shredded cabbage. Inch broke into a sweat and grunted
as he threw his two-hundred-and-forty-pound might behind the strokes.

"Nine . . . ten . . ."

He stopped, gasping for breath as one of the tails broke, turned to the stand and selected another cat-o'-nine. As he did, the rest of the observers stood fast except for the doctor, who bent under the frame in order to look up into the victim's face.

"Fuck off," Conor said.

"Continue, Mr. Inch."

"The count was ten," Hugh Dalton said. "Eleven . . . twelve . . . thirteen . . ."

Conor spit out the rubber piece. . . . "Oh, they're hangin' men and women for the wearin' of the green . . ."

"What the hell is he doing!"

"I think you might say he's singing, Governor. . . ."

"Mr. Inch, if you apply your strokes properly, he'll stop it. . . ."

"When we were savage, fierce and wild,
Wack fol the diddle lol and di so say,
England came as a mother to her child . . ."

"Fourteen . . . fifteen . . . sixteen . . ."

"Gently raised us from the slime,
Stopped our drinking and our crime."

"Nineteen . . . twenty."

A red tide had erupted, a blood field, a site of a massacre. The governor snorted his displeasure, the whipper knew his whipping days were numbered. The doctor hastily felt pulse, heard heart, popped light into his eyes.

Conor Larkin smiled at him.

He stood and faced them all. "Keep your fucking stretcher, I'll walk," he said.

*

"Are you all right, sir?" the constable asked.

Inspector Holmes turned his eyes away from the sight. He was faint and reeling. He leaned against the wall for support. "God Almighty, God in heaven," he groaned.

The red hair that had been shorn from Shelley's head lay strewn on the ground glued up with a thicker, deeper red of her blood. Her face grotesquely ballooned from hundred hammer blows. She was found tied to a lamppos at the middle of an alleyway behind the hospital.

"Never seen the likes of this. . . not in my thirty year . . ." the inspector whispered. "It's the work of a lunatic."

"More than one," Detective MacCrae said. "I'd say half dozen or more different weapons were used. I'v counted over fifty stabs. All right, cut her down."

There was terrible screaming at the narrow end of th alley where a dozen constables held a gawking crowd a bay. One of the police rushed back to Detective Mac Crae.

"What's going on down there?"

"It's her brother trying to get through."

"For God's sake, don't let him through. He can't se this."

Another detective came from the blind end of the alley "We found one of her arms in the dustbin."

Inspector Holmes's eyes fixed on the words scrawled o the wall. PAPIST WHORE.

CHAPTER TWENTY: Governor Greenleaf called meeting of warders the instant Conor learned of Shelley' murder. Portlaoise held the other Sixmilecross prisoner and extraordinary pressures were expected.

Warder Hugh Dalton was ordered to keep personal an intense watch on Larkin on the usual Catholic-to-Catholi logic. In his time Dalton had seen a hundred men lear of an ultimate tragedy on the outside. It broke a ma quicker than any other calamity. After that first week o complete void and numbness during which the mind sim ply closes down operation and shuts out thought and pain the sufferer will usually give off survival signs or deat signs.

Conor did not utter a single word or shed a single tear He sat on the edge of his cot, back to the cell door. His sole movement other than necessity of relief was to take spoon or two of food, an occasional sip of water or fal back on the cot for a moment's sleep. It never varied, day or night. He rejected all visitors, all messages, all orders

He sat, dawn, day, evening, night, wordless, dead of eye.

Hugh Dalton had watched men go on in a like manner for several weeks, then burst apart when containment was no longer possible. Although Larkin showed the slightest of life signs, he gave no clue that he was heading to an explosion. A week, a fortnight, two weeks, three, four, five, six, seven, eight. He sat, he stared blankly. It never varied.

*

The *New Republican*, a four-page newspaper spewed out of the Liberties of Dublin, was apparently the work of Seamus O'Neill but with no way of proof. Distribution was meticulously timed to reach beyond Dublin into every corner of Ireland and over the water to the Irish slums from Manchester to Glasgow to London. It created a furor.

The *New Republican* led off with Conor Larkin's devastating speech from the dock at the kangaroo court at the Aghavannagh Barrack. The inner pages carried a detailed account of the violation of the agreement between the Irish Republican Brotherhood and Sir Lucian Bolt. The final page dissected the articles and meaning of the Detention and Emergency Powers Act, Larkin's agony, and the betrayal of the Sixmilecross men.

As the ink dried on the *New Republican*, Atty Fitzpatrick led a parade of republican orators in the halls and to the streets, addressing huge and flaming rallies in Dublin, Cork, Galway, Derry and Limerick. She was heading into the teeth of the hurricane, announcing a march on Belfast, when she was taken into custody, ostensibly for her own protection, and held aboard a prison ship anchored in Kingstown Harbor south of Dublin.

*

So long as the issue stayed hot it was incumbent on Governor Greenleaf to see to it that nothing further happened to Larkin. He was moved to a cell isolated from the main body of the prison with Hugh Dalton assigned as a sort of personal watchman.

And then the murder of Shelley MacLeod.

At the end of the third month it was still the same. Conor refused to cry out and there was no indication if he had even plumbed the bottom of his grief. Neither Hugh Dalton nor anyone else had seen the like of it. He began to wonder if Larkin had gone insane and he decided he had to force a contact.

For days on end he tried to talk to Conor without answer but each day there was the slightest hint that Conor was aware of his presence and knew him. A spoonful more of food, a minute or two of pacing . . . tiny, tiny clues.

After a few weeks of this Dalton tried again. He put a chair across from Larkin and leaned close to him one more time.

"You know who I am," the warder said, "I see that you know me. I see you lift your head when you hear me open the door. I know you can hear me now."

Conor turned his head away, a good sign, Dalton said.

"When you heard your woman was gone, something told you you were going to continue to live. If it hadn't you'd be dead by now. People who want to die, die. Something kept you from dying then and from dying now. So if you're going to live you'd better get started on it."

Conor heaved several telltale sighs.

"I'm under orders to get you cleaned up and start exercising you with a walk in the yard. Don't worry about anybody being around. It'll just be me and you when the others are back in their cells. I'll escort you personal."

The sighs became grunts and heightened in intensity, the first audible sounds from him in nearly four months.

"Man, you've taken enough punishment. Don't force me to add more. Are you going to walk with me, Conor?"

Conor's mouth trembled open.

"Tell me what you've got to say, Larkin!"

"Dalton," he moaned as though he were speaking in a hollow tube. "I'm ready to go . . . take me to the pit . . . don't let anyone see me . . ."

Conor was quickly removed down to a padded cell in solitary and made secure with chains so he would not destroy himself.

Hugh Dalton alone heard it. Conor Larkin screamed out his torment for thirty consecutive hours, repeating her name in agony a thousand times, flailing at his bonds, gagging on his tears and vomit. "Shelley! Shelley!"

Hugh Dalton had never lived through such an experience. At the end of an entire night and half of the next day of it, he was driven to his knees and he prayed Larkin would pass out. . . .

But the screams went on . . . weaker . . . weaker . . . weaker. . .

"Shelley . . . Shelley . . . Shelley . . ."

With a day and a night done, Conor's voice left but he continued to cry out, coming to life on the brink of darkness again and again. Then a stupor descended, followed by total collapse. Complete, total exhaustion.

*

By late spring a whisper of life returned to Conor during the days he went walking with Warder Dalton. Some color, some strength returned. He continued to remain isolated from the main prison body and was refused visitors. The public outcry continued and he remained an object of quandary for the authorities.

He and Dalton spoke very little during the exercise walks but Conor began to look forward to the daily turns about the courtyard.

"I'm off your case as of today," Dalton said as they passed the last guard gate into the stone court.

Conor remained silent but was disappointed. They paced the long diagonal way to the base of the wall, turned and started back.

"They're going to keep you isolated. You might want another person to talk to once in a while. Maybe you ought to start going to church on Sunday."

"You're talking to the wrong Roman," Conor answered.

"You're tough, Larkin. Looking back on thirty years in this business, I only remember one or two like you, before. They're always republicans somehow. Old Long Dan Sweeney, now there was a hard number, and Brendan Sean Barrett as well."

Conor slowed his gait and eyed Dalton suspiciously.

"Matter of fact," the warder said, "I had dinner with them last night."

Conor stopped and sat at a bench. The sight of prisoner Larkin and Warder Dalton walking, talking and sitting in the prison yard had been commonplace for the past days, so nothing was made of it either by the guards on the wall or the men in their cells.

"I'm listening," Conor said.

"We had to wait until I would be taken off this assignment with you. We want to let enough time pass by so suspicion doesn't come back to me."

"I've heard the names of those men but I don't know them," Conor said. "How does a person like yourself find people like that?"

"Through Seamus O'Neill."

"Sure, I didn't know old Seamus knew those men."

"I thought it was possible," Dalton said, taking off his cap and wiping the sweatband inside. "Just a hunch on my part."

"Really think I ought to attend mass?"

"Put in a request to begin serving the mass this Sunday. Father Dermott will send your name up to the office as a matter of routine."

"What's in it for me?"

"On the first Sunday of each new quarter there's a sort of open house. That would be Sunday, July 5, four weeks from now."

"What happens?"

"A few hundred prisoners on good behavior and in the honor cells are allowed visitors. They all go to mass together family style. On each quarter there are usually a dozen or more priests in from around the country visiting inmates, reporting back home, counseling, giving letters."

"Interesting."

"The chapel is small. On that particular day there are maybe eight or ten masses held. Some of the visiting priests spell Father Dermott and rotate giving mass. Others are floating about doing the visiting and guidance activity. There's lots of movement and security is loose. It's apt to get as confused as an Irish wake. If you start serving mass now it will appear natural for you to do so four weeks from now."

"My records show I'm not a churchgoer."

"A lot of men find religion here. They won't refuse your request to serve the mass."

"What happens?"

"You'll get further instructions when you go to the sacristy for the last mass of that day."

"Ever hear of *ley fuga*, Dalton?"

"What is it?"

"An old Spanish custom, quote, prisoner shot in the act of escape, unquote. Gets rid of a lot of unwanted deadwood. How do I know you're not setting me up?"

"Seamus O'Neill said to give you this message. He said the booley house was visited that summer by Mr. A.I. and Miss E.L. He said the message was signed with the name Runt."

"What about the other lads?"

"They're tunneling out the same day."

"Why are you doing this, Dalton?"

"I don't know, really. I guess I never got used to watching them kick the shit out of republican lads. I got to thinking, what the hell's my thirty years amounted to? Kissing British asses. The pet Catholic warder to keep the lads in line. I was curious about you. I read a copy of the *New Republican*. After, I went up to Derry so's nobody would recognize me and heard Atty Fitzpatrick speak. What's so strange about it? I'm an Irishman. We'd better start walking again."

*

SUNDAY, JULY 5, 1908

During Saturday, Great Southern trains stopping at Maryborough dropped off an unusually large number of passengers for the quarterly visits to inmates of Portlaoise Prison.

The prison gates cracked open at half five Sunday morning for some two hundred family and a few dozen priests on duty calls.

The final mass began at noon. Prisoner Larkin, who had served the mass since ten o'clock, went back to the small sacristy adjoining the chapel to assist the last priest with his robes.

As he knocked, he was jerked inside and Father Dary Larkin clamped a hand over his mouth. A second priest quickly locked the sacristy door.

Conor let go his first smile in months.

"This is Father Kyle," Dary said. "He's agreed to be the victim of some foul play which we are about to perpetrate."

Dary dug into his vestment bag and pulled out a rope, a hood, a mouth gag and a club. Father Kyle peeled off his clothes down to his underwear. The plan was obvious

and simple. Father Kyle, a close friend of Dary, would
act the role of having been attacked by Larkin, who
took his clothing and escaped dressed as a priest.

"In order to make this look authentic, I'm going to
give Father Kyle a rap on the head with this club," Dary
said. "God forgive me for what I'm about to do, Kyle."

The second priest closed his eyes and girded. "Do your
duty, Dary, and good luck to you, Conor," he said.

Dary clenched his teeth, lifted the club and whacked
the taller priest on the forehead with a fine shot destined
from impact to knot up and discolor.

"I've drawn blood. Are you all right, Kyle?"

"A bit woozy, but otherwise fine."

Conor dressed in the priest's clothes, then helped Dary
tie him up and gag him. In a few moments Father Kyle
was shoved into a closet which was locked after him.
All of the priest's papers were in Conor's hands and he
quickly sorted them out. He helped Dary dress in his
vestments to give the last mass of the day.

The noon whistle sounded.

"Remain in the sacristy," Dary said. "I'll be right
back after the mass and change. We will assemble with the
other priests and visitors in front of the chapel."

"Won't some of the other priests miss Father Kyle?"

"Those who know him are also my friends. Shove the
hat down over your eyes . . . that's better. You make a
fine-looking priest, Father Conor." Dary sucked in a deep
breath. "I hope I can get through the mass without giving
myself away." He opened the sacristy door and entered
the chapel from the rear.

A half mile away Sterling McDade had made through a
classical tunnel and emerged in a covering of thicket by a
stream. Carberry, Darren, McGovern and Gorman of
Sixmilecross were behind him. McAulay and Gilroy had
elected to remain.

They were immediately snatched up into the false bottom of a hay wagon and on the way to a safe house on a
farm outside of Abbeyleix.

At that moment Conor Larkin walked through the front
gate of Portlaoise Prison in the middle of twenty priests.

END OF PART SIX

PART SEVEN
A Terrible Beauty

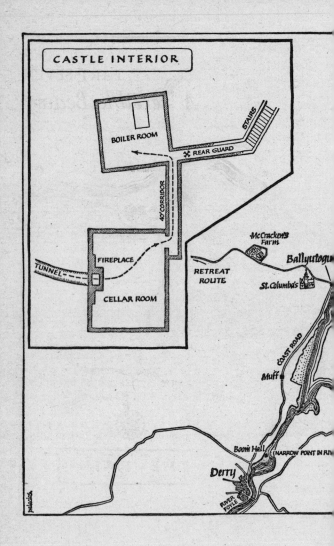

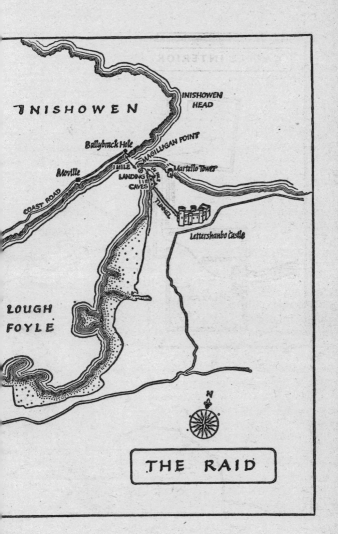

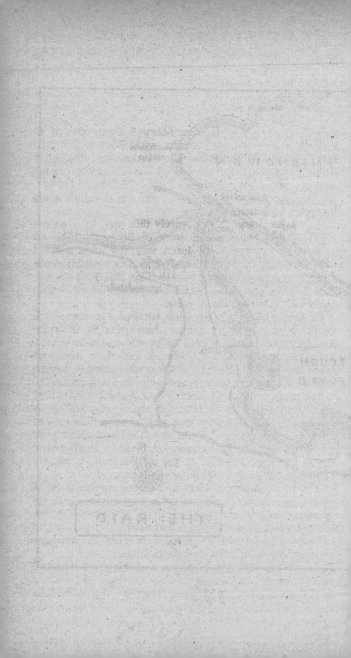

CHAPTER ONE: Brigadier Maxwell Swan arrived at Hubble Manor in grim consort with Warren Wellman Herd. After brief amenities they locked up with Lord Roger in the library, arrayed before the great marble fireplace beneath the portrait of King William of Orange, site of a thousand Hubble ponderings and decisions down through their generations.

W. W. Herd was unimpressively thin and drab, an appearance that belied his mastery of his craft, a silken private investigator. Until lured into the Hubble-Weed combine, he had earned a lucrative income by fixing scandals for scoundrels. Swan had to offer him a small ransom to wean him away, but he had proved he was worth every quid in the past seven years.

Sir Frederick had often been enraged and humiliated by competitors getting a jump on him either by an invention he should have invented or by some ingenious marketing. It occurred to Sir Frederick that there should be some manner by which he could obtain advance knowledge of the competition's thinking. W. W. Herd responded to the problem famously. Setting up a small but incredibly efficient unit, he was the founder and forerunner of industrial espionage. Herd's unit had gone undetected for five years and time and again had taken the thunder out of Sir Frederick's fellow ship and rail builders. Lord Roger, likewise, was able to get his hands on a number of patents, particularly for his power looms.

When Swan assigned Herd to a seemingly simple bit of fluff, Herd knew it carried more importance than appeared on the surface.

Roger drummed his fingers impatiently on the arm of the chesterfield as W. W. Herd unsnapped his briefcase and withdrew a report several pages thick.

"You'll find that Mr. Herd has been his usual thorough self," Swan said.

The investigator set the report on the tea table. "I'm

afraid your lordship's suspicions have been fully justified," he said in a raspy sort of whisper.

Roger allowed himself an awful sigh of resignation and took up the report. It was dated February 15, 1909, and bore a title page that read: ACTIVITIES OF MR. JEREMY HUBBLE. HIGHLY CONFIDENTIAL. TWO COPIES ONLY.

Roger set it back down without opening it. "I think we'd better have Caroline here, straight off," he said, punching the button for a servant and ordering the man to fetch her.

The atmosphere was apparent to Caroline the instant she set foot into the library.

"Darling, I'd like you to meet Mr. Herd, Mr. W. W. Herd."

Caroline nodded as the little man bowed slightly.

"Mr. Herd has been in our employ for a number of years," Maxwell Swan said.

"In what capacity?" Caroline asked directly.

"Some special duties regarding industrial relations," Swan evaded. Caroline knew that could cover a multitude of sins.

"What duties?" she pressed.

"Mr. Herd is a private investigator by trade," Roger said.

"And what have you been investigating that brings you to Hubble Manor?"

Roger handed his wife the report. She glanced at it, set it down and looked from one to the other. Herd knew from Lady Caroline's reputation it might be a very long afternoon.

"Just what has Jeremy gone and done? Is he a raving deviate, a flouncy homosexual, taking opium, bribing professors, or has he run up a monumental gambling debt?"

"No, no, no, no. Nothing of that sort," Swan said.

"Worse," Roger interceded. "He's sleeping with a girl, a Catholic. Background: daughter of a tailor, one of eleven children, all street urchins in the Liberties. The girl herself is an illiterate, a seamstress in her father's sweatshop. We are confronted with a potentially disastrous situation. The girl might be pregnant. God knows who did it but Jeremy is taking the responsibility. So, you see, we are about to have a proper earldom now, complete with bastards."

Roger shot off the chesterfield and fortified himself with a jolt of brandy.

"How did you find out?" she asked.

"I became suspicious over a number of things," Roger said, "and certainly Jeremy's past affairs of the heart wouldn't indicate a thing to the contrary. His continued absences over weekends and holidays, the dismissal of the manservant, Donaldson, whom I personally assigned to him, and other reasons led me to conclude some skulduggery was going on behind our backs."

"I see," Caroline said, "and so you commenced a secret investigation of your son."

"Our son," Roger corrected.

"Did it occur to you that you might have spoken to me first?" Caroline said.

Roger's cheek muscles flexed as he clenched his jaws. Oh, there she goes, he thought, rising to the defense of Jeremy even though he had committed the indefensible. How dare she! But why should this time be different?

"Lord Roger was extremely upset," Swan interceded. "He didn't want to upset you as well until he was absolutely certain."

Caroline turned from her husband to the investigator. "Just what did you find out, Mr. Herd?" she said.

W. W. Herd cleared his throat officiously. Imparting bad news to stunned relatives afforded him his one moment in the center of the stage. "I understand how much of a shock this comes as to your ladyship."

"No one is shocked, only curious, Mr. Herd," she said, and the investigator knew that neither he nor his profession held any favor with her. "What did you find out and how did you find it out?"

As an air of discomfort and tension settled in, Herd stood before the portrait of King Billy, eying the guardedly distraught father and the strangely irate Countess.

"The job itself was rather routine," he began. "As you know, your son has a flat on Merrion Square within walking distance of Trinity College. Being a rather gregarious chap, your son's digs were a social center of sorts for his chums. When he dismissed his manservant, Mr. Donaldson, whose loyalty belonged to Lord Roger, it was a dead giveaway the young gentleman wanted to be . . . well . . ."

"Away from prying eyes?" Caroline said.

"One might say that, yes," Herd concurred. "With Mr. Donaldson out of the way, certain activities might be pursued, unencumbered."

"What sort of activities?" Caroline snapped.

"Oh, the usual for university lads. Drinking parties. Sexual encounters. Being on the rugby team and otherwise popular, Jeremy generally had a crowd around him. He was generous in letting his friends borrow a room for trysts, et cetera, et cetera, et cetera."

"Just what do you mean by et cetera, et cetera, et cetera?" Caroline said.

"Well, er, your ladyship, it's all in the report in great detail."

"You wrote the report, Mr. Herd. I'm sure a man of your skill would remember every word."

W. W. Herd realized that it was he who was on the carpet. Far from being distraught, the Countess was going at him like a barrister in the throes of cross-examination. He cleared his throat again, this time out of mounting uneasiness.

"As you know, Countess, it is a large flat containing five bedrooms. His lordship's, a room for his manservant, a room for his two maids, and two spare bedrooms. Over the weekends there were numerous overnight occupancies by his gentlemen friends cohabiting with various ladies. In addition, the premises were used for the purpose of cohabitation on occasion in the afternoons. Some one dozen times in the past several months."

"That's interesting," Caroline mused. "How did you arrive at the figure?"

W. W. Herd licked at dry lips.

"You appear distressed, Mr. Herd," she said. "Should I ring for some tea or perhaps you'd care for something a bit stronger?"

He reckoned as he could do with a drop of whiskey, took it fading from stage center and slipped to the edge of a chair and looked for help from Swan, who offered none.

"Please continue," Caroline said.

"I arrived at the figure quite simply. Once Mr. Donaldson had been dismissed and returned to Hubble Manor, I befriended Lord Jeremy's new manservant, a Mr. Wordlock, as well as the two live-in maids."

"By befriending them, you mean you put them on your payroll."

Again Herd looked to Swan for respite.

"That's right," the Brigadier answered.

"And in that manner you were able to get an accurate count, or should I say, body count," Caroline said.

The investigator nodded.

"And Jeremy's friends were more or less lads from good families. Ascendancy people."

"Yes, m'lady."

"Whose families might be a bit upset if they knew their sons were being watched."

Herd held up his hand quickly to piously defend his professional honor. "I can assure you that everything, but everything, is entirely secret and only two reports exist."

"And you're equally certain the maids will never discuss any of this . . . body counting."

"They are sworn to secrecy," he said, but crimsoned as he did.

"What about the girls doing the, how do you put it, cohabiting?"

"Therein lies the problem," Herd said.

"Whores?"

"Uh, no, m'lady, not exactly. You see, a number of them were Catholics."

"Does that alarm you or surprise you in any way, Mr. Herd?" Caroline asked.

"I have no opinions," Herd answered. "I merely investigate and report my findings."

"What were your findings?"

"Well, some of the girls lived about Trinity or worked in places college students would frequent."

"Loose?"

"Yes, some of them."

"And perhaps other girls were having their first affair or were deeply in love. And perhaps, Mr. Herd, some of the couples were secretly married?"

The tic which W. W. Herd had mastered suddenly began to act up after a decade of silence, and his left eye twitched out of control. "Your ladyship, I must protest. I have no personal interest and no quarrel with anyone."

"Aren't you going a bit hard on Mr. Herd?" Swan said.

"I'm sorry," Caroline said. "Of course you were only doing your job, isn't that right?"

"Yes, m'lady."

"Let me get it all straight. In the past few years Jeremy has become popular with his mates at Trinity, has had drinking parties in his flat and has allowed some lesser endowed chums to use the place to have an occasional romp in the sheets."

"Yes, m'lady."

"Sort of the normal thing one might expect from a normal healthy college boy in his circumstances," Caroline said.

"Although I don't give opinions, I would agree to that," Herd said.

"You wouldn't call it a sporting house?"

"Nothing of that sort, m'lady."

"And being a thorough chap, you investigated Jeremy's studies, I presume, and you found that he applied himself rather diligently and did not go to bribing teachers or seek to cheat by getting his work done by honor students."

"I found nothing of that sort."

Roger watched the performance with growing but contained fury. At a number of points he was about to break in and call it off but decided to let Caroline complete her game and not create one scene on top of another. Yet he wished she would show a bit more anger over what Jeremy had done and get a little less pleasure out of tormenting Mr. Herd.

"Now then, Mr. Herd," Caroline continued, "I should like to know about this girl Jeremy is mixed up with."

At this point Herd wanted to hold the report in his hand but he knew the Countess was not going to permit it. Resigned that he'd have to go through it step by step, he withdrew a small notebook from an inner pocket and worked on a pair of eyeglasses.

"The girl's name is Molly O'Rafferty. She is one of seven daughters and eleven children of one Bernard O'Rafferty, proprietor of a tailoring establishment on Duke Street, about two blocks away from Trinity College."

"Did I understand you to say the man owns his own business?"

"Yes, m'lady. The establishment has been in business

over twenty years and is extremely popular for attiring the young gentlemen at Trinity."

"Is it a profitable business?"

"Quite," Herd said, flipping the pages of his notebook to support his statement.

Maxwell Swan had his icy eyes fixed on Caroline. He had known her since she was a young girl and watched with fascination as she built a case in behalf of her son. He wondered what her private scene with Roger would be like when she had polished Herd off. Roger and Sir Frederick might well win the fight against the girl but if they earned Caroline's wrath in the process it could be a costly victory.

"Ah, here it is," Herd said, clearing his throat one more time. "O'Rafferty is netting well over three thousand a year. He's trained all of his children as tailors and seam-stresses. The business is run as a family enterprise. A high-class cottage industry, one might say. The work is creditable by Irish standards. Seems that he takes them in-to the trade once they finish their schooling."

"Did I understand you to say schooling?"

"Yes, m'lady."

"Not meaning to contradict my husband, but they are educated then?"

"Yes, m'lady."

"How much education?"

"Well, the girls have received from a minimum of four up to eight years of schooling."

"Private?"

"Yes, m'lady."

"Convent?"

"Yes, m'lady."

"And the boys?"

"One graduated from Maynooth. He's a priest now in Kilkenny. Of the other three . . . let me see . . . yes, they've all completed schooling up to college."

"Are they all in the business?"

"No, m'lady. In addition to the priest, one owns an es-tablishment in London and another has emigrated to Chi-cago. He also owns his own business. The remaining son, Bernard, Jr., acts as manager and heir apparent to the business here in Dublin."

"And the seven girls?"

"Five are married and two have brought their husbands into the business. Molly and the younger girl, who is still in school, are unmarried."

"All told, then, the O'Rafferty family is a responsible, educated, prosperous and respectable family."

"I don't give opinions but one would conclude that."

"Then Bernard O'Rafferty is not a typical feckless, lazy Irishman, not one who drinks or gambles his money away."

"No, m'lady, he doesn't even have a bookmaker."

"Or a wretched home in the Liberties?" Caroline said like a well-fired shot.

"No, m'lady, they've quite a proper address in Harold's Cross."

Roger burst out of his seat. "We appreciate your thoroughness, Caroline, but I fail to see what this has to do with the problem."

"But, darling," she answered softly, "it was you who initiated this investigation and up to now I'm not quite sure what the problem is. Please go on, Mr. Herd."

Roger sank back to the chair ashen-faced as a telling silence turned on him. Could it be possible, imaginable, that Caroline was going to approve of this disaster?

"Please go on, Mr. Herd," Caroline repeated. "Tell me about the girl."

At that instant she softened visibly, staring out past the long high stacks of books to the great stained glass at the far end of the library as the sun empowered its colors.

Herd played with his notebook, scanning a handwriting so small as to be nearly unreadable. "Here we go. She stands five feet and two and a half inches in height. Her weight is . . ."

"No, no," Caroline interrupted. "Just tell me what your impression of her would be if she walked into the library this moment."

For the first time W. W. Herd seemed humanized and without his burden of office. "I would say she is quite beautiful. Yes, ravishingly so."

"When did Jeremy meet her?"

"Seventeen months ago. There's a students' pub on the banks of the Liffey called the Lord Sarsfield. Molly O'Rafferty sings ballads there in the evenings. She is extremely popular."

"Nice voice?"

"Yes, ma'am. I'd go into the Sarsfield myself now and again just to listen to her," he said, speaking with touches of intimacy.

"How old was she when she met Jeremy?"

"Sixteen."

"With a reputation for sleeping around?"

"No."

"You investigated that thoroughly, did you not? Was she a virgin when my son took her?"

"As far as I can ascertain."

"And in the months they've been living together has she slept with any other men?"

Herd balked. He knew where his duties lay but he knew as well he'd better not play the Countess for a fool. "No, m'lady, she has not," he said, turning his eyes down from Swan and Lord Roger.

"I know you don't like to venture opinions, Mr. Herd, but would you say that Jeremy and Molly O'Rafferty are truly in love?"

"Just a moment," Roger interrupted. "That sort of thing is entirely out of Mr. Herd's domain. I have been extremely patient, Caroline, and I know exactly what you have been getting at. I think these things had best be discussed between you and me privately. Is there really anything further you need ask that you can't find in the report?"

"Just one more thing," Caroline said. "There is a suspicion that this girl is pregnant. How do you know?"

Herd paled.

"Can I find it in the report?" Caroline asked.

"No," he rasped.

"I'm waiting for an answer."

"I prefer not to divulge this information. Brigadier Swan will attest to my loyalty to your family, Countess, but as a private investigator there are means of ascertaining information that must remain strictly confidential."

"I suggest you are not leaving here until I find out."

"I think you'd better tell Lady Caroline," Swan said.

"I'm sorry but I shall have to refuse."

"Then I'll tell you," Caroline said. "You went to this

girl's priest and coerced him into betraying the confidence
of the confessional by threatening her life, isn't that so,
Mr. Herd?"

Silence devoured the library.

"Oh, God," Caroline cried, "don't act so shocked,
Roger, you either, Max. It's so unbecoming."

"How did you find out!" Roger shrieked crazily.

"Our son told me, that's how."

"Jeremy told you! Jeremy!"

"The priest was distraught to the point of insanity for
what he had been made to do and he came to Jeremy for
forgiveness, then turned himself in to his Bishop. What a
bunch of gangsters!"

"But . . . but you've known all along. You've known and
put us through this whole charade . . ."

"Yes, I've known, Roger. I've known about Molly
O'Rafferty from the day Jeremy met her. You see, gentlemen, you've gone to a lot of trouble for nothing."

At that, Caroline stalked from the library and left
them gaping.

CHAPTER TWO: Atty Fitzpatrick closed the cottage
door behind her. She walked over the room and stopped
before the rocking chair where Conor sat limply as he
sat for most of his waking hours. He glanced up to her
for an instant, then lowered his stare to the floor.

"We've all been worried sick over you," she said.
"We've spoken of little else."

He made no reply.

"I'm going to stay with you for a while."

"You'd clear out if you were wise," he mumbled.

"I've not been accused of that particular quality," she
answered.

"Don't moon over me, Atty. I'll not have anyone bray-
ing in sympathy. Take your motherly love elsewhere. I'm
nae worth the trouble any longer."

"Live if you can, Conor, die if you must, but you cannot go on in limbo any longer."

"You don't know what's going on in this room, Atty.

The agony and sickness of it will murder you if you stay."

She held her ground, showing no iota of intention to turn back. Since his escape from Portlaoise Prison he had flooded her thoughts. Strange, strange, strange. Atty Fitzpatrick, the righteous champion who exhausted herself giving to causes and causes and causes. Yet in all that giving she had never really given herself to a single person unabashedly. No true emptying of oneself to another human. She craved to give it all to Conor Larkin without hope of reward, self-fulfillment or even so much as a thank you. Why?

"I'm not going to let you sink, man," she said strongly.

Conor looked up to her curiously.

Oh, Lord, she cried inside, the pain in him. One of his eyes danced off wildly in another direction, the stare of a madman. I must do something about it.

"I am going to touch you, Conor," she said. "It will not be the touch of Shelley MacLeod. You'll not feel her again. But what you will feel from me is life. The life inside me begs to transfuse to you. Don't fight me, man, please don't fight me."

She reached out tentatively and, frightened, placed her hand gently on his head. He accepted it, registering neither joy nor resentment. Ever so slowly Atty pressed closer until she stood above him within whispering distance. Her hands drew his head to her belly and she held him hard against it.

For a time he remained rigid, then he closed his eyes and groaned and brought his own arms about her waist and buried himself in the compassion that flowed out of her every pore.

*

The Baron Louis de Lacy's estate, Dunleer, lay hauntingly in the lunarscape of Connemara in County Galway. His barony stretched thousands of acres, encompassing dozens of the hundreds of lakes that pocked the area. The land drifted up into the Twelve Bens, mountains of naked stone mass, Benbaun, Bencorr, Benbreen, Benbrack and the rest, hovered over a moorlike bog and a fairy coast of hidden coves and strands and plunging fjords. This mystic De Lacy domain was all but hidden to the human

eye, a wonderment of emptiness. Once out of the foothills
an island-inundated archipelago peppered a water world
from bay to open sea.

The De Lacys were old Norman Catholic aristocracy
of the vaunted "Tribes of Galway" eccentricized by generations of Connemara wilderness. Dunleer demesne was
part of that tragic heritage, the land to which Oliver
Cromwell had condemned the Irish into exile.

The present Baron, affectionately called "Lord Louie,"
had recently closed out a distinguished career in the British Navy and consular service and retreated to Dunleer
to breed Connemara ponies and continue his mania as a
Gaelic scholar.

Lord Louis was also an ardent republican and made no
bones about it. Secretly, he was a member of the Irish
Republican Brotherhood. Although he remained outside
of the Supreme Council, he was in constant communication with Long Dan Sweeney and Dunleer figured heavily
in Brotherhood plans.

On the day Conor Larkin made his escape he was
spirited to Dunleer and hidden. Gored and within himself,
the only human presence he allowed or even recognized
was Atty Fitzpatrick.

But even Atty could not reach him. Truly reach him.
There was only enough contact between them to keep hell
from devouring him. She was able to force him out of the
cottage where the gloom was not so consuming and she
would ride behind him at a safe distance as he blurred
off into the foothills of the Twelve Bens where he contemplated endlessly above the scatter of lakes and islands
and the morbid flats of granite and bog. In that bitter-
sweet wilderness he was in places and things unknown to
Atty.

She asked nothing and gave everything. Her patience
was endless and she rewarded herself in fractionary
signs that he was returning to life. Bits and pieces, but life,
nonetheless.

Although Conor touched her, lay down beside her,
broke often in her arms, he showed no inkling of desire to
make love. Atty wondered if that was dead in him forever.

As Conor inched back it was also time for him to
move on from Dunleer. Lord Louie was dispatched by

the Supreme Council to see the German ambassador in London, where a working contact had been established. Both the Brotherhood and the Germans were in the business of disrupting the British and so they had grounds for mutual cooperation. An arrangement was made for a rendezvous at sea.

Months later on a night in October of 1908, Lord Louie de Lacy and Conor Larkin made their way to the nearby fishing village of Roundstone where his yacht *Gráinne Uáile* was docked. At sunset they slipped from the harbor and sailed past Slyne Head where a meeting at sea was kept with a small German freighter, the *Baden-Baden*.

Two weeks later Conor crossed over the Canadian border into the United States to contact Joe Devoy, leader of the American Clan of the Gaels. His mission, to raise money for an underground newspaper and arms, those two most vital instruments of insurrection.

*

In Conor's absence, growth of the Brotherhood remained stunted, weak and without the ear of the masses. It had but a single canon, freedom from England. As a revolutionary movement it made its own legitimacy by infiltrating the Gaelic League, the Athletic Association, the labor unions, Sinn Fein Party, the boy scouts, the intellectual societies and even the Church.

Yet the Brotherhood meticulously wrote the textbook for future revolutionaries of the century and Conor Larkin had indelibly inscribed his name in it. His principle of non-recognition of British institutions on Irish soil and disobedience to British authority became a universally accepted cornerstone for breaking the yoke of the colonizer.

It was largely the hold of the Church on the Irish people that deterred them from rising against their masters. A few priests here and there, acting on their own, identified with the movement, but the bishops deplored the Brotherhood no less than the Devil hated holy water.

What the Church really feared was the free thought that emanated from the urban society. Dublin of the era was the cesspool of Europe, owning the highest mortality rate, with Moscow running a distant second. Yet the

Church was the bitter enemy of the trade unions, the Gaelic revival and all that intellectualism that challenged their stranglehold. Moreover, the cities fomented secret societies whose members were not divulged in the confessionals. The Church deplored secret societies although none was more secretive than the Church itself.

The cities bred dangerous ideas such as freedom from England. Obviously, any movement which won Irish independence would seek liberation from the totalitarianism of the Church as well. In church politics, the British had bestowed privileges and exclusive domains which had to be protected.

Its essential grip on the people was locked into an agrarian culture. Out in the small villages and towns the parish priest was able to impose a doctrinaire hold with little question or opposition.

In 1908 the Vatican poured queer oil on the troubled Irish waters, hastening unrest by the decree of *Ne Temere*.

It had been the custom to accept mixed marriages with the sons following the father's religion and the girls taking after the mother. After centuries of holy wars, inquisitions, crusades, Reformation and Counter Reformation, the twentieth century was greeted as a coming of light. It was not to be.

Ne Temere in a fell swoop invalidated all mixed marriages except when performed by the Catholic Church with the coercion that children of such marriages be signed away at birth to be raised as Catholics. *Ne Temere* plunged Ireland back into a dark age. The bigotry of it fell right in line with the most dire predictions of Ulster's frothing Protestant clergy. The Oliver Cromwell MacIvors lost no time in reacting and no St. Bartholomew's massacre could have supplied more fuel for their paranoia.

*

Two months after Conor Larkin arrived in America the first trial and execution of the Irish Republican Brotherhood took place halfway around the world in Australia. A special task force located, abducted and tried Doxie O'Brien, finding him guilty of the most heinous of Irish crimes, informing. After a written confession he was dispatched by a single bullet to the brain.

CHAPTER THREE: Hubble Manor lay in a week-long coma. The upstairs maids who changed bed linens gossiped down the news that the Earl and Countess had not slept together during this period, which coincided with them not eating together and canceling all joint engagements.

It was Roger who crossed no man's land into his wife's boudoir. Caroline showed pasty effects of the silent warfare. She had gone over her arguments again and again, justified her anger, tossed sleeplessly, brinked on surrender, then stiffened each time.

What would she say now? Should she explode on him or adopt an attitude of conciliation? She knew how rooted his feelings were. She toyed with the idea of capitulation. At any rate Roger would be the epitome of calm, that was for certain. Roger never brooded this long on a problem without becoming deadly. Listen, don't leap, she told herself. Don't let him egg you into a rage.

"I think we'd better have a go at it," he said, "bearing in mind that a single misdirected spark is liable to blow this place apart. This is serious, Caroline, terribly, terribly serious. The worst that's happened to us in our twenty-five years."

Caroline unfolded herself slowly from the chaise longue. Her hair was down, long and sensuous as she wore it to bed, and she was without cosmetics. Lines of aging had deepened in the past week. Still, she looked hauntingly lovely.

"You humiliated me," he said. "Made a complete ass of me not only in the eyes of the Brigadier and Herd, but in your own eyes as well."

"Is that what's bothering you, that you were made to look foolish?"

"It's damned well part of it. What really hurt was you and Jeremy in this conspiracy behind my back."

"Conspiracy? What conspiracy? The boy wrote to me months and months ago that he had fallen desperately in love but begged me not to tell his father. I told him he had to but he was afraid. Father wouldn't understand,

711

that's what he said, Father wouldn't understand. It's the understatement of the decade. Father has never understood, not from the first day of his life. Father has made a career out of not understanding."

"Are you done?"

"Company spies in your son's bedroom, Roger. Why didn't you get photographs of them making love as well!"

Roger held up his hand for her to stop. "I shall overlook the insinuations you've built into your remarks."

"Insinuations, hell," she snapped, "they are accusations. Second-story snoops taking a count of sheets and towels. It's the most despicable, utterly disgusting thing I've ever heard of."

"Jeremy Hubble is not some greengrocer's son. Nothing on God's earth can change the fact that he will become the Twelfth Earl of Foyle. He is the logical and legitimate inheritor of lands and factories valued at tens of millions. I have not only the right but the duty to protect the interests of this family . . . your father included."

"Perhaps, if you had given the boy some sense of friendship, he would have sought you out when he had a problem."

Roger laughed sarcastically. "Lovely how all of this has been twisted around to being my fault. I suppose it is also my fault that I'm his father and he was born to be Viscount Coleraine."

"What's that to do with a boy falling in love with a girl?"

"Everything, Caroline. The boy has had obligations all his life that preclude this kind of romantic nonsense."

"Yes, poor Jeremy, through no fault of his, or ours, is the Viscount Coleraine. Alas, he is not so cunning as his father when he was Viscount. Lord Roger would fathom nothing less than a suitable marriage calculated to razor's edge. Jeremy just went out there and fell in love like some untitled slob. Well, Roger, he's in love and he didn't ask his daddy's permission. What on earth are we going to do?"

Roger allowed her sparks to fizz out and waited for her to calm. "I suggest that Jeremy hasn't the faintest notion if he is in love or baying at the moon like a dog in heat."

"Not entirely unlike his mother used to be," Caroline cracked. "Isn't it strange that you found my Paris attic capers so wildly exciting but see the same thing in your own son as vulgar. Or maybe you'd care to strike me off the list as well."

"Stop distorting things, Caroline. The point of it is that his mother's skirts have shielded him through his entire life from his responsibilities."

They glared, both realizing they were peaking their anger too harshly and too quickly and knew it had better come under control, for they were reaching a plateau where permanent damage could be inflicted.

Caroline paced, wrung her hands and tears welled in her eyes. "Roger," she pleaded in a whisper, "what do you want from the boy? He's a plain, simple, loving sort of young man whose friends adore him. He hasn't a mean bone in his body. The reason you're alienated is because you've tried to make him into something he isn't. He's neither a driven tycoon like Freddie, a righteous Ulsterman nor pretender to any ancient thrones. He's not his brother Christopher, all perked up to assume the family glory. Why in the name of God can't you accept him for what he is and love him?"

Roger stared from the window to the great stretch of green below, then turned slowly. "I'll tell you what Jeremy is," he said grimly. "He is the recurring nightmare that has cursed the Hubble family."

"All right, you've said it," Caroline snapped. "Jeremy and your father, Arthur, are one and the same. Dear old stuttering Arthur living on the dole, terrified of the drums and marching, terrified of life. Resolved: Jeremy is Jeremy is Arthur."

Roger slumped and held his head for a moment. "I've fought it," he said, "but there is no use fighting it any longer. Do you know what it means to give up on your own son?" he moaned. "I know he'd destroy in a decade what we've taken generations to build, I know that. And so he will become Christopher's ward . . . just as my father was mine."

"Make an arrangement that will let the boy live in peace," she pleaded. "He's known all along that Christopher will run things. He accepts that and doesn't resent it."

"Oh, Lord, if it were only that simple," Roger answered. "What diabolical quirk of fate made Christopher the youngest? No arrangement can ever change the fact that

Jeremy will become the Earl of Foyle. Caroline, understand this clearly. I and I alone am responsible for the
continuation of our line. I shall not permit some trollop
carrying someone's bastard to become the Countess of
Foyle and have . . . that . . . become our future Earl."

"Stop it, Roger!" Caroline cried. "Stop it! Molly O'Rafferty is an exquisite, delicate little creature blindly in love
with our son. Don't speak lies. Speak to her, meet her, but
for God's sake don't speak lies."

"Is it a lie that she's a Roman Catholic?"

"She'll convert in a minute."

"She'll convert! She'll convert! How decent of her! We're
not Belfast shipyard workers swapping wives, neighborhoods and religions."

"Find it in your heart to bend, Roger, I beg you."

"No," he said bluntly, "no."

"Roger . . ."

"Even if it were in my heart . . . even if she were half of
what you claim, it would still be out of the question."

"But why!"

"We have entered the arena for the death struggle. War
for this country will crash down on our heads within our
lifetime. Do you think I can impose upon the people
whose loyalty is vital to our existence a debauchery of
their beliefs?"

Caroline gaped and saw the man for the first time in her
life. There seemed neither a shred of compassion for the
two young people caught in his web nor an iota of ability
to yield. Caroline was frightened.

"Somewhere along the line"—her voice quivered—"we
are going to have to make peace. If we don't, Jeremy and
Christopher and their children will have to fight this whole
thing over again. All we'll have managed in the end is
to delay an Armageddon and pass this madness down to
another generation. Can't we make our own little start
by the simple human act of letting two young people in
love show that there can be love in this place?"

"You're being a bore, Caroline . . ."

"Roger, you're frightening me."

"And a hypocrite!"

"How dare you!"

"This latter-day Gladstonian liberalism is highly out of
character," he said, coming to his feet and waving his arm

in a sweep. "If my recollection does not fail me it was the Lady Caroline standing in the rear of the Long Hall cheering us on while Randolph Churchill played the Orange card. Where were you when your father and I and our cronies sliced Ireland up like a pie? Where were you when we were covering our dung after the shirt factory fire? Oh, you were there, all right, clear up to here, because you believed in what we were doing. And why? Because you wanted your million quid to gussy up Rathweed Hall and Hubble Manor and acquire art and culture and become a great and powerful lady. Oh, you were there all right, because your precious money and your precious power came from the same imperial experience that now makes you hold up your hands and wail . . . 'Oh, Roger, why can't we get along with these people?' You, madam, in your heyday spending more money a week than the wages of every man in Weed Ship & Iron and the shirt factory combined. You and your token little house Catholics can neither absolve you of your sins nor transfer them conveniently to your husband and your father."

Roger had crossed the line from which there could be no return, now or ever. . . .

"What are you going to do with them!" she cried.

"It's already done."

"Roger . . . what . . ."

"The Brigadier and Mr. Herd, whom you found so disgusting, have faced Jeremy with the fact that two of his friends have sworn to have had sex with Molly O'Rafferty."

Caroline's body trembled uncontrollably and she looked around the room half mad, then plunged to the phone. "Freddie . . ." she gasped.

"Don't bother to call. Freddie quite agrees with me. He is also aware you will probably become sentimentally hysterical over Jeremy."

"But that girl . . . Molly . . ."

"Adequate compensation is being arranged."

"The child, Roger! Your own grandchild! You know what happens to foundlings. They can't survive! And Molly! That precious girl! She'll be condemned like a common whore, all but burned at the stake as a witch."

"If the young lady is sensible she'll accept our offer to

leave the country where arrangements will be made to have the child put up for blind adoption. She will have enough money to remain quite comfortable for a long period."

"Who are you? God? Manipulating your son's life as if he were some sort of dumb animal. Roger, you're a bloody monster!"

"Am I, Caroline? Am I? Your darling boy Jeremy chose to believe that Miss O'Rafferty had been unfaithful to him. Is that how deeply his love runs? You see, Jeremy might have stood up like a man for once in his life and told us all to go to hell. At that point we would have had no choice but to accept the girl. So lump Jeremy in with the rest of the pack you suddenly find so indecent."

Caroline broke, weeping long and hard and without his comfort, only his statue glaring down on her. "What about us?" she said at last.

"When I knew what I had to do I realized the risk to you and me. All I knew was that in the end I could not be responsible for destroying my family. After we're gone, what does it really matter how we ended our time together?"

His completely detached cold incisiveness chilled her.

"There's something I don't know," she said. "I cannot have lived with a man for twenty-five years and not have sensed the power of hatred I feel from you now. You hate me and you hate Jeremy. I want to know why!"

"What difference does it make now?" he said softly.

"I want to know why. What have we done? Why . . . when . . . I have to know, Roger."

He walked to the bedroom door as if in a trance. His voice was far away, as though speaking in a tunnel. . . . "It happened in there . . . on that bed . . . you lay there . . . glistening with sweat and writhing with birth pains . . . and then there was a burst of blood between your legs and you screamed the instant Jeremy was born. . . . You screamed . . . for your father. . . ."

CHAPTER FOUR: The turf fire glowed aromatically delicious, whiskey was in my glass and Conor Larkin

stood before me. On the surface of it he had entered
middle life with all the strength and beauty that had
marked his boyhood and manhood. No woman would turn
away and few men would care to challenge him. There
was a softness, a mellowness that only comes to a man
who has endured enormous suffering. So much of his ways
and speech now reminded me of his daddy, Tomas.

But what of the scar? Did it still leak blood in his
brooding hours? Had scar tissue formed so thickly as to
lock in hurtful memory? What defenses had risen to
detach himself from our sorrowful land? Had Conor
numbed into a new person, not apparent on the outside,
whose spirit, poetry, rage and awesome will power had
fled?

Was he still Conor after his year in America?

"It was a long way to go for a few bags of gold," Conor
said, "but it was worth the journey. A hell of a land,
Seamus. Can you imagine a single country with four
different zones of time and forty-six states, each one larger
and more populous than our four paltry provinces? It bent
my mind riding over that land remembering that Irish
navvies laid down every mile of the railroad track. Aye,
but there it is, the worst shantytown was better than what
they left here. Then, of course, the American dream is
held up before them like a vision of the holy grail. 'Just
reach out and grab it!' That's what they're told from
birth. 'It's yours! Take it!' Ah, and all those self-made
tycoons all trying to fart higher than their Irish asses filling
up obscure churches with vulgar stained glass windows to
the memory of fathers and mothers they truly want to
forget."

I had slurped my glass dry and himself promptly
refilled it.

"My problem was that those few who did remember
their beginnings want to buy their way into heaven by
their donation to the Brotherhood. They don't like giving
secretly. They want to shout about it, as though God
were not aware."

"For my own selfish purposes, I'm glad to see you back,
even though it means your having to live on the run," I
said. "The underground paper comes out biweekly, thanks
to your fund raising, and the British haven't found our
presses."

"Is anyone listening to you, Seamus?"

"Maybe. We're getting attacks from sources that used to ignore us. We're annoying someone, sure enough."

Conor bit his lip thoughtfully and set his glass down. "Why was I ordered back?" he asked.

"Dan Sweeney has given the word to start forming units. He's going to have you arrange friendly farms around the country and take over charge of organization and training. You'll command everything outside the Dublin area."

Conor whistled softly.

"Lord Louie has agreed to let us use Dunleer here as our primary training base."

"Aye, that's good, but why me? You've a number of more qualified men on the Supreme Council."

"Alas," I said, "that august body is notably devoid of knowledgeable soldiers as well as practical politicians. Dreamers hold high rank. Dan gets sick of them in regular cycles of two weeks. Not once but a dozen times he's hit his fist on the table over a thorny problem and wished out loud that you were back in Ireland."

Conor shrugged and said something unfittingly modest.

"I detected a look of disappointment when I entered the cottage today," I said.

He broke into a defensive smile.

"Like maybe you expected Atty to show up with me?" I said.

"If I burned you for a fool, I'd have wise ashes," he said.

"Funny. Atty had the same expression on her face when she saw me off at the train station. I thought to myself as I pulled away from the platform, Isn't it strange for a woman to look like that in light of the fact she hasn't had a letter from you in six months?"

"All right, runt," he said, "I hear you."

"Well?"

He studied the fire for a time. "There was a wise old jailor by the name of Hugh Dalton who was with me when it happened to Shelley. After I reached bottom he told me that all men in that instant of ultimate agony make the decision to live or die. It's not a conscious decision, but one your spirit makes. Apparently I made the decision to go on living . . . in one form or another. The question since then has been . . . how much can you live? How much of me lies in Shelley's grave? I don't know the answer."

"It might need more testing," I said. "You did miss Atty?"

"Aye, sorely."

"That tells you something, doesn't it?"

"It does. Look, man, Atty and I shared an uncommon, horrible experience. She refused to let me die. She saw me in dark moments nae man nor woman has or will again. In one form or another, I'm Conor again and she is Atty again. Here at Dunleer at that time we were two different people."

"Or perhaps the same people just grown taller?" I suggested. "The total person, all of you revealed, not a studied person who presents a calculated version of himself to the world."

"God knows I thought of her a great deal in America," he said. "What Atty found so attractive in me in the beginning was my strength and my hold over her. I think that no man ever had that before. When she came to me at Dunleer after Shelley, she saw a weak groveling little cur. Weak, like any man and every man she had ever known. Having seen me in such a state, she knows I am capable of weakness again. I believe that once Atty smells weakness in a man it's no less than a wolf smelling the blood of a wounded elk. In time it would become my strength against hers. Even so, what is in it for either of us? Half the man she once knew? The ghost of Shelley rankling around over the both of us?"

"As a practical matter, my friend," I said, "the two of you are going to be locked into each other's lives from here on out. Don't you think the woman knows she is not going to replace Shelley?"

As he became uneasy I pressed him.

"All right," he said at last, "what do you think?"

"I think you're the one man I know capable of going from one great love to another great love. An entirely different kind of love, but a great one, nonetheless. There is so much that binds you and Atty together. Even knowing that every moment could be your last binds you. You'd be the worst kind of a fool not to find out."

"Perhaps I will," he whispered.

"Will you let me take a message back?"

"Nae . . . I'll know when the time is ready. . . ." Conor took another long drink and I think the whiskey found its mark. I'd not often seen him drunk but the trip back, the transfer at sea, slipping into Dunleer, the confusions of America, all ganged up on him now.

"Aye," he mused, "so I'm back in Ireland . . . really back and alive . . . only you know, Seamus, nothing ever happens here in the future. It's always the past happening over and over again. We and the British are like two comets streaking through the universe and leaving tails of cosmic dust a thousand miles long trailing after . . . we orbit through the heavens, each in a different direction, and then we inevitably move at one another . . . we bear down for a head-on collision . . . sometimes we barely miss one another, coming so close that the dust in our wake brushes and tumbles through the skies and the heat from our bodies stifles the planets in our wake . . . steaming . . . hissing . . . swirling into invisible infinites. We disrupt the order of the heavens. And we pass and go our separate ways, screaming off into space and circling, circling, circling until we once again have made our individual sweeps of the universe and have come full circle into each other's path again. . . . What will happen this time? Do we merely brush close or do we smash into one another at last?"

CHAPTER FIVE: Never having penetrated the innards of Dublin's Liberties, Lord Jeremy Hubble entered as though he intended to hold his breath the entire time. Stares followed him. He was obviously so out of place in the squalor, his discomfort heightened with every step. Turning off Bridgefoot Street into the narrow confines of Tyndall's Alley, he walked as if on eggs in unpaved muck bounded on either side by hovels where poverty had bottomed out. Jeremy pulled himself together and rapped heavily on the door, then lowered his eyes to avoid the sight within.

"What do you want?" a man answered.

"I'm looking for Molly O'Rafferty."

"She ain't 'ere."

"She is here," Jeremy insisted. "I intend to see her."

"If you are who I thinks you are, she don't want to be seein' the likes of you."

"Look here, my good man . . ."

"I ain't yer good man."

Jeremy couraged himself, called up his reserves and made a move. "I'm coming in and I'd advise you not to stop me." He caught the door before it slammed in his face and shoved it back open.

"It's all right, Finn," a voice called from inside. "Tell him I'll be right out."

The man sneered and turned away. In a moment Molly O'Rafferty passed through the door into the alley. Jeremy had not seen her in over a week. The past days had driven him to the brink of hysteria. Molly looked beautiful, even in this sordid background. She made her own clothing. He had always been so proud to have her on his arm. Jeremy glanced to her belly. She didn't show yet. All he had seen of the coming baby was her breasts enlarging and that had excited him. Her voice was tiny and pure when she spoke and, when she sang, a springtime of innocence that matched big black eyes and long raven hair.

"I'll not ask how you found me," she said, "but I'm telling you to say what you're after saying and be on your way."

"Who are they?" he asked, nodding toward the house.

"Old friends."

"Look, can we go somewhere and talk? Down by the river?"

The figure of a man lurked protectively in the window. Molly thought about it for a few seconds. "I'll be back soon, Finn," she said.

Molly tightened a shawl about her shoulders, refusing Jeremy's arm. They walked apart down Bridgefoot Street to Usher's Quay along the River Liffey and found a bench. The greened copper dome of the Law Courts loomed over the way past the browned slow-moving water. Jeremy gathered himself again near the rail.

"I hardly know where to begin," he said nervously, flailing the air, scraping at his hair and wringing his hands. He sucked in gasps to fight off tears. "They came to my flat with Mal Palmer and Cliff Coleman. Each one in turn recited how they had made love to you, swore it, feigned sympathy, said there were others. Something in my mind just snapped. Plain violent, purple jealousy. The entire atmosphere of it was unreal. Once Mal and Cliff were dismissed, Brigadier Swan and the Herd chap went at me, pounding into my brain. You've got to understand, Molly, this kind of thing is their job. They're masters at it. First the business about disgracing my family. Then the other thing . . . about you and the others."

He gritted his teeth and looked to her but was unable to hold his eyes to her.

"When they had finished, my father came down from Londonderry. He said I'd been bringing them nothing but grief since I was a boy. He said, 'God knows whose baby she has.' At any rate, they said they'd do the proper thing for you. Even my brother Christopher. I looked to him for some sort of sympathy, but the bastard waved the flag of Ulster in my face and pounded slogans in my ears I'd been hearing since childhood."

Molly remained immobile, her hands quietly in her lap, a vast sorrow in her eyes fixed on the tormented young man.

"Your family," he said, "did they throw you out? I mean, have you been . . . you know what I mean."

"No, they didn't throw me out. But they're divided and broken. I've brought the ultimate shame to them. When a girl goes up the pole, the rules of the game are quite clear. I have to leave my home and chances are my name will not be spoken again."

"Oh, Molly, I've done a frightful thing. When we had the fight and you left . . . after the fall . . . I began to piece it together. First I was consumed with overpowering loneliness and then I realized fully what I had done by believing them. I went out and found Mal Palmer and I tore the truth from him."

"You might have asked me, Jeremy, I would have told you the truth," she said.

"I know, you tried, but I was crazy. Well, the bloody truth is Mal Palmer and Cliff Coleman were bribed, two hundred quid each."

"You've a very generous family, Jeremy. They spread goodness wherever they reach. They've gone and made all sorts of arrangements for me as well."

"What kind of arrangements!" Jeremy's voice quivered.

"It seems there are some very fine clinics in Switzer-

nd to take care of bastard children of the aristocracy. I'm
ld everything is done under sanitary conditions. And, if
ou insist on having the child because of religious rea-
ns, you are assured of a splendid adoption."

"Molly, for God's sake!"

"I was only saying how considerate your family is."

"Listen to me, darling. I'm sick inside. I'm sick at myself.
can't even beg forgiveness. But I want to earn it and
ll prove to you every day and every night how much I
dore you."

"What do you mean to do, Jeremy?"

He puffed up a large chest full of air and beat his fist in
is hand to mark the depths of his determination. "Father
as ordered me to quit Dublin and take a year or so of
ublic duty. Colonial Office, consular service or some
uch sort of thing. From there it will be the family regi-
ent. Fine with me. I mean to say, I've known all along
hat this would be in store."

"I know how important family duties are," she said.

"See, I'm a fool, Molly, an utter fool. All during this
rdeal my mind was allowed to stray from a single devas-
ating piece of reality. I am the Viscount Coleraine.
There is nothing on God's earth my father or anyone else
an do about it. The succession to the earldom is mine and
nine alone. He can bully me all he wants, he can threaten
ne, but he can't take away my birthright. I shall quite
imply go to him and inform him that Jeremy Hubble is
oing to marry Molly O'Rafferty and he can lump it if he
oesn't like it. Don't you see, he has no choice but to ac-
ept you then."

Molly smiled tinily and let out a little peep.

"I say, you don't seem terribly pleased," Jeremy said.

She patted the bench. "Sit here beside me, Jeremy, and
old my hand." Doing as he was bid, Molly ran her fingers through his hair and traced his cheeks and chin
delicately with her fingers.

"I love a boy, a kind and gentle boy trying so hard to
be a brave man . . . but not quite able to make it. I love
you, Jeremy, for what you are and nothing else, lad, and
I'll go any place in the world with you, except Ulster."

Jeremy looked at her puzzled and shook his head.
"What do you mean, Molly?"

"It doesn't matter to me if you're delivering ice for a

living or dressed in a business suit or tending bar in a public house. I'll take you as you are any place, but I'll not share you with that family of yours."

"You . . . you want me . . . to . . . to renounce my title? Give up my inheritance?"

"It's not what I want but it's the only way for Jeremy and Molly. I know plain old Jeremy and I know how to take care of him, sure enough."

"But, darling, I don't believe you understood me. Once we are married and they have to accept you, then they will."

"I don't care whether they accept me or not, Jeremy. I don't accept them."

"What?"

"They are sick people living in a sick place. Do you really expect me to live within their walls after offering me money to destroy our child?"

"But . . . but . . ."

"Do you expect me to spend my entire life trying to become a woman who, in the end, will destroy Molly O'Rafferty?" she said. "If I go up there and adopt their ways I'll come to hate. I'll adopt their hatred and their cunning and I'll wait around for your father to die and then I will have become just like him in the end."

"You're confusing me, Molly, you're confusing me."

"I'll put it plainly. I'm afraid your family is too common and low a breed for the daughter of Bernard O'Rafferty."

Jeremy gaped. Molly got up and took his place at the rail and became consumed for a moment by a passing barge.

"What do you want me to do?" Jeremy croaked.

"Just go along your way, lad. Do what your father tells you. You've not the strength for anything else."

As the moments ticked off, the truth sank into him as truth. He was ashamed to look at her. She was so God-awful strong, this little girl. Where did she find it? It was there, all the treachery of his family laid out in simple view. Yet he had no iron to rebel. Any notion of running off with her became totally squashed by visions of muddy alleys and peeling rooms.

With all his tugging and hauling with his father, he liked being Jeremy Hubble, Viscount Coleraine. He liked

he well-cut tailored suits, all three dozen of them. He
iked riding in his grandfather's opulent car and buying
rounds for the crowd. He liked being good old sporting
Jeremy. He liked that more than anything . . . Molly . . .
heir child . . . anything. . . . To go with her, to pretend it
could work, would only delay disaster.

"I can't go with you," he mumbled.

"I know, Jeremy."

It was done. He dared lift his eyes. "You'll go to Switzer-
land, of course."

"I think not," Molly said.

"But you've got to get it taken care of."

"Not to bother," she said, walking away.

Jeremy raced up behind her and turned her about to
face him. "Look, I've got to know!"

"I'll not be a party to a murder along with everything
else. I'll have my child and I'll raise it."

"Oh, my God, Molly!"

"If you're worried about yourself and your own twinges
of conscience I suspect you'll get over it in time."

"But you'll take the money . . ."

"Jeremy, please . . ."

"Molly . . ."

"My family will see me through. Even though I've
brought them shame, we do love one another. I'll certainly
go to where our existence will be of no bother to you or
your lovely family. I have my hands and I have my voice.
Bearing a child will do nothing to harm either."

"Let me help. Promise to let me help."

"I give you only one promise. You'll never see or hear
from either of us again."

Molly O'Rafferty, touching upon her eighteenth year,
left Jeremy at the bank of the River Liffey. She departed
from Dublin and Ireland a few days later . . . forever.

CHAPTER SIX: In the year that followed Conor
Larkin's return to Ireland he took on his new role with
the same studious zeal that had made him an ironmaster, a
great rugby player and the Brotherhood's best fund raiser
in America. His immediate goal of setting up training

camps on "friendly farms" was achieved. Outside the Dublin area a major site was established in each of the provinces of Connaught, Munster and Ulster. The Connaught friendly farm of Dunleer was the most important.

A training regimen was established in small arms weaponry, dynamite, urban tactics and rural ambush along with sabotage. In this period Conor all but wrote the military textbook of the Brotherhood.

He traveled underground constantly, keeping control of the units from Cork to Derry, establishing a coherence of commanders, communications, intelligence, supplies, weapons, medicine and political indoctrination. It was an army of tiny magnitude with only a few hundred men in each province, but secrecy and dedication had been meticulously preserved. Fanaticism was expected to compensate for lack of growth.

Conor's home of sorts was a remote cottage in the backwater of the Dunleer barony. The main manor house and farms stretched along Lough Ballynahinch and forest where it met the bottom of the Twelve Bens. Bits and pieces of an original fifteenth-century Norman castle remained, including a keep in total preservation. A mile into the woods a natural draw along Lough Fadda hid the Brotherhood training area and Conor's cottage from all outside view.

Men were trained at odd times and in odd numbers depending on when they could get away to Dunleer. These were barracked at an ancient, restored monastery around the lough from Conor's cottage.

He set up a forge where he manufactured a reasonable replica of the British Army Webley revolver and made the ammunition for it as well.

He met Atty infrequently, always in the midst of Brotherhood business, and they seemingly avoided personal contact out of mutual design.

*

One evening at twilight early in autumn, the intercommunication signal from the manor house rang in the forge, signaling Conor that a safe person had been passed through into the training area.

He went outside to the lake front and sighted a lone horse and rider through his field glasses. As horse and rider circled the lough against a backdrop of pines and the first reddening of the water by a plunging sun, they came clearly into view.

It was Atty Fitzpatrick.

Her posture on the animal was magnificent, of one who had spent many hours at it. Of course she had been Lady Royce-Moore once, out of the same County Galway, and she had spent a good part of her growing days astride a Connemara.

As she came within shouting distance Conor called and she spurred, galloping the mount along the water's edge, sending her hair flying back in a brown cascade. She pulled up and leaped down into Conor's grasp.

"What a grand sight at sunset," Conor said.

"I'm terribly out of practice and out of shape. I used to be very good at this," she replied, gasping for breath.

"Don't get too close to me," Conor said, holding her back at arm's length, "I've the dirt of the forge on me. Before I find out what brings you here, are you game for a nice sobering swim?"

"Where?"

"In the altogether in that lough," Conor said, getting out of the leather apron, peeling off shirt and trousers and running, then leaping into the water, emitting a yowl of painful delight in the boyish flash that seemed to overwhelm him the instant he saw her. He beat himself on the chest, dunked and hollered.

"Well, are you joining me or not?"

"I think I'd follow you anywhere, Conor, except that lake."

"Then go into the cottage and fetch me a towel."

Atty returned with a towel in hand and another wrapped about herself, flashed it off and jumped in, sending up an icy spray. It was an unabashed surge of joy, holding hands and jumping up and down screaming and splashing. He picked her up in his arms and flung her, then both crawled breathlessly up the bank filled with blue goose bumps of cold, applying the towels vigorously.

"Jaysus!" Conor said. "I forget from one night to the next how desperate that lake is. Jaysus, let's get inside."

It was a good Irish cottage in that the turf was always smoored and ready to flare and it soon glowed, warming them along with a fiery measure of poteen while the sun seered violent into the ocean. They dressed wondering about the crazy exhilaration on seeing one another. Both of them had pondered long about such a meeting and felt it would be filled with guilt and evasions and half-spoken truths.

"Well, what grievous tidings do you bear?" Conor asked as the leading edges of night crept down from the Twelve Bens.

"Dan Sweeney sent me. He wanted to send Seamus but Seamus is apt to become gullible when dealing with big brother Conor. The two of you rarely fail to set off on flights of Celtic fantasy."

"And at this moment I'm thanking Long Dan," Conor joked.

"Besides, I asked him if I could come."

A wind rushed through the cottage. Conor studied the sky outside, feeling the first tiny drops of rain ride in on the winds. The peaks of the Bens were suddenly covered beneath massing clouds and these would be rolling down on the loughs.

"There's a head beetler on the way," Conor said. "It moves in here as swiftly as it moved in from Scotland up in my home. I'd better get you back to the manor house before the storm."

"Lord Louie's in London and you've no men training here now. If I remember, the cottage does have an extra bedroom."

"Aye."

"Why don't we button in and see what the cupboard holds in store?"

"Sure," Conor said. He secured the barn and the windows, barely beating the rain, which swept down in a single hard stroke from Benlettery. Atty fired the turf stove and applied odds and ends to a stew after proper appreciation of the contents of Lord Louie's larder and pantry. She knew her way around a peasant's cottage among other things the woman did without flaw. He had seen her in the same room two years before but so much of that had been in a haze that this was like watching her here for the first time. He hovered between a desire to wrap his arms about her and a feeling of being trapped.

The meal was unlike any since he had left America.

The storm cracked in for fair. Atty sat before the turf,

knees tucked close to her chin and her arms draped around them. Conor was above her on a creepie lightly filing and oiling four new pistols he had completed at the forge.

"Dan's angry with you," she began.

"The usual state of affairs between himself and myself."

"Louie set up to meet a German freighter off Slyne Head and take on a load of guns. You countermanded the order."

"Aye, I did," Conor agreed.

"We want to know why."

"I don't want his yacht used for that purpose any longer."

"I'm afraid we don't understand. The Germans are willing to make offshore rendezvous on a regular basis. They're even considering running in a submarine with arms."

Conor aimed the pistol at an imaginary target, cocked it and clicked the trigger. He filed softly, blew, squeezed the trigger again.

"The risk isn't worth the gain," Conor said.

"I don't consider that a sufficient answer," Atty said.

"Gunrunning with that particular yacht in this particular area will quickly lead Lord Louie to the scaffold and we'll end up losing the finest and most secluded and irreplaceable training site the Brotherhood will ever have on Irish soil."

"Sorry, Conor, we don't accept it," Atty pressed.

"Louie is aware of the risk and accepts it. He also accepts the decisions of the Supreme Council. Perhaps, I should say, a little better than you do."

"He's a nice aristocratic gentleman, a noble Gaelic scholar, but otherwise apt to be a bit of a clod from too much Connemara moonscape and too much inbreeding with the Court of St. James's. I'll make Louie's decisions, at least the ones concerning his boat and his home."

"I suggest that the Supreme Council will and has," Atty said.

"Well, I suggest that Seamus work up a good speech for Lord Louie to deliver from the dock prior to his hanging."

"Conor, dammit, you're being both obstinate and disobedient." She unraveled herself and stood above him, taking the pistol from his hand and tossing it on the table.

"Sit down, Atty, and listen. There are informers in both Roundstone and Clifden who mark down every time the *Gráinne Uáile* leaves and enters port. They have watchers on every cove and beach in the area. Commander Weatherton of the Royal Navy is just champing to knock him over. It takes a party of ten to twenty men to transfer and beach a load of guns. You can bet your last quid that one or more will be on the British payroll."

Atty fumed. "Why in the hell didn't you tell us this in the first place!" she demanded.

"Oh, mind your tone, Atty. You're not at a Council meeting. If I am commander here, then you've got to allow me to use my judgment. I'll not have Dublin overriding me on a whim. They've got to convince me first I've made a wrong decision. Otherwise, don't bugger me just because you have a set of Irish maps to play with."

She loathed his arrogant softness. Of course he was dead right, and had he not interceded the Council would have blundered into a tragedy. But more than his self-confidence, Conor remained among the two or three men she had ever known whom she could not control. After the initial urge to conjure up a scene, she accepted it with amazing quiet.

"Anything else on Dan's mind?" he asked.

"Yes," she said, reorganizing herself for a calmer discussion. "It's between you and Dan. He asked me to speak to you in his behalf because he has trouble speaking for himself. He detests your independence, which in many ways goes against the grain of Brotherhood discipline."

"Oh, Dan knows how to say that for himself."

"What he can't bring himself to do is beg you to join the Supreme Council. He has to have you, Conor. He simply has to have you. Independence, arrogance be damned. The man needs you."

Conor gathered up the pistols slowly and wrapped each in a cloth. "What would I be doing debating with all those fine Dublin intellectuals?" he said.

"You're running half the Brotherhood now."

"Sure the Council's not for me, Atty."

"We're overloaded with mystics and scholars. Dan tells me that I'm the only practical one he can rely on most of the time. He also says you've learned more about weapons, tactics and training men in a single year than he has in a lifetime."

"I'd only be a pain in everyone's ass," Conor fenced. "I know my job here. I've no stomach for arguing in endless circles."

"Dan's wearing out. Conor, it can't leave this cottage but he told me he's looking around for his successor."

"Me?"

"You."

A shutter blew open. Conor watched it beat under a whiplash of wind for many moments. "I'd have to respectfully refuse him," he whispered.

"That needs an explanation."

"I'll tell you something that also cannot leave this cottage. To become the commander of the Irish Republican Brotherhood I would have to be a liar and a traitor to things I know to be the truth. The truth is . . . we cannot win. We cannot defeat the British with arms in a hundred years, we cannot defeat them at a conference table and we can never reconcile the Ulstermen. Those are truths. Brutal truths that no wild-eyed revolutionary's fantasy can change."

He came over the room to her slowly and gripped her arms hard. "All we can ever hope for is a glorious defeat. A defeat that may somehow stir the dormant ashes of our people into a series of more glorious defeats. Every man in the Brotherhood must defy, scream, kick, die hard, bloody, shake consciences. You see, the true job of the Brotherhood is not to expand to win but to sharpen its teeth to die hard."

"What would you do, Conor?"

"See to it that not a single death can go silent and unheard. Destroy British will by our will." He dropped his hands from her arms and turned away. "So you see, Atty, I can never be the maker of dreams, for there is no dream, only a nightmare. Do you understand that, lass?"

He walked off and she followed him, touching his back, and he turned and they stared at one another.

"Oh, man." Atty Fitzpatrick's voice shivered. "I've missed you so."

"Myself as well," he whispered.

"I made myself a fool over you once and it mattered to me. I'm going to make a fool of myself again and I don't care. I've not been right for any man or myself since I met you."

They held their places rigidly.

"I cannot help but batter you, Atty, and bring you to pain. At times, I'm frightened, you're so strong. I don't know how damaged I am. I don't know what's left for me to give or if I've already given it all. I've even got scars from our damned Church . . . aye, that as well . . ." he said.

Atty's face was locked and pale. She closed her eyes and let the tears fall as they might.

"I've never forgotten what you did for me, Atty. Each night coming to that room in the darkness, opening your robe, laying beside me, holding my head to your breasts and letting me weep. Only by your mercy am I alive. I was glad when they sent me to America in a way, for I was becoming ashamed of my tears and ashamed of needing you so desperately."

"Do you think I did what I did out of mercy, Conor? All of a sudden I was able to do that for a man! Knowing for the first time I owned that capacity was like the first day of life for me. And then you took it away. Do you know what it is for a woman to realize she has this much to give and be spurned by the man who has opened it all to her?"

"You should never have come, Atty . . . I'll hurt you . . ."

"Conor! Because Shelley died doesn't mean you'll kill me! I'm trembling for you, man!"

He slumped at the table and turned his back to her.

"God Almighty, I don't know what's in it for either of us," she said, coming up behind him. "But I've got to know. I'm worn out from waiting. I won't go beyond this day. Conor . . . my door will be open and this night it is I who needs you to come to me. If you don't, it will never be open again."

"Run if you've got the brains!"

"No!"

He bolted out into the rain and let it beat at him.

Oh, Shelley, he cried to himself, I cannot hold onto you any longer. . . . I want to live, Shelley . . . please let me live . . . please let me live . . . please let me live. . . .

He opened the door of her room and filled the frame. The light of the best room fell over her. Atty stood beside the bed and unloosed the drawstring of her blouse and pulled it over her head proudly and freed her breasts and unbuttoned her skirt and let it fall to the floor. Conor moved into the room slowly and kicked the door shut behind him.

CHAPTER SEVEN: A decade of relative political tranquillity came abruptly to a halt when a constitutional crisis brought on two elections in the year 1910.

Herbert Asquith had taken over leadership of the ruling Liberal Party and attempted to pass a "people's budget" which called for heavy taxation on the gentry and their holdings. It was smashingly rejected by the House of Lords. The Liberals had long realized that legislation for ordinary people could be accomplished only if the House of Lords had its powers curtailed. The Parliament Act was finally introduced for this purpose containing a provision enabling Commons to override a Lords veto if a bill was passed during three successive sessions.

To win the act, the Liberals threatened to create five hundred new peerages into Lords from their own ranks. Specter of this number of men ennobled from common sources was too much for England's aristocracy to stomach and to avoid it the Parliament Act was accepted.

Although the Liberals still ruled, their majority had severely shrunk and history repeated. Asquith required John Redmond's Irish Party to form a coalition government and once again the price for such cooperation was a Home Rule Bill. Redmond held a strong trump card but as the battle lines shaped up he vacillated and showed willingness to accept watered-down legislation calling for continued allegiance to the British Crown, a repugnant dose to almost all Irishmen.

If John Redmond had a single glaring flaw it was that he had dwelt in the House of Commons too long and knew the Irish people too little. He selected his arena of combat foolishly by pitting a hundred Irish members against five hundred and fifty of the "foe." Even though Redmond was allied with the Liberals, the Liberals were apathetically lukewarm to Irish aspirations. Yet John Redmond was

the best the Irish people had to follow, for the voices of
Sinn Fein and the Brotherhood were still too small and
distant to hear.

*

Not so naïve were the Ulster Unionists, who were
strong, rich, united, knew what they wanted and counted
on fanatical support from their own people. The Unionists
had depended for decades upon a House of Lords veto as
their principal bulwark against Home Rule. With this gone,
their reaction was instant and traumatic.

Great leaders are always created by their times. Few men
illustrated this point more succinctly than Sir Edward
Carson. A brilliant barrister who fought some of the great
court cases of the times, his cross-examination of Oscar
Wilde was a landmark of courtroom devastation. As a
member of Parliament, he rose to high government office.
Although Dublin-born and Trinity-trained, Carson was
the complete Ulsterman, the epitome of imperial man, the
total servant of his own aristocratic class. A grim, hatchet-
faced hypochondriac, his ruthless tactics demonstrated the
qualities needed of a leader in such a fight. Like most great
men, he was obsessed with a single idea. His was to keep the
union with Britain.

When the dust and consequence of the 1910 elections
settled, a third Home Rule Bill loomed with no veto of
Lords to prevent it. Roger Hubble, who operated best
behind the scenes, fell in naturally at Carson's side as
the Unionists closed ranks like a fist. Lord Roger was
delegated to stay in quiet contact with the Whip of the
Liberal Party, Alan Birmingham, a relationship he had
kept up off and on for years. The maneuver was designed
to have inner access to the Liberals and at the same time
free Edward Carson to lead the public and parliamentary
fight against Home Rule.

*

Time had eroded much of Alan Birmingham's naïveté
about the intent, arrogance and ruthlessness of the Ulstermen. It was Roger Hubble who had formed and run the
Unionist Information Bureau after the 1906 election to
"educate" middle class England. He unleashed a flood of
rotating preachers and Irish baiters at schools, county

fairs, churches and town halls. Sermons, slide lantern shows and an inundation of books and leaflets poured out of Ulster with a repetitive message until it saturated the English mind. The old fiddle played the old tune so often that most Englishmen came to regard it as gospel. THE ULSTER PROTESTANT FIGHTS FOR THE BRITISH IMPERIAL CAUSE AND THEREFORE MUST BE SUPPORTED. THE IRISH CATHOLIC IS DISLOYAL AND HOME RULE WOULD LEAD TO THE DESTRUCTION OF THE EMPIRE.

Herein lay Alan Birmingham's sticky wicket. His party was in a forced marriage to the Irish Party and pledged to Home Rule. Nevertheless, most individual members of the Liberals and most of the English people supported Ulster.

The Conservative Party used this division to their own ends. Committed to continuation of the Empire, they argued that any measure of freedom granted the Irish would be apt to have a chain reaction throughout the colonies. They kept the Irish pot fomenting because they were on the popular side of the issue and hoped the Liberal Party would destroy itself over it. At the bottom of the Conservative alliance with the Ulster Unionists was a plot to regain power, reverse all that liberalism and return England to the old imperial-oriented order that was fading from the scene.

*

When Alan Birmingham received Lord Roger into his study he realized there was far more at stake than Irish Home Rule. The very existence of his party hung in the balance and the man opposite him was one of those bent on its destruction.

Alan Birmingham was a product of the merchant class, a relatively new sort of figure in British politics who had been replacing the monopoly of aristocrats. Birmingham had come into the national limelight when he led a near rising in Commons against the imperial policy during the Boer War. He was known as a decent man, moderate and skilled to push through the social reform which the Conservatives despised.

Noticeable coolness prevailed in the disheveled, booky den on Cadogan Square as the two men fenced with small talk. Birmingham had aged portly. His hair was flecked with gray as was a trim mustache and his face was rather good-natured and devoid of suspicion. Roger had enjoyed dealing with him, for he was a good adversary with whom one could fight and then enjoy the theater with afterward.

"I rather think we will be in close quarters for some time over Home Rule," Roger said. "My door is open to you, Alan, and I trust it's the same for me."

"Yes," Birmingham replied, "good idea to know what the other chap has on his mind." He fished chubbily into his humidor, peeled and lit a cigar.

"Carson's public posture is necessarily going to appear inflexible so our liaison can keep things from getting too muddy, the sort of thing that can happen if we both depend on secondhand reports and the press," Roger said. "We realize that Redmond has a noose about your neck and introduction of a Home Rule Bill is inevitable. You can likewise assume that the House of Lord will reject it on each occasion and force three passages, so nothing will be ready for royal assent for some two to three years. It will be a long haul. We should remain friends."

"What are you chaps after?" Birmingham said directly.

"Well, the end result of any Home Rule Bill must exclude Ulster," Roger said.

"All of Ulster? Even those counties with a Catholic majority?"

"Well, let's say we haven't gotten around to drawing a map but certainly all of Ulster for the moment."

"Obviously none of this comes as a great surprise, Lord Roger."

"Yes, Alan, right. But what we want to know is whether or not you agree to the principle of a separate Ulster."

Birmingham grunted, working his cigar in a slow circle of digestive contemplation. "Winston Churchill certainly doesn't agree to dividing up Ireland and I dare say the party is split down the middle on the issue. In any event, John Redmond is a member of our team and I'm not willing to divulge anything that would jeopardize his bargaining position."

"Oh, come now, we know you chaps haven't got your heart in this," Roger answered. "Isn't it better if we understand each other's intentions?"

Fox played with fox. Indeed, Birmingham did want to know how far Roger Hubble and Sir Edward Carson were willing to go to get their demands. "At the moment," he said, "I am prepared to introduce and fight for a Home Rule Bill. I am ready to go through three sessions and this would be a bill including all of Ireland. That is our position. It might ease in a month or a year or it might harden. I'm not clairvoyant."

"And I can say in all candor that if Ulster isn't excluded Carson is going to pull out all stops," Roger answered.

"Just what do you mean by that, old chap?" Birmingham asked.

Roger leaned over the desk, trying to show neither too much menace nor too little. "All stops, Alan. Eighteen eighty-five all over again, only this time we won't be using wooden rifles."

"Civil war?"

"I didn't say that."

"But you are ready to tear the country apart." Birmingham stood, slipped his hands in his jacket and mulled heavy-footed about the room. "There is a small church in my constituency up north which I attend regularly when I'm there. During the last campaign there was a guest preacher, a chap from Belfast who had come over through sponsorship of the Unionist Information Bureau, which, I believe, is headed by yourself, Lord Roger. This vile little creature stood on God's pulpit and denounced me as a traitor. Me, Alan Birmingham, seventeen years in the Royal Navy, ten years in the Colonial Office and twenty years in the House of Commons, suddenly a traitor."

Roger threw up his hands in mock horror. "I know how zealous they can be at times. Try as we may, there are bound to be a few unfortunate isolated incidents."

"Really? Well now, these horror stories abound against members of the Liberal Party. Oh, don't act so shocked. Read some of your own literature, my dear fellow. I say, what in the name of God is happening when the ruling party of Great Britain is characterized as a gang of godless, mindless turncoats? Political character assassination in a democracy? Now you have the utter cheek to sit in my study and out of the other side of your mouth tell me, 'See here, Birmingham, either you traitors give us what we want or we'll rebel against the King because we'll only agree to obey laws we like.'"

Roger reddened. "My dear chap, you are taking this too seriously . . ."

"Oh, I know you, Lord Roger, and I know Edward Carson. I've regretted it from the moment you bullied me into that dreadful Detention and Emergency Powers Act. You chaps are table thumpers in the name of some warped ideas about loyalty. You know, when all this Home Rule business started I didn't give much of a damn but now I'm rather looking forward to ramming this bill down your throats because, old boy, I've my own notion of who the traitors are in this game."

He returned to his chair, plopped into it and fought to contain his trembling, for he was not given to these sorts of outbursts.

Roger had gotten control of himself and actually nodded that he understood. "Trouble is, Alan, this issue never fails to inflame men who usually have a grip on their common sense. I suggest that we cannot lose ours. What you must realize is the fanatic determination of our people to remain in the Union."

"See here, Lord Roger," Birmingham said, shuffling through the papers on his desk. "Here is the fiendish Home Rule Bill in all its infamy. Why, the Irish aren't even allowed to have their own armed forces much less collect their own taxes. Treaties, trade, navigation, foreign relations, patents, legal tender all remain under British control. Not only is there an oath to the King, but Westminster retains the right to cancel legislation enacted by the Dublin Parliament." He flung it over the desk. "Is this what is driving you people so wild?"

"At the risk of suggesting you are naïve," Roger hissed, "this merely constitutes their first step. The Irish will use it as a springboard to continue their pressure."

"Then I say it is you who are naïve," Birmingham retorted. "Any simple-minded parliamentary tactician can use this to tie up the Irish for a hundred years. They'll never get out of the terms of this act. Why do you people fail to see that if we deny the Irish this crumb we will really induce them into a rising? The Home Rule Bill we have fashioned here is the most positive instrument imaginable to pacify them." He smacked his fist on the desk for emphasis, then laughed a bit sadly. "Truth be known, this act doesn't even start to cancel our debt of oppression to the Irish."

"That kind of statement only proves that you have no sympathy for our determination to stay out of a Dublin Parliament," Roger said testily.

"I've had enough of that, Lord Roger!" Birmingham snapped abruptly and angrily. "Before you make me swoon with your lofty ideals, let me tell you that Ulster Unionism is nothing more than Protestant materialism. Your epoch of greed has gone on for three hundred and ten infamous years of classic misrule and classic injustice. You have bled and raped Ireland. You have imposed abnormal taxation. You have manipulated to keep the Irish farmer the most impoverished in the Western world and the Irish laborer the most underpaid in Europe. You have destroyed the vitality of the land so as to expose it to cancerous famine. Why, you've driven more Irishmen out of their own country than populate it today. You and your entire parasitic band are in it for the pound sterling. I suggest you have been milking a big fat tit, sir. All of this has been done while nobly wrapping yourself in a Union Jack. Love of England, indeed. Love of English law, indeed. Reformation, indeed. Poppycock. I say good day to you, sir, good day."

CHAPTER EIGHT

CRAIGAVON RALLY DRAWS 100,000. SIR EDWARD CARSON OFFICIALLY NAMED LEADER OF UNIONIST PARTY. TERMS PENDING HOME RULE BILL "NEFARIOUS CONSPIRACY."
        by Seamus O'Neill
September 23, 1911, Belfast (Irish Overseas Press Service)

Upward of 100,000 Orangemen and Unionists gathered today at Craigavon, the estate of Captain James Craig on the south shore of Lough Belfast. Units representing all Belfast and County Antrim Orange Lodges, Unionist Clubs and Women's Associations marched to

Craigavon from downtown Belfast in a wet morning.
The throng assembled on the vast lawn of the estate,
which formed a natural amphitheater. The meeting was
presided over by the Earl of Erne with the speakers'
platform holding a who's who of Ulster ascendancy.

Thomas Andrews, a well-known Orange figure, introduced the crowd to their new leader, Edward Carson,
with the words, "We will never bow the knee to the
disloyal factions led by Mr. John Redmond. We will
never submit to be governed by rebels who acknowledge no law but the laws of the Land League and illegal societies."

Sir Edward Carson, 57, appearing bulldog grim, accepted the resolution proclaiming him as their leader,
with fighting words.

"I now enter into a compact with you, and every
one of you, and with the help of God . . . we will yet
defeat the most nefarious conspiracy that has ever
been hatched against a free people.

"We must be prepared . . . the morning Home Rule
passes, ourselves, to become responsible for the government of the Protestant Province of Ulster . . . we
ask your leave for a meeting of the Ulster Unionist
Executive Committee to be held on Monday . . . so
that at no time and at no intervening space shall we
lack a government in Ulster, which shall be a government either by the imperial Parliament or by ourselves."

Carson's proclamation was greeted with delirious
cheering and was taken by most political observers
present to be a declaration of independence should the
Province not get what it wanted. Others, however, felt
Carson was setting the tone for a monumental bluff. A
third opinion among observers was that Carson's words
constituted a treasonous statement.

*

ULSTER UNIONISTS COMMISSION A CONSTITUTION IN
BELFAST MEETING
        by Seamus O'Neill
September 25, 1911 (Irish Overseas Press Service)
    On the heels of their massive rally at Craigavon,
some four hundred and fifty delegates representing
the Unionist Party's Executive assembled in Belfast's

Rosemary Hall. The meeting was chaired by Lord Londonderry and unanimously voted to establish machinery for a Provisional Government in the event of Home Rule passage.

A second resolution was adopted to establish a Commission to "take immediate steps to frame and submit a constitution for an independent Ulster." This body will be headed by the Earl of Foyle, Roger Hubble.

*

SIR EDWARD CARSON THREATENS ARMED RESISTANCE IN SWING AROUND ULSTER
by Seamus O'Neill
September 30, 1911, Portrush, Co. Antrim (IOPS)

Touring the province in his new role as Unionist leader, Sir Edward Carson repeated the anti-Home Rule message he had been delivering at loyalist meetings for the past several days.

"We are not going to fight the Army and Navy, but if the Army and the Navy under a British government come up to displace us, they will displace us at their peril. It is not that we mean to fight them. God forbid that any loyal Ulsterman should ever shoot or think of shooting the British soldier or sailor. But, believe you me, any government will ponder long before it dares shoot a loyal Ulster Protestant, devoted to his country and loyal to his King."

*

ANDREW BONAR LAW SUCCEEDS BALFOUR AS LEADER OF CONSERVATIVE PARTY—ALLIES WITH CARSON AGAINST HOME RULE
by Seamus O'Neill
November 12, 1911, London (IOPS)

Canadian-born Andrew Bonar Law assumed leadership today of England's Conservative Party, and the Unionists picked up a powerful ally, long dedicated to the Ulster cause.

Law, who has Ulster-born parents, can be expected to join actively against Home Rule. In the event of a future Conservative victory Law stands the chance of becoming Britian's first foreign-born Prime Minister.

*

MILITARY DRILLING "LEGALIZED" FOR UNIONIST CLUBS
EXCLUSIVE by Seamus O'Neill

January 25, 1912, Belfast (Irish Overseas Press Service

Ulster Unionist Clubs quietly reactivated under "crisis" conditions by Lord Templeton last year have received licenses "legalizing" their activities. In a decision handed down by two Belfast magistrates, leave was given to "drill and practice military exercises, movements and evolutions."

This bizarre and quasi-legal granting of licenses was based on an obscure section of a century-and-a-half-old statute which had primarily been used to allow the formation of community defenses and militias during the peasant land wars in the late 1700s.

Following the lead of the Belfast magistrate's precedent, twenty more licenses were immediately granted to Unionist Clubs throughout Ulster on the premise that . . . "such authority is sought and will be used by them only to make them more efficient citizens for the purpose of maintaining the constitution of the United Kingdom as now established and protecting their rights and liberties thereunder."

Although the licenses were granted to establish a legal basis for operation, it has been an open secret that paramilitary units have been drilling for months throughout the province.

Heading up the over-all program is Colonel R. H. Wallace, prominent in Orange circles and former commander of a battalion of Royal Irish Rifles during the Boer War. Ranks of the clubs are filled with ex-officers and enlisted men of the British armed forces.

*

SECRET UNIONIST ARMS FUND OF ONE MILLION POUNDS UNCOVERED
EXCLUSIVE by Seamus O'Neill

February 3, 1912, Belfast (Irish Overseas Press Service)

This reporter has learned that wealthy backers of the Ulster Unionist Clubs now engaged in paramilitary activities have established a banking credit of one million pounds sterling for the purpose of purchasing arms.

Operating under the general guise of the Provisional Emergency Fund, it is headed up by Sir Frederick Weed, prominent Belfast industrialist and member of the governing bodies of the Unionist Party and Orange Order.

It is somewhat ironic that Weed should be placed in charge of these particular monies in that he was the scapegoat in a gunrunning scheme by the Irish Republican Brotherhood several years ago in the renowned Sixmilecross incident. When questioned as to whether he was seeking vengeance for that humiliation, Weed snapped:

"Revenge is not in my nature."

It is known that Weed and his son-in-law, the Earl of Foyle, each personally contributed £25,000 to the fund, an amount matched by Sir Edward Carson. Other contributors read like the directory of Burke's Peerage with much of the money coming from English Conservatives. It is rumored that Rudyard Kipling is listed among the £10,000 class of donors.

When pressed for details of the fund, Weed flatly denied the monies were being used to buy guns.

"Poppycock," Weed declared. "The Provisional Emergency Fund is being established in the event of a civil war to take care of evacuations, hospitalizations and hardship cases."

Despite Weed's denials, some pertinent collaborating facts have been unearthed. The importing of weapons is close to impossible under existing laws. As in the case of "legalizing" the paramilitary clubs, Unionist lawyers have found a loophole in the statutes.

Licensed "Hunting and Shooting Clubs" are permitted to import limited numbers of weapons for "sporting purposes." An investigation of the records of the customs bureaus and city halls around the province reveal a set of startling statistics.

New licenses have been granted to alleged "Hunting and Shooting Clubs," increasing their numbers by three hundredfold since the onset of the Home Rule crisis. In every instance the membership of these clubs is identical to the membership of the Unionists' paramilitary units.

Moreover, a dozen new import/export licenses have been granted by customs to individuals and firms in

Derry, Belfast and other ports about the province with "authority to receive shipments of weapons."

Although drilling and practice have continued with wooden replicas, it is estimated that two to three hundred rifles a week (mostly of Italian vintage) have been getting through.

When queried about this, Sir Frederick Weed shrugged it off.

"It just so happens that the province is going through a period of unusual interest in hunting," he claimed.

When asked just what could be hunted so massively in Ulster's sparse woodlands, Weed commented, "Fairies, woodkerns, God knows what."

It is known that banks throughout the province have been notified to cover overdrafts of cheques drawn by any paramilitary club without question. Such money has been replaced by cheques drawn from the Provisional Emergency Fund.

To this, Weed answered, "The clubs are engaged in medical and other activities of a humanitarian nature that might occur in the event of civil war. It certainly does not indicate the overdrafts went into arms purchases."

However, cheques from the Fund have matched, quid for quid, cheques written to the newly licensed arms importers.

*

THE ULSTER UNIONIST PROVISIONAL EMERGENCY FUND. GUNS OR HUMANITARIANISM? DUCHESS OF SOMERSET CONFIRMS SIR FREDERICK WEED'S ASSERTION
EXCLUSIVE by Seamus O'Neill
February 4, 1912, London (Irish Overseas Press Service)

The Duchess of Somerset announced today that an organization has been established to come to the assistance of Ulster's Protestants in the event of civil war. The Humanity for Ulster Committee is seeking to find refuge in England for tens of thousands of "our loyal subjects in Ireland."

Existence of this committee was revealed rather suddenly in light of yesterday's uncovering of a million-quid fund allegedly for arms purchase and corroborates Sir

Frederick Weed's claim that the Provisional Emergency Fund was for other purposes.

*

WINSTON CHURCHILL SCHEDULED TO COME TO ULSTER FOR PRO-HOME RULE RALLY
EXCLUSIVE by Seamus O'Neill
February 5, 1912 (IOPS)

It was learned by this reporter today that Liberal Party M.P. Winston Churchill, First Lord of the Admirality, has accepted an invitation from the Ulster Liberal Party to speak in Belfast. The province's Liberals constitute a small minority and have been all but swamped since the Unionist Party offensive against Home Rule.

Lord Pirrie, the Belfast shipbuilder and leader of the Ulster Liberals, confirmed the arrangement. "It is hoped," he said, "that Churchill's appearance will do something to bring light and reason to a situation gone totally out of control by a frenzied overreaction to a very mild piece of legislation."

Pirrie further went on to say, "I think the people of England have mistakenly come to believe that all Protestants here are speaking with a single Unionist voice. In addition to the Liberals there are tens of thousands of plain, unorganized people without a voice who consider Home Rule by a Dublin Parliament as a viable and desirable idea."

Ulster Hall, property of the Belfast City Corporation, has been booked for the event. Churchill's appearance will complete a family circle of unique involvement in Irish affairs.

It will be almost thirty-four years to the day that Churchill's father, Lord Randolph, spoke from the very same platform but presented a diametrically opposite point of view. In playing the historic "Orange Card," Lord Randolph delivered his famous "thief in the night" speech to the embattled Unionists of the previous century.

*

ULSTER UNIONISTS MOVE TO BLOCK CHURCHILL APPEARANCE
by Seamus O'Neill

February 7, 1912, Belfast (IOPS)

Reaction to the announcement of Winston Churchill's proposed pro-Home Rule speech in Belfast's Ulster Hall was swift and angry in Unionist circles.

A hastily assembled quorum of the Unionist Executive gathered at Rathweed Hall, home of Sir Frederick Weed, and passed a unanimous resolution to deny him use of Ulster Hall.

Colonel R. H. Wallace, titular head of the paramilitary Unionist Clubs, warned bluntly that riot and bloodshed could not be prevented. He threatened to have his forces seize the hall.

"It is lamentable," Sir Frederick said after the meeting, "that this man deliberately comes to this loyal city under sponsorship of the John Redmonds to speak treason and defile the very same platform his father spoke from so gloriously in behalf of our liberty.

"Free speech," Weed continued, "is not extended to turncoats. Churchill gave up his birthright and bolted the Conservative Party to consort with those who would destroy the Empire. He is the most provocative orator in Britain and this is nothing more than an arrogant exercise and an insult at a time and in a place where the magnificent words of his revered father still ring in our ears."

When asked if his estimation of Winston Churchill wasn't excessive and brought on by the climate of the moment, Weed replied angrily, "In my frank opinion, sir, Winston Churchill is no Englishman."

•

CHURCHILL BACKS DOWN. ULSTER MEETING FIZZLES.
by Seamus O'Neill
February 12, 1912, Belfast (IOPS)

Landing today at Larne, some thirty-four years after his father, Winston Churchill, First Lord of the Admiralty and foremost spokesman of the Liberal Party, met with a far different reception than had been accorded the elder Churchill.

Large crowds on hand gathered in a mood that could only be described as ugly. Booing and shouting anti-Home Rule slogans, they lined the route from the Mid-

land Railway Station to the Grand Central Hotel. Every
few feet Churchill was greeted with an insulting placard
or a dummy of himself being hanged in effigy.

Moved time and again to the brink of violence, the
way was continually impeded by men storming his car,
shaking fists, spitting, rock-throwing and otherwise menacing him. At one point they overwhelmed his Constabulary escort and lifted two wheels of his vehicle
off the ground, shaking it violently.

After a hasty consultation with Lord Pirrie and other
local Liberals, it was decided that in the interest of
avoiding bloodshed the meeting site had best be
switched. At the last moment Parnell Field, a rugby
ground in the Catholic Falls section of the city, was
chosen for the rally.

*

JOHN REDMOND PLEADS FOR HOME RULE BILL, WARNS
BRITISH AGAINST TRICKERY.
          by Seamus O'Neill
March 31, 1912, Dublin (IOPS)
Under growing pressure from Ulster and discontent
within his own party and about the country, John Redmond addressed a mass meeting in St. Stephen's Green
as the moment pressed closer for the introduction of the
third Home Rule Bill.

Speaking in Gaelic in an impassioned voice, Redmond
laid bare his position and placed his tarnishing political
future on the line with a mixture of pleas and veiled
threats.

"There are many men here who would destroy the
British Empire if they were united . . . we have no wish
to destroy the British, we only want our freedom."

Redmond went on to say that he, personally, would
never pay homage to the King of England but at the
same time stated that the pending bill was good for
Ireland despite the fact it retained allegiance to the
Crown.

". . . if we are tricked this time, there are parties in
Ireland, and I am one of them, who will advise the
Gael to have no further counsel with the foreigner ever
again, but to answer them henceforth with the strong

hand and the sword's edge. Let the foreigner understand that if we are cheated once more there will be red war in Ireland."

In light of Redmond's conciliatory behavior in Westminster his "fighting words" were viewed as strictly for home consumption but with a tinge of desperation for his Liberal allies not to pull out on him.

*

BULLETIN!
April 14, 1912, London (Rueters)

After acceptance of the third Home Rule Bill in the House of Commons by 110 votes, it was immediately rejected in Lords by a vote of 326 to 69.

A second reading of the bill is scheduled by the next session of Commons either late this year or early next year. Three passages are required to override Lords, according to the recent Parliament Act.

*

ANTI-HOME RULE/CATHOLIC RIOTS SWEEP OVER ULSTER.
July 4, 1912, Belfast (Rueters)

"Belfast Confetti," an iron disc about the size of a two-shilling piece punched out of ship plating, has been introduced as a semi-lethal street fighting weapon as hundreds of shipyard workers swept into the Catholic Ballymurphy District, hurling their missiles at people and windows. By noon over seventy people required hospitalization.

*

ANDREW BONAR LAW AND SIR EDWARD CARSON DECRY HOME RULE BILL IN MOST POWERFUL AND OMINOUS STATEMENT TO DATE AT BLENHEIM PALACE RALLY
by Seamus O'Neill
July 11, 1912, Blenheim Palace (IOPS)

In the largest demonstration to date on English soil and in support of Ulster's Protestants, a Conservative Party rally on the grounds of the birthplace of both Winston Churchill and Randolph Churchill drew upwards of a hundred thousand people.

The ancestral home of the Duke of Marlborough was in full bloom, a floral and wooded wonderland greeting the multitudes whose vibrations were of combative intensity.

Bonar Law made the most powerful statement yet against Asquith's Liberal Government. Referring to Liberal rule as "a revolutionary committee which has seized upon despotic power by fraud," he declared that his Conservatives would not be bound by the restraints of British law that would influence them in an ordinary struggle. Bonar Law threatened that if Home Rule for Ireland were eventually passed "there are things stronger than a parliamentary majority."

"As for Ulster's Protestants," said Law, "if an attempt were made to deprive these men of their birthright as part of a corrupt parliamentary bargain, they would be justified in resisting such an attempt by all means in their power, including force. I can imagine no length of resistance to which Ulster can go in which I should not be prepared to support them, and in which, in my belief, they would be supported by the overwhelming majority of the British people."

In answering questions as to the treasonous nature of Law's statement, Sir Edward Carson replied, "If this is treason, so be it. At least we'll take the best in England along with us."

●

ALAN BIRMINGHAM QUITS AS LIBERAL WHIP IN PROTEST AGAINST CONTINUED APPEASEMENT OF CARSON AND LAW. EXCLUSIVE INTERVIEW by Seamus O'Neill
July 20, London (Irish Overseas Press Service)

Alan Birmingham, Liberal Whip for the past decade, tendered his resignation to Prime Minister Herbert Asquith tonight in protest against his government's inaction concerning the "obvious seditious behavior of Conservative leader Andrew Bonar Law and Unionist head Sir Edward Carson," citing Bonar Law's "despotic power by fraud" speech at Blenheim as the final straw.

"Carson and his bully hordes have unsheathed a sword of naked political terrorism," Birmingham said angrily. "He and Bonar Law continue to flaunt British law and hold the Liberal Party up to public ridicule over our failure to enforce it. It's all being done by design, bit by bit, to see what the traffic will bear, and as we stand by idly, they continue to become bolder and bolder.

"There is indeed a conspiracy," he continued, "not of our making but by those who seek to destroy the Liberal Party and return England to class rule.

"If they wish to make martyrs of themselves, we should accommodate them. If they wish civil war, we should accommodate them on that, too. What we cannot permit is the continuation of bald-faced treason to go unchallenged. If they are allowed to get away with this, I predict we shall still be paying the bill for it in Ulster fifty years from now."

CHAPTER NINE: Although no one liked the idea of Conor Larkin returning to Belfast, the scheme required organization and a deft hand only he could bring to it. Conor was known on sight in Belfast by thousands of rugby fans and dozens of old friends. The Council only reluctantly let him return to Belfast.

When Conor had first presented his plan to the Supreme Council, the reaction was one of shock. Yet the plan was so simple and logical they became quietly convinced of its feasibility.

In early summer of 1912 office space was rented on the second floor of a building on Royal Avenue, the main central thoroughfare near the General Post Office. A sign lettered on the door carried the inconspicuous inscription: B.R.I. IMPORTS-EXPORTS, F. Clarke-MacCoy, Customs Broker.

B.R.I. stood for the Baptist Revival in Ireland and seemed, on the surface, a thinly veiled purchasing agent for a dozen paramilitary Unionist Clubs in the Inishowen region of County Donegal. B.R.I. was among the dozen or more operators who had received certification as customs brokers. Everyone knew but rarely spoke about them, for their principal reason for going into business was to obtain guns for the Unionists.

B.R.I. gave every appearance of being another supplier for the clubs, from their stationery down to an office filled with religious supplies needed in a revival movement. F. Clarke-MacCoy was treated with a nod and wink by the customs officials when he picked up his weekly consignment of two to four cases of rifles. Documents were passed rapidly and his goods passed through automatically and without inspection.

What the customs service was unaware of was that by reversing the initials of the Baptist Revival in Ireland one would read, the Irish Republican Brotherhood. The ploy continued to work week in and week out without a hitch. Main concern was for Conor's safety. He was still very much of a fugitive, as well known in Belfast, and had to rotate between a half dozen "safe houses" in an unscheduled pattern.

One flat was kept in the mixed neighborhood out in Finaghy which was used only occasionally when Atty was able to slip into Belfast. Her visits were necessarily too infrequent and too short in duration. Conor's days were personless and lonely for the most part and he waited for her visits like a cooling shower on a scorching day.

By autumn the latest cycle of riots had died down but Sir Edward Carson continued to raise the ante in light of meek opposition from the government. The Unionists meticulously planned to cap off the year in a crescendo and named September 26 as the day to unleash the greatest political demonstration in the history of the British Isles.

Atty was due in the day of the demonstration and so was a shipment of rifles. The B.R.I. office had a view down to Royal Avenue, heart of the parade route, and after finishing his paperwork deep in the night, Conor stretched out on a cot in the office. He wanted a first-hand look at the Unionists in action to draw his own determinations.

It was a still autumn day of soft beiges, a quiet day like the Lord's day although it was only Saturday. Ulster was stilled from the hubbub of the mills and factories along Lough Belfast, a hush that rolled over the land clear to County Londonderry. No hay was mown in the fields and the traditional Saturday market stalls stood near empty as a subdued holiness flowed ahead of the righteous thunderstorm.

Sunday's pants were pressed and Sunday's boots were polished. The Orange sash, the medals for service and valor, the bowler hat, the rolled black umbrella, were ceremoniously laid out in fifty thousand row houses and fifty thousand farm cottages.

All movement flowed gently to the call of church bells. On this unusual Saturday, Methodists, Baptists, Presbyterians and Anglicans interchanged preachers, but the message was as old as the imperial experience in Ireland.

If one stood on Cave Hill in the highest place in Belfast and listened closely he could surely hear fifty thousand voices from ten score churches all singing a single hymn.

Oh, God, our help in ages past,
Our hope for years to come,
Our shelter from the stormy blast
And our eternal home.

Under the shadow of Thy throne
Thy saints have dwelt secure.
Sufficient is Thine arm alone
And our defense is sure. . . .

This instrument of ultimate defiance was to be a Covenant of Resistance, a blood oath concocted from an old Scottish vow. Ulster's Solemn League and Covenant, an epic document, pointed out the evils of Home Rule, declared it a conspiracy and swore allegiance to God and King. After having stated such allegiance, the Covenant continued to say: "And in the event of such a Parliament [Dublin] being forced upon us we further solemnly and mutually pledge ourselves to refuse to recognize its authority. In sure confidence that God will defend the right, we hereto subscribe our names . . ."

Men, teachers, preachers, children who all had memorized that Kipling poem, repeated it often this morning. At the great Presbyterian Assembly Hall it was read in unison in response from the pastor.

"We know the war prepared
On every peaceful home,
We know the hells declared
For such as serve not Rome—
The terror, threats and dread

In market, hearth, and field—
We know when all is said,
We perish if we yield.

Believe, we dare not boast,
Believe, we do not fear—
We stand to pay the cost
In all that men hold dear.
What answer from the North?
One Law, one Land, one Throne.
If England drives us forth
We shall not fall alone.

With the tone of the day set early, the great white cathedral and those other ships of Belfast's armada of the Reformation emptied their cleansed congregations.

Heartstone was the Belfast City Hall: St. Paul's Cathedral and the Parthenon rolled into one, where an honor guard of two hundred and twenty Orangemen arrayed with white staves and another twenty-five hundred marched solemnly behind the faded silk flag that William of Orange carried at the Battle of the Boyne.

Into all this solemnity rolled the entourage of Sir Edward Carson flanked by the mighty, Captain James Craig and Sir Frederick Weed and a small legion of noblemen, aristocrats, gentry and Orange, Conservative and Unionist leaders. They trod majestically up the steps behind macebearers into the rotunda where the sacred Covenant lay on a round table, and above it hung the world's largest Union Jack. Behind the table itself was the great wrought-iron screen, depicting Ulster's grandeur, as designed and executed by Conor Larkin.

The Anglo world tensed as the great moment drew close at hand. Top-hatted leaders tapped nervously with silver-headed canes as clouds of flashpowder exploded. At the precise instant, Sir Edward Carson stepped to the desk, unsheathed a square silver pen destined for immortality and affixed his signature to the document. One by one the great ones sanctified the Covenant and marched out.

The gates were thrown open to the common man. It was all quite orderly and exquisitely organized. If something was intended to be shown this day it was that Ulster was

one, humble and mighty alike. In they poured. The City
Hall corridors held a half mile of desks able, to accommodate five hundred persons at a single time and fifteen hundred a minute.

The first of the wrists were cut, and there were, hundreds on that day, and names were written in blood.

Now all of Ulster throbbed alive with the spectacle.

At Hillsborough the Covenant was signed where King
Billy had stopped to rest.

At Templepatrick it was signed on the head of a Lambeg drum.

At Derry the Guildhall, scarred with bullets from anti-
Catholic riots, was under the protection of soldiers at
fixed bayonet as the Earl of Foyle and his Countess led
the signers.

The sick and aged were carried up to the Covenant on
stretchers and rolled up in wheel chairs like a second coming to Lourdes.

At Ulster Hall of Orange Card fame the women signed
their separate pledge, no less zealously, no less massively
than their menfolk.

At the Shambles in Monaghan the green flag and effigy
of Carson were torn down at the pork market by Coven-
anters.

By noon in Belfast the early hours of discipline faded as
thousands flooded Royal Avenue, waiting to get to the
City Hall.

From Conor Larkin's vista at the B.R.I. office he could
watch the frantic chanting for Edward Carson to make an
appearance from the Reform Club over the way. As Carson and Sir Frederick Weed and Craig strode out to the
balcony the day's first frenzy erupted. Now the holy Boyne
flag was brought to the balcony and, as it was hung, ten
thousand heads bared in reverence and men and women
broke into unabashed weeping.

The air was pocked by a thousand motorcar horns
pushing toward Royal Avenue down North Street, leading legions of Orangemen, Purple Marksmen, Black Pre-
ceptories, Royal Scarlets, Garters, Crimson Arrows, Link
and Chains, Red Crosses, Apprentice Boys and the rest all
swaggering eight abreast behind thumping Lambegs and
war-singing bagpipes.

Another line merged down Howard Street, another over the bridge from the stronghold of East Belfast, another up Dublin Road as all of Belfast seemed to converge now on the manger, the center of the universe.

On they poured like an enraged waterfall, a thousand signers a minute, and this was repeated in every town and hamlet over the province.

The scene in the streets had turned to pandemonium with ancient tribal signals of bonfires erupting from Cave Hill, then Divis, then Stormont, then in an unbroken necklace around the lough and over the hills to every town in Ulster. With night, searchlights raided the sky and fireworks illuminated the bay.

The crowd clung to Edward Carson's footsteps as he whisked from place to place. They hung from lampposts and tiptoed to rooftop edges to get a glimpse. They pulled his carriage by hand in boundless admiration for their new King Billy and Orange Christ rolled into one. All binds on emotions blew wild as Carson and his entourage made to the docks massed with bands and booming cannons.

As he boarded the overnight ship to England he attempted to shout over the mob to keep the old flag flying and promised to return in peace or war.

Conor Larkin had watched much of this scene for the entire day, transfixed. When Carson's boat pulled away from the dock, everything burst forth, lighting the sky in a single ultimate violent illumination, and for an instant Conor thought he was either before the gates of hell or had witnessed the hand of the Lord destroying Sodom and Gomorrah.

CHAPTER TEN: "Atty!" Conor cried. Receiving no answer, he made up the stairs two at a time, entering the flat with a strange sensation of panic.

"Atty!"

"I'm here," she called, entering from the kitchen.

Conor allowed himself a heave of relief. She studied him and frowned. He looked clear gaumy, knocked off his rails, a rare state for himself.

"What's this all about?" she asked.

He shook his head, flopped his arms and sank into the big chair. Atty handed him a drink of whiskey. He did it in and held up the glass for another.

"Did you see any of it?" he asked.

"I tried to get to your office but Royal Avenue was impassable. Will the government do anything about it this time?"

Conor shook his head. "What are they going to do, Atty? Throw a half million Protestants into prison? How many thousands of them who signed that Covenant were in the military, the Constabulary and the government itself? Here, give me another belt of that stuff . . . that's a good girl. The bloody Unionists are shrewd. They've got the English people on their side and the opposition party split in half."

Atty came around behind him. Her fingers went to work to massage the back of his neck and shoulders. Although he wanted to submit, he was a tight wall back there and she was not able to penetrate.

Conor reached back and patted her hand, took up a pace and drank some more. "It was a masterpiece of organization and resolve. What is so terrifying is the way they can wind up a half million people like mechanical dolls and march them in neat little rows on a given signal, then push another button that says, 'Break into mass hysteria.' Why in the hell don't our people stand up like that? Because we're beaten, that's why. The only time we can attract a crowd is for some pilgrimage up some goddamned holy mountain to chase the snakes and banshees out of the country."

"They came for Daniel O'Connell once," Atty said. "They came by the hundreds of thousands."

"Yes," he retorted, "but that was before the Irish people died."

"What the hell do you want, man?" Atty snapped. "Your daddy, Tomas Larkin, or a potato-faced Orange Grand Master for a father? If we acted like them, we'd become like them. Is that what you want? We're Irish, messed up, superstitious and unorganizable . . . but, by God, you don't see any poets coming out of Ulster."

"I suppose you're right," Conor mumbled, reaching for the bottle again. This time he did so with Atty's disapproving eye. He glanced at her an instant, then un-corked it anyhow.

"Besides," Conor said, "if it were Catholics marching today in Dublin to sign that Covenant, we'd have been shot down in the streets. Sons of bitches!" he yelled suddenly. "Dirty sons of bitches!" Down went the drink and another was poured.

"You're in a fierce mood and you're drinking too much," Atty snapped.

"I don't need your advice on my drinking habits."

"I think you do. You're getting unpleasant."

"And I suppose you're sorry you came up to see me!"

"I didn't say that, Conor."

"You implied it," he said.

"Draw any damned inference you want. God knows how frustrating and terrifying it is to see that pack of animals out in the streets today. Calm yourself, man . . ."

"Aye . . . I'll try."

"Do you suppose you'd like something to eat?"

"Nae. You go on," he answered. "I've no appetite myself."

"I'll put everything into the icebox. It will keep," she said, retreating to the kitchen. She returned in a few moments and approached him tentatively.

"I hate to bring things up when you're in such a state, but I've brought orders. You're to return to Dunleer right off, tomorrow."

"Who takes care of the guns?"

"O'Leary will take charge."

"He'll muck it up," Conor said.

"He's been right good acting out the role of F. Clarke-MacCoy up to now . . ."

"He'll muck it up," Conor repeated. "I have to reinstruct him line by line every time he goes down to customs."

"That's the orders, Conor. Dan wants you out of Belfast. You've been here too long. We know you almost got picked up twice in the past months."

"Seamus O'Neill blabbers too much."

"Are you going to give me trouble about this, too?"

"Nae, what the hell's the use? All I'm doing here is getting the scrapings of the pot, anyhow. For every gun we manage, the Prods are running in a hundred . . . what the hell's the use?"

"Shut up for a minute about your own sorrows!" she yelled.

"Get the guns, don't get the guns, I wish to hell Dan would make up his mind."

"If you helped Dan a little more with the Council maybe he could make his mind up better."

"Dan, Dan, Dan, Dan," Conor snapped. "I think sometimes it would have been better to stick with Jesus and Mary. Some bloody god I picked for myself."

"Your god has cancer," Atty said.

Conor glared at her stunned.

"You heard me right," she repeated.

He put his face in his hands, closed his eyes and rocked slowly. "How long?" Conor croaked.

"Who knows?"

"When did you learn?"

"I found out quite by accident. At any rate he admitted it to me. No one else knows on the Council."

Conor spun out of the chair, all but enfolded himself in the drapes by the window as he stared out unspeaking. At last Atty came behind him, tapped his shoulder and took the glass out of his hand, standing in such a way as to invite his arms. "I'm looking forward to having you back in Dunleer," she said softly. "We used to get awful wild in that little cottage."

Conor turned from her abruptly. "The earth is caving in and all you want to think of is making love!"

Atty straightened up, hurt. "I'm going out for a breath of air," she said.

Conor heard the door slam and fell back into the chair and remained motionless for ever so long, then lifted his head as though he were in a daze, retrieved his drink and the rest of the bottle.

He awoke stink-mouthed and head busting, groaning himself upright. Somehow, Atty had gotten him undressed and into bed. He fished around in the darkness. Her back was to him and she was bundled close to her edge of the bed, awake, stiffly awake, but unyielding in a pretense of being asleep.

Conor wobbled into the loo, dunked his head, brushed his teeth, then subjected himself to a long look in the mirror. He did not like what he saw. He glanced to the bedroom, grunted in shame, tiptoed in sheepishly, slipped between the sheets and wiggled up close against her back.

Atty neither budged nor acknowledged his presence. He played his fingertips down her back and over the curve of her hip. No response. He rolled away, over onto his back. He knew she was awake, stuffing it in, would never show a tear.

"You're mad at me and you've every right to be," he said.

For a time she continued to lie immobile. As he moved away in defeat, her hand reached out to touch him ever so slightly. He rolled back up against her, relieved.

"Are you furious?" he, asked.

"A little, not too much," she answered.

"I don't know what the hell's the matter with me," he said. "For three weeks I've been looking forward day and night to seeing you and the, last time and the time before that. Then I always manage to go and make a balls out of it."

"It's natural enough," Atty said. "You're all pent up with no one to let it out on. You've got to cut it loose on me, I suppose. I understand."

He found the bed lamp, scratched a match and lit it and then opened his arms. She came to him freely.

"I don't know how much of this guff you have to take," he said.

"Just because you get drunk once in a while, I'm not letting you go, man. Besides, I've poor little pride where you're concerned."

"I need a smoke," he said.

"Me too."

She knotted her dressing gown loosely with much of her luscious woman showing as she lit up. He tied on his disheveled bathrobe and trailed after her into the parlor. They drew hard on their smokes, going their own ways for a moment, then she snubbed hers out.

"When we first made love," she said, "I have to admit some mean thoughts crossed my mind. The bastard has kept me waiting for two years and I had to all but go to him on my hands and knees, even then. And, I thought, now that he wants me as a woman I'm going to give him some of his own medicine. Just plain old-fashioned pride filled with revenge in the battle between boys and girls . . . a battle I had never lost till then. But don't you know,

Conor Larkin, I've not the will to fight you. The minute you put your hands on me, it's all over. No man's ever come within light-years of doing what you do with me . . . not Desmond Fitzpatrick, not any of them. You see, lad, I was never really woman until you cried in my arms. Love I didn't know I possessed poured out of me. I was determined to wait until the sickness of Shelley had been closed inside you."

She was close on him now, filling his face with touches. "I was going to wait . . . half of forever, if necessary. But once I realized I was able to open up and then you wouldn't let me . . . it was enough to kill me at first. Sometimes you may get the notion you're only half a man and riddled with weaknesses but you're twice the man in my eyes since the first day you let me hold you and you wept. Anyhow . . . you're all I want and I can't fight you when you touch me."

"That's bad luck for you, Atty. You deserve better."

"Conor, we're not breaking up, are we?" she said with a touch of desperation.

"Not as long as you can stand me."

"Oh, that will be a long time then," she sighed. "Can I fix you something to eat?"

"Nae . . ."

"The doings today got to you very deeply."

"Aye," he said, "they did. Anyhow, it will be good to leave Belfast. Once you're out of this place you can play little games with yourself that it doesn't even exist or that somehow it's all changeable. But on days like today you have to know what the reality of Ulster is."

They sat across from one another and Atty waited until he opened his own door and let it all pour out.

"If there's a God," he whispered at last, "and I surely think there is, He will have looked down on the Catholics and Protestants of this province and shaken his head sadly in realization it is the one place the Devil has beaten Him thoroughly."

She nodded.

"I've always believed," he continued, "there was no such thing as total good or total evil and that good and evil must live side by side, even within a single human cell, but today I think I truly saw the Ulstermen for the first time. God knows that the Catholic Church has done all the, wrong things to fuel their fears of Rome but the British aristocracy has done the real job. They've created a mongoloid race. They'll never rise here above the level of self-imposed ignorance. Their minds have become vacuums that shut out light and air and ideas and beauty. They are robots who will never be able to see themselves as pitifully enslaved . . . oh, Lord, I'm rambling."

"Ramble, Conor," she said.

"Look, you've told me, about Dan because he wants me to take command of the Brotherhood. That's right, isn't it?"

"Yes."

"Well, I can't."

"Your fear of not being able to win is not reason enough," she said. "As commander you will be able to arrange the glorious defeats you seek. I think Dan understands that."

"Nae, Atty, nae."

"Why, Conor?"

"Because I keep seeing truths that destroy my illusions."

"What are they?"

"Cover your ears, woman, because I speak blasphemy that runs against the grain and enrages the soul of every republican concept. Even though it is the truth, no one among us dares speak it. The truth is that there is as much chance of bringing reason, much less love, to that mob out there today as trying to draw blood from the wind. So long as we continue to hang onto an illusion of a single, unpartitioned Ireland, the Ulstermen will drench that illusion in blood. Oh, I've made you turn pale, woman," Conor continued, "but what the hell do we want with a million fanatics? You said yourself they are not us and we are not them. They are the tragic orphans of this Irish trilogy, they are His Britannic Majesty's royal lepers and, by God, woman, we Irish are a civilized people and civilized people do not let a million lepers walk among them and poison their wells. I say, wall them off in their goddamned leper colony and let them sing their bloody hymns and beat their bloody drums and fly their bloody Union Jacks till hell freezes but keep them out of our lives

. . . or we'll end up diseased by their hatred. The Ulster-man is the one who needs an illusion to survive. If we leave them to themselves how long will they last before their hatred has to seek out something to destroy? Who will they have to hate with us gone? They will turn on one another like a sea filled with bleeding sharks. In the end, they'll turn on the aristocracy who brought them to this and follow maniacs like Oliver Cromwell MacIvor.

"Ah, Atty. Why do we continue to hang onto this false dream? I say give them their filthy province, for if we don't we will have condemned the Irish people to eternal damnation."

It was not until this moment that Atty Fitzpatrick truly knew that Conor Larkin was never going to lead the Brotherhood. Yet who but Conor Larkin would stand up and shout truth into a hurricane of illusions?

CHAPTER ELEVEN: I was on a continuous treadmill these days between Dublin, Ulster and London as the year 1912 came to a close, and the government prepared the Home Rule Bill for its second round in Commons.

Rhetoric had grown furious, with both Prime Minister Asquith and chief spokesman Winston Churchill decrying the move to partition Ireland as undemocratic. At the same time we knew that the fury and daring of Carson's tactics had eroded much of their iron. Although Unionist attempts to tack on wrecking amendments had been turned back, the door to compromise had been opened.

The Liberal Party remained in the struggle because they were hostage to the Irish Party and John Redmond was in a last-ditch fight to save his credibility. Yet bitter-ness mounted around Ireland. Carson, Hubble, Weed and gang had gotten away with every affront. Redmond him-self squashed talk of jailing Carson in secret conferences as he feared a backlash in Ulster that could break his fragile hold on the bill. By now even our reluctant bishops were ready to concede the government façade at evenhandedness was a farce.

We knew the Unionists were going to pull something soon and we didn't have to wait long. I received a call

at my Belfast bureau office for a press conference at
Rathweed Hall on January 15, 1913.

Nothing was more welcome to the expanded press corps
than a summons to Rathweed Hall. It usually denoted a
major story and also free booze and a caviar-type spread
in Sir Frederick's opulent manner. My colleagues arrived
at the Sunhouse an hour early and were well oiled and
softened by the time Weed made his appearance.

Sir Frederick was in his seventies but had lost little of
his spark or spunk. I had a strange sort of adverse
relationship with him. He referred to me as his "favorite
Fenian," rarely failing to joke about my one-upsmanship,
and at times gave me messages to deliver to the
Brotherhood while kidding on the square.

The twinkle in his eye this day told me that the
Unionists were going to come up with a corker. He gloried
in the paper he held in his hand as he called us to attention
before him.

"Gentlemen, your attention, please," he said. "I am
going to read you a brief announcement."

He placed his glasses on with all the paused skill of a
mighty barrister, cleared his throat, and looked up to the
fifty journalists arrayed before him, singled me out and
told me to make certain my pencil was sharp.

"The Unionist Executive," he commenced, "as of this
date hereby declares the formation of the Ulster Volunteer
Force. Our goal is to recruit an army of one hundred
thousand men between the ages of seventeen and sixty-
five under a unified central command for the purpose of
defending the liberty of this province."

Weed paused pregnantly to allow that to be digested.
The murmurs about the glassed room ranged from
disbelief to audible comments of astonishment.

Sir Frederick tapped for attention and continued to
feign reading from a paper he had memorized.

"We have canvassed the one hundred and seventy
Unionist Clubs in existence and are happy to report that
all such clubs are transferring their entire memberships en
masse to the Ulster Volunteer Force and will form its
nucleus so we will have some seventeen thousand men
bang out of the bag. Further recruitment will begin
immediately. It is our intention to have a full range of
activities and departments, a transportation corps, a

medical corps, intelligence, communications, et cetera, et cetera, et cetera. Finally, gentlemen, we are in contact with Lord Roberts, who, as you all well know, was a leading general in our Indian Army. Lord Roberts and Colonel H. H. Pain, also of the Indian service, have both indicated their readiness to assume command of the Ulster Volunteers."

Darwin Dwight of the London *Times* was, as usual, first to his feet. "Am I to understand correctly, Sir Frederick, that this is, in fact, to be a private army sponsored by a political party?"

"In a manner of speaking. However, the Unionists are only acting in accord with the wishes of the overwhelming majority of the population."

"And this Ulster Volunteer Force is to hire the services of former British officers?" Dwight pressed.

"Yes," he was answered bluntly.

"Sir Frederick," Tenley of the *Mail* picked up, "who holds the allegiance of the Ulster Volunteer Force? The Crown? The Unionist Party? Just who are they committed to, sir, and in what priority?"

"They are pledged to the continued freedom of Ulster as a part of the United Kingdom," Weed answered.

"But I say, Sir Frederick, is it possible that this Ulster Volunteer Force might be used against the British Army?"

"God forbid it comes to that, but we will shoot anyone who denies us our British heritage."

"In other words," I said, coming to my feet, "you will fight the British Army in order to remain British as well as ignoring British law that isn't to your liking?"

"Ah, my favorite little Fenian," he quipped. "Well, as odd as it seems, Seamus, that is the situation we have been forced into and I dare say a majority of the English people will do likewise in our behalf."

"Then why did the English vote a Liberal Party into power pledged to a Home Rule Bill . . . by that I mean, aren't you exaggerating your English support?"

"Come now, Seamus," he countered, oozing with familiarity. "You know where the English people stand on this issue. You also know the only reason this obscene piece of legislation ever saw the light of day is because Redmond and his pack forced it. Any more questions?"

"One more," I said. "Have you discussed the legality of

this so-called Ulster Volunteer Force with Sir Edward Carson and your Executive?"

"We have."

"Well, is it legal or not?"

"As you know, the Unionist Clubs and drilling were considered illegal and arms importation was considered illegal. I suppose that certain quarters may also consider the Ulster Volunteer Force as illegal. The government knows it is illegal but I rather suspect they're not going to do a damned thing about it."

"Sir Frederick," a half dozen jumped up shouting simultaneously.

"That is all the questions, gentlemen," he said tersely, coming to his feet. "Good day to you all."

As the journalists broke for the General Post Office, to file their stories, Darwin Dwight pulled me aside.

"I think they've gone and done it this time," he said. "The government has to act."

"Want to bet?" I said.

"You're on for a dinner. If they don't crack down on Carson on this one, Asquith will fall in a fortnight."

*

A series of furious conferences ensued between the Prime Minister's Office, the Cabinet, the War Office and Dublin Castle. At the same time thousands of those who had marched on Covenant Day kept right on marching into Orange Halls and signed up for the Ulster Volunteer Force.

Both John Redmond and the Liberal press attempted to play it down as Carson's bluff and folly but behind closed doors the concern grew grave. Credence to the charge that the Liberals were incapable of ruling reached an all-time high. Yet a severe crackdown in Ulster ran the risk of creating a wave of sympathy in England and Scotland that could spell the fall of the government.

The Conservatives squeezed and Asquith opened up more avenues of compromise. With screams of sellout by the Irish ringing in his ears and with the Ulster Volunteers growing larger and more brazen by the day, the Prime Minister finally summoned his generals to 10 Downing Street. As the meeting broke, the assistant chief of operations acting as a personal courier departed for Ireland.

He made immediately for Camp Bushy outside of Roscommon on the River Shannon where the King's Midlanders were barracked.

Orders: TO PLACE THE KING'S MIDLANDERS ON TWENTY-FOUR-HOUR ALERT TO MOVE INTO ULSTER WITHIN THE WEEK.

Mission: TO SECURE PORTS, RAILWAY DEPOTS, ARSENALS, BRIDGES; REINFORCE ROYAL IRISH CONSTABULARY STATIONS AND OTHERWISE PROTECT ALL GOVERNMENT PROPERTY LISTED HEREIN.

CHAPTER TWELVE: General Sir Llewelyn Brodhead had paced his office dry. Beyond his window the grounds of the century-old Armand Bushy Barracks lay in pastoral solitude where the River Shannon widened into the bulrushes and willows of Lough Ree. Old Camp Bushy had been one of the most desirable commands in the Empire, what with England so close at hand.

Brodhead had whipped his Midlander Division into wartime sharpness for eventualities on the Continent. If war did come, they would be ready. He was particularly keen that the Coleraine Rifles, a crack Ulster regiment, had been made part of the division. Infusion of the Earl of Foyle's home regiment had perked up the entire command and given a sense of needed competition among the units.

It all crashed down on Sir Llewelyn overnight. The order to move into Ulster had been vague, deliberately vague, Brodhead thought. It was almost like invading one's own country. The way the orders read, his troops might come into conflict with the Ulster Volunteers here, particularly in the Constabulary posts. All up and down the line the silence was ominous and seemed to say that "old Brodhead really got a hasty one hung on him this time."

He called his officers together and relayed the order matter-of-factly but secretly anticipated a number of resignations from the Coleraine Rifles. They did not disappoint him as thirty-four of the regiment's thirty-five officers offered to quit when the division crossed into Ulster.

So be it. He'd do his utmost to keep a non-military posture when they deployed. After all, British troops in the province had always indicated a visit of old friends. The Ulster folk would realize the Midlanders were only doing their duty. What threw General Brodhead totally off guard was that, in addition to the Coleraine resignations, half the division's other officers resigned as well.

With the order to go into effect in seventy-two hours, his dilemma became sheer agony.

*

Captain Christopher Hubble entered the General's office and snapped off a salute before his desk. Brodhead seemed positively ashen as he waved young Chris to a chair.

Christopher was prepared for anything from an appeal to a tongue-lashing to come storming through the General's mustache.

"Chris, I'm caught in a bit of a bind, you know. Nasty damned business, what? Hoped to be able to go about it without any bother."

"I'm certain the General recognizes my own particular situation. The Coleraines are the family home regiment, you know, sir."

"Indeed I understand, Chris, indeed I do. I have your resignation here in the middle of this pile."

"I can assure the General that my action was solely of my own doing. I discussed nothing with the others, sir, and have no idea who or how many followed suit."

"Tea?" Brodhead asked, loading up a pipe.

"No, thank you, sir."

He flicked out the match, sucked and billowed. Brodhead's penetrating blue eyes met Christopher Hubble's penetrating blue eyes. "Cardinal sin in the military to involve oneself in politics, you know . . . unless the Army were being used by radicals as a political instrument against our own people. Do you agree with that, Chris?"

"Quite, sir."

"Shall we let our hair down, you and I?"

"Yes, sir."

Llewelyn Brodhead leaned over his desk, his large knuckle wrapping it with a thump on every second word. "I did not serve in His Majesty's forces for thirty-six years to come to this." He hunched up, spreading his fingers wide as though he were about to leap over the desk. "For years we've stood by watching the Liberal Party set about to dismantle the Empire, piecemeal. Our imperial forces have created and taken on a system of universal order second to nothing the world has ever seen. Now these bloody bastards have the affront to try to turn us against loyal British citizens. And all of this in behalf of these people down here who would defile the Union Jack, destroy the Empire and stab us in the back in the middle of the night."

Brodhead got a grip on himself. "In three days we cross into Ulster, unless . . ." He stopped deliberately. "Shall I go on, Chris?"

"Please do, Sir Llewelyn."

"Unless," Brodhead continued, "we do something here at Bushy to force them to rescind the order. Of course, a thing like that would require some very special dedication as well as some risk."

Chris nodded.

"Suppose, shall we say, that by tomorrow at noon I have received resignations from every officer in the division, all hundred and forty. Suppose I add my own resignation as well, take this to London and face the Chief of Staff with it as an accomplished fact."

Chris dabbed at the perspiration that suddenly appeared on his face.

The General got up from his desk and resumed pacing along a well-worn track. "Call it what you will, insubordination, mutiny, call it what you will. But the Liberals have to know that if they want this filthy business done, then they'd better scour about for some nigger troops to do it. If they attempt to court-martial us all it could well mean an open rebellion by the entire officer corps of the Army. At best, I think we can get them to call off this madness of occupying Ulster. At worst, I believe a reprimand and removal of the Midlanders from Ireland. I'm not totally sure of the consequences but we've strong friends all up and down the line. Do you think we should give it a go, Chris?"

"I do."

"Good man. Obviously, I think you're the one."

"I'll try not to disappoint you, sir."

"It has to be to a man. One hundred and forty resignations by noon tomorrow. No exceptions. It's the only way we can win. If anything goes wrong, I'll take the responsibility off you."

"It will be done, General."

"All right, Chris, good luck, get cracking, lad, get cracking."

*

Jeremy Hubble was never the same from the moment Molly O'Rafferty disappeared from Ireland. He made a fool's lunge at trying to locate her about the time he knew the baby was due but he was met by a wall of silence and hatred.

For a time he fared better when he joined the Coleraine Rifles, then the military unfolded much the same as the other life patterns. His younger brother was cut out of the proper mold, ambitious and brainy. Christopher followed his father's ways from physical appearance to wit in what was a near duplication of personality. Christopher soon won promotion to Captain and stood at the side of General Brodhead, the epitome of a proper aide.

On the other hand, Lord Jeremy was generally characterized by a lack of distinguished qualities. Yet Jeremy was roundly popular as a member of the division rugby team and among the junior officers. He remained easygoing, a good touch for a loan and certainly the pleasanter of the two brothers. He was particularly suited to the role of the good fellow when it came to time away from camp, hosting a perpetual party at Daars or Rathweed Hall or Hubble Manor. It was good fun to hang around with Lord Jeremy and good food, good drink, lots of girls and good sport.

So long as there was a crowd around he was jolly enough, but there were times he drifted off to Dublin alone and wandered in a kind of tragic nostalgia, haunting the pubs that bounded Trinity College. He'd go into a funk that spilled over into days-long drinking bouts terminating in someone's brothel. Jeremy kept himself totally mediocre. He never rose above the rank of second lieutenant nor was there much hope that he would make any kind of inroad.

After a time his adoring grandfather became painfully convinced of Jeremy's incompetence. He and Roger went about snipping away everything that wasn't in the original entailed holdings of the earldom's charter from the Crown. What would be left for Jeremy would be the title and the original lands around Hubble Manor. These were not self-sustaining so he would be put on an income, a high-class dole for all his days, as Roger had done with his own father.

Jeremy would earn his passage by performing public duties as the Earl of Foyle and for producing a suitable male heir. The rest of it would be in Christopher's hands. The only resistance Jeremy seemed capable of mounting was to ward off subtle pressures that he marry and assure a family. There was a finality to it that spelled an end to even the fantasy of Molly O'Rafferty. Roger and Weed decided to let it go until he finished his military service, then settle it with a suitable marriage.

Christopher and Jeremy neither loved nor hated one another, but came to accept the queer fate of the order of their birth and priority of their abilities. The younger man had once coveted the title he would never own but he realized the awesome power and wealth he was coming into and that he could acquire a title of his own.

Among the immediate family only Caroline remained as Jeremy's intimate. He did not see his mother often these days as she spent more and more time in London away from Ulster in what was an unofficial and unspoken separation from Lord Roger.

*

It was well past midnight when Christopher made it to Jeremy's quarters. Captain Christopher Hubble had returned from General Brodhead's quarters with the balance of the resignations. It was a bit sticky at first but as the fever grew the holdouts succumbed. Everyone had their quid in now, except for one, Lieutenant Jeremy Hubble.

He was awake, for he knew Christopher would be coming back, and he got himself well pissed in anticipation. He lay on his back staring ceilingward as Chris contemptuously studied, then flipped the empty bottle into the trash basket, pulled up a chair next to his cot, planted a foot in its seat and hovered over him. Jeremy blinked in red-eyed discomfort.

"Well, what's it all about?" Christopher demanded.

"Father will just have to hang my portrait facing the wall in the Long Hall."

"Turn around, I can't talk to your back."

Jeremy came to sitting.

"All right, Jeremy darling. You've got me here in the middle of the night pleading with you. I know it looks lovely on paper if the Viscount Coleraine of the self-same Coleraine Rifles is the single officer in Camp Bushy who chose not to resign. I know how incredibly humiliated Father and Grandfather will be. I realize how amusing it will be for you to bring us all to eternal shame . . . but, Jeremy . . . who is kidding whom? You haven't got the guts to go through with it."

"Oh, haven't I?"

"No, you haven't. I know that all you're in it for is to have me standing here, half the night shouting and begging. By the light of the new day you will forthwith hand in your resignation, so why don't you be a good lad, do it now, and let me get some sleep?"

"Fuck off . . ."

"I've a notion to and let you see what it's like tomorrow when all your mates have a good go at old turncoat Jeremy."

"You'll not force me to sign the bloody thing . . . I don't believe in it . . . I don't share your hatred of Catholics."

"Oh, you don't believe in it. Well, that's different then."

"No, I don't believe in it," he said, weaving off the bed and staring down at the parade ground.

Christopher stomped to the door. "I'll advise General Brodhead we'll just have to go in one short of unanimous." He opened the door and slammed it but did not leave the room. Jeremy whirled about in panic.

"You bastard!" Jeremy said.

Christopher withdrew a folded paper from his inner pocket, tossed it on the desk and unscrewed the cap of his fountain pen. "Sign it," he said.

Jeremy's face tightened. He glared at the letter, then at his brother.

"You know, Jeremy, if you succeed in holding out alone, the worst possible thing might happen to you. You might have to go out on your own and attempt to earn your own living."

"Can't you understand just once?" Jeremy cried. "I've reasons . . . deep reasons . . . I mean them. Just once, can't you see that . . ."

"What reasons?" Christopher asked coldly.

"It's like . . . well, signing something against my own son."

"Molly O'Rafferty isn't coming back, not now or ever," Chris said.

"Stop it! Stop it!"

"Not coming back," he repeated.

"You've no . . . bloody feelings . . . you fucking ghoul . . ."

"Oh, stop your whimpering, Jeremy. If you'd cared about your child, you would have made your stand four years ago. I'm getting a little sick of this role of the scorned, broken lover dwelling in the haunts of his beloved. It's nothing but a bloody crutch and you know it. You know the consequences of not signing this as well as I do. Now, let's get it over with."

Jeremy slumped in the chair before the desk. "I suppose your resignation was first in," he grunted.

"That's right. Mine came two minutes after the order to occupy Ulster."

"That's us, isn't it? Christopher is always number one and Jeremy is one hundred and forty." Jeremy laughed sickly. "That's what is between us. Sign this, sign that. All my life you'll be standing over me sticking papers in front of me."

"For the compensation you're getting, you should be the last to complain."

Jeremy chewed at his lip, trying to muster up courage for a final defiance, breaking into a sweat, looking for something more to drink, avoiding Christopher's stare.

"If I open your door again," Christopher warned, "I'll go through it this time and leave you with the consequences."

Jeremy began to sniffle, then sob. He looked up in teared and glassy-eyed hatred, snatched the pen and scrawled his name to the resignation.

*

"Who was that, Alan?" Matilda Birmingham said, half asleep.

"Winston," her husband answered.

"Churchill? Good Lord, it's three o'clock in the morning."

"Yes, I know," he said, tumbling out of bed, padding to the closet and fishing for his lounging jacket. His wife was up after him, prepared a tray of tea and left it with him in his study.

Since his resignation as party Whip, Alan Birmingham had become one of the most vociferous back benchers, applying a continuous needle over his party's vacillation on Home Rule. In fact, Birmingham had taken over as ringleader of a group of young turks in ridiculing Asquith's timidity. Although a lid of secrecy had been clamped on the Camp Bushy mutiny, Birmingham had gotten wind of it and knew that General Llewelyn Brodhead had been locked up in meetings in London with other military leaders.

Churchill greeted him postured in his best crisis manner and apologized about the hour.

"We have reason to believe you know about this dreadful business with the King's Midlanders," Winston said.

"I do," Birmingham answered.

"And the Cabinet suspects you're going to have something to say about it tomorrow in the House."

"Your suspicions are well founded."

Churchill grunted and regrouped himself as Birmingham poured them tea. "Alan," he said slowly, "I'm going to appeal to you to let the matter pass over."

"I'm not sure I understand you, Winston."

"Let it die."

"Do nothing?"

"That's right," Churchill said.

"A hundred and forty British officers, including their General, have staged a mutiny. You're not suggesting we condone mutineers along with everything else, are you?"

"It's not a question of condoning them," Churchill answered. "Alan, we've been going around about this for twenty solid hours. Asquith and the Cabinet, and myself in concurrence, have concluded that if we attempt to discipline these people we may be opening a Pandora's box."

"I suggest you're opening a Pandora's box by ignoring it. Just where do we draw the line with these people, Winston? The next thing you know they'll be running guns in broad daylight."

"Come now, Alan."

"Well, I can tell you what I'd do," Birmingham said testily. "I would have Brodhead arrested and relieved of his command this instant, send a new commander to take over the Midland Division and give the rest of those ruddy bastards precisely one hour to withdraw their resignations or face a general court-martial."

"Your point of view was expressed quite adamantly at the meeting," Churchill said.

"But it's the only course of action."

Churchill held up his hand like a traffic officer. "Not all that cut and dried."

"What are you suggesting?"

"Far from being received as a mutineer, Brodhead is being looked upon as some sort of hero at the War Office."

"But of course," Birmingham retorted. "The old imperial military machine is out to cut the Liberal Party's throat, we know that. They've got to know here and now who is ruling this country, Winston."

"We have been advised by the Chief of Staff," Churchill said, "that if we prosecute this bunch we can anticipate resignations of a third of the entire officer corps. In addition, we've a dozen or more Ulster-born generals in tremendously important positions."

"But, my dear chap. That's just ordinary blackmail."

"With the possibility of war in the near future, Alan, it is no time to risk losing half our commissioned officers."

"I say let the beggars resign. If we can't control the military in a minor crisis in Ireland, how the devil are we going to control them in the conduct of a major war?"

"Alan . . ."

"No, dammit, there is a right and a wrong, Winston. What would happen tomorrow if the Conservative Party also decides to raise a private army and the day after that we Liberals decide to do the same? By God, political parties in a democracy just don't go about raising private armies!"

"I'm going to have to appeal to you on the basis that it is our appraisal, our astute appraisal, that we cannot run this risk. It will simply destroy our foreign policy as well as the confidence of our allies. Berlin would love nothing more at the moment than to see half our officers chuck it."

"Indeed," Alan mulled. "Do you have any idea of what

we're buying? If the province of Ulster is eventually excluded from the Home Rule Bill, and I suspect you've not the guts to do otherwise, those Unionists are going to establish a tyranny there, a tyranny with our stamp of approval."

"There's a war almost on us, Alan. Our imperative duty is to see to it that we're prepared and that we win that war. We can't risk our officer corps over a tempest in a teapot. We are all coming to the notion that the Irish solution will have to be delayed anyhow."

"I see. Then you intend rescinding the order to move the Midlanders into Ulster."

"We do."

Birmingham shook his head in disbelief. "We've built a catalogue of mistakes eight centuries long in Ireland. In the end, we are going to be sucked into Ulster. I beg you, don't come to me two decades from now and tell me I was right out of hindsight. If we don't take the bold action required this moment, then we shall be placed in molasses up to our necks and wallow about in it helplessly, unable to extricate ourselves from Ireland for time immemorial."

Six hours before the King's Midland Division was to cross into Ulster, the order was rescinded. The division remained on duty at Camp Armand Bushy. General Sir Llewelyn Brodhead and his officers did not receive so much as a mild reprimand.

*

The Ulster Volunteer Force established its own legality by government refusal to act and it burgeoned in size and arrogance. By midsummer of 1913 over fifty thousand men had enlisted and they continued coming in at a rate faster than they could be absorbed.

The three provinces of Catholic Ireland watched all this with growing resentment until spontaneous brush fires sprouted about the country.

In late December of 1913 a mass meeting was called in Dublin to form a counterforce against the Ulster Volunteers. The outpour was enormous. Seven thousand men filled the rink in the Rotunda Gardens, overflowed into the adjoining concert hall and another five thousand were turned away.

The Irish Home Army was declared and four thousand men enlisted on the spot. At the core of this new group were a number of legal organizations with heavy republican leanings such as the Gaelic League and the Gaelic Athletic Association. Dublin Castle and London were eager to move against this Home Army and outlaw it but were unable to do so in light of the Ulster Volunteers.

So there it was, England on the verge of 1914, with two private armies existing in her Irish provinces. London was able to draw small comfort in that the Catholic army was pitifully unarmed and without the professional overseers who guided the Ulster Volunteers. It seemed organized with traditional Irish raggedness.

But for the Irish Republican Brotherhood formation of the Irish Home Army was the key to open the golden door. This tiny clandestine group of two thousand men was entirely ready. Long Dan Sweeney gave the command and the Brotherhood members joined the Home Army in total and quickly infiltrated its upper echelons, seizing key positions and commands.

The Irish Home Army grew beyond expectations until London became alarmed. Then, and only then, did Asquith declare an end to all gun importing into Ireland. The Unionists waged no protest, for by this time their weapons larder was well stocked and they held a fifty-to-one gun superiority over the Catholics in the south.

CHAPTER THIRTEEN

HAMBURG, MARCH 1914

Herr Ludwig Boch flipped through the pages of documents, singing softly beneath his breath as he did. Satisfied that everything was in order, he gathered them all up, stuffed them into his briefcase and snapped his pocket watch open. It was a time until the meeting. He lit a cigarette and puffed contentedly, watching the rings expand as they drifted about his office.

Ludwig Boch, a short plump sixty, had reason to be

pleased with himself. He had not been among the large weapons traders, those mystical international figures who flitted covertly about the Continent, but he had carved his own unique niche and he verged on closing the arms deal of his life.

Boch had the usual chain of contacts in the military, the Foreign Ministry, customs and the Armament Board. What he had done differently was to play the Irish fiddle with consummate success. More than any other arms dealer, Boch had sold the idea that it would be to Germany's advantage to get arms into Ireland for both sides and let Protestant/Catholic conflict become a thorn in England's side.

It had proved a windfall. Recently Protestant agents were offering to buy in large quantities and at premium prices. It had to be deft sleight-of-hand, because on the surface the Ulsterites seemed fanatically loyal to the British King. However, the political analysts in the Foreign Ministry confirmed his own conclusion that guns supplied to the Ulsterites had every chance of being used against the British. Their stated loyalties were paper-thin. Berlin believed that. Good luck for Boch.

He did have fears he wouldn't be able to deliver the most recent order. The Ulsterites were asking for automatic weapons and mortars which were in short supply and the German Army now had a priority on all production. He was both delighted and amused when approval came down from Berlin, as well he should be. There were eight hundred thousand marks clear profit in it for him.

Boch knew that arms exports from Germany would come to an abrupt halt when war broke out on the European continent and war was a foregone conclusion. He and the others in his trade rushed about madly to fill their orders before their grisly markets dried up.

With this shipment his nest was feathered for life. He would close shop, emigrate to Argentina and reap his rewards.

*

A few miles removed from Ludwig Boch's inconspicuous office in the St. Pauli waterfront district, Christopher Hubble paced his suite at the Four Seasons Hotel. Until this moment it had all been a lark, but now he was growing nervous. There was an hour to go until rendez-vous. Perhaps a walk. He donned the tweed Norfolk jacket and matching shooting cap that earmarked him as an Englishman and stepped out of the hotel, strolling along the Inner Alster Lake watching the sailboats until the Rathaus bells chimed the hour, then he grabbed a taxi.

"Shuemans Austernkeller, Jungfernstieg," he said in passable German.

*

By the time Christopher had completed his active ser-vice, he had been promoted to major, one of the youngest in the Army, and a high personal favorite of General Sir Llewelyn Brodhead. As tradition required, he remained in the active reserve in the Coleraine Rifles.

After talking it over with his father and grandfather, all concluded that Chris could best serve for the present on the general staff of the Ulster Volunteer Force and he was received there with open arms by Lord Roberts.

Chris proved to be Johnny on the spot when a minor crisis came at the end of 1913 with the government order to cease all arms shipments into Ireland. At the moment the Ulster Volunteers had expanded to upward of a hun-dred thousand men and their arsenal held a rifle per man. What caught Lord Roberts and his staff short was a shortage of automatic weapons and light artillery in the form of portable mortars. Chris convinced his commander to talk things over with his father and grandfather despite the arms ban and they, in turn, took it up with the Unionist Executive.

They reached a decision to get the weapons despite government orders to the contrary. The purchase was underwritten by the industrialist and gentry establishment and Maxwell Swan traveled to Germany to contact Lud-wig Boch. At first Boch, their most reliable supplier, felt the order would be impossible to fulfill because of the German army's priority on weapons but to his own amazement the permits came through. Young Chris was then personally dispatched to Hamburg to personally bring the weapons to Ulster.

*

Otto Scheer disliked Christopher Hubble the instant they met, but the money was too good to let that interfere. Small pangs of conscience had invaded Scheer, who was a reserve officer in the German Navy, a U-boat man. He knew that if he and the young Englisher met again they would do so as enemies and most likely through the cross hairs of a gun sight.

For the time being, Scheer had been hired as a mercenary, a gunrunner for the same British they would be fighting. Boch said it had the approval of the German government. Well, such was the crazy world of Ludwig Boch. A firm hand as a North Sea and Baltic ship's captain, Herr Scheer had dragnetted the St. Pauli district collecting a scavenger crew lured by the bonus money.

He grunted reluctant approval of the arrangement that made Christopher Hubble titular captain of the ship even though he would be sailing it under a German flag.

They went over the entire plan from Ludwig Boch's acquisitions and manifests and the journey route. Schnapps, which Christopher considered a vulgar drink, was ordered by Herr Boch to toast consummation of the deal and halfhearted handshakes completed the luncheon.

Word had been spread about Hamburg that a shipment of arms was about to leave port to deposed ex-President Díaz of Mexico, who planned a coup to retake the government, but the ploy fooled almost no one. The entire deal had Ulster Volunteer Force written all over it.

On the evening of March 24, 1914, Christopher Hubble boarded the nine-hundred-ton grain steamer, the S.S. *Prinz Rudolph*. Her sister ship, the S.S. *Prinz Oscar*, was docked in the adjoining berth. He inspected the cargo of some three thousand machine guns, twelve hundred mortars and several million rounds of ammunition, then ordered the hatches sealed and to be shown to his quarters, thus establishing the manner of conducting business by speaking to no one except for terse instructions to Otto Scheer.

At daybreak the *Prinz Rudolph* slipped up the Elbe River trailed by the *Prinz Oscar*. By the time the two ships reached the North Sea, they were picked up and shadowed by a destroyer of the Royal Navy, H.M.S. *Battersea*. Christopher ordered the two ships to continue

on a southwesterly course through the English Channel
as though they were heading into open sea.

When he instructed Scheer to veer north into the St
George Channel and the Irish Sea, the German balked
He didn't like Hubble, Hubble's youth, his cargo or walk-
ing a tightrope on the edge of British territorial waters
But the bloody Englisher was unflinching and the thou-
sand quid for the job was more than a year's wages.

*

URGENT. ALERT TO FIRST NAVAL PERSON, ADMIRALTY,
FROM H.M.S. BATTERSEA. S.S. PRINZ RUDOLF AND S.S.
PRINZ OSCAR STEAMING DUE NORTH AND STILL FLYING
GERMAN COLORS. RUDOLPH BELIEVED BEARING UVF
WEAPONS. REQUEST INSTRUCTIONS FOR SEARCH AND
SEIZURE.

First Lord of the Admiralty Winston Churchill was
looking at a possible act of piracy if he boarded the vessels in international waters. He quickly returned a message for the observation destroyer to continue to trail the
pair and went into consultation with his own staff and set
up a late meeting with the Prime Minister.

War was imminent but England's position vis-à-vis her
treaties with France and Belgium had not been publicly
stated. There was tremendous pressure on him against
committing an act that would make England a party to
the conflict before she was ready. As midnight conferences ensued, first at the Admiralty, then at 10 Downing
Street, a consensus mounted to let the Ulstermen get
away with their latest little gambit rather than offend the
Germans at the moment.

Only a final plea effort by Churchill was able to keep
the *Battersea* watching the two ships as he set up contingency plans to board if they dared enter Irish waters.
The *Prinz Rudolph* and *Prinz Oscar* continued to steam
into the North Channel which separated Ireland from
Scotland. On their fourth night out of Hamburg they
edged close to Ulster and the moment for the "make or
break" decision was at hand.

*

Otto Scheer knocked and entered Christopher's cabin as
night fell.

"The destroyer is still following us," he said.

"Yes, I know. Well, carry on as planned."

"Herr Hubble, the crew is getting extremely nervous."

"What of it? They'll just be thrown into jail."

Otto Scheer sneered. "That's not funny."

"I didn't mean it to be funny. You agreed to the plan, did you not, Herr Scheer? I mean to say, you Germans are supposed to be crackerjacks at carrying out a plan. Not losing your nerve, are you?"

The German crimsoned. Christopher seemed unflappable.

"The minute we enter Irish territorial water . . ."

"Stop your bloody sniveling, Herr Scheer. You all liked the color of the quid when we signed you on, now go about your job." Scheer glowered at the man half his age, then snapped off a salute-like bow of the head and turned on his heels.

"Scheer. You can tell your people that by morning the *Battersea* will be nowhere in sight."

"What makes you so damned sure?"

"They're just trying to bluff us out. And by the by, tell that chef of yours . . . well, never mind, we've only one more meal together. I'll manage through that stuff, somehow."

Alone, Christopher blew a long breath and hunched over pale and shaky. Everything had looked so cut and dried on the planning board. The entire operation was based on the fact that Sir Edward Carson and the Unionist Executive had gotten away with every bluff against the government so far. Afraid of risking an unscheduled confrontation at sea, they had gone to great lengths to make certain the Royal Navy knew about the ships and their cargo. In that way they could put the ball in the Liberal Party's court, so to speak, force them to make the decision. Their scenario called for grim, all-night meetings in London and by morning the escort would be gone. Well, that was the plan, anyhow.

He lay back on the cot. There would be poor little sleep until daybreak. Then, who knew? Visions of a clammy prison cell awakened him every time he dozed.

Mustn't let the bloody krauts see me in a state, he mumbled to himself, must keep up the old front. . . .

Chris was snapped out of his sleep by loud jabbering.

They were speaking so fast he couldn't make it out.
Dawn light slivered through the porthole. He went to the
sink, heart pounding, and meticulously washed his face,
combed his hair, brushed his teeth and gained rigid control
of himself.

He stepped out on the deck arrogantly, up the ladder
to the bridge. As he did, crew members below him broke
out into applause and cheers. Rathlin Island lay off the
starboard bow and the *Battersea* was nowhere to be seen!

Chris clasped his hands behind him.

"Morning, Herr Scheer," he said gingerly.

Scheer smiled and nodded.

"Have you contacted the *Prinz Oscar?*"

"*Ja,* I have."

"Then proceed to rendezvous as scheduled."

Rathlin Island, a semi-deserted boomerang-shaped piece
of land, lay within sight of County Antrim's north coast.
Site of centuries of bloody struggles from Scottish and
English invasions, the island became the demesne of the
Viscounts Gage, then fell into dereliction, left to the
migrating flocks who alone held court amid its spectacular
cliffs and caves.

A day earlier a replacement crew of former British
Navy men in the Ulster Volunteer Force had been
dropped on Rathlin and awaited the ammunition ship.

By early afternoon on their fifth day out of Hamburg,
the *Prinz Rudolph* and *Prinz Oscar* pulled into the
sanctuary of Church Bay, dropped anchor and contacted
the crew on land by semaphore. Within minutes, they
rowed out and boarded the *Rudolph.*

In a brief but proper ceremony the ship was turned
over by Otto Scheer, the German flag was struck, a flag of
Ulster raised and the ship renamed *Glory of Ulster.*

Lifeboats from the *Oscar* came alongside and took the
German crew to their own ship. Last to leave, Otto Scheer
clasped Christopher's hand with a strange flush of affection.

"You're nervy, Hubble," Scheer said.

"Yes, well, good show, good journey home," Chris replied.

Once aboard the *Oscar,* the Germans lifted anchor and
sped back for Hamburg as the *Glory of Ulster* moved due
west in the opposite direction. By evening they dropped

anchor near Inishowen Head where Lough Foyle entered the sea and radioed to prepare for their entry into Londonderry the next morning.

Throughout the night all units of the Ulster Volunteer Force went on emergency duty, executing a plan to take and guard key points around the province and move units of the transportation corps into Londonderry.

At daybreak, Ulster Volunteer "seizure" of Londonderry had been completed, the waterfront sealed off and a fleet of seventy lorries on the Strand alongside the main Caw & Train dock.

The *Glory of Ulster* steamed down the River Foyle under the hand of Christopher Hubble, past the Pennyburn Light and to the dock where port master D. E. Swinerton, an off-duty UVF officer, waited with all the necessary documentation. He boarded immediately and scanned the ship's manifest, which read, "Communications and Medical Supplies," signed and sealed all papers and within two minutes unloading proceeded.

By broad daylight and with no Constabulary or British troops in evidence the *Glory of Ulster*'s treasure was transferred to the waiting lorries and within two hours the convoy sped out to a predestined dump. In a later announcement to the press Lord Roberts characterized it as an exercise to test the efficiency of certain UVF units, declared the exercise a success and vehemently denied the presence of weapons aboard the ship.

*

Lord Louis de Lacy's republican sentiments boiled over. Against Conor Larkin's advice, Louie urged the Supreme Council of the Brotherhood to counter the *Glory of Ulster* affront with a daylight gunrun of their own, this one with weapons for the "legal" Irish Home Army.

Three weeks later, in what was to be Ludwig Boch's final arms sale to the Irish, a small German freighter precariously anchored off Inishmore, the largest of the Aran Islands in the mouth of Galway Bay. A thousand rifles and a hundred machine guns were transferred to Lord Louie's yacht, the *Gráinne Uáile*, with no attempt at secrecy.

Commander of the Home Army in County Galway instructed units to report to the docks in ranks, unload the

yacht with ceremonious fanfare and thence parade into
the center of the city.

Orders from Dublin Castle were conveyed to General
Sir Llewelyn Brodhead at Camp Bushy to move one of his
regiments into Galway, "to prevent disorders." The
Fusiliers of the King's Midland Division arrived at the
waterfront at the same time as units of the Irish Home
Army.

Cheering and bands that greeted sight of Lord Louie and
Gráinne Uáile soon turned to bullying and herding by
soldiers with fixed bayonets being personally led by a
mounted General Brodhead.

The pushing and shoving turned to hooting and stone
throwing. As the yacht was being unloaded, shots rang
out on the unarmed gathering. Within minutes five members of the Irish Home Army lay dead and another twenty
wounded.

The subsequent investigation and report stated that
"upon receiving weapons from the *Gráinne Uáile,* several
members of the Irish Home Army activated them and
opened fire on the troops. The Fusiliers returned fire only
as a last resort and for the purpose of defending themselves."

*

June 28, 1914, Archduke Franz Ferdinand was assassinated in Sarajevo. Five weeks later England was at war
with Germany, Austria-Hungary and Turkey.

The Home Rule Bill was cleared for final passage and
royal assent but Lords had successfully attached crip-
pling amendments to suspend enactment for the duration
of the war. Moreover, Carson had gotten his provisions
for a future Ulster exclusion.

Despite this, Redmond rose in an emotion-packed
House of Commons and urged Irishmen to join in England's war. He begged for arms for the Irish Home Army
to defend its own country and free British troops on Irish
soil for combat duty.

While many greeted the speech with relief, the War
Office greeted it with suspicion. They did not want a
strong Irish Home Army.

*

The bill was passed shortly after war began and immediately went into cold storage . . . the dead letter file. John Redmond eclipsed fighting, seizing control of the Home Army as his future guarantee for a Dublin Parliament.

At the same time, Sir Edward Carson moved astutely to protect Unionist claims in the postwar era and offered up the Ulster Volunteers to the British Army. Lord Kitchener and the ruling generals greeted this warmly. An all-Ulster Division was formed with their own officers, insignia and flag.

When Redmond attempted the same sort of thing for the Home Army, the War Office was not so inclined to put Irish Catholic units into the field and bogged Redmond's appeals in red tape. Even with this affront, Redmond continued to urge loyalty to the Crown and what shaped up as a contest to see which side would sacrifice the most blood for the British to support their respective positions at the conference table after the war.

Tens of thousands of Irish Catholics enlisted in the British Army and were accepted and treated as second-class troops, as indeed they had lived as second-class citizens in their own land. They were dispersed with deliberate, methodical bigotry. Fervor for England's war dimmed.

By mid-1915 the republican message began to get through: Ireland and the Irish people had no enemies among the nations of the world except for the British themselves, and Irishmen were dying by the thousands in British uniform.

The Redmond era was done, in consummate failure. The day of the republican was begun.

CHAPTER FOURTEEN: Dan Sweeney had thinned out like a scarecrow. It had been months since he had set foot out of Dublin and the trip to Dunleer through a network of safe houses had worn him out.

The two men sat outside the cottage a short distance from the lough. It was a warmish evening. Dan lit a cigarette and hacked in pain. The sickness ravaging his body had tempered his acid. He spoke softly and meditatively these days as Dan Sweeney was turning into the ghost of Dan Sweeney.

"At the last meeting of the Supreme Council," he said, "we declared ourselves as the provisional government of Ireland and passed the resolution to stage a rising sometime during this war."

"So say you all?" Conor said.

"So say us all, myself and Brendan Sean Barrett as well."

"Strange, I thought it would come with celestial fanfare and angels and their harps all floating over a scene with choirs singing ancient Celtic litanies."

"Have no fears, Conor. When the Irish people learn of our decision I am certain Seamus and our new poet brother, Garrett O'Hara, will encase the moment in a proper hallelujah chorus."

Dan coughed again and stole a glimpse at the bottle resting at the tip of Conor's fingers. He held it up to Dan, who resisted. "Go on, Dan, you never made any temperance vows I ever took seriously."

Dan grunted and accepted the bottle, knocked off a swig with the gusto of a man who had been nipping in secret. After the first rush of fire the pain eased and he indicated with a smile that whiskey was what he needed now.

"I'm sure you didn't travel all the way to Dunleer to let me know we're the ruling body of a non-existing government of a republic yet to be declared," Conor said.

"Well put, well put. We've got to stop the Protestant momentum," Dan said. "John Redmond is finished. Asquith is finished. Carson is the belle of the ball. Nothing is too atrocious for him to get away with. The time has come to let them know we're in business."

"Aye, I agree."

"In a year or so we will be commanding our men to stage a rising," Dan continued. "Before they go into battle, I believe they have to have gained faith in themselves. They have to know they are capable of winning. We need a victory now to fortify ourselves, Conor. Not poetry or rhetoric. We have to whip somebody, Englishmen,

Ulstermen. The Brotherhood must know that it's a good force."

"Those are my sentiments entirely," Conor said.

"But what to do? We've argued ourselves dry. Most are in favor of an assassination. We've spoken of British Chief Secretary Augustine Birrell most often, and the rest, Carson, Weed, Hubble, Bonar Law. We even spoke of taking out John Redmond. We spoke of bridges to be blown, raids, even a robbery on the Treasury."

"Where does it stand, Dan?"

"It stands with me coming to you to ask for help. Whatever we decide on and execute will be my last act as commander."

"What do you mean?"

"For a time Atty and I kept my imminent demise secret. When the obvious became obvious to everyone, I sent her to you in Belfast. Having thrice been offered the crown of Rome and thrice refused, I suggested Garrett O'Hara as my successor. He's not much of a military man but as a zealot and scholar he'll embellish the rising with flourish and mystical flavor. Maybe that will catch the fancy of the Irish people, who knows? But for now, I am here with my old friend and adversary Conor Larkin, the one link of steel in our otherwise flossy chain of command. I want you to give us the victory we need so desperately."

"I see," Conor whispered.

"Victory is such a lovely word," Dan said. "No matter how temporary, it will grow larger each year in our fanciful minds and warm us for ten thousand nights. We've had so few. They've had so many."

Dan seized up into another coughing fit and chucked away his cigarette angrily. It was strange to hear him talk like a poet, Conor thought. Blunt old Dan who had always put it cuttingly on the line. He really wanted the exhilaration of victory once so he could die without considering himself a failure.

"I've a notion or two," Conor said.

"That's why I came. I knew you would."

"Lord Roberts and the mucky-mucks of their imported British staff have put a true army together in the UVF. Yet they've some sloppy habits carried over from the old days. Part of the reason is that they've no respect for us as a fighting force. The Brotherhood is ignored and the Home Army is disdained."

"Namely?"

"I'll get to that in my own good time. Despite their bragging about the masses of ordinary Ulstermen being the backbone of their force, neither the British staff nor the gentry completely trust their own people. They're not putting the guns they've collected into the hands of their own rank and file. Likewise, they don't consider us a threat so their guard is down."

"Namely, Conor, namely."

"Namely, they've stored all their eggs in one basket. Everything that came off the *Glory of Ulster* and probably half the Ulster Volunteer Force arsenal is stored in a single place . . . Lettershanbo Castle."

"Sure, Castle Lettershanbo," Dan mused. "Why don't you plan an attack on Gibraltar as well?"

They were speaking of an eighteenth-century bulwark guarding the entrance to Lough Foyle. A single road over a large musty dune constituted the only entry and that could be seen from the castle walls for miles. The entry road was blocked with defenses four deep. Once at the castle, an attack force faced twenty-foot walls ten feet thick covered by machine guns and searchlights. Rumors abounded that it held an enormous arms cache but it was utterly impregnable for the likes of the Brotherhood.

"You're daft," Dan said. "I asked for a simple little victory, Conor, not Wellington at Waterloo."

"Sure, you know me by now, Dan, always looking for back doors."

"Give me another drink of that stuff," Dan said. It hit the mark. "I think we're a couple of old Irish drunks playing with the fairies. For a moment I thought you said something about blowing up Castle Lettershanbo."

"There's an old poem I learned during my travels in America that goes something like . . . one if by land and two if by sea . . . I'm thinking in terms of number two."

Long Dan Sweeney's torn old eyes narrowed to slits. He stared at Conor for a full three minutes. "You've my undivided attention," he said at last.

Conor returned from the cottage with a map of County Londonderry and pointed it out as he spoke.

"Lettershanbo sits right of Magilligan Point at the entrance of Lough Foyle to open sea."

"I know where the hell it is," Dan said crustily.

"I agree the defenses cannot be penetrated by land, scratch that. Here at Magilligan Point, the way over to Inishowen at the narrowest point is about a mile. There are coves on both sides to take off and land."

"You're speaking in terms of crossing behind the castle?"

"Aye."

"How? The coast on the castle side is a treachery of reefs."

"Well, you know those stupid Irish and their stupid little tar and wood curragh boats that ride right on top of the water?" Conor said slyly.

"Curraghs . . . go on, go on."

"Right. There's an abandoned Martello tower where we can hide the boats. It's about a quarter-mile hike to Lettershanbo."

"All right, we've crossed the channel by curragh. We've hiked up behind the castle. Now what? Parade around the walls for seven days and seven nights waiting for the Lord to tumble it down?"

Conor closed the map and smiled. "My village used to have wrack rights just over the lough from the castle. Lettershanbo was abandoned in those days. We'd slip over, a few boatloads of boys and girls, and picnic in the ruins. I got to know the old place right well. As kids adventure, we found a cave with a secret tunnel into the castle. In later years, when I was an ironmaster, Lettershanbo was restored. I did a goodly part of the ironwork. The tunnel is still there."

"Let me see that map," Dan rasped. His bony hands opened it and trembled, then he stared at Conor with a begging curiosity.

"Sure, I wouldn't be fooling a kind old gentleman like yourself," Conor said.

"But wouldn't they know about the tunnel?"

Conor shook his head. "It's bricked up and there's no access visible to the naked eye. Only the fairies could have found it. It leads into a fireplace, of all things, in the basement."

"Jesus," Dan whistled, "Jesus!"

In a manner true to himself, Conor laid out a plan that was a masterpiece of simplicity and Dan knew now why he had traveled to Dunleer to see this man. Dan questioned long and hard but Conor seemed to have the answers.

"Why didn't you tell us about this before?"

Conor shrugged. "I knew the Council would ask for ideas when the time came."

Dan shook his head in disbelief. They went over it all again and again. This was beyond Sweeney's wildest hopes. Not only would half the Ulster Volunteers' weapons and ammunition go up in a single blast, it would win the Brotherhood credence. Such an accomplishment would establish its own esprit de corps, give it a sense of winning. It was that kind of blow from which the British would never fully recover. It was epic, the most daring undertaking since Wolfe Tone over a century before.

"What will you need and how much time?"

"Twenty or so hand-picked men and one month to prepare them."

"You'll have it," Dan said, "and I'm going to be one of them."

"Sure, Dan," Conor said knowingly. "You'll be in my boat."

It took an hour for the magnitude of it to settle. They sat in the endless twilight, drinking and dreaming. Long Dan, not terribly attuned to whiskey, mellowed and became more and more lucid.

"You should have told us about it," Dan repeated. "But I see you now, Larkin, with all your puzzling aloofness disassociating yourself from players and games because you've already figured out who the winners and losers are going to be and you refuse to ignore your own honest conclusions."

"Maybe it's something like that, Dan."

"But I know the same things," Dan said, "and I go on playing the games. That's all of it for me, the illusion of a rising. So I ask which is the better? Is it easier for someone like myself to be a player and keep up a pretense that he doesn't believe in the ending? Don't all men deceive themselves in one way or another, cling to vestiges of the dream, no matter how unreal? Or is it easier to be a

Larkin, know the ending and disassociate yourself from the dreamers?"

"All I know is that I could never knowingly lead men to their defeat."

"Blistering question," Dan said, "blistering indeed. See, the problem with reality and the Irish is an inbred failure to analyze our defeats. All John Redmond had to do was read the life of Parnell to know how far he'd get with a British Parliament and what his end would be." Dan downed another belt of whiskey and his voice blurred instantly. "However, in the end, the oppressor inevitably bumbles into unifying and angering the oppressed. Sure as I sit here drunk, the British are going to make a blunder that will finally arouse the Irish."

"They've done that already," Conor said. "It doesn't seem to help."

"I mean a monumental blunder, a thundering, disgusting blunder. I want to press them into that blunder when we rise . . ." Dan suddenly cried aloud with pain.

"Do you have anything for that, Dan?"

"Some pills."

"Can I get them?"

"No. I don't take them. Pills cloud my mind. At least with the pain I know I'm still alive. You piss me off, Larkin. You'd have made us one hell of a commander."

"We've a lot to get started," Conor said. "I'm after getting some sleep."

"Sleep? Who sleeps?" Dan laughed in irony. "We'll both have time for that in eternal measure soon enough."

Conor got up and strolled to the water edge, grabbed up a handful of pebbles and flipped them into the still pool, watching their circles widen. Dan came up alongside him. The old man looked awful, suddenly shriveled.

"What do you think about these days?" Conor whispered.

"A girl. I think about a girl a lot," Dan said. "I even forget her name."

"Aileen," Conor said.

"That's her, Aileen O'Dunne. Funny you should remember. But don't you know, with all the lovelessness and life on the run and dirty little rooms, I was there on the night we declared ourselves a free people. Beyond this raid and this rising I am now a part of Ireland's story. No one can take that away from me."

"Is that enough, Dan? Is it enough for this nagging burden of emptiness we've carried, knowing we are not natural men and can never have normal lives?"

"It has to be enough. It's all I have. All I know is that fools like you and me were walking toward a prison cell the day we were born."

"Well now, this talk is becoming grim," Conor said. "Let us consider the positive side. Atty can travel about with our bones from town to town eulogizing us and raising funds and my sister will only have to wait for my brothers Dary and Liam to have a churchyard filled."

"Conor, I'm about to ask yourself a personal favor."

"Sure, Dan, anything you want except to ask me to take absolution."

"Before we go tearing up that castle, say something handsome to Atty. I think I'm the only man alive, including yourself, who knows how much she loves you. Tell her a lie, if you must, but don't go off without leaving her something."

"Aye, I should and I promise I will."

Dan braced for another shooting pain that passed without striking, then retreated to the cottage for another bottle. When he returned Conor was at water's edge looking off into infinity. The hours of night darkened, making a challenge at the sun. The Twelve Bens and the lough became muted fires in harvest hues.

Conor looked to Dan strangely as he approached, as though he were looking at someone from another time and another place.

"What is it?" Dan said.

"For a moment . . ." Conor began in a harsh voice not totally his own.

"What?"

"Dan, what is death like?"

"I don't know, Conor. You seem to see it more clearly than I have. You seem to be looking at it half the time."

"You don't want to come back from that raid, do you, Dan?"

"No," Dan answered. "Tell me, Conor, who did you just see?"

"My daddy . . . Tomas . . . I see him often. It's always

me down by the village crossroad running up the path
when he's coming down from the fields. He takes me up
in his arms ... Dan ... Dan, I'm scared."

"Sure, I know that feeling. We are men of little consequence and less property. Once you were a man of
substance. You were heir to forty acres of Larkin land ...
and then ... you left Ballyutogue."

CHAPTER FIFTEEN: For five weeks I was a member
of a hand-picked task force of twenty-two men and Atty
Fitzpatrick training at Dunleer for an undisclosed mission.
We lived at the monastery, eating, drinking, breathing and
sleeping the drills our taskmaster, Conor Larkin, beat into
us.

I was among the chosen, not because of my size or
prowess, but to chronicle the event. The target was a
tightly held secret known only to Conor, Dan and Charley
Hackett, a dynamite man of considerable skill.

We trained by night, always racing against a clock with
a forty-pound pack on our backs and an emphasis on
rough-water drills in curraghs with a lot of belly crawling
through caves of the Twelve Bens. A "silent" communications system was built by hand signals, with discipline
broken only when we were out of sight of one another,
then we went to bird and animal calls.

This much was known:

Atty was in charge of a lorry which contained a first aid
station.

Lord Louie stressed navigation and handling of the
fragile little boats.

Gilmartin, an old hand from the Boer War and member
of the Supreme Council, worked in league with Dan
Sweeney at manning a machine gun. Gilmartin was somewhat of a blowhard but the most military among us as
well as a competent seaman.

Charley Hackett and his team of Jennings and Pendergast were going through a lot of wiring drills, ostensibly
on dynamite.

Any time we felt we were getting razor sharp, Conor
kicked the notion and pushed us beyond our previously

known capacities. He was a martinet, an ugly man, during those weeks, striving for perfection beyond perfection. Whatever Dan and Conor had up their sleeves, we felt from their vibrations we were going to something gigantic.

In the beginning of June 1915 we broke camp and in twos and threes made our way to Derry where we contacted Darren Costello, Brotherhood commander of the area, and disappeared into the sanctuary of the Bogside. Conor, Dan and Charley Hackett were all on the run and needed a few days longer to reach Derry.

When we had all assembled, we were still told nothing, loaded aboard a pair of lorries and whisked from Derry into territory familiar to me as we headed in the direction of Ballyutogue.

Just after nightfall we came to a stop in a clump of trees off the road between Ballyutogue Township and the Upper Village and were whisked into St. Columba's Church, which was strangely deserted. The only villagers present were Boyd McCracken, the older brother of Myles, who had inherited one of the worst farms in Ireland, and his son Tim, a lad of fourteen whom I scarcely knew.

Some benches had been moved, some bedding was on the floor along with a makeshift kitchen. The windows were covered to block light. Twenty back packs of the sort we had trained with were stored in a corner behind the pulpit.

We milled about, reaching new bounds of curiosity and not a little tension, with orders not to leave the building. There were a number of consultations between Conor and some of the others in the vestry and, at last, we were called together.

A semicircle of wrought-iron candlesticks was placed around a slate board near the altar. As we gathered in close, Conor scratched out a map of some sort in chalk, then turned to us.

"From here on out you are all under stringent security," he began. "You will remain inside the church during the day. You may go out into the yard as long as it's dark. There are guards outside with orders to shoot to kill if you go any farther."

Sure, this was Conor Larkin the military commander speaking! There was not a tinge of warmth or humor in his voice but a continuation of the authority the situation required and it was entirely welcomed.

"We are in the village of Ballyutogue," he continued, "it is the village of Seamus O'Neill and myself. Most of the villagers are off harvesting kelp on the annual wrack rights. No contact is to be made with anyone remaining. Father Cluny and Boyd McCracken have been using this church and Boyd's home as safe houses for years."

The loudest noise was the flickering flames. The church was bathed in mellow light, giving an orangeish glow to the sorrowful Virgin and the bleeding Jesus.

"You have all assumed a number of things by now," Conor said. "Our target is somewhere in this area, we must cross water to reach it and we will do it by night. All three assumptions are correct."

He turned to the slate and encircled a point on his diagram. "We are going to destroy Lettershanbo Castle," he said.

My God! My God Almighty! I felt the sweat come right through my palms, my tongue go dry and my stomach tighten in a grip of sheer unadulterated fear. I was afraid to look at the others but I suspected it was likewise with them.

"All right, your attention," Conor called. "What we're after is fifty thousand rifles, three thousand automatic guns and mortars and a stash of three hundred tons of dynamite." He X-ed a place on the board. "This is Ballyutogue, our present location. Tomorrow at dusk we move up the coast in two lorries. The first will be driven by a local brother, the second by Atty, which is outfitted as a first aid station."

She nodded.

"We proceed to this point just beyond Ballybrack House to a small cove known as Ballybrack Hole. Lord Louie will give you your compass points there. Boyd and the brothers in the area have five curraghs hidden at Ballybrack Hole for the crossing. Tomorrow was selected because of moon, tides and probable weather. Obviously we want as little light on the subject as possible. Questions so far?"

There were none.

"Lord Louie and Gilmartin were advised of the crossing just before this meeting. Louie?"

Always looking strangely out of sight in our company,
Lord Louie came to his feet. "It should all go just as it
did during practice. We've done enough rough-water
maneuvers to know what to expect. Perhaps a bit more
weather here. But even under adverse conditions the
crossing should be negotiated in no more than a half hour.
Mind your drifts, keep a good eye on the compass, wear
your life belts."

"We cross in the teams we've been working with,"
Conor carried on. "We move out in the order we've been
practicing. Dan, Seamus, myself, Charley Hackett in boat
number one. Gilmartin's team in number two. Lord Louie
in number three, and so forth. Boyd will join Gilmartin's
boat."

Conor marked another X on the board. "We head for
this Martello tower," he said. "The landing should be
similar to the ones you've practiced at Slyne Head, hard
surf, tricky undertow, rocky footing. Get your boats up
on dry land, assemble at the tower. Questions?"

"Are you certain the area isn't patrolled?"

"Aye," Boyd McCracken said. "I've made three dry
runs including one last night. The tower is abandoned
and the landing area unguarded."

"What about the Royal Navy? Isn't there a patrol boat
on Lough Foyle particularly moving against poachers at
night?"

"Darren Costello and the lads in Derry will be conducting a supporting maneuver to make certain the Royal
Navy is locked up in port and unable to enter the lough,"
Conor answered. "Likewise there will be a diversionary
movement against the Greencastle Barracks, although
most of them will be up in the hills on maneuvers. So we'll
only have a skeleton force of three or four to contend
with."

Murmurs of concurrence greeted Conor as we all
realized the thought that had gone into the plans.

"As you know, the Martello towers were built by the
British as coastal defense points against a possible Na-
poleonic invasion. Although they can't stand up under
today's naval guns, they're still formidable. Dan and
Gilmartin will establish a machine gun post to cover our
return crossing."

He walked to the pulpit, picked up a back pack and

held it aloft. "The packs you practiced with held forty
pounds of rocks. The rocks have been removed and
replaced by dynamite. They're waterproof and hold no
danger of going off by themselves . . . but don't go around
lighting any matches."

Nervous laughter.

"From the Martello tower we move down the beach to
this point . . . here into a cave and cliff area. By low tide
you'll enter the designated cave in waist-high water.
Thirty yards into the cave it's belly crawling for some fifty
yards. Then a tunnel into Lettershanbo."

Another round of comment stopped him for a moment.
As Conor talked I had remembered it as well from our
own wracking days as young lads chasing that girl . . .
what was her name now?

"We estimate no more than a half hour from cave
entrance to the castle. I will remain in the cave to unreel
the wire and set up the detonators. Charley and Boyd will
lead you to the castle. When you reach the end of the
tunnel you'll find a brick wall. Boyd, do you want to take
over?"

"Aye." The pre-aged angular brother of Myles still
showed faint family familiarities even with the passage of
so much time. "I went over and lived in the cave and
tunnel for three days," Boyd said. "Conor gave me the job
of chipping away the mortar from the brick wall. He
reckoned I was eminently qualified due to my off-season
work in the stone quarry. Working silently and with nothing larger than a penknife, I loosened everything so the
bricks can be removed by hand and provide a sufficient
crawl space. When we go through the hole we will be
coming in by a fireplace to a basement room. From there,
the target is just down the corridor. I was able to move
around without detection. The basement seems to have no
regular guard or patrol. Nevertheless, don't stomp
around."

Boyd held up a pair of pampooties, rubber-soled shoes
for negotiating slippery rocks around the surf which
would also deaden footsteps on the stone floors of the
castle. "We've a pile of pampooties in the vestry. Find a
pair that fits you."

"Charley," Conor said.

Charley Hackett, a grizzly number, erased the slate and

drew a diagram of the castle basement. "The boiler
room is it," Charley said. "In the renovation, a central
heating plant was installed with large warm air ducts to
every room in Lettershanbo. I am betting that the ducts
will carry the blast like a telephone wire. God willing, our
dynamite will find its way to three hundred tons of UVF
dynamite and their own stuff will blow the place to hell."

"What if it doesn't work, Charley?"

"We'll have come a long way to blow out a few
windows."

"Have you ever seen it work?"

"No, and I won't give you my opinion," Charley said.
"However, there is a dynamite man I know whose opinion
I value highly and I agree with him. All right now, once
you enter the castle, move behind me quickly and quietly,
dump your packs in the boiler room and get the hell
back to the cave. Jennings, Pendergast and myself are
giving ourselves ten minutes to wire everything together."

Conor took over again. "There is a junction of two
corridors at the boiler room. Boyd knows it. Seamus will
man the submachine gun in case we draw unwanted
company. It's the stickiest spot in the operation. If you'll
recall, you all drew lots one night back at Dunleer and I
wouldn't tell you what for. Well, Seamus, you drew the
short straw . . ."

"As usual," I said.

"You are the last one back into the tunnel. You've got
to move like fury, for when you leave, the detonation
wire will be unguarded for some ten minutes. If it's
discovered and cut, we've come here for nothing. If
there's an attack, Seamus has to protect the wire."

I wouldn't say this was the most frightened I'd ever
been in my life. I was saving that for tomorrow but I
knew, despite Conor's frowning on the subject, I was
going to have a confidential talk with Jesus and Mary. . . . I
got a grip on myself, said something funny to alleviate the
tension, but I almost threw up with fear as I spoke.

"We have regrouped at the Martello tower," Conor
said, "and crossed back to the Inishowen side of the lough,
hopefully leaving a shambles and a confusion at Lettershanbo to make pursuit impossible. Atty and one of the
brothers from Ballyutogue will remain at Ballybrack Hole
with the two lorries. She will stay until one hour before

daybreak or when she is certain all are back who are coming back. You will be taken back to the church. We will move up to Boyd's house."

"Conveniently located high in the heather," Boyd interrupted.

"From there, young Tim will fade us back into the hills. Believe me, you won't be found. Atty has and will issue you your disbursement instructions. We go out of the hills one at a time, in different directions."

Conor beat his fist into his hand and re-covered most of the points slowly, then became a grim mask.

"We go tomorrow. There will be no postponement. The operation has been constructed to move in concert with Darren Costello's raid in Derry and we will be out of communication with him. If we hit rough water and you swamp, we'll not stop and search for you. If you are wounded on the castle side to such an extent you slow us up, you're going to be left. If you require medical attention here, you will be left. You have all volunteered on the basis of taking on a suicide mission. We have done everything possible to get you back alive. Anyone caught is sworn to secrecy. If you spill to the British and they don't kill you, the Brotherhood will . . . all clear?"

It was brutally clear.

"Dan," Conor said.

Long Dan Sweeney had steeled himself beyond his capacity to make the trip without being a burden but the pain was destroying him before our eyes. "Lads," he rasped, "and lassie, I never thought I'd live to see the day that twenty Irishmen would ever prepare such a mission without creating utter chaos. But . . . here we are . . . and here it is . . . over there. We don't care if this shot isn't heard around the world so long as they hear it in London. This war has been used by the mother of parliaments as their latest excuse to further deny the legitimate claims of the Irish people. It is entirely and poetically fitting that we use the very same war to advance those claims. The success of this mission could well spell the achievement or denial of our goals for this generation of Irishmen. Do your jobs well. This moment belongs to all of us and to the Irish people as well . . . but to one in particular. Do you have words for us, Conor Larkin?"

So, there it was, round and round the universe, round

and round the circle of life. It all begins and ends in the same place, doesn't it? Conor and me in Ballyutogue. We all come home eventually. As he stood before us now he was no longer the stern commander, but he bore the look of a young boy, smoldering . . . far away from us . . . how strange, how very strange. He was surrounded by men who worshiped him and a woman who loved him beyond loving. He seemed unaware. Was he fulfilled at last? Had he reached so much as a single answer to his long, sorrowful journey? Ah, Conor lad, Conor lad. It is so good to be here with you at this moment. I would not have missed it for anything. Not even for the day of the rising.

"If there are some among you who do not come back, I am sorry I was not good enough or thorough enough. As for words? Well, there is too much magnificent literature and too many pedantic ballads as well that spell out our longing for freedom. What can a fool like myself add to all that? As Catholics we learned to accept mysteries as children. Some of those who questioned mysteries found that they weren't mysteries at all. But there is a mystery that defies all attempts to explain it. There is no mystery more intense than a man's love for his country. It is the most terrible beauty of all. No greater tragedy has befallen our people, who, through generations of suffering at others' hands, have lost this furious love of country. Tomorrow, we open our case to rekindle that flagging spirit."

*

The air was sweet and cool beside my daddy's grave. I sat next to him pretending I had a flute in my hands and was fingering a dancing tune to make him smile.

I heard movement nearby at the Larkin plot, then saw the figures of Conor and Atty. I became transfixed by them and committed the unpardonable sin of eavesdropping.

"Oh, God," she whispered, "hold me, man."

Atty cried softly in Conor's arms, then he spoke to her above the tombs.

"I have seen another truth," he whispered. "It only came to me here and now. If you love your country, then you must try to make it live beyond your own paltry

mortal moment. Here I am among them all and perhaps I
am to join them soon. My ma . . . Greatgrandfar Ronan
. . . my Grandfar Kilty . . . and my daddy. I was wondering, have we Larkins come to our end in Ireland? Brigid
is sterile, Dary is a priest, and Liam's wanes will never
know their Irishness. I realize that I have tried to commit
the crime of not daring to need you but I always have and
I do now. I want to come back and I fancy you carrying
my baby."

"I'm as fertile as the plains of Kansas," she said, "but
not to wait too long."

"Aye," he said. "I'll be back from this one all right, for
I know truth. Of all the hazy ghosts, the wandering and
the hells of doubt, it comes down to a single thing. It
is you, Atty. . . . It is you I'd call for at the moment of
my death."

CHAPTER SIXTEEN: Our equipment was checked
and rechecked. Rendezvous points, routes, elapsed times,
details of duties were gone over throughout the day. Every
hour a weather report was brought in from an observer at
a high point overlooking the lough.

By late afternoon the British patrol boat was seen
steaming southward toward the mouth of the river into
Derry. We knew it would remain in port until darkness,
then make its night run against poachers.

Most of us had been thrown out of the Church because
of our republican leanings but, let me tell you, there was
a lot of unabashed praying at the altar as the hours
droned on. We tried to sleep but it was impossible and the
late meal was largely uneaten.

Our first shock came when Conor tersely ordered us to
clean up the church and remove all trace of our presence.

Lord Louie came back from weather observation
grunting unhappily. It was clouding up fast outside. That
much was fine, for we hoped for cloud cover. But I knew
this place and Conor did as well and I could see from
the way he received the news he feared a storm behind
the moving front.

*

The first dullness was on the sky. Darren Costello and five members of the Derry Irish Republican Brotherhood unsheathed a stolen delivery van from its hiding place in an abandoned potato warehouse at Quigley's Point on the coastal road. KNOCKDARA LIVERY COMPANY, the repainted sign on its side, read. Costello drove with his son Cassidy at his side and the other four tucked in the rear. They headed to the Derry waterfront and the Caw & Train Dock where the *Glory of Ulster* was berthed.

Since, its renowned daylight gunrun the German grain ship had become a celebrity in its own right. As a new symbol of the besieged, thousands of Protestant school children and Orange Lodges came to the shrine. An enterprising gentleman, Mr. Edwin Cowley, himself a past Grand Master, converted the *Glory of Ulster* into a day cruiser around the lough for charter by Orange and Unionist groups.

The waterfront was virtually deserted at this hour as the Knockdara Livery Company van pulled to a halt alongside the ship. Costello knew there would be but a single watchman aboard. He and Cassidy grabbed a pair of tea chests out of the back and made up the gangplank.

"Hello there," Darren called, "is anybody aboard?"

In a moment the ancient watchman reluctantly stuck his head out of the wheelhouse window.

"Who's down there?" he demanded.

"I've two cases of tea, sir," Darren called back.

"Tea? Who the hell ordered tea?"

"Mr. Edwin Cowley, sir. It's for the temperance ladies' cruise next Sunday."

"Hell of an hour to be making a delivery."

"Sorry, governor. My van broke down."

"Well, just leave it there on the deck. I'll take care of it later," the watchman called.

"Sorry, governor. I need your signature. I'll bring it up to you."

Darren dashed up the ladder with his son behind him and went into the wheelhouse. Cassidy shoved a pistol into the man's belly as his father applied the pipe, to the back of his head.

Darren stepped out and whistled and three of the lads in the rear of the van boarded. One headed to the engine room and the other two cast off the docking lines, then jumped on. The remaining man drove the lorry off.

In a matter of moments the *Glory of Ulster* was under steam and cruising slowly up the River Foyle. St. Columba's Park on the Protestant side of the river was filled with late picnickers and strollers. On seeing the *Glory of Ulster* they waved and cheered. "Captain" Darren Costello tooted the boat's whistle in response.

They had glided past the Naval Docks and the patrol boat, which was receiving its crew for the night run around the lough. When the river widened past the Clooney Light, the watchman was carried down to the engine room. Costello didn't want it this way but the man could identify him and his son later. He was killed with a single pistol shot through the head.

A mile upriver it narrowed dramatically at a point known as Boom Hall. The site was named for the place where the forces of King James had thrown down a boom to block entry during the siege of 1689 and prevented relief supplies by sea. Borrowing a passage from history, Darren Costello maneuvered the ship sideways in the narrow channel, then opened the valves, scuttling her in the same spot the ancient boom had been lowered.

The *Glory of Ulster* settled in the shallows in a neat piece of work, making passage from the docks into the lough impossible and sealing the patrol boat in Derry. They rowed ashore to the waiting Knockdara Livery Company van on the Limavady Road and fled.

*

Ten minutes later the three-man guard at the Greencastle Barracks was quickly and efficiently dispatched.

*

At the same moment the *Glory of Ulster* met its ironic fate, the two lorries pulled into the cove at Ballybrack Hole where the five curraghs had been hidden in the tall grass. We moved them to water's edge, loaded our equipment and waited for darkness. Conor gathered us about, explained Darren Costello's part in this and reckoned we could now scratch one British patrol boat.

He went off, checking his watch every minute or so, sneering at the sea, worried by its mounting anger. It was getting very choppy with thickening clouds emptying the first sprinklets of rain. We could usually see Letter-shanbo from this point but it had faded ominously from view.

I had been in a fearful state on the drive up the coast, not daring to so much as budge. As Lord Louie gave us our compass points I felt a strange bliss. What kept me from breaking into an open sweat was a sudden sense of unreality about the whole thing. I was detached from danger, in some kind of euphoria that left me untroubled. Had I found the secret of brave men under fire?

Conor put his arm about my shoulder and pulled me aside.

"Sorry about you drawing the short straw," he said.

"Somebody had to get it."

"Well, don't go waking up the guard over there and haul your ass down that tunnel fast," he said.

"Not to worry. Look, Conor, I've a bit on my conscience," I said. "I overheard you and Atty in the churchyard last night."

"I've only been able to keep one secret from you in my life," he said, referring to our destination during the training at Dunleer. "I almost spilled that. So, you heard."

"Aye. Did you tell her the truth?"

"I want to come back, Seamus, and I want to have children with that woman."

"That's grand." Euphoria or no, I looked at the darkening water and almost doubled over with fright. Conor's hand gripped my shoulder.

"You're not alone," he said.

Funny, I had never thought of Conor Larkin being scared . . . funny. . . . He turned from me and went to Atty.

"I'll see you in a little while," he said to her.

"I'll be here," she answered. Her eyes cried out that she loved him so much she'd forgive him even if what he had said was a lie.

"Stand by," Conor ordered.

"I love you, Conor," I heard her call but he did not hear because he was at the water's edge. He slapped me on the backside and got to one side of the curragh.

"Get in, Dan. Let's go, Charley. Hang onto the reel of wire while we cast off. Good luck, lads!"

We slid the boat in, climbed quickly over the side and picked up the oars. In the strange manner of curraghs, the oars had no blades but were constructed to skim above tide and currents. In a few seconds the raised bow cut into a whitecap, split it and oozed out of sight of the cove.

The crossing should have taken no more than twenty minutes but the wind in mid-channel blew in from the open sea and began to push us around fiercely as well as whip up the waves. We were bouncing and crashing, bouncing and crashing with every stroke. Charley Hackett held the compass, redirecting us every third or fourth stroke. Dan peeled his ancient eyes for the others but he could not see them. Every team was struggling on its own. It became a mess with Charley and Dan bailing to keep us from swamping, ourselves drenched and in the dark and the curragh bobbing like a cork.

At dead center of the strait we heard chilling screams.

"Someone's swamped!" Charley cried.

Cries followed the screams.

"Let's have a look, Conor!" Charley broke.

"Sit down and shut up," Dan ordered. "Sit down, Charley!"

"Pull, Seamus," Conor yelled, gritting his teeth and shutting out the desperate cries for help. A wave nearly bent us in half and we were in a struggle to keep upright. Water poured into mid-boat as the tar and canvas stretched and grunted to the ripping point.

"Quarter into the waves, Seamus!"

We spun in a convulsed circle. Conor grabbed me and shoved me out of my seat, taking over my oar. He brought the boat under control as I bailed with Dan and Charley, then he played agilely with the swells and chops. He danced and tiptoed through it like his daddy would have done.

"I see land!" Charley cried.

"We may have to ride a wave in like a shot," Conor cried. "Charley, Seamus, prepare to jump when I tell you, grab the bow, hold it high. Don't let it crash straight down!"

Suddenly we tore at the shore atop a high, hard-moving breaker. The boat catapulted . . . closer . . . closer . . .

"Now!"

Charley and I went in up to our necks, then lifted to hold the bow high and keep the boat from smashing up. I was lifted off my feet, then dunked, then lifted. I clawed with my feet at the rocks, gagging from water and with shots of pain from the bashing. Conor was at my side adding his strength.

"Run at the beach!" he screamed.

We hurled ourselves. The curragh eased onto the sand as though it had been riding on glass. Dan tumbled out and all four of us dug, dug, dug, getting the boat up to safety. Out came the machine gun, out came the ammunition box, out came the wire reel and the stretcher to carry it.

We sank to our knees, allowing the luxury of a minute to double over and gasp.

"All right, up. Dan, Charley, set up the gun. Seamus, take the boat up behind the tower!" Somehow we had landed within fifty yards of our destination. Conor was in the water, scanning for other boats.

In they limped. A second curragh was a quarter of a mile off target. We could see them stagger and reel. The boat was shattered on landing and broke apart.

Conor herded them into the tower.

Then came Gilmartin, who, along with Lord Louie, was the best of the sailors. He mastered his craft in safely, then collapsed face down. Conor dragged him up the beach with my help. We knew that one boat had swamped but one more was due. Conor ordered me to get Gilmartin to the tower.

"I'm going back down and find the other boat," Conor said.

"Wait . . ." Gilmartin gasped. "We're it. . . ."

"There's one more out there."

"No, they're both gone. I saw it. Pendergast flipped over and swamped. I fished him out while passing. He was dead."

"The other . . ."

"Lord Louie. He almost ran over the top of us, then broke in half . . . oh, Jesus . . . Jesus . . ." Gilmartin screamed.

"Shut up, goddammit!" Conor bellowed. "Shut up! All right, let's get up to the tower."

*

A curious, cautious boarding party inched on the *Glory of Ulster*, consisting of naval personnel, port authorities and Constabulary. A search of the ship turned up nothing. The dead watchman was well hidden in an inaccessible flooded part of the hold.

Amid the head scratching, Mr. Edwin Cowley, the owner, finally boarded. There was a confused consultation. Cowley ranted right off that it was obviously the work of thugs from the Catholic side of the river. It was also obvious to Edwin Cowley that it was an insult to all that was good in Ulsterism and to the Crown as well. He stormed off his half-sunken ship in quest of Orange fellows. There would be a riot on the Bogside to pay for this.

The authorities were more concerned at the moment with the mess. For all practical purposes the Londonderry harbor would be out of business for at least a week.

*

"We've got about three hundred pounds of dynamite left," Charley Hackett said after the survey.

"Will it be enough?"

"We won't know till we spark it."

"All right," Conor said. "Saddle up. Everyone goes except Dan. You're going to have to handle the machine gun by yourself for the time being."

"Sure," Dan said, drying his glasses, placing them on carefully and failing to see very much in front of him.

"We've got a potful of time to make up," Conor said. "Let's go."

The storm, which had been both killer and tormentor during the crossing, was now our ally with its protective cover. Conor chucked the original plan, which called for us to crawl down the beach to the caves. Instead, he ordered everyone to run standing up as far and fast as they could go.

Conor and Charley Hackett bore the brunt of it, packing a two-hundred-pound spool of wire on a stretcher. Boyd McCracken found the proper cave. We sloshed in after him, got deep and onto dry ground, then fell and lay panting.

A candle was lit. Glistening icicles of rock revealed a fairy's den. Boyd pointed to a minuscule opening. Conor tied a rope to the stretcher, then around himself like a harnessed horse. We followed Boyd, one after another on our stomachs. The crawl was agony. With forty pounds of dynamite on my back and a submachine gun and ammunition the space narrowed in places to two feet by two feet. Jagged rock clawed my flesh and tore at my pack. Blackness added to the horror.

I could hear Conor grunt as he pulled the stretcher a few inches at a time . . . grunt, gasp, grunt, gasp.

"Cave-in," Boyd called in the blackness. I saw the faintest light from his torch as I lay entombed in rock and swooning into a nausea of claustrophobia. Boyd called back again that he could get it clear with bare hands. I crossed myself in thanks as the line began to slide forward again.

The path of torture widened into a cavelet room. No time to collapse again. Conor, still in the passage, passed the rope forward and all of us tugged in unison to get the stretcher through. No ounce of strength was left untapped. It came into the cavelet just in time, for although it had been sewn four layers thick it was badly ripped.

Conor's torch played over the den, then stopped. "That's it, the tunnel entrance," he said. "Gather in. We're going to have to improvise some changes. Boyd first, Charley in a one-minute interval, then Seamus, then Pete. If the wire fouls, the front man begins to work back until he finds the snarl. I'll have to handle the reel here by myself."

Conor had again saddled himself with a brute-strength job that would have sorely tested two men. He braced to balance two hundred pounds in his hands as Boyd entered the tunnel with the wire. One after the other we took the wire into the tunnel on hands and knees.

*

"There it is, lads," Boyd said, flashing his light on the brick wall. "I'll carry the wire in. Follow me, Charley. Gilmartin, stay and keep it free. We've a sharp bend. I'll jerk the line three times to let you know when I reach the boiler room."

Working like a safecracker defting a combination lock, Boyd McCracken slipped the bricks away like a Chinese puzzle and opened up a man-sized hole. Boyd drew his pistol. The others followed suit. He inched through the opening, doubled up and slid headfirst through the rear of a fireplace flue, then down through the fireplace itself.

We followed. It was a vast room in bluish-black darkness pierced by the single torch light in Boyd McCracken's hand. He turned the light on our smutty faces, taking count. All were in except Gilmartin, who was feeding the wire through. We stole over the stone floor to a great wooden door and slid the bolt. A light cracked into the room from the corridor as we bunched up behind Boyd.

He peered out. The hallway was clear. He pointed to another door some forty feet down the line and slipped out, hugging the wall. One by one we oozed after him, ganging up again before the boiler-room door.

Boyd handed the end of the wire to Charley Hackett, darted to the door, pressed his ear to it, flung it open! He stepped in, brandishing his pistol. Nothing. Another signal and we poured in as he lit up the single bulb. We dumped our packs, placed them together before the largest of the pipes and duct, then moved out. With Pendergast gone in the crossing, Charley had only Jennings to wire the stuff into the ducts.

As the others fled back, Boyd and I took up our rear-guard post at the junction of the corridors. It was a perfect position with a clear view to the only entrance to the cellar. Anyone trying to get to the wire would have to turn a corner blind and right into my path of fire.

The moments went by with brutal slowness . . . eight . . . nine . . . ten . . . fifteen . . . sixteen. Come on, Charley, for God's sake! Jennings bolted past me, giving a signal that it was about done.

Another three minutes . . . Charley showed. The instant he did we all froze. A shadow fell over the stairs at the end of the corridor. Someone was coming down!

We gaped. I froze an instant and then . . . somehow, I knew what had to be done.

I signaled for Charley Hackett to get back into the tunnel and I nodded for Boyd McCracken to do the same.

*

Gilmartin had held a position near the fireplace, counting everyone as they went through. Charley and Boyd reached him at the same instant.

"Let's go," Charley said.

"Where's Seamus?"

"Someone's prowling around. He's got to stay."

Gilmartin winced aloud, started back over the room. Boyd grabbed him.

"No use getting us all killed. Get in the tunnel, Gilmartin."

He wavered a moment, then turned and fled with the others. Feeling the wire lightly as they tore back, tears of agony fell down their cheeks for the man left guarding the line. Several minutes into the passageway, they heard it and stopped. Machine gun fire!

"Oh, God!"

"Move, goddammit, move! We've got to get back to Conor . . . move . . . move . . . move . . . move!"

Crouched and in a dead run, they hurled themselves back to the cave in half the allotted time.

"Blow it!" Charley screamed to Conor at the detonator.

"Seamus!" he cried.

"Blow it, Conor! Blow it!"

Conor crouched over the box, hand on plunger, eyes wild . . . "Seamus! Seamus! Seamus!"

"He hasn't got enough ammunition to hold more than a minute. Blow it! They'll cut the wire!"

Charley Hackett came at the detonator. Conor rose like a crazy man, leveling his pistol at Charley's forehead. He took a step back and whirled the pistol around, menacing the others, then dropped it to the cave floor, fell to his knees and emitted a hideous scream . . . "Forgive me!"

He lay over the plunger, making contact.

Everyone looked up in hushed terror. Nothing happened. And then they were hurled around the cave like matchsticks!

*

Dan Sweeney's eyes widened, for no man had seen the half of it before. The land about Magilligan Point leaped and jumped as though it would be torn off and thrown into the sea. The light was the light of a thousand hells, a rage of oranges. Debris hurled against the Martello tower like a shower of hailstones.

Another explosion . . . and another . . . and another!

The wrackers on the opposite shore fell to their knees in fright. They saw it on the coast of Scotland and it lit the heavens at Derry twenty miles away. The sea heaved wildly from it and heads rang from its terrible sound.

The storm was done. Dan Sweeney sighted over the open field before the tower. Minutes passed and then he heard distant sirens.

There! Up the beach. He swung the gun around.

"It's us, Dan!"

Dan left his post, hobbled down the steps and flung the tower door open. In they limped, Gilmartin, Conor Larkin, Charley Hackett, Boyd McCracken, Jennings and four others bashed up from the impact, even at their distance, from three hundred tons of freed dynamite.

They swabbed at their gore, tied tourniquets, shot morphine, wrapped bandages. Distant flashes of torchlight and barking dogs were heard.

Conor lifted his bloody head.

"Take them back over, Gilmartin," he said. "Take them back. See . . . I made the waters calm for you."

"It's my position to stand here with Dan," he answered.

"Sorry. Orders have been changed."

"Dan," Gilmartin protested. "Tell him to take them back."

Dan seized Conor and shook him. "Take your people back, Conor!"

Blood spurted out of Conor's mouth as he opened it to speak. He wiped it with the back of his hand. "Poor little runt. He had to come. He just had to come."

"What of Atty!"

"That is the cruelest joke of all, allowing myself to believe for a single crazy moment there was a life before death. I've done what I came for and that will have to be enough. I can't take any more."

"Aye," Dan whispered. "I know that feeling well." The old man turned to Gilmartin. "Kindly make your departure as swiftly and quietly as possible. Mr. Larkin and my good self have had our fucking fill of terrible beauties."

As the first shots rang out in the direction of the tower, Long Dan Sweeney and Conor Larkin positioned their gun. Gilmartin pulled back swiftly through the grass, dragging the large curragh over the sand and dumping in the half-dead remains of the raiders. As he slid into the water, they sighted in.

"We are all absurd actors on the stage of the diabolical," Conor whispered. "The English killing Germans for the freedom of Belgians and us killing Englishmen for our own freedom."

He put a flare into the signal gun and shot it. It arched away from the tower, lighting the field of sea grass and exposing the advancing enemy. Red tracer bullets streaked from their machine gun. Startled men keeled over like a scythe cutting wheat. Others dropped to their stomachs and inched forward respectfully. The tracers streaked out again in deadly red fingers.

*

GALLIPOLI, TURKEY

The tracers streaked out as a flare turned the battlefield to daylight again. Christopher slid into the muddy hole, collected his thoughts, then crawled over to the fallen officer and rolled him over. The pyrotechnics glowed over the man's face. It was Jeremy. His brother was dead.

He closed his eyes for a moment as the racket above him set up near solid sheets of fire.

"Major Hubble," his sergeant major gasped, crawling alongside. "They're cutting us to pieces. I say, sir, what are the orders?"

"I say we give it a go."

"But, sir, we'll never reach those machine gun nests."

"One more charge, man, one more charge." He crawled to the lip of the shellhole, looked to his right and left to what remained of his battalion, raised his pistol, jumped out into the field and rushed forward. They followed. The Turks had them in a cross fire. The massacre heightened.

THE KING AND QUEEN DEEPLY REGRET THE LOSS YOU AND THE COLERAINE RIFLES HAVE SUSTAINED BY THE DEATHS OF YOUR SONS, MAJOR CHRISTOPHER HUBBLE AND LIEUTENANT JEREMY HUBBLE, AT GALLIPOLI IN THE SERVICE OF THEIR COUNTRY. THEIR MAJESTIES TRULY SYMPATHIZE WITH YOU IN YOUR SORROW.

PENBURTON, Private Secretary
Buckingham Palace

*

The door of the Martello tower creaked open cautiously. A line of soldiers slipped up the circling stairs, tensely alert. Suddenly the platoon leader signaled them to halt. He inched closer, lowered his pistol, held it on the pair and studied them.

"Get the company commander up here," he said shakily.

In a moment the company commander dashed up the steps and stopped alongside him.

"Only two of them?" the company commander said.

"Yes, sir, only two. They ran out of ammunition."

The platoon leader knelt first by Dan Sweeney, then Conor Larkin.

In ... out ... go ... dusty bluebells ...
In and out ... dusty ...
In ... bluebells ...
I'll be your master.

"The old one's dead but this one still seems to be alive, sir."

Follow ... Londonderry
Follow me ... Cork and Kerry ...
... so light ... and ... airy ...

"Look, sir, he's opening his eyes."

"Can't talk, can you, fellow?" the company commander said. "Well, you ought to be proud of yourself ... that was quite a show. ..."

Shelley ... bluebells ... Shelley ...

"Shall I get a stretcher for him, sir?" the platoon leader asked.

The commander's boot reached beneath Conor and flipped him over on his back. "No, poor devil's cut in half. Half his guts are on the floor."

Daddy ... daddy ... daddy ... daddy ...

"Here, give me your pistol. I'll put him out of his misery."

Daddy ... daddy ...

The report echoed sharply off the stone walls.

Daddy ... daddy ... Atty ... Atty ... atty ... aty ... at

EPILOGUE

When the British returned the bodies of Long Dan Sweeney and Conor Larkin, Garrett O'Hara, commander of the Irish Republican Brotherhood, seized upon the moment.

Defying an order from Dublin Castle, the two were placed in state in the rotunda of Dublin's City Hall. Dan Sweeney had been remembered in household, pub and school as an Irish martyr of the Fenian Rising of the last century. Conor Larkin had no small measure of fame from the Sixmilecross incident. All of that was overshadowed by the enormity of the destruction of Lettershanbo Castle.

Casketed under a finely lighted dome, twelve sentries from the Irish Home Army stood by each of the pillars as an honor guard.

Thousands passed in homage. After three days in state, Dan Sweeney's procession was joined by a hundred thousand Dubliners who marched in ragged dirge step to the grounds where Daniel O'Connell and Charles Stewart Parnell lay. Sweeney, "the unforgiving Fenian," was not set down until Garrett O'Hara delivered an oration destined to change the course of Irish history. Speaking in the ancient tongue, he lashed the millennium of tyranny with exquisite rage. And over the land, long-dormant republican stirrings were heard at last.

Conor Larkin was accompanied back to Derry by Atty Fitzpatrick in a simple cortege of a hearse and a single car. Yet in every town along the route it was stopped and children laid flowers on his coffin, women wept, and Brothers and members of the Irish Home Army escorted it as an honor guard to the next town. Then, at last, Father Dary Larkin put his brother to rest alongside their father in St. Columba's churchyard in Ballyutogue.

Ten months later, members of the Brotherhood leading

a few hundred Home Army men staged an aborted rising in Dublin. It was on Easter Monday of 1916 that a terrible beauty was born by a declaration of independence.

The leaders of the rising were sentenced to death by a secret tribunal and they were shot by firing squads at Kilmainham Jail. Kilmainham Jail, the Irish hall of martyrs which had housed Parnell and Wolfe Tone and Emmet and a hundred more of that pesty ilk. By execution of these men, the British blundered into outraging the Irish people and converted the rising into Ireland's most glorious defeat.

When all of this was done, a republic eventually came to pass but the sorrows and the troubles have never left that tragic, lovely land. For you see, in Ireland there is no future, only the past happening over and over.

THE END

ABOUT THE AUTHOR

LEON URIS, born in Baltimore in 1924, left high school to join the Marine Corps. In 1950, Esquire magazine bought an article from him—and it encouraged him to begin work on a novel. The result was his acclaimed bestseller *Battle Cry*. *The Angry Hills*, a novel set in war-time Greece, was his second book. As a screen writer and then newspaper correspondent, he became interested in the dramatic events surrounding the rebirth of the state of Israel. This interest led to *Exodus*, his monumental success which has been read by millions of people. From one of the episodes in *Exodus* came *Mila 18*, the story of the angry uprising of Jewish fighters in the Warsaw Ghetto. *Exodus Revisited*, a work of nonfiction, presents the author's feeling for the land and the people of Israel. Mr. Uris is also the author of *Armageddon, Topaz, QB VII* and his latest, *Trinity*—all sensational bestsellers.

At present, Leon Uris lives in Aspen, Colorado, with his wife, Jill.

BANTAM BOOKS

#1 around the world
Leon Uris
TRINITY

a novel of ireland

Don't Forget These Other Famous Leon Uris Novels

SPECIAL
MONEY SAVING
OFFER

Now you can have an up-to-date listing of Bantam's hundreds of titles plus take advantage of our unique and exciting bonus book offer. A special offer which gives you the opportunity to purchase a Bantam book for only 50¢. Here's how!

By ordering any five books at the regular price per order, you can also choose any other single book listed (up to a $4.95 value) for just 50¢. Some restrictions do apply, but for further details why not send for Bantam's listing of titles today!

Just send us your name and address plus 50¢ to defray the postage and handling costs.